THE SINS OF
THE MOTHER

By the same author
and published by Bantam Books

No Sad Songs
(writing as Sarah Lyon)

A Woman of Pleasure

THE SINS OF
THE MOTHER

Arabella Seymour

BANTAM BOOKS

LONDON · NEW YORK · TORONTO · SYDNEY · AUCKLAND

THE SINS OF THE MOTHER
A BANTAM BOOK : 0 553 404830

First publication in Great Britain

PRINTING HISTORY
Bantam edition published 1996

Set in 10/11pt Monotype Times New Roman
by Phoenix Typesetting, Ilkley, West Yorkshire.

Bantam Books are published by Transworld Publishers Ltd,
61–63 Uxbridge Road, Ealing, London W5 5SA,
in Australia by Transworld Publishers (Australia) Pty Ltd,
15–25 Helles Avenue, Moorebank, NSW 2170,
and New Zealand by Transworld Publishers (NZ) Ltd,
3 William Pickering Drive, Albany, Auckland.

Reproduced, printed and bound in Great Britain by
Cox & Wyman, Reading, Berks.

For M.C. and C.H. who inspired the characters of
Curt Koenig and Fritz von Ehrlich. And for my
daughter Keturah, who is always there for me.

Arabella Seymour
August 1995

PROLOGUE
Beverly Hills, California, April 1933

One by one, the handful of mourners filed in silence out of the chapel to the daylight outside. Past the hearse, now divested of its elaborate coffin and floral wreaths, past the waiting limousines, through the white petrified forest of monumental masonry. Heads bowed, not speaking, they took their places around the open grave.

The bright sunshine overhead was deceptive, like almost everything in Hollywood – ironic, appropriate; the blue sky, the innocuous smattering of cloud, hid a cruel breeze. Elynor shivered, grateful for the protection of her sable coat and the reassuring clasp of her husband's hand. Her brother Gene, a few feet away, glanced up and caught her eye; next to him, wearing a heavy veil and clinging to his arm, their younger sister Alice was crying uncontrollably. On her other side, Walter Oppenheim, her mother's attorney for twenty years, looked grave.

Elynor stared back across the yawning space in front of her, to the ornate white marble headstone; erected on her father's death more than twenty years before, no expense had been spared: festooned with winged angels, cherubs and scrolls, it was a monument in itself to the stonemason's art. The lettering for her mother was fresh, like ink on parchment that has not yet had time to dry: a poignant reminder of mortality to everyone present.

MARIANNA EASTBRIDGE KOENIG
Born January 1st 1876
Died April 7th 1933

Only she and Gene, of all of them, really knew a hint of the truth about the years in between.

She gripped the hand that held hers more tightly; leaned against the tall man standing by her side. The strong, self-confident woman she'd become, released from her mother's stifling clutches, was his creation. As yet, there was no lump in her throat, no burning tears waiting behind her eyes. Her mother was already 'beyond the need of weeping, beyond the reach of hands'.

The minister's robes billowed in the wind; he cleared his throat. *Ashes to ashes, dust to dust.* The earth fell upon the coffin with a soft thud. The timeless ritual was over. After a few moments of respectful silence, the little group turned away and began to disperse. Then Walter Oppenheim walked towards her across the damp grass.

'Elynor . . .' He held out his hand in a conciliatory gesture, and smiled: a lawyer's smile. She had always regarded him as her mother's creature, and she'd never trusted him. He was the cleverest and the most expensive lawyer in Los Angeles, and also the most devious: Oppenheim and her mother had fitted as perfectly together as a hand in a glove. 'I wish we could have met again in happier circumstances.'

'I think that was unlikely, don't you?' She had nothing to fear any more; not from Oppenheim, not from anyone. That other strong presence in her life had completely transformed her.

'I had to speak with you . . . before I read the will.' Oppenheim refused to take offence at her polite coldness. In his line of business, what other people thought about you didn't matter, so long as they paid. Marianna Koenig had been one of his best clients. He cast a glance towards Gene and Alice, getting into the back of one of the limousines. 'You see, your mother entrusted a package to my care before she died . . . with the specific instruction that it was to be the one item of her estate excluded from the will . . . and handed to you personally on the day of her funeral. It's in the safe, in my office. I suggest that after the will's read this afternoon at the house, you come by and take delivery of it.'

'A package? But what is it?'

8

'I'm as wise as you are. Your mother never told me.' Could she really believe him? 'All she'd divulge was that it contained something very important to her, and that you were to have it. As far as the rest of the estate goes, the package in my safe doesn't officially exist.'

'Are you saying that my mother didn't want Gene or Alice to know about it?'

Oppenheim smiled his smooth lawyer's smile a second time. He shrugged. 'If she had, she wouldn't have instructed me to hand it over to you, and only you . . . would she?'

She'd lapsed into reflective silence for most of the journey from the Whitley Heights mansion into central Los Angeles, where Oppenheim's smart, ultra-modern offices were situated on Wilshire Boulevard. Going back to the house, being forced to confront the past again, had unsettled her far more than she'd realized it would, far more than she'd been prepared to be. Only the presence of the man she loved – the man who had walked into her life and changed it for ever – had enabled her to find the strength to do it.

The will in itself meant nothing to her; she was here only out of a sense of duty, to attend her mother's funeral. She'd already decided – before they'd left England, even – that whatever had been bequeathed her, she wanted no part of it. When the will had gone through probate, it could all go to charity. Only the contents of the mysterious package she was on her way to collect intrigued her.

The receptionist in the lobby of the Oppenheim building was brisk and efficient; she telephoned to his seventh-floor suite to say that they were on their way up in the elevator. Oppenheim himself was waiting to show them into his private office.

'We could have driven back from the house in my limousine,' he said, as he closed the door behind them. 'But then the others would have wondered why you were coming back here with me.'

'Walter, whatever my mother said to you, if what you

9

have in your safe is something I feel my brother and sister should know about, then I intend to tell them.'

'Of course.' He flicked the combination dial back and forth, and the safe door came open. 'That's entirely your privilege. And a matter for your own judgement.' He reached inside and took out the mysterious package at last: it was larger, much heavier than she'd expected; but then, what exactly had she expected? It weighed too much to possibly be any of the things she'd guessed at – jewellery, photographs, letters; and, even if it did contain any of those things, then why hadn't her mother wanted them to be included in the property and inventory of the estate itself? 'For my part, I've carried out your mother's instructions to the letter; this belongs to you now.'

'You don't want me to sign a receipt?'

Oppenheim closed the safe door, moved the picture back into place again. 'A receipt? For what? What you're holding in your hands doesn't officially exist.'

Elynor sat on the couch in their hotel suite, the package still unopened on her lap. There was a layer of brown paper wrapping on the outside, carefully tied with string. Where the string had been fastened in the centre, a large blob of dark red wax held it to the paper underneath; beside the seal, the date was written in her mother's unmistakable, strong, bold hand. *October 12th, 1925.* Eight years ago, three weeks after she'd left America for good, to make her new life in England. Elynor had never seen her mother again.

Her mind travelled back in time: 1925. The year of the first transatlantic broadcast, the year the Locarno Treaty had been signed in Europe. The year Warner Brothers had bought out the old Vitagraph company where her father had made his first film, the year Cecil B. DeMille had left Paramount to go independent and F. Scott Fitzgerald had written *The Great Gatsby* . . . the year she'd finally broken free and found herself with a future in front of her away from her mother's vice-like dominance. But without her fateful meeting with the man who had changed her life, would she ever have found the inner strength to do it?

He came into the room now from the adjoining bedroom and stood behind her, his tall, imposing frame casting a long shadow across the opposite wall. He touched her shoulder lightly with his fingers; there was almost no need for either of them to speak aloud. With that uncanny gift he'd always possessed, she knew that he had already sensed exactly what she was thinking. She turned her head, pressed her lips against his hand. Then, slowly but determinedly, she began to untie the string.

The wax seal came away from its anchorage beneath the string, the brown paper crackled. She tore it open, pushed it aside. When she saw what it contained she caught her breath, glanced up in silence to where he stood behind her.

The manuscript was handwritten, each sheet meticulously numbered: more than a thousand pages. There were smudges in places; words struck out and replaced, spillages that had made the ink run, some of the corners missing or turned down from constant handling; slowly, Elynor turned over each sheet from the beginning.

There were precise dates, times, places. And names. The first date when her mother must have been little more than a child, long before she'd met their father, long before any of them had been born. The final page had been written on the night that she'd seen her mother for the very last time, the night when she'd found the courage to walk out of her life. Until now, Elynor had had no idea that this manuscript existed.

She glanced up once more at her husband, then back at the contents of her lap. She could see by the expression on his face that he, too, realized the significance of what she held in her hands. Her mother's story from beginning to end, with no detail of herself, their father, her life with him, or Hollywood and its secrets spared.

There was no last letter, no note, no final instructions

inside the package. Only the question that Elynor asked herself now.

Knowing the sensation the contents of the manuscript would create if it were read by any other eyes than hers, what had her mother wanted her to do after she herself had read it?

CHAPTER ONE

'Young men have filthy minds.'

Of everything that happened to Marianna that fateful summer in New Hampshire, those words from her mother stayed etched in her memory for the rest of her life. Years later, looking back, long after she'd left home to marry, long after her mother was dead, she realized that that afternoon at the Lake Winnipesaukee house had been a turning point in her life. Afterwards, she'd never thought of men in the same way again.

It had been warm and sunny when she'd gone down to the edge of the lake by the boathouse in her white muslin dress and straw boater hat, and caught sight of their neighbours' son Luke Waad, paddling in the water. He'd glanced up as he saw her running down the grassy slope from the trees, and waved at her: Marianna had called out a greeting and gaily waved back. She was happy to see him again. Ever since her father, Frederick H. Eastbridge III, had bought the big white clapboard house five years before as a peaceful holiday retreat and out-of-state weekend home, Marianna had known the Waads' three sons; Luke, at nearly fifteen, was the nearest in age to her.

An only child, she looked forward to his company after spending weeks on end in New York City, where her father's business interests lay, and where, to the elegant brownstone house on Fifth Avenue, few young people ever came.

She'd taken off her shoes, then her hot black stockings, and tucked her petticoat inside her frilly bloomers so that she, too, could stand in the cool lake water with Luke, when her mother suddenly appeared at the edge of the belt of trees, and called her sharply. Marianna turned and began to tiptoe slowly across the stones to the place where she'd left her shoes and stockings, wondering what had happened to make her mother so angry. Picking them up, she ran across the grass to where she stood, cold-eyed, arms folded stiffly in front of her like a schoolmarm.

Marianna squinted, shaded her eyes from the sun. 'What is it, Momma? Am I late for tea?' Why else would her mother, hostess to a dozen out-of-state weekend guests, have especially come looking for her?

'Cover yourself up this minute and follow me back to the house!'

The parlour was cool and shady after the bright light and warmth of the afternoon sun, and all the windows in the room had been opened. The net curtains moved gently in the breeze, voices and laughter drifted in from outside, where white wicker armchairs for her father's guests had been set out on the lawn and everyone was taking tea.

'What's wrong, Momma?'

'You're never to be alone with that boy again, do you understand me? Never!'

'But, Momma, what has he done?' She stared uncomprehendingly. 'Luke's my friend!' For the last five years they'd been neighbours: inseparable at vacations and weekends. They'd paddled, fished, gone boating, butterfly hunting and kite flying together. Luke Waad was the big brother she'd always wanted, the big brother she'd never have. Why should she suddenly be forbidden to see him? 'Momma, I don't understand!'

'Then I'd better make it plain to you. Luke Waad isn't a boy any more . . . he's fourteen, going on fifteen, at least . . . not a suitable companion at all! Young men can't be trusted alone with innocent young girls after they've reached a certain age, and you might as well know that. They have feelings towards females that aren't pure, feelings that no respectable young woman knows anything about. Young men have filthy minds. From now on, you stay well away from them, do you hear?' Marianna cowered beneath the onslaught of her mother's anger. 'Have you any notion what people would think if you'd been seen down at were tell-tale streaks on her cheeks where the tears had been; for some reason, that made him even sterner and angrier, and Father's anger was terrifying. No matter how many times she washed her face, no matter how many times she soaked a handkerchief in cold water or eau de Cologne and held it against her eyelids, he always knew.

She closed the door and looked around the room: it was neat, clean, tidy; almost clinical. Her mother inspected it personally every day – as she inspected every other room in the house – and woe betide Marianna if there was a single shoe, a book, an ornament out of place; for her mother, tidiness was almost an obsession. There must be no disorder, no dust, no smeared mirrors; the frilled white cotton nightgown must be laid just so neatly across the pillows.

Marianna sat down on the floor with a sigh; to sit on her bed would only crease the counterpane, and then it would have to be tidied all over again. Cross-legged on the rug, she propped her chin in her hands. Who would be her friend, if Father sold the New Hampshire house and they moved back to New York City for good? She had no friends there. Mother and Father were very strict in regulating whom she could or could not be permitted to mix with – no Roman Catholics, no children from tradesmen's families, no Southerners – and life in the elegant brownstone on Fifth Avenue was, not surprisingly, lonely. Though there was a fine upright piano in the drawing room, Marianna was never permitted to use it if Father wanted to read the newspaper or work in his study, and, for lack of constant practice, had never learned to play well; mortifying to her, when she loved music, and as she sat sewing needlepoint in silence would gaze longingly at the keys, in vain.

She got up, gazed out of the window. In the distance she could see the gleam of the lake beyond the belt of trees, the distant rooftop of the Waad house almost a mile away. What had Luke thought, when Momma had appeared and sharply called her, when she'd gone without waving to him or even saying goodbye? Maybe he was still down on the shore, paddling in the water and aimlessly peering down at the pebbles on the bottom, watching for fish, waiting for her to come back. Maybe he'd get tired of waiting and make his way home again, maybe he might walk up to the house to find her. If he did, Momma or Father would almost certainly send him away again, with a white-lie excuse, and then Marianna would never be able to see him, never be able to explain. If she secretly wrote him a note, could she trust Ida to deliver it for her on her day off, or would she take the note straight to Momma? What Momma would do with it, Marianna could guess only too well; better to forget it.

She opened her wardrobe and took out a clean, beautifully pressed white frock from the row of 'summer things' hanging inside; like almost all her clothes, it had been purchased from the smart dress department in R. H. Macy's department store in Herald Square, New York, but she was too preoccupied and too miserable now to feel any pleasure in wearing it, with its graceful pleats and flounces, the little puff sleeves decorated with tiny satin ribbon bows and fancy pin-tucking; mechanically, she undressed herself and then laid the frock she'd spoiled down at the lake neatly over the chairback for Ida to take away for washing. She took clean underwear from the chest of drawers: camisole, petticoat and bloomers; she put them on, pulled the fresh white frock over her head and managed to fasten all the buttons at the back except the top two, which she could never reach, leaving only her hair for Ida to brush: though Father employed three servants – Mrs Hobbs the cook, a manservant and a maid – Marianna had been brought up strictly to understand that they were there to help run the household smoothly, not to wait on her. Father had fully indoctrinated his only daughter in the desirability of self-sufficiency from an early age.

She sat down ready on her dressing-table stool, stared at her unhappy reflection in the mirror. A sad, large-eyed little girl with a waterfall of dark hair stared back, the beginnings of a tear forming in the corner of one eye. Defiantly, she brushed it away. Father always knew if she'd been crying; Father always did.

CHAPTER TWO

Frederick H. Eastbridge III settled back comfortably in his chair, opened the *Boston Gazette* in front of him at the financial pages, then helped himself to a choice Dutch cigar from the box on his desk.

The soft breeze coming from the partly open window behind him was warm and pleasant still, and the silence, now the guests had left and his wife had gone up to bed, was soothing; as a young man, even as a boy, he'd valued his solitude – and used it profitably. Like everything else, it could be turned to advantage; it had pleased him to think that, while others slept, he was getting ahead of them, putting those night-time hours to good use. A first class honours degree when he eventually graduated from Harvard succinctly proved his point. By the time he was twenty-one he was already going up in the world and well on the way to following in his father's footsteps and, as anyone in the ruthless, cut-throat business world could have testified, Frederick Harrington Eastbridge II was a tough act to follow.

At twenty-five, he was already within a hair's breadth of reaching the top of the ladder; groomed to succeed his father as president of one of the biggest and most powerful stockbroking firms in New York, at twenty-nine he was one step closer as vice-president with his own office and a fleet of underlings. A month before his thirtieth birthday he announced his engagement to one of the most well-connected heiresses in New England.

The Ayres of Massachusetts could trace their lineage back to the early pilgrims and it was said, by the family's friends as well as their enemies, that Millward K. Ayres was a man prouder than Lucifer, and brought up to believe in the maxim that like should marry like. His uncle was a

21

senator and his wife a Winthrop, with a small fortune of her own as well as an immaculate New England bloodline, and their daughter Edwina had been paid court to by the wealthier and better-connected young men from five states. She chose – predictably, as groomed by her ambitious mother – the richest and best-connected of them all, Frederick Harrington Eastbridge III. After a high-profile society wedding at New York's fashionable Trinity Church off Broadway – and a reception that cost the bride's father more than ten thousand dollars – they set up home in smart Washington Mews, an elegant three-storey townhouse with the luxury of its own private stables – a wedding present from the bridegroom's father. Within the year, company profits had soared even higher and 'F.H.'s' reputation along with them: there were invitations to charity galas and important dinners with city bigwigs, evenings at the theatre or the opera, a second house upstate for summers and weekends when the heat and bustle of Manhattan grew too much, and his first child on the way. When the news was announced, the Ayres family immediately set up a private trust fund for the benefit of their first grandchild; on that New Year's Eve of 1875, it had seemed to F.H. that the world was at his feet. Until the early hours of New Year's Day, when Edwina had given birth to a girl.

He could remember that night with startling clarity, every moment until twelve o'clock; afterwards, everything was a blur.

Since his wife had gone into labour hours before he'd paced the hall floor restlessly, waiting for the sound of his son's first cry, then the doctor's footsteps coming from her bedroom down the stairs to the hall to bring him the news for which he was waiting so impatiently. The names had already been chosen: Frederick Harrington Millward Eastbridge; the nursery, with every imaginable luxury, had been prepared months in advance. A wetnurse had been engaged through an exclusive New York agency; a week before the baby was due, he'd sat down at the desk in his study and written out the birth announcement for publication in the *New York Times*. He'd gone from the hall into the drawing room to pour himself a brandy to calm his nerves when he'd heard the sound of footsteps coming towards him, and when the doctor appeared in the open doorway smiling broadly he'd almost dropped both the glass and the decanter in surprise.

'Congratulations, sir. Mrs Eastbridge has given birth to a fine strong girl.'

The words stunned him, struck him like a blow; his mouth fell open. Nine months of waiting, nine months of elaborate preparation and at the end of it all, a girl. Just a girl. He was too shocked, too bitterly disappointed for a moment to speak a word, even to say, 'Thank you.' The doctor – who had delivered Astors, Ryersons, Stuyvesants and Vanderbilts and had one of the most prestigious practices in the whole of New York – put his reaction down to what he privately called 'the first-time father syndrome'. It would take some time, no doubt, for the reality of parenthood to sink in.

'Mrs Eastbridge is well but she's had a very difficult birth and she needs to rest as much as possible,' he said gently, in his best professional manner, 'but naturally you can see her and your daughter for a few moments first.' *His daughter*. F.H. had forced a smile, taken the doctor's extended hand, accepted his congratulations with as good a grace as he could muster. He had to pull himself together, put a brave face on it. His wife was young and strong, after all, the child was healthy and a good birth weight: in a year's time, he told himself as he mounted the stairs, he would have the son and heir he'd expected today, that he so passionately wanted. That was well worth waiting for.

Edwina stared up at him from her capacious bed, her face drained of colour and her eyes dull from the effects of the chloroform. She knew that whatever he said, however much he pretended not to mind, a daughter was a terrible disappointment, and she'd failed. Instead of the radiant glow of motherhood, the expression she wore was almost shamefaced. When the nurse brought the baby to show him, she could barely meet his gaze.

'I'm sorry, F.H.'

He patted her hand stiffly, kept the tight smile in place.

'Nonsense, my dear; she's a fine, healthy child. God grant her a brother next time round.'

'Yes.'

God never did.

Twenty minutes past midnight, and Edwina Eastbridge still sat reading in bed. It was a Charles Dickens novel, *A Tale of Two Cities*, and she'd reached the part where Sydney Carton had exchanged his identity with the husband of the woman he loved, and was waiting in the prison to meet his fate. Though her eyes were beginning to feel tired now, she somehow couldn't bring herself to put down the book: the tale of romance, sacrifice and heroism in Dickens' pages were the closest she would ever get to experiencing any of those things in real life.

Every now and then, her eyes would glance up from the book and look towards the bottom of the door that separated her bedroom from her husband's dressing room: but still no light seeped from under it. So, he was still downstairs, smoking and reading his newspaper in the study. Or, perhaps, still mulling over in his mind the information she'd imparted to him that afternoon about their daughter Marianna.

Marianna. For a moment, her mind wandered away from the novel and the heroism of Sydney Carton and back into the past; the past, where a younger, softer Edwina had lain in another bedroom, though much like this one with its paintings and sumptuous carved furniture, desperately trying to focus through the haze of agonizing pain and chloroform.

She could remember the moving silhouettes about the room, the midwife's voice, the doctor's expert hands, willing her to use the last of her fading strength to rid her body of its intolerable burden, a son and heir to inherit the Eastbridge fortune. But at the end of the exhausting travail and the pain that had made her feel her entire body was being torn in two, there was no son, no heir; just a wailing, useless girl and her husband's cold eyes staring down at it in the midwife's arms, pretending that it didn't matter, that he wasn't more disappointed than he'd ever been in his entire life.

'I'm sorry, F.H.' She could hear her voice now, echoing down the years; after Marianna's birth almost fourteen years ago, then eighteen months later, when she'd produced a son who had died of whooping cough before his navel had healed, and the three stillbirths after that. It was then that the family physician had told F.H. that there must be no more pregnancies, that if there were then she would be seriously endangering not only her health, but her life. To both of them, it had been a devastating blow. Had it dated from then, she wondered, the resentment they'd slowly begun to feel towards Marianna, whose difficult birth with instruments had left her mother internally weakened, never able to bear a healthy son?

Her eyes drifted back to the dressing-room door; still no light shone underneath it, so he was still shut away in his study downstairs. F.H. rarely came to her bedroom now, and that suited Edwina very well; by nature she was cold and the physical side of marriage repelled her, just as her elder sisters and her mother had warned her that it would. Sex was a tiresome and distasteful duty, a burden that, like all burdens, simply had to be borne; she was fortunate indeeed that F.H. had always been considerate in that way, and had never pressed his attentions on her more frequently than once a week. His passion in life was power, not women.

Edwina laid down her book, reached across to the bedside table for her marker. Her eyes were sore now; time to turn out the light. She closed her Charles Dickens with its beautiful scarlet calf binding and gold-edged pages: Sydney Carton and the unspeakable fate that awaited him at the guillotine would have to wait until tomorrow when there were no guests for tea and she could read under the apple tree alone.

Before she slept, she thought of her problematic daughter. Innocent now, but, exposed to the nastiness of teenaged boys, not innocent for long: for an Eastbridge female, unthinkable. F.H. had frowned ominously when she'd gone to him after the guests had left and told him of the episode down at the lake that afternoon. As she'd expected, he'd agreed that the childhood friendship must end abruptly with the onset of dangerous adolescence. He would send for Marianna tomorrow and give her a lecture on female modesty that she would never forget.

The Waads, naturally, would never learn the truth; for the remaining two weeks before their departure to New York, Marianna would be 'unwell' if any of the Waad boys came up to the house to see her; but they would be tactfully turned away. No sense in offending respected neighbours who had kinship with a US senator: the Waads were important people around these parts.

How much easier her life would have been if she'd never had Marianna, if she'd not been cursed with a daughter but had been blessed with a son.

Marianna hesitated outside the door of her father's study, steeling herself to pluck up enough courage to go inside. Since the scene with her mother yesterday she'd been on tenterhooks, worrying when the axe would fall and the dreaded summons from her father would come; but when, at breakfast, he said nothing, she'd begun to breathe more easily: was it possible that her mother had decided – for reasons of her own – not to tell him at all? For a little while, she'd almost felt happy, in spite of being forbidden to go down to the lake again on her own. But then he'd laid down his white damask napkin, got up from his place at the head of the table and fixed her with a long, penetrating stare before he'd said ominously, 'I want to see you in my study in half an hour,' and she'd known that she was in trouble.

He was standing by the window when she let herself in, gazing across the lawn. The sunlight cast a bright glow across his profile and picked out the amber shades in his thick hair, the immaculate handlebar moustache and meticulously pomaded beard. He reminded her, in fact, of the lifesize portrait of her grandfather that hung in the hall in their house on Fifth Avenue, and she wondered if as a boy he had been as afraid of his father as she was of him.

At last, after what seemed an interminable time, he turned and looked at her.

'I'm ashamed of you, Marianna.' With that brief sentence he managed to make her feel dirty, guilty, utterly wicked. She hung her head.

'I'm very sorry, Father.'

He sat down in his hide, button-back chair. 'You're almost fourteen now; old enough to have a sense of dignity. Old enough to know how a young lady should behave in public.'

'I was only paddling in the water. Luke and I have paddled in the water hundreds of times!'

'Children paddle in water. Young ladies do not.' He was staring at her from beneath straight, bushy eyebrows; the effect was terrifying. Those penetrating eyes were exactly like the eyes in the Fifth Avenue portrait of Frederick H. Eastbridge II. Marianna trembled. 'Young ladies do not remove their shoes and stockings in public. Young ladies do not show their underwear. Young ladies at all times are expected to adhere strictly to the accepted codes of propriety . . . particularly if they bear the name of Eastbridge. To bring shame, even the smallest breath of scandal on the name of Eastbridge is something that I will not tolerate . . . do you understand me?' He never shouted, never once raised his voice, but that soft, deadly tone struck terror into her in a way that nothing else could. Forty years later, Marianna could still remember that voice.

'Yes, Father . . . I understand.' The words were a whisper. The door behind her seemed far away and she was desperate to escape from him, from the harsh glare of those pale, pitiless grey eyes. 'I'm very sorry; I promise, I'll never do anything wrong ever again.'

He turned away abruptly, as if he could no longer bear to look at her. 'I'm sending you back to New York tomorrow. Go up to your room and start to pack.'

Outside the study door she leaned against the wall and closed her eyes, breathed a sigh of relief; so banishment from the summer house to Manhattan was to be her punishment: to her surprise, far less than she'd expected. In New York it would still be stiflingly hot and the housekeeper and the governess would no doubt have received strict instructions to keep her occupied, but as she ran up the staircase her heart sang. She could dance, sing, play the piano as loud as she liked and Father wouldn't be there to stop her, her mother wouldn't be there to object. Bounding into her room where Ida was already packing her trunk Marianna was just beginning to think how lightly she'd been let off when her eyes caught sight of the empty cage.

'Where's my canary?' she asked, as the smile faded from her lips. But somehow she already knew.

PART TWO

New York, September 1897

CHAPTER THREE

It was ironic that the day her whole life changed for ever should have started like all the others in her ordered, predictable and chaperoned existence; mundane and boring.

In the morning after breakfast, when her father had left the Fifth Avenue house for his office on Wall Street, she'd helped her mother address invitations to members of her Ladies' Guild for a charity lunch, then accompanied her by cab to R. H. Macy's department store for a morning's shopping, followed by lunch at Muschenheim's on 31st Street, east of Broadway. At two o'clock, there was a short round of calls to make at the homes of various acquaintances: the Havemeyer house on Madison at 38th Street, Mrs Depew, at 27 West 54th, and Mrs Lauterbach on East 78th before taking tea with yet another Ladies' Guild acquaintance in the Green Teapot tearoom on Lexington Avenue. While her mother spoke across her as if she was invisible, Marianna gazed round uninterestedly at their surroundings, bored by the Ladies' Guild gossip and wishing she was a hundred miles away: anywhere, to escape the drone of women's conversation and the infernal clatter of plates and teacups.

There was delicate plasterwork along the low ceiling, and a plate rail displayed a varied assortment of china pots, decorative plates and knick-knacks. There were framed engravings on the walls and a working fireplace, Victorian rose-back chairs, and a crystal candlestick and real flower and fern on each table: and not a single man in sight. The total effect, the waitress in her spotless white frilled cap and starched apron and the well-dressed patrons taking tea, exuded an atmosphere of unqualified respectability.

'And you, my dear,' Marianna looked up suddenly,

startled that her mother's companion had condescended to include her in the conversation at last, 'do you also enjoy the theatre?'

'Yes, very much . . . when I go.' A resentful glance in her mother's direction now: how many plays had there been in the past that her parents had vetoed because they were deemed unsuitable for a young lady? Only since she'd turned twenty-one at the beginning of the year had they relaxed their vigilance a little, begun to treat her in a way slightly more befitting an adult; but even now, if she wanted to leave the house for any reason – even an innocent shopping trip in downtown Manhattan – her mother demanded to know exactly where she was going, exactly how long she intended to be. Her lack of freedom irked her. No young man, even within their own circle, had yet received her parents' approval to accompany her to any venue unless they planned to be present; likewise, since it would have been unheard of for a young woman of her class to go to a theatre alone, she could only go with her parents, to plays that they chose; her preferences were never catered for. She suppressed a sigh and forced herself to smile out of politeness. She was tired of a strict diet of intellectual drawing-room farces and innocuous comedies that had her yawning halfway through the first act, yearning for the intermission when she could alleviate the boredom by a trip to the ladies' cloakroom where the conversations she overheard were often much more interesting than the play. She longed for something that was exciting, controversial, energetically different, a story and acting to match that would have her sitting on the edge of her seat. There had been several tantalizing reviews in her father's newspapers that she'd read avidly and secretly when he was out, but dared not ask about, plays like *Octoroon* or *Humanity* by Sutton Vane, produced barely eighteen months ago, which, the critic in the *New York Times* had enthused with bated breath, featured a scene with mounted sword combat that was pronounced by all who'd seen it to be the most realistic ever produced on stage. Marianna would have given almost anything to have been among the audience that night; instead, she'd had to accompany her parents to an Oddfellows' benefit dinner.

She excused herself, so that she could escape to the ladies' room and get away from the monotonous chatter at her mother's table.

She splashed her cheeks with cold water and washed her hands to kill a little time, then sat down at one of the mirrors and adjusted her hat. It was the first hat she'd been allowed to choose for herself and, since her mother hadn't approved of her choice, had been obliged to pay for from her own personal money – the interest from her trust fund – and not have charged to her father's account. That first, small act of independence, the knowledge that she had a tidy sum invested under her own name at the New Amsterdam Bank on Broadway, had given her more pleasure than she'd ever thought possible. Little by little, she'd tried to assert her newly acquired adulthood in small, unobtrusive ways that her parents wouldn't notice: the choice of a hat, a gown, an afternoon's shopping by herself in the Manhattan department stores; but she'd soon realized that, twenty-one or not, neither of her parents had relinquished any real power over her; in fact, little had changed.

She was still required to give an account of her movements, the names of anyone she might meet. Though she was permitted to go out in the mornings or in the afternoons unaccompanied, to travel anywhere alone after six o'clock would have been unthinkable. Along with her twenty-first birthday cards and gifts had come an uncompromising lecture on behaviour and morality from her mother. This time, much more graphic than the one she'd received that day eight years before at Lake Winnipesaukee.

'The most important asset any lady ever has is her good name . . . and I don't just mean that you always have to remember you're an Eastbridge; that goes without saying. What I'm talking about is a lady's personal behaviour . . . the way she talks, the way she conducts herself in company. And, when she's married, in private with her husband.' Marianna had been utterly fascinated, but deeply embarrassed. 'There are private parts of a woman's body that are only ever seen by herself . . . on marriage, she has to do her duty and surrender herself to her husband for the sole purpose of having children to carry on his name. She takes no pleasure in that. She never enjoys what happens between her and her husband in that regard . . . no lady, no decent woman would. Only hussies, fallen women with no morals, no self-respect, take pleasure in that act, and they're despised, ostracized by everyone; especially men.' She'd tilted her chin, narrowed her eyes. 'Always remember how to conduct yourself when you come into the company of men; a gentleman would be truly shocked at any young woman who behaved in a forward manner, laughing too loudly, staring too boldly into his face in an unseemly way, or flaunting herself to invite male attention. Never forget this: if a girl wants a man to respect her, she must never flirt like a common shopgirl or allow him to become over-familiar with her, never commit the smallest indiscretion that would tarnish her good name.' After that, Marianna had started to take more notice of how other women behaved around men; and it was quite true, she saw, that there was a definite distinction between the behaviour of women of the lower sort and the ones from good families like her own. Whereas she would always look away sharply and lower her eyes at once if a strange man happened to glance in her direction, she had noticed only a few days before how a female shop assistant had spoken pertly to a male customer, fluttering her eyelashes and giggling when she handed him his change. The strange thing was, contrary to what her mother had told her, he hadn't seemed to take offence at her behaviour at all.

'Men might pretend to enjoy being flirted with, but underneath they know the girl is cheap. If they met her again in the street, they'd look the other way, pretend they didn't know her. If she so far forgot herself as to go up to them in some public place, they'd run a mile.'

Marianna stood up, straightened her dress and went back to the tearoom, where she caught the name of Mrs Leslie Carter being whispered as she approached the table;

but the moment her mother and friend caught sight of her coming towards them, their conversation was hurriedly curtailed.

Marianna had heard that name before – and seen it, in huge letters on the billboards outside the Lyceum Theatre. About to enter the family drawing room one evening, she'd overheard that intriguing word 'notorious' and, instead of opening the door and going inside, had stood for several minutes listening at the keyhole: the conversation had been muffled but very enlightening.

'It's disgusting. A disgrace. Why, the woman's no better than a tramp.' Her mother's voice: strident, full of indignation. 'No wonder her husband went through the divorce courts to get rid of her. *Five lovers!* She committed adultery with five men and she was found guilty on the evidence, so it must have been true. And this is Belasco's new leading lady!' The voice faded a little as her mother must have moved to another part of the room, but Marianna could still hear her plainly. 'It's a public scandal that such a shameless creature should be allowed to flaunt herself on a Broadway stage!'

'My dear, it's all Belasco's doing . . . he'll stoop to any depths to create a sensation and get cheap publicity. After all, what else can you expect from a Jew?'

'I'm shocked that a man of Daniel Frohman's reputation would have anything to do with her!'

Marianna had read about the playwright David Belasco and Daniel Frohman, who managed the Lyceum Theatre, and his brother Charles, who had staged one of the few plays she had really loved, *Shenandoah*. She had been too young to see it when it had first been shown in New York, but there had been a revival with John Drew in the leading role and Marianna had enjoyed the performance so much that she'd begged her mother to take her to the matinee the next day. As they'd been leaving the theatre she'd caught sight of John Drew in the foyer, and had wanted to ask him to autograph her programme, but her mother had refused to allow it.

She pulled back her cane chair and sat down again, well

aware that her mother had changed the subject deliberately the minute she'd come within earshot. But Marianna had overheard enough. David Belasco had written yet another play – this one especially for Mrs Carter to star in – called *The Heart of Maryland*, and the theatre where she was appearing had already been sold out for weeks.

'We really must be leaving.' Edwina raised a kid-gloved hand and imperiously beckoned to the waitress. 'I have another call to make before we go home . . . and of course there's the theatre tonight to get ready for.' Marianna kept a straight face: not *The Heart of Maryland* starring Mrs Leslie Carter, she'd warrant.

'How splendid – we're going to the opera. *La Forza del Destino*. Caruso and Patti.' The waitress had come to their table as soon as she'd been summoned and presented the bill. 'What are you and F.H. going to see?'

'Edward Rose's new romantic drama, *Under the Red Robe*. At the Metropolitan.' Edwina opened her handbag and took out a dollar bill. 'F.H. was impressed with his adaptation of *The Prisoner of Zenda* – we saw it in Boston when he had business there last fall. When it came here in January, we saw it three times.' She took her receipted bill and left a five-cent tip on the plate. As they said their good-byes at the door, her companion turned a bright, impersonal smile on Marianna.

'And you're going too, my dear? You enjoy yourself, won't you?'

Marianna smiled back and made the obligatory response, but all the way back to Fifth Avenue she was wishing that she could have gone to the Lyceum and seen the notorious Mrs Carter instead.

It was halfway through the second act when he suddenly walked on stage and the whole play, the entire evening for her, changed. She sat up, moved to the edge of her seat and held up her opera glasses almost guiltily, terrified that her parents would notice that her hand was shaking, and somehow read her mind. But she couldn't tear her eyes away from him.

36

He was tall and beautifully proportioned, with long shapely legs made even shapelier by the tight-fitting costume he wore, and his bright golden hair was a thatch of curls. When he spoke his lines, a zing went through her: she leaned forward, rested her hands on the edge of the box. It was then that she realized they were trembling. When he disappeared from the stage at the end of the act and didn't reappear in the next, her disappointment was so intense it felt almost like a physical pain. During the intermission, she fumbled with her programme to find the list of *Dramatis Personae*, and there, more than halfway down it, was his name. Curt Koenig.

She kept staring at it until the intermission was over and the lights dimmed. She kept repeating it to herself over and over again. Curt Koenig. After the play, when they'd left the theatre and were on their way home to Fifth Avenue, all she could think about was seeing it, him, again.

Curt Koenig had left the Metropolitan by the backstage entrance two acts before the play ended: not much point in staying for the encore when he was just another insignificant member of a large supporting cast and would not be missed. It was Maud Adams and Otis Skinner that the audience had packed the theatre to see.

He'd changed back into his street clothes and hung his costume in wardrobe – only the stars had their own dressers – and gone out into the street where he began walking in the direction of Queens instead of taking the tram: four more days till payday; wiser to save the fare. It was nearly eleven when he reached the one-room apartment he shared with a friend – Shawn Duchovsky – who had already eaten supper alone and not yet bothered to clear away, judging by the state of the kitchen.

'Coffee?' He was boiling a blackened kettle on the temperamental old stove, surrounded by unwashed pans, dishes and crockery. 'Guess you can sure use one, huh?'

Curt threw himself down on one of the beds and rested his head behind his hands. 'How come you can make so much mess cooking one plate of sauce an' spaghetti? No wonder your old man threw you out.'

'Hey! Don't worry about it; I saved some for you. Just wait till you taste it. Anyhow, we can clear up later . . . tomorrow'll do.' Clouds of steam started to belch from the kettle spout into the air until the kitchen was full of it. 'How did the play go? Was it a full house?'

'Yeah . . . a full house.' Curt yawned. 'Adams an' Skinner can sure draw the crowds.'

'It'll be your turn someday . . . don't tell me they were born famous!'

'Maybe. But it's a long climb up that ladder. And with every other guy trying to get ahead of you to the same place.'

'Aw, c'mon . . . drink this.' He handed Curt the coffee and sat down himself. 'You're tired out now. Long week. . . rehearsals . . . first night. You gotta keep thinking ahead to the next time and the time after that. The next part'll be bigger, and the one after that'll be bigger still. Hey! This is New York, remember? Where it's all happening! You just need that one break and you've cracked it.'

'Sure . . . sure. I just wish that there was a short cut, that's all. That I could get the chance to show someone like Belasco or Frohman what I can really do.' Curt raised himself on one elbow and looked pensive. 'I need something with more guts than a few lines in act two.'

'So you gotta wait awhile . . . hell, Curt, you got your toe in the back door; in a few months or so, you'll have the whole foot. You got talent. You got stage presence. You got good looks. Why don't you stop complainin', for Chrissake?'

Curt grinned. He raised the cup in his right hand. 'This coffee tastes like shit.'

They'd known each other for more than fifteen years; for fourteen of them, they'd lived on the same street in Minneapolis, Minnesota; their parents had gone to the same church, they'd gone to the same school – and been friends ever since. Lorenz Koenig was a second-generation

American and, after his German-born family had settled in Minneapolis, he'd married local girl Martha Randolph, who helped serve the customers in her father's downtown general store. He was hardworking and ambitious – qualities that had rubbed off in liberal quantities on his second son – and by the time he was twenty-eight he owned the biggest livery stable for fifty miles. Because of his splendid physique, he'd been a prize-fighter in his youth, and had only given up what had proved to be a very lucrative living when he'd married, mostly on the insistence of his wife. He'd expected his sons to work in the livery stable business when they were old enough, and all of them had – except Curt. After taking a girl to the local theatre in town one evening when he was twenty-two, he'd had stars in his eyes ever since.

His whole family had disapproved; just what he'd expected from them. He'd had a blazing row with his father and eldest brother who'd told him in no uncertain terms that if he left to try his luck in New York he'd be back with his tail between his legs before the year was out. But they'd all reckoned without his tenacity. He'd had more bitter disappointments and gone hungry more times since coming to the big city with Shawn Duchovsky than he'd ever done in his life; but he was determined never to give in. A week after Shawn had found a job as a desk clerk with the Hamburg–Amerika Line at 45 Broadway, he'd managed to land a small part in a major production, and after that had never been out of work for more than a month. For a rookie actor from Minneapolis without any theatre connections, Curt Koenig reckoned that that wasn't bad going. It was only on nights like tonight, when he was tired and irritable after a long day, that he felt a touch of despondency setting in. That was when Shawn would kick his butt and remind him of how much he'd achieved already.

The pots and pans were still piled up in the little kitchen, with their baked-on sauce and spaghetti setting harder by the minute. Swinging his long legs off the bed, he got up and began pumping water into the sink so they could soak all night. He opened the larder and peered inside to see if there was anything left for supper that was edible.

'Hey . . . what about my spaghetti?' Shawn, coffee cup in hand, was at his elbow now. 'I cooked extra for you, special.'

'Shawn, you have it, OK?' Curt took out cheese, and what was left of a loaf of bread. There was no butter and no beer. 'You know I can't stand that fuckin' Iti stuff.'

Duchovsky smiled. He shrugged. 'You're an ungrateful sonofabitch, Koenig . . . you know that?'

CHAPTER FOUR

It was already getting dark and the wind turning cold when detective Roy Delucca came on duty at his precinct on 14th Street; he was in an ugly mood tonight. His wife had been out at her mother's in East Flatbush all day long, and had got back so late that she hadn't had time to cook his supper before he left for work. Delucca was hungry, and when he was hungry he was mean.

'Momma's sick, Roy, and she's all alone. She needs me. I couldn't just up and rush away, you know that. Not till Mrs Fachetti came to sit with her; and she was late today.' Momma was sick; Momma was always sick. She'd been sick since the day they'd got married and whenever she wanted anything – like her daughter to come running – she knew just how to get it. Trouble was, he was the only one who could see it. 'She looks forward to seein' me and the kids once a week; she gets lonely by herself. Anyhow, you can grab a bite to eat somewhere downtown, can't you? I got to get the boys washed and put to bed.'

'Downtown? I'm not goin' downtown. Chief Rawlins wants Mac and me to finish that business in Little Italy.' He bent down and started lacing his shoes. 'You shoulda told me you was goin' to be home this late, Maudie . . . I could have eaten at Joe's place. Now, I got no time to do nothin'.'

'I'm sorry, honey . . .' He could tell that she wasn't really listening; the boys were tired out from the train ride from Flatbush and the little one was blubbering; all she wanted to do was get them to bed so she could put her feet up when he'd left the house. 'Tell you what. I'll fix you somethin' real nice for breakfast.' She shooed the boys into the bathroom. 'You take care, you hear?'

'See you in the mornin'.' Delucca pulled on his overcoat,

stuck on his hat and slammed the apartment door behind him. His footsteps echoed loudly on the stone floor and stairs. As he went down the steps and out into the street all the depressing sounds of humanity assaulted his eardrums: women crying, kids screaming, couples yelling at each other; what he wouldn't give to move away from it all further uptown, to a better district, to maybe some nice, neat little house near a park with its own backyard, where his boys could grow up without hearing fighting and cussing going on all around them twenty-four hours a day. Fat chance. On a sergeant's pay in the New York City Police Department, the best he could do was a three-room apartment two floors up in Brooklyn Heights.

It was getting colder. The wind cut into him like a knife. He pulled up his collar, quickened his step. His belly rumbled, reminding him of his missed supper and how goddam hungry he was; he cursed Maudie's mother. Hell, hadn't that old bitch lived well over her time? With all the things she reckoned were wrong with her, she should have been six feet under years ago. She was a thorn in his flesh; always had been, always would be, with Maudie wrapped right around her little finger; fetching and carrying, taking the elevated railway train over to Flatbush to see her two, maybe three times a week. If he had the money to move right uptown, it would be too far away for Maudie to get over there even once a month. If only.

At last, he reached the precinct steps and rushed up them two at a time, grateful for the sudden warmth of the building. As usual it was a hotbed of activity, the honeycomb of corridors and warren of offices always full of people coming in and going out, clutching sheafs of paperwork, questioning suspects and witnesses, hustling Lower East Side prostitutes or drunks down to the cells. Delucca found his partner already in their poky, shared office, sifting through a stack of files on the untidy desk.

'Hi, Mac, how goes it?' He tore off his hat and overcoat and hung them roughly on the peg on the wall. 'Jeez, it's fuckin' freezin' outside. Tonight, I don't mind pushin' paperwork around the desk.'

'Forget it. Chief Rawlins is spittin' blood over that bust down in Little Italy . . . he wants it wrapped up, watertight, this week, all ready for the DA's office next Monday. Looks like we'll be out on the street most of tonight. An' tomorrow, too, if we don't get results. Betcha.'

'Fuck Chief Rawlins! I just about had a gut full of that guy!'

MacKenzie shrugged. 'Heads'll roll if we don't get right on it, Roy. What you say we head down there now and take statements; maybe Lombardi and his brother have thought things over and decided to be a little more co-operative this time.'

'The fuck they have.' Delucca snatched his hat and over-coat back off the peg; he might as well have kept them on. 'Whatever, I'm not comin' back here tonight till we've nailed 'em.'

'OK. Let's go then.'

There was only one thing more depressing than the Lower East Side in the daytime and that was the Lower East Side at night. Walking south-east from the precinct towards Delancey and East Broadway, they'd stopped at a late-hours eating place halfway, so that MacKenzie could have the hot coffee he was gasping for and Delucca could get himself something hot to eat. While they waited for their order and MacKenzie gabbed on about the case, he watched the shabby, dirty, hopeless-eyed hotchpotch of humanity come and go, and felt nothing but contempt.

His grandfather had come to America nearly forty years before Ellis Island had even been heard of as an immigrants' processing station, and married a girl in Philadelphia, where his father was born; despite his name, Delucca considered himself a full-blooded American and despised the flock of immigrants who'd mostly come over in the 1880s – not from the traditional western European countries like England, Germany, Ireland and Scandinavia, but south-east Europe: Russians, Poles, Czechs, Slavs – filthy hordes of ragged, resourceless people fleeing from poverty or political persecution, sometimes both. In the last forty years immigration had quadrupled, and the south-eastern Europeans were arriving at a hundred times their former rate, crowded into the port cities along the whole of the east coast. In New York, whole families, most not able to speak a single word of English, were crammed into run-down tenement blocks with no windows, no proper sanitation, often more than eight or ten to a single room. Chief Rawlins reckoned that there were at least one and half million living in forty-three thousand tenements in the lower Manhattan slums – streets like Baxter, Hester, and Mulberry – and Delucca had already found out that most of the crime he had to deal with was concentrated in that area – Chinatown, Little Italy, and the Lower East Side. It gave him the creeps just to look at it.

He only grunted between mouthfuls as MacKenzie put him in the picture about the previous day's happenings when he'd been off duty: though the meat and potato pie with onion gravy wasn't Maudie's home cooking, it was sure a hell of a sight better than an empty gut: 'Never go to work on an empty stomach,' his father had always said. He wiped his mouth on the back of his sleeve appreciatively. But then, his father hadn't been a cop, just a shoemaker, a man who wanted his only son to get on in the world, to do better than he had; he'd been a craftsman, good at his job, and taken pride in it, but he wanted his son to have a job that got him respect. Be a cop, son, Delucca senior had told him over and over again. A cop, he gets respect. And, if he works hard, he can get on in the world, rise up the ladder. Delucca grimaced to himself. He was thirty-six, with more than ten years' service behind him, and he was still just a sergeant in the detective division; and no matter how hard he worked he never got on or got higher: Chief Rawlins had seen to that. 'Some guys' faces don't fit,' a cynical beat cop had told him once, a long time ago – clear as glass that in Rawlins' eyes, his didn't. Rawlins bawled him out in front of the whole department if he made the slightest mistake, and sent him on crap cases to places he hated like Chinatown or the slums on the Lower East Side. Delucca, always a man to harbour a grudge, wouldn't forget that.

No, he was never going places, never in with a chance at the big time while Chief Rawlins was in charge.

'Hey, Roy.' MacKenzie was plucking at his arm. 'It's a quarter before nine already. Reckon we'd best be headed on down to Little Italy.'

Yeah, yeah.' Delucca had been miles away. He was warm and he was full and he didn't want to move from where he was. 'Say, Mac . . . you got a cigarette on you? We got a little time left yet.'

They'd finished in Little Italy earlier than they'd expected, and got names to follow up – but no firm addresses. The time they'd saved at the start of their shift soon evaporated as they went from door to door in the Lower East Side. More than once, Delucca wondered if they'd been sent on a fool's errand, fed a pack of lies just to get rid of them while the guys they'd questioned back in Little Italy did a runner upstate. Delucca cursed. This was the typical kind of case Chief Rawlins liked sending him and his partner on – what had started out as a simple, straightforward job of getting to the bottom of the who and why of a knife fight on Spring and Bowery was turning into a night-time runaround.

With their local knowledge, asking here and there, they got a lead on a possible witness by a quarter after ten. Neither MacKenzie nor Delucca liked the look of the dark, narrow alley that led to the front of the tenement building on Allen and Bowery Street: simultaneously, they reached inside their overcoats to feel for their Smith and Wesson pistols; second nature to a New York City cop venturing into the labyrinths of the Lower East Side after dark.

'We'll knock on this door first, ask some questions, OK?' No point in wasting time traipsing six floors up if their potential witness was out or wasn't here at all. Delucca just hoped that his hunch was right and they hadn't come, as he'd feared, on a fool's errand: it wouldn't be the first time some shit-scared Polak had given them the wrong information just to get them off his back – come to think of it, what was a Polak doing living in Little Italy anyhow? He didn't like the smell of things.

'C'mon, c'mon,' MacKenzie hissed between clenched teeth when there was no instant response to his loud pounding on the door. Eventually, they heard footsteps on the other side, the sound of bolts slowly being drawn back. Then the door opened a few inches and an old woman peered around it, her sunken eyes full of suspicion and fear. No good ever came from strange callers this late at night.

'English? You understand English?'

'Little.'

'Grozinski . . . you heard that name before? Anyone of that name live here?'

'T'ird floor . . . up there . . .' She jabbed a crooked finger towards the stairs. They turned away without thanking her and went up the filthy stairwell, Delucca first. They struck lucky at the fourth door they tried.

The stench inside the one-room apartment made both of them gag; MacKenzie started coughing and reached for his handkerchief; Delucca, with two years' more experience of hassling immigrants, was more inured to their appalling living conditions than his partner.

It was obvious from even a cursory glance around the windowless room that the family was subsisting by doing piecework at home: the whole place was filled with lint and thread from the minute sewing and weaving operations they performed for probably only pennies a day at most. There was a battered stove, barely alight, and beside it a basket which MacKenzie saw, to his horror, contained what looked like a newborn baby. He could see only a single bed. In the bed, lying among filthy and tattered blankets, was a woman, her face turned to the wall, her dark hair streaked with grey and badly matted. At the sound of their voices she turned her head with painful slowness, as if even the effort of something so small was too much. Her skin was prematurely lined and yellowish; she stared at them with hopeless, almost lifeless eyes – eyes that reminded Delucca of the old woman downstairs. She could have been thirty or sixty; it was difficult to tell.

'We're detectives from the New York City Police Department.' Delucca addressed his questions to the man

46

who had opened the door to them. 'We understand that your son – Ladislav, is it? – could be an important witness to a stabbing incident that took place outside an eating house at the corner of Spring and Bowery, two weeks ago. Is he here now?'

MacKenzie's eyes were just becoming used to the dinginess in the room, lit by a single kerosene lamp. Besides the man and the woman in the filthy bed, he counted six children under the age of ten dotted around the room.

'My son, he do nothing wrong . . . we want no trouble . . .'

'I said, is he here now?' Delucca wore his mean look; he narrowed his eyes. Grozinski junior no doubt had wind that the cops were looking for him and had gone to ground somewhere, most likely, Delucca took a shrewd guess, with relatives elsewhere on the Lower East Side; unless he was invisible, or under the rickety bed, he certainly wasn't in the room: with three sticks of furniture in the whole place and no window to jump out of, there was nowhere for him to hide.

'He go out . . . he come home later . . . I tell him you call.'

Delucca went over to the bed and looked under it. For a brief moment, the woman lying there stared up at him, and her sunken eyes met his. He screwed up his mouth in disgust; Christ, but the bitch stank! 'This your wife? These kids . . . children . . . they're yours too?'

'Yah. My wife, she is sick. The baby, it sick, too . . .'

'Ladislav. How old is he?'

'Twenty-one.' Delucca and MacKenzie exchanged glances. Delucca raised his eyebrows.

'So you're tellin' us he's twenty-one, while the oldest of these can't be more than nine or ten at most . . . why the big age difference?'

'Ladislav, he son of my first wife . . . she die in old country. Ladislav, he born in old country. I marry again before we come here . . . Ladislav, he only son from my first wife . . .'

'So, you come to America, and all these kids were born here?' Delucca turned aside to his partner. 'They come here, bring nothin', just turn lower Manhattan into a sewer

47

and breed like rabbits. Some guy gets knifed in Little Italy and you want some co-operation to make life easier for yourself, and what do you get? The runaround.'

'Wherever he is, he ain't here, Roy. We're wastin' our time.'

'You wanna bet?' Delucca lifted his voice to its normal pitch and turned back to Grozinski senior. 'You expectin' Ladislav back tonight? Do you know where he is now?'

'He go out . . . he meet with friends. I don't know where.' He started to cough. 'I not know when he be back. Maybe soon, maybe not.'

'Now you listen to me, Polak, and you listen good.' Delucca went as close to him as he could bear to; he smelled like he hadn't washed for a week. 'We're not takin' no more shit from you – you lie to me, an' I'll have you downtown behind bars sooner than you can say chutzpah . . . you got that, schmuck?'

'I no lie . . .'

'I ain't finished talkin' yet.' Delucca looked at him as if he was something he'd just trodden in. 'You fuck me around, I can make life real difficult for you people . . . you push it, an' I'll have immigration on your back investigatin' a list of charges you never even dreamed of . . . lyin' to get your papers rubber-stamped at Ellis Island, ineligibility for US citizenship, harbourin' a suspected criminal, evading police questioning . . . and that's just for starters!' The man was really terrified now; he started to blubber but Delucca cut him short. 'You got any idea of the penalties for evading police questioning, for harbouring a criminal? You know what could happen to you and your family if you're caught? Guess. That's right . . . you get kicked right back where you came from.' He sneered with a perverted sense of satisfaction as the threat went home: deportation was a fate far worse than prison to a family like the Grozinskis.

'No, no, mister! We do no wrong! My son, he done no wrong! He saw a fight . . . yes. But he nothing to do with it, he take no part, he want no part. No trouble. I tell him, always I tell him . . . son, you keep out of trouble. He good boy. He do that. Please, mister, you believe me. I tell truth.'

'OK. That's better. Now, we're gettin' somewhere. The boy saw the fight in Little Italy. We need to talk to him about exactly what he saw. That's why we're here.' He nodded at MacKenzie. 'When he gets back . . . the minute he gets back, we want to see him. You got that. Right away. We want him down at the precinct to make a statement.'

'You tell him if he doesn't show up,' MacKenzie put in, 'you're all in big trouble. Got it?'

'Yah, yah, I tell him. I come with him and he make statement.'

Delucca cast a last disparaging glance around the filthy, cramped little room before turning on his heel and walking out. Halfway down the stairwell, he spoke.

'Dirty Polak bastards . . . filth like that, they come here with nothin' and get made American citizens!' He spat on the ground. 'I tell you, Mac, that sticks right in my guts!'

'Ain't nothin' we can do about it, though.'

'You see the *state* of that fuckin' room? Jesus, you *smell* it? I reckon they all go to the can in there!' They'd reached the bottom of the stairs now. 'And you see that baby? You ever see or hear a baby like that before? I mean, babies – they scream, they cry, they move . . . that one sure as hell wasn't like any baby I saw before. It just laid there, like a dead thing. Not a whimper, not a wriggle; nothin'. Just like the woman.' MacKenzie nodded. 'How old you reckon she was, huh? Couldn't tell, just like me. But you see her face, you smell her? And that Polak guy sleeps with her! How you figure that?'

'She's his wife.' MacKenzie shrugged. In all the time he'd been a cop and hassling suspects down on the Lower East Side, he'd been in plenty of tenement buildings and most of the women looked exactly the same, wherever they'd come from. First time he'd been involved in a bust, coming east of Manhattan had been a culture shock for him, like entering another, alien world. He'd heard every language under the sun except English; the great metropolis was a mare's nest, its slums as awful as anything he'd heard about in Russia, or Warsaw, in some places much worse. There was terrible poverty at every turn, the most crowded living conditions he'd ever seen. Communities of immigrants speaking their native tongues, with pushcarts and small shops, thrived as though entire city blocks from eastern Europe had been set down there. Newspapers seemed to be in every language except English. A whole world away from the elegant mansions on Fifth Avenue and the smart, fashionable shops in upper Manhattan, the theatres, the private carriages. 'So, what now?'

'We wait, that's what. Till the Grozinski punk comes back . . . then we grab him.' Delucca indicated a suitable hiding place near the top of the opposite alley. 'You think I believed that Polak bastard when he said he'd send him down the precinct to make a statement about what he saw? No way.'

'But you scared the shit outa him, Roy. I reckon he'll make sure the kid toes the line.'

'You wanna bet on that? I know these Polak sonofabitches. Soon as they find out what I said'd happen to 'em if they didn't co-operate is a bunch of crap, chances are the whole fuckin' family'll disappear. And then I'll have Rawlins screamin' down my neck! We stay.'

'The state of that woman and that baby, I don't reckon they're goin' anywhere . . . except maybe six feet down.'

Delucca took out the cigarettes he'd bought on the walk downtown and offered the packet to MacKenzie before lighting up himself. He tossed the spent match irritably on the ground.

'Best place for 'em. Fuckin' Polaks.'

It was almost two hours later before a thin, shadowy figure came into view and, casting a furtive glance across his shoulder, let himself into the tenement building across the dark, deserted street. Silently, finger to his lips, Delucca threw away his half-smoked cigarette and gave his partner the nod; together they followed the young man inside, up the stairwell, careful to walk on tiptoe, careful not to make a sound, even an indrawn breath, in case he turned round suddenly and saw them. It was only when he'd reached the third floor and had called softly through the keyhole for his father to let him in that Delucca and MacKenzie pounced.

'Ladislav Grozinski junior?'

'I done nothing, I done nothing wrong!'

Delucca stuck the muzzle of his Smith and Wesson brutally into the small of Grozinski's back. 'You're comin' with us downtown to make a statement about the knifing you saw in Little Italy. Get movin', you piece of garbage.'

CHAPTER FIVE

For Marianna, it was a curious feeling of elation mixed with nervousness as she walked into the entrance hall of the New Amsterdam Bank on Broadway by herself, for the very first time. This was her third visit; the first, on her twenty-first birthday, when she'd been accompanied by her parents and had received great deference from the manager, had been to hear in detail the conditions of her trust fund; the second, only a few weeks ago, to make her first personal withdrawal so that she could buy a hat that her mother disapproved of. Though her father had summoned her to his study the day after her birthday and given her a long lecture on recognizing the importance and value of money, having financial independence was a comforting feeling. No longer would she have to submit to having her choice of clothes overruled by her mother on shopping expeditions; now, she could simply please herself. On her last visit, her mother had been with her and she'd withdrawn only enough money to enable her to buy the hat they'd disagreed about; today, she wanted money for something else. Even more frivolous, her parents would no doubt have criticized, if they'd known. She was determined to attend the matinee at the Metropolitan. Almost three weeks after she'd first seen the play with her mother and father, she still hadn't been able to get the image of Curt Koenig out of her mind.

She walked to a free table in the Ladies' Department, and sat down. She looked around her, to where another customer was seated, writing out a deposit slip at a neighbouring table. On each table, there were two stacks of slips: one for deposits, the other for withdrawals. There was also a clean, hide-edged blotter, a brass inkstand and two pens. The room was long and narrow, quite unlike any other part of the bank; almost cosy, with carpet on the floor and real Persian rugs, comfortable chairs and potted plants, and even a Negro maid to serve refreshments at one end of the room, in a white starched apron. But Marianna was in too much of a hurry today to be tempted to take advantage of the New Amsterdam Bank's modern refinements; the matinee of *Under the Red Robe* began in less than half an hour.

She filled out a withdrawal slip, blotted it carefully, and took it to the counter in the main banking hall. No doubt she'd drawn out far more than she really needed, but a hundred dollars would last her for the entire month. It was a heady sensation, knowing that she had a hundred thousand dollars in her trust fund account, and could do almost anything she wanted, buy anything she saw that took her eye. She smiled at the clerk as he counted out the money in ten-dollar bills, then folded the crisp new notes in half and slipped them into her handbag. As she turned to leave, she glanced up towards the large clock in the banking hall: almost a quarter after two. She could reach the Metropolitan in time for curtain up if she dispensed with ladylike conventions and ran.

She bought her ticket at the box office and sat as close to the stage as she could; somehow, it seemed the height of daring to come here completely alone and sit among total strangers because she was longing to see a young actor called Curt Koenig who had completely captivated her. Once she was seated, she fidgeted nervously with her gloves, stealing glances to left and right just in case there was anyone sitting close by whom her parents knew; but she was blissfully anonymous. As the curtain rose, her heart began to race with sheer excitement and anticipation. She was here, she was close to the footlights, within feet of her new-found idol, a world away from the remoteness of her father's splendid private box. Moments before she knew Curt Koenig would come on stage during the second act, tremors of delight ran through her; when he appeared, the sheer thrill of it all was almost too much to bear. He seemed so close that she felt she could reach out and touch him.

The play, the costumes, the scenery, the others on stage might have been invisible: Curt Koenig was the only thing that seemed real to her. When it was over and she was making her way towards the exit at the back of the auditorium, she felt peculiarly self-conscious, as if everyone around her could guess by her over-bright eyes and flushed cheeks why she'd come here today; in truth, she was just one of hundreds who wanted to see the matinee because it was possible on matinee days to sit closer to the stage than for evening performances when the audiences were much larger and contained far more men: afternoon performances were attended almost exclusively by women.

Outside in the street, Marianna felt strangely disorientated, coming from the dim auditorium out into the light. To her annoyance, it had begun to rain; not heavily, but enough to feel unpleasant, and since it had been fine when she'd left home she hadn't brought an umbrella. She also felt a little sick and a little dizzy, and her stomach growled as she began to walk along, in no particular direction; she realized, almost as an afterthought, that that was probably because in her rush to get to the theatre she'd completely forgotten about lunch; she hadn't eaten anything since breakfast.

She stood on the edge of the pavement shading her eyes from the rain, which was coming down more heavily now, but there wasn't a single cab in sight. With some difficulty because of the volume of traffic, she managed to cross the busy main thoroughfare to the opposite side of the street, where the entrance sign of a chop and oyster house caught her eye. A little uncertainly, Marianna peered in through the large windows; though it was certainly not the type of eating establishment that either of her parents would be likely to patronize, and unlike any she'd been inside herself, it looked spotlessly clean and completely respectable. Hunger and the ever-increasing volume of rain finally decided her; she'd go in, find a table and order a meal, and then she could leave as soon as the rain had stopped.

Inside, it was much busier than she'd realized, and she had difficulty in finding an unoccupied table; there was no attentive waiter ready to conduct her to a specially reserved seat, no damask tablecloth and elegant silver condiment set, no place settings on the tables as there always were in the elegant, fashionable restaurants of upper Manhattan where she lunched with her mother – just plain starched white tablecloths, salt, pepper and seafood relish in pewter containers and a napkin in a glass. After sitting for a minute or two she was spotted by a harassed waitress who hurried over to take her order.

While she waited, Marianna discreetly looked around her. The other tables were mostly crowded, and there was a loud volume of chatter, laughter and clattering knives and forks, a far cry from the refined surroundings of the exclusive Broadway restaurants she was used to. The clientele, she observed, were mostly shoppers and office workers, certainly not the types to be seen in places like Muschenheim's or Del Monico's; not that they could have afforded their prices. As she ate her meal – surprised at how tasty it was – Marianna reflected that her parents would certainly be shocked that their daughter was eating lunch in a chop and oyster house in the company of folk they usually had very little to do with.

She had almost finished eating – she'd left more than half a plateful, since the helpings had been so generous – and was looking in her handbag for change, when a fresh batch of customers came in out of the rain. Without glancing up, Marianna could hear them laughing and complaining how wet they were, and that there didn't seem to be a free table. She half stood up, still trying to fish in the bottom of her leather drawstring bag for the elusive cent pieces, when another voice, a voice she recognized instantly because she'd heard it on stage only an hour or so ago, spoke across the din around them.

'Hey, Shawn! Looks like there's a table free over here . . .'

She looked up in disbelief, and there he was, walking

towards her. Out of costume, he looked different but was as striking, more handsome, than he'd seemed on stage; this was the real flesh and blood man. His strong athletic build was even more noticeable than it had been before and, up close, there was an earthiness about him that hadn't been evident when she'd watched him on stage because, then, he'd been someone else. He was very wet; rainwater dripped from his clothes and had turned his fair hair into a mass of tight little curls all over his head; this near, she could see his face clearly: he had the bluest eyes Marianna had ever seen.

'Excuse me, are these seats taken?' He was looking directly at her, speaking to her; she drew in her breath sharply. Curt Koenig was speaking to her; to *her*. He was standing on the other side of the table, just two feet away. It scarcely seemed possible, after his remoteness, his inaccessibility of an hour ago.

'No . . . no, they're not. Please, have this table . . . I was just leaving anyway . . .' But she didn't want to leave, she didn't want to stop looking at him and listening to him speak. She cursed her bad luck; why couldn't she have come in later, or they earlier, so she would have had the perfect excuse to stay and talk to him? It was a chance in a thousand that he'd come in while she was here, an ironic twist of fate.

'Say, you haven't finished your meal,' said Koenig's companion, smiling at her. 'You don't have to rush off on our account.'

'No way.'

She felt foolish, tongue-tied; she wasn't used to having social conversations in public places with strange young men, only the false, stilted chit-chat at the carefully selected venues her parents meticulously chose, so that their daughter would only ever mix with those of their own kind, those that they considered to be 'suitable'. Compared to someone like Curt Koenig, how dull and boring they all seemed.

'Thank you.' She sat down, nervously twisting her hands together beneath the table, trying desperately to hide her lack of composure. Then she realized that both of them had caught sight of her theatre programme.

'You were at the performance this afternoon?' Curt Koenig said, with genuine surprise; he seemed startled to have come suddenly and unexpectedly face to face with a member of the audience. 'Did you like the play?'

'I thought it was marvellous. Wonderful.' They were the only two words that had come into her head and they sounded so stilted, so clichéd, so inadequate to describe what seeing him on stage had meant to her, but face to face with her idol her mind had turned to stone. She could scarcely believe that here she was, within touching distance of him, that he was looking at her, speaking to her. The crowded tables, the babble of conversation and laughter and the harassed waitresses going up and down with plates of food, all faded into insignificance. The only person she saw was him. 'I've seen the play twice; the first time, at one of the evening performances, with my parents. But I just had to see it again.' She remembered the programme in her hand. 'I wonder . . . could you, would you, sign this for me? Oh . . . I don't even have a pen!' She was fumbling clumsily in her handbag when Koenig's companion produced a fountain pen from his top coat pocket. 'Thank you.'

Curt Koenig opened the programme to the page where the names of the cast were displayed, then glanced up at her with his bright, charismatic blue eyes. 'What's your name, Miss . . .?'

Marianna coloured. 'Marianna Eastbridge.'

'Marianna Eastbridge.' He smoothed down the page and wrote something in his large, upright, flowing script, then handed back the programme. Her hands were shaking slightly as she took it from him; they briefly brushed against his. 'Thank you. Thank you so very much.'

'My pleasure.'

They stood up when she did, squeezing her way past the tables towards the front of the restaurant, where she paid her bill; when she looked back, they'd both sat down and were giving the waitress their order.

Marianna put her change into her handbag, willing him

to turn round and look at her, but he never did. Most likely, he'd forgotten her face and her name the minute she'd said goodbye and got up from the table.

Outside, she opened her precious programme and eagerly turned to the page he'd written on. *To Marianna Eastbridge . . . Cordially, Curt Koenig, 1897.* She touched the signature, traced it gently with the tip of her finger. To shield it from the rain, she slid the programme under her coat and began to walk in the direction of upper Manhattan. After several minutes of fruitless searching, she caught sight of a cab and hailed it.

Her mother was waiting to pounce on her the moment she reached home.

'Marianna! It's almost five o'clock . . . where on earth have you been? Ada Depew called to invite you to make up a foursome for the theatre, and she's waiting for you to call back. Really, you might show some consideration . . . I didn't know what to say to her.' Her strident voice echoed around the hall. 'They're going to the Metropolitan, for *Under the Red Robe* . . . do you want to go, since you've seen it already?'

'Nice girl,' Shawn Duchovsky said, laying down his knife and fork on a plate so clean that it looked as if it had been washed and polished. 'She sure liked you . . . wish I could get the broads to look at me that way! Jeez, but did you give her outfit the once-over, huh? That stuff she was wearin', that was top-drawer upper Manhattan. That was real class. Hey, I wonder what a girl like that was doin' eatin' in here?'

Curt shrugged and finished off his coffee. For the last five minutes, he'd been trying to catch the waitress's eye to ask for their bill. 'Shawn, she just wanted her programme signed, that's all. Why make such a big deal out of it?'

'I'm just sayin', I'm just sayin' . . . anyhow, don't you reckon she was good-lookin'?'

'If you like your girls stiff and starchy. She wasn't my type.'

* * *

The Depews and the Eastbridges had known each other since Jefferson B. Depew had run for Governor eight years before and Frederick H. Eastbridge III had been one of the major backers in his campaign. Though he hadn't been elected and had had to settle for deputy status, the two men had been united in various business ventures since, and F.H. was a major shareholder in the Depew railroad company, responsible for the building of the New York City elevated railway. From similar social backgrounds – F.H. was Harvard-educated, Depew had graduated from Yale – they'd both married into respected old New England families, and their wives were both daughters of wealthy men. In their well-to-do circles, it was tacitly understood that they expected their offspring to follow in their footsteps: like to marry like. Since the age of eighteen, Marianna had known that her parents would welcome an alliance between their only daughter and one of the Depew sons.

Since Jefferson junior had recently become engaged – indeed, he and his fiancée were one half of the foursome destined for the Metropolitan that evening – Marianna correctly surmised that his younger brother Thomas would be her escort: personable enough to look at, but otherwise one of the biggest bores she'd ever met. Invited to his brother's engagement party, Marianna had found him standing at her elbow every time she turned round, and he'd talked of little else except baseball and his father's companies: she'd escaped into the ladies' powder room to get rid of him. Faced with having to spend a whole evening with him again, she would have told her mother she had a headache or stomach cramps and asked her to telephone Mrs Depew with her excuses, but a chance to see Curt Koenig on stage at the Metropolitan for the third time was something she just couldn't miss. Ignorant of the real reason behind Marianna's eagerness to accept the invitation, Edwina Eastbridge reported to her husband in his study while their daughter was getting ready upstairs.

'They seem to get on well together, F.H. Even Ada

Depew's noticed how taken he is with her. And she likes him, I'm sure. When she went to Jefferson's engagement party, Ada said that every time she saw her Thomas was just two paces behind all evening.'

'Pity he isn't the eldest . . . though I dare say Depew's arranged things so that the companies are equally shared. Jeff has no real head for business . . . Thomas is the one with all the drive.' F.H. put away his stock market papers and closed the desk drawer; he might envy Depew his two sons, but the elder was living proof that even great men can breed mistakes: Thomas had the bigger share of brains out of the two of them, younger son or not. 'You could be right . . . after all, it's early days yet. This birthday party at the Hotel Astor . . . the invitation from the Lauterbachs . . . you've seen that she's accepted?'

'She didn't seem overly enthusiastic about it.'

'See that she does.' F.H. had opened another ledger and picked up his gold Waterman fountain pen, a sure sign that he still had important business papers to read over and wanted to be left alone. 'When his father dies, Jerry Lauterbach's going to be one hell of a powerful man in this city.'

After almost a quarter of a century of marriage to a man like F.H., Edwina knew exactly what she was expected to say and do.

'I'll speak to her about it before she goes out this evening.'

Marianna already knew just what she would wear; for the first time since her aunt and uncle had brought it as a twenty-first birthday gift back from Worth in Paris, she took the evening gown from her huge wardrobe and held it against herself in the floor-length mirror. It was an exquisite thing, of ivory satin with an overlaid garniture and bodice in matching ivory tulle, the centre of the bodice and the overskirt all embroidered in tiny brilliants. Though she needed her maid Betty's help to be laced tightly into her waist-minimizing corset, the moment the gown was on and fastened she sent her away.

She sat down in front of her dressing-table mirror and opened her jewel box.

She rejected the gold and opal necklace with matching bracelet and earrings that her Ayres grandmother had given her; somehow, it detracted from, instead of enhancing, the effect of the gown. Her single rope of pearls also looked wrong; they hung too low down the bodice, almost to her waist; she returned them to the box. The emerald choker was also no good; green clashed with the brilliants sewn on the overskirt of her gown. Finally, she chose a collar of pearls and diamonds, also with matching bracelet and earrings, which her parents had given her when she'd come of age. As she was studying the overall effect, her mother entered her bedroom without knocking.

'You're ready, then?' Though Marianna knew that she looked her best, striking, even, she also knew that she could expect no kind of compliment from her mother; personal vanity, any drawing of attention to oneself, had always been strictly frowned on. She realized, meeting her mother's cold eyes in the mirror, that Momma was frowning now.

'Yes, Momma. I'm all ready. Except for my cape.' She picked up her long gloves and began to draw them on.

'That neckline is too low for a young unmarried girl like you', Edwina said critically. 'You should have tried the gown on before, when your Aunt May first brought it back from Paris. I'll have to get Betty to sew a piece of lace or satin around the top of the bodice . . . your father won't allow you to go out to the theatre dressed like that.' She rang the bell.

'But, Momma . . . you'll ruin it! This is a Worth original, you can't have bits of material sewn on, they won't match!'

'You either do something to cover yourself up or you take it off and put on something else. When men see women showing too much décolleté, what, exactly, do you suppose they think? That she's a hussy; a tramp. Do you want them to look at you and think that?' Marianna's face flushed scarlet with embarrassment. 'I always did think that gown was far too old for you . . . it's much more suitable for a woman of thirty than for a young girl of your age. May never did have any judgement about clothes . . .' She was interrupted by Betty coming into the bedroom in answer to the bell. 'Betty, help Miss Marianna off with that gown and then fetch the sewing box. I'll go to my room and see if I can find some material or a piece of lace to match. I shan't be long.'

'Yes, ma'am.' Betty did as she was told and kept her thoughts to herself. There was nothing wrong with the way the gown looked that she could see, in fact she'd never seen Miss Marianna look so handsome. Hanging the gown away after she'd unwrapped it on her birthday, Betty had seen the Worth label stitched inside and had been very impressed. After all, everyone knew that gowns that came from famous couturiers in Paris were the best, the most fashionable, the chicest in the world. No doubt about it, with or without an extra bit of lace sewn across the top of the bodice, she'd turn more than a few heads at the Metropolitan tonight. Going to fetch the sewing box, Betty pondered on her six months' employment in the Eastbridge household and decided that within the next week or two she'd tell a few white lies about her mother being taken ill, so she could leave, and with a good reference; six months' service in a place as strict as the Eastbridges' was more than enough for her liking. She'd stay for a while with her married sister in Queens while she looked for something else, and with a reference from the Eastbridges on Fifth Avenue she reckoned she could pick and choose. But she'd had her fill. The maid she'd replaced six months ago had been fired because Mrs Eastbridge had seen her kissing her sweetheart outside on the sidewalk.

She took the sewing box back to Miss Marianna's bedroom and stood holding out the Worth gown while her mistress held pieces of lace against the bodice to see if they matched.

'None of them is the right colour, Momma!'

'Nonsense. Betty, hold that bodice higher up, towards the light.' Finally, a piece was selected. 'This will do. Now cut it to size and then sew it across here, so there's a ruched effect . . . it's almost a perfect match.' She ignored the expression on her daughter's face. 'Details are so important. . . make sure it's your neatest stitching. Then you can help Miss Marianna dress again.' She went out, brooking no further argument.

'It'll look fine when I've finished it, Miss Marianna.' Marianna was standing there miserably in her petticoats.

'It's a Worth gown, Betty! The whole look will be ruined!'

'Best do as Mrs Eastbridge says.'

'Wait a minute. Just use loose stitches, stitches that can be unpicked again easily . . . and give me the smallest pair of embroidery scissors that you've got.' A flash of rebellion. She was twenty-one now, a grown woman with her own money, her own ideas about what she wanted. Although women's suffrage hadn't yet been achieved in New York, if she'd lived in Wyoming, Colorado, Idaho or Utah she would have been old enough to vote. It seemed an outrage that her mother was still insisting on controlling almost every aspect of her life, even down to the clothes she wore.

'What are you goin' to do, Miss Marianna?' asked a wide-eyed Betty, although she'd already half guessed.

'I'm going to go to the ladies' cloakroom when we get to the theatre, and unpick it all. I'll be wearing my cape when I come home and Momma won't even know what I've done, because I'll get undressed straight away and you'll hang the gown back in my wardrobe.'

Betty handed her the smallest pair of embroidery scissors she could find in the sewing box. 'I'll make the stitches as easy as I can for you to unpick, Miss Marianna. I just hope Mrs Eastbridge never finds out.'

The atmosphere in any theatre before an evening performance was a world away from the atmosphere before an afternoon matinee. The matinee audiences consisted almost exclusively of women, come chiefly to admire the costumes, the romantic theme of the play and the popular actors of the day; few, except perhaps William Gillette, Edwin Booth or E. H. Sothern in his prime, could fill a theatre like Otis Skinner. By contrast, an evening performance was a social occasion, to which the ladies came resplendent in their jewels and evening gowns, and their escorts always wore formal evening dress.

Garlands of fresh flowers – hot-house flowers in autumn and winter – as often as not festooned the private boxes around the crowded auditorium; diamonds winked and glittered in the soft muted light and ladies fanned themselves as they waited in eager anticipation for curtain up. After unpicking the superfluous insert of lace Betty had tacked along the top of her neckline, Marianna had hurried from the ladies' cloakroom and made her way to the Depews' private box, where the others were discussing their invitations to the Lauterbach birthday party at the Hotel Astor.

'You know, old man Lauterbach's always been a big patron of the theatre . . . word is, he's one of the chief backers for the next Frohman production . . . a stage version of *The Count of Monte Cristo*, so I heard. I also heard that Charles Frohman is going to be one of the guests at Jerry Lauterbach's party. Unconfirmed, but the two things together are too much of a coincidence for it not to be true.'

Marianna pricked up her ears; she sat down between Thomas Depew and his brother's fiancée. 'Oh? I hadn't heard anything about that. Has it been cast yet?'

'Frohman most likely has principal players in mind – probably John Drew as Edmond Dantes and Maud Adams for Mercedes – but I doubt if the script has even been finished yet. I expect he's commissioned either Clyde Fitch or David Belasco to write it.' Thomas Depew lowered his voice as the lights dimmed and the curtain went up. 'People in the know are predicting that it'll be the biggest sensation of the year . . . particularly with an actor of Drew's stature and drawing power in the title role.'

Marianna fell silent, turned her attention to the figures on stage. Curt Koenig wouldn't make an entrance until the second act, and meanwhile she let her mind absorb the possibilities opened up by their discussion of Frohman's next play – and something else, that had concerned her all week.

Until recently, her parents would never have permitted her to accept an invitation to the theatre unless they themselves intended to be present; latterly, her father had been doing business with Jefferson senior, and there had been several visits to the Depew house on West 54th Street; did it mean anything significant, Marianna wondered? True, Ada Depew and her mother had been on calling terms for a number of years, but this was the first time an evening foursome to the theatre had been suggested, and Mrs Depew would never have made the suggestion if she knew that her mother would disapprove of it. Marianna stole a sideways glance at Thomas: did he know something about their mothers' machinations that she did not? It would have been unthinkable to ask him outright, almost as unthinkable even to hint; and, if she was wrong, the sheer embarrassment would be so great that she'd never be able to look him in the eye again and her parents would be furious. One thing she knew for sure: the last thing on earth she wanted to be was Mrs Thomas Depew, no matter how rich and important and powerful the Depews were in New York City, no matter how high Thomas stood in her father's esteem. To move from Fifth Avenue to West 54th Street would merely be to exchange one kind of gilded imprisonment for another.

She turned her attention back to the play, impatiently counting the minutes till he appeared on stage. When he did, she could feel her heart racing again as it had at the matinee and afterwards when she'd met him face to face; she could feel the strange hot flush all over, the burning sensation in her cheeks; she was thankful that the lights were low, so that the others couldn't see her. She felt unbearably excited, elated, almost guilty – what if he had a sweetheart, what if – unbearable thought, but perfectly possible – he was married? She couldn't bring herself to even think about it. But he was handsome, charming, charismatic . . . was it likely that a man as powerfully attractive as Curt Koenig could still be single? And even if he was, what then? They inhabited such totally different worlds – his, she knew virtually nothing about at all – that the chance that they might meet again seemed so remote as to be almost impossible. Yet as she sat there with her eyes riveted to the stage, watching his every movement and hanging on his every word, something – refusal to accept the obvious, some faint glimmer of hope – made her think of what might lie beyond the barriers that separated them.

It was as the party was coming down the main staircase from the upper floor at the end of the evening that she spotted a face she remembered at once – the young man who'd been with Curt Koenig in the chop and oyster house that afternoon. Almost simultaneously, he saw her too and smiled, but he was too far away, and too hemmed in by the dispersing crowds to come over to her. He was close enough, none the less, to overhear someone else greet her escort, and catch the name Depew. That was when he suddenly made the connection. Eastbridge. She'd said her name was Marianna Eastbridge. But it couldn't be the same Eastbridge, could it?

'That wasn't who I thought it was, was it?' he asked the doorman, when the foyer had cleared and almost everyone had gone.

'The Depew brothers . . . their old man ran for Governor a few years ago. Didn't get elected, but with their dough, what did it matter? Eldest one's just got engaged to Senator Sutton's daughter.'

'No, I meant the other young lady . . . the one in the cape and the white dress.'

'That was Miss Eastbridge. Frederick H. Eastbridge's daughter. She's bin to see this play three times in a single week.'

'Frederick H. Eastbridge? The financier? You kiddin' me or what?'

'Now why'd I want to do that?'

'Curt, it's true . . . hand on my heart! I just seen her. Miss Eastbridge, old George said . . . F. H. Eastbridge's

66

daughter. You know who F. H. Eastbridge is? Just one of the biggest financiers in New York, that's all . . . and his daughter asked you to sign her programme! I told you, didn't I? That girl was class.'

Curt looked thoughtful. 'What would Eastbridge's daughter be doin' in that place? I'd have thought those fancy Manhattan restaurants where they charge a week's wages for a steak were more her style. Did she recognize you?'

'Yeah, I smiled at her and she smiled right back.' He chuckled. 'That stuffed shirt she was with sure gave me a filthy look. The Depews, old George said; when some guy spoke to 'em as they were leavin', I recognized the name straight away.'

Curt went on taking off his greasepaint. 'She must be gettin' married to one of 'em.'

'That's what you oughta do . . . marry money, someone whose family name can make things smoother for you. It happens. When you got a name like Depew or Eastbridge people sit up and take notice; you don't have to stand on a ladder and shout to make yourself heard.' He pulled a stool towards him and perched on it. 'You take this new production of Frohman's . . .'

'The *Monte Cristo* adaptation that Clyde Fitch and Belasco are working on?'

'Yeah. Now, I know Frohman's most likely got John Drew earmarked for the big part, but you'd make a great Mondego. Just take auditions for that as a small example. If you had clout, a family name people remembered, you'd be more likely to get picked than if your name was John Doe.'

'So what are you suggesting I do? Change my name to Astor or Guggenheim? Anyhow, Frohman isn't that kind of producer . . . he cares about talent, not pedigree. And even if I went along and auditioned for Mondego's part, he'd probably tell me that I didn't have enough experience for a role that big.'

'You're not hearin' me, are you, meathead? George said that the Eastbridge girl had been in to see the play three times this week . . . so what does that tell you? She likes the play and she likes you. A little subtle name-dropping never did anyone any harm, is what I'm sayin'. Do I have to spell it out? If Frohman hears the word "Eastbridge" even he's bound to sit up and take notice.'

'You're crazy!' Curt went behind his screen and peeled off his stage costume. 'Hey, do something useful and throw me my clothes! Look, what difference does it make if Eastbridge's daughter liked the play . . .? Maybe she had other reasons for coming. Maybe she had nothing better to do, maybe she just saw someone in the street she wanted to avoid and came in here so they wouldn't see her . . . who knows why women do anything? In any case, it doesn't matter one way or the other; as far as I know F. H. Eastbridge isn't a patron of the arts and he's certainly never put any of his money into the theatre.'

'OK, OK . . . point taken. But who's to say that that couldn't change in the future? I mean, she bein' his only daughter an' all . . . the blue-eyed girl . . . she could maybe persuade him?'

Curt finished dressing, came out from behind the screen. He picked up a comb and began smoothing down his unruly, curly fair hair. 'Shawn, that's too many "maybes" for me. She's simply a spoiled society girl with time on her hands who just happened to spend it coming to this theatre three times in one week. So next week, she'll be interested in something else. Those kind of girls are like that.'

Shawn Duchovsky shrugged. 'Hey, what you say we go down the village, have somethin' to eat and find us a couple of swell-lookin' broads to have fun with? I could sure use some!'

'Yeah . . . why not?'

'And this new production of Frohman's? You taking my advice and going for the Mondego part? Remember. Nothin' ventured, nothin' gained.'

'What do you think? It could be my big break.' Curt reached for his coat. 'I didn't have a big fight with my dad and leave Minneapolis just to spend the rest of my life sharing a room in Queens with you – and giving him and that big-headed brother of mine the satisfaction of saying, "I told you so" when I don't do all the things I set out to do. No way. When . . . if I go back, I want them to admit that I was right about the stage and they were wrong.' There was a hard, steely purpose in his eyes now. 'I want to make it, Shawn . . . no matter how hard it is, whatever it takes, whatever it costs.'

Outside the theatre, the Depew carriage was already parked and waiting.

'Who was that just now, Marianna? I didn't recognize him.'

'You wouldn't. He's a friend of one of the actors in the cast.' She smiled, deliberately making light of it. 'I bumped into them yesterday, when I was having lunch.' Her heart was beating very fast again. Even to think about him, how close he'd stood to her, the thrill it gave her that he knew her name, made her feel incredibly excited, something none of them could ever understand in their dull, insulated world of finance and city politics. But she was quick to change the subject. If either of the Depews realized that she'd struck up a conversation in public with two strange men to whom she'd never been formally introduced, they'd almost certainly mention it to their mother; and Ada Depew, busybody that she was, wouldn't hesitate to stir up trouble by telling hers. When the portals of the Fifth Avenue house came in sight, Marianna almost breathed a sigh of relief.

'I'll see you inside,' Tom Depew said, and held out his arm. He asked no more awkward questions, did not mention the incident in the foyer to her mother when Edwina wanted to know if they'd run into any friends at the theatre. He'd forget, Marianna thought, as she undressed later and gave the Worth gown to Betty to hang away, by the time he got back to the Depew house on West 54th Street. She should have known a Depew better.

CHAPTER SIX

It had been another hell of a day at the precinct. A murder one suspect had escaped when the only witness they'd had had done a runner upstate, the downstairs cells were fit to bust with last night's drunks and Chief Rawlins was bawling his head off about sloppy paperwork and inefficiency. After a whole week working nights down on the Lower East Side, Delucca felt as if he was sleepwalking even when he was awake.

Ready to go off duty at last, he'd tidied his desk, finished writing his report, put his feet up and lit a cigarette, when someone stuck their head around his door.

'Hey, Roy . . . Chief Rawlins wants you in his office . . . like right now.'

'What the fuck does that guy want with me? I'm outa here in a couple of minutes!'

'Don't bank on it.' The head disappeared and the door closed.

Delucca let loose a string of oaths, stubbed out the cigarette butt and made his way reluctantly to the chief's office, five minutes' walk away in another part of the building. Delucca could hear him shouting down the telephone on the other side of the door, ranting at some poor sap who probably didn't understand what had hit him. He had to count to ten before he knocked and went in.

'You wanted to see me before I go off duty, sir?' The 'sir' definitely stuck in the gullet; and Delucca emphasized the words off duty'. It was as well to remind a slave-driving bastard like Rawlins that his overworked men had homes to go to, even if he didn't.

Rawlins slapped a bunch of papers down on his desk.

'That bust I sent you and MacKenzie on, the one in Little Italy. You said you had the guy, the witness, the statements to tie it all in . . . I wanted it all signed, sealed and delivered for the DA's office this Monday. Now there's another witness, ready to swear that the guy you got down for the knifing was somewhere else when it happened.'

'They're lyin'!'

'Course they're lyin' . . . do you think I don't know that?' Why did Rawlins always manage to make everything he said sound as if Delucca was stupid? 'But I'm not interested in how you make 'em tell the truth, just that you do. I want results, quick. OK?' He sat down in his chair, shoved the top sheet of paper across the desk towards Delucca. 'Forget goin' home till you've sorted this one. I want a retraction from this so-called witness within forty-eight hours, or the suspect walks.'

'Hell, sir . . . I've been on nights for over a week . . . what'll I tell my wife?'

'Tell her what I tell mine. That I'm too busy. Get on it, Delucca. And no fuck-ups over this.'

Delucca sighed angrily and rubbed at his eyes. He picked up the piece of paper with the witness's name and address scrawled across it. S. Mazzoli, Canal Street. Another goddam trek down to Little Italy. 'What's this guy tryin' to say, chief? That he was playin' pool with the suspect while the knifin' took place? Huh, they think we'll fall for that one!'

'It's a she, Delucca. Sophia Mazzoli. And she's sayin' she was in bed with him. Get down there and get me a signed statement that says she wasn't.'

Sophia Mazzoli. Delucca scowled as he pushed his way through the busy corridors back to his office, grabbed his hat and coat and then left the precinct. Most likely, he told himself as he went down the steps and headed south-eastwards downtown, some cheap little tramp who had been paid to give Joey Fabrizio a false alibi just to save his stinking neck. He was in the foulest mood yet; and when he got to Canal Street he fully intended to take out his anger on the lying bitch for sabotaging his free evening off. He'd had it all planned out, and now, because of her, it was ruined.

He'd intended to spend some time with his boys before

Maudie bathed them both and put them to bed, then they'd have sat down to Maudie's roast beef dinner, the hot, home-cooked meal he'd been tasting in his imagination all week, with fried potatoes and onion gravy, and after that, with the boys asleep, they could have gone to bed themselves and made love, something else he hadn't done for so long that he couldn't remember when the last time was. Now all he'd be good for when he finally came home in the early hours was sleep.

He stopped at a roast chestnut stand in lower Manhattan and bought a bag of chestnuts, peeling off the shells and throwing them on the sidewalk as he went. It was a far cry from Maudie's roast dinner, but it was the closest thing to hot food that he was likely to get. It took him almost an hour to find the address in Canal Street that Chief Rawlins had written down for him, another twenty minutes to find the right apartment house. The further he walked, the more he could sense hostile eyes watching him: resentful, wary, suspicious; down in the Lower East Side, they knew that he wasn't one of their own kind, that just by the way he walked, the way he looked, he was a cop. They co-operated because they had to: they knew it and so did he. They wanted to be American citizens and they wanted to be left alone; most of them didn't want any trouble. But Delucca knew, like any other cop back at the precinct, that when you got thousands of immigrants crowded together – poor, unemployed, most of them not even understanding a few words of English – there was always bound to be trouble somewhere along the line.

He kicked back the entrance doors and went up the dingy stairs; they were cleaner than the stairs in the tenement where he and MacKenzie had gone to find the Polak boy, Ladislav Grozinski; a middle-aged Italian woman he met halfway up looked shabby, but her clothes looked clean and she was almost what he might have called respectable, at least for the Lower East Side.

'You know Sophia Mazzoli?'

'Yes. She live in room at top of stairs.' She pointed, and then hurried on. Delucca pummelled on the door.

He heard soft footsteps, a moment's hesitation, then the sound of a chain falling away on the inside. The door opened about half a foot and a young girl's face framed with frizzy dark hair peered out at him.

'Sophia Mazzoli?' She nodded, wordlessly, her eyes full of suspicion and fear. 'My name's Delucca, detective, New York City Police Department.' He stuck his foot in the door in case she tried to close it. 'You know why I'm here. I suggest you let me in so we can talk.'

She did as he said. Inside the apartment, Delucca looked round and found it surprisingly neat and tidy, with a table and chairs, a cupboard, and an iron bed. 'You live alone here?'

'Yes.'

He remained standing, towering over her tiny frame to intimidate her. Though she was small and slender, she had large, rounded breasts, the shape clearly visible through the thin stuff of her blouse; Delucca found himself staring. He'd always liked big-breasted women, and sometimes when he'd been off duty he'd spent time in the nickelodeon parlours on Broadway, where you put in your five cents and, for a few minutes, could peep through the kinetoscope holes to see a dancing girl, or, more daring, a woman undressing. Most department stores, hotels and saloons had had the novelty machines installed for the amusement of passing strollers in the last year or two, and Delucca had often taken his sons to see the more innocent 'flickers' of runaway trains, slapstick comics or performing dogs, much to their delight. With the new advances in the development of the machines, talk was of inventing one that could show real moving pictures on a screen to a whole audience of people, not just one. It seemed incredible to him, as incredible as the bare-faced nerve of this big-breasted Italian broad, who thought she could bust up his whole case by claiming to be Joey Fabrizio's alibi.

'I haven't got time to waste, so we'll make this quick. You say you were with Fabrizio the night Tommy Bellini got knifed in Little Italy? You're sayin' he was here, with you, in bed . . . all night?' She nodded slowly. 'Funny, you never came forward before, when we first busted him. Even more funny, he never even mentioned your name when we hauled him in.'

'He didn't want to involve me! He say, just keep quiet. But I can't, when he's in big trouble. I tell my brother Ricky to come to you and say what happened . . . that it couldn't have been him, because he was here, all the time, with me. He stayed all night . . . from before it get dark to eight o'clock the next morning. I swear it!'

'Anyone else vouch for that? They see him come in, or leave the next day?'

'No, no-one. But he was here. I am telling you the truth.'

'How much is Fabrizio paying you to tell me this pack of garbage? Huh? Or has he got somethin' else on you that you want to tell me about?'

The girl looked horrified. 'He no pay me nothing! I love him, he love me! I tell you, it is the truth!'

'I get it. You love the guy . . . you lie for him to get him off the hook. Forget it, honey. I heard that sob story a thousand times!' He took her roughly by the wrist and shook her, hard. 'Now it's your turn to listen to me; so listen good, you got it? I bin workin' every fuckin' night this week, chasing trash like Joey Fabrizio all over the Lower East Side, and I'm dog sick of it. I haven't seen my wife, or my kids, and the last hot thing I ate was a bag of fuckin' chestnuts, so don't try and waste my time by playing me for a sucker.' She cried out as he tightened his grip on her wrist but he just laughed. 'There's a report on my chief's desk back at the precinct that says Joey Fabrizio's guilty and two witnesses' statements to prove it . . . all nice and tidy till you come along and say different. Now I don't like that; I don't like that at all . . . and I as sure as hell don't feel like tearin' up that report and startin' on it all over again . . . you readin' me?' Tears began rolling down her cheeks. 'I'll give you a day to think things over. Either you change your mind and say Fabrizio was never here – that he offered you money in exchange for an alibi – or I hit you with a rap for prostitution. You choose.'

The girl was trying to talk in between sobs.

'No . . . no . . . it's a lie . . . you can't do that!'

'Honey, I'm a cop in this city and I can do anything I want.'

A sudden thought, another glance at her breasts. Maybe he hadn't wasted his time coming down here, after all. 'Like I said, I'll be back tomorrow. If you're nice to me, I just might make things easy for you. Know what I mean?'

He decided to call in home before he reported back to Chief Rawlins at the precinct; the thought of one of Maudie's hot dinners and the chance to lie back in his easy chair for five minutes was too tempting to resist. If he was late back there were plenty of excuses that he could throw Rawlins' way – like the Mazzoli girl had been out when he'd got to Canal Street and he'd had no choice but to wait around. Hell, Rawlins could go stuff it anyhow.

He gave Maudie a weary kiss and threw himself down on the couch.

'I expected you home earlier than this, Roy. What happened?'

He grimaced and picked up the newspaper. 'Chief Rawlins happened. Called me back in his goddam office just as I was puttin' on my coat to leave.' He flicked over the pages without really reading them: the immigration processing station on Ellis Island had finished being rebuilt from the ramshackle wooden hall it had been to an edifice of brick and iron; Vice-President Hobart was dining with the financier J. P. Morgan; some kid had drowned off the beach on Coney Island; Thomas Edison, the man who had invented the kinetoscope, was bringing a lawsuit against Charles H. Webster, for violating the Patents Act. 'I tell you, Maudie, I'll swing for that guy one day.'

'Don't let him get to you.' She dropped a kiss on the top of his head as she passed by on her way to the kitchen. 'Can you stay to eat, or what?'

'Yeah, why not? Rawlins can bawl me out when I get back to the precinct late, but what the hell? I'm starved.' The bag of hot chestnuts he'd bought on his way to the Mazzoli girl in Canal Street hadn't even started to fill the hole in his belly. 'That dinner sure smells good.'

Maudie brought the food to the table and Delucca tucked into it with relish, but when she didn't start to eat straight

75

away he knew there was something on her mind that he didn't want to hear.

'Roy? I went to see Momma today . . . she was poorly again, real poorly . . .'

'Look, honey . . . I told you before. She puts it on when you visit. When it's time for you to go, she turns on the tears, rolls out the list of aches and pains . . . aw, you should be wise to her by now!'

'It isn't just that, Roy . . . she's lonely. The neighbours look in when they can, but she spends hours on her own, just gazing at Daddy's picture and crying . . . I can't bear to think about it . . . and she says she doesn't see enough of the boys . . .'

Delucca laid down his knife and fork. Now he couldn't even swallow a mouthful of grub without aggravation. At work, it was Chief Rawlins, at home, it was Maudie's mother. He guessed where all this was leading. 'Maudie . . . if she's anglin' to come and live here with us, she can forget it. I told you before . . . no way!'

'I know, Roy . . . but I can't help feeling guilty. After all, me and the boys are all she's got.'

'You're forgettin' that no-good brother of yours! He wasn't stupid, moving out of state to Philadelphia! Why don't you write him and tell him to get off his ass? Tell him you're all washed up lookin' after the old lady and now it's his turn . . . bet he wouldn't even want to know!'

'That's the trouble when you're old; no-one does.' Maudie was just picking at her food. 'Roy . . . I've been thinking . . . how about we all go and see Momma on Sunday, the four of us? She'd love that, wouldn't she? You were going to take the boys over to Prospect Park anyhow, and Flatbush isn't that far away . . . if it's fine, we could take a picnic, sit Momma on one of the benches under the trees . . .'

Delucca wiped his mouth on his napkin. Sunday was the one day off he had coming to him this week. 'You've already told her that we'll take her, right?'

'Well . . . I did kind of promise . . .'

Delucca pushed away his plate, swigged down the rest of his beer and stood up. 'OK, Maudie. OK. If that's what you want, you go sit with her under the trees. With the case we're on now, I don't reckon Rawlins'll let me take Sunday off anyhow. Now, I gotta go back to work. Don't wait up.'

Back at the precinct, Chief Rawlins' office was empty.

'Where's smart-ass? Gone to the can again?' Delucca asked a couple of passing uniformed cops.

'Rawlins? He went home hours ago. Why, what you want him for?'

'It'll keep.' Delucca wandered into the office he shared with MacKenzie at the end of the corridor and took out his cigarettes.

'Hi, Roy. Don't mind if I do.' MacKenzie sat back in his chair as Delucca perched himself on the edge of the cluttered desk and struck a match. 'Thought you was off duty a couple of hours ago. What gives?'

'Tell me about it. Rawlins called me back. Gave me this garbage about our case against Joey Fabrizio bein' busted wide open 'cos a new witness had come forward to give that lowlife an alibi . . . so I had to forget about heading back home and go traipsing all the way down to Little Italy instead to check it out. Asshole.' He inhaled the smoke from his cigarette.

'And?'

'Like I said, it was garbage. This broad, she reckoned Fabrizio had spent the night with her so he couldn't have done the killin' . . . turns out, he paid her to say that. Soon as I laid it on the line about what would happen to her if she was lyin' to me, she spilled her guts.'

'That figures. So now what? I got an hour or so before I'm outa here . . . if you want to stick around and write up your report, I'll shout you for a couple of beers. What you say?'

'You got it.'

When he reached home just after eleven thirty, he saw that Maudie had taken him at his word and already gone to bed; only the light in the lobby was still burning. Delucca took off his hat and overcoat, turned it off and went into the bedroom, half hoping that she hadn't been in bed long and was still lying awake, waiting for him. Hell, they hadn't made love for more than a week – two, almost – and the sudden thought of the Mazzoli girl's big breasts pushing against the thin stuff of her blouse and the effect of the beers he'd drunk made him want to now. But as he pulled back the covers on his side of the bed, he could see that Maudie was already fast asleep.

He climbed in, lay there in the darkness with his hands behind his head, too frustrated to sleep and too tired out to do anything else. In this restless frame of mind, his thoughts often turned to his father. Be a cop, son. A cop, he gets respect. You represent law and order, and people, they look up to you. He hadn't found that, in his experience . . . most people hated cops; leastways, the trash that he had to deal with, day in, day out, hated him, because they were afraid of what he could do. That gave him a buzz, having a kind of power over some people, deciding if he'd turn a blind eye and let them go free – for a price – or let them rot in the city jail. All the backhanders he'd taken in the past had been small time; but other cops that he'd known reckoned that if a guy was patient, some nice little racket on the side more often than not had a way of coming along. Not always in cash. He thought of the Mazzoli girl and had an erection. Yeah, he'd grab himself a piece of that action. She was too stupid, and too shit-scared to cross him; he liked it that way.

He turned over, settled his head into the pillow. Behind him, he could hear the soft rise and fall of Maudie's breathing; when she was asleep, the roof could cave in and she wouldn't hear a sound. He was already thinking of the excuse he'd give her in the morning for being late home again tomorrow night, when he intended to take a little detour to Canal Street and cash in on his investment in Little Italy. Fabrizio's girl would no doubt try to twist and squirm her way out of going to bed with him, but Delucca knew just how to make little tramps like her do what he wanted. He was looking forward to it.

CHAPTER SEVEN

For a moment, Marianna hesitated outside her father's study door before knocking; then she heard his voice and let herself inside. A flash from her childhood came back again: she could remember the study door at the Lake Winnipesaukee house with startling clarity, even though her father had sold it almost nine years ago; maybe it was the way the light reflected on the grain of the wood that reminded her, how the brass doorknob and the elaborate fingerplate would gleam like gold in the morning sunlight. So many times, she'd been summoned peremptorily to her father's presence to answer for some fault or transgression, the image of that study door had never been completely erased from her mind.

She wondered why he wanted to see her now.

Her mother was with him. Perhaps it was her trust fund money – what else? Twice now, she'd gone into the New Amsterdam Bank on Broadway and 59th to make withdrawals of the interest so that she could go shopping, but now that she'd reached twenty-one, surely her parents didn't expect her to ask their permission before every transaction?

'You wanted to see me, Father?'

'Who was the young man you spoke to at the theatre the other evening?' The question took her completely off guard. They were both staring at her intently, critically.

'I didn't speak to anyone.' The old nervousness, the butterflies in the stomach, the thudding heart, all came back; he was treating her just like a naughty child again. 'I did catch sight of someone I met by accident just the day before . . . they smiled at me and I smiled back, just from politeness . . . why, Father?'

'They?'

'He.'

Her father got up from behind his desk. 'Marianna, I think you understand well enough that young women in your position, young women who come from highly respected families, are expected to behave in a certain acceptable way. Society has rules and civilized members of it abide by them. Since your twenty-first birthday, your mother and I have given you a much greater degree of personal freedom, and you now have your own money. I'd expected to see you conducting yourself in a more responsible fashion . . . and remembering that unless someone has been formally introduced to you, you do not simply strike up conversations with them in a public place or in the street. Do you understand what I'm saying to you?'

'Father . . .'

'Now, if you please, kindly answer my question: who was the young man at the theatre?'

'I don't know. Really, I don't even know his name . . .' She tried to make light of it, but they both continued to look at her with faces of stone. 'You see, I went shopping. . . after I'd withdrawn some money from the bank. I thought it would be pleasant to see the play again – *Under the Red Robe* – just because I'd enjoyed it so much the first time. I remembered the matinee performance started at half past two, and as there wasn't time to have lunch before I bought my ticket, I found a restaurant near the theatre afterwards. I'd eaten my meal and I was just about to go, when one of the actors from the cast came in with a friend . . . I didn't know him to speak to, of course . . . but it was, well, a little like knowing someone. It was very crowded, and the table I was leaving was the only table free, so they came towards me as I stood up. I said how much I'd enjoyed the play and I asked him if he'd be kind enough to sign my theatre programme for me. He signed it and I left.' Why were they looking at her like that, as if she'd done something terribly wrong? 'When we were leaving the theatre the other night, Mr Koenig's companion just happened to be in the foyer, and he smiled in my direction. It would have been very impolite to have ignored him, don't you think?'

Her father went back to his desk; there was a theatre programme lying on the blotter. He turned the pages. 'Mr Koenig? You're referring to Curt Koenig?'

'Yes.'

'You, an Eastbridge, behaving like an off-duty maid, striking up a conversation in a public restaurant with an actor! Have you no thought whatsoever for who you are and what your name means in this city?'

'I didn't think! I just acted on impulse! Is there anything wrong with that?'

'Thoughtlessness and impulsiveness are two failings no lady can afford to be guilty of!' Now her mother entered the fray; that was what Marianna remembered from that day whenever she looked back – her father's icy disapproval and her mother's furious anger. 'Have you any idea at all – do you care? – what people who know us would have thought if you'd been seen?'

Marianna was suddenly as angry as they were.

'Curt Koenig was perfectly charming, if you want to know! And as for what other people might have thought if they'd seen us, I don't really think it's any of their business, do you?'

'How dare you speak to your mother and me in that fashion?' His voice was deadly soft, but it struck a chill through her: pictures from her childhood that she'd thought had been long buried and forgotten came back again, like sequences in a nickelodeon: the hand-carved musical box, the treasured scrapbook of cuttings and pressed flowers, the beloved canary that had vanished from its cage – all taken away to punish her for trivial misdemeanours. For the first time, she looked at her parents and realized just how cruel, how callous, they really were. The uncritical child she'd once been had been unable to judge, seeing only figures of respect and authority; the respect that all adults were accorded, authority that was never questioned. The grown Marianna saw something else, something very different.

'Father, why are you and Momma making so much out of such a little thing?'

He got up, hands tucked stiffly behind his back. He walked over to the window and looked down into the street, to the traffic passing to and fro along Fifth Avenue towards midtown Manhattan. Despite her bold words she was suddenly apprehensive, afraid almost, because when she'd been a little girl and he was going to discipline her for something she'd done that he thought warranted punishment, he had always turned his back on her and adopted that very same stance. But what, now, could he do to hurt her?

'You've been brought up to conduct yourself like a lady, as people expect an Eastbridge, and my daughter, would.' He turned round now, and fixed her with those cold, grey, pitiless eyes that had never held even a glimmer of love in them, and she realized that although she wasn't a child any more she was still afraid of him. 'Let me tell you this. A lady's most precious possession is her reputation. Once it's lost, you can never get it back no matter how hard you try. It takes only "a little thing" to lose it.'

For the past four months, Sophia Mazzoli had worked for ten hours a day in a shirt factory upstate, where she and her fellow seamstresses had been reduced to hapless pieces of machinery with only daydreams to keep themselves human; hers had been of Joey Fabrizio, a better life, pretty dresses and a decent home to live in, away from the foul and dirty alleys of the Lower East Side, the disease, the poverty, the hand-to-mouth existence that was a way of life.

She missed her family, whom she'd quarrelled with when she'd taken up with Joey and left in a fit of anger after her father and brothers had said he was nothing but trouble, a thriftless waster who'd bring her nothing but misery; that if she didn't stop seeing him, she could pack her things and move out. She already bitterly regretted it, especially when she woke in the early hours alone and lonely, terrified of the trouble Joey had dragged her into, even more terrified of bringing any trouble or shame on her familly. Whatever happened now, she was too proud, as well as scared, to go back home and tell them that they'd been right about Joey all along; that he was a no-good no-hoper who'd used her and abused her love and trust, dragged her down to his level, got her into big trouble with the cops. This was a mess that Sophia Mazzoli had to cope with alone.

Desperate, she'd confided in a workmate, a Jewish girl who shared a couple of rooms with a cousin somewhere in the Bronx; the girl had offered Sophia a sympathetic ear and a place to stay for a while, in return for a quarter of the rent, and she'd accepted gratefully: the Bronx was much closer to the factory where they worked and she'd be saving on fares. She was moving out today. The moment she'd got home she'd frenziedly packed what little she owned into a canvas bag, taken out the remainder of last week's pay packet from under her mattress, and was ready to leave as soon as it got dark. In a few days' time the rent was due and the landlord would be calling as he always did on Fridays, but he'd find her gone; she felt guilty. Dishonesty went against the grain – her parents were poor but they would rather have starved than cheat anyone of a cent – but there was no help for it; she needed the money more than he did. She was just closing the door on the dimly lit landing outside when – too late – she heard footsteps on the stairwell and a hand gripped her from behind like a vice.

'You're not plannin' on runnin' off somewhere, honey?' Delucca leered into her terrified face. 'Don't even think about it. You and me have got some unfinished business.' He kicked open the door, shoved her and the canvas bag through it. Then he locked it behind him.

'No, please!' She backed away. 'Leave me alone, mister. I do what you want, I make a statement about Joey. The truth. He was here that night, but only for a little while. After that I don't see him no more.'

'I'm not here about the statement.' He grasped her by the wrist and swung her onto the bed; when she tried to fight him off he punched her in the face. 'Let's make it look authentic, sweetheart . . . some of Joey's lowlife pals worked you over to try and persuade you not to talk . . . but you decided to be a nice, law-abidin' citizen and talk anyway . . . how's that?' She was sobbing hysterically as he slapped her around and then ripped off her clothes. Half naked, the little tramp sure was a sight for sore eyes, with her big, firm breasts and that tantalizing bush of black hair between her legs, all there for the taking. He grabbed at her, biting and sucking while she pleaded for him to stop. Taking no notice, he unfastened his trousers and pushed her legs wide apart. 'Come on, honey, don't play the coy virgin with me! You and me know better, don't we? You're just beggin' for it. What about all the times you let that little creep Fabrizio stick it up you?'

She was still crying when he left her, lying face down on the bed among the bloodied sheets, her face and body a mass of cuts and weals. He looked back over his shoulder and felt an overwhelming contempt for her. She represented everything he hated and despised, the droves of foreign immigrants who were overcrowding and polluting New York, with their babel of languages and strange customs, trash who were stealing American jobs by working at half-price rates and turning huge chunks of the city into ghettos. Perversely, the fact that she'd excited him to fever pitch and he'd enjoyed sex with her more than he'd ever enjoyed it with his wife made him furiously angry. His Maudie was worth a million of her kind.

He strode over to where she lay and let loose a string of the vilest invective he could lay his tongue to. Then he urinated on her.

CHAPTER EIGHT

Marianna decided on the Worth gown again for the Lauterbachs' party in the Hotel Astor ballroom; this time, there'd been no need to stoop to subterfuge and tamper with the neckline: her mother had had it sent to her own dressmaker to have the offending décolleté expertly altered, and subtly raised.

She chose the same white ermine cape, the same evening shoes, the same accessories. The only difference this time was her jewellery. For an occasion her parents deemed as important as this one her father's safe had been opened and the Eastbridge diamonds brought forth to adorn her neck, her wrists and her earlobes. While Betty dressed her hair and helped her to fasten them on, Marianna sat in front of her mirror wondering how many Eastbridge employees had sweated over the decades to pay for them.

Tonight, there'd be no chance of enjoyment for her as there'd been at the theatre: no play, no opportunity to escape her parents' scrutiny, no handsome Curt Koenig. Though her father would drift away, no doubt, to talk business with old man Lauterbach for most of the evening, her mother would probably stick to her like a shadow, steering her towards all the most eligible, suitable and boring men in the room. Only the thought of what she intended to do if she could shake off her mother for long enough to approach the impresario Charles Frohman made it all bearable.

There was a freezing silence in the carriage almost all the way along 44th Street, until they reached the junction with Broadway; after the scene in her father's study she was still in disgrace. While she stared from the window her parents carried on a conversation across her, as if she was invisible, but she was happy to be left to her own thoughts. She was back in the Depew box at the Metropolitan, watching the beginning of act two with trembling excitement because any second Curt Koenig would make his entrance from the wings and walk to the centre of the stage. She could remember his exact lines, the way his voice projected each word, his every movement; the sense of disappointment and desolation when he left the stage at the end of the act and she knew that he wasn't coming back again. As they arrived at the Astor and made their way into the sumptuous ballroom Marianna's mind was still miles away.

Jerry Lauterbach, his widowed mother and his grandfather, J. Lauterbach senior, were standing at the entrance to the ballroom greeting their guests. Edwina gave her daughter a little nudge in the small of her back.

'Don't forget. Be extra nice to Jerry. Lauterbach business is very important to your father.'

'How could I forget, Momma?' Marianna said sweetly, with an undertone of sarcasm her mother was already too preoccupied to notice. She handed their host the expensive gift-wrapped present that her father had chosen a week earlier – a solid gold French antique fob watch, from one of the most exclusive jewellers in Manhattan. 'Happy birthday, Jerry. Thank you so much for inviting me.' The most dazzling smile she could muster, and the sentiment, were both false: there was only one reason why she'd wanted to come, only one purpose now she was here – she had to find Charles Frohman and get herself introduced to him. The hawk-nosed widow and Lauterbach senior smiled approvingly, while eligible Jerry insisted that she save him a dance later; her parents smiled.

As she passed through the entrance and into the crowded ballroom she congratulated herself silently on her deception; when push came to shove she could be quite an actress herself.

It took her almost half the evening to throw her mother off the scent and engineer a few minutes when she was able to be alone. Jerry Lauterbach turned out to be her saviour. After their dance, when he offered her his arm and took her to the buffet table, she knew that her mother was watching

86

but would certainly not follow. She turned and scanned the crowded balconies above. There were groups of guests standing and talking together or sitting at small tables; downstairs, couples took to the floor again as the orchestra played.

'Jerry, Tom Depew told me that Charles Frohman, the theatrical impresario, is here tonight. Is that true?'

'Why, yes.' He handed her a glass of champagne punch. 'My grandfather wanted me to invite him . . . ulterior motive, of course.' He laughed and she laughed with him. 'He's one of the backers for Frohman's new play, an adaptation of *The Count of Monte Cristo* . . . a bit ambitious, I thought. It's a lengthy book, and to fit everything in you'd need to have about a dozen acts . . . far too long for an audience to sit through without at least three intermissions.'

'I think it's a wonderful idea! I've read the book – I love Dumas – and a story like that would make a really exciting play . . . something that would have the audience sitting on the edge of their seats biting their fingernails!'

'That would depend on the playwright and the cast. Nothing's apparently been decided yet, except that Frohman's commissioned Clyde Fitch and David Belasco to collaborate on the script.' He sipped his champagne punch thoughtfully. 'Grandfather's convinced that when it finally goes into production, it'll create the stage sensation of the decade . . . and I'm sure it will.' He smiled. 'If he wasn't so completely sold on the idea, he would never have put his money into it.'

Marianna's eyes were still roving across the crowded ballroom; her mother was deep in conversation on the other side of the floor, and, moreover, she had her back towards them; this was the opportunity Marianna had been waiting for.

'Jerry, I'd love to meet Charles Frohman . . . but I don't even know what he looks like. Even if I did, it would be like looking for a needle in a haystack here tonight . . . and I'd feel awkward unless you introduced me . . . would you mind?'

'Of course not.' He gazed round the floor, then to the

balconies above. 'Ah, I think I've spotted him . . .' He held out his arm and she took it. 'Let's squeeze our way through here.'

Edwina Eastbridge smiled as she watched Jerry Lauterbach with Marianna on his arm. No need now to follow discreetly in her daughter's footsteps; they made a fine couple. The Lauterbach boy had spent more time in Marianna's company during the evening than he had with anyone else, and that was a good sign.

She sipped her champagne punch and carried on with her own conversation. Though they'd now disappeared among the guests who thronged the balcony, it was no longer necessary to keep a careful eye on what her daughter was doing, no need to be concerned . . . until twenty minutes later when she caught sight of Jerry Lauterbach laughing with a group of friends, but of Marianna there was no sign.

'You're a devotee of the theatre, then, Miss Eastbridge?'

'Just a theatregoer, until recently. Until I saw a play called *Under the Red Robe* at the Metropolitan. That was the moment I became a devotee.' He looked nothing like the imposing figure of her imagination, but his eyes were shrewd and his smile was kind. He was much shorter than she'd thought he'd be, and much older, but he was genuinely interested in what she was saying to him and that was all that mattered.

'Yes, I've seen the play, naturally. I make it my business to see every play in New York. A fine production, masterfully directed – Julius Cahn, the director, is a personal friend of mine – and masterfully acted by a fine cast.'

She smiled and took a deep breath. 'Mr Frohman, I know that you're producing *The Count of Monte Cristo* in the very near future, but that it hasn't been cast yet . . . people are saying that it'll be a sensation, the biggest production ever mounted on Broadway . . . please, don't think me very forward, but there's something I simply have to ask you . . .'

The shrewd eyes twinkled. 'My dear young lady, I think

I know what you're going to ask me . . . and I hate to refuse.' Her face drooped with disappointment. 'Believe me, you certainly have the poise and the good looks for the role of Mercedes . . . but I always make it an absolute rule to engage only professional actresses.'

Her eyes grew bright with hope again. 'No, please . . . you misunderstand me . . . I wasn't asking for myself. I was talking about someone else, a professional actor. Curt Koenig . . . you saw him in *Under the Red Robe*, so you'll know exactly who I mean. Oh, Mr Frohman, he'd be perfect for the role of Monte Cristo!' She was very excited, animated now. 'I know everyone expects you to cast someone famous like William Gillette or John Drew, but they just wouldn't be right . . . Curt Koenig was made for that part! He has the height, the stage presence, the charismatic aura, and this special way of casting a spell over you whenever he speaks . . . just as I imagine Edmond Dantes would! When he walks on stage, everyone else seems irrelevant . . . the only person you're aware of is him. All the others are fine actors, I know that; and they have far more stage experience than he does . . . they'd act the role as competently as you'd expect them to . . . but if you want a Monte Cristo who holds the audience spellbound, who takes that character right out of the pages of the book and brings him totally alive, Curt Koenig is the only actor who can do it.'

She was oblivious of their surroundings, of people who'd overheard her beginning to look their way.

'That's quite a speech. Are you a personal friend of his?'

'No. No, I'm not.' For the first time, she looked embarrassed by her passionate outburst. 'It's just that I don't believe anyone else could possibly play that role the way he would.' She lowered her eyes and her voice: had she really behaved so brazenly, so much out of character? Supposing someone who knew her parents had overheard her conversation with Frohman and told them? Whatever happened, she didn't regret what she'd done, not for a single moment: fate had handed her the opportunity to help him and she'd seized it with both hands. Even if nothing came of it, at least she'd done her best. 'I'm sorry. Not for anything I've said, because it was just the truth. But if I've embarrassed you at all. You're a guest here and I've taken advantage of that.'

'On the contrary, my dear . . . I prefer my ladies forthright. It makes them much more interesting.' He smiled. He had a rather nondescript, ordinary appearance, but his charm made his lack of looks irrelevant. 'In return, I'll be as forthright with you. I can't promise to cast Curt Koenig in the role of Monte Cristo . . . or, indeed, in any role at all. But I will consider him.'

Her face lit up. 'Mr Frohman, you're very kind,' she said, as they shook hands, though she knew that if he did cast Curt Koenig in anything it would have nothing to do with kindness, but everything to do with the fact that his success was due to his ability to perceive outstanding theatrical talent.

Dead beat as usual after another hard day's work in the shirt factory upstate, Sadie Sneiderman was pulling on her shabby coat ready to leave with the rest of the girls when word came down that the boss wanted to see her in his office. 'I'll catch ya up!' she shouted after her workmates as they filed out, most of them too tired after a ten-hour shift even to crack a joke. Ninety-five per cent of them were immigrant labour – factory bosses could hire them for two dollars a week, sometimes less – and all they wanted to do was go home and sleep. Sadie had been working in the factory longer than most.

'You'll miss your train!' somebody shouted. 'What does the boss want to see you for? You done somethin' wrong?'

'No I ain't.' But as she tramped up the steps to his office, Sadie felt worried; if it had been something trivial, the foreman would have spoken to her instead.

The boss was smoking a short cigarette inside the poky ten foot square room that served as his office. His fingers were stained with nicotine. And he was scowling.

'You know that Mazzoli girl better than most of 'em here?' She nodded. 'Why ain't she showed up for work?'

'I dunno, Mr Bloomfield. She just ain't showed up. I

think maybe she's sick. Last time I spoke to her, three days ago, she said she was leavin' the place where she is now, and movin' in with Rachel and me.'

'An' you ain't seen her since?'

'No, I ain't seen her at all. She was goin' to bring her things to work the day before yesterday, and come home with me when we finished. But she never turned up.'

'When you see her, tell her she's fired! She ain't no use to me if she don't turn up when she's s'pposed to. I need workers I can count on.' He fished in the cash box and then banged four dollars down on the cluttered desk. 'Here, that's what's owin' to her. Give it to her when you see her, and tell her not to bother to come back.'

Outside, Sadie looked down at the money in her hand. She wasn't sure what she ought to do. When Sophia hadn't turned up for work two days ago, she'd just thought, like everyone else, that she was sick and she'd be in the next day; but she hadn't turned up then, either. At first, Sadie hadn't worried too much about it; girls sometimes took days off if they were really ill; not often, because they needed the money, and if you didn't work then you didn't get paid. But what Sophia had told her a few days before about being frightened because the cops were giving her a hard time sounded warning bells now – what if she wasn't sick at all, what if something had happened to her? Though Sadie's instincts were to mind her own business and keep out of it, she liked the Mazzoli girl and felt sorry for her. Maybe someone should take a ride down to her place on the Lower East Side and check that she was OK.

She started to run, so that she wouldn't miss her train, though after ten hours on her feet operating a machine with one half-hour break she could barely summon up the energy. She caught it by the skin of her teeth. When she got home to the Bronx she'd talk it over with her cousin Rachel and then they'd decide what to do. First, though, she needed to put her feet up and eat a hot dinner.

She didn't like the idea of going to find Sophia Mazzoli on her own, down on the Lower East Side; Rachel would have to come with her. But one thing she did know, and that was that she had a bad feeling about all of this, a suspicion that the reason Sophia hadn't turned up for work for two days in a row had nothing to do with her being sick.

All the way home to the Bronx she tried to tell herself that she was wrong. But the nagging feeling that Sophia was in trouble just wouldn't go away.

Joey Fabrizio grabbed the bars of his police cell for the fiftieth time and rattled them, screaming at the top of his voice for someone to come. But just like all the other times during the last two weeks, nobody answered, nobody took any notice. When the uniformed cop who'd brought him the plate of pigswill they called dinner came down to the cells two hours ago, he'd yelled about being held without evidence and prisoners' rights, but the bastard had just shoved the plate through the hatch and gone away laughing.

'Quit wastin' your time yellin' out,' someone from the next cell had called. 'You think those guys gonna listen? Why don't you shut up and save your breath?'

'I ain't done nothin' they can charge me with and they won't let me out!'

'If they won't let you out, sonny, they must have somethin' on you. Either way, you ain't gettin' outa here till they're ready.' Fabrizio had paced some more, lain down, got up again and yelled some more, but in the end he'd decided the guy in the other cell was right, and he sat down on his bunk, his chin in his hands. It was almost dark when he heard the clang-clang of keys, and then footsteps.

'He's bin shoutin' his mouth off all day,' Fabrizio heard the uniformed cop say to whoever was with him. Then he heard that hated voice and Roy Delucca came into view.

'Well, well . . . who was it said we couldn't keep him here for more than a couple of hours?' he sneered to his companion, another plain-clothes cop Fabrizio hated almost as much. 'How long has it been, Mac? Two weeks?'

'You sonofabitch! You ain't got no right to keep me here without evidence!' He grasped the bars and his eyes were full of hate and impotent rage. 'I already told you, I ain't done nothin' and I don't know anythin' about any knifin' in Little Italy!'

Delucca sneered again. 'And we got two witnesses who say otherwise. Thought you'd like to know, Joey . . . they signed statements today. You stay.'

'They're lyin' to save their own necks!'

'That's not the way they tell it.'

'I got another witness. I told you – Sophia Mazzoli – you said you guys was goin' to see her to check it out. She promised me she'd make a statement to say where I was that night, and that was right there with her!'

Delucca made a sign to the uniformed jailer and he unlocked the cell door. The detectives walked in. 'That rat won't run, Joey . . . your girlfriend's chickened out. Way she tells it, you tried to pay her to keep her mouth shut. But she don't want to be involved no more. Says she should have listened to her family when they told her you was bad news.'

'You're lyin'!'

MacKenzie shrugged. 'Why should we, Joey? We're just tellin' it how it is. The Mazzoli girl won't lie for you . . . smart kid. After we put her wise about the penalty of committing perjury, she thought better of it. Tough.'

'You bastards! You threatened her!'

'Better watch that big mouth of yours, Fabrizio. Could get you in a whole lot more trouble than you're in already. Tell you what.' Delucca sat down beside him on the hard bunk. 'We'll leave you to think it all over, and come back later. Give you time to make up your mind. Here's where it's at. You plead guilty and do yourself a favour, or you plead not guilty and you go down . . . there's too much hard evidence against you. And you know what? Judges don't like guys who try to fool juries, like wasting the court's time and public funds pleading not guilty when all the evidence shows they are. Take some good advice. Plead provocation and they might go easy on you.'

'OK, OK. I was there, sure . . . but I never knifed no-one. We was playin' pool, me and some other guys, and this argument broke out over some broad. Tempers got heated up, fists started flyin', then someone pulled out a knife . . . but it wasn't me. Hell, I just went there to get a game.'

'But when the blood started runnin', you were outa there! You didn't even stop to see if you could help the guy.'

'So I didn't wanna get involved! It wasn't my fuckin' fight. We all got out as quickly as we could before the cops came.'

'But someone remembered your face . . . and they reckoned you were the one with the knife in your hand.'

Fabrizio ran a hand through his hair. 'Look, how many more times? I told you, they was lyin'.'

Delucca stood up. MacKenzie shouted for the guard to come back and unlock the cell door. 'Don't fight it, Joey. Face reality – you're goin' down. Give us the runaround any more, and we'll make things real uncomfortable for your nearest and dearest . . . you got that? When we come back, you better be ready to play ball.'

'Lousy cops!' His bitter voice rang out after them. 'Too fuckin' lazy to find the real killer . . . so any guy'll do!'

'You think he'll finally admit he did it?' MacKenzie turned to Delucca upstairs.

'When he's had all night to think about what we said, he will. Most of 'em do.' They walked along the corridor, into their cramped, untidy office. 'Hey, what about a cup of coffee? Put your feet up, relax a little . . . it's Chief Rawlins' day off.'

'Don't mind if I do.' MacKenzie sat down and lit up a stub of cigarette. 'Say, what happened about the Mazzoli girl? Didn't you say you'd broken the alibi she'd given Fabrizio and she'd agreed to admit he forced her to do it?'

'Yeah. But she's scared of Joey's pals when word gets around that she didn't come through . . . know what I mean? I told her to keep her door bolted and watch her back for a while, maybe even move out somewhere else, till it all dies down. That's why she hasn't been here to make a statement. See, the way I figured it, if she shows her hand and gets called by the prosecution, everyone'll know that she helped put Joey away. We already got two witnesses to identify him and get a conviction. I didn't want to involve her unless we had to. Besides, I already told Rawlins that because of her reputation, she wasn't reliable. I mean, if a tramp stands up in court, who's gonna believe her anyhow?'

'You got that right.' Mackenzie downed the stewed coffee. 'So, what's Rawlins got lined up next?'

'Cargo gone missin', down at the docks. Looks like an inside job . . . warehouse heist. Now we've got the Fabrizio case more or less wrapped up, what you say we make a start on that tomorrow, after he's come through with the guilty plea?'

'And if he doesn't?'

'It's his funeral. With all the evidence we got against him, the prosecution case is watertight.'

They finished their coffee and discussed the next day's case for a few more minutes before MacKenzie went off duty. Half an hour later, while he was leafing through the mound of papers on his untidy desk, Delucca came across the memo Rawlins had left him about Sophia Mazzoli the other day. Until now, he hadn't even thought about her, much less about what he'd done to her. He tore it up, tossed it in the waste paper basket. Down in the Lower East Side there were a thousand girls like Sophia Mazzoli; he'd lost count of the number he'd threatened, bullied, framed and forced himself on over the last few years, ever since he'd been a cop. Though he despised them all for what they were – poor, ignorant and foreign – he enjoyed using them; that's all they were good for. Immigrant trash. Like the Mazzoli bitch, they'd all been too scared, too weak, too unimportant ever to be a threat to him.

It was dark by the time Sadie Sneiderman had got home to the Bronx from the shirt factory, put her aching feet up for a while and then cooked tea with her cousin; another hour or so went by before they'd eaten and cleared everything away; over dinner, she'd confided her worries about Sophia Mazzoli, asked Rachel what she thought they should do.

'When she never turned up this mornin' – that's three days she ain't showed for work – I thought, well, maybe she's sick . . . maybe she's upped and gone back to her family . . . after all, that'd figure.' She broke off a piece of bread and wiped it around her plate. 'She only left home when they were givin' her a hard time about Joey . . . now she reckons he's no good, that they were right all along, maybe she figured it'd be best to make up with 'em.' She shook her head slowly. 'But you know . . . I just keep gettin' this bad feelin'. When I left work today, I made up my mind to go down there, check up on her, just see she's OK. But I ain't goin' down there alone . . . you'll come with me, won't you?'

'You sure got some chutzpah! I'm dead beat!'

'Aw, c'mon, Rachel . . . we can ask Danny and Mikey to come with us . . .' She smiled, knowing her cousin would say yes if the two young men who lived downstairs, one of whom she was sweet on, said they'd come too. 'Let's heap the dishes in the sink and do 'em when we come back; it'll take too long if we do it now. Besides,' a sly note came into her voice, 'if we hang around too long, those two just might make other plans for the evenin' . . .'

'OK . . . but I say we don't go unless they come too. You'd have to be a real schmuck to go down the Lower East Side at this time of night without a guy with you . . . agreed?'

'Agreed.'

'Either way, I got mixed feelin's about all this. You think it's really a good idea that we get involved?'

'Look, I told you, she's a good kid . . . and you agreed to her comin' here for a share of the rent . . .'

'From here on in, she ain't got a job no more. Not unless Bloomfield takes her back. You think he might do that?'

Sadie shrugged. Zak Bloomfield was a real tough cookie. Usually, when he fired someone, they stayed fired. 'Not unless she's got a real good excuse for not showin' up at work, he won't. And even then I wouldn't give much for her chances. He's a mean sonofabitch.'

'Let's go get Danny and Mikey, and we'll go see.'

It took them less time to get downtown than any of them had reckoned on; by seven, most of the city workers who used the elevated railway had already travelled home and it was much quieter than it would have been an hour earlier. They could even choose their seats. Sadie had the address in Canal Street written down on a scrap of paper and, after asking around when they got to Spring and Bowery, it didn't take them long to find the building. On the way in, they even bumped into some guy who lived on the floor below hers, on his way out to his nightwatchman's job down in Coney Island.

'Sure, I seen her, once or twice. I ain't lived here long. We don't often speak . . . she's always in a big hurry. But I ain't seen her for a couple o' days. Gotta go.'

The four of them went in single file up the dirty stairs, and found the right door. Sadie knocked and called out, but there was no answer.

'Maybe you was right, maybe she's gone back to her folks after all. Maybe she never turned up for work 'cos she's got herself some other job, closer.'

'She'd have let me know.' Sadie went on knocking, louder this time. 'Sophia, you in there? It's me, Sadie.'

'Looks like she ain't at home . . . hell, all this goddam way for nothin',' Mikey grumbled.

'Wait . . . I can hear somethin' . . .' When she called out again there was a faint but unmistakable groan. 'I knew it, she's sick! You boys, put your weight against that door!'

But there was no need. When one of them turned the handle, it opened easily; Sophia Mazzoli hadn't even bothered to keep it locked. When they let themselves into the room, they realized why.

She was lying there on the unmade bed, what remained of her dress sticking to her bruised, battered body in bloodied tatters. She had a black eye, someone had punched her repeatedly in the face and her lips were split, and hideously swollen.

Deeply shocked, Sadie went down on her knees beside the bed and held her cold, limp hands in hers. There was a sickening stench of stale urine coming from her torn clothes and the cover on the bed.

'Sophia . . . what happened, for Christ's sake? Who did

this to you?' She glanced back at the others. 'Was it Joey's pals?'

The slumped figure on the bed groaned, and turned her battered face towards her friend. Now Sadie could see that the black eye was so swollen that it had almost closed, that there were bite marks all over her neck and what she could see of her exposed body. There was no expression in her right eye, and her voice was so hoarse that Sadie could barely hear her whisper, brokenly, 'I . . . can't . . . tell you.'

CHAPTER NINE

The letter from Charles Frohman came ten days later, when Curt knew the date that *Under the Red Robe* would close: in three months' time, just as rehearsals for Frohman's *Count of Monte Cristo* were due to begin. He was stunned, delighted, puzzled, ecstatic, almost speechless as he read it again and again: it was rare, almost unheard of, for a barely known, middle-of-the-road young actor like himself to receive an invitation from a leading Broadway impresario to audition for a part in a major production. Suddenly, he was suspicious.

'Shawn, I don't get it.' He frowned. 'There's somethin' about all of this that just doesn't sound right . . . you think it could be somebody's idea of a joke?'

'Somebody who's used Frohman's headed stationery and signed his name?'

'Yeah . . . but . . .'

'Think about it. You get the letter, you go see Frohman; if the letter's a fake, then he'd want to know who it was who had access to his headed paper and was forging his signature, wouldn't he? He can't have that many people working under him who'd have the free run of his private office. Or who'd dare sign his name to a letter he doesn't know the first thing about. I've never met him, but I shouldn't think he's the type of guy who'd be amused, even if it was meant as a joke. Anyhow, who'd want to play a joke like that on you, of all people? It stinks. Besides, you don't know anybody who works for Frohman, do you?'

'No.'

'Well then . . . quit worrying and go see him right now! He must have seen you on stage and liked what he saw. No other explanation.'

'I still don't get it.' Curt looked thoughtful. 'And he doesn't say what part he wants me to audition for.'

'Maybe he has more than one in mind.'

'Could be.' He started pacing now. 'It's just . . . I can't figure it out . . . I mean, I was going to go along when the auditions were announced. But to get a letter from him, from Charles Frohman . . . I mean, why me?'

'Don't you think you're good enough for him to have noticed you, then? It's common knowledge, you told me, that he makes a point of watching every production on Broadway so he won't risk missing anyone with special talent . . . chances are, he's been to the Metropolitan and he's spotted you.' Shawn Duchovsky said what he knew would shake his friend out of his illogical mood. Curt might not have the experience, the connections, the fame and adoration of the theatregoing public like Otis Skinner, William Gillette or John Drew, but anyone who'd watched him on stage could see he had what it took. It wasn't like him to doubt himself, or that Lady Luck had finally spun the wheel of fortune and it was his turn to win.

'Of course I don't think that, what d'you take me for?'

'Don't look a gift horse in the mouth, then.'

He met the impresario in his office at the Lyceum the following morning; the letter was genuine after all. Shawn had been right. No actor who wanted to succeed could ever afford to question his own ability, or his worth to other people. Frohman was famous for discovering theatrical talent and then nurturing it until it flowered at the very top of the tree. Suddenly, he felt unbearably excited. Was it really happening to him, all the things he'd longed to happen, the things he'd dreamed of, that he'd quarrelled with his family over and left home for, vowing never to return – he'd have starved, rather than have gone back a failure – until he'd proved to his scoffing and cynical father and brothers that he had the ability to act, and earn a living at it? Success – and everything that went with it, which he wanted perhaps even more than the success itself – was such an elusive thing. He remembered how, when he was a boy, he and his brother Jesse had gone butterfly hunting, and how, when they'd chased their quarry for so long and waited so patiently for it to settle so they could pounce on it with their nets, it had suddenly darted away and they'd been left with nothing. He had that desperate, helpless feeling now, face to face with Charles Frohman; he felt so close, so near to what he wanted and what he longed to be, that in its very nearness it was yet as elusive as the butterfly that had escaped from them that day. Frohman might have summoned him here for an audition in his production of *Monte Cristo*, but there was no promise that he would give him a part in it.

'I was very flattered to have you write me and ask me to come here today . . . but even more than that, surprised that you'd written me at all. I'd intended to come to the auditions for the play when they were announced in the press . . . I'd like to play Mondego . . . but I never expected a personal invitation from the producer.' Despite Frohman's easy manner, Curt was still a little on edge: was it just his imagination, or was Frohman holding something back? The impresario smiled.

'It is a little unusual, yes. You're interested in the role of Mondego, you say? That wasn't quite what I had in mind, of course . . . but we'll see. You'll most likely have realized that the actual script hasn't been finished yet, so we'll improvise. You know Dumas' original work, of course?'

'I bought a copy of the book when I first heard that you were producing the play. And I've memorized a passage at the end, the scene where Monte Cristo's identity is revealed and he and Mondego have a final confrontation.'

'That was very enterprising of you. Please . . .' He stood up, motioned Curt towards the door. 'On our way down to the stage, maybe you'd tell me something about your early career . . . and how you come to be in the theatre at all. I like to know as much as possible about my actors . . . so do forgive me if my interest borders on the extremely inquisitive.' They continued on down the steps, side by side. 'A long time ago – around the time I was producing *Shenandoah* – I asked the same question of·a pretty young actress . . . and she told me to mind my own business.' They both laughed; Curt decided that he liked him. 'I told her that if I gave her a part in my next play and it made her famous, what I asked her would be nothing compared to the kind of questions she'd be asked by the press.'

'And did she answer your question after that?'

'She walked out on me.' A dry smile. 'Unfortunately, it's a point to bear in mind . . . the press. I was about to say "the gentlemen of the press", but I don't think that would be the correct epithet; modern journalists are almost invariably anything but gentlemen. A regrettable fact of life. The unrecognized often dream of what it would be like to be famous; invariably, they think it something they would revel in. Although some do, the reality can be very different.'

'I hadn't thought about it.' It wasn't entirely a lie: he'd thought more about the rewards of fame than its drawbacks. An ample supply of money, flattery and recognition from strangers, doors that had once been firmly shut in his face suddenly opened. A smart house, a private carriage instead of a streetcar or the elevated railway. Nothing any journalist might ask him bothered him at all; why should it, when he had nothing to hide? So what, if he'd been born the second son of a prize-fighter in Minneapolis, who'd married a store-keeper's daughter and now ran a livery stable, with no connections with the stage? His beginnings just showed how determined he'd been to succeed against the odds, how far he'd come without any help except his own talent and ambition. Let the press dig all they wanted. 'I don't see anyone else here to audition,' he said suddenly, as they entered the auditorium and found it deserted except for two men sitting in the front row, leafing through what looked like a script and talking in undertones. 'Am I the first one to arrive?'

'You could say that. Let me introduce you to my playwrights. The script isn't finished . . . we don't expect a final version for some time. Perfection is of the utmost importance in any field of art, as I'm sure you of all people would appreciate. David Belasco is not only co-writer of the

Monte Cristo script, he's director of the play.' He made the introductions, and they chatted about the production. Curt knew little about Clyde Fitch except that he'd written several successful plays for Frohman, but of the flamboyant David Belasco he knew a great deal more.

A native of San Francisco, Belasco was well known within and outside theatrical circles for his spectacular showmanship, and his brilliance as an innovative, adventurous playwright and producer – the very qualities that had attracted the attention and then the patronage of Charles Frohman. Money, fame and power were his goals in life – goals Curt could readily appreciate, since they were almost identical to his own – and he'd lost no time in pursuing all three with awesome zeal. He'd enjoyed some success in Chicago several seasons back with his own work, *Hearts of Oak*, but though the play had had a respectable run and been well received by the critics, it had never made it to New York. To gain a toehold there, Belasco had taken a job as stage manager at the Madison Square Theatre – a job he did not plan to remain in very long – and it was there he'd met Frohman's elder brother Daniel, one of the theatre's financial directors, and Henry De Mille, an actor, playwright, and, with his wife Beatrice, a play reader for the company, at a salary of $1,500 a year. Belasco's flamboyance and original ideas had appealed to Frohman, who was sympathetic to his ambitions to direct. But it was his brilliant and realistic staging in *The Main Line* that riveted audiences and shot him to almost instant fame – 'A triumph of originality and stage mechanism', the critic from the *New York World* had eulogized, and since then Belasco had never looked back. To Curt, his career was an inspiration – it proved his point that a combination of talent and ambition could take anyone to the heights of success and fame – with, of course, the ability to recognize a lucky opening when you saw it. This was his. Just as he'd felt an instant affinity with Charles Frohman, so he felt a similar enosis with Belasco.

'He's it, he's perfect, he's everything you could want for the part!' The director waved his arms wildly. 'Except he's

103

not a face that the audience know! Even better . . . you'll take them entirely by storm!' Curt was more than a little taken aback: Belasco certainly lived up to his reputation for eccentricity. 'He has this incredible presence . . . this aura . . . you feel it?' He turned to Fitch, then Frohman. 'Of course you do! Otherwise, why would he be here?'

His confidence rising, Curt mounted the steps to the stage and went through the scene he'd memorized and rehearsed a dozen times or more over the past few days. He blotted out everything but the character of Mondego, the lines in his head that he'd learned, refined, practised and delivered in the confines of his room every hour since he'd received Frohman's letter. He blotted out Frohman now, sitting benignly in the front row of the stalls with Fitch and Belasco, the stagehands and behind-the-scenes workers who'd heard about the audition and come to stand around at the back of the theatre to watch. With a sixth sense, he felt that now was the moment he'd been waiting in the wings for: if he failed, if his performance fell short, there would never be another chance quite like this one.

He left behind everything of himself at the foot of the stage steps; he was no longer Curt Koenig. In a stroke, within the space of a dozen strides across the stage he'd assumed the personality of the villain Mondego: lying, cheating, scheming; utterly ruthless, utterly contemptible, utterly believable. When at last he'd finished, he felt drained, almost dazed. He was suddenly Curt Koenig again. He walked to the edge of the stage and looked towards the others, as from the depths of the auditorium the handful of workers who'd gathered to watch him gave him a round of applause. He smiled.

'Can you come down, please, Mr Koenig?' Frohman called.

'I knew it, I felt it . . . even with those lines, that incredible persona shone through.' Belasco was ecstatic. 'We'll need you to come back again, when the script is finished and you can read the actual lines you'll be speaking in the play itself.'

'Mr Koenig has another six weeks at the Metropolitan,' Frohman said, while Curt tried to come to terms with the fact that they'd liked him, that his performance had impressed them to the extent that they were offering him a part. 'By that time, the script should be complete, and any rough edges smoothed out.' He turned to Curt now. 'For an impromptu performance, without proper lines, you certainly rose to the occasion . . . Miss Eastbridge was right.' Curt stared at him, unable to believe his own ears.

'*Miss Eastbridge?*'

'You know the young lady?'

'If meeting someone by chance in a chop house and being asked to sign her theatre programme is knowing her, then yes, I do.' He was stunned, flabbergasted. 'I'm sorry, but I don't understand. What has she to do with my being here?'

'I attended a function at the Hotel Astor recently, and she was also there. She made herself known to me.' He smiled. 'She's a great admirer of yours . . . and since she'd heard about the production of *Monte Cristo* she wanted to bring your talents to my attention. Unusually, I agreed to have you audition. She's certainly a very persuasive young woman.'

Curt's exuberant smile had faded a little now. 'Do you mean that if she hadn't asked you, you wouldn't have sent for me?'

'Don't be too hard on yourself. Let us rather say that it took an inspirational touch of feminine intuition to guide me towards your talent sooner rather than later. For that, you do have Miss Eastbridge to thank. But that takes not one iota away from you . . . you've just given us an incredibly inspired performance. I think you were made for this role – and that I would be amazingly shortsighted if I failed to give you the chance to portray it on stage . . . little-known actor or not.'

'I don't know what to say.'

'I made no promises to Miss Eastbridge. I agreed only to have you audition for me. I told her that I couldn't possibly undertake to offer you the part of Monte Cristo or indeed any other part. And she understood that.'

Curt stared. '*The part of Monte Cristo*? She wanted you to audition me for the part of Monte Cristo?'

'My dear young man . . . you gave an admirable rendition of Mondego, and it will be very difficult indeed to find anyone to do it with anything like your fire. But that isn't the part for you. No. The moment you walked on stage and transformed yourself into Mondego, I knew we'd discovered new treasure . . . and I'm offering you the chance to play a leading role. With the amount of money invested in this production, believe me, I wouldn't be offering it if I thought there was the slightest doubt that you could do it. All my instincts, all my judgement, tell me that you can. Yes, that's right,' Frohman said as Curt continued to stare at him in disbelief. 'I want you to play the Count of Monte Cristo.'

'I was stunned. In shock. And then Belasco said, "Do you realize how vital a part timing plays in our lives? Sometimes we're too early, sometimes too late. But you're here now. The right time, the right place. This play is going to be a sensation. This play will take New York audiences and critics by the scruff of the neck and shake the hell out of them! You can believe it. They'll be enraptured, they'll be agog, they'll be trembling with excitement and gasping for breath. Fastened to their seats, hanging on your every movement, your every word; stunned, stupefied and smitten. When the final curtain comes down they'll be desperate, longing for more . . . have you any idea what it feels like to hold the audience of an entire theatre in the palm of your hand?" That Belasco, he's some guy!' Shawn had poured Curt a drink and he swallowed it in one gulp. 'I don't know which was the biggest shock today. . .being offered the lead in a Broadway play or finding out that it was F. H. Eastbridge's daughter who was responsible for Frohman getting me to audition for it.'

'Hey, don't you realize what this all means? Haven't you even thought about it? That girl, she's treasure trove! One day, you're strugglin' uphill, grateful for any crumb that comes along . . . then all of a sudden some bigshot financier's daughter takes an interest, and everythin' starts happenin'. Curt, you gotta see her, cultivate her. Listen, with F. H. Eastbridge's daughter on your arm, you're goin' places, you're goin' to get noticed by all the right people!'

'I got that part on my own merits, Shawn!' He was suddenly angry. 'Frohman said that.'

'Yeah, yeah, tell me somethin' I don't know. Hell, I know how good you are! But use your head, Curt. That girl made Frohman sit up and take notice . . . because the name Eastbridge means somethin'. You said you wanted to get where you aimed to be whatever it cost, whatever it takes. So take it. For Chrissake, Curt, don't let a girl like that slip through your fingers . . . I never took you for a fool.'

Curt was thoughtful for a long while. All the way back from his meeting with Frohman, he'd actually thought a great deal about Marianna Eastbridge.

'You think I should arrange to meet her? Take her to dinner, maybe, as a way of showin' her my thanks? What about old man Eastbridge? What I heard about him, I don't like.'

'She's his only daughter, isn't she? Probably the apple of his eye . . . I'll bet she can twist him right around her little finger.' Curt looked uncertain. 'Either way, you can't afford to let a girl like that go. Hey, you lucky son-ofabitch . . . grab her with both hands!'

'But I told you before . . . she isn't my type.'

Shawn laughed and shook his head in exasperation.

'With the kind of dough her old man's got salted away, and her set to get the whole goddam caboodle, I wouldn't give a busted nickel's worth if she had two heads. Come on, Curt, I always thought you was real smart.' He went to the untidy writing table on the other side of the room and picked up some paper and a pen. He put them in Curt's hands. 'Make a start right now. You always did have a way with words and women. And show her how grateful you are, how much you appreciate her taking such an interest in your career. Send her some flowers. Joseph Fleischman's on Broadway is swanky enough to impress even an

Eastbridge.' He opened the inkwell for him. 'Curt, just do it.'

The basket of expensive hothouse flowers arrived for her that afternoon, only moments after her parents had left the house to attend a charity function at the Hotel Prince George.

She'd been halfway down the staircase when the front door bell had rung, and she'd heard the delivery boy's voice say, 'Flowers for Miss Marianna Eastbridge.' At first, she'd assumed that Jerry Lauterbach had sent them; since the night of the birthday party there'd been invitations to dinner and tea at the Lauterbach house, and Mrs Lauterbach had dropped hints about her staying for the summer at their cottage in Maine. She'd given the flowers to the German maid to put in water, then taken the sealed note up to her room. When she'd opened the envelope, it had been a shock.

She'd sat down on her bed. Her hands and legs shook. She felt a thrill of excitement run through her. Curt Koenig wanted to see her. Curt Koenig was inviting her to lunch. He named a restaurant on Broadway at one o'clock the next day. Her mind had raced wildly ahead: could she get away without her parents being suspicious?

The address he'd given on the note was the address of the Metropolitan Theatre, not where he lived; she wondered why. Perhaps he lived some distance away, and thought a reply to the theatre, where he went every day, would be quicker; whatever the reason, if she was to accept in time she needed to send her answer straight away. Though she was in a hurry, she was careful to use her best handwriting; there were postage stamps in the drawer of her little desk. When she'd sealed the envelope and addressed it, she stuck on the stamp, quickly changed to her outdoor clothes and rushed out to post it along the street. Walking back home again, she felt she was walking on air.

She could barely contain her excitement and curiosity until the next day: had Charles Frohman offered him the part of Monte Cristo as she'd begged him to, or some other role? Looking back, she wondered at her own effrontery in approaching the impresario at all. Had she really summoned up the nerve to ask a complete stranger to give the leading part in an expensive Broadway production to a virtually unknown actor, simply because she had an enormous girlish crush on him? Clearly, Charles Frohman had listened to her, otherwise why would Curt Koenig be inviting her to lunch, why else had he sent her flowers? She looked down at the brief note again: there was no clue to what had happened when he'd met Frohman, no hint of what the part Frohman must have offered him might be. Whatever it was, it was an important advance in his acting career, and he knew it: Frohman's production of *The Count of Monte Cristo* was going to be the biggest on Broadway for years.

Gerda knocked on her bedroom door a few moments later, with the flowers in a vase. Marianna set them down on a little oval table, and gazed at them almost reverently. They were beautiful, and filled the room with subtle scent, but that was not the reason they were so special to her. He had sent them. Had he chosen them himself, she wondered, or had he asked the assistant at Fleischman's to choose them for him? Suddenly, a small question like that seemed desperately important. She passionately wanted him to like her for herself, not because she'd gone to Charles Frohman for him, not because she was F. H. Eastbridge's daughter . . . but did he? From elation she was suddenly plunged into anxiety and despair. Tomorrow seemed an unbearably interminable time away, and soon she'd have her parents to deal with. Her mother would see the flowers and ask questions, and Marianna would have to lie about whom they'd come from, about where she was going tomorrow. She prayed that her mother hadn't accepted any invitations for her for the following day, arranged any surprise outings with the daughters of her Women's Charity Guild friends. She also hoped that nobody who knew her or her parents would see her with Curt Koenig; though she was proud to be going to lunch with him, she knew they'd be horrified if they found out she was associating with an actor.

'There are flowers in your room,' her mother said, when she came back from her charity function. 'Who are they from?'

'Jerry Lauterbach sent them.' It was a stupid lie and Marianna instantly regretted it; but she couldn't take the words back. Her parents had come home earlier than she'd expected and there hadn't been time to think of another plausible lie.

At dinner, she prepared the ground for the following day by inventing a mid-morning trip to an art exhibition on Sixth Avenue with daughters of families her parents knew and approved of; when neither of them questioned it, Marianna breathed an inaudible sigh of relief.

After dinner, her father went to his study and her mother retired to the drawing room to read and drink coffee; Marianna went into the parlour to play the piano, thinking that since she'd first seen Curt Koenig at the Metropolitan, she had never told so many lies in her life.

A bleak, cold morning. Early shift. Streaks of light flecked the dawn sky outside the window in Brooklyn Heights, promising maybe the hint of sunshine later. Delucca pushed back the covers and swung his legs out of bed, taking care not to wake Maudie as he dressed; she'd been up for most of the night with their youngest boy, who'd sicked up the candy and chocolate cake his grandma had plied him with the afternoon before. Woken from a deep sleep at two a.m. Delucca had let rip.

'Hell, why you let her stuff him full o' that crap, anyhow? Every time you take 'em over there to see her, one of 'em's sick when you get back!'

'Roy, you know how kids can't resist sweet things, an' Momma likes to spoil them . . . '

'Just tell her if she don't stop, then she don't see 'em at all!' He'd rubbed his eyes irritably. 'Jesus, I gotta be up by five thirty!'

'I'll fix him some bicarbonate of soda to settle his stomach. You go back to sleep.'

Delucca went into the bathroom and splashed cold water on his face from the jug. He felt like shit. On his way to the kitchen to fix himself some bread and dripping and hot coffee, he caught sight of the clock. Was it really three hours since he'd been woken up? The way he felt, it might have been five minutes ago. Sleep. Sleep. He just craved sleep. He'd have given anything to have been able to tell Chief Rawlins to stick his lousy job and just crawl back into bed. If only.

He was too tired to taste what he was eating and drinking; the bread tasted like chaff and the coffee like someone had pissed in it. He spat it out in the big stone sink and wiped his lips on the back of his sleeve. A glance at his nickel pocket watch; time to go already.

It was barely light when he let himself out the front door, pulled it to and began walking along the street in the direction of the bridge. When he reached the other side he found he'd got some time in hand, so he paused at a corner news stand to buy himself a paper. He cast a brief glance over the front page before flicking it over in disgust – he was sick of reading that political crap! Hell, he could tell those newspaper guys a few choice things about politics, and the kind of stuff that really went down at City Hall. Like Chief Rawlins, for instance, and his predecessor, who turned a blind eye to some of the gambling dens and whorehouses in certain parts of the city for a backhander, and made sure those lower down kept their mouths shut, hinting that if they didn't they'd not only lose their jobs but find very unpleasant things happening to them, or their families. Delucca had been in the force long enough to know the score. He turned over another page and skimmed it. It wasn't the rackets from the top down that bothered him, but the fact that he was too low down the scale to get in on them; thanks to the bastard Rawlins, who'd taken a dislike to him, he'd been shunted over to detective duties in the Lower East Side, where most of the residents were too poor to have anything to pay cops on the take with. When he thought about how much others in the better districts were making on the side – bribes, protection rackets – he seethed with anger; always getting the short end of the hush money stick made him frustrated and bitter. Be a cop, his father had said!

Being a cop in the right district was what counted. Didn't he know it. Police commissioners could never quite control the force: hadn't Theodore Roosevelt complained a year ago that policing was 'a business of blackmail and protection'? That had certainly caused one hell of a stir and for a while there'd been a well-orchestrated attempt by the Governor's office to put its city police house in order; but nobody in the know was fooled. Soon things were back more or less exactly as they'd been before all the self-righteous ballyhoo, with the cops working their neighbourhoods like local bully-boys, quicker with a night-stick than a warrant: who gave a shit about legal niceties? Delucca's beef was that of all the cops on the take around the city, he'd got only the crumbs from the table, thanks to that sonofabitch Chief Rawlins.

He folded the newspaper and stuffed it in his pocket. It was another half-hour's walk down to the docks where he and MacKenzie had arranged to meet. After a process of elimination, they'd narrowed down their suspects to a shortlist of three. A little pressure, a promise of going easy on them if they came across thrown in, and they'd be able to chalk up another case solved.

He arrived at the meeting place five minutes early and, since MacKenzie wasn't there, leaned against a wall and took out the newspaper again to pass the time until he showed. A couple of paragraphs near the bottom of one of the inside pages caught his eye. Thomas Edison, the man who'd invented the kinetoscope, had just received his letters patent for the revolutionary machine, and was taking legal action against anyone marketing their own versions of the motion picture equipment. Delucca read on with interest, the seeds of an idea already forming in his mind. He could be on to something. He noted names, addresses: Edison's laboratory was out at West Orange, New Jersey – a fair trek from the city but not impossible to reach on a free day. He looked thoughtful. Court action was being brought against American Mutoscope and the Biograph Company for infringement of the patents law, but the article said that Edison suspected others besides these were pirating his invention. This was something worth looking into. Maudie had mentioned seeing a studio near her mother's place over at East Flatbush where people were making 'moving pictures'; could be a piece of information Edison might pay for, if Delucca made a few unofficial enquiries of his own and struck up a deal on the side. While he waited for MacKenzie, who was now two minutes late, he ran over what he already knew about the booming 'flickers' business.

Three years ago, the world's first kinetoscope parlour had opened its doors at 1155 Broadway, and curious people – himself included – had paid their cents to look through peepholes in amazement at the short filmstrips that showed runaway trains, dancing girls and slapstick comics; the novelty had quickly caught on and soon nickelodeon parlours were springing up everywhere – in department stores, hotels, saloons – in major cities all over the country, always with the same gratifying results: curiosity, amusement, patronage and profits. Although the public response was enthusiastic, Edison's kinetoscope had its limitations, mainly the fact that only one viewer could look through the peephole at a time. Delucca remembered how, when he'd taken his two boys to a phonograph parlour on Bergen Street, they'd squabbled about who was going to look through the peephole first. People began asking, what if pictures could somehow be projected onto a large screen for an audience; and no sooner had entrepreneurs dreamed of such an advance than technology turned the dream into reality. Through the work of Robert K. Paul in England and the Lumière brothers in France, as well as Edison's technician Laurie Dickson at the West Orange lab, the motion picture projector had become a commercial reality in only two years. Edison had first introduced his to the public at Koster and Bial's music hall on Herald Square – Delucca had got a neighbour to mind the boys and taken Maudie for the night out – and soon after the Lumière brothers had launched theirs at B. F. Keith's vaudeville house at the Union Square Theatre. Other vaudeville managers followed suit, and soon other houses began including motion pictures on their cards, along with dog acts, lyric tenors and slapstick comedians. With the appearance of the Biograph projector, which was capable of showing bigger, clearer and sharper pictures than its rivals' machines, the 'flickers' business spread, bringing instant success and Edison's wrath. With Edison's competitors riding roughshod over the patents law to grab their share of the profits, and lawsuits flying, Delucca could see a chance to make a quick buck.

He folded away his paper, looked up to see MacKenzie coming hurriedly from the opposite direction.

'Where the fuck have you been? I bin waitin' ten minutes already!'

'Sorry, Roy. I was held up leavin'. What's the score?'

'We've narrowed the list to three names. One of 'em's been on the take, losin' the cargo . . . so today, we get him. I thought it over last night. OK. Here's how.' They began walking side by side in the direction of the docks. 'We interview each one on the list separately, tell each one that the other two have squealed, an' pointed the finger. They'll get mad, tell us everything they know, and then we'll find out which one of 'em's bin milking off the cargo. Trust me. It'll work like a dream.'

Marianna had chosen one of the smartest outfits in her wardrobe for her lunchtime assignation with Curt Koenig – a walking suit in two-tone aubergine velvet, with the stylish hat her mother had so disapproved of to complete the ensemble. It was black, with an enormous brim and deep crown, decorated with a wide ruched band of rainbow velvet and masses of matching feathers; worn at an angle with one side of the brim subtly turned up, it was the perfect complement to the austere chic of the costume skirt and tailored jacket that fitted like a glove. Alone in her room, she studied the effect in the mirror, wondering if he would like it, if he would think she looked elegant and sophisticated, if he thought she was pretty. Now that it was almost time to go and meet him at last, she was nervous, tense, unsure of herself. She looked at herself critically.

True, she was what most people regarded as a good-looking girl, without being a noted beauty; at least, nobody had ever told her that they thought she was beautiful. She had dark, luxuriant hair with a natural wave, clear skin, regular features, fine eyes. Good looks ran in the Eastbridge genes, and in her mother's family: grandmother Ayres had been a noted belle in her native Massachusetts; her great-aunt, a Winthrop, had been much admired not only in Boston society but in London and Paris, where her father had sent her to acquire 'European polish'. Though she hadn't the benefit of that, Marianna had had the finest private tutors, music and dance teachers money could buy. But if Curt Koenig didn't find her attractive, what did any of that matter?

She slipped his note into her handbag, went downstairs and out of the house. Her father was at his office on Wall Street, her mother was entertaining friends in the parlour. No-one to see her. She hailed a cab and got out a whole block before she needed to, so that the walk to the restaurant would give her time to calm her nerves. Although she arrived exactly at the time he'd given, he was already there and waiting for her.

'Miss Eastbridge!' He rose from the table and they shook hands; the pressure of his fingers over hers sent all her pulses leaping. He was smartly dressed, handsomer than ever. His eyes seemed bluer, more intense than she remembered. Or was that because he was paying her so much more attention now? When they'd met before he'd barely glanced at her. She gave herself a reason for that. It was the height of vulgarity for a man to show too much interest in a woman he didn't know, had never been formally introduced to. It was different now. They sat down, and the hovering waiter – who'd recognized her – handed them the menu cards. Curt couldn't believe the prices, even for the hors d'oeuvre.

She thanked him profusely for the flowers. He was amused, even taken aback, by her intensity. Her, thank him? Was she serious?

'A small enough thing to do for a girl who persuaded Charles Frohman to audition me before anyone else.' His smile dazzled her. 'He offered me the part of Monte Cristo. Even now, it hasn't sunk in.'

'Oh, that's wonderful!' Her face lit up. 'I knew he would, he just had to, the moment he saw you! When I heard he was producing the play, I knew you were exactly right for that part! And that's what I told him.'

'I'm glad you could make it today . . . I thought maybe you wouldn't be able to, not at such short notice. But I had to tell you the news first.' Keep cool, don't gush, Shawn had advised him; gushing was vulgar, unsophisticated. It betrayed raw edges, and that would never do. Even though a stage career and mixing socially as well as professionally with the theatrical middle classes had put polish on the boy from Minneapolis, Minnesota, when you were dealing with the Eastbridges of this world caution was the key. The trick was to take things slowly, not yield to the temptation to talk up to her, even if she did live on swanky Fifth Avenue, even if she was F. H. Eastbridge's daughter. He didn't even have to try very hard because she already liked him. Could any other girl have proved that so spectacularly as she had?

'I hope you didn't think I was interfering when I asked Mr Frohman to see you.' Interfering? Was she kidding him, or what? She'd got Broadway's major impresario to audition him for the leading part in the biggest production for years, and now she was apologizing for it? 'I heard that John Drew would probably be cast in the part, and I knew he'd be all wrong for it. That's what really decided me. When I found out that Mr Frohman was going to be at a party we attended at the Hotel Astor, I got a friend to introduce me . . . and I just asked him.' Even now, she could scarcely believe that she'd had the nerve. 'He was very kind, and he didn't seem to mind at all. At first, I thought he'd only agreed just to humour me. But I knew when he saw you on stage he'd soon change his mind.'

What could he say to that? That he was indebted to her? That would only be half true: she'd got Frohman to see him, yes; but it had been his performance at the audition that had secured him the part. He compromised instead. 'Whatever, however, I'm very flattered that you did what you did.' Another smile; his smile worked miracles on women far more worldly, far more experienced than she was. 'I didn't realize my performance in Julius Cahn's play had impressed anyone so much.'

'It did.' While they paused in their conversation to order the meal, his own remarks raised a question in his mind. It was well known that Charles Frohman watched every play produced on Broadway, no matter how short a run it had, no matter how small; no man was more adept than he was at perceiving theatrical talent. Why, then, had it needed a besotted girl, with no theatrical connections, to bring his abilities to the impresario's notice? Curt wasn't sure that he liked the answer. In a second or two, while the waiter brought the champagne he'd ordered – Shawn had staked him a fifty-dollar loan in case he needed it – he had a more comforting thought to console himself with: Frohman was a busy man and had only seen *Under the Red Robe* once; Marianna Eastbridge had seen it three times, to his knowledge. There lay the answer. The more she'd seen him, the more convinced she'd been that he was worthy of greater things; all she'd done was to open Frohman's eyes a little wider, and focus them.

'You're not eating,' he said, pouring more champagne, then remembering that the waiter was supposed to do it for him. He cursed inwardly, but she hadn't even noticed.

'I don't think I could eat very much. I'm far too excited.'

He caught the tone of her voice, the look in her eyes. Time to risk something.

'Why, because you're here with me?'

'Yes.'

'It's gratifying to think that you'd place having lunch

with me so high on the list of things you find exciting.' The
colour rushed to her cheeks, and he wanted to smile. He
was used to women wanting him, but a millionaire's
daughter was an entirely different ball game; this was heady
stuff to handle. Could Shawn have possibly been right
when he'd said that Curt was holding her in the palm of his
hand? Maybe. He had only to look at her now to know that
what she'd done for him had been motivated by something
far more than simple admiration for his acting talent. But
he was on shaky, even dangerous ground encouraging her;
this was F. H. Eastbridge's daughter, for Christ's sake! 'Is
your father interested in the theatre?'

'Only as a socially acceptable means of entertainment.'
Was that a harsh note he could detect in her voice? 'If it
were possible, I think he'd prefer to spend his evenings on
Wall Street rather than on Broadway.'

'You get your love of the theatre from your mother,
then?' His sharp eye caught the guarded expression, the
sudden withdrawal; this was a subject that she didn't want
to talk about.

'I don't think either of them has a deep feeling for
anything.' It was a bold statement, and he was almost
shocked. Here was a turn-up for the books. The picture
Shawn had surmised, the heiress, the spoiled, cherished
only daughter, wasn't borne out by reality; this was a
bitter young woman. 'We don't have very much in
common at all.' Her upbringing had taught her to be
self-possessed, composed, how to conduct herself in any
company, and she brought all three to bear now, out of
habit more than anything else. Her parents had always
taught her never to reveal her innermost feelings to
anyone, least of all strangers, never to themselves. To give
way to any emotion was a sign of weakness, a lack of character. No Eastbridge worthy of the name would ever yield
to such a thing.

She seemed barely to have touched her meal. 'Is there
anything wrong with that?' He nodded towards the food.
'If you don't like it, I can get the waiter to bring you
something else.'

'No . . . oh, no . . . it's fine. Really.' She was smiling again now. 'I'm just far more interested in talking to you than eating.' She sipped her champagne. 'Please, tell me more about yourself . . . where you come from, about your family. How did you come to be on the stage? Do you live in Manhattan?'

He laughed, very softly. 'Which do you want me to tell you first?'

'I'm sorry . . .'

'That's OK.' He should have said 'all right'. That's what Shawn would have told him. OK was considered slang in Eastbridge circles. But, what the hell, he wasn't on stage now and he couldn't pretend he was something he wasn't. 'I was born in Minneapolis. My father runs a big livery stable there.' He gave her a brief account of his family, his past, his quarrel with his father when he'd left home to head for New York and a career on the stage. He sensed an understanding when he mentioned how he and his father had fallen out; clearly, family arguments were something she identified with. Interesting. 'When my folks get to hear about this . . . me, landing the lead in a big Broadway play like *Monte Cristo* . . . they just won't believe it. But I told my dad I'd make it, whatever it took. As a pal of mine said – Shawn Duchovsky, you met him with me that day in the chop house – success is the best revenge.'

'Yes, you're quite right. It is.' She was astonished when he told her that his father had once been a professional prize-fighter. 'I can't imagine anyone wanting to fight for a living. I just can't. I don't think I could bear even to watch it.' So that was where he'd got his splendid physique from? 'Is that what he wanted you and your brothers to be? Is that why you quarrelled?'

'He taught us all how to handle ourselves. I could walk down to the Lower East Side any time and not have to worry that someone might try to jump me.' She was fascinated, awestruck. She'd never met anyone like him before. The young men in her own narrow circle, Lauterbachs, Elliotts and Depews, would run a mile from any physical confrontation. Curt Koenig was a real man.

119

He gave answers to her other questions. 'Right now, I live in Queens . . . I share an apartment with Shawn Duchovsky. It's cheaper when you split the rent.' That smile again. The blue eyes twinkled. Was this what it felt like, being in love? She'd read about it, wondered about it, never quite imagined it happening to her. Surrounded by Lauterbachs and Depews, was it any wonder? But she felt giddy just gazing across the table at him. 'And what about you?' he was asking her suddenly. 'You've asked me a lot of things. But you haven't told me anything about yourself at all.'

'There isn't that much to tell.' Her life seemed so unexciting, monotonously predictable compared to his, where almost every day was different. While she described the daily routine on Fifth Avenue, Curt took the opportunity to study her.

Shawn was right; she was a good-looking girl. She had an attractive face, a slim figure under the stylish outfit which was worth anyone's second glance; and that outfit, he'd wager, had come from one of the most exclusive shops in Manhattan, with a price tag to match. She was intelligent, well educated, undoubtedly she had class. Curt had noticed straight away how the waiters treated her with deference and respect, how they'd recognized her the moment she'd come in. 'Good day, Miss Eastbridge.' Like Shawn said, when you lived on Fifth Avenue and your father was a millionaire on Wall Street, people sat up and took notice. Would Charles Frohman still have sent for him if Jane Doe from the Lower East Side had asked? He didn't kid himself about the answer. With an Eastbridge on his arm, doors opened; did it really matter that she wasn't his type?

'Could I see you again?' He saw her look of surprise. 'It isn't easy arranging a social life around performing in the theatre. There are matinees twice a week, and I have to be on stage every night except Sunday.' An idea now. 'Tell you what. I'll take you to lunch again, the day after tomorrow, and we could have dinner on Sunday night.'

Her mind was racing wildly. She could get out of the

120

house easily enough to meet him for lunch downtown, but her parents were always at home on Sundays.

'Is that a problem?'

'No . . . no, I don't think so . . .'

'I think there's a "but" coming here somewhere . . .'

'It isn't that . . . I'd love to have lunch with you again.' He sensed an edge to her voice now. 'It's just that my parents are very old-fashioned about Sundays . . . they have definite ideas on how the day *shouldn't* be spent.'

'I understand. Hey, I have a much better idea. Why don't you come to the evening performance on Friday, and we can go on to dinner from the theatre?'

'That would be lovely!' Friday would be the perfect day for her to slip unnoticed out of the house; her father always spent the evenings at his club and her mother played bridge with Mrs Gardener, Mrs Elliott and Mrs Depew. Like Cinderella, she was free till midnight.

He beckoned to the waiter to bring the bill and helped her from her chair. They shared a cab until it was time for her to get out at Fifth Avenue. Once she was out of sight, Curt got the driver to put him down at the corner of Lexington and Central Park; after paying the bill in the restaurant, he had just enough left to cover the fare.

'Hey, how did it go?' Shawn was all wild enthusiasm. 'Bet you had her eatin' right out of your hand!'

'Shawn, she's a lady, not a carriage horse.'

'An' you know what they say about ladies . . . the colonel's lady and Rosie O'Grady!' He slapped him on the back. 'Come on, loosen up a little and let's hear it! Didn't I tell you she'd be a walkover?'

'Pity you didn't tell me about the prices in that fancy restaurant you checked out.' He showed him the bill and Shawn whistled.

'Hey, what you do . . . buy the place?'

'That's what it felt like. Can you imagine what it'd cost to eat at a joint like that every day?'

'Curt, you gotta pay for anything classy.'

'Tell me about it. I invited her to lunch again the day

after tomorrow, and then dinner after the performance on Friday. That was before I saw the bill.' Suddenly, he saw the funny side and they both laughed.

'Listen.' Shawn was en route to the untidy kitchen. 'Let me fix us some coffee and then you can tell me about it. And don't worry . . . I can lend you somethin' if you're strapped for a few extra bucks. I know you'll pay me back.'

Curt flung himself down on the nearest chair and took the weight off his feet. It had been a long walk back from the wrong end of Central Park to their apartment in Queens. 'It sure comes expensive impressing an Eastbridge.'

Shawn was back now, coffee pot and cups in hands.

'Hey, you quit that kinda talk, you hear me? You know how the sayin' goes . . . you gotta speculate to accumulate. Her old man would say just the same. Curt, you just *had* to do it . . . it was her who put the word in with Frohman. Look. I know you would've got there without that . . . eventually . . . but that could be a long time. You gotta grab chances in this life, make things easy for yourself. Sometimes, it's smarter to take the short cuts.'

'I know.'

'What's your problem, then? She likes you, you like her . . . don't you?' He poured the coffee. 'She's smart, she's pretty, she's got class. And, most important of all, she's F. H. Eastbridge's daughter.'

'I got the feeling she isn't the apple of daddy's eye like you thought she'd be.'

'Oh? How come? What did she say?'

'Not so much what she said as what she left out. Every time I brought his name up – and her mother's, come to that – she didn't bite.'

'Why worry?' Shawn shrugged. 'As long as she's sweet on you, it don't matter about anyone else.'

'A guy like F. H. Eastbridge has probably got some prospective husband already lined up for her . . . she's his only daughter, remember?'

'But she's got a mind of her own. And he won't turn sour and disinherit her. Think about it. At the end of the day, however hard a guy he is, he'll just want his sweet little girl to be happy.'

'I guess.' Curt was thoughtful for a minute or two. 'She did let something slip, when she was telling me about herself. Not that she told me very much at all. She has her own trust fund money, an account at the New Amsterdam Bank on 39th Street . . . it was set up for her by her grandparents. It set me thinking. Even if there was a rift with her folks for a while, she'd be independent of them till they came round.'

'Wish my grandparents had set a trust fund up for me. Trouble was, they never had a bean to spare for anyone or anything. Besides which, there was five of us to think about.'

'Same here.' Curt stretched and yawned. He ached all over. 'Jesus, I feel like hell. And I have to be on stage in two hours.'

'Just think of Friday.'

Marianna let herself into the house and, without taking off her outdoor clothes or even her hat, went straight into the parlour and began to play the piano.

It was one of her favourite pieces, a Liszt sonata, one that she had always loved to play loudly but which she never did because her father and mother would have disapproved; and when her father was in the house she never permitted to play at all because he complained that the noise disturbed him.

She pressed her long, graceful fingers down hard upon the keys, let her joy express itself through the lilting, exhilarating melody. Liszt had composed the sonata when he was a young man and, she guessed, had been in love. Now, she understood exactly how that felt.

CHAPTER TEN

Delucca's official day off; things to do that he didn't want Maudie, or anyone else, to find out about. In this world, it paid a man to keep his mouth shut, to keep his private business to himself. Waiting for the ferry to cross Newark Bay, he smoked what was left of his last cigarette.

It wasn't that he didn't trust Maudie: a cop's wife knew better than to gossip over the back yard fence; it was his mother-in-law he wouldn't trust any further than he could throw her. And that couldn't ever be far enough. She had nothing better to do than jaw with her neighbours, anyone who came into the house to pass the time of day. There was Mrs Fachetti from down the street, who ran errands and kept her company as a favour to Maudie, Mrs O'Flaherty from next door and Mrs Olovski from the house next to that, and Delucca knew that once he told Maudie something she'd tell her mother even if he'd sworn her to secrecy, and that was just what he didn't want to happen. With Maudie's mother's mouth as big as the Long Island Sound it wouldn't be five minutes before the whole of Flatbush knew.

It was the newspaper article about Edison's patents war that had first given him the glimmer of an idea, and the more he'd thought about it, the better it seemed to sound. Edison was a smart guy, and he was a businessman; after a word in his ear, Delucca didn't have any doubts that he'd see it that way too. Fact was, his invention wasn't the five-minute wonder some people reckoned it would be; with the new advances in kinetoscope technology that he'd been reading up about, seemed as if a whole load of guys were getting ready to jump on Edison's bandwagon; with the 'flickers' shows moving up a notch from a peephole in the nickelodeon parlours to moving pictures projected

124

onto a screen, those same guys could see the possibilities . . . and there were dollar signs in their eyes.

Delucca took a last deep drag on his cigarette and flung down the stub. This was what this little out-of-state trip was all about. Edison couldn't have his eyes everywhere, find out just who was violating the patent on his invention, and where; but a smart cop who knew his way around the city was in a prime position to discover a lot more. That was the deal: Delucca unearthed the names, Edison paid a flat fee, no questions asked. Delucca was certain a man as obsessed with his rights as Edison was would want to do business.

He already had answers for any arguments Edison might hit him with – such as if a violation of the patents law was committed, the police had to act anyhow. Anyone in the know down at City Hall would tell him that it just didn't work that way. With all the murders, robberies and prostitution rackets the cops had to deal with in the city, who cared if a few mavericks were making copies of Edison's machine, and improving on his original design? Delucca's way, Edison got his own eyes and ears on the ground, and stamping out the pirates meant keeping his moving pictures developments a one-horse race.

Delucca peered over the side of the ferry into the muddy, swirling water. He wondered what MacKenzie was doing just about now. Late last night, as they were coming off duty, Chief Rawlins had put him on a fresh case – some body dragged up from the East River a few hours before.

Not uncommon, as any cop in New York City knew – bodies were always being dredged out of the East River or the Hudson, usually some drunk, some whore, or some vagrant who'd got high on cheap booze and toppled over the bridge; but Chief Rawlins suspected possible foul play because of the condition of the body.

Maybe MacKenzie would have cleared it up before Delucca was back on duty tomorrow; maybe it would take them both a few days. Either way, Rawlins was most likely wrong and it'd turn out to be no-one who mattered after all.

* * *

Edwina Eastbridge had first become suspicious about Marianna during afternoon tea at the Lauterbach house on 78th Street; mentioning the flowers Jerry Lauterbach had sent to her daughter she was astonished, then perturbed, when his mother said that she knew nothing about it, that she was sure he would have told her first, and that Jerry wasn't paying special attention to any girl right now. To cover her embarrassment, Edwina had swiftly steered their conversation on to other things, but inwardly she'd seethed. Whatever Marianna was up to – and by now Edwina was convinced that she was up to something – her deceit had come close to making her mother look a fool. That Edwina would never forgive.

Back at the house on Fifth Avenue, she'd kept her suspicions to herself, but watched and waited. Marianna seemed to be more out of the house than in. Edwina had also noticed a subtle change in her, a change that, when she cast her mind back, seemed to date from the time she received the flowers. One afternoon, when Marianna had gone shopping in Manhattan, Edwina went up to look round her room.

She went straight to her daughter's dressing table; every drawer except one was unlocked. No sign of the key; she went to fetch the spare from her husband's study, where duplicates were kept of every key in the house. The drawer contained only a theatre programme, almost three months old, and nothing else; but when she took it from the drawer it fell open at a page that had been signed, and an envelope fell out.

Edwina read the inscription: *To Marianna Eastbridge . . . Cordially, Curt Koenig, 1897.* Her name, written across the envelope in a large artistic hand not dissimilar to her own, was in the same handwriting. Edwina took out the letter inside.

The date was interesting. The same day as the delivery of flowers. She quivered with rage: this Curt Koenig, this actor, had had the temerity to invite her daughter to have lunch with him.

She took the programme, and the letter, straight downstairs to show her husband.

He was writing a company report for the Title and Guarantee Trust Company in his study when she came in, neat stacks of papers showing growth charts and projected investment figures all in precise order on his desk. He didn't speak, make any comment at all while she ranted about their daughter's duplicity, about her lies and deceit. He merely put aside his pen and glanced down at the incriminating objects Edwina had placed in his hands. Then he turned back to the papers on his desk. Only someone who knew F. H. Eastbridge as thoroughly as she did could have told that the outward appearance of calm was a façade that hid the real depth of his anger.

'Take those back where you found them and lock the drawer again. For the time being, say nothing at all.' He glanced up at her. 'Leave this with me. I'll deal with it.'

'Curt, there's a place showing moving pictures on a screen – a big screen – down on Union Square . . . I saw the advertisement hoarding when I was passing in a cab just the other day . . . please, do you think you could take me there?' They were on first name terms now, and she was meeting him two, sometimes three times a week, still without her parents' knowledge. It would be different when rehearsals for *The Count of Monte Cristo* started and there were articles in the New York newspapers about Charles Frohman's surprise choice for a leading man, and his name became well known enough for her to risk introducing him to them; until then, Marianna was taking no chances. Only successful men were likely to find favour with her father. 'Curt?'

'Sure, if that's where you want to go . . . there's another place on 14th Street. The little vaudeville theatre there. Two Englishmen, I heard – used to be in a vaudeville act together – started it up, rigged their own projector and are calling it the Vitagraph. Shawn's been there. He said they keep running out of subjects to show on their screen, so they're looking for a studio to rent where they can make more pictures to put on the bill.'

'Do you think they make very much money doing that?'

Curt shrugged. 'Hard to say . . . must be somethin' in it. The kinetoscope caused somethin' of a sensation when Edison first invented it, but interest dropped off after a while . . . could be these longer little films, moving pictures you can show to audiences on a large screen, will catch on too. Then again, maybe not. They only last a few minutes.'

Marianna moved a little closer to him, thrilled by the gentle pressure of his arm against hers as they strolled. 'Wouldn't it be wonderful if they could film an entire play? Just think. *The Count of Monte Cristo* on a screen, so everyone could see it! Even people who'd never been inside a real theatre.'

'Only because they can't afford the prices of the seats.' He realized that sounded like an admonishment, and he hadn't really meant it to; it wasn't her fault she'd been born an Eastbridge, that she had no idea what it felt like to be poor. Cushioned as she was from the harsh realities of life behind the walls of a smart brownstone on Fifth Avenue, he'd wager there were huge chunks of the city that a girl like Marianna never even realized existed, like the slums on the Lower East Side where deprivation, overcrowding and disease were rife, the Jewish ghettos, the dens of vice. No, she wouldn't know about places like those, or the people who lived in them. 'I guess the moving picture parlours are a novelty,' he said, to change the subject. 'People always flock to see anything that's different. But one thing's for sure: nothing'll ever replace the theatres. Flickers are just a passing phase.' They'd arrived at the restaurant where he was taking her for lunch; most of his pay from the Metropolitan went on lunches. But then, as Shawn was constantly reminding him, heiresses didn't come cheap. And it was all a means to an end. He held back the door for her. 'This time next year, those parlours on Union Square and 14th Street'll be out of business, all shuttered and boarded up. Or showing the next craze to hit town.'

'I suppose so.'

The waiter showed them to their table and they sat down. While they waited for the meal they discussed the last night of *Under the Red Robe* which closed at the Metropolitan that Saturday, and the start of rehearsals for Frohman's new play. Curt thought that there were bound to be a lot of pressmen and critics at the final performance, now that news of the starring role he'd landed in *The Count of Monte Cristo* was out.

'I'm not used to all the attention . . . things being written about me in the press. In the beginning, there were just rumours flying around that Charles Frohman had cast a little-known actor for the lead in his new play, and critics speculating about who that might be. Frohman enjoys playing his cards close to his chest; when they sent someone from the *New York Times* to his office at the Lyceum to interview him, he wouldn't be drawn. He told me he didn't think it'd be fair if he made an outright announcement, and I got pressmen hounding me night and day, asking crazy questions . . . you know how they do? He said I didn't realize it now but I would as soon as rehearsals started . . . that there's a lot of pressure on the leading players, and I wasn't used to handling it. I told him I didn't mind at all.'

'I'm going to cut every piece they write about you out of the newspapers and make an album of them.'

He smiled. 'You and my mother both. I wrote her a while ago and told her the news . . . but I don't think it's quite sunk in yet. My father and brothers have never heard of Charles Frohman . . . come to that, they've never even been inside a theatre.' Marianna could hardly credit it. Didn't they have theatres in Minneapolis? 'I don't think any of my family quite understand what it means to have the lead part in a big Broadway play.'

'They must still be very proud of you.'

Curt shrugged. 'I guess. When they read about it. But we haven't talked about Saturday yet . . . it's the last night of *Red Robe*. Will you have dinner with me after the performance? Somewhere special?'

Marianna's face fell. 'I'd love to, Curt, but I can't. Not Saturday. I have to go with my parents to the Hotel Prince

George . . . some boring function. I don't want to . . . I'd much rather be with you.' She smiled at him. 'But I can't get out of it.' A pause. 'I could come on Friday instead. That's the one night I know both my parents will be out. In any case, won't there be some sort of celebration at the theatre, it being the last night and all?'

'There's a big party planned, but not everyone in the cast has something to celebrate. At least, those that haven't got more work haven't. I'm one of the lucky ones.'

'You deserve it.'

'You and Charles Frohman might be in the minority in thinking that. I don't have any illusions about how some people in this business will see me . . . or how ready they'll be to stab me in the back if the play doesn't do well. They'll say I shouldn't have been given the lead because I haven't really proved myself . . . that it should have gone to someone well known like William Gillette or John Drew.'

'They'll only say that if they're jealous.'

'You're very perceptive.'

'You are too.'

There was a pause, while the waiter came to take their order. Curt didn't speak again until he'd gone.

'You haven't told your parents about me, have you? About us?'

Us. A thrill ran through her. He was speaking about them as a couple, for the first time; until now, Marianna hadn't dared to see their relationship that way. Part of her had always wondered if he had been so kind, so attentive to her over the past few weeks, simply because he was grateful that she'd gone to Charles Frohman about the play. Now, she wondered if she'd been wrong. Was it, could it be possible that he felt the same way towards her as she did about him? Even now, she was afraid to ask him outright. A lady, a well-brought-up girl from Fifth Avenue never would.

'My father's very strict . . . I told you that when we first met. My mother, too. They'd never approve of anyone I hadn't been properly introduced to. But when the play opens at the Lyceum and everyone knows who you are,

130

everything will be different.' Shawn Duchovsky's words exactly.

'I think I can bear to wait till then.' He gave her the charming smile that would have melted stone. 'So, Friday it is?'

'Friday it is.' Three days. It seemed an eternity away. But well worth waiting for. She would wear her favourite Worth gown.

F. H. Eastbridge left his Wall Street office at the usual hour, then took a cab home along Broadway to Fifth Avenue. When he entered the hall, his evening newspaper was waiting for him, and the afternoon delivery of mail. What he'd been expecting for the past few days was at the bottom of the pile, a long brown envelope that bore the postmark Chicago.

Edwina was still not back from her afternoon meeting of the New York City Women's Guild, at the Ladies' Lunch Establishment on Broadway at 24th Street; Marianna was either out, or somewhere else in the house. F. H. strode to the sanctity of his study, closed the door, sat down at his desk and reached for his paper knife. He slit the brown manila envelope open along its top and let the contents slide out onto the blotter.

There were three sheets of typewritten paper, a personal letter, and an account for forty dollars. He read the typewritten pages slowly, carefully, before putting them back into the envelope. Then he wrote a cheque for forty dollars and pinned it to the account.

He rarely, if ever, drank before dinner. Today was one of the rare occasions when he did take a drink of bourbon before eight o'clock. One and a half inches up the glass; he knew the exact measure by heart. He sipped it slowly, sitting at his desk, until every last drop had gone. His mind slipped back, unusually, into the past: if only he'd had a son.

He picked up the brown manila envelope and held it for a moment in his hands, deep in thought. Then he unlocked his private safe on the other side of the room and placed the envelope inside.

The penultimate night of *Under the Red Robe*. Only two more performances at the Metropolitan Theatre. His last matinee performance had come and gone. In two weeks he'd be rehearsing for *The Count of Monte Cristo* at the Lyceum and all his worries would be over. When Charles Frohman had told him what his salary would be, starting in the first week of rehearsals, Curt had drawn in his breath. No more borrowing from Shawn to take Marianna out on the town, no more scrimping and saving. At last, he was going places; his faith in himself, despite all the past trials and tribulations, was vindicated. He couldn't wait to go back to his family in Minneapolis and make them eat their words. He'd already planned the trip by train for the following week.

Knowing Marianna was in the audience, he gave one of his finest performances. In between scenes, he chatted with Shawn Duchovsky in his dressing room; when he came offstage Shawn helped him get off his make-up and change into his evening clothes so as not to keep Marianna waiting.

'What restaurant is it tonight, then?'

'I let Marianna choose . . . she's picked some swank place with a French-sounding name, east of Broadway.' His face was clean again. He poured some water from the jug on one side into a basin and began to scrub vigorously. 'Jesus, don't think I've ever gotten used to this greasepaint!'

Shawn perched on the edge of a chair. 'Chalk it all up to the price of fame.'

'No fame yet . . . but give it time. Just give it time.' He grabbed a towel and dried his skin, then darted behind the screen to change from his stage costume into evening attire. There was a howl from Shawn.

'Hey, you gone shy on me all of a sudden? I seen your butt before, remember?'

'This is a theatre dressing room, Shawn! People are just liable to walk in at any time . . . get me my shirt studs, will ya?'

Shawn found them among the clutter on Curt's dressing table. 'Hey, have a good time tonight, you hear?' Curt came out and started combing his hair. 'When you goin' to meet old man Eastbridge, then?'

Curt stopped what he was doing and made a face in the mirror. 'Gettin' round him, from what she's said about him, just might take a little longer than that fame we were talking about.'

Marianna gazed across the table at him, barely conscious of the discreet glances coming their way from other diners; he looked so handsome tonight, the black suit only emphasizing his fair good looks, the startling blue of his eyes. She was so much in love with him that it was impossible to look at him without wanting to reach out and touch him; but that was something she knew she'd never do. No lady would.

'Curt, what are you thinking?' Unbidden, echoes from long ago, that last summer at Lake Winnipesaukee. Her mother's voice. *Young men have filthy minds.* Why think of that now? 'There's nothing wrong, is there?'

He smiled. 'No. No, of course not. I was just thinking of that long train ride to Minneapolis to see my folks, and wishing that I didn't have to do it.'

'But you want to see them, don't you?'

'Yeah . . . I guess. It seems so long since I was home.' He shrugged and smiled again. 'It's just that finishing at the Metropolitan tomorrow night and starting rehearsals for *Monte Cristo* the week after next doesn't give me much free time. Almost none at all, in fact.' He toyed with his dessert spoon. 'If I don't go to Minneapolis next week, I won't have time to go at all. Once the play opens, I'll have to stay put in New York.'

'They could make the trip here instead.' He surprised her by laughing. His folks, in swanky New York City! Talk about fish out of water. Not that he was ashamed of them, or his own origins; far from it. But they were small-town folks and always would be, while he'd always been the one who was different: he felt completely at home in elevated company. Rubbing shoulders with high-fliers and the theatrical élite would just make them feel uncomfortable.

Not easy for a girl brought up on Fifth Avenue to understand.

'I don't somehow think that would work out.'

'But surely they'll want to see you on stage? In a play like *Monte Cristo*? Curt, this is the lead in a major Broadway production we're talking about!'

'Yeah, I wrote them and explained all that. Sure, they understand. And they'll all want to see me in it. Momma, so she can go back home and say, "That was my boy up there!" and Dad and those crazy brothers of mine so they can poke fun at me for getting dressed up and struttin' across a stage!'

'Poke fun?' Marianna looked shocked, then angry. 'Don't they realize the prestige attached to playing the leading role in a Charles Frohman play?'

Curt covered a sigh; she'd missed the point completely. Not all that surprising, since she'd never had any brothers of her own. The Koenig boys had always teased each other; in a close-knit family, it was something that just happened and you never really grew out of it. 'You got me wrong. They don't mean anything by it. In their own way, they're as proud as Momma . . . and they do understand how important it is to be playing a lead role on Broadway. Even in Minneapolis they've heard of Charles Frohman.' He smiled. 'When you've been around horses and livery stables all your life, seeing your brother on stage dressed up in fancy clothes takes a little getting used to, that's all it is. No offence meant. None taken.' Marianna still wasn't sure she liked the sound of them.

'I'll miss not seeing you, after you've gone.' It would only be a week, but seven days without him was like an eternity. And she wouldn't even be at his last performance in *Red Robe* tomorrow night. 'You said there was a big party planned after the play's finished tomorrow . . . you're still going?'

'I guess. But I won't be able to stay at it for very long.' Somehow, that thought comforted her. 'I have to get back to the apartment and pack my things, get some sleep. My train to Minneapolis leaves first thing the next morning.'

He paid the bill for their meal, and the doorman called them a cab. It was relatively quiet along Broadway and Fifth Avenue now, with the after-theatre traffic already gone and even late night shops closed. As the cab drew up outside her door, he took hold of her hand. Then he leaned over, took her chin in his hands, and kissed her.

'Marianna, I'll see you the minute I get back.' She stared at him, speechless, breathless. No man had ever kissed her on the lips before. She was confused, not even certain if she liked it. Part of her was thrilled, because she loved him so much, but her total lack of experience made her uncertain what she should say to him now, how she should act. He forestalled her by speaking first. 'You always look beautiful . . . but you looked especially beautiful tonight.' He raised her limp hand to his lips and kissed it, without taking his eyes from hers. 'I just want you to know that all the time I'm away in Minneapolis I'll be thinking about you.'

She restrained her sudden urge to fling her arms around his neck and kiss him back. 'I'll be thinking about you, too.' She smiled. 'Curt . . . will you see me to the door?'

He told the cab driver to wait. He helped her out, and waited with her at the top of the steps while she looked in her evening bag for her key. 'Can you come inside, just for a moment?' She opened the front door and he followed her into the hall. He caught his breath – what a place! He'd never been inside a house on Fifth Avenue before. So this was how a millionaire lived? He saw the marble floor, the gold-framed oil paintings, the gleaming furniture and the huge chandelier. But before he could say anything at all, a door to their left suddenly opened and they were confronted by Marianna's parents. She turned visibly pale.

'Father . . . Momma! I didn't think you'd be home till later . . .'

'That is very evident.' They were both staring coldly in Curt's direction. Her father went on. 'May I be permitted to know who this is, since I don't believe we've ever been introduced?'

Curt extended his right hand, in vain. 'Good evening, sir.

135

Ma'am.' At that moment, he was grateful for his theatrical training. But to no avail: their eyes remained hostile. He could see at a glance that his charm wasn't going to work on either of these two.

'Father, this is Curt Koenig, the Broadway actor.' There was pride in her voice, in her eyes; he looked so handsome and imposing standing there. Her parents couldn't possibly dislike him. 'Charles Frohman has cast him for the leading role in his new play, *The Count of Monte Cristo*.'

'Indeed? Perhaps he should also find a suitable role for you, my dear, since your aptitude for deception is remarkably akin to the art of acting.'

'*Father . . .*'

'May I ask just where you think you've been?'

Curt took a step towards her. This wasn't at all how he'd wanted things to be, but it was too late for him to follow his original plan now. F.H. was a bully, a man clearly used to getting his own way and crushing underfoot anyone who dared cross him. Curt sensed that if he didn't stand by Marianna now, he'd lose his chance with her for ever.

'Mr Eastbridge, I'm sorry that you and your wife don't seem to approve of us . . . but I love Marianna and I want to marry her.' He didn't know if he'd shocked her more even than her parents. She stared at him. For a moment, there was utter silence.

A sneer appeared on F.H.'s lips. 'Did you decide this before or after you realized she was my daughter?'

'Father, how can you say such a thing?' Marianna moved close to Curt and gripped his arm. He loved her. He wanted her. He was the first person she'd ever seen who wasn't afraid to stand up to her father. She gazed up at him adoringly; this was one thing that neither of her parents was going to take away from her. 'I love him and I want to marry him.'

'Mr Koenig, I should be grateful if you would leave my house.'

Curt looked at Marianna. Her eyes were shining. Whatever they said to her when he had gone, however they tried to browbeat her, he knew that she wouldn't listen now. He smiled back at her. 'Marianna, I'll see you before my train goes.' He squeezed her hand and she felt strong. 'Take care.'

'You're taking a trip to Minneapolis?' How could her father possibly know that? Curt didn't answer him.

'Meet me tomorrow afternoon, three o'clock, in the Hamburg–Amerika Line office, 45 Broadway. Shawn works there. He'll show you where you can wait, if I'm held up.' He went out, and the front door closed behind him. She was alone again. When she looked back on that moment years later, she could remember the sudden horrible silence between the three of them, broken only by the loud ticking of the hall clock.

'Marianna, I want you in my study, if you please.' F. H. turned away from her abruptly, without giving her the chance to say a word. For a moment she hesitated; she was tempted to run up to her room and lock the door. But her mother was standing directly in front of the staircase, barring her way, and the old pull of fear and obedience was still strong. Head bowed, face white, Marianna followed her father into his study.

'Whatever you're going to say to me, Father, I won't change my mind and you can't make me! I love Curt and I want to be with him. And he loves me.'

F.H. had sat down at his desk; he leaned back in his chair. 'If that is what you choose to believe, my dear, then you are quite right . . . I can't make you change your mind. Only point out, perhaps, that your ridiculous infatuation and naivety in these matters hardly qualifies you to make a rational judgement. Of the deceit you've practised so assiduously over the past few months in order to meet this man, I'll say no more for the moment . . . after all, you're scarcely experienced enough to see him for what he really is: an ambitious main-chancer who doesn't care for you at all.' A cruel smile touched his lips, as if he took a perverse pleasure in hurting her. 'Do you really suppose he'd be so anxious to marry you if your name wasn't Eastbridge and you weren't my daughter?'

Marianna bit back angry tears. 'You still don't understand, do you, Father? That you can't manipulate me any more. That none of these insults are going to make the slightest difference to what I think, or what I intend to do. Curt doesn't care about my name, or your money. He loves me for myself. Not that you or Momma know the first thing about him!'

'That is where you're wrong.' He got up, went to his safe and unlocked it. He took out a folder, brought it back to his desk. He laid it down, opened it to the first of several typewritten pages. 'Shall I read it for you, or would you prefer to read it for yourself?' He sat down again. 'Curt Koenig, second son of Lorenz Koenig . . . a professional prize-fighter and livery stable owner. Mother, Martha Randolph, daughter of a local store-keeper. One of four sons . . . the youngest, Gene Koenig, died in infancy. Born April fourteenth, 1871, in Minneapolis, Minnesota.' He glanced up. 'Shall I go on?' he flicked over the pages. 'It's a completely comprehensive report, I can assure you . . . schooling, early stage career, addresses in Minneapolis and here, in Queens County, where he shares an apartment with a friend by the name of Shawn Duchovsky.' For a moment she was too shocked to speak. 'I know about his movements, that he's recently been offered the leading role in Charles Frohman's new play – long before you told me this evening, I might add – and even that he purchased a return ticket to Minneapolis at Grand Central Station three days ago, to travel on Sunday. I can even tell you the time his train will leave.' So, that was how he knew! 'You look surprised, Marianna. Quite taken aback that I should be in possession of so much information. The explanation is simple. When your mother and I found out that you were seeing this man – how we found out, I won't waste time by going into – I commissioned a full report on him from the Pinkerton Detective Agency in Chicago.'

Slowly, Marianna rose to her feet. '*The Pinkerton Detective Agency?* You paid a firm of private detectives to compile a dossier about Curt?' She was outraged, furiously angry. '*How dare you!*'

F.H. snapped the folder closed. His eyes were as cold as ice. Never in her entire life had Marianna dared to address him in that way, dared to defy him. 'I think your emotional state has made you forget to whom you are speaking. I would advise you to remember it.' Behind her, the study door opened and her mother came into the room. 'It's perfectly clear to me and your mother that this young man is a totally unsuitable companion. Whatever his professional achievements might be in the future, he's just an actor. I will not have any daughter of mine associating with such a person, and I forbid you to see him or have any further communication with him . . . do I make myself absolutely clear?'

She felt deadly calm, more in control of herself, more certain of what she wanted to do, than at any time in her life. Curt loved her, and that made her strong. She wasn't afraid of her father any more. 'I'm sorry, Father . . . I won't do it.' She saw how stunned he was by her open defiance. 'I love Curt and he loves me. And I intend to marry him, whether you approve of it or not.'

'You stupid little fool!' her mother shouted angrily. 'Haven't you realized yet that he's only interested in your money? Do you think he'd even look at you if it wasn't for that hundred thousand dollars in the New Amsterdam Bank?'

Marianna turned to her, determined not to let herself down and cry. She looked at them both, thought of all the things in her life that they'd deprived her of. Ironic that, though they'd never shown her any love, they were now doing everything in their power to prevent her from finding it elsewhere.

'Money . . . that's all you really care about. It was never me. All my life, you've controlled me, pulled the strings, and I've always done what you wanted me to. But now I'm doing something for myself. If you won't accept Curt, or that I love him, I'll walk out of this house tonight. I have my own money, I can do exactly what I want. Until I marry Curt I can stay in a hotel.'

F.H. surveyed his only daughter coldly; how right he'd

been all these years to mourn the fact that Edwina had never given him a son. A son might have sown a few wild oats or had discreet affairs with showgirls, but he would have known exactly where to draw the line: no scandals, no unsuitable marriage to cause his parents social embarrassment; whatever he might have done in his private life he would have bowed to family duty and married where the Eastbridge interests lay. More now than at any time in his life, F.H. regretted the fact that his only child had been a girl.

'If that is what you wish to do, then by all means go ahead. Neither your mother nor I will detain you. But remember one thing, Marianna . . . and I mean what I say . . . if you walk out of this house tonight, I shall never permit you to come back again.'

She knew that he meant every word of it. F.H. never made idle threats. He was asking her to choose between them and Curt, and her choice had already been made.

'Goodbye, Father.' She hesitated at the study door where her mother stood, then walked past her without another word and went upstairs. It took her less than half an hour to pack. The study door was closed and the hall was empty when she came downstairs again with her baggage; no sound, except for the relentless ticking of the clock.

She opened the front door, looked behind her for the last time. The cold grey eyes from the portrait of her grandfather, Frederick H. Eastbridge II, stared out from their heavy gilded frame, as if to admonish her. But in her last act of defiance, she turned away from it abruptly, slammed the front door so hard that it was heard all over the house. *Cast aside thy shackles, cast off the chains that bind thee*; appropriately, she recalled the lines from a play that she'd almost forgotten. Turning her back on Fifth Avenue and all it represented, she felt free for the first time in her life.

CHAPTER ELEVEN

Her message came hand-delivered first thing the next morning, before either he or Shawn was even dressed. He stared down at it, still rubbing the sleep from his eyes, trying to take it all in. So there'd been a big scene with her parents after he'd left last night, and she'd packed her bags and moved out to a suite in the Hotel Marie Antoinette on Broadway at 66th Street? Not surprising, he supposed, when he remembered the hostile way they'd received him, and that old man Eastbridge had refused even to shake his hand.

He'd sat up into the early hours with Shawn, telling him about it. 'That place . . . you should have seen it, no kiddin'! Pictures in gold frames, clocks, French furniture, big mirrors, this chandelier, four foot wide! You imagine growin' up in a place like that?'

'Nope.' Shawn had poured them both another half-glass of bourbon. 'But you gotta remember that that's what she's used to.' He hadn't known quite what to say when Curt had blurted out that he'd asked Marianna to marry him, and F. H. Eastbridge had told him to leave the house. True, Curt had been working up to it, in his own good time; there was the visit to Minneapolis and then the start of the rehearsals for *Monte Cristo* to get over, before he'd have time to sort out where he was going in his personal life. Work had to come first. When the play had opened in two months or so, and he'd got himself a name, Marianna's stuck-up family would most likely have seen the whole thing differently. Now the plan had gone wrong and she'd walked out of the Fifth Avenue house before he'd had the chance to start building bridges.

'What am I goin' to do?' Curt appealed to him. 'I was plannin' on takin' it easy today, finish my packin' and goin'

141

for a drink before the performance. My train leaves first
thing in the mornin'. Now there's this crisis with
Marianna.'

'Why don't you just take her with you?' Shawn sat down
among last night's dishes and poured coffee for both of
them. 'Send a wire to your folks, tell 'em you'll be a day or
two late, change your single ticket to a double, and go get
a special licence from City Hall. Marry her on Monday,
take the train to Minneapolis Tuesday. Now she's had the
big bust-up with her folks, you might as well do it sooner
as later . . . what you lookin' at me like that for? You want
to marry her, don't you?'

'Shawn, Eastbridge is a name that means somethin' in
this city. Whether she's talkin' to her father or not, if I got
F. H.'s daughter as my wife, closed doors open. Course I
want to marry her. She's rich, she's smart, she's pretty. And
she's got class.' He started to drink the coffee. 'Besides, how
often does any ordinary guy like me have an heiress head
over heels in love with him? You know what you said –
don't look a gift horse in the mouth. By my reckonin', she's
a pretty fancy horse!'

'So what you beefin' about then?'

'I just had this next week all planned, and now I have to
change it all at a minute's notice. I mean, after what's
happened, I can't just go off and leave her here all alone til
I get back . . . what would that look like? Anyhow, what's
done is done. I guess we'll just have to make the best of it.
I'll pick up the licence, go meet her at the hotel, and plan
things from there.' Another thought. 'Hell, where we goin'
to live when we get back? I can't bring her here!'

'Why not?' Shawn teased. 'These rich Fifth Avenue girls
like a little slummin'!'

'Be serious . . .'

'OK. Here's a suggestion. You get dressed and washed
go fetch the licence. Then on the way to the hotel you
change the train tickets and send the wire. Tell her the
score, then you can leave together first thing Tuesday
mornin'. One, you can either leave her with your folks while
you come back at the end of next week and find another

142

apartment; or, two, you can come back together and stay at the hotel while you both look for a suitable place. It'll be more expensive that way, but she's got that trust fund money of hers, didn't you tell me? A hundred thousand dollars sure does go a long way!'

'That's just the tip of the iceberg, Shawn. You care to make an educated guess as to how much F. H. Eastbridge is worth?'

'Doesn't matter now. She's gone an' turned her back on all that. If I was you, I wouldn't bank on gettin' my hands on any of it. She's gone and made old man Eastbridge mad as hell . . . from what I heard about him, when he's mad as hell, he's real mean.'

'He'll come round, no question.' Curt was the eternal optimist; theatre people were made that way. 'When we're married, when he's had time to get used to the idea. When the play's a big success and Marianna gives him his first grandchild . . . you'll see what a difference that'll make.'

Shawn looked doubtful. He guessed he'd better make a start on breakfast, if Curt was going to fit in everything he had to get done today. 'I wouldn't hold your breath.'

The Hotel Marie Antoinette on Broadway at 66th Street. As he got out of the cab, Curt caught his breath; this was sure a real swank place to stay at. He was impressed but not surprised; everything about Marianna had style and, as he'd seen for himself last night when he'd taken her home, she was already used to the very best. This place, built less than two years ago in the Nouveau Louvre style – that was Second French Empire to the uninitiated – had elaborate ironwork details on the outer doors and tapestry serving as portières inside in the tradition of the fifteenth century; the uniformed doorman, in a swallow-tailed coat and gaiters, was dressed exactly like an attendant at an eighteenth-century English manorial estate. Inside, it looked richer still.

A bellboy took him up in the elevator to Marianna's suite on the second floor, where he found her impatiently waiting for him.

'I'm sorry I couldn't get here sooner,' he apologized, kissing her and handing her the little leather box that had cost him more than half his savings. Couldn't be helped. It just meant that now he'd have to take his family in Minneapolis cheaper presents. 'I had to stop by and arrange a few things . . . and get you this.'

She opened it almost gingerly. 'Curt, it's beautiful!' It had been the least expensive ring in the jeweller's window, and what he'd paid down had been only a deposit: he'd bought it on a month's approval, with a matching wedding ring as well. It was only when he'd paid for the rings and left the shop and was halfway along the street that he'd realized his mistake: he should have told the jeweller that his fiancée was F. H. Eastbridge's daughter. The man would have been falling over himself to let him take away the best merchandise in stock, probably without even a deposit at all. Then again, would he have believed him? It didn't matter. In a few days' time most of New York was going to know they were married, and when people heard the name Curt Koenig they'd look up.

'You really like it?' She nodded wordlessly, almost too overcome with emotion to say anything. It was all happening too quickly. 'Here, let me put it on . . .' He slipped the ring on her finger and kissed her hand. 'This wasn't anything like the way I planned it . . . that business with your parents last night. . .the last thing I wanted was you to have a showdown with them over me. It's all my fault that now there's a rift between you.'

'No!' Her voice was strong. She wouldn't allow him to blame himself. It was her father. 'I won't let you talk that way. They were both insufferably rude to you. Momma staring at us both and not saying a civil word; my father refusing to shake hands with you. They were just making you their whipping boy to punish me. They've always manipulated me, one way or the other, all my life. They've always expected me to conform. Now that I'm old enough to make decisions for myself, they don't like it.'

'Maybe now they've had time to cool down a little, you should write them a letter and explain things.'

144

She wouldn't hear of it. 'I've already explained things, Curt. I said all I had to say last night. Father gave me an ultimatum, and I gave him my answer.' She told him what had happened after he'd left. 'I just packed my bags and came straight here. I'll never go back, and he'd never have me.'

'I can't believe that! When all this blows over, he'll want to see you. You're his daughter, Marianna!' She almost laughed; how little he knew F. H. Eastbridge.

'Curt, when my father says something, he always sticks to it. He never changes his mind.' They'd see about that. He didn't believe it for a minute; wasn't blood thicker than water?

'I know this is all a rush, but I couldn't stand the thought of being away from you – especially after what's happened – for a whole week or more. If we get married first thing on Monday, we can leave for Minneapolis by the afternoon train . . . I got the licence, I got the ring, I got the tickets. What do you say?'

'Curt!'

'We could look for an apartment today, together . . . somewhere that's easy for the theatre, so when the play opens I won't have to spend all day going backwards and forwards. It's beautiful here, but until I'm on the payroll for *Monte Cristo* we'll have to economize.'

'But, Curt, why? I told you, I have my trust fund money. Let's go to the bank today, and I'll draw out what we'll need and you can take care of it. I'll sign a co-signatory paper, so you can have whatever you like at any time.' It was even better than he'd hoped; he could buy his folks some expensive presents after all. 'We'd better go and see a real estate agent, and a domestic agency downtown. We'll have to have a cook, and a maid.'

'Whatever you say.' These were things that he hadn't even thought about. But he could see the practicality. Brought up on Fifth Avenue, Marianna had never been taught to either cook or clean house; the very idea for F. H. Eastbridge's daughter would have been unthinkable. Even if she'd been willing to do the household chores like any

145

other newly married girl, she wouldn't have known how to. She was certainly going to be a big surprise to his family in Minneapolis; on his way to the hotel, he'd already wired them.

'Curt?' In all the excitement of the moment, there was still something she wanted to ask him, a question she'd thought about constantly since last night. 'When you told my father that you loved me, did you really mean it?'

He held her gently by the shoulders, leaned down and kissed her. 'Why would I have said it if I didn't?' he said with a touch of gentle admonition, and drew her towards him so that he didn't have to look into her eyes. She laid her head against his chest, more happy than she'd ever been in her life; forgetting the past, the last angry scene with her father, and that the man she was marrying in two days' time would be one of the most accomplished actors ever to appear on the American stage.

They found the perfect apartment on West 59th Street, a cab ride away from the Lyceum Theatre. To Marianna, it was 'a sweet little place for the time being'; to Curt, the height of domestic luxury – though a long way below Fifth Avenue standards, it was a world away from the home he'd grown up in where he and his two brothers had all slept in one room, and the cramped untidy quarters in Queens that he shared with Shawn Duchovsky.

Already furnished, even down to the potted plants, it had an entrance hall, a dining room, a drawing room, a small library that could double as a study, and two bedrooms. There was a spacious bathroom with modern plumbing and hot water, a basement kitchen, and two small boxrooms adequate to serve the needs of the small staff they'd need to run the place. After signing the lease, they called in at the downtown offices of a highly respected domestic agency, to engage a cook and a maid, where the mere mention of the name Eastbridge got them the manager's personal attention and assurances of the highest standards of service. They met Shawn for lunch in Manhattan.

146

'Hey, don't worry about that extra witness you'll need for Monday. I got just the guy.' He tucked into his lobster with relish. 'He used to work at the Hamburg–Amerika offices when I first went there, but he's a desk clerk now in the foreign currency office at Thomas Cook on Broadway. And get this. If you could find time for a honeymoon, he could get you discount on a ten-day trip to Bermuda . . . it's usually forty-seven dollars fifty apiece, but he could get it for twenty-five per cent less. Interested?'

'It'd be nice,' Curt said, sipping his wine, 'but it's not possible. When we get back from Minneapolis next weekend, we only have one day together before rehearsals for *Monte Cristo* start on Monday. Maybe another time.'

'OK. I'll tell him.' He checked his watch. 'Hey, I been here too long already . . . some of us have to work! I'll see you later, Curt. Marianna.' He smiled at her, 'I'll see you on Monday.'

'Is he always in such a hurry?' Marianna watched him weave his way through the well of the restaurant towards the door, then disappear. 'He didn't even finish his meal.'

'That's Shawn, always in a rush. But he does have things to do, since we're both quitting the Queens apartment on Monday. He's found another pal to share with, on 116th Street. It's much closer to his place of work and we can meet easier at lunchtime, after rehearsals begin.' He noticed that she suddenly looked anxious. 'What is it? Caught sight of one of your parents' friends?'

'No, it isn't that. It was just that I was thinking . . . the rehearsals, the play. Isn't it traditional to hold some kind of party before the first night?'

'Does that bother you? We'll be married by then.'

'Jerry Lauterbach senior is one of the production's financial backers . . . it's an odds-on certainty that he'll be there. He's also a friend of my father's.'

'Do you think he'll withdraw his backing for the play just because you've gone against your family and decided to marry me?'

'No. He's far too astute a businessman to do anything like that, and in any case he's been associated with Charles

147

and Daniel Frohman for several years. He wouldn't. But if Mrs Lauterbach is there, she might cut me deliberately, to humiliate me. She's a close acquaintance of my mother's, and it's exactly the sort of snobbish, petty thing she would do.'

Curt thought for a moment. 'We'll just outsmart her. Leave Mrs Lauterbach to me. I'll have a quiet word with Charles Frohman, and make sure that if she comes face to face with us he'll be right there too. She won't dare cause a scene if she's presented with a *fait accompli*. Besides, whether the Lauterbachs are friends of your parents or not, what you do is none of their goddam business.'

They parted in midtown Manhattan. Curt had more packing to do before the final performace of *Under the Red Robe*, Marianna wanted to go shopping for a suitable wedding outfit. It was almost six o'clock by the time she got back to the Hotel Marie Antoinette with her packages. Wanting privacy, not to have people around her, she ordered dinner in her suite.

Afterwards, she lay on the bed, stared up at the ornate ceiling and reflected on how different her life had become since she and Curt had met, how different her wedding would be to the old fantasies that, as a lonely little girl at Lake Winnipesaukee, she'd created in her mind. A gleaming carriage and a fashionable church, a white flowing gown with a never-ending train held by a dozen bridesmaids; pageboys, flowers, crowds of smiling people, all there to wish her well. The reality, the day after tomorrow, would be very different – no carriage, no church, no gown or bridesmaids, no pageboys and no smiling people; no gown, just a smart costume with hat and veil because just twenty minutes after the ceremony their train to Minneapolis left Grand Central Station, and there was no time to go back and change – but that didn't matter, only her passionate love for Curt.

Her father had dared to call her feelings for him a 'ridiculous infatuation'. But what did he – a man who'd married for family name, wealth and power – know about love?

Not for an instant did she regret what she'd said to him, that she'd turned her back on Fifth Avenue and everything it stood for. Married to Curt, Marianna would feel loved, safe, secure. That night before she fell asleep, thinking of all she had to look forward to, she thought that the happiness she felt at that moment could never possibly be matched.

Just before nine thirty on Monday morning, the cab drew up outside City Hall. Curt jumped out, paid the driver and asked him to wait. Then he helped Marianna climb out. She wore pale ivory silk and Maltese lace, and a broad-brimmed hat with a long flowing veil. When the wind tugged at it and Curt helped her to hold it on, she laughed.

Shawn Duchovsky and the friend he'd brought with him as the second witness stood waiting at the top of the steps. They'd arrived several minutes before and had been watching for the bridal cab, smoking cigarettes to pass the time. On the way, Shawn had stopped to buy a posy of violets from a street flower seller, and he handed them to Marianna as she and Curt reached the top of the steps.

'Tom an' I have already found the room where you have to go . . . you just give your names to the clerk in there. Better move it if you want to catch that train.'

Inside, they found the clerk and he took their names, then directed them along the corridor to a room at the end. Marianna didn't have time to feel nervous. Ten minutes later, they were all standing outside the room again, and she was Curt's wife. He lifted back her veil and kissed her.

'How do you feel, Mrs Koenig?'

Mrs Koenig. How strange that sounded. 'To tell you the truth, I thought it would all take much longer . . . it didn't seem like a proper ceremony. Everything happened so quickly that I don't really feel married at all.' They all laughed, but it was true; she felt no different from how she'd felt yesterday, or half an hour ago. Except that they had the certificate to prove it.

Shawn and his friend shook Curt's hand and kissed Marianna; they were both late for work and were in a hurry to go.

'Say, congratulations again! We'll toast you later over a glass of Fidelio's draught beer! Don't wanna rush you, but you've still got that train to catch. Say hello to all the folks in Minneapolis for me!'

When the two of them had gone, Curt kissed her again. 'We really do have to hurry, Marianna.' He took her by the hand. 'Traffic's pretty heavy, heavier than I thought it'd be. We've got just about twenty minutes to get to Grand Central Station.'

'I know. Let's run then.' She longed to be away from the crowds, she just wanted to be alone with him. They rushed along the corridor and out of the double doors, down the flight of stone steps towards the waiting cab. The driver was ready, reins in hand. But as they reached the bottom of the steps Marianna caught sight of a man just a few feet away holding a camera on a tripod; there was a sudden blinding flash, a puff of smoke, and then from nowhere a horde of journalists with notepads swooped down on them.

'Miss Eastbridge, have you just gotten married . . .?'

'Mr Koenig, can you say anything at all about the rumours that Charles Frohman has cast you as the lead in his next big Broadway play . . .?'

'Who the hell are you?' Curt was completely taken aback; he hadn't spotted the newspaper photographer when Marianna did.

'Matthew Jones, *New York Herald* . . . ma'am, is it true that your father strongly disapproves of your marriage to a Broadway actor . . .?' As they all converged on her and Curt like a pack of wolves, shouting questions from every side, Marianna clung to her husband's arm so that they wouldn't be separated. Then to her astonishment Curt grasped the nearest reporter by the lapels and thrust him hard against the side of the cab behind them.

'I'm only sayin' this once, so you all better listen. Neither of us has anything to tell you. You want to know who Charles Frohman's cast in his new production, you go ask

150

him. You want to know what F. H. Eastbridge thinks, then you go ask F. H. Eastbridge.' He opened the cab door and helped Marianna inside. She was so proud of him! 'You want to know if we just got married, you go check the public records. We've got a train to catch.' He climbed in beside her and slammed the cab door. The driver already knew their destination.

They didn't arrive in Minneapolis until late on Wednesday evening, after travelling virtually non-stop from New York City for three whole days. Without Curt, the journey would have been a nightmare to Marianna; though they had first class sleepers, there was scarcely enough room to turn round and the constant lurching movement of the train made it very difficult for her to sleep. It was a curious 'honeymoon' of sorts: no wedding reception, no flowers and rice, no traditional wedding night; until they reached Minneapolis and Curt's home where they'd have a proper double bed, they were obliged to spend the first two nights of their married life apart. But the closer they got to their destination, the more anxious Marianna became. What did she know about being married, about men, about what was expected of her? Her mother had never spoken of such intimate subjects and never would; to talk about physical things was considered gross, unladylike. Edwina would never have offered; Marianna would never have dared ask. What happened between man and wife after the wedding ceremony was over and the guests had gone away was a no-man's-land, something every girl was expected to find out for herself, like her sisters, mother and grandmother before her. All Marianna knew but would never admit was that when Curt kissed her and held her she liked it, but was too shy, too embarrassed and too well brought up to either tell him, or kiss and hold him back. For the last few miles of the journey, when it was getting dark, she fell asleep with her head against his shoulder. The train pulling to a halt jolted her wide awake again.

'That's it, we're here!' Curt was already on his feet, throwing the compartment door open and calling for the porter to help him with the baggage. 'Hey, there's Jesse with the buggy out there!'

She sat up, rubbed at her eyes. She stumbled up and straightened her hat in the mirror. Meeting Curt's parents, his brothers, maybe unexpected family and friends, she wanted to look her best. 'Curt, wait for me!' But he was already out in the corridor, shouting greetings to his brother from the open window.

She followed him from the train onto the platform and stood a little way away, not wanting to intrude into the brotherly reunion, watching them while the porter loaded their luggage onto the back of the buggy. Finally, Curt turned to see where she was. He smiled and beckoned to her.

'Marianna, come on over! This is my youngest brother Jesse.' She did as he said and held out her hand politely. He was a little shorter and more slightly built than Curt, but just as blue-eyed and fair. 'How do you do?'

'Hey, she's pretty, just like you wrote us! Ma and Pa can't wait to see her.' He shook her hand vigorously and plonked a kiss on her cheek, then helped her into the buggy. 'Say, you must be tuckered out, travellin' for three days. But don't worry none. Ma's got the spare room all fixed up, and supper on. They're all waitin' back at the house.' Marianna's heart sank. Though she'd half expected a big family welcome when they reached Minneapolis, all she wanted was to wash and go straight to bed. But that would be impossible. Somehow, she'd have to get through it all.

'Let's go then,' Curt said.

Robbinsdale was a half-hour's buggy ride from the station, on the south road from town, and nothing like Marianna's expectations. It was a fair distance from the hub of Minneapolis, more like a rural backwater than the outskirts of a city; she peered out from the window of the rocking buggy in surprise when they finally came to the end of the ride. It was a big, sprawling house of clapboard, with a low verandah out front, a barn on one side and the livery stables on the other. As the buggy came along the bumpy road the front door flew open, and the entire Koenig clan, with some of the neighbours, poured out. When Curt climbed from the buggy first, they all surged around him, and it took several minutes of hugging and handshaking all round before he could extricate himself. Finally, he turned round.

'Ma, Pa . . . Larry . . . this is Marianna.' He opened the buggy door and helped her out. 'Marianna, this is Ma and Pa, and my eldest brother Larry.' He smiled. 'It's liable to get a little confusin' around here, 'cos Pa's called Larry too. But we've always seemed to manage somehow.'

'How do you do?'

'Say, she's real pretty, ain't she, Ma?' Jesse said with enthusiasm. He was untying the luggage on the back of the buggy. 'She looks that good, an' she's bin travellin' for three days already!'

'Welcome to the family, Marianna.' Curt's mother kissed her. 'I hope you're not too tired?'

'A little.'

'Come on, come meet some of the neighbours!' Marianna kept the tight smile in place while she endured umpteen handshakes and introductions: why did they all have to be here? She was exhausted. It seemed an eternity before all the goodbyes were said and the family moved back inside the house. She looked around uncertainly, at the chintz curtains and homely furniture. 'I wonder if I might go to your bathroom?' There was a loud guffaw from Curt's brothers.

'Bless you, honey, there's no bathroom in this house,' Mrs Koenig said, seeing Marianna felt awkward. 'If you want to get washed up, there's hot water in the jug in the room I've made up for you and Curt. If you need anything else, the privy's out back in the yard.'

'Hey, I'll go fetch you a lamp if you wanna go outside!' Jesse offered, humping in their luggage. Curt had taken the largest trunk into their room already.

'Thank you, but the hot water will be fine.' She wanted to be alone, just for a little while, so that she could lie down and close her eyes, change her travelling clothes before the

153

ordeal of dinner. Supper, Jesse had called it. Curt's mother took her to their room.

'It's a good soft bed . . . feather mattress.' She smiled. 'And if you're wantin' more blankets, you just holler. Now you just take your time. I'll be out back, fixin' supper. Curt'll come and call you when it's ready.' She went out and closed the door behind her, leaving Marianna mercifully alone at last.

She took off her hat, sat down on the bed. She had the beginnings of a terrible headache. She looked round the bedroom; spotlessly clean, cosy and neat by rural Minneapolis standards; in New York, it was the kind of bedroom she'd expect to give a servant. But she couldn't say anything to Curt. Secretly, she would have much preferred to have booked into a hotel in the centre of town, where they would have had more privacy and a slightly greater degree of the comfort she was used to, but she hadn't dared to suggest it for fear of offending him; after all, they were his family, and they'd welcomed her with open arms. When she thought of how hostile her parents had been when she'd introduced Curt to them, she felt ashamed.

Her headache – it had started just after the train left Milwaukee – was getting worse. She felt rather sick. She poured herself a glass of cold water, lay down on the bed with her eyes closed. So tired out that she almost drifted off to sleep there and then, she didn't hear the footsteps on the stairs, the bedroom door open or Curt come over and lean across her. When she felt the pressure of his body on hers, her eyes flew open. She struggled to sit up quickly; she wasn't used to anyone coming into her room without knocking. 'Curt! I didn't hear you come in.' She straightened her hair, pulled away from him. 'I should get changed.'

'Hey, what's the hurry? You look fine. Nobody around here bothers about things like changing for dinner. Just relax.'

'I can't go downstairs and sit at the table in the same clothes I've been travelling in all day.'

'Marianna, you're not on Fifth Avenue now.' He moved towards her. 'You don't need to worry about things like that.'

'I'm sorry, but I have to change . . . the quicker you go back downstairs, the quicker I'll be.' He astonished her by bursting out laughing.

'We're married, for Christ's sake! You don't need to be shy about lettin' me see you in your underwear. I do know what women's underwear looks like. Come on, Ma's already puttin' the food on the table for us. It'll spoil.'

'Curt, *please*. I said I'll be down in a minute.' As she spoke, they both heard Mrs Koenig's voice calling up to them from the bottom of the stairs. 'Why don't you go down and tell them all about the new play?'

'Is she all right, Curt?' Martha Koenig asked when he came down into the kitchen alone. 'She looked mighty pale when you first got here . . . just tuckered out. It's down to all that travellin' from New York, I guess.'

'She's OK, Ma. Just changin' her clothes.'

'What for? The clothes she had on looked fine to me!'

'Ma, she's from New York. Fifth Avenue. I wrote you about that in my letter. That's what people from families like hers do there . . . they always change their clothes before dinner.'

'So that's why you brought all those trunks with you! I was wonderin' why there was so much luggage, and you only stayin' till the end of the week.' She laid her hands on his shoulders and kissed him. 'It's so long since we saw you, Curt . . . if only you could stay just a little longer.'

When Marianna came down, they were all talking about the play, and his leading part in it. He stood up and helped her into her seat. Though they'd given her a warm welcome, she still felt awkward, out of place, ill at ease; there were certainly no refinements at the Koenig dinner table. Dishes that had been brought out of the stove were placed straight on the table. Large tureens of vegetables and a dish of potatoes were left in the middle, so that everyone could help themselves. Though the food was surprisingly good, Marianna ate very little. Her headache was worse, and Lorenz Koenig's home-brewed red wine had made her feel giddy.

Curt had moved on from the play to their new apartment on 59th Street. 'It was already furnished, so we didn't need to spend time choosing things to put in it. With rehearsals starting Monday, there wouldn't have been time. Ma, Pa, you two . . . you've just got to make the trip to New York for the first night.'

Martha was all smiles and Marianna could see how proud she was. 'Of course we will! You think we'd miss somethin' like that? When we first got your letter, I just couldn't believe it had happened. My Curt, the leading man in a big Broadway play! I tell you, darlin', I've just about told *everyone* in this town!'

He smiled, and reached for Marianna's hand. 'I've got Marianna to thank for it, really and truly. She went up to Charles Frohman himself and asked him to audition me for the part. I thought it was a cinch to go to John Drew.'

'You know this Charles Frohman?' Jesse asked. 'Is he a friend of yours?'

'No.' She managed to smile, even though by now she felt quite sick and her headache was getting worse. 'He just happened to be at a party at the Hotel Astor that I was also invited to. I didn't even know what he looked like. I got a friend to introduce me and he took it from there. I knew that once he'd seen Curt audition he wouldn't offer the part to anyone else.'

'Hey, what do you think of these new-fangled moving pictures, Marianna? Those flicker parlours downtown sure are fun! Me and some pals of mine went to the one on Dawson Street, and they was showin' the Bob Fitzsimmons heavyweight title fight . . . it ran for a whole eight minutes, too . . . only five cents apiece to go in.'

'They're amusing, and I agree, a novelty . . . but that's really all they are. They can never be art, like the theatre. Just a cheap form of entertainment.'

'This new machine they're writin' about in the papers,

156

though . . . somethin' called a Vitagraph . . . you read about that, Curt?' Curt nodded. 'Invented by these two English guys . . . a double vaudeville act. One of 'em was handy with mechanics, and he played around with the basic Edison design until he improved on it. Paper reckons they're on to somethin' . . . making the moving pictures last longer, and turnin' out pictures of better quality. Quite a few studios springin' up around New York, with others tryin' to improve on the original machine design.' He polished off the last morsel of apple pie on his plate. 'There must be money in it, don't you reckon, Pa?'

'I guess. But it's still like Marianna says, just a novelty. Novelties wear off. Moving pictures'll fizzle out in a year or two, when folks are tired of 'em, like everything else.'

Curt spoke up. 'One thing I do know, there's a lot of lawsuits flyin' around because of the Patents Act. Edison has pounced on at least half a dozen of these new studios that have sprung up overnight since he invented the kineto-scope, claimin' that they're infringin' on his original design. He's got a point, too. Look at it this way. Think of how many moving picture parlours there are all over the country, and how many people put their five cents in every day, just to see a few minutes of film. Add it all up . . . that's a tidy sum. But Edison doesn't make his profits on the flickers, just the projecting equipment . . . his patented design. If mavericks are coming along and making and leasing out their own machines, he loses out. That's what these lawsuits are all about.'

'It's all beyond me.'

Martha Koenig stood up at last. 'And me, I dare say. But now we've eaten, I think we should have a thought to Marianna and Curt. They've been travellin' here for three days, and I know Marianna's real tired out. We can talk tomorrow. For now, I reckon they ought to head upstairs to bed, and you boys go with your pa down to the saloon while I clear away here. Go on, off you go!'

'OK, Ma.'

'Won't you come and have just one drink with us, Curt?'

'Maybe tomorrow.'

'It's all right, Curt.' Marianna stood up now. 'You go. I don't mind, really.'

'You sure about that?'

'Yes, I'm sure.' Suddenly, she was apprehensive again, worried about what she was expected to do when she was alone with him. She needed just a little more time on her own to get used to the idea that they were married now, that from now on they'd be living together, sharing a bed. She said good night and went upstairs. She found a powder in her luggage for her headache. She took a silk nightgown from one of the trunks and laid it ready on the bed. That was when Curt's mother knocked on the door and came in.

'Marianna?' She closed the door behind her, sat down uninvited on the chair. 'The boys have gone down to the saloon with their pa . . . but don't worry, he'll make sure Curt doesn't stay too long.'

'It's all right, it doesn't matter. I know they must have a lot to talk about . . . really, I don't mind.' She picked up the nightgown. 'I'm so tired after the train journey, I'll probably be asleep when he comes back anyway.'

'But you two haven't had a proper wedding night.' Marianna could feel her face colouring. 'That's why I came.' Martha smiled. 'I didn't know if you needed any advice . . . how much your own mother's told you about such things . . . but I thought I'd best ask, in case she hadn't. Unless you have a little idea about what's expected, it can be quite a shock.'

'I'm all right, thank you.' Marianna was horribly embarrassed. She desperately wanted Martha to go, but she kept sitting there. 'I hope you sleep well.'

'Such a beautiful nightgown.' Martha was looking at it admiringly. 'I declare, just look at that fine embroidery . . . and it's real silk. I never saw such a lovely thing.'

'Thank you.'

'Remember, if there's anything you want, you only have to ask. Good night, honey.'

Marianna sat down on the edge of the bed. Her headache was beginning to wear off just a little, but she was still tense. Supposing Curt came back before she was ready, before she'd got undressed and gone to bed? The moment when they'd be alone together, the moment that a week ago she'd looked forward to so much, now seemed infinitely terrifying, something that she wanted to postpone until they were back in New York, until she'd had time to pull herself together. She loved him and she wanted him but it was all too soon, everything was happening far too quickly.

She undressed, hung away her clothes, brushed out her long dark luxuriant hair. She climbed into the feather bed, turned out the lamp. But though she was more tired than she'd ever felt in her life, somehow she could not fall asleep. Then she heard the sound of footsteps on the stairs outside.

'Marianna, are you asleep?' It was Curt's voice, calling softly from the door. Under the bedclothes, she stiffened.

'No. Not quite.'

'Sorry if I was a long time. I didn't even want to go. Not tonight, anyhow.'

'I didn't mind. I told you that. You could have stayed longer.' There was a pause, while she heard the sound of him undressing. 'Good night, Curt.'

Very softly, he began to laugh. 'Good night? On the first night we've got ourselves a proper bed, after that goddam train?' She felt the covers lift as he climbed in next to her, felt the shock of bare flesh against her body. Much as she loved him, she was almost appalled. She felt panic, the urge to jump out of the bed and run. He was drawing her towards him, and she was pulling the opposite way. She kept her eyes tightly shut. She had never seen, never even imagined what a man looked like naked; she had never seen her father without his tie on, let alone anything else missing.

'Curt, please . . . no!' Vehemently, she pushed him away from her. 'You can't. Not here. Not in your parents' house . . . they might hear us!'

'Christ, Marianna . . . we're married now! What the hell's wrong with you?' She heard the impatience in his voice.

'There's nothing wrong with me. I just said that we can't do anything here . . . it wouldn't be right. I'm sorry, Curt. But I'm tired and my head aches. I just want to go to sleep.'

He lay down and stared up at the ceiling, not knowing

what to make of her. Up till Monday she'd been utterly different. Shy, demure, but still affectionate, never drawing away when he'd kissed her. Though they'd been married almost three days now, the separate berths in the train sleeping compartment meant that they hadn't had the opportunity to consummate their marriage until now. He understood, sympathized with how she felt, but he was a man who needed physical relationships with women, and all day he'd been looking forward to being alone so that he could make love to her. If she didn't want to, he couldn't very well force himself on her. But the prospect of having to wait until they got back to New York was something he hadn't contemplated.

He turned to her in the darkness, kissed her lightly on the cheek. He had no choice but to make the best of things. He rolled over onto his side, trying to ignore the throbbing sensation between his thighs. It was a long time before he fell asleep.

He was up at first light, dressed and downstairs before Marianna was even awake. The big kitchen was just as he remembered it, warm, comforting, with the delicious smells of hot coffee and baking bread. His father and elder brother were already up and in the livery stable, seeing to the business of the day, but Jesse was in the kitchen with their mother.

'Hi, Curt darlin'.' She kissed him as she passed on her way to the stove. 'You and Marianna sleep well?'

'Fine.' He sat down, picked up a crust of bread and began to chew on it. 'This sure tastes good, Ma.' He managed to smile. 'Just like it always did.'

'Oh, you say that now . . . but soon you'll be sold on Marianna's cooking.' With her back turned towards him, Martha didn't see the expression on Curt's face. 'Now you go back upstairs when you're ready, you tell her there's no hurry for her to come down. You both just take things real easy while you're here with us.'

'Everythin' all right, Curt?' Jesse, not preoccupied with the early morning chores like his mother, caught on to

Curt's mood very quickly. 'Hey, you two ain't had a bust-up already?'

'Curt?' Martha swung round anxiously. 'Is Marianna OK?'

'Just tired after all the travellin' we've done, that's all. She's not used to it.' He gave his younger brother a warning glance. 'I thought I'd take her out in the buggy today, show her some of the scenery.'

His mother's suspicions were allayed. 'That's a wonderful idea! Tell you what. I'll pack you a picnic basket and you can stay out all day, if you want to. There'll be a hot meal on the table tonight.'

'So, tell us more about this fancy New York apartment of yours,' Jesse said. 'Don't think I'd care for livin' in an apartment. I'd hate not havin' a big back yard.'

'I got used to that, sharing in Queens with Shawn. He sends his regards, by the way.' Curt went on to describe all the rooms, and how convenient it was for the theatre. 'Once rehearsals start I have to show up every day, except Sundays. When the play opens, I'll have even less time to myself.'

'Won't that be a little hard on Marianna? And what about mealtimes? How will she know when to get dinner started if she doesn't know when to expect you?'

'We've employed a cook and a maid from one of the agencies, Ma. She doesn't need to concern herself with anythin' like that.' Martha and Jesse exchanged glances. Clearly, they were both astonished.

'You've employed a cook? But what for, Curt? Won't Marianna be takin' care of things like that?'

'Ma, you don't understand. She comes from Fifth Avenue . . . she doesn't do anything like that. Marianna was brought up with servants, a whole houseful . . . I told you, she's F. H. Eastbridge's daughter. Anyhow, she couldn't do it even if she wanted to. She can't cook.' They looked even more shocked now. 'She was never taught how.'

'I never in my life heard of a wife who can't cook her husband's dinner!'

'Ma, just drop it, will you? I explained it all in my letters.

161

Marianna comes from a different world to what we know . . . it isn't her fault.' This was more difficult than he'd thought it would be. 'Besides, would you expect ladies like Mrs Astor or Mrs Vanderbilt to roll up their sleeves and go down to the kitchen to baste a roast or peel potatoes? People like the Eastbridges pay other folks to do that kind of stuff for them. They were brought up that way. They're not like us.' For the first time, his mother looked seriously concerned.

'Curt, I know you love her an' all . . . but you're both so different . . . it worries me. I want to know that you're bein' looked after properly . . . I'd hate for things not to work out.'

'Of course they'll work out! You worry too much. Listen. Here, I'm me. The same Curt Koenig I always was. When I go back to New York, when I'm on stage, I'm someone else . . . Curt Koenig the Broadway actor. I even talk different then.' He smiled. 'Here, I can just be myself, forget all those elocution classes. It's the same with Marianna. Here, it's difficult for her . . . she's only used to Fifth Avenue living, the best restaurants, swanky hotels. Now we're married, got our own apartment together, it's a halfway thing, finding a middle ground. Her world and mine, coming together. It'll work out, you'll see.'

Martha laid her hands on his shoulders and kissed his fair curly hair. He reminded her so much of his father when she and Lorenz had first met, except that Curt was a little taller and even more good-looking. She was proud of him, of everything he'd achieved, yet despite all his assurances the niggling grain of doubt remained.

'I just want you to be happy,' she said.

It was sunny and bright, but cold, when they took their picnic basket and set off in the buggy after breakfast so that Curt could show her more of the Minnesota countryside. Compared to New York, Minneapolis itself seemed backward and provincial, and they spent only an hour or so window-shopping before setting off in the direction of

Golden Valley, then making southwards towards Medicine Lake.

'It's glorious out here in the spring and summer. Especially the summer. July, August. It gets real hot. When we were boys, Pa used to bring us all fishing.' He smiled, leaned against a tree, stared across the water. They were good memories. He'd often thought of being here as he'd stared from the window of the apartment in Queens. Another world away now. 'We'd maybe sit here all day, and none of us get a single bite . . . it happened sometimes. Most times, we'd be lucky, and take home a whole basket of fish for Ma to cook for our supper. One time, Jesse had this big fish on the end of his line and he lost it, just as he was reelin' it in. Boy, how he howled! All the way home.'

Marianna was gazing across the waters of the lake herself, remembering the summer house in New Hampshire, the shore of Lake Winnipesaukee where she'd laughed and played with Luke Waad. That afternoon when her mother had ruined their childhood friendship came back to her. Luke Waad and his brothers. Where were they all now?

'When did you decide that you'd outgrown the place, that there was more in life than summer fishing trips with your brothers and working for your father in the family livery stables?' She hadn't meant it to sound the way he took it, but it was too late to take back the ill-chosen words.

'Just because you grew up on Fifth Avenue doesn't mean you have to denigrate the way other people live. There are more ordinary people in this country than there are millionaires . . . in case you hadn't noticed.'

'I'm not denigrating anything. You misunderstood.' He was sorry, too, but he was still tense and irritable after last night. She didn't even like him kissing her in front of his family, as if any demonstration of affection was somehow shameful. 'What I meant was, when did you decide that you wanted to act for a living?'

'When I was still at school, I guess . . . we staged a play one Christmas and it kind of stuck in my mind. I got all wrapped up in it, wanted more than anything to get the leading part . . . a little like wanting to play Monte Cristo. Then my teacher told me she thought I had a lot of natural talent, and I ought to try to develop it.' Even then, women had been charmed by him. 'So that's what set me thinking, and that's what I did.' He put his arm around her and they strolled slowly along the lake's edge. 'I got taken on with a local stock company. . . just small stuff, nothing special. I asked around and watched and listened, and then I realized that I wasn't going to get where I wanted to be unless I took the plunge and came to New York.' He kicked a stone in his path and sent it spinning. 'It was hell at first, making the move, everything was so big, so different. It was hard to adjust . . . for Shawn too. He got a job straight away with the Hamburg–Amerika shipping line, and I got taken on as a non-speaking cast member in a small off-Broadway play. That's how it all started.'

'You're wondering what it would have been like if you'd never left Minneapolis?'

'No . . . why do you say that?'

'Just a feeling I get. That you left part of you behind when you came to New York, the part you take up again when you come back.'

'Marianna, I was born here . . . there'll always be a tie. My family are here. You can't mind about that!'

'That's the second time that you've completely misunderstood me.'

'I'm not doing very well on that score, am I?'

She was silent. She pulled her fur cape closer around herself, feeling the cold. It was deceptive, with the sun shining and so few clouds in the sky, but the breeze that came off the lake was icier than any they had in New York. It was so bare, so open here, not picturesque and idyllic like the scenery in New England and around Lake Winnipesaukee. She shivered. And there was something else on her mind. 'Curt, do you think we could leave earlier than we planned to . . . this evening?' He was shocked. 'I've been thinking about it. By the time we get back to New York, it'll be halfway through Sunday, and rehearsals for the play start on Monday morning. We'll have spent hardly any time together.' She looked up at him. 'I just want to be alone with you.'

He almost laughed. 'You didn't last night!'

'Curt, that isn't fair! I told you why . . . it's . . . different here, under your family's roof. I explained why I wanted to wait.'

'Marianna, with the rehearsals and then the play opening on Broadway, when exactly do you think I'm going to be able to see my family again, if I don't make the most of the time I've got now? What do you think they'd say if I went back and told them we're leaving tonight? They've gone to a lot of trouble to make us welcome . . . and they've been looking forward to my visit for a long time. I'm sorry, but no. We have to stop until tomorrow.' He felt her draw her arm away from his. 'I just won't hurt their feelings like that.'

She stopped walking. 'And what about my feelings? We only got married on Monday. Since then we haven't had any time to ourselves. Three days' travelling, then in a house surrounded by other people. We haven't had any privacy at all.'

'For Christ's sake, Marianna, they're my family! We agreed that we'd come to Minneapolis and visit.' Suddenly, he was as angry as she was. 'At least they gave you a real proper welcome . . . something your parents didn't accord to me!'

'I wasn't responsible for that, and you know it! You also know that when my father gave me an ultimatum that same night, I packed my bags and walked out of the house. I don't think I can give you any more proof of my love for you than that!'

'I wasn't asking you to prove anything. I was making a point.' It was their first quarrel and they were both upset by it. There was a few moments' silence before he spoke again. 'Look, the wind's turning cold and it's getting late. I think we should be heading back now.'

She climbed into the buggy in stony silence. Curt got in beside her and flicked the reins. She suddenly longed to be home in the city again, with the familiar sights and sounds, the big department stores, hotels and brightly lit theatre fronts, the streetcars and congested traffic. Most of all, she wanted to be in their new apartment, alone with Curt. Here, she felt like a fish out of water; unhappy, awkward, totally out of place. And he wasn't even trying to understand her. All the way back to Robbinsdale neither of them spoke.

'Anything wrong?' his eldest brother asked him when they came into the house, and Marianna hurriedly disappeared upstairs alone. 'Maybe it's just my imagination, but things seem a little cool between you two.'

Curt lowered his voice, closed the door between the parlour and the kitchen so that the others wouldn't hear him. 'She wants to head on back to New York tonight, instead of waiting till tomorrow. I said no.'

'You mean you've bin married just three days, and you're arguin' already? Brother, that doesn't bode too well.'

'It's nothing . . . and I do understand why she wants to leave a day earlier. If it wasn't for the rehearsals of *Monte Cristo* starting on Monday, we'd stay much longer. But it can't be helped. It's just that to her way of thinking, with three days' travellin' in front of us when we leave here, we'll just have Sunday evening together and that's all.'

'You've got every night together . . . that's the important thing!' A teasing note came into Larry Koenig's voice. 'Say, just between you and me . . . what's it like havin' a real life heiress in your bed?'

'I guess she'll be not much different from any other girl who's been there.'

Larry's eyebrows rose. 'You mean . . . last night, nothin' happened?' Curt shook his head. 'How come? And how come you don't even sound so enthusiastic. Hey, Curt, what's this all about? You love her, don't you?'

'Marianna's not like any of the girls I've been with before . . . Fifth Avenue females haven't really fallen across my path. Not a word of this to Ma, you hear me? Or anyone else for that matter . . . you're the only one who'd understand.' Even now, after so long away, the brotherly bond between them was still strong. He could always tell Larry anything, and trust him to keep quiet about it, just like Shawn. 'I care about her, I want you to know that. But getting married . . . it isn't the way Ma or Pa think.' He explained how he and Marianna had met, how she'd gone to Charles Frohman and he'd been auditioned for the part. 'It's the biggest production in years . . . everyone's saying it's bound to be a sensation. You understand what something like that means to me? But we're talkin' about New York, Larry . . . the hardest place on earth to get a big break. She made it clear how much she liked me, and things just took off from there. Shawn said it'd be good for my career, for everything, having an Eastbridge on my arm. It was easy to believe, easier to accept because she's pretty, she's smart, she has money of her own. Even though her family don't approve of me, I'm convinced it'll all change when the play's a big success, when I'm well known, when their grandchildren come along. It's just a case of waiting, biding my time. You know what Pa always used to say about patience?'

'Has she gone cold on you?'

'No, it isn't anything like that. She just wants to wait till we get back to New York.'

Larry laughed, lightening the atmosphere. Curt had always been smarter than any of them, and what he did was his business; it wasn't his place to pass judgement, or interfere. From what he could see, Eastbridge or not, the girl seemed pretty wrapped up in him. Most girls had been. 'She wants to go back to New York early, and you said no? What you complainin' about, then?' He gave Curt a playful swipe across the arm. 'Go out in the back yard and I'll throw a bucket of cold water over you. That'll cool you down.' A more serious note now. 'Look, I'm not tellin' you how you should run your life . . . but what happens if you meet a girl you really do love? You'll want to be with her, she'll want to be with you. What will you do about you and Marianna?'

'I'll cross that bridge when . . . if . . . I ever come to it.'

CHAPTER TWELVE

They arrived back at Grand Central Station at eight o'clock on Sunday night. For the first time since they'd got married almost a week before, Marianna felt truly happy: they were home in New York at last. The noise, the smoke, the steam, the cold when she stepped out from the warmth of the train onto the platform, might not have existed. She was so relieved to be away from Minneapolis, the suffocating presence of Curt's family and friends. Now, at last, they were going to their own home – no more living in hotels, in other people's houses – and tonight they would be well and truly alone for the first time; the cook and the maid engaged through the downtown agency weren't due to arrive at the apartment until the next morning. True, there was no food, no spare linen, no fires lit, but Marianna didn't care. Now she had Curt all to herself. In the cab as they drove towards 59th Street, she clung to his arm and rested her head against his shoulder.

Inside the apartment, he turned on all the lights and they made a tour of the rooms together. Curt found coal and wood down in the basement kitchen. He lit the stove, the boiler, then fires in the drawing room and the largest bedroom. In no time at all, with all the doors left open, the whole apartment became warmer.

'If there's enough fuel, you could light a fire in the library; it's cosier in there. Do you have to read through your lines for *Monte Cristo* for the morning?'

'I don't have the complete script. And it'll keep. After all, we have more than two months for rehearsals. Plenty of time.' He came towards her and took her into his arms. 'Besides which, you and I have some unfinished business.'

'Unfinished business?' Her naivety amused him; surely she understood what he meant?

'A little matter of an unconsummated marriage, if you remember.' He was teasing her now. 'Did you know that non-consummation is regarded in law and by the church as grounds for divorce, or annulment?' Instead of being amused, she was embarrassed and annoyed with him.

'Curt, that's a dreadful thing to say! And it's also very vulgar.' It took him a moment or two to realize that she was deadly serious.

'Come on, Marianna. Lighten up. I was only teasing you.'

'I don't care to be teased. I'm not a child.'

'No, you're not. You're my wife and I want to go to bed with you. So will you please go to the bedroom, get undressed and wait for me. I'll come in a moment when I've checked that it's safe to leave all the fires.'

She went away without another word, without closing the drawing-room door behind her. He heard her open the bedroom door and close it again, then there was silence. He knelt down, pushed back the hot coals with the poker, then held his hands out towards the blaze. It felt good to feel the heat of an open fire, after the artificial stuffiness of the train and the freezing cold of the station platform. But there were other things, other pleasures on his mind tonight.

He turned out the electric lights and followed Marianna to the bedroom. She had already undressed – remarkably quickly, he thought – and was sitting stiffly on one side of the enormous bed, a book in her hands, with her long hair spread across the lace pillows. In the soft lamplight she looked ethereal.

'You haven't got time for reading now.'

She looked up, almost with an expression of defiance; he remembered their first night in Minneapolis, and the protests she'd made. Now they were home in their own apartment, and there was nobody to disturb them, nobody to invade their privacy. But it seemed to make no difference. When he began to unfasten his tie and his shirt buttons, she looked at him, aghast.

'Curt, if you're going to get undressed, please wait till I've turned out the light.'

169

She reached over, turned out the lamp. The room was suddenly plunged into darkness. She heard him drape his clothes across a chair, the soft thud of his bare footsteps as he came towards her. Then he was on top of her, unfastening her nightgown, pushing her down on the bed. The pitch blackness all around them made it worse. One moment he was kissing her, then she felt, with horror, some unmentionable part of his anatomy thrusting hard between her legs. With a shriek of shock and disgust, Marianna wrenched herself free, desperately feeling for the lamp. Suddenly there was light again, and Curt was staring at her as she grabbed the bedclothes and pulled them protectively around her body.

'For Christ's sake, Marianna, what the hell's the matter with you?'

'Please . . . please don't come near me . . .' She was almost in tears. She put up her hand, as if to ward him off. 'I want to sleep in the other room.'

Curt could scarcely believe this was happening to him.

'Marianna, we're married now.' What could he say to her? She was almost hysterical. He'd known she was shy, a little naive, a little unworldly and very inexperienced, but he'd never suspected anything like this. It was almost as if she'd had no idea what was meant to happen. 'Why are you behaving like this?'

'It's horrible . . . ugly.' She was trying hard not to cry. 'I don't want to do it.'

He'd wrapped a blanket around himself. 'Marianna, I don't know what the hell to say to you. I'd go in the other bedroom but it won't solve anything. I know we're both tired, but we have to talk this out.' Whatever happened, he mustn't lose his temper with her. He had to remember just how strictly a girl like F. H. Eastbridge's daughter had been brought up. But was it really conceivable that her mother had never told her what mothers were supposed to tell their daughters? It seemed almost impossible to imagine. After the frustrated nights in Minneapolis, then the three-day journey by train through Milwaukee, Chicago, Detroit, Buffalo, then Rochester and finally to

New York, he'd expected more than a hysterical, frigid wife at the end of it.

He sat down on the bed, took her hand in his. She didn't pull it away; at last he was making progress. But he still had a long way to go. 'Marianna, I thought you loved me.'

'I do! I love you terribly!'

'Then why won't you let me make love to you?' Even in the dim light he could see how the colour had risen to her cheeks with embarrassment. 'It's what people do when they're married, when they're in love. I thought you understood that.' It still seemed inconceivable to him that she didn't. Or was it simply that because the thought of intimate physical contact was repellent to her she chose not to think about it? 'Everyone does it, married or not. That's why we're all here.'

'Do you have to put it quite so crudely?'

'How else do you want me to put it?'

'I'm sorry, Curt. I'm just not ready.'

'That's what you said in Minneapolis.'

'It was different then. We weren't really alone. We didn't have any privacy.'

'That's just an excuse, and you know it. Besides which, we're here now. We are alone. There's no-one in the whole of this apartment except us.' He got up, began to pace the room. Despite his earlier resolution, it was difficult not to feel angry, impatient with her. She was impossible. 'OK. I'll sleep in the bedroom next door . . . will that suit you? I'll wait until tomorrow, when you've had time to think it over. But just a second . . . the cook and the maid will be here then! Maybe you should contact the agency in the morning and tell them not to send anyone after all because once they move in here, you won't even contemplate sleeping in the same bed with me!'

'Curt, please don't be childish!'

He stopped pacing and stood still. His eyes caught sight of the mantelpiece clock: ten after eleven already. He tried to calculate how many hours of sleep he'd get – if he ever got to sleep at all – before he had to rise in the morning and get ready for rehearsals at the theatre. Would they have resolved their difference, or would they still be arguing then?

'This isn't getting us anywhere.' He ran a hand through his hair in exasperation. He'd never felt so helpless and so frustrated in his life; married to Marianna, how was he going to get through the rest of it and hold on to his sanity? 'Maybe you don't feel about me the way you think you do. Maybe you don't love me at all. Maybe that's it.' At last, something he'd said seemed to get through to her. She looked at him wide-eyed, almost afraid that he could doubt her love for him. Hadn't she left her home, her family, because she wanted to be with him, and they hadn't approved? Her father had forced her to make a choice, and she'd made it without hesitating for an instant.

'I know exactly how I feel about you.' She got a grip on herself. It frightened her when he talked about her not really loving him. She was desperate to make him understand. 'I do love you, Curt. You have to believe that. I thought I'd already proved it to you.' She was quiet for a moment. 'I'll turn out the light and you can come into bed.'

'Do you mean that?'

'Yes.' It was only half a lie; she was afraid of what would happen if she kept refusing him.

The darkness enveloped the room again. She let him come close to her, slip her silk and lace nightgown over her head. He wound his hands in her long hair, pulled her towards him and began to kiss her. She trembled when his hands touched her body, when something warm and very hard pushed against her, then slid between her legs. The pain was excruciating, almost unendurable; she bit her lip to stop herself from screaming. She screwed up her eyes, forced herself to think of something else: was it possible that any woman could enjoy this? The idea seemed unthinkable. Equally unthinkable, the idea of her parents doing anything as distasteful and undignified, and yet they must have done. How long was it meant to last, and how often was she expected to put up with it, were the next questions she asked herself. She had no idea. Was it every month, every week, every night? If so, she didn't think that she could bear it.

His physical needs spent, Curt lay on his back in the darkness. Neither of them spoke again, even to say good night. What else, after this ugly business, was there left to be said? After a few moments, he felt her edge away from him towards the other side of the bed, and for an instant he felt guilty. He should have made more effort, been slower, gentler, more patient. Perhaps if he'd really loved her as she loved him, it would have been different, easier. Together, they could have overcome the handicap of her naivety and inexperience. Love made such a difference; too late, he realized that now. Even without love, passion and desire would have made the experience a mutually fulfilling one – he'd had many affairs with girls, girls very different from Marianna, where there had been no love but a great deal of the other two things, on both sides. Tonight, on his at least, there'd been no love; on Marianna's, no passion, no desire: a foolproof recipe for disaster. As Shawn might have said with crude wisdom, masturbation would have served him just as well; as it was, he'd upset her and got his way for nothing. Ironically, at the end of it all he'd felt no real satisfaction, no real pleasure. How could he, when she'd just lain beneath him like a statue, when he knew by the way she'd bitten her lip and clenched her fists just how much she'd really hated it?

From the day rehearsals for *Monte Cristo* started at the Lyceum, she hardly saw Curt at all. He was up by eight, when he ate a cooked breakfast and scanned the early morning papers; by nine, he was out of the apartment and on his way to the theatre, from which he rarely returned before seven o' clock in the evening, sometimes much later. For the first two weeks, Marianna got up at the same time so that they could spend at least an hour together before being apart for most of the day, but she soon realized this was a waste of effort: Curt scarcely spoke to her, barely even acknowledged that she was there; when he'd finished eating, he was either reading the newspaper or memorizing his lines. Eventually she gave up, and stayed in bed till he was gone.

Even with the cook and the maid in the apartment – Mrs Dawkins, a widow, and Bridget O'Hare, an Irish girl – Marianna was lonely. Once she was ready and dressed and had eaten breakfast by herself in the dining room, there was nothing to do. The whole day, empty and devoid of any real purpose, stretched away in front of her. There was no point in shopping; she didn't need anything. No visits to family or friends; when she'd left her old life behind her at Fifth Avenue, she'd effectively cut herself off from both. When the boredom and purposelessness had grown too much, she'd asked Curt if she could come with him and watch the rehearsals, but he hadn't wanted her to.

'I'd feel kind of self-conscious with you there . . . it would put me off. I wouldn't be able to concentrate. Anyhow, I don't want you to see me until I'm perfect in the part.'

She'd smiled, and tried to sidle up to him. 'I think you're perfect already.' But he'd been studying some of David Belasco's changes to the script and he wasn't really listening.

'I'll see you later, OK? If I'm extra late home tonight, just start dinner without me.' Almost two months later when the rehearsals were coming to an end, Marianna knew little about what was going on with the production except for what she read for herself in the press.

Back from an aimless morning's window-shopping, she'd taken Curt's *New York Times* into the little library and turned straight to the theatre pages, as she always did, and learned something that Curt had either forgotten or not bothered to tell her. David Belasco, besides co-writing the script, had designed several spectacular stage sets for some of the most dramatic scenes in the entire production – the gaunt interior of the Château d'If where Edmond Dantes was imprisoned, the secret cave on the island of Monte Cristo where the lost treasure was found, and the hall at the very end of the play where Monte Cristo, identity at last revealed, engages Ferdinand Mondego in a swordfight to the death.

The enormous wardrobe department, the writer of the article asserted, had worked overtime to produce the one hundred and fifty different costumes needed by the cast, and in addition to the costumes – which ranged from the rags Dantes was consigned to wear during his imprisonment, to the most lavish ballgowns worn by ladies in Napoleonic France – four dozen wigs had been specially commissioned, more than ten thousand dollars' worth of props, furniture, carpets, mirrors and artificial jewellery had been bought, and more than one thousand dollars had been spent on flowers used in the play itself, to decorate the theatre and the President's private box. Marianna read the last line again; there was no mistake. President McKinley was to be present at the first night opening of the play.

She looked further down the page, read on. *Mr Charles Frohman, well-known theatrical impresario responsible for producing this much-vaunted stage version of Dumas' classic novel of intrigue, revenge, and thwarted love, is wholly convinced that his controversial decision to give the leading role of Monte Cristo to the comparatively little-known actor, Curt Koenig, will be vindicated beyond any doubt on the opening night of the play. Mr David Belasco, co-writer of the script and also the play's director, fully concurs in this.* There was a quote from Belasco himself. *'Originally, the role of Monte Cristo was envisaged as being played by Kyle Bellew, William Gillette, or John Drew, with Drew the most probable. But the moment Curt Koenig stepped on stage for the audition, we all knew that here, in front of us, was the only possible leading man. We were looking at our Count of Monte Cristo.'* There was no mention, no hint of the part she had played in bringing Curt to Charles Frohman's attention; an oversight? An accidental omission? In the only interview with Curt himself so far he had simply told the reporter that it was while he had been in the cast of *Under the Red Robe* at the Metropolitan that he'd heard about Frohman's production of *Monte Cristo* and decided to audition for the role of Mondego; he hadn't said a word about Marianna, not even that they'd been married just a week before the rehearsals began. Whatever his reasons, she was hurt by the fact that, as far as the newspaper reports were concerned, she did not seem to exist at all.

She folded the page, read more. Maud Adams would play opposite Curt as Mercedes; Richard Duvall, the villain Ferdinand Mondego. Her eyes moved down the list of supporting cast: E. J. Masterson, Gertrude Thomas, Gerald C. Bryant, Madeline Dupre. In one of the minor roles, she noticed the name of another recent Charles Frohman discovery, Maurice Chelfont – cast as Cavalcanti – and remembered something that Shawn Duchovsky had said about his transition from the English to the American stage.

'I heard it, the company he'd come over from London to New York with had suddenly gone bankrupt, and none of their players had gotten paid; also, they were all stranded. Word is that Frohman saw him hanging around outside one of his theatres, and thought he had the look of a matinee idol in the making, so he took him on, gave him a small role in one of his plays. Curt says that Frohman thought he looked a little Italian, so he was perfect for Cavalcanti in *Monte Cristo*.'

'When I was coming back from Macy's yesterday, I saw Frohman's advertising posters being pasted up all along Broadway!'

Shawn had seen them, too. 'Everyone at work's talkin' about it, everyone wants a ticket to the first night! You can't open a newspaper without seeing an advertisement for the box office, or some interview with Belasco or Frohman about the play . . . after it opens, Curt'll have his work cut out fending off the newspaper guys and the teenage matinee girls!' He'd chuckled with amusement, completely oblivious of Marianna's strained reaction. 'Stage doorman at the Lyceum says when there's a new leading man who's good-lookin' – never mind in a play as advertised as *Monte Cristo* is – they get hordes of young girls mobbing the stage door so that nobody can get in or out. When Maurice Barrymore was playin' in *Captain*

Swift a few years ago, he reckons it was so bad they had to disguise him as a woman to get him out of the theatre!'

'How grotesque.' She'd carried on pouring tea into the china cups, passing him the sugar, as if the thought of Curt being mobbed by crowds of adoring young women didn't bother her at all, but inside she was boiling over. 'Surely the management wouldn't allow anything like that to happen now?'

Shawn shrugged, still oblivious of the way she'd suddenly become very quiet. 'Not much they can do to stop it . . . and why would they? It's big publicity. To Frohman's way of thinking, and everyone's concerned with the production, the more the better.'

'I doubt if Curt would agree.'

'Oh, it doesn't bother him,' Shawn said blithely. 'In Minneapolis, in school, the girls were always swoonin' over him. He can take it all in his stride.' Only afterwards, on his way back to his new apartment at the other end of town, did it dawn on Shawn that Marianna might have been just a little upset by what he'd said. She'd seemed to have her mind on other things when she'd seen him to the door and said goodbye. Women were funny that way.

Left alone, she'd called for Bridget to take away the tea tray and then she'd gone into the library to read. There was a fire lit, and the room was comforting and warm. She'd chosen a book from the shelves and settled down in one of the big winged chairs, but she hadn't been able to concentrate. She'd stared down at the printed pages but all she could think about was what Shawn had said. She realized that she was jealous.

Jealousy was an ugly emotion, one that had never visited her before; and why should it have? She'd never envied anyone. Until she'd married Curt and left home, her father had provided her with all the material things any girl could want. She'd never been in love before she'd met Curt; the question of being jealous of someone else had never arisen. But what Shawn had imparted to her not only angered her, it alarmed her. The idea of other women – foolish young girls or not – swarming around him in great numbers, clamouring for his attention, was something she'd never thought about, something she hadn't been prepared for. But while she waited for him to come home from the final week of rehearsals, she forced herself for the first time to think about the implications of the play's success, and what it might mean to both of them.

With a month before the play opened on Broadway, the Frohman publicity machine had gone into full swing. For weeks now there'd been giant billboards all over New York, advertisements in every newspaper, every saloon, every department store. Everywhere she looked, there were artists' impressions of Curt, and, outside the Lyceum Theatre alongside the huge colour placards announcing the opening of the play, publicity photographs of all the major players in the cast – his and Maud Adams' the most prominent. Marianna had to admit that anyone living in New York would have to be blind and deaf not to have known about the *The Count of Monte Cristo* or Curt Koenig. But, she asked herself, wasn't that exactly what she had wanted? Why else had she gone to Charles Frohman all those weeks ago and begged him to audition Curt for the part, if she hadn't wanted this to happen? It was only the other things, the swooning women pursuing him, the crowds of autograph hunters, the sudden turmoil spilling over into their private lives, that she didn't want, that she hadn't even thought about in the beginning. Now, it was too late to stop it.

When she heard him coming into the apartment she ran out to meet him.

'Curt, you're so late! Wherever have you been? I was starting to get worried!' She meant to sound concerned, but the words came out like an admonishment. He frowned slightly.

'Christ, Marianna, it's only just after nine!' He hung up his hat and coat. 'I told you this morning I might be late back.' They went into the drawing room. 'I can't just walk out on the dot of seven. We open in three days' time. There were pressmen, interviews to give . . . and we've been

178

spending more time on the difficult scenes, just so that everything's perfect on opening night.' He went across the room, poured himself a drink. 'Belasco, he's a real hard taskmaster. And I thought I was a perfectionist!'

'Is he difficult to work with?'

'No, not at all. He just wants everything to be as good as it can be.'

She was anxious, on edge again; he seemed so distant. Was it because of the hard work of rehearsals, the thought of opening night coming closer, or was it something else? She couldn't get what Shawn had said out of her mind. 'I told Mrs Dawkins and Bridget to hold back dinner.'

'You shouldn't have done that. I told you to start without me if I wasn't back by seven thirty.'

'I didn't want to sit at that great long table and eat all by myself.'

'I'm not that hungry.' She was getting more alarmed by the minute. During the past few weeks, he'd changed so much. Almost every day, she found new excuses to explain it. He was working hard, he was preoccupied with the play, he was worried that perhaps it wouldn't be the enormous success all the newspapers were predicting, that if it failed and the reviews were bad it would all be his fault. Each evening when he came home she'd tried to talk to him about it, but he seemed increasingly unwilling to discuss anything with her. He either read the newspapers in the library after dinner, or disappeared to practise his lines.

'Curt, when we've had dinner, I thought it might be a good idea to get an early night. You look so tired.' He glanced up. 'You don't have to study the script tonight, do you?'

'I was planning to go to bed earlier anyhow. But you don't have to join me. You just keep me awake when you have the lamp on to read.'

'I'm not going to read.' It was the closest she could come to telling him that she wanted him to make love to her. *Hussy!* she could almost hear her mother's harsh, disapproving voice say. It wasn't that she wanted to; the physical act between them still deeply embarrassed her, but she'd already realized how important it was to him, even though he knew how much she hated it.

'That's up to you,' was all he said, but Marianna could sense that he understood. Over dinner, he made an effort to sustain a conversation with her; during the past weeks, he'd spoken only in monosyllables, sometimes barely at all.

'Curt? There's something I wanted to ask you . . . Shawn mentioned it a few days ago . . . it just seemed a little fantastic, that's all. I wondered if it was true.' He looked up.

'Oh?'

'There haven't been any crowds, waiting outside the stage door, have there? You haven't had any trouble getting out of the theatre after rehearsals?'

'There are always crowds when there's a big Broadway play. It's inevitable. But not so much after rehearsals; mainly because we don't always finish at exactly the same time.' She wasn't really reassured by his answer. 'There have been a lot of people waiting about on the pavement these last two weeks, but the doorman always tells them that the cast have left by another exit!' He smiled. 'We can't do that after the play opens . . . it wouldn't be right to refuse to talk to the press, or sign theatre programmes. Not good for business . . . and I don't think Charles Frohman would approve of that.'

'Does that mean that when the play opens I'll hardly see you at all?' There was an edge to her voice now. 'I scarcely see you now as it is.'

'That's the price of success, Marianna.'

She laid down her knife and fork. Though he'd almost finished eating, her food was barely touched. She felt a lump in her throat, an empty gnawing sensation in the pit of her stomach. She couldn't seem to reach him, couldn't make him understand that she was upset about the amount of time they were spending apart. She'd accepted that the rehearsals for the play were time-consuming, that when it opened press and public interest would take away some of their privacy, but she hadn't expected this, the feeling of being pushed aside completely. She was afraid of

180

what was happening but she didn't know what to do about it.

'Curt, I'm very tired.' She laid down her napkin and stood up. 'I can see you are, too. Let's go to bed now.'

He looked almost shocked, stunned even. 'But we haven't had dessert yet.'

'I don't want dessert.'

'OK.' He pushed away his plate and got to his feet. 'I'll tell Bridget to clear the table, then.'

She reached their bedroom first, while he was still in the dining room. She knew exactly how long he'd take. When he'd spoken to Bridget he'd go into the library and put away his copy of the script, then he'd go into the bathroom to wash. She could do that later. She unpinned her hair, undressed and climbed into bed. When she heard him coming, she turned out the lamp.

She saw him hesitate as he noticed her nightgown lying across the chair. 'You've forgotten this,' he said, lifting it up and bringing it towards her. She gazed up at him from the depths of the capacious bed.

'No, I haven't forgotten it. I don't need it now.'

She loved the warmth, the feel, the closeness of him; the texture of his hair, his skin, the rippling muscles; the sensation, more heady than strong wine, when he held her against him, and kissed her. Why, why, why did she hate and loathe the other part so, the messy, painful undignified part when it all ceased to be romantic and instead degenerated into something base and ugly? She'd tried so hard to like it for his sake, tried even harder to pretend. But though they never spoke about it, she sensed that he knew she was only dissembling, only going through the motions to hide the truth.

'Curt . . . I love you . . . so much,' she whispered to him, moments before the part she enjoyed changed abruptly to the part she found so coarse and degrading.

'I know,' he answered, before the yawning silence fell between them, but without saying that he loved her, too.

* * *

181

The evening before the play opened, Curt's family arrived in New York and he installed them in style at the Hotel Endicott, on Columbus Avenue, insisting that he foot the bill. Marianna could scarcely raise any objections, since it had been at her suggestion that the money from her trust fund be transferred into his account at the National Bank; besides which, with the play set for a long and very profitable run, Curt's salary would reflect his success accordingly. But she was hard pressed to hide her annoyance when he also insisted on spending most of the next day – when he should have been resting – with his father and brothers in Ives Billiard Parlour on 42nd Street, while she was left with the task of entertaining his mother.

'Really, Curt, I would have thought you'd have had more sense! It'll be gruelling tonight . . . more than two hours on stage, and you in almost every scene! You ought to have been lying down upstairs, taking things easy!'

'So my family travel across six states to get here for the opening night, and you think I should just ignore them and go to bed instead? This is a big occasion for them, Marianna!'

'And it isn't for me?' She'd become even angrier with him. 'I'm the one who's been sitting alone for the last two months, while you've been out all day rehearsing! And I was the one who went to Charles Frohman in the beginning and begged him to audition you!'

'As you never get tired of reminding me.' It was rapidly degenerating into a quarrel, the last thing she'd wanted. But she was tired of being pushed into the background, of constantly being forced to take second place to everything else in his life. All she'd wanted was to spend the day with him before they had to leave for the theatre, but instead he'd spent it in a billiard parlour.

'Curt, please, let's not argue . . .'

'Who's arguing? I just stated a fact.' He was already across the room, ready to go out of the door. 'Look, it's getting late now . . . almost a quarter before seven.' He sighed. 'I'm going to get washed and changed. I suggest you do the same. The cab taking us to the theatre will be here in half an hour.'

Disconsolately, when she ought to have been so happy, Marianna went into the bedroom where Bridget had already laid out her evening clothes. Her favourite Worth gown, her opera cape, shoes, silk and lace underwear, long white satin gloves. It took her much longer than usual to dress because she didn't ring for Bridget to come and help, not wanting the girl to see how dejected she was after the quarrel with Curt. As a result, when the cab arrived at the front door, she was barely ready.

'We'll have to hurry,' Curt chided as he helped her into the carriage. 'I telephoned the theatre earlier and they said it was difficult already for anything to get through the crowds.'

'I hope your family left early enough, then,' was all she said to him for the entire journey along Broadway. If she was waiting for him to apologize for upsetting her, or to kiss her before they parted in the Lyceum foyer, she was going to be disappointed.

'Curt . . . good luck . . . though I know you won't need any.' There was a lump in her throat; whatever happened, she mustn't cry. To become emotional in public, to embarrass him and herself in front of so many people when everyone was watching them, would be unforgivable, unthinkable.

'I'll see you afterwards, then,' he said, only giving her half his attention because at that moment he suddenly caught sight of his family, talking to Charles Frohman, and left her side to go to them.

Standing there alone, she watched him with them and the others who had milled around him; laughing, chatting easily, exerting the charm that he increasingly rarely bothered to display at home. Then he turned and kissed his mother, exchanged a few more words with Frohman, and disappeared to his dressing room to change.

Marianna took her place alongside Curt's parents in the centre of the front row. The whole theatre was alive with an electric atmosphere of anticipation; beautiful flowers, flashing jewels. The cream of New York society and the theatrical élite had come together this evening to witness the most talked-about Broadway production for years.

She had once been part of that same society. Behind her on the balcony, no doubt, the Lauterbachs and the Depews were ensconced in their flower-decked private boxes near the President's; in the dress circle, in the stalls, were many people who knew her father; some, perhaps, who also knew that the actor who played the Count of Monte Cristo tonight was married to F. H. Eastbridge's only daughter. She was no longer part of the world they inhabited.

She kept her eyes fixed straight ahead of her, on the orchestra pit, beyond it to the stage. Were her parents, perhaps, somewhere in the theatre tonight? If they were, she doubted that they would seek her out.

There was a sudden hush, almost a sigh from the packed theatre. The lights faded, the orchestra began to play the overture, the scarlet velvet curtains slowly drew apart with a majestic sweep, and Curt walked on stage.

Marianna knew that he'd act tonight as he'd never acted before. That he'd justify every ounce of belief she had ever had in him. That he'd vindicate Charles Frohman's judgement in the chance he'd taken in casting a barely known young actor in such a demanding, immensely important, part. Marianna had never doubted that he would do all those things. But at the end of the final scene, after he'd captivated, mesmerized, thrilled and stunned the entire theatre for more than two hours, she knew that even her estimation of his talent had come nowhere close to doing him justice.

He took curtain call after curtain call. The entire theatre was on its feet. She sat there – the only one not standing – with tears smarting behind her eyes. Not because she was suddenly overcome by emotion, not because she in any way begrudged him this glorious moment of triumph, but because she knew that, for them, it signified the beginning of the end.

PART THREE

The Rise and Fall of a Silent
Screen Idol,
Broadway and Hollywood,
1906–1913

CHAPTER THIRTEEN

Roy Delucca walked down the steps of the precinct, paused for a moment while he took out and lit a cigarette, then headed in the direction of lower Manhattan. He stopped on the corner of 2nd Street and bought the evening paper; off duty now, instead of making his way directly home – no point, since Maudie had taken the boys to visit her mother in Flatbush – he went into one of the eating houses that proliferated in the district, and ordered himself a meal. While he ate, he read. And he liked what he read. It had been an inspired idea, eight years ago, to take that little trip out to West Orange, New Jersey, and have a little covert tête-à-tête with Thomas Edison about the guys who were jumping on his kinetoscope bandwagon, using his ideas without his permission to start a little business activity of their own. Modern technological advances in the moving picture business had continued apace since then; now there were even more sophisticated projectors, capable of showing films of up to an hour in length, to which people flocked in wonder. He and Maudie, on his weekly day off, often took the boys to the Theatre Unique on 14th Street, where they'd seen such exciting features as *The Life of an American Fireman*, *Jack and the Beanstalk*, *A Desperate Crime*, and the boys' favourite, *The Great Train Robbery*. The movie craze seemed to have swept everywhere in New York City; up in Harlem, one of the guys at the precinct had told him, there were nickelodeon theatres five a block. Maverick film companies suddenly began springing up everywhere, eager to cash in on the ever-rising and lucrative market; and Edison's patent war took off with a vengeance.

Delucca smiled as he read the article in front of him: to put a stop to all the movie freewheelers who were trying to siphon off a slice of his profits – and to make a peace settlement with his chief rivals the American Mutoscope and Biograph Company – Edison was moving for the formation of a Motion Picture Patents Company, which would outlaw all the small producers, distributors and theatre owners out for a quick profit. Though that might take another twelve, maybe fourteen months to happen, it meant that in the meantime Delucca would be kept busy with his undercover informer service, weeding out the two-bit mavericks who were already violating the existing patents legislation – not only for Edison, but for his rivals American Mutoscope as well. Taking that trip to Edison's studios that day had proved a sound investment: in eight years, he'd almost doubled his police department pay with Edison and American Mutoscope payoffs; and, when the MPP became law in a year or so, he looked set to make even more. Either way, he couldn't lose.

With the sharp rise in income, his standard of living had risen too. Two years ago, he'd been able to afford to quit their Brooklyn Heights apartment and move to a bigger one, in a better neighbourhood; though still in Brooklyn, they were now in Marcy Avenue, closer to the East River Park for the boys, and a shorter journey to work for him across the Williamsburg Bridge. Not only that, but they were further away from Maudie's mother in East Flatbush, so that it wasn't feasible for her to go visiting more than once or, at most, twice a week. With the extra back pocket cash, Delucca had been able to pay a neighbour to look in on the old lady a couple of times a day, so that Maudie didn't worry, and indulge himself in a crap game with the boys from the precinct on Saturday nights. Naturally, he kept his mouth shut about where the money was coming from; if he hadn't, it might set them thinking about maybe muscling in on the action, and that'd be no good at all. Delucca was born smart. He dropped a few hints around 14th Street that an old aunt of Maudie's had died and left them a useful little nest egg; and as far as Maudie went, what she didn't know wouldn't hurt her. All in all, Delucca was happy with the way things were heading; all he needed now was for Chief Rawlins to get himself shot dead, or retire. Neither looked like happening in a hurry.

He finished his meal, ordered coffee, then smoked another cigarette. He went on flicking through the newspaper, stopped when he reached the entertainment pages. There was a long list of twenty-cent movie houses with various offerings to cater for the masses, a vaudeville section, and then, the top of the pile, the latest on-Broadway plays. An illustration of the famous stage actor Curt Koenig, appearing in *Rupert of Hentzau* at the Lyceum, caught his eye. Jeez, but he was certainly a handsome bastard! No wonder his Maudie and half the women in New York City flooded the theatre on matinee days, no wonder every play he'd been in since *The Count of Monte Cristo* eight years ago was sold out for weeks, sometimes even months ahead, and always ran for at least a year. Delucca, who knew almost nothing about theatres and even less about the people who worked in them, wondered how much dough a guy like Koenig made a week. Not that he reckoned he'd ever be short in the money department, what with being married to the only daughter of the millionaire F. H. Eastbridge. He turned back to the front page now; a bulletin about Eastbridge had already caught his eye; seemed he was lying at death's door after a heart attack at his East Coast home. Delucca stubbed out his cigarette. Pity it wasn't Chief Rawlins who was on his last legs. Koenig was probably putting his hands together over it right now; rumour was the swanky Eastbridges hadn't taken kindly to their little girl running off with an actor, even though he'd turned out to be famous, and had boycotted the Lyceum ever since. Whatever, when old man Eastbridge died, the daughter stood to get everything. What was it like, Delucca mused, for an ordinary guy to be married to an East Coast heiress?

He got up, left his money for the meal and a five-cent tip on the table. He winked at the waitress on his way out, ran an appreciative eye over her neat figure. Nothing he'd turn down, if it was offered, but he preferred his women to be a little more generously stacked.

He checked his pocket watch; by now, Maudie should be home from her mother's in East Flatbush. He hated it when he got home and she wasn't there. He walked on briskly, quickening his pace; at the end of the block he'd catch a streetcar that'd drop him at Delancey Street near Williamsburg Bridge. From there, it was only a twenty-minute walk on to the apartment on Marcy Avenue.

It was as he was settling back in his seat a few minutes later that the streetcar passed the corner of Second Avenue and he suddenly caught sight of the placards outside a newsvendor's stall. *F. H. EASTBRIDGE DEAD.* Talk of the devil. He'd bet his month's pay cheque at the precinct Koenig was counting his blessings now.

She only learned about her father's death when she read it in the evening newspapers; there was a Stop Press, with few details except the bald facts. He'd died following a heart attack at his East Maine home. That was all.

'I'm so sorry, Mrs Koenig, ma'am,' the maid who had brought the newspaper to her in the library had said awkwardly. 'I couldn't help noticing . . . it was right there, on the front page.'

'Thank you, Rosie. That's all.' Alone again, Marianna had sat staring at it, feeling neither sorrow nor joy, just a strange kind of emptiness. Since that night when she'd walked out of the Fifth Avenue house and he'd told her that once she left it he would never allow her to return, there'd been no contact of any kind; for her own part, she'd understood that. F. H. Eastbridge did not like anyone who stood up to him, anyone who dared cross him, even if that someone was his own flesh and blood. He had never forgiven her for marrying Curt. Even when the children were born – Gene, in 1899, Elynor in 1901, and finally Alice in 1904 – he'd never relented, never sent a word of congratulation, never replied to her letters. The fact that he had cut her off, banished her from his life, had neither hurt nor surprised her; she knew her father much too well for that. But to ignore the birth of a grandson, the male heir he'd always wanted, had shocked her to the core. No doubt F.H. had reasoned that if he sent for the boy the mother would come too, and to receive her after he'd sworn never to permit her to cross his threshold again would have been a sign of weakness.

She laid the paper aside, got up and paced the room. She wasn't quite sure yet what she should do. When she'd first read of her father's heart attack at the East Maine house – the brownstone on Fifth Avenue had been sold seven years ago – she'd sat down and written to her mother. Edwina Eastbridge had never replied. Maybe now that her father was dead, her mother would see fit to acknowledge the existence of the three grandchildren he had ignored completely while he'd been alive.

She could hear their voices now, excited, squealing with delight, as they ran downstairs to greet their father. So, at last, Curt was home. These days, she never knew when exactly to expect him; she'd long ago ceased even to ask. Life, for him, centred around rehearsals, performances, invitations to dine, and playing with the children. For her, there seemed scarcely any room in his life at all.

He went into the enormous drawing room laden with gift-wrapped packages; from the library door she could hear his laughter and the sound of tearing paper, then the gasps of pleasure as the contents were revealed. She hesitated outside the door, unwilling to walk in on them; when she did, she knew that the smile would disappear from Curt's face and the children would suddenly fall silent. Her strictness with them was her way of providing an antidote to his extravagant spoiling, and she knew that because of it all three of them resented her, but she felt compelled to do it for their own good.

She waited a few more minutes while the four of them laughed and examined the gifts he'd brought them, then she opened the door wider and went in. As she'd expected, there was a sudden yawning silence and then four pairs of eyes all turned towards her as she stood framed there in the open doorway.

'Gene, Elynor, Alice . . . go upstairs and find Rosie. It's

time you got washed and ready for bed.' She looked down at the toys and gift wrapping strewn across the floor. 'Take all that with you. Rosie and Bridget have enough to do in the house without clearing away after you.'

'Yes, Momma . . .' Heads down, all three did as they were told without a protest. Curt kissed each of them on the top of the head before they filed out of the room, little Alice last. When she got to the door she turned and gazed at her father; she was a carbon copy of him, with fair curly hair and enormous bright blue eyes. 'I love you, Daddy!'

Curt blew her a kiss from his fingertips. 'And I love you, too, sweetheart. Run along now.' He smiled. 'I'll come up and read you a story later.' The door closed, and they were alone.

'I heard about your father,' he said quietly. 'I'm sorry.'

'What is there for you to be sorry about? You only met him once, and he asked you to leave the house.' There was an edge to her voice, though she hadn't meant to sound acrimonious. But almost everything he did and said these days somehow provoked her to anger, or resentment, and for some reason she couldn't seem to help it. She desperately wanted him to show her that he loved her instead of lavishing every moment, all his attention, on the children; she longed for him to talk about just the two of them, instead of his latest play, what was happening in the theatre. But he never did. Because Marianna had never found it easy to express her deepest feelings, she withdrew into herself when he ignored her; as time went on, they'd become almost like strangers living in the same house.

'I know that, but to hear of any death is never pleasant. Whatever he was, he was still your father.'

'You're trying to make the point that blood is thicker than water?'

'Something like that.' He went across the room, poured himself a drink. Why couldn't they discuss anything, have an ordinary conversation, without it degenerating into a row? They seemed to argue about everything: the children, the time he spent away from home, even the choice of a restaurant to dine in on the rare occasions they spent time together during the day if he was free.

'I expect his attorney will write to me.' She sat down, but he stayed where he was on the other side of the room, drink in hand. She wanted him to come over to her, to sit down beside her, just be there. But even that seemed too much to ask. 'Father won't have left me a five-cent piece, but I expect he's made ample provision for Gene and the girls.'

'Yes.' He put down the glass. He went over to the door. 'By the way, I promised to have dinner with Clyde Fitch and his wife tonight, so I'll probably be back very late . . . no need for you to wait up. I didn't particularly want to go, not after doing the matinee and the evening performance, but I couldn't very well say no. He wants to discuss the script for his new play before he goes any further.'

Marianna didn't bother to ask what play it was. One play, these days, seemed very much like another to her. What each new idea, each new success meant, in fact, was that she'd see even less of Curt than she'd done before. If she objected, if she spoke her mind and told him that she thought he needed a rest from the constant treadmill of endless work commitments, it would just provoke another quarrel. The last thing she wanted. 'Are you dining at his home?'

'No, at Del Monico's.'

'I won't wait up, then.' She went out, into the spacious wood-panelled hall, and up the stairs. After Gene had been born seven years ago, they'd found the apartment on 59th Street too small; now they lived in a grand house on Madison Avenue, with another maid to help with the children, and Curt had an automobile. Yet, large and magnificent as the new house was, Marianna often felt homesick for the apartment on 59th Street, their first home together. Curt never mentioned it.

She went into their bedroom and sat down at her dressing table, stared at her reflection in the mirror. What do I see, she asked herself? She was thirty years old, still strikingly attractive, but the grey eyes, nowadays, were always sad. To the outside world, Marianna Koenig had everything – she was married to a famous Broadway actor with three beautiful children; she lived in a magnificent house in one of the best parts of New York, and they had plenty of money – to other women, she was an object of envy. But no-one in the outside world would ever have guessed the truth. That she was unhappy, lonely, neglected. That the audiences who packed the theatre every evening to watch her husband on stage saw more of him during the performance than Marianna did all day. Even before the children had come along there had been disagreements, tension building up between them because of her inability to express her love for him in the way he wanted; afterwards, he seemed to have transferred his affection, and all his time, to them.

From the beginning there'd been furious, sometimes even ugly arguments, often fuelled by the slightest, most inconsequential thing: what time the children should go to bed, how to punish them if they were naughty; that she was too strict, that he spoiled them and showered them with too many presents. He was always unrepentant.

'Marianna, I think I know what I'm talking about . . . I grew up in a family where we had discipline, but we also had love. You didn't, from all you've told me. In this instance, I think I know what's best for them . . . better than you do. As for the presents . . . I do it because I enjoy it and so do they.'

'I don't want them growing up and thinking that they can have anything just by asking for it.'

'Neither do I. But they won't. For Christ's sake, let them enjoy being kids while they can . . . they'll grow up soon enough.'

She could hear him coming up the stairs now; not coming to her, but going past her door to see the children. She heard Alice's voice, pleading for a bedtime story. No point in staying, when she wasn't needed; she went downstairs, sat down at one end of the long dining-room table, ready for dinner. Bridget had brought the first course and was ready to serve it before Curt finally appeared.

'Do the children know about your father?'

She looked up. 'I haven't told them, no. I'll wait, until either my mother or Father's lawyer contacts me. The funeral will probably be in Maine.'

Another long silence before he spoke again. 'You'll take the children?' She nodded. 'Do you want me to come with you?' That surprised her.

'Can you really spare the time? We couldn't make the journey in a day . . . we'd have to stay over, two or even three days.'

'I'll make the time. If that's what you want.' It had been so long since he'd said anything like that, since he'd actually asked her what she wanted. Was it really because he wished to be there to show his support for her, among the gathering of hostile relatives, or because he'd guessed that F. H. Eastbridge had left the bulk of his fortune to their son? Marianna could not bring herself to ask him.

'Will anyone else be there at Del Monico's tonight, or is it just you and the Fitches?'

He shrugged. 'There may be one or two others. I couldn't say. I didn't think to ask him.'

'And he didn't think to ask you to invite me?' Ever since he'd told her about the dinner, the question had been waiting on her lips. She'd tried to bite it back, not wanting to start another pointless argument, not wanting to sound as if she resented his going out to dinner yet again without her, but the more she'd thought about being left out the more incensed she became. It happened so often that she was beginning to think that Curt's theatrical friends had some special reason for excluding her.

'Marianna, it's no big deal . . . for most of the evening, all we'll be doing is talking shop. It isn't a social occasion.'

'I'd like to hear about the new play.'

'Clyde's already booked the table and told them how many people are going to be there. It'd be awkward for him if you came.' He poured himself more wine. 'Besides, don't you think it'd look a little strange for you to be dining out on the day you heard that your father had died?' Marianna had to admit that that was a point she hadn't thought of.

'Yes, I suppose you're right. It would seem that way.

195

Some eagle-eyed newspaper reporter would probably see me and write a story about it for the gutter press, and say that I was out celebrating while my father was lying in his coffin.'

Curt gave a rare smile. 'I doubt if you'd find any of the gutter press having dinner in Del Monico's; they couldn't afford the prices.' She smiled with him; it wasn't often, these days, that they could share a light-hearted joke together. 'So I'll see you later, then.'

'I hate sitting here and eating while you just have wine.'

'I'm sorry. I should have telephoned and told you that I wasn't having dinner with you tonight. I guess I just got caught up with the play.'

'It doesn't matter.' She'd hardly touched her food; she had no appetite. She got up, moved away from the table. 'Give my regards to Clyde.'

He kissed her on the cheek, but there was no warmth, no real feeling in it. Because he was preoccupied thinking about the new play, she made herself believe, because he was in a hurry. She heard the front door open and close, and he was gone, leaving her in the yawning silence.

She walked into the library and sat down with a book on her lap. The servants were down in the basement kitchen, the children were upstairs in bed; so why, she asked herself, did she feel so desolate, so alone? She opened the book, tried to focus her eyes on the pages, but her concentration kept wandering. She started to think about her father.

He was dead, and there was nothing she could do to change it. She felt no sense of loss, no sadness; to do so would have been hypocritical. She had never been close to him; he'd never encouraged that, never permitted it. All her life he'd kept her at arm's length. Even after his first heart attack, he hadn't sent for her; all the confirmation she needed that he'd never loved her, never cared. Impending mortality might have softened lesser men, but not Frederick Harrington Eastbridge. To his very last breath, he'd been unyielding towards his only daughter. Even at the end, he hadn't been able to forgive.

She turned back to her book again. The warmth from the

fire had made her feel tired, but she didn't want to go to bed. If she went to bed alone she'd just lie there, staring up at the ceiling and the ornate canopy, waiting, listening for him. Suddenly, there was a knock on the door.

'You've a visitor, Mrs Koenig, ma'am. Mr Duchovsky. Shall I show him in?'

'Shawn?' She was on her feet, surprised to have him calling at this time of night; he never did so, unless Curt was there. She wondered what he wanted.

'Marianna.' He kissed her on the cheek. 'Sorry . . . am I disturbing you?'

'No. No, of course not.' She invited him to sit down. 'But you do know that Curt isn't here tonight?'

'Yes, I knew. He's at Del Monico's with Clyde Fitch and the rest of the cast, discussing script alterations for the new play.' The rest of the cast? Curt hadn't told her that. 'Actually, it was you I came to see.' A pause. 'Curt told me about your father, and I saw the placards on my way here . . . Marianna, I wanted to say how sorry I was.'

'That was thoughtful of you.' She'd been quick to see that Shawn had a sensitive side under the levity and wise-cracks, a side people who didn't know him well never guessed was there. 'But did Curt also tell you that after everything that's happened I'm not exactly broken-hearted? I suppose that seems callous?'

'Not if you weren't that close to him, and he ignored you all these years. He was a hard man, by all accounts.'

She smiled. 'I found that out a long time ago.' She looked away, into the fire. 'He never forgave me for leaving home. For marrying Curt against his wishes. He was so used to manipulating other people . . . making everyone do exactly what he wanted them to. Employees. Servants. Me. It was only after I'd met Curt that I really found the courage to stand up to him. I don't think he ever got over it.'

'Will you still be going to the funeral, after what's happened?'

'I was waiting for my mother to write to me. Perhaps it's too soon. After Curt left tonight, I thought about sitting down, writing her just a short letter, to say I'd heard about my father and I wanted her to know that I was sorry . . . but that would have seemed so hypocritical. I don't think I could do it. I could just send a card, with "condolences", and my signature on it.' An acceptable compromise. 'I expect my father's lawyer will write to tell me about the final arrangements. I doubt if my mother can bring herself to do it. Perhaps I'm wrong. I can't believe that she wouldn't want to see her own grandchildren after all these years . . . especially now that she's lost my father.' Was that only wishful thinking? Edwina had always known how to hate with finesse. But eight years was a long time to bear a grudge.

'No, me neither.'

She forced herself to smile. 'Do you want some coffee? Some of Curt's bourbon, maybe?' She should have asked him straight away, but her mind had been elsewhere. And for the last half an hour or so she'd felt the tell-tale nagging pain, low in the pit of her abdomen, that heralded another debilitating bout of the dysmenorrhoea she suffered from.

Shawn shook his head. 'Nothing, thanks. I do have to go. I'm meeting some of the guys I work with downtown for a drink.' He stood up, and she went with him to the door. 'It's OK, Marianna, I can see myself out.'

'I wouldn't hear of it.' She went with him from the cosy library with its booklined walls and glowing fire into the huge, wood-panelled hall. There was a strong odour of beeswax and fresh flowers. 'I might sit down and write that card . . . or go to bed with a book. I wanted to wait up for Curt, but he didn't say what time he'd be home.'

'Oh, I wouldn't wait up if I were you . . . he probably won't be back till eleven or twelve. I had lunch with him today, and he told me that some big deal was going to be discussed at Del Monico's tonight, besides the script changes for the new play. Then afterwards he has to drive Madeline Dupre back home in that automobile of his.' He hadn't noticed the sudden change in Marianna's expression. Curt had said nothing about any of this. 'She lives right the other side of Central Park, so it'll take him a while to get there and then come back again.'

'Shawn, can you wait? Will you do me a favour?'

'If I can. Hey, you OK?' Her face was flushed, her eyes seemed unnaturally bright, almost feverish. Perhaps her father's death really had affected her after all.

'I want you to take me to Del Monico's.'

'What, right now?'

'I have to change first; I can't go dressed like this.' She was already at the foot of the staircase. 'But I'll be ready by the time you've called a cab.'

She barely spoke a single word, all along Broadway. In the end, Shawn fell silent too. He'd asked her if there was anything wrong more than half a dozen times since they'd left Madison Avenue, but all she'd done by way of a reply was to continue to stare straight ahead. When the cab drew up outside the restaurant, he paid the driver and helped her out.

'I'm grateful, Shawn. But you don't have to come in with me.'

'Marianna, are you sure that you're OK? If you want me to, I'll go inside and bring Curt out here.' It was delayed reaction to her father's sudden death that was making her act this way, he'd swear it. 'You won't get any privacy to talk to him, not in there.'

She gave him a strange look, as if she knew something that he and Curt didn't. 'Privacy to talk to him? That isn't why I came.'

She was wearing a dramatic black evening gown, no gloves; the cut of the gown was so close-fitting over her perfect hour-glass figure that she looked exactly like the famous 'Gibson Girl' prototype currently all the rage, and, as she walked into the restaurant, heads discreetly turned. A long white satin cape, flamboyantly embroidered all over in tiny beads of black jet, fell from her shoulders. She slipped it off and handed it to the hovering cloak attendant.

'Mrs Koenig!' The head waiter remembered her well; she had dined here frequently with her father in the old days. 'What a pleasure to see you.' He smiled at her. 'Your husband's table is this way, if you'll follow me.'

Halfway across the crowded restaurant, Marianna caught sight of them, before they could glance up and see her first. There were a dozen people at their table – almost nobody she recognized – and Madeline Dupre was seated next to Curt at one end. He had whispered something into her ear and she was laughing, leaning against him with all the ease of comfortable familiarity, and, as she laughed and chatted with the others around them, Marianna noticed that she frequently turned back towards Curt and touched his hand. A hot, searing flush of emotion that she'd never experienced before rose up and washed over her, diminishing even the growing agony of her dysmenorrhoea. For a moment she paused.

Someone had looked up from the table and seen her standing there. 'Hey, is that Camille Clifford?' She certainly made a breathtaking picture, with her upswept hair and minuscule waist. They were all looking at her now. Further along the table, Curt turned pale.

She walked straight towards him, with a bright, false smile. All the men stood up. Barely even acknowledging them, she looked directly at Madeline Dupre.

'How kind of you to entertain my husband until I was able to get here . . . but I believe you're sitting in my chair.'

A furious argument erupted the moment they got into his automobile outside Del Monico's.

'How could you just walk in there like that and humiliate me in front of all those people?'

'And how dare you lie to me!' Marianna was shaking with emotion and rage. 'If Shawn hadn't called by tonight to say he was sorry about my father, I would never have found out the truth. That far from the quiet little dinner with Clyde Fitch and "one or two others" that you claimed it would be, I find you enjoying a full-scale celebration for a dozen people, and that Dupre bitch all over you! 'She was too upset, too angry to care what she said. 'How dare you leave me at home all by myself while you have the nerve to go out in public with some other woman!' She wouldn't give him the satisfaction of seeing her cry. 'How dare you humiliate me, you bastard!'

Curt was as furious as she was.

'I didn't tell you the truth because I knew that you'd react to it just the way you're doing now! Inviting Madeline was Clyde Fitch's idea, not mine! One of the people at Del Monico's tonight was William T. Rock, president of the Vitagraph Moving Picture Company, and he wanted to meet Madeline . . .'

'Oh, yes, I can believe that! Those cheap moving pictures would suit her just fine!'

'You're like a lot of short-sighted people around, who think moving pictures'll stay the poor relation of legitimate theatre for ever! Well, you could be in for a big surprise, Marianna! From what Rock was telling us tonight, the future for the moving picture industry could be big . . . very big, with the technology for making better-quality pictures improving all the time.'

'Am I supposed to be impressed?' Her voice was mocking now. 'From all I hear, William T. Rock is some showman from Louisiana, and his marvellous technicians are a couple of ex-vaudeville failures!'

'Only someone raised with blinkers on Fifth Avenue could make a completely uninformed statement like that. Vitagraph have gotten so big that they moved from Nassau Street out to Flatbush a while ago, and they've constructed several glass-topped studios with more to come. For your information, they've become a real force in the industry. And the two ex-vaudeville failures as you call them are now producers – no longer acting in and directing their own films; they don't need to. They're hiring directors, actors, property men and other professionals to perform special-ized functions in a professional manner. They've left any trace of amateurism way behind them. Rock says that in a little over a year they expect to be turning out at least eight films a week . . . one- and two-reelers, and have a stock cast of around four hundred people.'

'Is there some point to telling me all this?'

'Yes. I'm explaining what Madeline Dupre was doing at

201

Del Monico's and why Clyde Fitch asked me to bring her.' He was slowing down; they'd almost reached Madison Avenue. 'Rock saw her in several Frohman plays and wanted to know if she might be interested in working for Vitagraph in the future. She was.'

The automobile stopped outside the front of the house. 'No self-respecting Broadway actor or actress would ever dream of demeaning themselves by appearing in those cheap moving pictures. Need I say more?' She got out, ran up the steps to the front door and let herself into the house, leaving Curt to follow. She went straight into the drawing room and poured herself a small measure of sloe gin; the only effective antidote she'd discovered to combat the spiralling pain of her dysmenorrhoea. He came in after her.

'Are you all right?'

'Don't bother pretending you give a damn about how I feel!' She put down the glass and cradled herself, bending forward to try to ease the pain. 'You're not on stage tonight.' He was about to say something when Bridget knocked and came into the room, a little gingerly; she'd heard the drawing-room door slam, the raised voices as she'd come downstairs.

'Is there anything I can get for you, Mrs Koenig, ma'am?'

'Just fetch me some aspirin, will you? You know where to find them. Then you can go off to bed.'

'Yes, ma'am. I'll go and get them for you straight away.'

'Do you think you should be taking pills and drinking that stuff at the same time?' Curt asked, when Bridget had gone. 'It can't be good for you. Hot milk, with some brandy in it, would be much better.'

'Why don't you just go upstairs to bed and leave me alone?'

'I think you should see a doctor about the pain, Marianna. It's getting worse instead of better. It can't be right.' He fell silent when Bridget came back with the aspirin bottle, and waited until she'd left the room before he spoke again. 'I thought you wouldn't have it any more after the children were born?'

'That's what I was told, but it hasn't made any

difference, has it? I've always suffered from it, even when I was a young girl.'

'Let me help you upstairs. You'll feel better when you're lying down in bed.' He came towards her, and she looked at him coldly; how different from the early days, when he could do nothing wrong. Whatever he did, whatever he said, Marianna would always somehow manage to turn it into a bitter quarrel. He wondered if her behaviour tonight was linked in some strange way to the terrible monthly agonies she suffered from, as if temporarily she went a little out of her mind. When they were first married – even as recently as a year ago – she would never have stormed into a public place like Del Monico's and tried to cause a scene. Only his quick thinking had saved him from a potentially embarrassing situation: when Marianna had forced Madeline Dupre to give up her chair, he'd suggested that they leave in consideration of the fact that her father had died that day. Fortunately, the others had understood. But at the first chance he got he intended to apologize to Clyde Fitch and William T. Rock.

'I'll come to bed in a minute.' Slowly, she got to her feet. 'I think I should write a card to my mother. Not a letter . . . I couldn't do that. There'd be little point, since I have nothing to say. And even if I pretended and wrote to say how sorry I am that Father's dead, it would all be lies. Why should I be sorry when he treated me the way he did?'

'Marianna, it's up to you. But do you have to write it tonight?'

'It could wait until tomorrow. But one more question I want to ask you won't.' He braced himself for another cross-examination. 'You said you only went to Del Monico's tonight because Clyde Fitch wanted to discuss his script for the new play. He could have done that with you any time at the theatre. Why tonight? Besides, I would have thought it's well-nigh impossible to discuss the complex-ities of a new script with ten other people present . . . surely you'd need peace and quiet?' The pain was searing into her like red-hot pincers; why, why, why wasn't the sloe gin and aspirin working this time, why wouldn't it go away? 'Curt,

I want to know the real reason Fitch invited you to Del Monico's tonight. And why all those other people were there. I didn't recognize any of them. Are they potential backers for Frohman's next play, or what?'

He leaned heavily against the door and sighed. He was tired, he was sick of quarrelling, but he knew that until he told her the truth there would be no peace. Besides, there seemed no point in trying to conceal something from her that she'd hear about soon enough.

'William T. Rock wasn't there just to meet Madeline Dupre. He wanted to talk to me as well.'

She frowned. 'I don't understand.'

'Vitagraph want to make a moving picture of *The Count of Monte Cristo*; they think it would be an enormous success . . . maybe even greater than the original stage play.' She shook her head in disbelief. 'They want me to play the leading part, with Madeline Dupre as Mercedes. They've had talks already with David Belasco, and he's agreed to their using the script from the Broadway play . . . with a few essential changes, of course . . .'

'No!' She was horrified. Her voice rose to a shout of protest. 'You can't be serious! How can you even consider stooping so low?' She was shocked, outraged. 'A stage actor with your reputation, sinking to the level of cheap moving pictures? No, Curt. You can't do it!'

'You don't understand what this could mean to me, Marianna! This is a whole new medium, reaching out to an audience of maybe millions . . . not just confined to the few hundred people who buy a theatre ticket on Broadway! Motion pictures are the future, and the industry's burgeoning . . . Vitagraph are living proof of that. They started with a shed and now their studios out at Flatbush are more than two city blocks long! The people who were at Del Monico's this evening are all connected with Vitagraph in some way . . . financially, artistically, technically, and legally. Their lawyer says that within the year a Motion Picture Patents Company will have been formed – it'll be called the Trust – consisting of the Edison Manufacturing Company, Vitagraph, and American

Mutoscope and Biograph. They've all been fighting each other to establish the control of their respective patents . . . see, together they hold all the important patents on motion picture film, cameras, projectors . . . and the idea is that, when it's formed, the Trust will issue licences to produce pictures only to its own members, and effectively stop just anyone who starts up with a little capital, looking to make a quick profit.

'What I'm trying to say is that once the Trust is formed, all the old stigmas attached to moving pictures will disappear . . . if not right away, then in a short space of time. Once it's legally regulated, the whole industry will take on a new credibility. Actors and actresses who appear in moving pictures will be treated with respect.'

'Is that what you think? That these cheap moving pictures, one step up from the peep shows and nickelodeons, are the entertainment of the future? That anyone with your stage reputation could sink to the level of appearing in them and not lose all respect?' She was so furious with him that she almost forgot her pain. 'Have they offered you a lot of money, is that it? Why else would someone like you be willing to identify himself with a cheap form of amusement that no-one could ever allude to as art?'

'Marianna, it isn't just the money that can be made out of moving pictures, don't you understand that? It's the challenge. It's completely new, it's exciting, it's pushing into unknown frontiers . . . it's a whole new medium – another dimension of the theatre – that can be used to tell a dramatic story in a way that no stage production ever can! Take *Monte Cristo*. There were scenes in that story, scenes that were in the book that we just couldn't use because they couldn't be reproduced on a stage. Like the part when Edmond Dantes throws himself over the cliff at Château d'If into the sea, and is rescued by the two fishermen. In a moving picture, things from the original story as important, as significant as that needn't be left out. That's the beauty of moving pictures.'

'But they have no sound,' she said, almost triumphantly. 'And how can you tell a dramatic story without that? Mime

205

it, with tacky subtitles? Nobody can develop a drama without words. When you've thought about it, you'll realize that. Or is it just the idea of having Madeline Dupre as your leading lady that you find so irresistible?'

'She has absolutely nothing to do with it, and you know it! It's irrelevant to me who they sign for the part, as long as she can act.'

'If that's the requirement, then what was she doing at Del Monico's tonight? Or is it simply that she's the only so-called actress Vitagraph could find who'd be willing to lower herself to appear in one of their pictures? Since she hasn't got an established reputation on the Broadway stage, she can hardly lose it, can she?'

'Madeline's a marvellous actress and you know it!'

'Perhaps it was your idea to put her up for this moving picture part? Then you could spend more time together!'

'For Christ's sake, Marianna, you're not jealous of Madeline Dupre because I've acted in a few plays with her, are you?' He was as angry as she was now. 'What the hell's the matter with you anyway?'

'How dare you shout at me!' Unnoticed by either of them in the heat of their bitter argument, the door behind Curt slowly opened, and little Alice stood there in her long white nightgown. She was clutching a toy dog in one hand, and her golden curls were ruffled. Her large blue eyes were full of unshed tears. Woken by the sound of her parents arguing, she'd climbed out of bed and come downstairs.

'Don't shout at my daddy!' She looked across the room at Marianna accusingly. 'Daddy.' She put up her arms towards Curt and he leaned down and hugged her to him. 'Why are you and Momma shouting at each other?'

'Alice, what are you doing down here?' Marianna went towards her, but she darted behind her father. 'It's long past midnight, you should have been asleep hours ago!' Curt scooped her up in his arms and she buried her face in his neck. 'Put her down, Curt.' The deep, low pain only increased her anger with him. 'Stop mollycoddling her, for God's sake!' She reached out to take Alice from him, but the little girl shrank away from her. 'You see what you've done now? You've spoiled her so much that I can't do anything with her!'

'That's garbage!'

'You seem to conveniently forget that I'm here all day with the children and you're not! It's so easy for you, isn't it? You just come and go as you please while I'm left with all the responsibility! Then you swan in with an armful of presents to bribe them with, and because you let them get away with whatever they want they think you're Mr Wonderful!'

'Stop yelling at my daddy!' Alice had started to cry again, and Curt began soothing her by kissing her and stroking her hair. He looked accusingly at Marianna over the tousled golden head.

'She's a baby, Marianna, for Christ's sake . . . she's just two years old! She's terrified of you!' He kissed her again. 'I'm taking her back upstairs to bed.'

'Daddy, I want you to read me a story!'

'OK, sweetheart. Let's go and tuck you up in bed nice and snug, and then we'll choose.' He went out with Alice in his arms, leaving Marianna drained and alone.

She was too tired, and too dragged down by the dual blows of emotional upset and physical pain, to write the condolence card to her mother, too weary even to think any more. She went upstairs, took off her black evening gown and hung it away. She was sitting on her dressing-table stool when, at last, Curt came in. She gave him a withering look, tugged the pins viciously from her upswept chignon, and let her thick, heavy hair tumble down around her naked shoulders. Irrationally, despite their heated argument downstairs, despite their bickering over Alice, he was suddenly aroused by the sight of her, half undressed, bare feet and lovely naked arms, luxuriant hair hanging down untidily to her waist. She stared at him in icy silence.

'Alice is asleep now. I don't think Gene or Elynor woke up.'

'Why bother to tell me? You seem to be the expert in how to deal with my children!'

'Marianna, I don't want us to fight all the time.' He came

207

across to her and laid his hands gently on her shoulders. But though she longed to reach up and touch them with her own, to press her lips to his fingers, she kept her hands firmly in her lap. He'd deceived her about the meeting at Del Monico's tonight, he'd infuriated her by his spoiling of Alice, and it would be a sign of weakness if she gave in to him, to her own hidden feelings. 'Marianna, come to bed.'

She stood up, and his hand fell away. 'I want you to sleep in the other room.'

'What?'

'I said, I want you to sleep in the other room tonight. And maybe tomorrow, and the night after that as well. Yes, that's right, Curt! Don't look so bewildered. What else did you expect?' She moved away from him. 'You spend the whole evening wining and dining in Manhattan with actresses and cheap moving picture producers, while I'm left here all on my own, then you just waltz back when you feel like it and deliberately encourage the children to flout my authority! No wonder I can't do a thing with Alice. If she doesn't want to do something, she thinks all she has to do is come whining to you!'

'That isn't true and you know it.'

'You've spoiled her since the minute she was born, Curt; don't deny it! More than either of the others. It's got to the stage where even Bridget and Rosie can hardly do a thing with her . . . the only person she takes any notice of is you. Well, it's got to stop right now. No more presents, no more letting her twist you round her little finger. There's nothing worse than a spoiled child, and I won't let you turn my daughter into a spoiled brat!'

'She's my daughter too.'

'Oh, yes, when it suits you to remember. If you spent more time at home with all of them, then you might start to realize that there's a hell of a lot more to being a good father than just showering them with expensive presents they don't need.'

He was silent for a moment. Marianna sat on the bed, pressing her hands to her stomach where the pain was. Why was he standing there looking at her like that, why didn't he just go away and leave her alone? 'Is this all because I didn't take you with me to Del Monico's tonight?'

'It has nothing to do with it. Except that it would have been nice to have been asked if I wanted to go. Why didn't you want me there, Curt?' Her voice was bitter. 'Was it because you didn't want me to see Madeline Dupre all over you like a rash, or because you thought I might cramp your style with Rock and his two-bit Flatbush cronies? It wasn't always that way though, was it? I can remember the time when you were only too eager to be seen with an Eastbridge on your arm!'

'I can't talk to you, can I?' He stalked over to the door. 'I'm going to bed.' He shut it behind him without even saying good night and she sat there in the silence trying hard not to cry. She threw herself across the bed and dug her nails into the pillows. She was unhappy, she was in pain, she wanted someone to come and hold her and comfort her but there was nobody. She drew up her knees, hugged them to her chest, trying to squeeze away the pain, but it clung on stubbornly. It had never been as bad, lasted as long, as this. Was there something wrong with her?

She rolled onto her back and stared miserably around the big room. It had every imaginable comfort and luxury but it might as well have been empty. Drapes, china, mirrors, pictures, the best linen, the richest carpets, the finest furniture, but nothing that really meant anything to her. She craved Curt's love and attention, but as each day passed she could feel everything she loved and cared about slipping away from her. She felt like the helpless driver of a runaway carriage careering downhill with no brakes, no control, no escape, disaster waiting at the bottom. It was a vicious circle. The more she loved him, the more possessive she became, resenting every moment he was away from her. In the beginning, she'd revelled in his success, the success she'd helped him to achieve; but success bred more success, and as more and more of his time was taken up with outside commitments she saw less and less of him. The less she saw of him, the more she became afraid. A vivid imagination worked overtime. Where was he? What was he doing? Who was he with? When she questioned him relentlessly and he gave her the answers she wanted, she couldn't bring herself to believe him: she'd seen the way women looked at him, and she couldn't bear it. Picture postcards of him in formal studio portraits, and in all his most famous stage roles, were on sale and displayed everywhere, and sold in thousands; she hated the thought of legions of unknown women owning them, having romantic fantasies about him. Having had them herself, she knew exactly what it felt like, to what lengths besotted women were prepared to go to meet their idol face to face. Each first night, each new production he appeared in was now something to be dreaded, with the swarming crowds packed like herrings in a barrel outside the theatre waiting to catch a glimpse of him when he arrived, the hordes of women who collected eagerly at the stage door, wanting to touch him and have him sign their programmes and autograph albums. She hated them all so much and loathed seeing them so much that she'd tried to persuade him to arrive for performances hours ahead of time. When he'd refused, and argued that since they bought tickets to see him it was his duty to make himself available to his fans, it had provoked another fierce quarrel. Sometimes, they would hardly talk to each other for days on end.

She sat up, ran her hand through her untidy mass of hair. The hated dysmenorrhoea was fading just a little now. All she craved was sleep. She was too exhausted, too full of anguish to be capable of thinking rationally about her and Curt. The children, the newly perceived threat of Curt's becoming involved with moving pictures. Her reasons for objecting so violently to that involvement were not solely because of the tainted image 'movies' had among the refined echelons of the legitimate theatre. They were much more basic, much more selfish, than that. As it was, she saw very little of Curt during the daytime. If he accepted Vitagraph's offer, what part of his already crowded life would he have left to fit her into? The answer terrified her.

It was a long time before she slept, between anxiety and pain. In the morning, Bridget brought in her tea and a letter from the Eastbridge family lawyer, informing her that she would not be welcome at her late father's funeral in three days' time. Neither would she, or any of his grandchildren, receive a bequest. Every cent of his five-million-dollar fortune, save for a lifetime annuity for her mother, had been left to charity.

'I'm sorry,' Curt said, as he handed back the lawyer's frigid letter. 'I guess the word forgiveness just wasn't in your father's vocabulary.'

'No.'

'Even so . . . I thought he might at the very least have left something to Gene. His only grandson. Maybe he would have been more inclined to if we'd called him Frederick, instead of Gene after my dead brother.'

'I doubt if that would have made any difference.' How could anyone bear such a relentless grudge, so enduring a hatred as her father had? Even when he'd been lying at the point of death and knowing, surely, that he could only have days, weeks at most, to live, he had refused to forgive her. And what, after all, had been the terrible crime she'd committed? She had loved Curt Koenig. She was glad, now, that she had never sent the card of condolence to her mother. To have done that and then received the post-humous rebuff would have been the most hurtful thing of all.

'I have to get to the theatre now.' Curt was already at the door. 'Costume rehearsals. I'll see you later.' He no longer kissed her when he left the house in the mornings; he never telephoned in the daytime any more. Why not, she'd often asked herself, but never him. Like so many things that had gone wrong in their marriage, it was never brought out in the open and talked about, never discussed. When you were afraid of the answer, it was best not to ask the question.

'Curt?' He turned round. 'About the Vitagraph offer.'

'Nothing's been decided yet, I told you . . .'

'I don't want you to accept. Please, Curt. Turn them down.'

'We'll see,' was all he said, and then he was gone. She

waited until she heard the front door slam and then she burst into tears.

Dressed in deepest black, Edwina Eastbridge stood at the huge bay window overlooking the landscaped gardens, gazing out to the rugged, scenic coastline, and beyond that, the sea. She could hear the rhythmic rolling of the surf, even from this distance; a sound that until a few days ago she had always associated with tranquillity and peace. Now, whenever she heard it, it reminded her of death; two nights ago she'd sat beside her husband's bed in this very room as Frederick H. Eastbridge III had died in his sleep.

Although Edwina had never been passionately in love with him, she felt a terrible sense of loss; it had been a highly successful marriage for more than thirty years. They had come from almost identical backgrounds, had identical temperaments, identical ideals. In all their three decades together, she had never disobeyed him, never disagreed with any of his decisions. Her only regret – and his, too, although he never put it into words – was that they had never had a son. F.H.'s last request – that Marianna should be barred from attending his funeral – Edwina had seen carried out within hours of his death.

She turned away from the window, gave one last look around the room. Everything was exactly as it had been on the day he died, everything in the house just the way he'd left it. Tonight, Edwina would dismiss the servants and travel to Boston, where she would stay with her nephew until the funeral in three days' time.

She closed the bedroom door behind her. Walked down the wide sweeping staircase, the magnificent picture-lined walls, for the last time. There was one single thought left to comfort her, as, no doubt, it had in some measure comforted F.H. just before his death: his vast fortune had been bequeathed to the setting up of the Frederick Harrington Eastbridge III medical foundation, in his home state, Massachusetts. Though there was no son to continue the family name, it had not died with him. There would be those who never knew the truth, who would wonder why

212

the millionaire five times over had left nothing to his only daughter, and everything to the medical foundation which would bear his name in perpetuity; Edwina would never reveal the reason; those closest to her could only guess. But the birth of the Eastbridge Foundation was F.H.'s – and her – perfect substitute for the son they never had.

CHAPTER FOURTEEN

Curt navigated his automobile through the horse-drawn traffic in midtown, then along 57th Street by the edge of Central Park, where it gradually became quieter. At the end of 57th he turned right, and headed in the direction of the Upper West Side.

It was still early – well before ten o' clock – and Madeline Dupre's maid took some time in answering the door. It transpired that Madeline was still not dressed, certainly not in any fit state to receive visitors, so he was shown into the parlour to wait.

It was a pretty, fussy, ultra-feminine room, festooned with swathes of lace and embroidered scatter cushions. Every inch of surface space had been utilized to hold photographs, ornaments, bowls of scented pot-pourri and theatrical knick-knacks, and pictures obscured most of the four walls.

He sat down and looked around him; though it was cluttered by his standards, it was undeniably cosy, almost intimate, so different from the wood-panelled splendour of his own Madison Avenue home, which, for the most part, reflected Marianna's decorative tastes rather than his own. The contrast between the two women's ideals was interesting.

He got up as the door opened and a smiling Madeline came into the room. He was a little taken aback by the fact that she was still not dressed; she wore a satin and lace dressing gown, with matching slippers, and her russet-brown hair was unbrushed and hanging loose. The dressing gown was flimsy, revealing rather than concealing her uncorseted shape beneath. He felt embarrassed now, wondering if it had been a wise idea to come.

'I'm sorry to call on you so early.'

'Nonsense, Curt! I'm delighted you did. I'm woefully late for the theatre . . . I overslept.' She sat down on the elegant chaise-longue and patted the empty space beside her. 'Do you think David Belasco will be able to find it in his heart to forgive me?' She giggled enchantingly. 'I've always found it almost impossible to arrive anywhere on time.'

Curt smiled. 'I should imagine he'd forgive you very easily.' They looked at each other for a moment; this was much more difficult than he'd imagined. 'Madeline . . . about last night . . . I wanted to apologize . . . Marianna . . .'

'Oh, that superb grand entrance of hers! I must say, it was terribly impressive. At least, every man in the restaurant thought so. I hate to have to admit it, since she obviously did it just to cause me as much discomfort as possible, but she really did look magnificent in that wonderful black dress. The Gibson Girl personified. She certainly has a divine figure, but I'm afraid that's the only praise I'm going to give her.' She reached out and laid her long, white, beautifully manicured hand on his. 'I know exactly what you're going to say, but you don't have to apologize. It really wasn't your fault.'

'She had no right to embarrass you that way.'

It was Madeline's turn to smile. 'She was quite a dragon, wasn't she? Almost breathing fire! I suppose she gets that from her father . . . hasn't he just died somewhere in Maine? Oh, I suppose that sounds dreadfully callous, doesn't it? Perhaps the fact that she was upset about his death made her do what she did last night? After all, she might have thought you ought to have stayed at home and comforted her instead of coming to Del Monico's.'

'That had nothing at all to do with it. Believe me, there was no love lost between Marianna and F. H. Eastbridge.' He hesitated, wondering if he should go ahead and say what wasn't yet public knowledge but the facts were bound to come out in the press over the next few days. 'Before I left home this morning, a letter came for her from her father's lawyers. It said that he'd requested she be barred from attending his funeral. And that everything he owned

215

was being left to set up a medical foundation bearing his name.'

'How cruel! No wonder she was in such a temper last night!'

'Last night she didn't have the slightest inkling about the letter. She was just mad at me because I didn't tell her about Vitagraph's offer.'

She gazed at him coquettishly from beneath her lashes. She had a mischievous streak – some, who knew her a great deal better than Curt did, might have called it something else – but her chattering, girlish, deceptively flippant manner always disguised it. 'That sounds ominous.' She let her hand fall from his and rest gently on his thigh. 'Are you saying that when you told her about it she didn't like the idea?'

'That's something of an understatement. In her view, moving pictures are just about the lowest depths that anyone could sink to. She doesn't want me to have anything to do with them.'

A serious note crept into Madeline's voice now. 'But the deal they've offered is so lucrative, Curt . . . unbelievably generous! And just think about it . . . it doesn't stop there. Once the film has been made, it'll be distributed through all Vitagraph outlets all over America, not just confined to one theatre in New York. People who've never had the opportunity of seeing you in the stage version of *Monte Cristo* can see you on film! That would only be the beginning. When the Motion Picture Patents Company becomes law – and that can't be more than a few months away at most – Vitagraph will be in the market for making even more money. There'll be more films, more opportunities, and even bigger financial rewards . . . but nothing if you turn your back on what they're offering you now. Please, Curt . . . don't turn them down just because your wife refuses to see the advantages of working in moving pictures.'

'I haven't made a decision one way or the other.'

She was silent for a moment. Her hand moved a little further along his thigh. 'I suppose if I was being brutally honest, I'd have to admit that I want you to accept the deal with Vitagraph for purely selfish reasons.' He looked at her intently. 'I want to play Mercedes opposite your Monte Cristo. Not just because I think your acting is pure magic and I admire you more than anyone else I've ever seen on stage, or worked with. But because I envied Maud Adams so much when she had the leading female role and I was just a minor member of the cast. I was so jealous of her . . . more jealous than you could ever imagine.'

'You're as fine an actress as she is . . . you don't need to be jealous of anyone.'

'That's not what I meant, Curt.' She moved imperceptibly closer to him. 'I meant that I was jealous of her because in the play she got to kiss you.'

'That didn't mean a thing.' He was suddenly doubting the wisdom of coming to see her. To lighten the sudden tension between them, he began to laugh. 'When we first started rehearsals for *Monte Cristo*, I'd only just come back from my honeymoon.' Madeline looked petulant. 'If you can call two days with my folks in Minneapolis and six days travelling across six states by train a honeymoon. We didn't get the chance to have a proper one until the play was over and by then we'd been married for more than a year!'

'Are you deliberately trying to upset me?'

'Upset you?'

'Curt, I don't want to hear about your marriage or your honeymoon. I can't even bear to think about them. Even less about your wife. Surely you know by now exactly how I feel about you? I've been head over heels in love with you since I first set eyes on you when we met on stage.'

'Madeline . . .' He tried to get up but she seized his hand and made him sit down again. 'I think I should go . . .'

'The question is, do you really want to?'

'It isn't fair of you to ask me that when I'm not free to answer it truthfully.'

'That's the point about life, isn't it? It isn't fair. It isn't fair to want someone so much that however hard you try, you just can't stop yourself thinking about them. Curt, you must have guessed why I was so eager to accept Vitagraph's

217

offer. Be honest with me, please. It wasn't really the excitement and the challenge of working in a brand new medium, of suddenly having the chance to have my face known to millions of people all over America . . . it wasn't even the money. I want to do it so much because it means that I'll be working with you, closer than we've ever worked together before. I want to be close to you, Curt.' A pleading note came into her voice now. 'What I want you to tell me is, do you feel the same way about me?'

He knew that the right thing to do was to get up and walk away from temptation. Because of his marriage, his family, what scandal would do to his career. Despite the fact that he'd never loved Marianna, he still felt a sense of obligation; and a strict upbringing in Minneapolis by two God-fearing, conservative parents had left him with a strong sense of right and wrong. He'd been wrong to marry Marianna for his own selfish and ambitious reasons; it would be even more wrong to betray her with another woman now. Yet he would have been less than honest with himself if he didn't admit that he wanted to.

'Madeline, there isn't a future for us. Whatever I feel, it's irrelevant. I'm not in a position to make you promises that I couldn't keep.' He took her hand in his. 'Look, I don't want to hurt you . . . and I don't want you to waste your time waiting around for someone who'll never be free. You deserve more than that. I admire your talent on stage and I enjoy working with you. For what it's worth, yes, I would like to accept Vitagraph's offer; in fact, I probably will.' Her face brightened. 'But you have to understand that there can only ever be a professional relationship between us.'

'If that's the way you want it.' The rebuff, however gentle, was like a blow in the face; but she hadn't finished yet. This was merely the first round. When Madeline Dupre wanted something, and wanted it badly enough, she never gave up trying until she got it. Let him think that she'd accepted his terms.

'I should be going.' He got reluctantly to his feet. 'I'm late for the theatre already. Do you want me to wait for you?' He smiled. 'I can drive you there in my automobile.'

'I thought you didn't want to be seen with me in public?'

'You know that isn't what I meant.'

'I'm sorry . . . I suppose I'm a little too sensitive right now. Not surprising, since I've just succeeded in making an utter fool of myself. And all for nothing.' She was gratified to see him look guilty.

'Madeline. I said that there couldn't be anything except a professional relationship between us. But that doesn't mean I don't want it to be something else.'

Five-year-old Elynor Koenig stood outside her mother's bedroom, listening to her crying. Uncertainly, her tiny hand hovered over the knob. Last night, she'd heard Daddy and Momma shouting at each other again, and so had Gene, but they'd both been too frightened to get out of bed and go to the top of the staircase as they sometimes did, in case Bridget O'Hare or Rosie Neale the maids came and caught them listening. Instead, Elynor had poked her fingers in her ears and, when she could still hear them shouting, she'd pulled the bedclothes over her head and Gene had too. But this time the argument they were having went on for so long, and their voices got so loud, that it woke little Alice and she'd started crying. Before either of them had been able to stop her, she'd climbed out of bed and run downstairs, and it was only a long time later that the terrible shouting had stopped and Daddy had brought her back up. Because they'd both been afraid that Daddy would be very angry with them if he caught them awake, Gene and Elynor had pretended to be asleep when he came in and tucked Alice up in bed again.

Gene was still getting dressed and Alice was being washed in the bathroom by Bridget when Elynor went to the door of her mother's room because she had heard her crying. She knew, too, that Daddy hadn't spent the night in the same room as Momma like he usually did, because she'd peeked round her door and seen him coming out of one of the guest bedrooms early this morning; no doubt that had something to do with the quarrel he and Momma had had last night. But when he'd gone into her bedroom Elynor had heard them talking to each other in normal voices, so they must have made up; but then, after Daddy had left to go to the theatre, she'd heard Momma crying again.

There was a large ornate vase full of flowers on the beautiful polished mahogany table on the landing. Reaching up on tiptoe, Elynor took one out – the one that looked the biggest and the prettiest – and then, taking a deep breath, knocked on her mother's door. When there was no answer, she turned the handle and let herself in.

Her mother was sitting on the bed, wiping her eyes with a handkerchief. A little way away from her Elynor caught sight of a letter, lying on the counterpane. Was that the reason she had heard her sobbing so bitterly? She was afraid to ask.

'Momma, I brought you something.' Marianna stiffened, put the handkerchief away. Elynor held out the flower towards her.

'Thank you.' Why did she find it so difficult, virtually impossible, to be close to her own children? Was it her own strict, loveless upbringing that had made her so inhibited and unable to express her emotions, or was it because all three of the children had always seemed to gravitate towards Curt? She didn't know. She'd spent so much time trying to counteract the effects of his spoiling them that it had left her the outsider; if any one of the children was hurt, or upset, or wanted something, they would go to their father to sort it out, not to her. 'Bridget's taking you all out for a walk in the park today . . . hadn't you best get ready? You haven't brushed your hair.'

'I won't go if you want me to stay here with you, Momma.' Marianna looked at her. Elynor was the one most like herself to look at; she had her luxuriant dark hair, her cool grey eyes. There was very little of Curt in that pretty, oval face. Gene was a mixture of both of them, while Alice was all Curt with her enchanting doll-like features, golden curls and bright blue eyes. She was also the most difficult of all of them because her father spoiled her so outrageously, and she sensed, despite her mere two years, that all she needed to do in order to get her own way in anything was to smile her beguiling smile, and she got it. Most of their bitterest arguments had been over Alice.

Marianna smiled. She reached out and touched Elynor's cheek with her hand. 'No, you go and get ready for the park; it'll be fun. I'm all right now.'

'Yes, Momma.' Elynor cast a last glance towards the open letter, still lying there on the bed. She wondered what was in it, if what it said had made her mother cry. But she did as she was told and went back to her own room. None of them would ever dare argue with Momma.

As they walked in the park later that morning, Gene fell into step beside his sister and they deliberately hung back so that Bridget, walking ahead of them holding Alice by the hand, wouldn't overhear what they said.

'Did you go into Momma's bedroom like you said you would?'

Elynor nodded. 'She'd stopped crying by then. I didn't like to ask her what had bothered her so. But there was a letter lying open on the bed.'

'Did you see what was in it?'

'No. But it wasn't writing . . . it was like a newspaper. That sort of writing.'

'You mean printing?' Elynor nodded. 'There's a special machine that does that. Daddy told me about it once. They use it in offices and banks. He showed me a picture. It's about this big . . .' he showed her with his hands, 'and at the front, there's a lot of real small bits of metal with all the letters of the alphabet on them. You wind a sheet of paper into the top . . . onto some kind of roller . . . and then you press the little metal things with the letters printed on them, and they come out on the paper. You can write a letter real fast using one of those. Daddy says they have them in the office at the theatre. I wish we could have one.'

'I wish Daddy and Momma would stop yelling at each other, Gene. I don't like it. It frightens me when I hear them shouting.'

221

Gene held her hand. 'I wish they would, too. But it's nothing to do with us, Ellie. It's grown-up things.'

Up ahead, Bridget turned round and called to them. Alice was pointing at some birds and trying to pull away from her.

'Come on, you two! Don't lag behind! Hurry up, will you?'

'Slowcoaches, slowcoaches!' Alice chanted in her high-pitched baby voice. She stopped walking, and held her arms up beseechingly to Bridget. 'I'm tired, Bridget. I want you to carry me the rest of the way . . . my legs are all tuckered out.' She smiled her enchanting little smile and put her golden head on one side. 'Please?'

Marianna opened one of the books lying at the side of her bed, placed the flower Elynor had brought her inside. It was wilting a little now; hothouse flowers never survived for very long out of water; by tomorrow, its fragile beauty would be gone. There was a lump in her throat as she pressed it between the pages and then closed the book. The impulsive childish gesture had touched her in a way that not many gifts, far more expensive, ever could. The value of something, she'd learned the hard way, couldn't be measured by cost.

She bent down, picked up the letter from the Eastbridge lawyers. She read it through one more time before screwing it up in her hand and throwing it away. Against her daughter's flower, the loss of her father's legacy suddenly paled into insignificance; what did F. H. Eastbridge's millions mean to her, anyway, whether she had them or not? Hadn't she walked out of the Fifth Avenue house more than eight years ago because she wanted to turn her back on all that? She'd never regretted it, not even when the endless quarrels with Curt had come close to breaking her, had almost dragged her down. Nobody knew what it was like to live in the same house as F. H. Eastbridge unless they'd done it.

The newspapers, no doubt, would run a story on her father's medical foundation, and the less scrupulous would almost certainly speculate why his five million dollars had been bequeathed to the setting up of a medical foundation rather than to his only daughter. It didn't matter now. What her father had chosen to do with his money was no longer any business of hers; she'd decided that more than eight years ago. It was the refusal to forgive, the cruelty of the slight even from beyond the grave, that really hurt her, not the loss of the money itself.

She could imagine her father, breathing his last in that enormous Maine coast mansion, smiling because he knew that, in spite of everything, he still had the power to punish her, to wound her, to disavow her to the last. Had he, she wondered, really died happy?

The bar of Fritz's café on Chambers Street was already crowded when Curt came in and edged his way through the lunchtime crush to where Shawn Duchovsky was standing over a beer at the counter. They exchanged greetings, Curt ordered a beer for himself, and they moved further back into a corner, waiting for one of the small tables to be free. It was a good meeting place, being roughly halfway between the theatre and the offices of the Hamburg–Amerika Line where Shawn still worked. He was chief counter clerk now, and in the last two years his pay had more than doubled.

'How's Marianna and the kids?'

'OK. And you?'

'Couldn't be better.' Shawn was far too shrewd and had known Curt for far too long to be satisfied with his answer. Something was seriously wrong here. 'You had a show-down with her over the Vitagraph offer?'

'Thanks for dropping me right in it.'

Shawn put down his beer. 'Hey, I never did that! You told me not to breathe a word about the guys from Vitagraph being at Del Monico's last night, and I didn't. But you never said not to tell her that Madeline Dupre would be there. Admit it.'

Curt pulled a face. 'Yeah, yeah, that's what I said. But I thought you might have used just a little discretion. You know that the sound of Madeline's name to Marianna is like showing a piece of red rag to a bull.'

'Curt, I'm not takin' sides . . . an' I know you have to act with her. But you can't blame Marianna for the way she feels. Hell, all the times I've seen you and Madeline Dupre offstage anyplace, the girl's always hangin' all over you. People talk. Especially people who like makin' trouble. Marianna's heard whispers and now even the name gets her hackles up. Wouldn't you feel the same?'

'If she wants to take notice of every piece of gossip that's going the rounds, then that's her problem.'

Shawn's sharp ears pricked up. He didn't like the sound of this at all. He smelt trouble brewing. 'You two had another fight? A bad one this time?'

'After what happened at Del Monico's, I didn't have any choice except to tell her about Vitagraph's offer. You can imagine what her reaction was!' He winced at the memory of it. 'I know I would have had to tell her about it sooner or later . . . but I wanted to do it in my own time, in my own way. I could have made a much better job of it then. But she was already giving me hell about going to dinner with Madeline when she hadn't been invited, and it just kind of all came out.' He sighed, and ran an exasperated hand through his fair hair. 'Jesus Christ, I've never seen her so angry! It turned into a full-scale row, so loud that it woke Alice up and she came down in tears.' He explained what had happened after that. 'I said I hadn't decided anything one way or the other, and that's how we left it.'

'And this mornin'?'

'We both behaved as if nothing had happened at all. Besides, she had something else to contend with.' He told Shawn about F.H.'s last snub. 'I reckoned with being told that she wasn't welcome at the funeral, and old man Eastbridge leaving everything he owned to charity, it wouldn't have been the right moment to tell her anything.'

'You'd made a decision on Vitagraph's offer?'

'Funnily enough, I hadn't. Not until about three hours ago when I called on Madeline Dupre.'

'What?' Shawn was rarely shocked, but he was now.

'After all that's happened, all the trouble she's caused between you and Marianna, you went to see her – alone – at barely nine in the morning? Supposin' some eagle-eyed newspaper snout was snoopin' around, tryin' to find some dirt someplace to use in his rag? Hell, Curt, you've been around long enough to know how those guys operate! You got a fuckin' death wish or somethin'?'

'That's not the way it was . . .'

'You think they give a shit about that? Sure, when you got turned into a big name after *Monte Cristo*, and they sat up and started takin' notice, all the newspaper reporters in New York wouldn't have found so much as a speck of dust on that lily-white image of yours, no matter how hard they tried!' He couldn't believe Curt could have been so careless or so stupid. 'Now, you're playin' right into their hands. With this news about F.H.'s death, and you rumoured to be considerin' goin' into moving pictures, they're goin' to get interested all over again! You get seen visitin' some actress at nine in the mornin', and the balloon goes up! Haven't you got more sense?'

'OK, OK . . . so I didn't think.' Curt was angry now; Shawn should have been on his side, not trying to lecture him on how Marianna felt. 'But what else could I do after last night? Marianna was so damned insulting to Madeline that I felt I just had to go and apologize . . . make sure she understood.'

'Don't you think you were apologizing to the wrong woman here?'

'What the hell's wrong with you today? Maybe it's the beer in here!'

'Curt. We've bin friends a long, long time. It was me who encouraged you to marry Marianna. We were a lot younger then . . . and it kind of seemed a good idea to go after some rich girl who lived in a big swank house on Fifth Avenue. I didn't see her as a human being with feelings in those days, just F. H. Eastbridge's daughter. I knew how much you deserved to get on, 'cos you worked so hard, and I thought someone like that would open doors for you . . . that was somethin' I was right about. Now, I just wish I hadn't been so glib about it.' He paused, finding it hard to talk about his feelings, even to Curt. 'What old man Eastbridge's just done – gettin' his fancy lawyers to tell her she can't come to the funeral, cuttin' her out of his will – just goes to show what kind of man he was, and how he must have treated her while she was living with him. Think about it. All these years, and he's not so much as written to her. Nor has that mother of hers. What kind of people can they be to treat Marianna that way? Now you give her a hard time just because she was upset at bein' left out of the dinner at Del Monico's! Hell, Curt. How many kicks in the teeth and rejections is she supposed to take?'

'I didn't kick her in the teeth, for Christ's sake. I just couldn't take her with me because the people from Vitagraph were there. Madeline was invited because they want to offer her a contract too. That was the whole goddam idea of the dinner!'

'Couldn't you have made somethin' up? Said you was havin' dinner with someone from the theatre at the Lamb's Club, somewhere ladies don't go?' Curt could be so dumb sometimes, and that wasn't like him. 'What the eye doesn't see an' all . . .'

'I guess. I just wasn't thinking. Anyhow, after I talked to Madeline, I decided.' He finished his beer. 'I'm accepting the offer from Vitagraph.' There was a long silence between them.

'Is it the dough they're offerin'? Or is it somethin' else?'

'Meaning?'

'You know as well as I do that people in the established theatre look down on movies as somethin' just one rung up from vaudeville. What's the attraction for someone as well known and well paid already as you are?'

Curt tried to explain. The novelty, the excitement of being part of the new medium everyone was talking about; the challenge of trying a different kind of acting, the appeal of becoming known to millions across the whole of America, not just the sophisticated theatregoers of New York. Vanity, maybe? He couldn't deny that. But Shawn was his oldest friend and it mattered to him that he understood. 'Madeline's accepting for exactly the same reasons as me. And, I guess, because instead of the minor role she had in Frohman's production of *Monte Cristo,* she'll be playing Maud Adams' original part opposite me.'

Shawn nodded slowly; he'd already read between the lines and hoped that his hunch was wrong. 'Have you slept with her?'

'No.' Curt was turning the empty beer glass round and round in his hands. 'But I want to.' It was almost a relief to say it, to unburden the weight of guilt on his mind to someone else. Shawn, of all people, understood. Hadn't they talked and joked and teased each other about the girls they'd had back in the old days?

'Curt, I'm not a judgemental person . . . Christ, you know that! I haven't exactly been an angel where women are concerned. But this is something else.' Curt glanced sideways at him. 'The difference now is that you're married, you have a family. This time, people can get hurt.'

'I said that I wanted to . . . not that I would. That's not quite the same thing.'

'But it's only a step away.' A pause. 'Are you in love with her?'

'No. I just want her. Like I've wanted Christ knows how many other women since Marianna and I got married. I always stop myself, before I start to get too tempted . . . but the temptation's always there. I wish it wasn't. Maybe taking up this offer from Vitagraph is a dumb thing to do just because I know I'll be working with Madeline every day. But maybe I need that, to make up for what I don't get back home.' This was the hardest part to tell Shawn. 'She's so cold, Shawn. So wooden. Not like a flesh and blood woman. And she hates it. She can't bear me to even touch her. You know how that makes me feel?'

Shawn put a hand on his shoulder. He was beginning to understand that this thing mightn't be all down to Curt's roving eye after all. But he knew Marianna loved him just by the way she looked at him.

'Maybe you and Marianna should take some time out and talk it through. It can't have been easy for her, growing up F. H. Eastbridge's daughter. I mean, what kind of guy stops his own daughter from going to his funeral, and disinherits her all in one stroke? Hell, Curt, we're talkin' serious stone-wallin' here. You think any girl could grow up normal with a father like that? And by all accounts, that stuck-up mother of hers wasn't much better. Maybe it isn't Marianna's fault she's the way she is.'

Curt looked at his watch. 'Guess it's time for me to go now.' He managed a smile. 'Thanks for the beer. Even more . . . thanks for listening.'

Shawn watched him make his way back through the crowd and disappear out of the door. He turned back to the bar, ordered another beer. He'd often envied Curt his extraordinary good looks, his talent, his success, and everything he had now. But after today, he wasn't sure there was much to envy after all.

He was back early from the theatre, much earlier than she'd expected. She heard him let himself into the front hall, then the delighted cries of the children as the three of them rushed down the stairs to greet him. She opened the door from the drawing room, where she'd been sitting, and he turned and saw her. For a moment they just looked at each other.

'Gene.' He turned back to his son. 'Take your sisters upstairs to the playroom for me, will you? I'll be up in just a little while.'

'But, Daddy.' Little Alice was reluctant, as usual, to do as she was told. 'I want you to come upstairs with me now!'

'Be a good girl and do as I ask you, Alice.' His tone of voice was firmer than Marianna had ever heard it when he spoke to their youngest daughter. Alice stared up at him in surprise. 'Go along, all of you. I have to talk to your momma.'

Alone in the big drawing room, Marianna took a seat. The dysmenorrhoea had gradually faded during the day, after liberal doses of aspirin, but she was feeling drained and tired still after their fierce argument last night, and the news about her father. What could he possibly want to talk about now?

'It isn't like you to send the children off like that.'

'I think we have things to discuss, don't you?'

'I'm listening.'

'Not here.' He crossed the room and poured himself a drink. Was it just her imagination, or did he seem to be drinking more than usual? Until recently, she had rarely seen him drink before dinner. 'I want to take you out to dinner tonight. I've already booked a table at the Ritz-Carlton, for eight o' clock. Does that give you enough time to get ready?'

'What's the occasion, Curt? Or is it that you're still feeling guilty about deceiving me?' Why, why, why did she always do this? He was trying to build bridges but she just wanted to turn every effort he made into a battleground. 'Is that the reason you're home so early?'

Keep calm, keep cool, he could almost hear Shawn advising him. Don't give up on it. 'Can't I take my wife out to dinner without having some ulterior motive?'

She was silent for a moment, as if his answer had thrown her off guard because it hadn't been the one she was expecting.

'All right. I can be ready by seven thirty.' She went towards the door. 'I'd better tell Mrs Dawkins that we won't be eating at home tonight.'

'Marianna? Wear the black dress you wore at Del Monico's.' That did surprise her.

'Any particular reason? Or is it just that you think black is appropriate because my father's died?'

'It's got nothing to do with that. I just want you to wear it.'

'You don't like my other evening gowns, then?'

'Yes, I like them. But I want you to wear the black gown for me, because you look absolutely beautiful in it.'

It was difficult, sometimes impossible, for Curt to go anywhere in New York without being instantly recognized.

For the most part, other people's attentions were confined to discreet smiling and guarded curiosity, at least in opulent surroundings like Del Monico's or here at the Ritz-Carlton on Madison and 46th Street; only if he was recognized in the street, or entering and leaving the theatre by any of his legions of female admirers, did problems ensue. Here, at least, they were virtually guaranteed a peaceful and uninterrupted evening. They were halfway through their meal before Marianna brought up the subject of Vitagraph's offer; something that, until they were home again at least, Curt had wanted to avoid.

'You haven't spoken about it all evening.' She laid down her silver dessert spoon and looked at him across the table. 'Does that mean you've come to your senses and turned it down?' There was no escape from being honest with her now, unless he told her an outright lie.

'No.' He'd intended to tell her later, when they'd finished dinner and he'd taken her home. After what had happened the previous evening, he was afraid that she'd create a scene. With the dining room crowded, who knew who might be watching and listening? He remembered what Shawn had said about muckraking newspapermen – wouldn't some ambitious reporter from the *New York Herald* have made a meal out of the little drama at Del Monico's? Coming hot on the tail of the news about F. H. Eastbridge and the sensation surrounding his will, what a tasty front page story a public slanging match between him and Marianna would make! He needed all his tact and discretion here. 'Marianna, we can talk about Vitagraph later. Let's enjoy the meal together, shall we?'

'What's the point of talking about it if you've already made up your mind?' She made no effort to lower her voice. 'You've gone behind my back, haven't you, Curt? You've struck up a deal with that cheap movie hawker William T. Rock, and agreed to take part in the pathetic farce he calls art?' She was about to throw down her napkin and get to her feet, but he reached across the table quickly and grasped her by the wrist.

'For God's sake, Marianna, sit down and lower your

230

voice! People are starting to look our way.' This was just what he'd wanted to avoid. 'This isn't the time or the place. As I just said, we can talk about it later.'

'We'll talk about it right now.'

'Please, don't do this . . .'

'Don't do what, Curt? Create a scene? Create a scandal in public? What exactly are you afraid of? Not your public image, surely?' Her voice was sarcastic. 'After all, once you sell out your integrity and appear in cheap moving pictures, you won't have a public image any more to worry about.'

'You won't even listen, will you? You don't know the slightest thing about the motion picture business, but you're still ready to carp and criticize. You only want to see the negative side. Did you know, for instance, that all the actors and actresses who appear in films are anonymous, that only the titles of the stories appear on the screen?'

'Really? Then why are Vitagraph so anxious to sign you? For two very important reasons, I should imagine. First, because your face is so well known from posters and picture cards – to people who have never even stepped inside a theatre in their lives – that you'd be recognized instantly, the minute you appeared on screen. And second, screen actors may be anonymous now, but can you really see that policy continuing into the future, even if the moving picture companies prefer it that way? Once any actor becomes popular, the audiences are going to want to know the name behind the face. Not that anyone would have any trouble in instantly recognizing yours!'

'Marianna, why are you so against my doing this thing? If I took the deal Vitagraph are offering, it would mean I wouldn't have to go on tour with the company outside of New York. I thought you'd prefer that.'

'Don't patronize me! And don't try to disguise an imposition to look like a favour.' She got up and swept out of the dining room, leaving him to find the waiter and settle the bill. When he rushed out to the foyer she had already retrieved her cape from the cloakroom attendant and was making towards the doors.

They drove home in stony silence. When they got back

231

to the Madison Avenue house, she left him without a word and went straight upstairs to bed. Disconsolately, Curt went into the drawing room and poured himself a drink.

He sat there by himself for a while, trying to think. Was accepting the offer from Vitagraph really worth all the trouble and aggravation he was going through with Marianna? Should he forget about it, ask William T. Rock to put the offer on hold while he tried to talk her round, or should he dig in his heels and make it clear to her that it was his decision and his career? If only he knew the answer.

He thought back to that morning, and the scene with Madeline Dupre. Now he felt more confused than ever. He'd decided to accept the offer from Vitagraph, just as he'd told Shawn, but now he found himself wavering yet again; if only Marianna could see his point of view. He knew what he wanted to do, but was it worth turning his private life into a constant battleground for? He had to have it out with her once and for all, he had to give it one more try.

He finished his drink and turned out the lights, then made his way upstairs. But when he tried to open the bedroom door he found that it was locked.

'Marianna?' There was no answer, though he could hear her moving about inside. 'Marianna, will you please open this door?' He glanced down. The light showing at the bottom of it suddenly went out, and then there was silence.

'OK, if that's the way you want it.' There was no point, no purpose, in trying to reason with her; if he made any more noise he would wake everyone in the house. But he had no intention of spending yet another humiliating night in one of the guest bedrooms. He went back downstairs, put on his coat and hat and climbed into his automobile.

His first wild impulse was to drive straight to Madeline Dupre's house on 79th Street, and he started off in the direction of Central Park. But halfway there he turned the automobile round and went, instead, to Shawn.

CHAPTER FIFTEEN

He telephoned William T. Rock at the Vitagraph studios out at Flatbush one week later, and told him that he accepted the company's offer. Shooting for the screen version of *The Count of Monte Cristo* was due to start twelve weeks later, after the final performance of Charles Frohman's current play. Frohman was totally sympathetic to Curt's decision to venture into the controversial new world of moving pictures: not only did his elder brother Daniel have substantial financial interests in American Mutoscope and Biograph, but he understood the enormous publicity value of using an established stage star like Curt Koenig in a moving picture. Though the norm was for screen players to remain anonymous as far as their vast audiences went, Vitagraph planned to use Curt's name and Madeline Dupre's to generate even more interest, and as far as Frohman was concerned it could only do both his stage career and the fledgeling moving picture business a power of good: Broadway audiences would be even more eager to see him appear on stage than ever; and his reputation and success in the theatre could only lend respectability and glamour to the silent screen.

But acting in front of a camera and acting on stage were two entirely different things, as Curt soon discovered during the first few weeks of shooting; without the aid of words, all the action, the story, the emotion, were dependent on mime. When he'd arrived at the Vitagraph studios on Elm Street, Rock's director Charles Kent – who also acted in some of their pictures – gave him some personal coaching, just so he could get the hang of it.

'What you got to remember, Curt, is that when the director calls "Action!" at the start of a scene, don't wait and look at the camera to see if it's going. That'll be taken care of. Never look towards the director when he speaks to you during a scene while the camera is running. He might be reminding you that you're out of the picture, or that there's somethin' else that you've forgotten . . . also, glancing at the camera at the end of a scene to see if it's stopped is another bad habit. The director'll always let you know when the action's over.'

'I know this is going to take a little practice, after stage work. But I think it'll be OK once I get the hang of it.'

'Eyes. Now, eyes are important to a screen actor. You have to remember to use 'em as much as possible. Remember, they express your thoughts much more clearly than just gestures or facial contortions. Don't squint. When you make an exit, make sure you're right out of camera range. Don't use unnecessary gestures or body contortions in fight scenes . . . it spoils the realism, and that's just what we don't want to happen. Kissing scenes . . . do it naturally, not just a peck on the lips and a quick breakaway . . . use your judgement about the length of a kiss. And remember to vary it by the degree of friendship, or love, that you're expected to convey. Any questions?'

'What about make-up?'

'Again, do some thinking for yourself; but just take in a few pointers, like don't redden your lips too much, as dark red takes nearly black on film. Likewise in rouging the face . . . whatever you do, don't touch up the cheeks only and leave your nose and forehead white. It'll look hideous when it's photographed.' He smiled. 'Hey, for a film like this, we're all goin' through a new learning process. Let's just get it together and take it through the script day by day.'

'That suits me just fine.' When he'd turned, Madeline Dupre had been standing there.

'Hello, Curt.' She smiled, in that teasing way she had. She had a copy of the *Monte Cristo* script someone in production had given her. 'So you managed to talk your wife round to your way of thinking at long last?'

'No, not really.' When Kent walked off they strolled through the various sets together, side by side. He looked unhappy, a little preoccupied. 'I wanted to go into this with her approval, but nothing I said got through to her. She's still dead set against it.' He shrugged. 'I said it was just an experiment, that because I'd agreed to do one picture it didn't necessarily mean that I'd agree to do others . . . but she still isn't talking to me.'

For once, Madeline seemed at a loss for words. 'I take it, then, that she won't be accompanying you here to watch while they shoot the picture?'

'You got that right! Wild horses wouldn't get her to set one foot in Brooklyn.'

'Poor Curt.' She twirled the script coquettishly in her hands. 'I know that she's your wife, and you don't want to upset her unnecessarily, but it really is unfair of her to keep trying to stand in your way. Doesn't she want you to have a successful career?'

Once Curt had mastered the art of screen acting, he never looked back; everyone on the Vitagraph set delightedly proclaimed that he was a 'natural', even more dazzling, even more stunningly charismatic than he'd been on stage. He'd watched the rushes of himself in disbelieving silence with Charles Kent, Madeline, and William T. Rock in the screening shed. Did this, he asked himself, bear any likeness, any resemblance, to the performance he'd given, the actor he'd been, on the Lyceum stage? It was so terrifyingly lifelike, with the vividly brutal scenes of Edmond Dantes' imprisonment in the Château d'If, the dramatic escape – that they'd gone all the way on location to Coney Island to film – from the clifftop fortress into the sea. On stage, the recreation of these components from the original story had been almost impossible to reproduce – Dantes' being tossed over the edge of the cliff in a burial sack, for instance – but on film, the potentialities were limited only to the camera's range and the director's ingenuity.

But it was the love scenes with Madeline Dupre that almost riveted Curt to his chair.

'Wow!' William T. Rock had gasped, at a startlingly realistic close-up of their lips, just a fraction of an inch apart.

'This is real great stuff, Charlie! Real great stuff.' He'd turned to a silent and stunned Curt, grinning from ear to ear. 'I knew it, from the minute you stepped on that set and the camera rolled. You're a natural. You've proved it in every scene from beginning to end . . . this is a classic!' Madeline appeared to be more than a little taken aback by the close-ups of them, too. 'You know what? With other stage actors we used, I've always had doubts. Sometimes a little, sometimes a lot. Like you've found out the hard way, acting on a stage is a whole lot different to doing it in front of a camera. But right from the start, when I saw you at the Lyceum, I knew you had what it takes. And I was right. Was I right!' He got up, called to the projectionist behind the screen. 'OK, we've wrapped it up . . . now let's go celebrate . . . the audiences are going to love it!'

'What is it, Curt? What's wrong?' He'd parked the automobile outside her house on 79th Street, and he was holding the passenger door open for her to climb out. But he'd been virtually silent all the way from Brooklyn. 'Don't tell me you're disappointed that now the filming's all finished you won't be able to see me every day?' Her voice was light, deliberately flippant; but he knew that she was half serious. After working with Madeline Dupre for weeks on end at the Lyceum and at the Vitagraph studios, Curt had come to understand her only too well.

'I suppose it's much too late to say this. But I think I made the wrong decision about signing with Vitagraph . . . I guess Marianna was right.' Her pert smile faded a little. 'I didn't realize it until today, when we were watching the screening. It was those close-ups that did it.' He couldn't get them out of his mind, the huge images on the life-sized screen. Seeing them magnified to ten times their normal size somehow made them seem so much more shocking.

He went with her to her door. 'I just didn't realize that they'd come out that way . . . so big, so graphic. I just sat there in that screening room thinking, "What the hell have I done?" It was so real. I couldn't believe I was watching myself up there.'

'Curt, please come in. Just one glass of champagne . . . to celebrate the end of the filming today. For me?' He hesitated, knowing instinctively that if he did as she asked he would be crossing a symbolic line that, up till now, had kept him safely separated from temptation; throughout the whole six weeks of filming, she'd used every last ounce of feminine guile, every trick in the book to get him alone. Until now, thinking of Marianna, his children waiting at home for him, he'd deliberately resisted. But as the weeks had gone on and Marianna's coldness towards him had only intensified, it had become more and more difficult for him to turn away from Madeline's gaiety and warmth. 'Curt . . .?' He hesitated for a moment, then followed her inside the house. He was struck by the quietness. Almost as though she could read his thoughts, she said brightly, 'Come in, and make yourself at home. I've given my maid the evening off. I think she has a sweetheart somewhere who's been dying to take her to the music hall . . . the Aeolian, on 42nd Street . . . she can't wait to see me in *Monte Cristo*! I told her she'll have to be patient.' She took off her cape and fetched two glasses. 'Now I'm going to propose a toast . . .' She smiled. 'See, I told you she was marvellous! Pink champagne left in the ice bucket just as I instructed.'

'Madeline . . .'

'Now, you're not going to go all serious on me, are you, Curt? You saw yourself up on screen today and you were wonderful . . . you shouldn't have any regrets. I know I don't. I was proud to be your leading lady. Not just because you're the finest actor I've ever worked with, but because I'm so madly in love with you that if you don't take me to bed this very instant, I think I really will die from disappointment.'

'Madeline . . .' He put down his glass, barely touched. 'We've been through all this before. I gave you my answer then.'

'Yes, you did. Then. But I want to know what your answer is now.'

'Nothing's changed, Madeline.'

'Hasn't it? Has your wife suddenly decided that she wholeheartedly approves of your acting in moving pictures after all, and stopped making your life a misery by picking a quarrel every time you speak to each other?'

He sighed heavily. 'No.'

'Then you've just answered my question, Curt.' She put down her glass of pink champagne and came towards him. She rested her hands lightly on his chest. 'When I saw those rushes today, they startled me, too. I think they startled everyone in the screening room. But do you know why? They were so real, Curt. So very real. Not because we acted those parts so cleverly for an audience . . . you know as well as I do that neither of us was acting at all. It looked so real because it was real.' Her hands moved from his chest to up round his neck. She moved her face so close to his that he could feel her soft, warm breath. 'Walk away from me and right out of that door if you don't believe that is the truth.'

Roy Delucca lay back in his favourite easy chair and closed his eyes, sniffed the air appreciatively as the smell of Maudie's cooking wafted in from the kitchen. Hell, what a bitch of a week he'd had, with three guys on the precinct reporting in sick, and Chief Rawlins giving him extra duty and bawling his head off because someone in Records had fucked up his paperwork for the District Attorney's office. Tomorrow was his first day off in almost two weeks, thank Christ.

He opened his eyes as Maudie came in carrying the dishes, ready to set the table for dinner. In a minute or two he'd get up and call in his boys, out in the back yard playing at cowboys and Indians, to come in and wash their hands. Tomorrow, he was taking the pair of them to the movie theatre in Union Square for a special treat, to see *The Count of Monte Cristo*, the new moving picture everyone was talking about. Maudie had wanted to come too, but her mother was playing up again and she'd agreed to spend the day with her out at East Flatbush instead. That had made Delucca as mad as hell when she'd told him about it.

'Jesus fuckin' Christ, honey, you know how long it is

since you and me spent some time together on my day off? I can't even remember! I had it all planned, just you, me, and the boys. They'd have popcorn and ice cream, and then we'd watch the movie in the best front row seats, and afterwards I'd take us all to dinner at Child's eatery on East 42nd ... we'd have a great time! Now you're sayin' you ain't comin' with us?'

'Please, Roy, don't fuss so. You know how bad Momma gets when she's had one of her dizzy spells. She gets panicky, and the doctor said that that's bad for her heart. It's not her fault.'

'What the hell does she think I pay that neighbour of hers four dollars fifty a week for? Just so every time she has a fuckin' giddy turn you can go rushin' over there to hold her hand?'

'Roy, you forget how old Momma is now, and how frail she is ... the doctor said that with that shaky heart of hers she could go off any minute.' Delucca scowled; chance'd be a fine thing. 'I'd never forgive myself if I didn't go when Momma needed me, and then something terrible happened!'

'You think that's likely, with the way she eats?' Irritably, Delucca had lit a cigarette. 'Holy cow, Maudie, that doctor o' hers is talkin' through his ass!'

'Roy, keep your voice down! You want the boys to hear you talk that way about Momma?'

Delucca had tried to talk Maudie out of rushing over to the wilds of Flatbush to hold her mother's hand, but she was as stubborn as a mule, just like the old woman. So he'd given up.

'Boys sure are excited over you takin' them to the movies!' she said, as she put the dishes on the table. 'And talkin' of movies, guess what Momma's next door neighbour told me, when I was there?' Delucca couldn't guess and he didn't particularly want to, but there was no stopping Maudie when she started jawing. 'The Vitagraph studios ... you know, the ones that made that picture you're takin' the boys to tomorrow ... well, they're not far from where Momma is ... and this neighbour of Momma's, well, it seems her eldest daughter has got work there . . . bein' paid five dollars a day as what they call an "extra".'

'Five dollars a day?' That had made Delucca sit up.

'Yeah . . . anyhow, like I was sayin' . . . all these people who go lookin' for extra work have to wait around to see if they're needed; if they don't get a call, they get paid fifty cents; if they get dressed up and made up and then don't get a call to go on set, they get paid one dollar fifty, and if they do get to go on set they get two dollars fifty. This girl got five dollars because they used her a lot one time . . . and they get lunch for free!'

'Maybe I should tell Chief Rawlins to go fuck himself and be a movie extra instead, huh?'

Maudie was on her way back to the kitchen to take the main dish out of the oven. 'Makes you wonder, though, doesn't it? If they pay extras up to five dollars a day . . . how much do they pay their leading players?'

Ever since he'd started working on *The Count of Monte Cristo* at the Vitagraph studios, Curt and Marianna had barely been on speaking terms. When he came home at the end of each day – tired, tense, emotionally drained – there was little relaxation at all. Once the children were washed and put to bed, the evenings were spent in chilly semi-silence; more often than not, Marianna would get up from the dinner table and shut herself in the library to read a book, rather than spend the evening talking to him.

For the first few weeks, he had tried hard to ignore it; between shooting the picture in the daytime and playing with the children when he came home, most of his time was taken up. But when even after the picture was finished Marianna's attitude remained as hostile and intransigent as before, Curt took to leaving the house straight after the children had gone to bed, and having dinner at 79th Street with Madeline Dupre, coming home only in the early hours. After a while, as he and Marianna continued to grow further and further apart, he didn't come home at all.

She withdrew more and more into herself, was stricter with the children than she'd ever been before. She never questioned him, never asked him when he stopped out all night where he had been; clearly, he told himself with growing bitterness and anger, because she no longer cared.

To the outside world – his adoring public, his fellow players and the press – the image of his private life could scarcely have been more perfect. Family-orientated articles, accompanied by smiling publicity pictures, appeared in every popular newspaper and magazine, and requests for information and signed photographs besieged the Vitagraph offices within days of the first New York City screening of *The Count of Monte Cristo*. Curt was more than a little bemused by it all, but he rose to the occasion. When the Vitagraph studio bosses offered to get a team of secretaries to write his name on the publicity photos they sent to members of the public who had asked for them, he was adamant that he autograph every one himself.

'It's up to you, Curt,' J. Stuart Blackton said, as he took him into one of the offices near the lot and pointed at the mounting heaps of mail. 'But with three or four girls working on this little collection, we could have it all cleared up in a couple of days. Who's to know any different?'

'I will. They want a signed picture from me and that's exactly what they're going to get.'

Blackton laughed. 'Well, if you haven't got better things to do with your spare time . . . be my guest. I'll get someone off the lot to stick it on the back seat for you.'

Ironically, it was his scrupulousness in insisting on signing his publicity pictures himself that brought his relationship with Madeline Dupre to an end. To his surprise, she agreed with Blackton that Curt should let specially employed secretaries do it instead.

'Curt, it's madness. The people who sent those letters wouldn't know what your handwriting looks like. What does it matter if someone else signs the pictures or not?'

'Blackton offered to get in three or four girls to do the job, right? So if I said yes and they did it, all the girls would sign the pictures – with four different styles of handwriting.'

'So?'

'So maybe two or three people compare the pictures and the autograph, and on every one the handwriting's different. They'd know that I hadn't signed the pictures at all.'

'I can't see that that matters. They've got what they wrote to the studio for. They wanted a signed picture of Curt Koenig and they got it.'

'Sure, they wanted the picture. But they wanted me to sign it for them. That's the whole idea. Otherwise they could just buy a postcard and ask anyone to write on it.'

Madeline lost patience with his line of reasoning. 'Oh, you worry far too much about stupid little trifles. Just like a man.' She came to him and slid her arms round his neck. 'In any case, if you spend the whole evening autographing pictures, you won't have any time to spend on me.' He looked into her face. It was a very pretty face, almost but not quite beautiful, and when she was displeased about something it had a hard, catlike appearance, just as it had now. Curt was repelled by her cynicism. It was an unpleasant side to her character that she usually kept well hidden, and one that he hadn't realized existed at the beginning of their love affair four months before; she was rarely careless enough to let the mask slip out of place. But though she'd told him she loved him at almost every opportunity, Curt wondered if she was in love with Curt Koenig the man or Curt Koenig whose picture adorned the outside of every movie theatre in New York City. Perhaps he didn't really want to know the answer because it posed another worrying question: did everyone he met like him for himself or for what he'd become?

'I'd better be going.' Her face wore a scowl. 'I have all these to sign and I would like to see my children before Marianna puts them to bed.'

'I don't recall you being so anxious to rush off to see them before. Why the sudden change of heart?'

'Over the last few weeks, I haven't spent very much time with them. Working on scenes for the new script has swallowed up most of the day, as you know.'

'I think that's largely down to the inadequacy of the

actress Charlie Kent has chosen to work with you on the new picture. Although, to be brutally honest, I use the word "actress" in its loosest sense.' The mask was slipping again. 'Anyone who has an ounce of understanding can see that she's never had any proper stage training in her life.'

'Stage training isn't necessary for moving pictures, you know that as well as I do. In some cases – maybe most – it can even be a hindrance. They're wholly different things, acting for the theatre and acting in front of a camera. If we're being brutally honest, Vitagraph only chose you and me because we'd acted in a major Broadway success and our names were known already. Otherwise, those parts could well have been given to someone else.'

'Oh, is that what you think? Well, thanks for the vote of confidence.'

'I didn't mean it as a criticism. I'm just stating the facts.'

'I still don't think a so-called actress like Sonia Severny is right for this part, Curt. And I also think you should tell Charlie Kent so. After all, he's hardly likely to listen to me. You're the important name in the company, the one with all the drawing power.'

'You know that it's standard practice to team a well-known leading man with several different actresses. There's no slight intended here.'

'That's a matter of opinion.' Her eyes took on a malicious look. 'Are you going to speak to Charlie Kent about taking Sonia Severny off the picture and replacing her with me, or do I have to do it myself?'

'Madeline, I'm not the casting director. I just read the script, do what the director tells me to do and hope for the best. It isn't the same as being in the theatre.' It wasn't the answer that she wanted from him. 'Look, I really do have to go. I'm sorry.'

She hid what she was really feeling under a façade of coquetry, a façade that Curt, after four months of intimacy with her, had gradually begun to see through. 'So . . . what will you tell your wife when you get home? Will you tell her that you've been with me?'

'It would be untrue to say that I hadn't.' He smiled. 'We do both work for Vitagraph.'

'I'm surprised in a way that she hasn't taken a trip out to see you at the studios . . . maybe even brought the children with her. Has she still not even been to see *Monte Cristo*?'

'I told you, she doesn't want to see it. She hasn't forgiven me yet for leaving the theatre and going into moving pictures.'

Madeline looked thoughtful for a moment. 'Really? She certainly does know how to bear a grudge. But then, you ought to have expected that, Curt . . . after all, she is F. H. Eastbridge's daughter.'

He left her without a backward glance.

It had been a long time since Marianna had taken the children shopping in Manhattan. They'd set out early, taking a cab as far as Lexington and Third, then doing the rounds of the department stores where all three of them were fascinated with the huge displays of different types of merchandise, and Alice immediately demanded umpteen new toys.

'You have lots of toys back home, Alice,' Gene scolded her gently. 'Most of them you never even play with any more. Ellie and me haven't worried Momma for anything, have we? You're just plain greedy.'

'Am *not*!' Alice stamped her little foot and her blue eyes looked ominously ready to fill with tears. 'If Daddy was here, he'd buy me everything I wanted! I'll tell him you were mean to me!' Marianna took her youngest daughter firmly by the hand and shook her sharply; tantrums in the middle of R. H. Macy's department store were certainly something she didn't intend to tolerate.

'Alice, behave yourself this instant. Otherwise we go home right now and you go straight to bed. Do I make myself very clear?' There was no mistaking the tone of steel in her mother's voice; grudgingly, Alice fell silent. She'd learned, some time ago, that it just wasn't possible to get around Momma the way she so easily got around Daddy.

But she intended to tell him how hard done by she'd been, later on.

Marianna took them to lunch at Muschenheim's, where even Alice's behaviour was exemplary. But as they were shown to their table and she sat the children down, she wondered if, in coming to this particular place, she'd made a wise decision. For her part, there were too many memories, not only of Curt when she'd first met and fallen so passionately in love with him, but of her mother and father. They'd both frequently brought her here to dine with them, too.

'Momma, could we please go to the big movie theatre on Union Square and see Daddy in *The Count of Monte Cristo*?' Ellie's low, melodious voice, so different from Alice's high-pitched whine, broke into her unhappy thoughts. 'Momma?'

'Oh, yes, Momma!' Alice clapped her chubby little hands excitedly, her earlier tantrum in Macy's forgotten now. 'I want to see Daddy in a moving picture!'

'Please can we go, Momma?' Gene pleaded. 'I asked Daddy if he'd take us when it first came into the moving picture houses, but he said it was up to you.'

'I don't think we'll have time today,' Marianna said, pretending to study her menu but hardly seeing it. 'And in any case, I don't really want to go into one of those places.'

'Please, Momma, please, please, please!'

'Alice, be quiet. And sit up straight. We'll see. If you behave yourself and eat what I order for you, I might take you on the way home if we have time. *If* we have time, I said.'

'Will there be time to have ice cream?' Alice asked hopefully.

In Union Square, almost every moving picture theatre was showing *The Count of Monte Cristo* at the top of its bill. Feeling uncomfortable, and totally out of place, Marianna stood outside one of the largest of them and looked at the life-sized pictures of Curt displayed on the gigantic billboards and around the box office. It was an extraordinary sensation, looking at images of her own husband and yet not recognizing him; the dashing, vibrant, handsome figure in eighteenth-century French costume splashed across the vast theatrical posters bore no resemblance to the Curt Koenig she'd met and fallen in love with, married, lived with, borne children to; it was someone else. But still it hurt – why was that? – to see people, strangers, legions of curious, chattering, giggling women lining up in droves to see him, when he belonged to her. Somehow, it seemed so wrong, a terrible, unendurable intrusion. He was hers, and yet now he belonged to everyone. She was his wife, but here she was, standing in line like all the others, queueing up outside a cheap place of mass entertainment to see her own husband. She hesitated, drew back.

'Momma?' Alice was gazing up at her and tugging at her hand. 'Momma, you said if we were good, we could see Daddy's moving picture . . . Momma, you promised!'

She nodded slowly. 'All right. But you have to sit very still, and not talk while the picture's running. Moving pictures have no sound, but there's a pianist who plays while the film's going on.' She waited their turn, then paid at the box office window. She was glad that she'd chosen a concealing, deep-crowned hat that half obscured her face; if anyone had recognized her, she would have died with embarrassment. True, it was hardly likely that anyone who knew her personally would be among the audience in here . . . although you never knew. The elegant, sophisticated theatre crowds that Marianna was used to rubbing shoulders with would never have lowered themselves to set foot inside a common movie palace. As they made their way inside and took their places she looked uncertainly around her, hating the way the seats were crowded together, and everyone seemed to have little room to move comfortably. She settled the children on their chairs.

'Momma, when is it going to start?' Alice's high-pitched childish voice seemed to rise above the general din around them. 'I want to see Daddy right now, don't you, Ellie?'

'Hush up, Alice, and keep your eyes on the big screen.'

'Look, Momma!' Even Gene was getting excited at the

prospect of seeing their father up on the screen in front of hundreds of people. 'The lady who plays the piano. She's all ready to begin!'

Ellie stole a covert glance at her mother; something was wrong, she sensed with an uncanny intuition far in advance of her near-six years. Momma was upset about something. 'Momma? Is it like the Lyceum Theatre in here, when Daddy was there?'

'It couldn't be more different.' Indeed, there could scarcely have been a greater contrast than that between the elegant, sophisticated interior of the Lyceum, with its audience in evening dress and jewels, and this packed, vulgar, noisy, brash collection of humanity, smelling of sweat and stale tobacco, and munching popcorn and candy. Marianna almost succumbed to the temptation to get up and push her way out again, no matter how loudly the children protested. But it was too late to change her mind now. The bright lights suddenly dimmed, the plump matron at the off-key piano began to play, then the huge white screen flickered into life. There was a collective sigh, and everyone edged forward in wonder as the first picture, a harbour scene in Napoleonic France, followed on from the title. Marianna's heart began to race a little faster as a fair, familiar face came into view and then filled the screen, while a woman's voice whispered to someone behind her, 'Isn't he just so handsome?'

The children all craned their heads forward in silent wonder as the clever camera angles moved rapidly from startling facial close-ups to scene after scene: boat decks, galloping horses, inside a tavern, a château, a church. Though there was no colour and no sound except for the monotonous tempo of the piano, they were riveted by the sight of their father as he mimed his way through the part of Edmond Dantes with a flair and style that even Marianna, prejudiced against moving pictures as she was, had to admire.

'Momma, who is that lady Daddy's kissing?'

Marianna stared ahead of her, unable to believe her own eyes. She'd read Dumas' novel, years ago, as a young girl,

247

and she'd seen Curt and Maud Adams perform this very scene on stage at the Lyceum so many times that she knew it by heart. But this passionate, open-mouthed kiss that went on for ever, magnified in close-up on the screen, in no way resembled the live performance. It seemed to fill the screen, hurtle unmercifully towards her, until all she could see in front of her was their lips, reaching hungrily for each other. Why didn't they stop, she thought in panic, as her cheeks grew hot? Why had the director and the cameraman made that single moment go on and on and on? She felt like a voyeur. Under her gloves, she could feel the perspiration forming in the palms of her hands. She felt as if she'd come home one day unexpectedly and stumbled on Curt making love to another woman. It was horrible. Intolerable. Shocking. She had to get out. She got to her feet and yanked Alice from her chair by the arm, and she squealed in protest.

'Get up, we're leaving. Gene, Elynor! We're going home right now.'

The house was unusually silent when Curt let himself into the front hall. No sight nor sound of anyone. No Marianna, no children. Just the deep, resonant beat of the longcase clock.

He hung away his coat, his hat. He toured the ground-floor rooms. No-one was there, not even one of the servants. Upstairs was likewise deserted. Puzzled, Curt went down the basement steps and into the kitchen.

'Mrs Dawkins? Have you see my wife?'

She looked startled to see him. 'Mrs Koenig brought the children back at teatime, sir. Then she went straight out again; didn't even stop to take off her hat and coat. Bridget's taken them for a walk in the park, like most days. They ought to be back any minute.'

'Did Mrs Koenig say where she was going or when she was likely to be back?'

'Not to me, no.'

'OK. Thank you.' He went into the deserted drawing room and poured himself a drink. He sat down, cradling the glass in his hands thoughtfully. Marianna had been so distant, so cold, so strange for months now, ever since he'd gone against her wishes and signed with Vitagraph; what could he do to try to make amends? He'd already tried everything he knew in an effort to bridge the widening gap between them, for the sake of the children if nothing else, but she refused to compromise. She'd never forgiven him for becoming involved with the moving picture industry and, as she put it, squandering his talent. He belonged on the stage in a Broadway theatre, she'd argued, not in the cheap, draughty, purpose-built studio on the Vitagraph lot, churning out potboilers for the uneducated masses. She'd refused to listen to him when he'd tried to explain that as the industry grew, purpose-built moving picture houses with all the elegance and comfort of theatres like the Metropolitan and the Lyceum would become the norm, and that the middle and even the upper classes would be attracted to them.

'If you believe that, you'll believe anything.'

'I've seen the plans, in the Vitagraph executives' office. Marianna, I'm not just making this up. Not only for here in New York City, but for towns all the way down the east coast. For Chicago. Detroit. San Francisco. The motion picture business is an expanding thing. If you don't believe me, why don't you come to the studio with me one day and ask Bill Smith or J. Stuart Blackton?'

'Set foot in East Flatbush? Over my dead body.' She wouldn't even stay in the same room with him. 'I'll leave that to you, Curt. You seem to have grown so fond of a little slumming.'

He put down his bourbon and stood up as he heard the front door open at last, and Bridget and the children come in. They all rushed into the drawing room to greet him when they caught sight of his outdoor coat hanging in the cloakroom off the front hall.

'Daddy, Daddy!' Alice, as usual, was the first one to throw herself headlong into his arms. She hugged him like a vice. 'Daddy, Momma took us into town and we went in all the stores!' She slid down onto his lap. 'I saw lots of things I wanted, but she said I couldn't have them. Will you buy them for me?'

'If your momma said you couldn't have them, she must have had a good reason.'

'Please, Daddy . . . I've been good today . . .'

'And what about you two?' Curt pulled Elynor into the crook of one arm and Gene into the other.

'We saw your moving picture today! Momma took us.' Curt was visibly surprised. 'There were so many other people lining up to see it that we had to wait a long while before they let us inside.'

'Is that so?'

'Momma made us come out again, before it was finished.' Alice looked up appealingly with her large blue eyes. 'Who was that lady you were kissing, Daddy?'

'Just an actress I was paid to kiss.' He looked up sharply, as Marianna stood there in the open doorway. 'That's what we have to do, sweetheart, whether we're on stage or in front of a moving picture camera. We do what the director tells us to.'

'Daddy, why wasn't there any sound coming from the moving picture? I wanted to hear what you said . . .'

Curt rose to his feet slowly, gently disentangling himself from them. 'They haven't figured out a way to have sound yet, honey. But I expect they will, sometime. Why don't you all run along now, so I can talk to Momma?'

'But, Daddy . . . !'

'Do as you're told, Alice.' His voice was uncharacteristically firm with her. 'I've got something to tell you all a little later on.'

When they were alone, he turned to Marianna. 'Would you like me to pour you something to drink?'

'No, thank you. You know that I never drink before dinner.' She could barely bring herself to look at him. All she could see were his lips, in graphic close-up, a fraction of an inch from Madeline Dupre's on that huge white screen. 'And if you're going to ask me where I've been, don't bother. I have no intention of telling you. Just as you stay out all night and never bother to tell me.'

'That isn't fair, Marianna.'

She turned away from him, sat down stiffly beside the fire. It was a vicious circle that went on and on. He'd hurt her, and she wanted to hurt him in return. But because she loved him so much she succeeded only in hurting herself. She wanted to reach out to him, but all the bitter quarrels, all the things they'd done to each other stood in the way.

'What is it you want to talk to me about?'

'The children said you took them to see *The Count of Monte Cristo* today.'

'They press-ganged me into taking them, yes.'

'You came out before the picture was finished?'

'Have you ever sat in one of those awful places, Curt?' She blotted the crowded rows of bodies resolutely out of her mind; the stale tobacco smoke, the terrible off-key piano. But the picture of him and Madeline Dupre most of all. Why did it stand out so stubbornly in her mind, when all day long she'd been desperately trying to forget it? 'If you have, you wouldn't ask me why I didn't stay till the end. You take the children, if you're so set on it. Come to think of it, why haven't you taken them before? They've been worrying to go ever since you finished the picture.'

'I thought some of the scenes might upset the girls . . . the imprisonment sequences, and the swordfight at the end.'

Marianna spun round, unable to contain herself any longer.

'Oh, is that all? What about the love scenes, Curt? Did you think about them when you were filming the picture? That they might upset your daughters, too? To say nothing of what I felt when suddenly a close-up of you kissing Madeline Dupre hit me like a blow in the face!' All her pent-up fury came rushing out. 'Don't tell me that you were just acting. *Don't.* I've seen you on stage with Maud Adams in that same scene, and you never kissed her like that!'

'Marianna, we're professionals! We're paid to make it look realistic, for God's sake!'

'I sat there, in front of my own children, more embarrassed and humiliated than I've ever been in all my life. Can you even begin to understand how I felt?'

251

'You're blowing this up way out of proportion, Marianna.' Ironically, he and Madeline hadn't even been lovers then. If only he'd never succumbed to temptation. But it hadn't been entirely his fault, had it? 'The director gave us the script and told us what kind of scene he wanted. I still have a copy of the script someplace, if you want to see it. *Long, lingering, passionate kiss between Dantes and Mercedes.* That's what it said. Check it, if you don't believe me.'

'I believe my own eyes!'

'Is that why you walked out when it was halfway through?' He should have guessed.

She was silent for a moment. 'Are you in love with her?' He would never know how much it cost her pride to ask him that question.

'No.' That, at least, was the truth; he'd never loved Madeline. He'd been irresistibly drawn towards her, like a moth to a candle flame; he'd lusted after her and made physical love to her time and again, but she'd never touched his inner emotions. 'Marianna, I swear it.'

'But she's in love with you.' It was a statement and not a question. 'I thought so.'

'There isn't much I can do about that, is there?'

'This new film for Vitagraph . . . is she in it?'

He shook his head. 'They've cast a new actress to play opposite me. Sonia Severny. One of Bill Smith's discoveries. He'd used her in modern bit parts but he decided she was worthy of better things. He wanted a natural blonde to play the princess opposite the role they've given me, and she photographs so well. He just didn't think that Madeline was quite right for this picture.' He paused. 'She isn't very happy about that. In fact, she's been badgering me to talk to Charlie Kent about it . . . but I told her casting was nothing to do with me, which it isn't.'

'Does that mean you won't be acting in any more pictures with her?'

Curt shrugged. 'As I said, casting isn't what I'm paid for.'

She turned away again, towards the fire. The warmth of the flames was comforting. As a child, she'd loved to watch them, to find the colours – blue, and green, as well as the yellow and red – and watch the wood darken, then crumble into ashes. It was soothing, watching the flames of a fire.

'You said that there was something you wanted to tell us.'

'Yes. I had a call at the studio today . . . from *Success* magazine . . . their office is at Waverley Place, in mid-Manhattan.' She looked up. 'Their editor wants to run an article on me . . . well, us.'

'Us?'

'Most of the other stuff that's been printed about me over the last few years has just been on the career angle. They want something more personal . . . you know the kind of thing.' He poured himself another glass of bourbon. 'They'd like to come here and take some photographs . . . kind of one or two family portraits. Us and the children.' He hesitated. 'I said I'd need to check with you first.'

She almost laughed. 'Since when did you check anything with me first? Did you ever bother to give me advance notice all those times you never came home at all?' Her voice was bitter. 'Why don't you just admit that these days you prefer drinking beer with your theatre cronies than spending any time with me?'

'You never have been prepared to give me the benefit of the doubt, have you?' He could not bring himself to admit to her that for most of those nights he'd been in Madeline Dupre's bed. But not all of them. He'd turned up on Shawn Duchovsky's doorstep more than a few times. Though they didn't have time to meet as much as they once had, they were still close; when push came to shove, he knew he could count on his old buddy to lie for him. Shawn would understand. 'Ask Shawn, if you don't believe me.'

'You were at Shawn's place?' That did surprise her. 'He never said.'

'Shawn wouldn't.' That had given her something to think about. 'So, shall I give the editor a call first thing tomorrow? They were thinking of sending the photographer round some time this week, if you agreed.'

'OK. Call him.' She turned back, gazed into the fire.

253

'Why don't you go and tell the children? They'll be excited about it.'

Upstairs, as he played with Alice and listened to Gene talking about the lessons he'd had with his tutor, Curt became aware that Elynor was staring at him with a strange expression in her eyes; an expression one didn't expect to see in the eyes of a five-year-old girl. At that moment, she reminded him almost disturbingly of Marianna.

'What are you thinking about?' he asked her gently, when later that night he tucked her up in bed. 'A dime for your thoughts.' But she didn't smile and laugh as she usually did.

'Daddy . . .' She was thinking of her mother's expression in the moving picture theatre that afternoon, as she'd watched the close-up of Curt kissing Madeline Dupre. 'Do you love Momma?'

He smiled to hide what he was really feeling, bent down and gently stroked her hair. 'I love all of you,' he said, as he turned out the light beside her bed, knowing that although he couldn't tell an outright lie to his daughter, he was allowed just a tiny twisting of the truth.

CHAPTER SIXTEEN

The girl who'd borrowed her train fare to buy a ride out here from the Lower East Side was lucky today. For the past three days, ever since someone had told her that the moving picture company hired extras for up to five dollars a day, she'd made the trip out to the Vitagraph studios in East Flatbush and lined up with all the other hopefuls, waiting to be called. Each afternoon, she'd gone home disappointed. Her brother Stanislav was the only one of the family who had a proper job – sweeping up in the local bakery – and she knew that he couldn't really afford to lend her the money for her fare from his meagre wages. When she'd returned home disconsolately on the first day, and then the next, she'd felt guilty for borrowing from him. But when she'd told him that on her arrival at the studios there had been more than two hundred people already waiting, and she hadn't been picked, he'd smiled and made her cheer up.

'They will pick you, Klara. You wait and see. A pretty girl like you? Just be patient. It will happen.' He'd smiled. 'Maybe even sooner than you think.'

'I hope so. Then I can pay you back, and give some money to Mama and Papa.' On the elevated train ride from the Lower East Side to Flatbush the next day, Klara Kopek had wondered how many other eager hopefuls like her there would be outside the Vitagraph studios today. If only she could get one or two days' work as an extra on one of the film sets, she could earn as much as five or ten dollars. Ten dollars! That seemed a small fortune, almost ten weeks' wages for her Polish immigrant family, who, except for Stanislav, spent every daylight hour in their two-roomed tenement making cigars for a local shopkeeper, from her father to her youngest brother Tomas, who was only six years old.

Though she worried about not getting work as an extra at Vitagraph – whatever Stanislav said, she knew he couldn't really afford to lend her the fare – it was a treat to escape from the filth and poverty on the Lower East Side to the fresher air of rural Brooklyn, to get away from the stinking, unhealthy tenement building where the family had lived since they'd come to America from Warsaw when Klara was fourteen years old, one family among 400,000 others who thought that when they'd finally passed through Ellis Island into the Utopia they'd imagined, they would find the end of the proverbial rainbow – freedom from oppression, persecution, poverty. But the reality had been very different, as they'd soon discovered. Being poor and destitute in New York was not very different from being poor and destitute in Warsaw. In some ways, it was even worse. At least in Warsaw the family had been surrounded by friends and neighbours, a strong sense of community spirit; in alien America, they were just Polish immigrants with no money, no neighbours that they knew, no friends. With only the barest knowledge of English, it was difficult for them to find jobs: only the lowest, the most exploitative, the poorest-paid were open to them. Unscrupulous factory bosses cashed in on their ignorance and desperation to get work of any kind, often paying only half, sometimes even a third, of the wages paid to American workers. Eleven- and twelve-hour shifts were not uncommon. A year ago Klara had thought herself fortunate to find a job in an upstate garment factory sewing seams together, but her work had been too slow for the foreman's liking and she'd been sent packing after the first week. Since then, she'd helped her mother and sisters with the cooking and cleaning, and her father and brothers with the cigar-making, even though she hated it. It left ugly brown stains on her fingers and nails that no amount of scrubbing with hot water and carbolic soap would remove, and the smell of the tobacco clung to her hair and clothes. Every morning before she'd caught the elevated train to

Brooklyn and the Vitagraph studios, Klara had scrubbed herself all over and washed her hair in the iron tub, afraid that if someone smelled the stench of the cigar tobacco on her skin she would never get a job. But the girl who'd told her about the studio had assured her that it didn't matter.

'I seen lots of people smoking up there. Directors, actors, the men behind the camera. They won't take no notice if they smell tobacco on your hair. You worry too much. I told you, it's your face they look at. If you look right for what they want on one day, then you get picked. If not, you maybe don't get picked till some other day.' Klara still hadn't felt sure. And did they really pay as much as she'd been told they did? What would she have to do?

'I told you they pay real good money. When you get there, you line up with all the others. You might have to wait all day. If you get picked, they tell you what they want you to do. One time, I got picked, and they gave me a costume to put on, then somebody painted my face. But then they found they didn't need me after all. I still got paid, though . . . one dollar fifty.'

'One dollar fifty for doing nothing?' It seemed impossible. No-one got paid for doing nothing. 'So why aren't you going there now, if they pay that much money?'

'Because my mama is sick, and I have to stay home to look after her. When she feels better, then I go back and see if I can get some more work. It's easy. Maybe then, we can go together.'

Klara looked unhappy. 'If I don't get picked this week, I'll have no money for the fare to come again. I can't even pay my brother back the thirty cents he lent me.'

'Maybe you get picked today. Maybe not. But it's worth waiting.'

Klara couldn't believe her luck when, on the third day, a tall man with checked trousers and a white shirt and cap pointed to her and another girl. 'OK. You. And you.' He gestured towards a building that looked like a large shed. 'Give your names to the guy in there.'

Klara was bursting with excitement; the other girl, she

found out later, lived in Brooklyn and had been picked as an extra before; she showed her what to do.

'When we've given our names, they tell us which set they want us on. Then the director decides if he wants us in a particular scene or not.' She was friendly, and Klara felt an instant liking for her. 'Nothin' to worry about. It's as easy as fallin' off a log.'

Inside the shed-like building, a man took their names, and wrote them in a ledger.

'Cissy Carmichael.'

'Klara Kopek.'

'OK, girls . . . make your way over to set one. Ask for Harry Mayo in casting.'

That was the beginning. Harry Mayo gave both of them the once-over, decided there and then that he needed them for a crowd scene, and sent them into a large open space that served as a general dressing room, to change their clothes. A fat lady called Mrs Spedon, whose husband, Klara learned afterwards, worked in the publicity department, told them that they were appearing in a costume drama and here were their clothes. Klara was a little embarrassed at the idea of having to take off her street dress in front of so many strangers. But Cissy just laughed.

'Hey, if you're gonna work here you'd better get rid of those inhibitions, honey!' she chuckled as she gaily stripped off without a second thought. 'Anyhow, you ain't got nothin' no-one here ain't seen before!'

'But there are men working out there!' Klara was shocked.

'Don't let it worry ya! They're all too busy to stop an' peek at us. Besides, even Maurice Costello and Curt Koenig share a dressing room with the others!'

'Excuse me? Who are Maurice Costello and Curt Koenig?'

Cissy stopped buttoning up her costume and looked astonished. 'You mean you never heard of 'em? Not even Curt Koenig? Jeez, his picture's plastered over most of Manhattan! Where you bin lately, Klara Kopek? The moon?' The other girls standing around overheard, and they all laughed. Klara couldn't understand. 'Hey, I'm only kiddin'. But you sure got a lot to learn about who's who around movin' pictures. Those two are what you call the leadin' actors around here. Especially Curt Koenig . . . he's real dreamy.' There was an enthusiastic chorus of agreement from all around them. 'Wow, what wouldn't I give to be in a scene with that guy!'

'Dreamy?'

'Hey, Klara! You know what "gorgeous" means? OK. Well, that's just what he is. Goddam gorgeous!'

'You mean, he is a very handsome man?' More laughter from the other extras in the dressing room.

'Just wait till you see him.'

Klara saw no-one famous that day, or the next, or the week after when she was picked out again for crowd work for four whole days. In her excitement at being paid a grand total of fifteen dollars, everything else paled into insignificance. She repaid Stanislav and gave him an extra two dollars for helping her when she hadn't had any money of her own, and the rest she handed over dutifully to her parents. But her mother made her take back half of it, despite her protests.

'No, Klara . . . this money, you have earned it. You buy something nice for yourself, huh? A pretty ribbon for your hair . . . some new clothes? You want to create a good impression when you go to this studio.'

'Mama, I want you to keep it. You need it to buy food and pay bills. I can get some more if they pick me tomorrow. I just need my fare, that's all.'

'But what if they don't pick you?'

Klara smiled. 'Then I'll go back the day after. I'll keep going back, Mama. It'll be all right, you'll see.'

There was so much to learn, and Klara loved to learn new things. She was filled with curiosity about everything that was happening around her, from the work in the wardrobe department and the scenery shed to the mechanical miracle

259

of the film camera. At the beginning, there was so much to understand.

Sometimes, an entire picture could be finished in half a day – these were likely to be what was known as the 'one-reelers', consisting of a mere thousand feet of film; nine hundred feet or so of story and titles, the remainder for winding, advertising and so on. The studio's important pictures – epics which starred the leading players – usually took far longer to produce, because many of the scenes would be re-shot time and time again to ensure absolute perfection.

Almost nobody was considered too grand to turn their hands to anything that needed doing. Mrs Turner, the mother of one of Vitagraph's important actresses, Florence Turner, was in charge of the wardrobe department, a long room with poles stretched across it filled with rows of coats, dresses, and period gowns. Groups of players who might be waiting around to be called onto one of the sets would often lend a hand with other tasks that needed doing, like mending costumes or painting scenery. Personal maids, even for the leading actresses, were unheard of; everyone took a turn at buttoning everybody else's clothes, helped each other with make-up and dressing hair. Florence Turner even handed out the extras' salaries, which were made up and placed in envelopes each evening. Klara had asked some of the other girls if Miss Turner was the only important player in the company to do it.

'Well, she ain't ever bin in the theatre, so maybe that has somethin' to do with it. She came straight into moving pictures without any stage experience at all. Some of the other actresses they've had here – Madeline Dupre, Sonia Severny – they started out acting in the Broadway theatres and they think they're far too good to lower themselves by doin' menial chores like that. Lots of 'em who've worked on the stage just look down their noses at anyone who works in moving pictures.'

'But, why? I don't understand?'

'To them, movie players are like . . . well, poor relations. People to be ashamed of. They hold 'em cheap. Except the

260

actresses I just told you about, and actors like Maurice Costello and Curt Koenig. They were both already established stars long before they came here.'

'Star? That is someone very highly regarded by everyone, yes?'

'You got it.'

Klara sighed as she reached for her pot of cold cream to take off the thick white make-up; she stared into the mirror.

'I wish I could get close enough to see them.'

It would be another three weeks before she did.

The shooting for *The Scarlet Pimpernel* had finished late today, and Curt was tired. One of the last scenes they'd done just hadn't seemed to come right, and it had taken three separate shoots to perfect it, to the annoyance of Louise Larsen who was, Curt decided, one of the most difficult actresses he'd ever worked with. They constantly disagreed over exactly how any given scene should best be played, and, only days into the picture, she'd telephoned the studio to say she was suffering from nervous exhaustion, and progress had been held up for almost two weeks. Even a temperamental actress like Madeline Dupre had never displayed such tantrums.

Curt removed his make-up and washed, then changed into his regular clothes. His reflection in the dressing-room mirror looked weary. Between endless disagreements with Louise Larsen on set and even more heated arguments with Marianna at home, his nerves were worn ragged. Much as he longed to see the children at the end of the working day he'd taken to staying out until well past their bedtime to avoid Marianna, and meeting Shawn for a cold beer in one of the bars that proliferated along Broadway. Shawn had noticed the change in him the last time they'd met.

'Hell, Curt . . . you sickenin' for somethin' or what? You look like you left the studio and forgot to wipe your make-up off. You're as white as a goddam sheet.' He'd sipped his ice-cold beer. 'What gives?' Curt had spent the next three hours telling him.

'It all started when Charles Frohman called while I was

at the studio, and he talked to Marianna. He's producing a new Broadway play . . . some modern drawing-room drama . . . and he wants me to play the leading man. But after I'd read the script I just didn't fancy doing it; somehow, the part wasn't me. Marianna didn't agree.'

Shawn had fallen silent for a moment or two. 'You won't solve anything by keeping out of her way. When you get back, she'll still be waiting for you.'

'Don't I know it.'

'You told her why you turned down the part?'

Curt had nodded, slowly. He stared miserably into his untouched glass of beer. He was losing his appetite for everything. 'It all comes down to one thing, Shawn. Marianna wants me out of moving pictures and back in the theatre. She thinks Broadway is where I really belong.'

'And you?'

'If Frohman had handed me a script I'd liked, I would probably have gone back to the Lyceum in a minute.' He gave a short, tired smile. 'I s'ppose my heart's always going to be in the real theatre . . . *Monte Cristo* . . . that play was the best thing I've ever done in my life.'

'Give it a year or two, maybe . . . and Frohman could be thinkin' along the lines of a revival. It happens, doesn't it? Hell, Curt, that play sure made him a lot of goddam money!'

A wry smile. 'I didn't do so badly out of it either, come to think of it.'

He got up and went out of the dressing room, along the corridor. No need to hurry. Tonight he wasn't meeting Shawn till later, and, despite the children's liking him to be home early enough to tuck them up in bed and read each of them a bedtime story, the thought of yet another argument with Marianna made him determined not to go back to Madison Avenue first. He walked across the almost deserted studio lot, nodding to anyone he knew as he went, and made his way outside. Just as he reached the door opposite the wages office, it opened suddenly and a young girl clutching an envelope came out. For a moment she stared at him. Though he had no idea who she was – one of the extras, he guessed – he smiled at her and then continued on his way to his automobile, parked under the trees outside.

Klara stood there, staring after him. In all her life, she had never seen anyone so handsome, so perfectly proportioned, had never seen such startling blue eyes. And he had smiled at her. All the way home on the elevated train from Flatbush to the Lower East Side, she couldn't get Curt Koenig out of her mind.

'Mama.' She helped her mother wash the dishes after supper while her father and brothers made cigars by candlelight. 'You know what happened today? I saw a very famous actor at the studio. His name is Curt Koenig. When I first went there, someone showed me a picture of him . . . what they call a publicity poster . . . and I crept over to the set he was working on with some of the girls, just to catch a glimpse of him. But today he was just walking along on his own, on his way out, I suppose . . . he looked straight at me and smiled at me. I have never seen a man so handsome . . . his eyes, they were so very blue . . .' She stopped what she was doing momentarily. 'On the way home, I wondered what his family were like, about the house he lives in. I wondered why he looked unhappy . . .'

Mrs Kopek's red, chapped hands placed another pile of greasy dishes in the cloudy water. 'Klara . . . you be a good girl, you understand what I am saying to you? I know there are a lot of handsome young men working at those studios. Your father . . . me, too . . . we worry about you. You are very young. We may be poor, but we have always been respectable . . .'

'Mrs Joblinski has been tittle-tattling to you and Papa again!'

'Mrs Joblinski has only said what we think . . . your father and I, we don't like for you to travel all that way to Brooklyn on your own, and home again . . . sometimes, when it is getting dark early. Maybe it would be best if one of your brothers came to meet you.'

'No, Mama. I told you. I can take care of myself.' She

smiled. 'Let me help you finish this, then I have something special to show you. I bought you a present. That was why I was a little later back tonight. It's a scarf . . . your favourite colour!'

'Klara, you shouldn't! We don't expect it. Already, you give us half your money from the studio work.' She put her arms around her daughter and kissed her. 'You have a good heart.'

Late that night, Klara lay in her narrow bed listening to the sounds of her sisters' snoring, but in her mind a whole world away. She imagined what it might be like to be Curt Koenig's leading lady; one step further . . . what must it feel like to be his wife? The other girls at the studio had told her that he was married and had three children, that his wife's father had been a millionaire. *A millionaire*. That must mean that he had one million dollars at least; almost impossible to imagine. Klara had opened her pay envelope today and looked at the seven dollars in her hand: how could anyone have more than a million one dollar notes? How did they come by so much money? Had he married his wife because her father had been so rich, or because he loved her? Klara found herself feeling jealous and resentful of this unknown, faceless woman. Did his children look like him, or were they like her?

Klara turned over, gazed up at the ceiling. She suddenly longed for it to be tomorrow so that she could go back to East Flatbush and see him again.

She would get up early, before even her mother was awake. She'd take extra trouble with her clothes, and her hair. Just in case he crossed her path again, she desperately wanted to look her best.

She fell asleep, still thinking of his blue eyes and his smile.

The bar of the Casino Theatre was on the point of closing. Curt and Shawn finished their drinks and went out into the now chilly late evening air. Then, side by side, they began to walk along Broadway. Shawn stole a sideways glance at his friend. Curt hadn't been very talkative tonight, but it was what he'd left unsaid that concerned Shawn most.

'So, things are still no better between you and Marianna?'

'They were never worse.'

'Wouldn't it be better if you spent more time at home with her and talked things through?'

'What's left to say?'

'She's still your wife, Curt.'

'Try telling her that.'

'You have to make an effort. Bad atmospheres are no good for the children. They sense these things.'

'They don't need to sense anything. They can hear us shouting at each other.' They walked on in silence, past lighted shop windows, storefronts, Riker's drugstore on the corner at 23rd Street. 'Look.' He slowed down a little. 'I appreciate your meeting me tonight.' He managed a ghost of a smile. 'I'm sorry I seem to be laying it all on you lately. I'll have to stop.'

'What else are friends for? You'd do the same for me, wouldn't you?'

'That's something you never need to ask.'

They parted on the corner of 34th and Madison. 'I almost forgot to tell you . . . Marianna's invited you to a dinner party . . . the twenty-fifth of the month. If you can make it, I promise that there'll be a general ceasefire for the evening.'

Shawn laughed; at least Curt could still crack one of his dry jokes. It didn't often happen, these days. 'Yeah . . . tell her I'd love to come. Say hello to her for me.'

Marianna had already gone to bed when Curt reached home; he should have been used to spending his evenings alone by now. He went into the darkened drawing room, turned up the lights and poured himself a large glass of bourbon, despite the fact that he'd already had more than enough to drink during the evening with Shawn. Maybe a double bourbon – or was it a triple? – would knock him out. He found it difficult to sleep, most nights.

When he went upstairs at last he was passing her bedroom door when it suddenly opened, taking him completely by surprise. He stared at her as she stood there in her long white nightgown with her wonderful hair all loose; she looked almost angelic.

'Good night, Marianna.' He walked on, towards the end of the landing and the guest bedroom where he always slept now. He sat down on the bed, tugged at his shoes and tie. Why had she opened her door just as he was walking by it? What was it that she'd wanted to say, or had it just been his imagination, wishful thinking, that she'd wanted to say anything to him at all?

He lay there in the darkness. There were no sounds, except for the distant ticking of a clock and a solitary passing vehicle in the street outside. Eventually, he slept.

Elynor had found it hard to get to sleep tonight, like all the other nights when she'd waited for her father to come home before bedtime, and he hadn't. None of them had dared to ask their mother why; Momma was always in a bad temper these days, and even little things – like Alice whining or saying she wanted Daddy to read her a bedtime story – would make her fly into an ungovernable rage. Now even Alice had learned that it wasn't very wise to upset Momma when she was in one of her strange moods. Elynor and Gene had tried to work out when they'd started, but neither of them could really remember, only that, from what they'd overheard in the house and listening outside the door when Daddy and Momma were yelling at each other, they were sure it was something to do with Daddy turning down Mr Frohman's script for the new play he was planning to put on at his Broadway theatre. Whatever it was, it was something bad this time, more serious than all the other disagreements put together; for these past few weeks, instead of shouting at each other whenever Daddy came home, they barely spoke at all. Now, Daddy never seemed to come home until Momma had gone to bed.

Elynor turned over, strained her ears in the silence. She'd heard Momma come upstairs an hour ago, but Daddy hadn't even come back for dinner. She'd peered up at her little clock on the mantelpiece just now when she'd heard the front door open and Daddy come into the hall, and it had said half an hour past midnight. That was very late, even for Daddy. But sometimes she'd fallen asleep waiting for him to come home and it had been so late that she hadn't heard him return at all.

At least he had come home tonight. A few moments ago she'd heard the sound of his footsteps outside on the landing, the noise of the guest bedroom door being opened. They all knew, but never spoke about the fact that Daddy and Momma didn't sleep in the same room any more. Daddy had been sleeping in the guest bedroom for so long now that neither Elynor nor Gene could really remember when it had started. She just wished, with all her heart, that everything could be different, that Daddy could come home early enough to see them before they went to bed, and be there in the morning. She always said her prayers and asked God to make it happen; but, so far, He hadn't done that.

Maybe, if she said another prayer now . . .

CHAPTER SEVENTEEN

As he drove the automobile out of the studio gates and along the road, Curt braked suddenly to avoid the young girl walking slowly ahead of him, head down, dragging her feet disconsolately, not looking where she was going. He honked his horn at her and she looked up. He vaguely recognized her; one of the extras from Charlie Kent's one-reeler set that he rarely saw. As he stopped at the side of the road and she drew level with him, he could see that she'd been crying.

'Can I give you a ride someplace?' He smiled at her and she smiled back; that was when he remembered where he first saw her.

'That is very kind of you, Mr Koenig.' She stood there shyly, awkwardly. He got out, opened the passenger door for her. 'I was going to the station, if that isn't too far out of your way.'

'Right by Prospect Park. No problem.' He started up the engine again. 'You work at the studios?' She nodded. 'And you live where?'

'Varick Street . . .' A pause. 'It's on the Lower East Side.'

'I don't know the Lower East Side too well. But if you want, I'll drive you home.' She looked stunned. He smiled again. 'You want to tell me what you've been crying about? Or should I just mind my own business?'

'You're very kind.'

'Maybe it'd make it easier for you if I pulled over.' He slowed down and stopped the automobile. Then he turned and looked at her. She was embarrassed, very ill at ease. She dabbed at her reddened eyelids with a bedraggled handkerchief. He studied her more closely.

She was neither plain nor beautiful, but somewhere in between, with dark blond hair and brown eyes; an unusual combination. Her clothes were cheap, but spotlessly clean. 'I'm a good listener.'

'I can't believe that I'm here with you . . . except for once, when I almost bumped into you, I've only ever glimpsed you from a long way away, when you were on set filming, or leaving the studio. I admire you very much.'

Curt smiled; the remark was par for the course from starstruck young girls who didn't seem to understand that actors were just flesh and blood like everyone else around them. But he understood. He took out his own handkerchief and gave it to her. 'I'm still waiting . . . is it so hard for you to talk about, whatever it is?'

She looked away, down to some point on the automobile floor. 'They told me that they didn't need me at the studio after this week. That they might call me again, but if they did they would write and let me know. I'm afraid that they won't want me any more.'

'It's just standard practice. Nothing to worry about.'

'It's all my fault. I shouldn't have taken it for granted that I'd work regularly. I'd got used to having the extra money . . . it was so nice, after having almost nothing at all. I was able to help my family, sometimes buy them little presents. I even left home and found an apartment to share with two other girls . . . it was so crowded at home . . .' She dabbed at her eyes again. 'Now I shall have to tell them that I won't be able to stay any longer. I can't stay, if I can't pay my share of the rent. The landlord is very strict, you know? He tell us . . . no rent, no rooms.'

Impulsively, Curt took out his wallet and peeled off several ten-dollar bills. 'Here, take this . . . it'll help tide you over.' When she just stared at the money and wordlessly shook her head, he pushed it into her hand. 'Tell you what. I'll have a word with Charlie Kent when I get to the studio tomorrow. I think I can persuade him to keep you on.'

Klara was stunned. 'You would do that, for me?'

Curt laughed softly. 'When I was a boy, I was taught that I should always help other people if I could . . . I guess you never forget those kinds of lessons. It's my pleasure.'

'I don't know how to thank you.' Her eyes were shining

at him. 'You are the kindest person I've met since we came to New York.'

'I can't believe that! How long have you been here? You weren't born in New York . . . not with that accent.'

'I was born in Warsaw. We come to America six years ago, when I was fourteen. We were always very poor, but there was much persecution, and my mother and father were very unhappy . . . they wanted a future for us . . . that is why we decide to come.' She described the nightmare voyage from the port of Danzig, crowded together in steerage with hundreds of other immigrant families, then the arrival at Ellis Island. 'My parents were afraid that the officials there might find something wrong with us, and turn us back. We were all afraid. We saw many other people – old, sick – whom they would not allow in. It was horrible. I thought to myself . . . I wonder what will happen to them.' She stopped abruptly, as if she'd realized she was talking to a virtual stranger and these were things that should not be spoken about to a man she scarcely knew. Why, after all, should a celebrated actor like Curt Koenig want to listen to anything a girl like Klara had to say, a story that he was most likely only listening to from mere politeness? He was, she reasoned, probably waiting for her to stop talking so that he could start up the engine of the automobile again and continue his journey home, where – according to studio gossip – he had a beautiful house, a beautiful wife, and three beautiful children waiting for him. Was his wife very beautiful, Klara wondered? She half turned away her face to hide her swollen eyelids – she must look a fright – so that he couldn't see it clearly; why couldn't she have been looking her best? She so desperately wanted him to think she was pretty. 'I'm sorry . . . I've taken up so much of your time . . . Papa always said that I talk too much to people I like.'

'There's no need to apologize. People should talk to each other more.' He started the engine and they continued along the road; but when they reached the elevated railway station off 15th Street by Prospect Park, Curt drove on past. 'It's OK . . . I'm not going to kidnap you.' He smiled with amusement at her astonishment. 'You said you lived on Varick Street, so that's where I'm taking you . . . though you'll have to give me directions as I don't know the place too well.' Another smile that sent thrills through her. 'You might as well go home in style.'

'No, please!' Klara turned to him in panic. 'I'd rather you just put me off on the other side of Brooklyn Bridge.' The thought of him seeing those rough, filthy streets with piles of rubbish and lines of washing strung up between the houses was too humiliating for her to bear. 'I can easily walk from there.'

But Curt understood. 'Hey, look . . . I wasn't exactly raised in a palace myself. I haven't always lived on Madison Avenue.' An afterthought; he'd been so preoccupied with his own problems leaving the studio today that he'd forgotten to ask her. 'You didn't tell me your name.'

She blushed and smiled at him shyly. 'Klara Kopek.'

'Well, Klara Kopek, are you going to argue with me all the time or are you just going to sit back and enjoy the ride?'

'I would never argue with you. It would not be right.'

Her fair hair was blowing behind her in the wind; against Marianna's coldness her warmth and total lack of sophistication was like a breath of fresh air. He deliberately drove slowly so that the journey wouldn't come to an end too soon; when he'd met her twenty minutes ago he'd been feeling downhearted and depressed, and she'd taken him out of himself. A sudden impulse struck him.

'Are you in a hurry to get home tonight?'

'No, not really.'

'Would you like to have dinner with me somewhere?' She stared at him, as if she had trouble in understanding.

'Dinner . . .? Why, yes . . . I would love to . . . but . . . I couldn't.' The brown eyes looked sad. 'Not in these clothes.'

'What's wrong with them?'

'Everything.'

'Klara, there's much more to a person than the clothes they wear. You can take that from me.' Was that just a hint of bitterness? It set her wondering. 'I won't take no for an

271

answer . . . besides, I wouldn't take you to any place that made you feel uncomfortable.'

She was blushing again; he was touched, somehow, by the way she was so obviously in awe of him. He was used to women being attracted to him but she was different from American girls. They always clamoured around him, demanding to be noticed; brash, bold, even the coyest flirting with him. Perhaps it was fate that had put her in his path today because she was exactly what he needed at the moment; quiet, soothing, a panacea to the deep unhappiness in his marriage. Her modesty, her total lack of guile made him feel oddly protective towards her.

'If you want me to have dinner with you, then, yes . . . I would love to. It would be a great honour for me.' She looked thoughtful. 'But is your wife not expecting you now?'

His smile faded and Klara was quick to catch on to it. Was there, could there possibly be, a flaw in the fairytale marriage she'd heard so much about? Ever since she'd seen him on the Vitagraph set and become obsessed with him, everybody she'd eagerly questioned at the studio had told her how happy they were. She couldn't imagine any woman in her right mind being anything but happy, married to Curt Koenig. He turned and looked at her with his startling blue eyes.

'My wife isn't expecting me for dinner this evening, no.'

Shawn had been about to call it a day and go to bed when he heard the sound of an automobile drawing up in the street outside his apartment. Though there were more horseless vehicles on the streets of New York now than there had been a year ago, it was still relatively unusual in this part of the city; certainly, no-one – at least no-one he knew of – who lived in any of the apartments below or above him owned so luxurious a means of transport. He went to the window and peered out into the night from sheer curiosity. What he saw jolted him wide awake. Getting out of the driver's side was the unmistakable form of Curt, his bright halo of hair like a beacon in the darkness;

but ensconced in the passenger seat and as clearly visible was a young woman: a very young woman. Shawn frowned as he let the net curtain fall back into place and went to answer his front door.

'Been out slumming tonight?' he asked with a chilly edge to his voice when he opened the door and Curt's face appeared out of the darkness.

'I only came by because I saw your light was still on. Sorry it's so late.'

'I won't ask you to stay, since I happened to see that you weren't alone.' Curt still hadn't noticed that Shawn didn't seem his usual jovial self tonight. 'Do you have any idea of what time it is?'

'I won't even come in. I just stopped by to say I can't meet you tomorrow . . . something's come up. But I'll catch you at Marianna's dinner party next week. You're still coming?'

'Try to keep me away. How are Marianna and those beautiful kids of yours?'

'All looking forward to seeing you. Don't you dare be late. Must go.' He slapped Shawn on the shoulder and turned back towards the stairs. 'Sleep tight now.'

Against his better judgement, Shawn followed Curt out onto the landing. 'Curt? Who's the girl?' Curt paused on the stairs.

'Oh, she works at the studio . . . I found her crying her eyes out on the way home today . . . studio told her that they were laying her off for the time being.' It all sounded plausible enough but somehow, knowing Curt as well as he did, something didn't quite ring true. 'I said I'd have a word with Charlie Kent in the morning and see if there's anything he can do.'

'You're going to a whole lot of trouble for a run-of-the-mill extra, aren't you?'

'It's no skin off my back.'

'Why are you out so late with her? You do know it's gone midnight?'

Curt gave him one of his charming smiles. 'We just got talking . . . I offered to take her to dinner. To tell you the truth, I felt sorry for her. I'm just taking her back home now. Like I said, sorry about tomorrow . . . but I'll catch up with you next week. See you at Madison next Friday, OK?'

'OK.'

Shawn closed the door and bolted it, went back inside. He watched from his window as Curt climbed back into the automobile, started the engine and drove away. As it passed under a nearby street lamp the passenger window was lit up momentarily and he got a clear view of the girl's face. Maybe it was the lighting, maybe his eyes were tired and he wasn't seeing straight, but what he could see of her puzzled him; though she was certainly very young, she was as certainly not particularly good-looking. Perhaps it had just been his cynical, suspicious mind thinking Curt had had an ulterior motive in helping the girl; perhaps he genuinely felt sorry for her after all. One thing was for sure; whatever else she was, she certainly wasn't his usual type, the smart, the striking, the sophisticated. He came away from the window for the second time, yawned and turned down the lights.

It was only when he was undressed and in bed and almost on the point of falling asleep that he remembered something. He'd forgotten to tell Curt that he meant to call in on Marianna tomorrow. Not that it mattered.

CHAPTER EIGHTEEN

Shawn stopped off en route to Madison Avenue at Seigel–Cooper on Sixth and 19th to collect some packages from the music department for the children, then at Fleischman's florists on Broadway for flowers for Marianna. When he arrived at the house, Bridget let him into the front hall.

'Mr Duchovsky, shall I take your coat for you? I'll let Mrs Koenig know you're here.' She smiled as the children stampeded down the main staircase, having heard Shawn's arrival.

'Uncle Shawn, Uncle Shawn!' Little Alice reached him first and clung to his trouser leg; her blue eyes sparkled at the sight of the parcels he was carrying. 'Have you brought me a present?'

'Have I brought you a present? Hey, would I dare come here without one?' As he turned to Elynor and Gene, Marianna came out of the drawing room.

'Shawn! It's good to see you.' Her smile faded a little as she looked at Alice, now being carried high in Shawn's arms. 'Alice, what have I told you about asking for things? How many times do I have to tell you that it's the height of bad manners?'

'It's OK, Marianna . . .'

'No, it isn't.'

'I'm sorry, Momma . . . but Uncle Shawn did promise to bring me a surprise when he came!'

He handed Marianna the flowers and kissed her lightly on the cheek. 'OK, you three, we'll go in here and you can unwrap these . . . then it's back upstairs to those school books.' He winked at Elynor and Gene. 'You want to be the cleverest kids in New York City, don't you? Well, you can't do that unless you get your noses stuck back in those

275

books and do some learnin' . . . you just ask your momma if you don't believe me.'

'I hate books without pictures!' Alice batted her big blue eyes at him, and Shawn thought, shrewdly, that here was one precocious little girl who'd most likely do very well in life getting what she wanted without them.

'You're still coming to dinner next Friday?' They sat down while the children unwrapped the packages he'd brought them. 'You haven't called by to say you can't come after all?'

'Wild horses wouldn't keep me away.' It was a while since he'd seen her and he was shocked by the change he saw; there were dark circles beneath her eyes and she looked as if she hadn't slept for a week or more. 'Marianna, you sure you're OK? You look a little pale today.'

'I'm very well.' He doubted that. 'And you? You're still at Hamburg–Amerika on Broadway?'

'Curt would have told you if I wasn't.' A strange expression like a cloud passed over her face.

'Curt doesn't exactly confide in me these days . . . he's always so busy. You must see more of him than I do. He leaves for the studio straight after breakfast and after the studio there's always some meeting he has to go to . . . or a working dinner. He never comes home till late.' She looked away from him, towards the three children. 'Sometimes, I don't get to see him at all.'

'They sure get their pound of flesh from him at those movie studios!'

'It isn't like the theatre . . . after a play was finished, he'd have weeks of rest. Maybe even a month or two sometimes. With these moving pictures, the minute one's in the can – that's the expression they use, Curt says – another one's already in production. It's like a never-ending treadmill. When I came down this morning, he'd already gone, but he'd left a pile of new scripts that he must have brought home with him late last night. I suppose he showed them to you?'

'Me? No way.' Shawn laughed. 'I'm not up to readin' anythin' at twelve thirty in the mornin'. Anyhow, he only stayed a few minutes. He just caught me before I went to bed.'

'I see.' Marianna fell silent. Curt had told Bridget when she was serving him his breakfast this morning that he'd had dinner with someone from the studio yesterday, then spent the rest of the evening at Shawn's apartment; now her suspicions were aroused. Was Shawn lying or was Curt? Shawn would have no reason to.

'Look, Momma!' Gene and Elynor had pulled the wrapping paper from their presents simultaneously. 'It's a big book all about baseball!' Gene turned the pages over in delight. 'And it's got all my favourites, all the all-time greats, with lots of pictures! A. G. Spalding, Adrian "Cap" Anson, Cy Young . . . hey, look! It says Adrian Anson made the Chicago White Sox one of the best teams ever . . . how about that?'

'Thank you, Uncle Shawn!' Elynor cradled the precious phonograph record in her hands. 'Momma, can I play it now, *please*?'

'Uncle Shawn's given me a musical box that plays the *Merry Widow* tune!'

'Oh, Alice, let me see!'

'It's mine!'

Shawn stood up. 'Hey, you three, keep it down before you give your momma a big headache! Now listen . . . what about you wind up the Victrola and play that nice and quiet, and your momma and me'll go talk in the other room?'

'You can play the Victrola, but not too loudly. Gene, you know how to wind it up. Alice isn't to touch it.'

'Thank you, Uncle Shawn!' three voices said together.

'You sure you're OK, Marianna?'

She made her lips smile a false smile; he mustn't suspect anything; not anything at all. She tried to concentrate on what he was saying, but it was almost impossible. All she could think about was that Curt had deliberately lied and there was only one reason she could think of why he would. Another woman.

It seemed unthinkable, almost beyond belief; any man whose face was as publicly known as his would never, surely, risk open scandal that would threaten, maybe even destroy, his very high-profile career, let alone his marriage . . . would he? Marianna cast her mind back and was suddenly not so sure. When they'd first quarrelled so bitterly over his acceptance of Vitagraph's offer he'd taken to staying out late, even into the early hours; later, as they'd gradually become more and more estranged by irreconcilable differences, there'd been nights when Curt had never come home at all. All the time, she'd assumed that he'd been with Shawn at his apartment – where she'd thought he'd been last night. Now, it was clear that he'd lied about yesterday; had he lied about all those other times, too? Though she'd caused jealous scenes over his various leading ladies – and hadn't she been justified, when he'd gone to studio functions with them instead of her? – Marianna had never really believed that Curt would be physically unfaithful to her. Was it possible that she'd been wrong? When Bridget brought in the tray of tea and cakes she found she couldn't touch them; the thought of Curt making love to someone else upset her so much that she felt physically sick.

'Marianna, you've gone very white. You sure you're not coming down with something?' He smiled, trying to make light of it. 'Hey, don't you dare cancel that dinner party!' She made herself smile back.

'It's all right, really. As I said, I haven't been sleeping so well. Nothing a few early nights won't put right.'

Shawn sipped his tea. 'Curt mentioned that both the Frohman brothers were going to be among your guests. Is that right?'

'I was hoping that he'd be persuaded to think seriously about going back into real theatre. I know I'll never be able to talk him into it . . . but I thought someone who has as much influence with him as Charles Frohman might succeed where I've failed.'

'Marianna, I hear what you're sayin' . . . but Curt can be very stubborn when he wants to.'

'You've known him far longer than I have.' Marianna held the cup to her lips without drinking; there was a terrible gnawing ache deep inside her and she felt incapable of swallowing even a mouthful. Shawn went on, oblivious of the fact that she scarcely heard a word he was saying. She felt too stunned, too sick with misery.

'You oughta've heard the almighty ruckus Curt had with his ma and pa when he first told them that he wanted to leave Minneapolis and go on the New York stage! Jeez, sparks sure did fly in those days! But no matter what anyone said to him, Curt's mind was made up. He was goin' to do it, an' he was goin' to do it his way.'

She put down her cup. There was a thin film across the liquid where she had left it untouched. Impossible to confide in Shawn, no matter how much she liked him; he was Curt's friend, and the bond between them was too strong. If need be, Shawn would lie for him, she felt certain. Equally, she knew that whatever else she did, she must never let Shawn know that she suspected anything. He would be almost sure to warn Curt and put him on his guard. No. This was something that Marianna must do alone.

From the adjoining room, they heard the sound of ragtime on the wind-up Victrola, and the children's delighted shrieks as they danced to the catchy popular tune. When it was time for Shawn to leave they all crowded round him in the front hall as he kissed Marianna goodbye. She kept her face a smiling mask.

'I gave Bridget the flowers you brought for Momma, and she's putting them in water.'

'Well, thank you, Alice! How about a big kiss goodbye now?' Unsuspectingly, he turned to Marianna and unwittingly let slip the very thing she needed to know. 'I'll see you and Curt next Friday for dinner, then. Tell him I'm looking forward to it . . . and that I said hello.'

She closed the front door after him, walked back across the hall. So, he was not expecting to see Curt again for almost a week. Now Marianna knew what she had to do.

*　　*　　*

He surprised her by coming home early that night, early enough for them to eat dinner together. It would be the first time in months that that had happened, and she was puzzled by it. After a day spent at the studio, he was always busy – talks with various Vitagraph executives, discussions with script writers and directors, working dinners in Manhattan – it had become a regular pattern and, until Shawn's casual, unguarded remark had alerted all her suspicions, Marianna had grudgingly accepted the long hours he spent away from home as a part of his commitment to the new career in moving pictures. Perhaps, she pondered now as they ate dinner in virtual silence, she had been terribly wrong to doubt him; maybe her suspicions were groundless after all. If there was someone else in his private life, surely he would not have come home at this unusually early hour in the evening? He'd said that there were no after-working-hours meetings today because the picture was almost finished, and she desperately wanted to believe him.

'Will you be home early again tomorrow?'

'No, I don't think so.' There was a guarded tone to his voice that her sharp ears quickly picked up on. Suddenly she felt tense again. 'Charlie Kent and Bill Smith wanted to meet somewhere in town and talk about the scripts they gave me to look over. It could take a while.'

'Why not bring them back here?' She chose her words carefully, kept her voice deliberately light. 'They could have dinner, and you could go into the library and discuss the scripts afterwards. I wouldn't be in your way.'

When he hesitated and then fumbled for a way out, Marianna sensed that she hadn't been wrong after all. Her heart sank as he said stiffly, 'I don't think that would work . . . I think they'd prefer neutral ground. Maybe another time.'

'Yes.' Somehow, she managed to get through the rest of the meal and the evening. After dinner, she went into the library to read and Curt went upstairs to play with the children. When they were asleep, he came down again and stood a little awkwardly in the doorway. She sensed – correctly – that the children had shown him the presents from Shawn and that he was worried about what Shawn might have inadvertently let slip to her.

'You never said Shawn called by today.'

She glanced up coolly from her book; but her heart was pounding. 'It completely slipped my mind . . . besides, he was only here for a moment or two. He'd just called to say he was looking forward to dinner next Friday and to leave some presents for the children. I told him he shouldn't spoil them.'

'Did he say anything else?' She could see that he was on edge now; nervous.

'No, nothing else. Except that he'd be seeing you soon.' She pretended to be trying to remember. 'Tomorrow evening, was it? Or was it the evening after? I can't think now.'

'I'll most likely call on him on my way back from the meeting with Charlie and Bill Smith tomorrow. The night after, I thought we'd go for a drink together downtown . . . someplace quiet.' Marianna kept her face expressionless; now she was almost certain he was lying.

'Where is the meeting with Bill Smith going to be? Does he live in Manhattan?'

Curt went over to the fireplace and took out a cigarette. She was watching him intently. 'Oh . . . probably one of the hotel lounges . . . the Prince George or the Endicott. We can have dinner in the restaurant there and then spread out afterwards.' He lit his cigarette. 'He lives in an apartment on 113th Street and from what he's said, it isn't too big. The lounge of the Prince George or the Endicott is much better. And neutral surroundings always help . . . especially away from the cameras and the arc lamps.'

She kept her eyes fixed rigidly on the book in front of her. Her heart was breaking. 'I won't wait up for you, then.'

All the next day, time dragged unbearably. At eight o'clock, Marianna went to the telephone in the front hall and got the exchange to put through a call to the reception desk at the Hotel Endicott. Neither Charles Kent nor Bill

Smith nor Curt Koenig was anywhere in the building; and, moreover, none of them was expected. When she put a second call through to the Hotel Prince George, the answer was the same. Woodenly, she replaced the earpiece.

She thought back to the previous evening. What was the address of Bill Smith's Manhattan apartment? She remembered now: 113th Street. For the third time, she picked up the telephone with shaking fingers: it was hardly likely that a chief executive of Vitagraph Motion Picture Company had an apartment without a telephone. The exchange put through the call and, as she waited, her heart was beating so wildly that she felt dizzy. When a deep male voice suddenly said, 'Hello, this is Bill Smith speaking. Who is this, please?' she quickly replaced the earpiece again.

She went into the empty drawing room. She was trembling all over. *Liar, liar!* She paced up and down. She'd never felt like this before. She felt as if somebody had crushed every ounce of breath, every emotion except hate and rage out of every particle of her body. She was too shattered, too hurt, too anguished to cry. If she could cry, if she could let all the pain and misery out somehow, maybe she would feel better.

But there was no way out. Curt had lied to her, gone to considerable trouble to perpetrate his deception, and his reasons were obvious. Wherever he was, he was neither with Shawn, nor with anybody from the Vitagraph executive. He was with someone he didn't want her to know about; someone whose identity he had clearly kept secret, even from his best and oldest friend.

Marianna had to find out who that someone was.

He'd singled her out at the studio today; ever since, Klara had been walking in the clouds. When he said that he'd drive her home again – but that he had something special to show her on the way – she'd spent the entire day racking her brains to think what that something might be. For the first time since she'd worked at the studios, time had dragged; she counted the minutes till the working day was over and she could see him again. The envy from the other

282

girls when she'd mentioned that Curt Koenig was giving her a lift to the other side of Brooklyn Bridge in his automobile had only increased her pleasure in his company; for a poor immigrant Polish girl from the Lower East Side it was a new experience to be envied.

'You are very, very kind to me.' Hair blowing behind her, eyes shining, she'd gazed at him in uncritical adoration. 'I am very grateful. Mr Kent, he told me this morning that he will not lay me off after all. I think that is because you spoke to him about me, yes?'

Curt smiled. 'I did have a word in his ear, yes. But it's no big deal.' He glanced at her. 'I didn't think it was fair for them to just say "That's it" when you've had a hard time making ends meet. Anyhow, if you're not in too big a hurry to get home, there's somewhere I'd like to take you.'

She was as excited as a child. 'I don't know what to say.'

'Don't say anything. Not until we get there.'

He'd been thinking of taking a small apartment, or a brownstone terrace somewhere uptown, for quite a while; ever since he and Marianna had started to drift apart. He'd realized that it wasn't fair of him to inflict himself constantly on Shawn whenever they quarrelled and he needed a breathing space; Shawn had his own life to live. There were obvious limits to where else someone as well known and instantly recognizable as he'd become could escape to spend his evenings. All the smart Manhattan restaurants, the popular bars and hotel lounges – particularly places where he'd been with Marianna – seemed full of people who, on spotting him, would smile knowingly and whisper among themselves. He craved peace, anonymity, a bolthole away from the emotional pressures of home. Only late last night, after he'd left Klara Kopek, did he finally decide to put into action a vague plan that he'd carried around in his mind for some time.

'Where are we going?' she asked, full of wonder, full of youthful enthusiasm, as he drove through central Manhattan and turned in the direction of upstate New York at Central Park. 'This part of the city . . . it's all so very different . . .' The brightly lit theatre fronts, the department stores, the rows of elegant brownstone houses they passed left her open-mouthed; it was another world, light years away from the grime, poverty and hopelessness of the Lower East Side, up till now the only things she knew. But ever since he'd stopped to offer her a ride to the station yesterday – had it only been yesterday? – her life had been dramatically altered.

'We're going upstate a little way . . . a part of the city you won't know. Washington Heights. I've just rented a terraced brownstone there.' He smiled when she looked at him blankly, not knowing what he meant. 'A brownstone is a small row house – like those we passed just back there – I signed the lease today.'

'But . . . I thought you said that you lived on Madison Avenue. Are you moving to this new house?'

'The house on Madison is the family home. This is something else.' Were they a real family any more? The children were the only reason he went home at all sometimes; he and Marianna hardly seemed to communicate nowadays. 'It's difficult for me to work at home. Hard to concentrate. Reading scripts, learning and rehearsing lines. I need quiet.' Was it her or himself he was trying to convince? His excuse for renting the upstate brownstone was sounding hollower and hollower, even to himself. Wasn't the real truth that he couldn't bear those awful, near-silent evenings with Marianna, the endless quarrels, the going upstairs alone to spend each night by himself in the guest room bed? The truth was, ever since the end of the affair with Madeline Dupre, Curt had been looking for someone – anyone, why didn't he admit it? – to fill the void in his life outside the studio, and in his bed. That, too, was important to him. Why else had he taken Klara Kopek out to dinner the night before last – a nondescript little film extra whom he'd never have even noticed if he hadn't almost run her down – why else had he suddenly rushed from Flatbush today to a realtor in midtown and signed a lease on a secluded house so far upstate that it took more than an hour across the city to reach it? If he'd really wanted somewhere for peace and quiet, there were plenty of places nearer.

'This house is yours?' She looked at it in disbelief as they drew up in the street outside. It was one of the most beautiful houses Klara had ever seen. 'The streets here are so different from where I live. So clean, so tidy, so many lovely trees. No piles of rubbish, no lines of washing hanging in back yards . . .'

He smiled. 'I'm glad you like it. Would you like to see inside?'

Her brown eyes were bright. 'Oh, yes! I would like that very much.'

He climbed out of the automobile and helped her with the door on the other side. She stood on the pavement, gazing all around her. The air was so clean, so fresh here. She envied the people who could live in a street like this.

'Shall we go inside?' He took a key from his pocket and she followed him up a short flight of stone steps to the neatly painted front door; it was black and shiny, with a polished brass letterbox and a huge lion's head knocker. She reached out and touched it. 'After you.'

She stepped into a compact but roomy front hall, with a highly polished woodblock floor with rugs and potted plants. Several doors led off the hall, and Klara followed Curt as he opened each one to show her – there was a cosy parlour, a small dining room, a miniature library; on the opposite side, another short flight of steps led down to the kitchen. A front hall staircase led to the first floor where there were three bedrooms, and a large modern bathroom with hot and cold running water; Klara could hardly believe her eyes. At home, there was a long walk to the water pump in the back yard, and the return trek up four flights of stairs.

'Please . . . could I look at all the rooms again before we have to leave? It's such a beautiful house. You see, when I go back I want to remember everything about each one . . . all the details.' She smiled sweetly at him. 'You are so very lucky to live in a house like this . . . and you are right. It is the ideal place for being quiet and peaceful to work in.'

'Why do you think I brought you here?'

'To show me. And I do appreciate it.' She blushed. 'I think you are very kind to take the trouble of showing me parts of the city I never knew existed . . . there must be many other important things that take up your time. I want you to know that I'm very grateful . . . and also grateful to you for speaking to Mr Kent about taking me back again. I wish there was some way that I could repay your kindness.'

'There is.' He smiled. 'I want you to live in this house for me.' Now he had shocked her. She stared at him, without understanding. 'That's the reason I brought you here . . . why else would I? Really, if you'd stay here and look after things for me, you'd be doing me a big favour.'

'But I don't understand. You said that you took the house because you needed a quiet place to work in.'

'I did. And I do. But I realized when you told me what it was like living on the Lower East Side what a waste it would be for me to have somewhere like this standing empty for most of the time, while you had to live in a place like that. It seemed wrong to me.' Her guilelessness enchanted him. 'Well, do we have a deal or not?'

'I don't know what to say!'

' "Yes" would be a good start.'

Spontaneously, she sprang towards him and kissed him on the cheek. In another moment she was in his arms.

Afterwards, he could tell himself the half-truth that he'd never meant it to happen; that it was a mistake, a momentary loss of self-control. But that wasn't the way it had been. He was already strongly attracted to her when he'd taken out the lease on the house; though, it was true, he hadn't planned to seduce her there and then, he was honest enough with himself to admit that he'd hoped a physical relationship would develop in time. When she'd flung her arms around him in happiness and gratitude, something that had been holding him back had snapped.

Her utter lack of inhibition in bed had completely astonished him. Who would have thought that a girl as shy, as guileless, as self-effacing as Klara Kopek could change, with the mere act of taking off her clothes, into the passionate creature lying under him, writhing, kissing, sucking, crying out in pleasure? Getting dressed afterwards, Curt had felt disorientated and dazed. It was a long time since he'd enjoyed making love to a woman so much. He'd glanced back at her, lying there on the bed with all her hair spread across the pillows.

'Klara . . . you do understand that my coming here will be something strictly between us . . . nobody else can know about it?'

'Curt, I understand.'

'And that we can't arrive at the studio every day together?' She nodded slowly. 'I've arranged for a cab to collect you here every morning at eight thirty . . . and pick you up again at five o' clock. Some days, you can have a ride with me . . . but not every day. There can't be any kind of pattern to it. Otherwise, people would suspect.'

'Are you ashamed of me?'

'Christ, no!' He'd turned back towards her and taken her into his arms. She felt warm and comforting. 'You must never think that. But people talk. If I wasn't married, it might not seem so bad, not if we were fairly discreet. As it is, there can never be even a hint of scandal.'

'I won't tell anyone . . . not even my family.'

He'd lit the stove for her and left money on the table in the parlour. 'You'll need it for ordering groceries. There isn't a telephone here at the moment, but I'll have the landlord arrange to get one installed.' He'd leaned over and kissed her. 'Klara, I think you're very sweet, and I like being with you. I'll see you tomorrow.'

When he'd gone, she went to the front bedroom window and watched him drive away. It had been quite dark by then. She'd dressed and gone downstairs, turning on all the electric lights as she went. Electric lights, when all she'd been used to up till now had been candles, and one oil lamp when she'd lived at home! She wished so much that her family could come here, just to see how wonderful it was, how lucky she'd been to meet a man like Curt Koenig.

She looked around the cosy little parlour; it was like a

dream, except that she was still wide awake. Her eyes caught sight of the ten-dollar bills he'd left in the middle of the table. She counted them – a hundred dollars! And she still had the money he'd given to her yesterday. He was so thoughtful, so kind, so generous. And gullible, as she'd so far found most men; almost without exception, when she told them about her family's terrible trials and tribulations on their journey to America, they felt sorry for her. Surely, she reasoned, it wasn't so very wrong of her to sometimes slightly twist the truth, making everything seem just a little worse than it really was? Her thoughts turned dark now. What kind of woman could his wife be if he felt the need to do this, to form an intimate relationship with someone else, someone that only two days ago he barely knew? He was on his way home to her now, to the big grand house on Madison Avenue where he lived with this faceless person and his three children. Klara was suddenly filled with curiosity about her; curiosity, jealousy, resentment. She did not deserve him. She was not worthy of being married to him. If he was happy with her, he would never have been tempted to make love with Klara tonight.

Klara went to the large oval mirror and studied herself. He hadn't said she was pretty, but surely he thought so? Her face was flushed, her eyes were shining. There was a mark on her neck where he'd kissed her. She looked down again at the money in her hand: she must buy some new clothes as soon as she could so that when he came again tomorrow she would look her very best for him.

She went back upstairs, lay down on the bed. She took one of the pillows and hugged it to herself. It was so soft, so white; real linen. She had never had real linen pillowcases and sheets before; never slept in a real feather bed. God was good. God was kind. God was generous. He had rewarded her for all the suffering and all the hardships of her life. If she prayed hard enough and often enough, perhaps He would make Curt fall passionately in love with her . . . and leave his unworthy wife?

* * *

'Marianna!' When the drawing-room door had suddenly opened and he'd seen her standing there, he'd almost jumped out of his skin. 'I thought you'd have gone up to bed hours ago.' He felt guilty, defensive. 'You startled me.'

'I was waiting for you.'

'Is there something wrong?'

'No. Should there be?' He followed her into the drawing room. The room was cold, unwelcoming without a fire. He thought, inadvertently, of the cosy little parlour, the intimate bedroom he'd left behind him at Washington Heights. What was Klara doing now, he wondered? 'I wanted to ask you how the meeting went tonight . . . with Bill Smith and the others. At the Endicott, didn't you say? Or was it the Prince George?'

He rubbed his eyes. 'Oh . . . yes . . . the meeting.' He couldn't quite meet her eyes. 'We managed to talk through a few things . . . one of the scripts looked promising . . .' He was fumbling for words. 'Trouble is, part of the story would need to be shot on location. . . a long way upstate in mountain country . . . it would mean stretching the production budget a little. . .'

'That isn't a problem, is it?' Why was she standing there like that firing questions at him, why didn't she leave him alone and go up to bed? He needed some time to get himself together. Though he didn't really want a drink, he went and poured himself one anyway.

'No. No, it isn't. But as I said, nothing's been decided on yet.' He cradled the bourbon in his hands. 'Are the children all right?'

'They were disappointed that you didn't come home in time to read them a bedtime story. But then you rarely do these days.' She gave a small, tight smile. How could he stand there and calmly lie about everything he'd done this evening, when she knew full well he hadn't been with Bill Smith at the Endicott, the Prince George, or any other place? 'Bill Smith and his wife are still coming to dinner on Friday?' He felt a stab of alarm now; he would have to speak to Bill, and Charlie Kent, first thing tomorrow at the studio, and ask them to cover for him. Otherwise,

289

Marianna might ask either of them some awkward questions. Something was already forming in his mind: he'd say that he'd quarrelled with her about Frohman's offer to go back to the theatre, and had spent the evening with Shawn to avoid further dissension.

'Shawn always kind of takes my side, and Marianna wouldn't be too happy if she found out I'd been talking it over with him all night. So I said I was with you guys into the early hours. . .' Yes, that sounded feasible enough. But how many times could he get away with it? He swigged back the bourbon in one gulp; things were getting so complicated, so completely out of hand. He was already enmeshed in lies up to his neck and he felt as if he was drowning, unable to escape the net in which he was tied – an ironical parody of the part he'd played in *Monte Cristo* when Edmond Dantes had been tossed over the cliff of the Château d'If in a burial sack?

At last, Marianna went to the door. 'I'm surprised Bill Smith kept you talking so late. When you have to be up so early for the studio.'

He shrugged. 'Couldn't be helped. He likes to have at least one or two scripts in the offing when we reach the end of one picture. We get the last scenes in the can next Saturday.'

'I'd better say good night, then.' She went out, leaving the door ajar. He watched her go up the stairs, without looking back, without glancing over the stair rail at him. There was something odd about her behaviour tonight; something Curt couldn't quite put his finger on. Maybe it was because he was tired and on edge because he hadn't expected her still to be up, maybe it was just his imagination. He put down the empty glass, turned out the lights.

Alone in bed, he closed his eyes and stretched out. His body began to unwind, relax. It had felt so good to be with Klara Kopek tonight, to be kissed, caressed, stimulated, excited, to feel a woman's warm, yielding body in his arms, responding to his passion uninhibitedly. And yet, even at the height of his ecstasy, Curt had been conscious that something was missing. He didn't love her. Just as he'd never loved Madeline Dupre, only grasped the opportunity to express his frustrated physical desires when overwhelming temptation presented itself. Would any other flesh and blood man have done otherwise? But instead of falling asleep satiated and happy as he'd expected to do, all he could feel was a terrible guilt because tonight, yet again, he had betrayed Marianna.

As soon as Curt had left the next morning, Marianna went out onto Madison Avenue and hailed a passing cab. A large tip to the driver ensured that he would keep a respectably safe distance between his own vehicle and Curt's automobile; across Brooklyn Bridge, around the perimeter of Prospect Park; then, as she saw Curt drive through the tall iron studio gates, she knew that following him, this morning at least, had been in vain. She got the cab driver to take her back into Manhattan and deposit her in midtown.

She went shopping in some of the exclusive gown shops and R. H. Macy's department store, making purchases that she didn't really need: silk stockings, accordion-pleated petticoats, handkerchiefs, shoes. She wanted to keep herself feverishly busy until it was time to go out into the street, find another cab and lie in wait for Curt when he left the Vitagraph studios in Brooklyn.

She hailed one in plenty of time and arranged for the driver to station himself near the corner of Prospect Avenue hard by the park, so that there was a clear, unobstructed view of the road leading from the studios up ahead. Sure enough, at twenty minutes past five, she caught sight of Curt's automobile coming at speed towards them, followed by a cab which she'd noticed driving by empty a little while before.

'Follow that automobile. If you can, keep behind the cab in front so that it doesn't see us.'

'OK, ma'am. It may be a little bumpy.'

'I don't care. Just drive.' She opened her handbag and placed a ten-dollar bill on the seat in front of her.

Curt came to a halt on the other side of the Brooklyn

Bridge. 'Stop here, just for a moment. Not too near.' Marianna watched in astonishment as the cab in front of them, instead of gathering speed and passing Curt by, drew up alongside his automobile; as she continued to watch, a young woman climbed out – without paying the driver – and a smiling Curt helped her into his passenger seat. Beneath the tailored jacket of her smart walking suit, Marianna's heart began to pound wildly. Her driver glanced back over his shoulder.

'You still want that I should follow the automobile, ma'am?'

'Wherever it goes.'

'You're payin' the fare.'

Through midtown, uptown, towards Central Park. Onto 59th Street and into the Upper West Side, past Riverside Drive, between Riverside and High Bridge Park, the Hudson River gleaming in the early evening light. As they approached the smart district of Washington Heights, Marianna told her driver to slow down and keep his distance. Up ahead, Curt had parked his automobile in the tree-lined street, and was helping the girl with him from the passenger side. At the bottom of the steps leading to one of the mid-terrace brownstones, they paused to kiss on the lips; a hot, surging wave of anger washed over her. Her hands began to shake uncontrollably.

'I've made a mistake,' she managed to say in a barely audible voice. She fought to regain some of her composure. 'It isn't my brother after all.' Unbearable, unendurable, to have a cab driver knowing the truth. 'Will you please turn round and go back to Madison Avenue?'

'Sure thing, lady.' As the cab passed the now deserted steps of the brownstone, Marianna peered from the window and noted the number of the house Curt and the girl had gone into: number 228. No need to write it down, as she'd written down the licence plate of the girl's cab half an hour before. The number, the address, the picture of Curt and the girl kissing in the street outside it, would remain indelibly printed on her mind.

Back on Madison Avenue, she waited until Bridget had

taken the children for their tea, then she telephoned the cab company.

The information they gave her was more than a little interesting: they had been paid one month in advance to send a driver to collect a passenger from 228 Washington Heights each morning at the same time, and take her to the Vitagraph Motion Picture studios in Brooklyn. At five o'clock, they were to collect a passenger from the studios and leave her on the South Street side of the Brooklyn Bridge. Marianna thanked them, and replaced the earpiece.

She left the hall, walked into the drawing room. Though she never drank spirits before dinner – some days not at all – she poured herself a large glass of French brandy to steady her nerves. The rich, dark liquid burned her gullet as she swallowed it. She sat down, unused to the effect it almost instantaneously produced; for a moment, the whole room swam in front of her eyes. But it didn't matter; even the nausea and dizziness was welcome because somehow it helped to blot out the appalling anguish and pain. How could he do this to her – deceive her, betray her – after all the sacrifices she'd made for him, after everything she'd done?

No doubt he wouldn't come sneaking back from his little love-nest at Washington Heights until the early hours, hoping that by then she would already be in bed. So be it. When the moment of giddiness and disorientation had passed, Marianna got to her feet and went upstairs. She didn't want to see him. She didn't want to talk to him. She was afraid that if by some chance he came home early, it would be impossible for her to hide her feelings and she would betray herself.

All she needed now was to fit a name to the face; the face she'd glimpsed only momentarily. Two facts, at least, were obvious to her now. The first, that the girl worked at the Vitagraph studios. The second, judging by the clothes she wore, not in an exalted enough position by any means to afford the rent on an elegant brownstone in Washington Heights . . . was it reasonable to suppose that it was Curt who was paying it for her? The very thought of it filled her with almost uncontrollable fury. As she sat at her dressing table brushing out her hair, the reflection that stared back at her was bitter. How long, she wondered, had he and the girl been lovers?

At dinner, Marianna sat alone at one end of the long dining table, the only sound in the room the gentle ticking of the mantel clock. She thought ahead, to tomorrow, and the day after that, and the longer she sat there alone the greater her deep, all-consuming anger gradually became. She was obsessed with finding out the identity of her hated rival, but she realized that, because of her desire for complete anonymity, this was a task for which she would need discreet professional assistance, just as her father had all those years ago when he'd paid the Pinkerton Detective Agency in Chicago to compile a dossier on Curt. Tomorrow, she would do it.

She was not F. H. Eastbridge's daughter for nothing.

CHAPTER NINETEEN

The final day's shooting on the picture had finished at last and Curt was enjoying an ice-cold beer with one of the cameramen off set. 'Hey, Curt . . . bet you're real glad this one's in the can, huh? Now you can relax a little. Which reminds me.' He wiped his lips on the back of his sleeve appreciatively. 'I'm organizing a little party for some of the guys out on Long Island this weekend . . . why not come along? There's no dressing up, no formality, just plenty of booze, ragtime and pretty girls . . . what d'you say?'

Curt laughed and finished his beer. 'Doesn't sound much like a party I can bring my wife to.'

'Hey, who said anythin' about wives?' He winked. 'Come on . . . it'll do you good to unwind after all the filming. You know what they say about all work an' no play, Curt!'

Curt thought about it for a moment. After Marianna's dinner party tonight they had nothing special planned for the weekend, and he hated the thought of Klara having to spend all Saturday and Sunday alone up at Washington Heights. As he had to be so careful about where he took her, and it was too great a risk for them to be seen in central Manhattan together, the Long Island party on Saturday sounded an ideal solution. 'I'd like to come, if I can bring a friend.'

'Anyone I know?'

'Just a girl I met recently.' He placed a finger on his lips and his companion smiled knowingly. 'I think she'd enjoy herself.'

'Enough said . . . we all got to let our hair down sometime, huh? Here, got a piece o' paper on you? I'll write down the time and the address.'

Curt took it from him, read it, then put it away in his pocket. 'OK . . . thanks. I'll be there.'

Elynor lay in bed, wide awake, listening to the sound of ragtime coming from the Victrola in the room below. Momma and Daddy had had a dinner party tonight, and she and Gene – and then Alice, who'd woken up – had tiptoed to the edge of the landing after Bridget had made them wash and go to bed, to watch the guests arrive and come into the front hall. Elynor had recognized some of them.

There was Mr Frohman – or, rather, tonight there were two Mr Frohmans, Mr Charles Frohman whom Daddy used to act for at the Lyceum Theatre – and his brother, whose name was Daniel, who was involved in making moving pictures. There was a famous stage actress called Maud Adams, who looked very striking and very beautiful in a pale green satin gown with lots of jewels, and an older lady (who could have been Mrs Frohman, but Elynor wasn't sure which brother she was married to), who wore an incredible fur stole which fascinated Alice, as it had lots of little dead animals hanging on the ends of it.

There were other people from the Vitagraph Moving Picture Company whom Elynor didn't recognize; they laughed a lot, and made jokes, and everyone seemed to know each other. Of all the ladies who had been invited, Elynor thought that Momma looked by far the best, in her lovely pale lavender silk evening gown with cream lawn neck and sleeves, and her hair all piled up and wound with feathers, pearls and jewels.

The three of them – Alice was yawning by now – had stood on the landing until everyone had gone into the drawing room and the door was closed. Then, reluctantly, Gene had told his sisters that unless they wanted Bridget to come upstairs and catch them out of bed, they'd best go back to their rooms. Alice didn't want to go, and Elynor and Gene had had to make her.

'Why are Momma and Daddy all nice to each other when they have people home, and then yell at each other when everybody's gone again?'

'Because it's not polite to yell in front of guests,' Gene

had explained patiently. 'Anyhow, they haven't yelled at each other much these past few weeks. Daddy's not been home at all.'

'Is Daddy going to make another moving picture, Ellie?' Elynor had made her small sister climb back into bed and pulled the covers over her. 'I don't think Momma likes him doing that.'

'It's none of our business, Alice. Now you have to turn out your light and go to sleep, or Bridget will hear you, and she'll tell Momma.'

'Bridget always says she'll tell Momma . . . but she never does.' Already, Alice had mastered the art of twisting servants round her little finger. 'Anyhow, I want Daddy to come up and tell me a story.'

'Go to sleep, Alice.' Elynor got up and went to the door. 'Daddy can't come up and read to you now . . . you know he's too busy.'

'Daddy said he's never too busy for me.'

'He is when he and Momma have got guests downstairs.' She waved good night and closed Alice's bedroom door, ignoring the protest from the other side. Then she went back to her own room again.

But once she was wide awake, it was difficult to go back to sleep; from downstairs, she could hear the lively ragtime tunes coming from the Victrola, the sound of laughter and voices. Though it kept her awake the sound made her happy; it was so nice to hear people laughing, talking to each other in normal voices. But she knew, instinctively, that once all the guests had gone and Momma and Daddy were alone again, the quarrelling and the shouting would start. Sometimes, when it got very loud, it would make her cry and she'd bury her head beneath the bedclothes. Alice wasn't old enough to understand but she and Gene would often talk about it when she wasn't listening.

'Why do you think they yell at each other all the time? Is it something to do with us?'

'I guess it might be. Momma said that Daddy spoils Alice, and it makes her as mad as hell . . . maybe that's why they do it.'

'I think it's something else, Gene . . . something to do with Daddy acting in moving pictures. Momma wants him to act on the stage instead. But for some reason, he doesn't want to do that.'

'Maybe Mr Frohman will talk him into it. Maybe that's why Momma's invited him to the dinner party tonight. So he can talk Daddy into giving up moving pictures and going back on the stage again.'

'Maybe. But if he doesn't, they'll keep arguing and yelling at each other.'

Elynor turned over, closed her eyes; her eyelids were growing heavy now. The gay ragtime tune, the chatter and the laughter coming from downstairs seemed to grow fainter, until she couldn't hear them any more, and she fell asleep, dreaming that everything between her parents was all right again.

Marianna had watched him carefully, intently, from her place at the end of the dining table; she studied his face. He was laughing at something that Daniel Frohman had told him and his handsome, boyish features were creased with mirth; it was so long since Marianna had heard him laugh like that that part of her – the part that still slavishly adored him, the part that all the bitter arguments and estrangement had left untouched – weakened under the spell his charm and charisma could still cast. While everyone round the table was talking and laughing together, she sat there asking herself when, and why, she and Curt had gone wrong.

Had it been at the very beginning – although neither of them had realized it then – when her shyness and deep inhibitions had sown the first seeds of dissension between them? Sex had always been so important to Curt, while the physical side of their marriage had left her cold. Had it been when Frohman had cast him in the leading role of Monte Cristo and their relationship had begun to founder under the weight of his success and new-found fame? Or was it because she hated the idea of his involvement in moving pictures, becoming so well known that he was almost public property, that the fear she'd always had of losing him had become a reality? Perhaps she would never know for sure; that was the tragedy. Though they shared the same house, ate at the same table, though he was sitting here with her tonight, Marianna knew she had lost him. If she had doubted it before, the moment she'd glimpsed him and the unknown young girl together outside the brownstone in Washington Heights, she knew it for sure.

At that moment, he glanced up and their eyes met; involuntarily, she felt a lump rising in her throat; behind her eyes, the sudden smarting of tears. She kept her face as devoid of emotion as she could, but inside she was being torn apart. She would have given anything – except for her strong, inborn sense of dignity – to stand up in front of them all and denounce him for what he'd done to her, to let everyone round this table know how he'd lied, cheated and deceived her. It almost gave her a perverse sense of pleasure, knowing that, if she chose to, that was exactly what she could do. But she knew that she would not do it. Intolerable, to have anyone else knowing how deeply Curt had wounded her, unthinkable that other people should find out that his love for her was dead.

She wanted to hurt him back; to shame him, to humiliate him, to make him suffer. How easy, how much more pleasurable that would have been had she not still loved him with all her heart.

For the first time in months, they ate breakfast as a family. Neither of them failed to appreciate the irony.

Curt intended to lie to Marianna about where he intended to spend the evening – Shawn was already giving him an alibi. Marianna intended to lie to him about how she intended to spend the morning.

She sat there holding her coffee cup in her hands while he laughed and chatted to the children. Barely a morsel of food had passed her lips. And, when Bridget came into the room to clear the table and Marianna got up to leave, Elynor was the only one who noticed. She followed her mother into the front hall.

299

'Daddy's promised to take us in the park as he doesn't have to go to the studio today. Are you coming with us, Momma?'

'No, Ellie. I have some things to do in midtown.'

'Daddy said he has to go into midtown this morning, too, while we do our lessons. Are you going to go together in his automobile?'

'No.' She forced herself to smile. 'He isn't ready yet. I have to leave right now.'

Elynor hesitated, screwing up her courage. 'Shall I ask him to hurry up and go with you now?'

Marianna's smile was almost genuine this time; young as Elynor was, she could sense that there was something wrong between her parents. 'No, I don't think so. He's been so busy at the studios for so many weeks, I think he'd rather spend time with you now he has the chance.'

She went out, walked along Madison Avenue until a cab came in sight, and then she hailed it. She asked the driver to wait a while. Fifteen minutes later she saw Curt come out of the house and start his automobile, then head in the direction of Broadway.

He parked outside Joseph Fleischman's, the florist at 71, and then disappeared inside; five minutes later he emerged again, and set off in the opposite direction. He was headed, she could tell, straight to Shawn's apartment on 119th Street. She instructed her driver to take her back to midtown.

Fleischman's was busy at this time of the morning and, while Marianna waited to be served, she looked around her. It was a large, long, elegant interior, each of its four walls almost completely covered with ornate, full-length mirrors. Potted plants in exquisite hand-painted jardinières lined one side; on the other, huge urns holding almost every procurable flower were reflected in the mirrors behind and in front of them and, in the centre, beneath three rows of tiered glass chandeliers, a wide table with stacks of tissue and rolls of ribbon stood where each purchase was carefully wrapped.

After a few moments, an attentive assistant apologized

that she'd been kept waiting. Marianna smiled her blandest smile. Her story must sound utterly plausible; and at all costs she mustn't reveal her name.

'I asked my husband to call by and place an order for flowers for a friend . . . the address was 228 Washington Heights. Could you please check that order was placed for me?' Another smile. 'He can be a little forgetful.'

'I'll check our order book, madam, if you'd care to wait.' She was taking a chance; could she be wrong? Curt could have ordered the flowers for her, maybe as a sop to his guilty conscience. But when had he last sent her flowers? If she was wrong, it didn't matter. All she had to do was smile and say thank you and walk out of the shop. If she was right, and the flowers were destined for his cheap little whore, then she would have succeeded in discovering her name without recourse to outside help. Nervously, she watched the assistant turning the pages of the order book.

'Yes, there is an order here for delivery to 228 Washington Heights.' She was in luck. 'Three dozen red roses to Miss Klara Kopek.'

'Thank you.' Marianna's throat felt so tight from anguish and rage that she could barely speak the words.

Outside in the street, she began to walk. On and on, without purpose, without direction. She walked and walked until her legs and feet ached and she felt she couldn't walk any longer. She found a teashop and went inside, sat down at the most secluded table, as far away from the window, the street, the crowds, as possible. Afterwards, she couldn't remember what she'd ordered, if she had drunk anything at all. Three dozen red roses to Miss Klara Kopek. The words kept going round and round in her mind until she thought she would go mad.

She couldn't remember paying for her order, couldn't remember getting up and walking out of the shop. Klara Kopek. Klara Kopek. Klara Kopek.

What hurt most of all was that the first bouquet he'd ever sent her had come from Fleischman's, and when she remembered the thrill and joy she'd felt then, it seemed almost sacrilege that, callously and unthinkingly, Curt had ordered red roses for his mistress at that very same place.

'Curt, don't be a fool.'

'It's just a party.' What the hell was the matter with Shawn today? 'Just a little fun, a chance for everyone to unwind with the picture wrapped up . . . where's the harm in that? OK, so none of the guys will be bringing their wives along, but we all need to let our hair down once in a while.'

'I have a hunch that it'll be more than hair that's let down tonight. You lost your mind, or what?'

'Shawn, for Christ's sake don't go all puritanical on me. I need a break, OK?' He'd never known Shawn to be like this before; the last thing he'd ever have figured him for was a wet blanket. 'Look. Why don't you come too? I'll introduce you to some of the guys from the set.'

'Is that girl going with you?'

'Klara? Yeah, I'm taking her.' He began to drink the beer Shawn had given him. 'I thought she'd enjoy a night out with me someplace where we don't have to hide in case somebody recognizes me.'

'If nearly everyone at the party comes from the studio, all of them will.'

'Shawn, it isn't like that . . . you don't think they invited Charlie Kent or Bill Smith along, do you?' Curt laughed. 'This is just a little fun for the rank and file. Come on, loosen up! You don't begrudge me a little fun, do you?'

Shawn was silent for a moment. 'That's why you're here, isn't it? You want me to cover for you with Marianna?'

'I'd do the same for you.'

'You won't have to. I'm not married, remember?'

'Is this a moral lecture, or what?'

'Last night, at the dinner party. You hardly spoke a word to her all evening. Hell, Curt, do you want her to suspect something?'

Curt ran a hand through his hair. He was beginning to wish he'd never come with Shawn in this mood. 'Shawn, you know the way it is between Marianna and me. We don't even sleep in the same room any more!' He got up, started pacing the room. 'She's so cold, she never lets me come close . . . I just can't reach her any more.' He was a fraction away from losing his temper for the first time. In all the years they'd known each other, they'd never had even one serious falling out. But Shawn had always understood him, hadn't he? 'For Christ's sake, you don't expect me to live like a monk, do you?'

'No, I don't expect that. But I thought you had a little more discrimination, that's all.' He'd been holding his tongue ever since he'd found out about Klara Kopek and Curt, but he couldn't hold it any longer. 'Look . . . we go back a long way. I know the score. Marianna's gone cold on you, so you go looking somewhere else. I'd probably do the same. But Madeline Dupre and the like are one thing; a nondescript little extra from the slums on the Lower East Side is somethin' else.' Curt couldn't believe what he was hearing. 'You've known her for five minutes and already you've set her up in a swank brownstone in Washington Heights, paying for her food, her clothes, and a cab to take her backwards and forwards to the studio like she was the Governor's lady. Think about it, Curt. What happens when you get tired of her and you want out, huh? You think she's goin' to just let all that go and kiss you meekly goodbye? Forget about it.'

'Klara's a sweet girl and I won't get tired of her! Besides, you have any idea what kind of place she was livin' in before I moved her out of it?'

'Put the violins away, Curt – I'm not buyin'. Sure, it stinks on the Lower East Side. But any girl who can survive there is a real tough cookie. You're livin' in dreamland if you think for one fuckin' minute that she's goin' to let all you've bin throwin' her way slip through her little fingers, I'd bet my last cent on it. You walked right into this one, Curt . . . she's got you hook, line and sinker. Lie down with dogs, you get up with fleas.'

'So, you won't cover for me when I take her to Long Island tonight?'

'I'll cover for you. That's what friends are for. But that doesn't mean I like what you're doin' to Marianna.'

Now it was Curt's turn to be angry. 'Somehow, I don't think this would be her kind of party.'

'You sonofabitch.' So many times Shawn had called him that jokingly, and they'd laughed together. But Curt knew by the expression in his eyes and the tone of his voice that this time he really meant it.

The wail of ragtime from the Victrola, turned up as loud as it would go, had reached deafening point. Empty glasses and bottles were strewn everywhere – across tables, on ledges and window sills, stuffed down the sides of chairs – and, all around the room, couples now almost too drunk to stand staggered about giggling, clinging to each other as they tried to dance to the music, while others openly copulated in corners of the room and even on the floor.

Though it had all started out respectably enough, as the drink began to flow and inhibitions were lowered, it had degenerated into chaos; a troop of near-naked dancing girls, specially hired for the party, had performed on the table tops, then gone off with any men who wanted them into the adjoining rooms. Someone had brought out an Eastman Kodak and started taking pictures, to the hilarity of almost everyone present.

'Hey, Curt! Smile!' Pip Waldo steadied himself against the wall and almost doubled up as he tried to aim the lens in the right direction. He collapsed in a heap on the floor, rocking with laughter. 'Aw, shit! No flash. I've taken a whole reel of pictures with no fuckin' flash!' Curt led Klara into one of the adjoining bedrooms to get away from the worst excesses of the other party guests; when the dancing girls had first appeared, she'd been more than a little shocked.

'Curt, how can they do such things, and in front of all those men?' He pulled her down gently on the bed beside him, began unbuttoning her dress. 'I don't think they care much about modesty, so long as they get paid.' He slowly drew her dress, and then the frilled camisole beneath it, down to her waist. 'I'm sorry . . . things have gotten a little wild . . . but I think I'm too drunk right now to drive you home.'

Halfway through making love, Pip Waldo burst in on them with more drinks. 'Hey, you two! C'mon now . . . you gotta drink a toast . . . try this, Curt . . .' Hardly able to put one foot in front of the other, he slurped half the contents of the two glasses all over the floor. 'Try it . . . go on, try it . . . I put a real special secret ingredient in it. Kinda gives you an extra lift . .' He staggered out again, giggling insanely like a schoolgirl, singing a bawdy vaudeville song at the top of his voice. Curt pressed his lips to the glass and sipped the fizzy, colourless cocktail, and, as it burned his throat and rushed straight to his head, everything around him suddenly exploded into one long, numbing vortex of blinding light.

Delucca had been woken by the noise of his two boys playing in the back yard. He dragged himself up, propped himself up on one elbow and irritably rubbed at his eyes. Six o'clock. Maudie still wasn't back from her mother's place in East Flatbush and he was on duty in just four hours. Hell, he hated night duty!

He got up, pulled on a pair of pants and grabbed a clean shirt from the closet, then went outside. 'Hey, Bret, Clay! Keep it down, will ya? Sounds like the goddam second Civil War out there!' The two boys ran indoors, carrying their ball.

'Sorry, Dad! Gonna have a game with us before Momma comes in?'

'Forget about it. I'm on night duty tonight . . . maybe the weekend.' He went into the kitchen to make himself some black coffee; he could have done with sleeping for another couple of hours. Fuckin' kids! He was just finishing his second cup of coffee when Maudie came back, with a complaint that the elevated train had been late leaving west Brooklyn and another sob story about her old lady. Delucca had heard them all fifty times before.

'Poor Momma, it wasn't one of her good days today . . .

305

when I got there, she'd brought out all her old pictures of Poppa and she was crying again.'

'What for? He's better off not bein' around her! She'd drive him crazy. Anyhow, just tell me when she last *had* a good day.'

Maudie bustled around in the kitchen. 'Roy, you can be so mean when you talk about Momma sometimes. She's old and lonely. We all gotta get old someday.'

'Every time you go over to see her, she puts the squeeze on. Somethin' she never tries with me . . . 'cos she knows you're a soft touch.'

'You're just sore because you're on night duty again this week!'

'Fuckin' Rawlins!' Angrily, Delucca lit up a cigarette. He'd already done his night shift, but then one of the other guys on the precinct had reported sick, and Chief Rawlins had given the extra duty to him. Pure spite, what else? He got up, pushed away the cup and kissed her on the cheek. Time to start getting washed up and ready. Might as well. Even if he went straight back to bed, Delucca knew that he'd never sleep.

He was in a foul mood as he made his way across the Williamsburg Bridge and headed in the direction of the precinct; the street ahead of him was bathed in darkness, almost deserted. The whole night stretched monotonously ahead, like a road with no ending.

God help anyone who crossed his path over the next few hours.

He'd just got back from a futile trip to Chinatown in the early hours when the desk sergeant handed him a message.

'Got a report of a disturbance out at Long Island while you was down on East Broadway, Roy. Better take a couple of the uniform division guys and look into it.'

Delucca let loose a string of oaths. Long Island, at this time of night! Hell, the place would be blacker than a nigger's arse.

'What kind of disturbance? Disturbances are uniform's line, not mine.'

306

'Could be illegal hooch . . . gotta be looked into. You know Chief Rawlins' brief a few weeks back about upstate distilleries . . .'

'Yeah, yeah . . . so give me the details and I'll get on it.'

'Telephone complaint, from a resident . . . some kinda wild party goin' on by all accounts. I've taken down the address . . . here. Seems the house where the party is belongs to some guy from the Vitagraph moving picture studios.'

'You don't say.'

It took Delucca and two patrolmen from uniform division more than an hour and a quarter to reach the house out at Massapequa; by the time they got there the party was over and there was hardly a sound.

Most of the revellers had already left – if they could stand, Delucca thought, as he gazed around at the glasses and empty bottles that littered the floor – in hire cabs, according to the owner of the house, who was nursing a vicious hangover and barely able to answer the front door at all.

'The police . . . ?' He fell back against a wall and rubbed his eyes. 'What is it, what's the matter? Someone crash their automobile on the way back?'

'I'm not in the mood for jokes, buddy.' Delucca signalled to the two men with him to go through the house, looking for evidence of illegal hooch or anything else he could slap on a charge for. 'We got a complaint about the racket that was comin' from this house, and I'm here to take a look around, OK?'

'Help yourself, officer.' Pip Waldo staggered along the floor in front of him and sank into the nearest chair. 'Sorry, it's a hell of a mess. Nobody was in much shape to give me a hand clearin' all this trash away . . . but I guess it'll keep.'

'I want a complete list of everyone who was here tonight, you got that?' He walked around the room, kicking glass and bottles out of his way. 'You got any thought for the neighbours around here?'

'It was just a party . . . we were just havin' a little fun, you know how it is. We'd just finished a picture and were

307

unwinding a little, having a kinda celebration. Didn't realize the music got that loud.'

'Only 'cos you were all canned outa your minds! As well as the list of names, I want to know where you got all this booze from. Suppliers' names and addresses, how many bottles and what of . . . am I coming over loud and clear?'

Waldo put a hand to his throbbing head. 'Look, that stuff all came from legitimate sources. I swear it. I even got the receipts somewhere.'

'Well, you better find 'em then, hadn't you?'

Delucca carried on prowling around the downstairs rooms among the debris, hoping to find something else that would merit a charge on Waldo; disturbing the peace looked like just about the only thing he could throw at him so far. He kicked open the door of a little room that led off the main room, and something lying on the bed suddenly caught his eye. He went over and picked it up. A woman's camisole.

The bed was untidy and rumpled; he grinned. From the tell-tale stains on the top of the coverlet, Delucca had a good idea of what had been going on in here. He folded up the garment and stuffed it in his pocket. Things could be beginning to fall into place, after all.

'What else has bin goin' on here tonight, Waldo? Loud music, booze, women. What I wanna know is . . . what kind of women?'

'What the hell do you mean by that? They were people from the studio, I already told you. Friends, guys I work with. Sure, most of 'em brought along a girl. Any law against that?'

'If they was prostitutes that might put a whole new complexion on things, wouldn't you say?'

Waldo's aching head was clearing rapidly with alarm.

'Just what are you tryin' to accuse me of?'

'You tell me. For instance, I just found evidence in that room off there that two people used one of your beds for something other than sittin' on.'

'OK, OK . . . so things did get a little wild . . . a lot of us got drunk. But that's all. Like I said, it was just a party.

Take a look around all you want to. I ain't got nothin' to hide.' Delucca stalked off without answering.

He was on his way out when he noticed the Eastman Kodak. He picked it up. Strange, he thought, turning it over in his hands, to have a camera in a room where there'd been a wild party. From the little he knew about photography, he was sure that if Waldo had used the camera that evening – for whatever reason – he would have needed to use some kind of artificial light to get a picture. But if he had taken some, Delucca could use the prints to identify who had been at the party, match them with the list of names Waldo would give him and see if he'd been telling the truth. It was a long shot, admittedly, but worth a try: if Delucca spotted the face of any known prostitute, he could push for a conviction. With the reputation moving pictures had with the 'respectable' elements in the city, it wouldn't be difficult to persuade a judge that a cameraman from the Vitagraph studio was using his hideaway for immoral purposes. Delucca chuckled as he tucked the Eastman Kodak under his arm. Even if he couldn't make the charge stick, it would sure frighten the shit out of the guy. Serve the bastard right for dragging him all the way out here to fucking Long Island when he could have been snoozing in his warm office back at the precinct.

'You use this tonight?'

'When the party first started, sure. Got a few group shots. Just a souvenir, that's all. Like I said before, we was celebrating the end of the picture shoot.'

'How can you take indoor pictures without light?'

'Easy. I got a portable arc lamp. Rigged it up myself. You want to see it? I'll show you how it works.'

'I'll take your word for it. But I'm hangin' on to this baby. I'll get the pictures developed and let you have 'em later. I'll keep 'em while I check the faces with that list of names you haven't given me.' He signalled to the two patrolmen outside that he was just about ready to leave. Dawn light had started to streak the dark night sky. 'Waldo, I want those goddam names . . . every single one of 'em . . . you hear me? Delivered to the precinct by this time tomorrow. Otherwise I'll be back on your doorstep . . . and this time, I won't be so nice.'

Waldo nodded slowly. Hell, his head felt three times its normal size. He couldn't remember the party beginning or ending, he couldn't remember who'd been there or what anyone had done. Coffee. Strong. Black. Later, maybe some of his memory would come back.

Marianna had been awake when she'd heard him come back and quietly let himself into the house, just before dawn. So, he'd decided to come crawling back from his little whore's bed, thinking that she would be fast asleep and that, if he was there when she came down the next morning, she'd be fooled into supposing that he had come home much earlier last night. She lay there in the semi-darkness, with the bitterness growing like a canker inside her, thinking of that hated name. Klara Kopek.

She knew, now, exactly what she would do. Give them a little more rope, give them a little more time to enjoy their secret fornicating together, and then she would strike. At dinner on Friday evening Bill Smith had mentioned travelling with Curt and some of the production crew to a location site upstate to check it out for the next film, but no date had been decided on; Marianna could wait. When Curt was out of the way she intended to take a little unannounced trip to 228 Washington Heights and let Miss Klara Kopek know exactly what she thought of her. She knew just how to deal with Curt when he returned from his trip, and for the first time since their marriage he was going to discover the hard way that nobody played an Eastbridge for a fool and got away with it.

She was to get her chance far sooner than she thought. 'Bill Smith's OKed the script and we're leaving to check out the location at High Point midday next Tuesday,' he suddenly announced to her almost a week later. 'It's quite a way so we'll have to stop overnight.'

She was sitting at the writing desk in the library and even without turning round she could tell by the agitated way he was hovering in the doorway that he was anxious to be gone. To her, no doubt. The Kopek whore. She barely paused with her letter writing.

'I'll tell Bridget to pack a bag for you.'

It was only when she reached the junction of 191st Street and Washington Heights that the first tremor of nervousness began to hit her. Until then, she'd fed on her boiling anger and simmering outrage at what Curt had done to her, at the humiliation of being supplanted in his life by a cheap little bit-part player, from her foreign-sounding name no doubt from a Lower East Side immigrant family, not even born in America. For someone with as much pride as Marianna, it was the ultimate insult.

At the bottom of the steps to 228, she hesitated for a moment to regain her composure. Whatever happened, she was determined to hold on to her dignity at any price. She took a deep breath, went up the steps and reached for the knocker on the door.

In the hire cab that day when she'd first seen them together, Marianna had only caught a fleeting glimpse of the girl. Not enough to be able to recognize her again, not enough to see how young or how pretty she was. The reality when the door opened and she saw her face to face for the first time was a shock. Was this mousy-haired, insipid little nobody really the kind of woman Curt found attractive? The girl stared at her with round, questioning eyes.

'Klara Kopek?'

She smiled. 'Yes.'

'My name is Marianna Koenig.' The smile vanished instantly and her mouth, a wide, full-lipped mouth, fell open. She even had the audacity to look angry.

'What do you want with me?'

'What the hell do you think I want?' Klara tried in vain to close the door on her, but Marianna's foot was already inside. With a strength she never knew she had, she shoved it forward so hard that Klara Kopek was catapulted backwards into the hall and halfway through the open door of the parlour, losing her balance in the process. She struggled to her feet as Marianna followed her into the room. The first thing she saw was the red roses that Curt had had sent from Fleischman's, wilting a little now, and the sight of them only inflamed her furious anger. Klara looked at her as if she hated her.

'I have nothing to say to you!'

'Really? I have plenty to say to you.' Now that she was here, now that they were face to face, she felt icy calm. 'I came here to see for myself just what kind of creature would stoop to sleeping with a married man who has three young children, behind his wife's back . . . now I've satisfied my curiosity. I can see exactly what you are. A cheap, common, miserable little slut with all the moral fibre of an alley cat.'

'*You* . . . you have no right to come here! This is my house, mine and Curt's. He loves me, not you. He never loved you.' The girl's dark eyes were full of spite. 'He only married you because you had money, because your father was an important man. But he wants me for myself . . . just myself.' Marianna's elegance, her beauty, had startled Klara. She had not expected Curt's wife to look like this. More than anything, she wanted to hurt her. 'When he comes back, I will tell him that you forced your way in here and insulted me . . . and he will be very angry.'

Marianna harnessed her pain, her anguish. What the girl was saying, could it possibly be true? The thought of it, and of Curt telling her so, utterly devastated her. But this was no time to show emotion, or weakness. 'When he comes back, he'll come back to his home and his children . . . Madison Avenue. And to me. After what I shall have to say to him, I can assure you, Klara Kopek, that he won't be honouring you with his presence here any more. Except to tell you that unless you find yourself somewhere else to live – or some other fool to keep you – you'll be out on the street. Do I make myself perfectly clear?'

A sneer began to spread across the girl's round, flat face. 'You think he will stay with you because you have his children? That he would turn his back on me because you say so? Well, you are wrong about that.' A taunting note came into her voice. 'You see, I am having Curt's baby.'

The words hit Marianna like a knife-wound. 'It will be born in the spring.'

'I don't think so.' A terrible numb pain, heralding one of the crippling headaches which so often afflicted her when she was under stress, began to throb across her forehead. 'I happen to know exactly how long my husband has been seeing you, and if you are pregnant, then it certainly isn't by him.'

With a shout of rage, the girl sprang at her, tearing at her clothes, spitting, screaming insults in Polish. Marianna stood back, then retaliated with a stunning slap across the face. Klara Kopek rushed at her like a wild animal.

For a few desperate moments they struggled with each other, reeling back and forth around the room, until Klara grasped one of the fire irons and came towards Marianna menacingly. To defend herself, she quickly picked up a tray on the nearby table and hit the girl full in the face with all her might. The fire iron clattered from her hand into the grate, she lost her balance completely as she tripped over the fireside rug, and went sprawling headlong into the brass fender where she struck her head with a sickening thud.

Marianna stood for a moment breathing heavily, paralysed by shock and fear. The girl wasn't moving. She called her name. Bent down and touched her. There was no pulse, no movement, no sign of breathing. A pool of dark red blood was slowly oozing from the gaping wound in her head.

Marianna backed away in horror, staggered back towards the door. Then she turned and ran.

313

CHAPTER TWENTY

Delucca made his way through the narrow, dirty labyrinth of streets in the no-man's-land between Chinatown and Little Italy, until he came to a small, narrow-fronted shop with a battered front door and filthy windows. Going inside, he closed the door behind him and pushed the 'Closed' sign against the dirty glass.

'Long time no see, Russo.'

'Mr Delucca!' The look of dismay was quickly covered by an expression of false pleasure. 'It good to see you again.'

'Like fuck it is! You'd stab me in the back as soon as look at me, and we both know it.'

'No, no! That not true!'

Delucca smiled. He looked around, at the grimy shelves stacked with cheap, battered boots and shoes, and thought that the only thing that had changed since he'd been here last was that Russo's shop had gotten darker and even filthier, and he looked more shifty and more shit-scared than Delucca remembered. 'So, how's business? Or shouldn't I ask?'

Russo shrugged nervously. Delucca always made him nervous.

'It OK, Mr Delucca . . . I can't complain. I make a living.'

'Only 'cos I chose not to bust you over what I found out was goin' on out in your back room.' Russo hung his head. And he'd thought Delucca wouldn't come back because it had been so long since he'd seen him. He should have bent his ear to the whisper around the streets in these parts, that Delucca was a real mean bastard who you just never got rid of, once he had the finger on you. 'OK. I haven't come here to give you a hard time . . . let's go out back and do us a little business.'

In the dark, dingy little back room, Delucca perched himself on a chair and took an object from his pocket. He held it out in the palm of his hand. 'You see what this is? Yeah, sure you do. A roll o' film from an Eastman Kodak. That no-good brother of yours ever use an Eastman Kodak for those dirty pictures he takes of underage girls? Well, I ain't here for that stuff. I want this developed and I want it done by tomorrow . . . you got that?'

'Yes, Mr Delucca . . . I get it done for you . . . no trouble. I get it done right away.'

Delucca stood up. He smiled. Slowly, he took Russo by the collar and pulled it tight until he started to gag. 'No extra copies. Just one set. And whatever you find on this roll o' film, good or bad, you keep your mouth shut, you got that?'

'I got it, Mr Delucca. Would I double-cross you? Would I open my mouth?'

'If you ever did, I don't have to tell you what I'd do to you . . . do I? Tomorrow. This time. Don't let me down.'

The house was cool, shady, quiet when she reached home; she let herself into the hall with trembling hands, slammed the front door behind her and rushed into the drawing room to pour herself a stiff brandy. She was shaking from head to foot. She sank down on the couch, cradled the glass in both hands. When she drank it, the brandy went straight to her head and made her feel sick.

She thanked God that the house was empty. Bridget had taken the children to the botanical gardens, it was Rosie Neale's and Mrs Dawkins' afternoon off. Curt wouldn't be back until early tomorrow. But when other people were around her, would she still be able to hide her panic and terror, would she still be able to pretend? For the first time in her life, Marianna understood the real meaning of fear. Supposing someone had seen her entering the brownstone at Washington Heights, supposing someone had seen her leave and remembered the time? She got up, unsteadily because her head was still swimming, and began to pace the room.

For once, she was almost grateful for the crippling headache whose onset she'd first felt when she'd confronted Klara Kopek an hour ago, for the pain somehow helped to dull her senses, to blot out everything she desperately wanted to forget.

Hal Goldenthal lit a Havana and smiled as he turned over the balance sheets of his accountant's report for the last quarter: things were looking up. Not only were the figures healthy, but there was a forty per cent growth rate in net receipts over the last twelve months; more, much more than either he or any of his business partners had expected. How right they'd been, he mused now as he glanced up out of his office window at the golden Californian landscape, when they'd left Philadelphia for the west coast on the tide of the moving picture boom, and staked almost every last dollar they owned on forming Telluric Universal: from a single wooden shack, on the corner of Sunset and Gower, with one cameraman and rented equipment, the studio buildings had mushroomed almost as fast as their profits, to two large brick buildings, offices, two directors and two cameramen with French Pathé cameras, who were turning out one-reelers at a rate of four to six movies a week. Goldenthal, born Heinz Goldblum on the Prussian–Lithuanian border forty-nine years before, was the true-life example of the poor eastern European immigrant made good.

The youngest of eight children, he'd become restless and intractable at the age of sixteen, wanting more out of life than toiling from dawn to dusk on the estate of the local landowner. With almost nothing in his pocket except a few coins and a letter of introduction to distant relatives in the north of England, he'd set out one day and walked, literally, from Ostralenka to Bremen, where he'd stowed away aboard a ship bound for Liverpool. When he'd arrived at the house of his father's relatives, they'd taken him in and given him work but, always looking to better himself, he had decided there and then to save enough for steerage fare to America. Fifteen years later, he'd worked himself up from an odd-job boy to a respected salesman in upstate New Jersey, and from there he'd gone on climbing steadily until an out-of-state business trip had brought him to Philadelphia. The nickelodeon craze had been in full swing then, and Goldblum, who had changed his name to Henry Goldenthal shortly after his arrival in New York, had toured the local nickelodeon parlours and five-cent theatres around the town, had instantly seen the possibilities. With the improving technology, coupled with the enormous surge in public demand for the new 'moving pictures', it was only a matter of time before a man with Goldenthal's vision got together with a group of like-minded friends and decided to climb onto the bandwagon.

The move to California, and a sleepy, sparsely populated little town called Hollywood, had been timely: with the formation of the Motion Picture Patents Company in 1908, a cartel formed between the Edison Company and American Mutoscope, with Biograph bringing up the rear, a legal restraint had been imposed on anyone else who wanted to get in on moving pictures. Ignoring the power of the Trust, as it was known, was only at the small independents' peril; when push came to shove, the Trust proved that in the battle for exclusivity and profit, it could get as down and dirty as anyone else. In order to scupper rivals' productions, it thought nothing of hiring heavies to sabotage buildings, equipment, and film; neither was distance any object. The Selig Polyscope studios in Chicago were forced to move their base to the west coast after a 'visit' from the Trust.

Hollywood had grown steadily from as far back as 1887, when Harvey Henderson Wilcox had registered his 120-acre ranch located just northwest of Los Angeles, and the name Hollywood had been given to it by his wife Daeida. Fifteen years later, exhibitor Thomas Tally had opened his electric theatre with seating for two hundred people; one year later, the fast-growing village of Hollywood had been incorporated as a municipality, and construction had begun of what was now a local landmark, the Hollywood Hotel. With the vice-like grip of the Trust in New York, the small independents had fast seen the economic sense of upping sticks and moving west, where the ideal climate, and the exceptional variety of settings for filming – deserts, mountains, villages, seaside and the large metropolis of Los Angeles – were all within easy reach. Not only that. Labour costs were significantly lower than they were in New York City, and extras were cheap to employ: the local population presented a useful mixture of different races and nationalities, including Mexican and Oriental. Hollywood made sense. Though the place itself was primitive and underpopulated by comparison to Los Angeles – a bridle path ran down the centre, and few of the roads were paved at all because the horse was the most sensible method of transport – when he'd arrived there, Goldenthal had immediately seen the potential for development. Another six months, a year maybe, and that palatial ranch-style home he'd dreamed of since he left Philadelphia more than two years ago would become a reality.

What he needed, what Universal needed, was someone special. A name that would add not only prestige, but a touch of magic to their next production. For the past few weeks he'd been turning the question of who that someone might be over and over in his mind. In fact, for days Goldenthal hadn't thought of very much else. A contact from the old days he still kept in touch with in New York regularly sent him studio gossip from the various upstate moving picture companies, and one name always kept coming up; Goldenthal looked at the newspaper cuttings on his desk that his friend had sent him in his last letter, which had taken almost two and a half weeks to arrive. Curt Koenig.

The name spoke for itself; this guy had it all, by every account. Good looks, charisma, photogenic quality second to none. Star appeal. And, most important of all, bankability. Goldenthal made one of his instant decisions; when he had a gut feeling about something or someone, he was never wrong. He wanted Curt Koenig for Universal at any price.

Delucca returned to the dingy little shoemaker's shop between Little Italy and Chinatown at exactly the time he'd said. It was after hours. He gave three sharp raps on the filthy glass window and, within seconds, there was a scurrying sound on the other side and the door was opened for him.

'Well, you got 'em done for me?'

'Sure thing . . . would I let you down, Mr Delucca, sir?' Delucca kicked the door shut behind him and shot the bolt across.

'You're too fond of your own fuckin' skin to do that. OK. Let's see 'em.'

Russo led the way into the back room, and turned up the oil lamp. Christ, it stank! No more than the rest of the place, though. He watched the little man open a drawer and take out a flat package wrapped in grubby brown paper. 'I think you'll be pleased with these, Mr Delucca. I already looked at them.' A knowing look came into his shifty dark eyes. 'They good, yes?'

Without bothering to answer him, Delucca flicked through them. The lighting could have been better but they were remarkably clear otherwise, the top half dozen or so taken before Waldo's party had gotten too wild. The group pictures were innocent enough, with everyone smiling, smoking cigarettes and holding drinks in their hands; there were two or three exposures of a couple of pretty girls pulling faces at the camera; nothing unusual. Until the last three.

'You see what I mean, Mr Delucca? I say they good, yes? My brother done good, huh?' Delucca saw. He saw all right. And he knew that face. It had looked out from a thousand picture postcards and smiled down from theatre and moving picture playbills all over New York City. Delucca wondered what his legions of fans, and the critics from the *Herald* and the *New York Times*, would say if they could see what he was holding in his hands now. A naked Curt Koenig, far gone in drink, making passionate love to an equally naked and equally uninhibited young girl.

319

Delucca smiled. He tucked them away inside his jacket. An idea was already forming in his mind; but it'd keep awhile.

He took out his wallet and extracted a few dollar bills. True, Russo's no-good brother already owed him one, but he was in a generous mood today.

'Thank you very much, Mr Delucca. You very kind.'

'Yeah . . . ain't I just?' He tapped his breast pocket and put a finger to his lips. 'You never saw these, and neither did your brother. You got it?'

Russo knew from past experience just what Roy Delucca was capable of when he was crossed. He shook his head. 'Mr Delucca . . . you was never in here.'

'So I wasn't.'

Curt had taken a hire cab from the station to the brown-stone at Washington Heights. But he felt guilty. He hadn't seen the children for almost two days, and half of him wanted to go back to Madison Avenue first. But against that, he weighed the fact that Klara had been completely alone since he'd left to go upstate, and once he went home it would be almost impossible for him to make a plausible enough excuse to get away. Seeing Klara first, just for an hour or two, was best.

He used his own doorkey to let himself into the house. Strange. When he called out her name there was no answer; had she gone out? He'd told her what time he was getting back to New York and that he'd come to her straight from the station. He shrugged, and went into the parlour; maybe she'd fallen asleep by the fire.

'*Klara!*'

She was lying full length across the rumpled hearth rug, one hand stretched out as if she'd been trying to reach something; her clothes torn, her face disfigured with a large, mottled bruise. There was a long gash in her head and the blood that had poured out of it as she'd hit the heavy brass fender was already congealed in a sickening, sticky pool. '*Klara . . .!*' He knew she was dead before he even touched her; no living human being looked that way. He had just about enough presence of mind amid the anguish and the shock to realize what would happen if he was connected with her; as fast as he could he gathered up every picture of himself and every memento he'd ever given her, and fled from the house.

She lay there in the darkness, still trembling. She'd taken pills to try to knock herself out, but all she'd succeeded in doing was making herself sick. Since yesterday, when she'd come home alone, Marianna hadn't been able to eat a thing. When Bridget came to tell her that Curt was back from the trip to Philadelphia, she had to fight a battle with herself to get up, behave normally, and go down.

He looked ghastly. 'Did you come straight here from the station?' She needed all her self-possession, all her strength of mind to pretend normality.

'Yes.' His voice was dead and flat. 'Are the children OK?'

'Why shouldn't they be? They missed you,' she added, in a softer voice. He was pouring himself a large bourbon; larger than usual. 'How did the trip go?'

'Bill Smith said that if I agree to do the picture, we'll go upstate on location.'

'And will you?'

'I don't know. I just don't know.' Why was he acting so strangely, as if his entire attention was somewhere else? Had he lied to her about coming home directly from the station – had he gone to the brownstone to see Klara Kopek first? He looked in a state of shock. The bourbon was already almost gone and he was topping it up, neat, from the bottle.

'Curt, Bridget is bathing the children right now. They've been asking what time you'll be home . . . so will you go up and see them when they're ready?'

'In a minute.' That, too, was totally unlike him. When he came home, even from the studios each day, the first thing he would always do was see the children. *He's been there*, she told herself, trying to stop the shaking in her hands. *He's been to that house and found her lying there!* A terrible fury seized her. Would he look like this – pale, haggard, unbearably unhappy – if something had happened to her?

Klara Kopek's cruel words came back to haunt her. Had Curt ever really loved her, or had it just been the money and the Eastbridge family name? Would she ever find the courage inside herself to ask him?

'Are you sure nothing's wrong?' He turned to look at her now. 'You seem so far away.'

He couldn't even bring himself to smile, he felt so wretched. Klara. Klara. 'I'm all right.' He swallowed the bourbon and strode out of the room, leaving her too devastated at his coldness even to cry.

He was at the studio in Brooklyn when the news of Klara Kopek's death broke.

One of the girls she had shared the apartment with on the Lower East Side had called to visit and, getting no answer, had peered through the front window. What she'd glimpsed of the room had caused her to raise the alarm and, within the hour, the police had been called and Klara Kopek's body discovered. The news spread through the Vitagraph lot like wildfire.

While everyone was talking about the sensational news, studio staff were trying to keep the swarm of journalists away until Bill Smith could appear and make a statement. He'd been occupied since eleven o'clock that morning talking to the police, who wanted to question anyone who'd known the dead girl.

Curt had broken into a cold sweat when two detectives had come looking for him in his dressing room.

'Mr Koenig, I'm Detective Roy Delucca and this is Detective MacKenzie. You'll have guessed why we're here.'

'Yes.' The single word stuck in his throat; he felt as if he was choking. 'It's terrible news. Unbelievable.' Delucca and MacKenzie exchanged glances. 'I'll help in any way I can.'

'Glad to hear that, Mr Koenig . . . you see, I think you could be more help to us than most of the other people we've talked to this morning.' Delucca was enjoying himself; he thought of those pictures Russo's brother had developed for him and he wanted to laugh out loud. This was going to be fun; cat and mouse. But Koenig didn't know it yet. 'Fact is, Mr Koenig, we're a little curious about 228 Washington Heights, where Miss Kopek's body was found yesterday. Our enquiries have revealed that you not so long ago signed a three-month lease for that very house.' Curt stiffened. So they'd discovered that already; of course, they would. 'What we'd like to know is why Klara Kopek was living there . . . in some luxury, I might add.'

'The explanation's very simple.' Curt told them that he'd needed a place away from home, to study scripts. But how feeble, how hollow that sounded now. 'I guess I offered her the place for the time being on impulse . . . I felt sorry for her, after what she told me about her family, how they'd come from Warsaw when she was fourteen years old. She'd had things kind of rough. That's all there was to it.'

'You must have felt real sorry for her, to lay out seventy-five dollars a month in rent.'

'I paid the first quarter in advance when I signed the lease.'

Delucca perched himself on a chair. 'You signed the lease on the same day she moved into the brownstone, Mr Koenig.' Curt had begun to sweat badly. 'Isn't that kind of a coincidence?'

'It is a coincidence. Fact is, it was the day after I gave her a ride to the station. I'd been thinking about how tough a time she was having, and I wanted to help.'

'It's a pretty roomy house,' MacKenzie put in, getting out a hand-rolled cigarette and lighting up. 'I'm sure there are more than a few girls here who'd like the chance to live in a place like that. Washington Heights is real swanky. I mean, a lotta girls who work here must come from poor backgrounds . . . don't you feel kinda sorry for them, too? A place that size, you could have fitted three or four in comfortably, at least. That'd make more sense.'

'Just what are you getting at?'

Delucca grinned. 'We're just doin' our job, Mr Koenig. And this is a murder enquiry, you do realize?'

'Yes. I'm sorry.'

'But just to get it on record, what we'd like to come straight out and ask you is if your relationship with Klara Kopek was just the way you describe it, or a little something more than that.' Curt looked up sharply. 'Did you sleep with her?'

'Of course not!'

'Did she ever put herself on offer? Kinda like in lieu of paying the rent?'

'She was a nice girl. I don't know who would want to kill her.'

'Nor do we, not right now. But we'll get there in the end.' Delucca got up. 'We'll need to talk to you again, Mr Koenig. You weren't thinkin' of going out of state at all?'

'No, of course not.'

'We have a lot of other lines to follow up, other people to see . . . and we haven't had the pathologist's report yet. When we've done all that, we'll get back to you.'

Curt stood up too, but his legs felt like jelly. He was sure they suspected him.

'One more thing.' Delucca hesitated. 'Did your wife know that the girl was living in the brownstone?'

'No, I didn't mention it to her . . . it didn't seem all that important.'

'You weren't afraid that she might get the wrong idea?' There was a smirk on Delucca's face now.

'It did cross my mind.'

'Mr Koenig . . . when we speak to you again, we may have to do it at your home on Madison. But don't worry. We'll be discreet.'

'He was lyin'!' MacKenzie tossed his cigarette stub away as they walked back from the Vitagraph buildings. 'You see how nervous he was? Seventy-five dollars a month out of charity . . . hey, come on! He must have bin fuckin' her!'

'He was out of state when she was killed. We got statements. We got the witnesses. There's no way he could have gotten back from that trip and killed her. No way.'

'Someone else could have done it for him.'

'Sure, but then he took the risk of them rattin' on him

324

when the heat was on. OK. So I agree with you . . . he was lyin'. I reckon he took the house just so that he could put her in it, and visit her when the fancy took him; that makes sense. Take it from me . . . I can smell if a guy's a killer . . . and he ain't. All he's guilty of is fuckin' some cheap little broad from the Lower East Side behind his wife's back. Oldest story in the book, Mac.'

'Girl could have gotten greedy, wanted more . . . you know what I mean? Threatened to sing to the wife. Happens all the time. Koenig lost his temper . . . get my drift?'

'Mac, he was upstate when she was killed. I don't need the pathologist's report to tell me that. Hell, ain't I seen enough fuckin' stiffs in this job to know what I'm talkin' about?'

'I guess. So, what now?'

'We wear shoe leather. Friends, guys she knew. People she worked with. Before she got the studio extras job, she worked in a factory upstate. That's the startin' place.'

'Sure, she worked here. Not for long, though. Too much like hard work for the pay she was gettin'!' Delucca's sharp, well-trained ears caught the note of unmistakable resentment. So, Klara Kopek mightn't be the sweet, amiable little immigrant girl from the deprived Lower East Side that everyone they'd talked to at the studio knew and loved? He moved in for the kill.

'I'm all ears. So tell me about her.'

The girl wore a sulky look. 'All she talked about was the hard time her family were havin', makin' ends meet! So what! What about my family? I was born in this country, and my folks never had things easy, neither. What she think, huh, that the streets in New York City were paved with gold? Always blabbin' about how short of dough she was, and how much she wanted to help her goddam family. She borrowed five dollars off my guy . . . gave him some sob story and he just handed it over!'

'Did she pay it back?'

The girl scowled angrily. 'You gotta be kiddin'! I told

him he'd never see it again – and he didn't. Served him right! She upped and left at the end of that week, and we never saw her no more. But I tell you one thing. He wasn't the only guy she took money from.'

'You care to elaborate a little on that statement, ma'am?'

'Like I said, she was always givin' out sob stories. The guys were suckers for that poor-little-immigrant-girl routine. You know what us girls used to call her? Shovel-face. Yeah, that's right. Shovel-face. 'Cos she had a flat face that just looked kinda like a shovel!'

'You didn't like her, I take it?'

'You take it right, mister. I don't like little tramps who try an' get their filthy claws into my guy!'

'She was tryin' to latch onto him?'

'Used to keep askin' him things about the machine she was s'pposed to be operatin'. Makin' out that she didn't understand how it worked. You think I don't see through that kinda shit? I had her number in a minute!'

'She wasn't popular, then?'

'Like I said, we thought she stunk. But the guys . . . oh, yeah . . . they felt sorry for her.'

MacKenzie and Delucca looked at each other across the girl's head. 'Did she have intimate relationships with any of the men who worked here?'

'Most of 'em, I wouldn't mind bettin' on it! But she was too sly to let on.'

'It's names we're after.'

'Then take your pick.'

After a whole day's work, they had a list of suspects but nothing really solid to go on. The possibilities were as endless as the list of men's names.

'It could have bin any one of these guys. She gives 'em a sob story and they lend her cash, then they see the light and ask for it back . . . but she doesn't give.'

'If it was one of the guys on this list, he must have kept in touch with her after she started working at the Vitagraph studios . . . he knew she was living at 228 Washington Heights. Whoever the killer was, Kopek let him in . . . there was no sign of forced entry, no open windows. She knew her killer. And she trusted him enough to invite him into the house. You saw that room, Mac. That was one hell of a struggle that went on in there! Broken glass, busted ornaments. Flowers all over the goddam floor. And about those flowers. Red roses. Three dozen of 'em. You know how much a bouquet like that costs? Way beyond the means of any of the guys on this list, you can bet on that.'

'One more possibility. Maybe it was someone she knew from the Lower East Side, someone who was into some racket . . . some illegal racket. Then he would have been able to afford to make gestures like that.'

'Mac, I've bin workin' the Lower East Side ever since I bin in this fuckin' job. Guys who crawl around that sewer don't do things like sendin' red roses, even if they got the dough to do it. It just ain't their style. Get it checked out. I want to know where they came from, how much they cost, who sent 'em, and when they were delivered. You got that?' He checked his pocket watch. Eight o'clock. Koenig would be home on Madison by now, sweating it out. 'We'll head on back to the precinct and find out what the medical report said. Then let's go grab a bite to eat and a beer.'

A maid answered the door to him when, a couple of hours later, Delucca arrived alone at the Madison Avenue house. Stepping into the enormous front hall, he was immediately impressed. This was another world. Any one of the clocks, pictures or pieces of porcelain in here would have cost more than five years of Chief Rawlins' pay, let alone his.

He looked up as he heard movement on the staircase. A beautiful woman was standing in the middle of it, wearing an evening gown and pearls. 'You've come to speak to my husband?'

'Yes, Mrs Koenig, ma'am.' She was class all right, and it showed. But cold. No wonder Koenig had fancied a little slumming on the side with a cheap little tramp like Klara Kopek. He introduced himself. 'I'm sorry to call so late . . . but I was on my way home from the precinct, and I kinda thought droppin' by here might save me some time . . . I got

327

about two weeks of taking statements as from tomorrow...
and I figured I needed all the short cuts I could take.'

She came down the rest of the stairs and opened a large
door that led off the hall. 'He's in here.' Delucca went
through and Koenig was standing there.

'Detective Delucca.'

Delucca grinned. The door closed softly behind him.

'I was just sayin' to your wife, Mr Koenig, that I was
sorry to disturb you at this time of night. But it was on my
way.' He was going to enjoy this. 'As you can see... I came
alone. See, I figured that what I got to say to you would be
better if there was nobody else around to hear it.'

'I don't know what you mean by that.'

'I've just come from the morgue. And from readin' the
report on Klara Kopek's body.' Koenig was nervous now.
'The girl was killed by a heavy blow to the head. She was
also three months pregnant.' Curt's face was white;
Delucca could almost feel sorry for him. 'I have to ask you
this... was it yours?'

'No, for Christ's sake! I didn't even know her then!'

'But you did lie to us yesterday when I asked you if you
ever slept with her?'

There was a long pause before Curt finally answered.

'Yes.' His voice was very soft. 'I'm sorry. It was just the
shock of hearing what had happened to her. OK. I was
having an affair with her but I didn't kill her.'

'I got two witnesses who saw you go into 228
Washington Heights on the day she was found dead. They
also saw you coming out again... in a hell of a big hurry.
You want to tell me what really happened or would you
rather come downtown and tell it to someone else?'

Curt sank down onto the nearest chair. He put his head
in his hands. There was no way to turn, no way out. God,
why the hell did he get involved with her? 'Look. I'll level
with you. This is the absolute truth. I went straight from
the station when we got back that evening to see her. I let
myself in with my own key. I found her lying there,
sprawled out in the parlour. I knew she was dead without
even touching her. I just knew. I panicked, I guess. I

thought of all the terrible implications if I reported it . . . why was I there, why had I let her live in the house, why hadn't I told my wife about letting her stay there . . . all those things. I didn't even think about afterwards. I was in a state of shock. I just ran.' He looked up, wretchedly. 'I should have called you right away . . . I know that now. But I wasn't thinking straight. All I wanted was to run.'

'I can sympathize with that, Koenig.' Delucca had dropped the veneer of politeness now. 'Just for the record, I don't believe for one minute that you killed the little tramp. And she was a tramp, you take my word for it. See, I bin makin' enquiries about her, and it seems you weren't the only guy she ripped off. She had a little habit of givin' out sob stories to any sucker who'd listen to her . . . they lent her, she never paid it back. So I reckon she made a few enemies . . . not to mention the girls she worked with who saw her sweet-talkin' their guys out of their hard-earned bucks.' Delucca was taking something from his inside pocket now. 'I got a list as long as your arm of possible suspects . . . and any one of those guys could have killed her. We know it was someone she knew because she let him into the house herself . . . unless someone else had a key that neither you nor we know about.' That surprised him. 'I see that possibility never occurred to you before? Not that it matters right now. See, I think we have better things to do than worry about who did or who didn't kill the little tramp. Lower East Side trash like Klara Kopek . . . they're a dime a dozen, just like I was sayin' to my partner today. There'll be a few days' big headlines like there is for killings like this, then it'll all blow over. Your name doesn't even have to be brought into it. I might even make an arrest or two to throw the press boys right off the scent. See, Koenig, I'm on your side. I know just how much you got to lose if the truth came out . . . scandal stinks. You got a reputation, people's respect, not to mention a wife and kids to think about. Lose all that, over a cheap little Polish slut who'd lie on her back for any guy who'd give her five bucks? That's what I call a waste!'

'I have told you the truth . . . all of it. Besides, I was

upstate when it must have happened . . . do you know the exact time of her death?'

'It could be stretched to just about cover you returning if I wanted it to. But I ain't vindictive. Like I said, I know you got a lot to lose.' Curt felt numb; his brain wouldn't function properly. Klara had told him she was a virgin, that there had never been anyone else. It was as if Delucca was talking about another person, not a girl he'd trusted, a girl he'd thought he might come to love.

'I appreciate all this. I'm very grateful.'

'Oh . . . I shall expect you to be grateful.' Delucca was unwrapping the flat package he'd taken a moment ago from inside his coat. 'See, it's like this, Koenig . . . there's just one more little matter that you and me gotta get cleared up.' He handed Curt the photographs and the whole room reeled.

'Where did you get these?' he asked, in barely a whisper.

'You took Klara Kopek to a party out on Long Island last weekend. I'd say that by the look of those pictures, things had gotten a little out of hand. The guy who took 'em – and a few more besides – was so canned he didn't even remember doin' it, except for the first one or two. Good thing. Like I said, now it's just between the two of us.'

Slowly, the thick fog around Curt's brain began to clear. He understood. 'What's your angle, Delucca?'

'I'll lay it right on the line, Mr Big Shot movie star. So you listen up and you listen good, OK? 'Cos with those pictures I can bust your career and that goody-two-shoes image of yours wide apart! This is the deal. I sit on 'em and keep my mouth shut. In return, you hand over a little good-will remuneration once a month. Oh, I figured five grand would do for starters.'

'*Blackmail!*'

'Blackmail's an ugly word, Koenig.'

'You bastard!'

'Sticks and stones.' Delucca picked up the photographs, placed them back inside his coat. 'I bin called worse names. In this job, you get a thick hide real early. I'll be in touch,'

330

he said as he opened the door to let himself out. 'Nice doin' business with you.'

Left alone, Curt poured himself a double bourbon, sank down onto the couch and tried to think. There was no way out, nobody he could turn to. Turn Delucca in, and he destroyed himself.

He had alienated Shawn Duchovsky, his oldest and most valued friend. Besides which, he was too angry with himself for his blindness and his stupidity, too ashamed, to confide in Shawn now. He had frozen Marianna out of his life; cynically used her love and trust to further his own ambitions, his own private ends. He had wanted everything her name and her money could buy for him and, when he got it, discovered how empty fame and material possessions could be. He'd turned his back on the unconditional love she'd held out to him, he'd lied, cheated and deceived her. Could he really blame her now that he'd succeeded in making her hate him? It was no less than he deserved.

In the front hall, he heard the telephone ringing. He got up mechanically and went outside. It was not, as he'd hoped, Shawn's voice on the other end of the line. As he was replacing the earpiece he glanced up at the rustle of taffeta, and saw Marianna standing at the foot of the stairs.

'Is something the matter?' It tore her apart, to see the haggard, haunted look in his eyes. Had he really loved the girl that much, then? 'Who was that?'

'Bill Smith . . . he was telephoning from home.' He forced his voice into some semblance of normality. 'He got a wire from Hal Goldenthal at the Tellurian Universal Studios in California . . . they want to buy out my Vitagraph contract if I'm willing to do a deal.'

'What does that mean, exactly?'

'Leaving New York and moving out there to the west coast.' She would never agree to it, not in a million years. 'To a small place called Hollywood . . . between Los Angeles and Beverly Hills. It's very primitive . . . provincial.' It was a lifeline, and he was desperate to grasp at it. Except that Marianna was a city girl, born and bred.

Maybe that would be the solution, for her to stay here with the children while he tried to carve out a new life, a new beginning for himself. If that was possible. 'Bill Smith says that it's up to me.'

'It is.'

She got the hire cab to set her down a block from Shawn's apartment on 119th Street. His door was the first door at the top of the stairs. He was astonished to see her. That made her smile.

'Shawn. Long time no see.' How her mother would have been appalled by such slang. A lifetime ago. 'Are you going to invite me inside or do I have to say my farewells standing out here on the doorstep?'

'Farewells?' She went inside. 'I don't understand what you mean, Marianna.'

'It's good to know how glad you are to see me.'

'Aw, come here . . .' He kissed her on the cheek. 'I'm sorry. It's just that I wasn't expecting you to show up, not like this. No call. No warning. But I'm always glad to see you, you know that.'

'We're leaving New York . . . that's what I came to tell you. Curt's signing a contract with a moving picture company on the west coast . . . some place called Hollywood.' She sat down. 'I don't know for what reason . . . and I'm not even going to ask . . . but I know that you two have had a fight over something. That's why we haven't seen you for so long.'

Shawn looked awkward and Marianna instantly knew that she was right. 'Look, Marianna . . .'

'I said I wouldn't ask. And I meant that. All I've come for is to say goodbye and tell you that whatever's happened between you and Curt, it isn't too late to make it up.'

There was something different about her; something he couldn't put his finger on right then; she seemed stronger, somehow. Unemotional. Self-confident. There were only traces of the sweet, shy, naive Marianna who'd fallen desperately in love with his best friend more than ten years ago. What had happened to change her?

332

'I guess we're both stubborn,' was all he could think to say to her without telling her the truth behind their last quarrel.

'Curt's going to Minneapolis the day after tomorrow, to stay with his family for a week or two while I arrange for the house to be sold.' She was so businesslike, so decisive. 'No point in keeping it on. We don't intend to come back again.'

'I'll miss you.'

She smiled, her smile a little like the old Marianna he remembered. 'California isn't at the ends of the earth, Shawn.'

'Just try to keep me away.'

She got up. So much both of them still had to say, but for their own separate reasons held back; for now, it would have to remain unsaid. Angry as Shawn was with Curt, he was even angrier with himself; with those two thoughtless, foolish young men they'd both been. Neither of them had mentioned Klara Kopek; neither of them would, though her murder had been front page news for the past week and a late edition of the *New York Herald* lay face up on the table. How much did Marianna know of what had really happened, Shawn wondered? Another question that he would not, dare not, ask her.

'We're leaving on the morning train the day after Curt gets back. Maybe we'll see you before then. The children miss you.'

'Give 'em my love and tell them to be good for their momma.'

She wanted to go to him and put her arms around him. But if she did that, she knew she would weaken and begin to cry. If she started to cry, she might not be able to stop. And what was it her father had always instilled in her as a child? Displays of emotion were a pitiable sign of weakness. Instead, she stayed where she was. 'I think Curt's been very lucky to have had a friend like you. Take care.'

'Marianna . . . don't forget. I'm your friend, too.'

*   *   *

Two in the morning. No moon, no stars. The water from the Hudson off Dyker Beach glistened black, like crude oil. Russo's brother edged his way nervously from behind a pillar of the old derelict building as he heard approaching footsteps. Then a man's silhouette emerged from the gloom.

'Mr Delucca!'

'Hi, Benito. You got my message?'

'Yeah, sure I did.' He grinned. 'You like the pictures I did for you, Mr Delucca?'

'Real nice, Benito. In fact, that's why I got you here. I wanna give you a little token of extra thanks.' He took out his wallet and the other man's eyes glistened at the sight of the ten-dollar bills.

'You could have left it at the shop.'

'Yeah, I guess. But I don't trust that brother of yours. I figured he might get a little greedy and keep back some for himself.'

'He wouldn't double-cross me, Mr Delucca. He's family.'

'Better to be safe than sorry.' He handed him fifty dollars. 'See you around sometime.'

Russo's brother walked away, counting the money as he went and muttering his thanks. He was still counting it when Delucca pulled out his Smith and Wesson revolver and shot him at point blank range in the back.

He stooped down, picked up the five ten-dollar bills from Benito's outstretched hand. He rolled him to the edge of the bank and then kicked him, hard. He toppled over and down into the murky water with a splash.

Somebody would discover Russo's body tomorrow, slumped behind the counter of the little shop where Delucca had left it, the skull crushed like the shell of a pecan nut by the iron shoe Russo used in his work. Whoever Chief Rawlins sent down there to clear things up would, no doubt, put both murders down to some gangland killing.

Delucca quickened his step. It felt good, tying loose ends. And with a five grand rake-off from Curt Koenig once a month, things were looking up.

He'd read in the paper a few days ago that Koenig was leaving New York and going to California, that he'd signed a contract with some west coast moving picture company; that didn't bother him at all. Koenig had the number of his poste restante box in New York and he knew what the price would be if that five grand a month failed to show up.

Delucca headed on back to the precinct. He smiled as he walked. Working nights wasn't so bad after all.

In the first class reserved compartment, Curt and Marianna sat on opposite facing seats, gazing from the window, neither speaking a word. Alice had clambered onto her father's lap and was chattering incessantly as always, while Gene and Elynor vied with each other to point out the different engines.

It was as the train slowly began to pull out of the station, amid the deafening noise and the hiss of steam, that they caught sight of Shawn standing at the end of the platform.

'Daddy, Momma, look! It's Uncle Shawn!'

Curt half stood up, pressed his face against the window. As the train gathered speed and thundered past, their eyes met for a fraction of a moment. Shawn smiled and raised his hand as the children waved to him; then, he was gone.

Without a word, Curt got up and opened the door of their compartment. An hour later, he was still standing outside in the corridor, staring from the window.

Marianna would have given anything to have found the courage to get up and go to him. But the hateful thoughts of him and Klara Kopek together were too powerful for her to forget, the stark, ugly fact of his infidelity was still like an immovable wall between them.

PART FOUR

Full Circle
1915–1925

CHAPTER TWENTY-ONE

Within six months of arriving in California, they had moved from a temporary home close to the Universal studios to a huge, Spanish-style villa in the Hollywood Hills, with fourteen rooms. Since none of their New York staff had moved with them, Marianna had engaged a cook and a maid, and Curt had bought ponies for the children. When he wasn't filming at the studios, he would get Consuelo the cook to make up an enormous picnic hamper and the four of them would drive out into the vast countryside for the entire day. Even when he was working, Curt would often bundle all the children into the back of his roadster and let them watch him on set.

Gene had quickly made friends with the cameramen, fascinated by the workings of the hand-cranked camera, and the way the different directors approached the task of guiding the actors and actresses through each separate scene. One day, in between breaks, one of the cameramen on set showed him inside the wooden camera box.

'At Universal, we use the Debrie-Parvo – it's a French design, and I reckon just about the best. This here's what we call a footage counter, and you can see how much film you've got left just by peeping through it. A dial on the back . . . here, see? . . . tells me how fast I should crank. Now, there's an art to that, and you can only develop it by practice.'

'When you look through this eyepiece, is that what you see on the set?'

'You got it. It shows you exactly what part of the scene you're recording on camera. Now, that's real important.'

'And what's this lever here for?'

'That, that operates the lens aperture, controls the amount of light that reaches the film. Now that's

339

important, too. You gotta get it just right. If you don't, you get the exposure wrong, and the film comes out too dark or too light. The reel'd get wasted . . . and I don't reckon Mr Goldenthal'd take too kindly to somethin' like that.'

'You know what? I asked my dad if I could have my own camera for my birthday, and he said yes! D'you reckon you could show me how to take real good pictures when I get it?'

'Sure thing. What kind you figure on gettin'?'

'Oh, anythin' that takes real good pictures. A Kemper Combi, maybe, or a Kodak. There's so much to take pictures of out here . . . the mountains, the beaches, the orange groves . . . and people! I'd like to take some pictures of my sisters to send to my Uncle Shawn back in New York.'

'Your Uncle Shawn, huh?'

'I miss him real bad. So does my sister Ellie. He used to come visit us all the time when we lived in New York, but then he stopped. I don't know why. My dad said it was because he'd gotten promotion at work and he didn't have so much time. I wish he'd come visit us out here. He could even pick his own bedroom to sleep in, we've got so many!'

'Why don't you write him and ask him to come stay awhile?'

Gene's face lit up; why hadn't he thought of that? But would Uncle Shawn be too busy to make a long trip west? People didn't have to work all the time in New York, did they? 'Yeah, that's a great idea! I'll get my sister Ellie to write it . . . she's much better at writing letters than me. Thanks, Chuck!'

Gene was astonished to find that his father was less than enthusiastic about his idea. 'But, Dad, Uncle Shawn would love it out here! And we could take him to see a new place every day!'

'I doubt if he'd be able to get the free time from his job, Gene. Maybe later.'

'But, Dad . . .'

Passing the open door, Marianna had overheard the

conversation. Later, when the children were in bed, she cornered Curt in the huge marble-floored drawing room.

'Just how long is it that you and Shawn have been friends, Curt?'

'Like since forever . . . you already knew that.' He'd half guessed what was coming next, and steeled himself. 'I meant to drop him a line, after we arrived down here . . . when I'd gotten settled at Universal. But then Goldenthal had problems with the script writers and there were some other hitches, and I got side-tracked somehow.'

'They're just empty excuses and you know it!' He looked up, stung by the tone of her voice. 'Something happened between you two long before we left New York and you never made it up. Isn't that a little closer to the truth?'

'Just what the hell are you saying, Marianna?' They shared a house, but that was all; he was no longer part of her life, nor she of his. Though they kept up the myth of the happily married couple in public – for the sake of appearances, for the children – it was no more than an empty façade; even the servants knew it. When there were no cameras, no press, when the front door was shut, they reverted to their separate selves again. They occupied different bedrooms, when they spoke to each other it was only to disagree, or quarrel about the children.

'You know damn well exactly what I'm saying!' Her loud, angry voice echoed around the room. 'I heard what you said to Gene. And I know why you don't want Shawn to come here. Because you're afraid that he might let out the truth!'

Curt tried to make light of it. 'I don't know what you're on about. I said I'll drop him a line when I find the time.'

'If you were serious about getting in touch with him, you'd have made the time. Besides which, isn't the telephone a rather useful invention?' Her voice was sarcastic. 'You had one installed two weeks after we arrived!'

'Shawn knows where I am if he wants me.' He was about to walk out of the room and away from her when her voice stopped him in his tracks. 'I went to see Shawn just before we left New York.'

She knew by the way his face suddenly drained of colour that that had shaken him. 'What did you say?'

'You heard me well enough.' She wanted to punish him for hurting her, for his infidelities, for all the deceit and lies. But she still loved him, in spite of everything. By hurting him, she also hurt herself. 'What's the matter, Curt? Don't tell me that the great actor is lost for words.' She hated herself, but some demon inside her drove her on. 'What are you afraid of? That I might have asked Shawn the real reason why you stopped speaking to each other?' She had all his attention now. 'Don't worry. He's far too loyal to betray your confidence. Even to me.'

'Why didn't you tell me you'd seen him?'

'Why didn't you tell me you were paying the rent on a brownstone at 228 Washington Heights so that your cheap little Polish whore could live there for free?' He was shocked, stunned. 'You look surprised. I wonder why. You should never have underestimated me, Curt. I may not have inherited my father's money, but I did inherit his brains. You made some stupid mistakes and aroused my suspicions . . . I worked the rest of it out by myself.'

'How long have you known?'

'It really doesn't matter any more, does it? After all, the little tramp's dead.' The demon was in her now, goading, goading, goading. She could hear the lapping water on the shore at Lake Winnipesaukee, the soft, deadly tone of her mother's voice. *Young men have filthy minds*. Edwina hadn't been so wrong, after all. Mental pictures of Curt and the Kopek slut together, in bed, tortured her, as they had almost every night since she'd first known. 'That's why the New York police department sent that detective to see you, wasn't it? Because they found out that you knew her.'

'I didn't kill her!' The anguish in his voice was like a knife twisting in her heart. She wanted to go to him, hold him, have him hold her. Tell him that she loved him, that she knew he was innocent, but the demon whispering in her ear held her back. 'Marianna, I swear it!'

'It wouldn't matter very much to me one way or the other if you had. Whatever my other failings are, hypocrisy isn't one of them. I'm glad she's dead. Whoever killed her did the rest of society a favour, wouldn't you say?' She wanted him to lose his self-control, to start shouting at her so that she could retaliate, but he just stood there, staring at her as if she was a ghost. 'There are too many trash like her in this world, parasites riding on the backs of others. You're well rid of her!'

'She was a human being.'

'And you'd know all about her so-called qualities, wouldn't you, Curt? Tell me, just for the record . . . did you meet her at the studios? Did you make the first move or did she do it? Did she offer herself to you in return for the rent?'

'Marianna . . . for Christ's sake stop it!'

'I'm interested, Curt. Why don't you want to talk about it? She must have meant something to you, for you to have kept her for so long. Was it her cute little Polish accent, or was it the pathetic sob story she spun you? Poor little Klara Kopek from the Lower East Side whom nobody loves. Did you just fancy a little slumming? Was she good in bed? Tell me.'

'Marianna, I don't want to talk about it.'

She was silent for a moment. 'You never loved me at all, did you? What was it, Curt? The family name? The trust fund money? You thought my father would leave his fortune all to me? I thought so. You haven't got the guts to look me in the eye and be honest with me, even now. How many other women had there been before Klara Kopek? Two? Ten? Fifty? How many?'

Suddenly, the door behind them opened and eleven-year-old Alice stood there in her nightgown, blue eyes round with fear, golden curls tumbling down over her shoulders. Her bedroom was closest to the reception room and the noise of their shouting had travelled up the stairs. She went over to her father and put her arms round him.

'Daddy, why are you and Momma fighting?'

'It's OK, sweetheart . . . we're just talking, that's all. Why don't you go on back to bed? It's late now.'

'I want you to take me.'

Alice's sulky face and whining voice made Marianna's

patience snap. Curt was always spoiling her. 'Your father and I were having a private conversation. You do not walk into the room without knocking first and then waiting to be told that you can come in . . . do you understand me?'

'Daddy, Momma's shouting at me!'

'Look, I'll take her upstairs . . .'

'You will not. Alice, leave the room this instant and go back to bed. Unless you want me to put you across my knee and give you the hard spanking you deserve.' Alice burst into floods of tears and Curt scooped her up in his arms.

'Marianna, she's just a child, for Christ's sake! Can't you see she's upset?'

It was happening all over again; he was shutting her out, taking sides against her. 'You really can't see the damage you're doing, can you? Giving in to her every whim since she was old enough to work out that she had you right in the palm of her hand! Whatever she does, you find an excuse for. Whatever she wants, you give her. Without any help from you, I've tried my darnedest to teach her that in this life, you don't always get all the things you want. But you just have to keep on undermining me!'

'I'm taking her back to bed right now, Marianna. I thought we'd agreed that we wouldn't argue in front of the children.'

Marianna walked away, stood by the enormous window that looked out onto the orange-blossom trees, the rolling landscape beyond the wild garden. The window was open slightly, and the sweet scent of the blossom and bougain-villaea drifted towards her, soothing her anger, her raw, frayed nerves. 'You do that, Curt. You do exactly as you please. After all, that's what you always do, isn't it?'

She heard him leave the room with Alice in his arms, their voices, as he carried her back to her bedroom at the top of the stairs. No doubt Alice would beg him to stay with her for a while and Curt, never able to deny her anything, would be gone for at least an hour or more; though the favouritism was unconscious on his part, he paid more attention to Alice because she was the most demanding of all their children, constantly clamouring for other people

344

to take notice of her. From almost the first day, Curt had got into the habit of taking her to the studio with him to watch the filming, and because of her enchanting doll-like looks she was petted and spoiled not only by her father but by most of the cast and crew as well. By sharp contrast, her elder sister Elynor, with her reserve and unfashionable dark hair, largely went unnoticed.

'Just guess what Mr Goldenthal called me the other day!' Alice had boasted to her, as she preened herself in front of the mirror in the marble entrance hall, ready to drive to the studio with her father. 'His little golden girl, that's what! I'll bet nobody'd ever call you that, Ellie!'

'If that swollen little head of yours gets any bigger,' Gene had called from the stairs on overhearing them, 'you won't find a hat to fit it!'

'I will too! You're just jealous!' Alice had flounced out of the house and climbed into the passenger seat of her father's new Pierce-Arrow.

'Don't pay any attention to her, Ellie,' Gene had said. 'Her mouth'll always be bigger than her brain.'

'It's OK. It doesn't matter.' It had mattered, but Elynor would never confide her feelings to anyone, not even Gene.

Marianna turned away from the window as she heard Curt come back into the room. For a moment, they looked at each other.

'You still haven't answered my question.'

'Whatever I said, would you really believe me?'

'I've already heard it, Curt.' She was back in that parlour at 228 Washington Heights, listening to Klara Kopek. The words were engraved in her memory, imprinted in her mind like the brand on a steer's hide. She could see the vase full with the red roses he had sent her, smell their cloying, slightly rotten perfume. For the rest of her life she would hate red roses, never allow them to be brought into the house. 'But now I want to hear it from you.'

In the late evening light, she was silhouetted against the deepening sunset; a bright golden halo cast a soft glow against her creamy skin, her rich dark hair. She was wearing black taffeta, and the cut of the gown reminded him of the black evening dress she'd worn that night when he'd dined at Del Monico's with Madeline Dupre without telling her, and she had stormed in and confronted him. Had it begun then, he wondered, the gradual, almost imperceptible change in the way he felt about her? If she'd been different, shown him just a flicker of warmth, a sign that she wanted him, could things between them have turned out differently? Something he'd never know because now it was too late. Ironic – and only Shawn would have understood the depth of the irony – that in the beginning he hadn't loved her; now that he realized he did, in spite of everything, his indifference and neglect had turned her love into hate.

'All right.' His voice was soft, barely a whisper. 'I admit it. When we got married, I didn't love you. It was just the way you said. What's gone wrong between us, it's all my fault. Except that things were never helped by how much you hated being in my bed. I accept all that. I've got exactly what I deserve. You hate me now, I know that. But I want you to believe me, Marianna, when I say that although I didn't love you then, I do love you now.'

She had longed so much, so much, to hear him say those words. But Klara Kopek's face, the scent of red roses cancelled them out, darkened them to irrelevance. He had told her so many lies so many times that she could never believe him again. The demon was goading her, laughing, baiting, taunting inside her head. It was another trick, another attempt to manipulate her. But the young, naïve, unworldly girl he'd married bore no resemblance to the bitter, cynical woman she had since become.

'Did you love her? Any of them? I know there were others, Curt. No more lies, please. Don't insult my intelligence by pretending.'

'No.' Their bodies. All he'd wanted was their bodies. He'd chosen them, not her. *Young men have filthy minds.*

'She was different from all the others. She was the one you were willing to risk everything for.' He shook his head. 'Scandal. Family. Career. You didn't care, as long as she kept opening her legs for you. Why, Curt, why? Why were you willing to risk it all? Tell me. She wasn't important. She wasn't pretty. She wasn't even a lady.' Her voice was bitter. 'How could you sink so low?'

'I could never explain to you in a way that you'd understand.'

A pause, while they faced each other. 'Would you have left me, as she wanted you to? Did she mean so much to you that you would really have gone that far?'

He stared at her without understanding. 'Marianna, I'd never leave you for anyone! What makes you think something like that?'

'She did.'

'What are you saying?' He took a step towards her. 'You never met Klara!'

'I was the last person to see her alive.' She felt nothing, only icy calm. 'I found out about the house, and I went there. Does it matter how? She tried to slam the door in my face when I told her who I was. She grossly underestimated how much strength someone has when they're boiling with anger.

'The first thing I saw when I walked into the parlour of your sordid little love-nest was the three dozen red roses you'd had sent to her from Fleischman's. And she, the little slut you'd given ideas far above her station, stood there hurling insults at me as if she owned you. I wish you could have been there, Curt. That was the only thing that was wanted to make it perfect. I was almost glad when she spat in my face and then attacked me, to have the excuse I needed to hit her back. When she tripped over the rug and fell onto the fender, I knew she was dead. I hadn't meant that to happen. I was nowhere near her when she fell and gashed her head. And I was sorry . . . I didn't want her to be dead. I wanted her to get up and face me so that I could hit her again!' A tear welled up in the corner of her eye and rolled slowly down one cheek. 'I wanted to hit her so much, Curt, for causing me so much pain. I wanted to beat her senseless! But I never wanted her to die. . .that would have been too easy, and she didn't deserve that. When you're dead, then there's no more

347

pain, no more suffering. Dying was far too good for a cheap, scheming little slut like her.'

'Why didn't you tell me, Marianna?'

'Don't come near me, Curt.' She held up her hand as he moved towards her. 'I don't want you to touch me. Not now, not ever. Not after her. No more lies, Curt . . . I've heard more than enough of them from you already. I don't believe anything you tell me any more . . . not after what's happened. So save your breath.' She mustn't break down and cry in front of him; she wouldn't. 'No big speeches. No trying to change my mind. I'm all through listening.' As she spoke, the front door bell rang shrilly, echoing through the house. 'The play's over. The curtain's come down. You're a brilliant actor . . . I always knew that. What I didn't realize was that it was the actor I'd be living with all these years, not the man.'

He couldn't reach her. There was no way he could make her believe that what he'd said was true. He'd lied too often. And she knew it. Just then, there was a knock on the door and their maid Colleen came into the room.

'Mr Koenig, it's Mr Goldenthal and his new director; Garrard Flair. Shall I show them in?' He was too shocked, too crushed, to answer her. Marianna spoke instead.

'Yes, of course, Colleen! Show them both in here.' She went forward to greet them, smiling brilliantly, her hands extended in welcome. 'It's wonderful to see you . . . you couldn't have arrived at a better time . . .'

348

CHAPTER TWENTY-TWO

The moment she set eyes on Garrard Flair, Marianna instinctively distrusted him. For the whole evening, while they sat and listened to Hal Goldenthal describing for the twentieth time how he had literally walked from the Lithuanian border to America, she tried to find a logical reason why. But there was none.

On the surface, there was absolutely nothing to dislike about him; he was tall, slim, attractive – though not in Curt's league – with impeccable manners and infinite charm. Why, then, she asked herself as she listened to the tortuous details of how Goldenthal and the other burgeoning Hollywood producers intended to thwart the latest restrictions of the Trust, was there something about Flair that she found totally repellent? Deliberately, she kept her eyes from meeting Curt's; instead, she concentrated on Flair.

She understood, she said, that he'd just come straight from England; what was the state of the film industry over there? His answer, without being exactly evasive, really told her nothing at all. Without the interference of an official body like the Trust it seemed they were enthusiastically making longer films; far longer than the films currently in production in America. He reeled off a list that he'd been 'directorial adviser' to; all sounded impressive. *Ivanhoe*, *David Copperfield*, *Queen Elizabeth I*. He mentioned work in France, Germany, Sweden; but when pressed for greater detail managed to avoid telling her the personal things about himself that she was anxious to know. She concluded that he was hiding something, and wondered what exactly that something might be: a family, an abandoned wife, perhaps? Flair was undoubtedly a charmer and there was nothing women were attracted to more; something she knew from bitter experience.

'What do you intend to do about the interference from the Trust? Can they legally stop you from producing and distributing longer films?'

'Look. The public wants feature films . . . longer films, films that tell real stories, know what I mean? In Europe they're doin' two-, three-, even four-reelers, but the Trust's standardization policies are standing in the way of our producin' the same film lengths. Hell, the exhibitors have bin screamin' for better and longer films ever since Curt did *Monte Cristo* . . . they want to attract a more intelligent, more sophisticated clientele . . . just like us. OK. So we'll still turn out slapstick comedies and one-reelers of Bronco Billy for those who want them – cheap films for cheap people – but you gotta move on and move up. The Trust, see, think that your average movie audience doesn't have the mental capacity to understand, let alone appreciate, longer films. Just tell me what the hell those guys know about makin' movies, huh?'

Curt desperately tried to focus himself after the shattering revelations from Marianna. 'You were saying, the other day, about organized resistance to the Trust. So, what's happening on that score, Hal? You've had meetings with Fox, IMP, Keystone, Thanhouser, Rex and Mutual. . . has any real progress been made about how the problems with the Trust ought to be tackled?'

'The Trust are like ten years behind in the way they think . . . if those peabrains know how to think at all! They don't wanna listen to reason, about what the public wants. They don't see things like people who go to the movies are startin' to want to know more about the players . . . they think the bigger the public acclaim, the bigger the demand for salaries is goin' to get. And that that, in turn, is gonna siphon off profits away from them. It ain't dawned on those pinheads yet that there's an enormous potential in movies for mass entertainment . . . all they care about is seein' that we supply standard length films to theatres at a cost based on theatre size rather than on the actors, directors or content. Hey, look! We've tried to play it their way, but they don't wanna listen.'

'They've filed lawsuits against the smaller independents by the hundred,' Flair put in, 'employed private detectives to search all over for patent violation, even called on federal marshals to arrest offenders, confiscate their equipment, and throw them in jail. That's why so many of the independents packed up and moved west from New York. The Trust has a stranglehold on the whole business up there. And it's not just on the east coast that these things have been happening. Selig Polyscope in Chicago had an entire feature film sabotaged – ripped to bits – by someone acting for the Trust.'

'But how the hell can they get away with something like that? They accuse the independents of breaking the law, but they're breaking it, big time. They just gotta be stopped!' At that moment, the telephone rang, and Curt stood up. He needed to get out of the room, to compose himself. When Colleen told him it was a person to person long distance call from New York, his heart leapt with anticipation. There was only one person it could possibly be; and that was Shawn. Uncanny, that Shawn should finally decide to ring him when he'd already made up his mind to sit down and pour his heart out to him in a letter tonight. He took the earpiece eagerly. But it wasn't the voice he was expecting.

'How you doin' down there in sunny California, Koenig?' Curt stiffened; his fingers tightened around the stem of the telephone. 'Real interestin', all the stuff I bin readin' about you up here ... like the big fat signing fee you just got from Universal. So I figured I'd just give you a little call ...'

'What the hell do you want, Delucca?' Curt glanced behind him, into the empty hall. He kept his voice to a whisper in case he was overheard. 'I sent the money. Just like we agreed. Every cent of it!' He felt the anger boiling up in him. 'Are you out of your mind, telephoning me here? My wife could have picked up the receiver ...'

There was laughter from the other end of the line. 'Now, you should know me better than that, Koenig. Would I rat on you, after you've bin so all-fired generous?' There was another laugh. 'I got more sense. Course, if you go an' upset me, well . . . then there's no knowin' what I might do . . . Hal Goldenthal might just be receivin' a little somethin' interestin' in his mornin' mail real soon. . .'

'What do you want?'

'That's better! Now . . . when I read about that fat signin' fee, I just figured it was time you gave me a little bonus for keepin' my mouth shut . . . after all, Koenig, if I hadn't done that, Universal wouldn't be signin' you up at all, you gotta admit that.' There was a pause; Delucca wanted to make him sweat a little. 'So, how about doublin' the five grand on next month's payment? Let's call it . . . a little gesture of continuin' goodwill, huh?'

'You're out of your mind!'

'Hey, Koenig . . . you ain't in no position to shout the odds, so cut the crap. You're the guy with it all to lose . . . and don't you forget that, Mr Big Shot movie star!'

'I can't take ten grand out of my bank account without my wife getting suspicious . . .'

'Double the payment, Koenig, you got that?' The voice at the other end of the line had changed now; there was a hard edge to it that told Curt Delucca meant what he said. 'Here's the deal, pal. You listen and you listen good. I wanna see ten grand in that mail box on the first of the month, or I talk.' Before Curt could say anything else, Delucca had hung up.

He stood there in the cool of the marble hall, trying to collect himself. There was absolutely no doubt at all in his mind that Delucca would carry out his threat if he failed to pay up. But how could he explain the enormous withdrawals from his bank account to Marianna, if she ever found out? That possibility wasn't the remote one it had been a few months ago; at a dinner party only last week, Hal Goldenthal had started talking about professional accountants, and the advisability of Curt's engaging one once the new contract was signed. Marianna had agreed. Even if, somehow, he could keep the truth from her about the payments to Delucca, how could he possibly explain the shortfall in his finances to a professional adviser? He felt trapped. When he reluctantly returned to the others in the marble drawing room, he let most of their conversation flow over him.

It grew more difficult by the minute to keep up any pretence of normality; when, half an hour later, Flair and Hal Goldenthal stood up to go, Curt almost breathed a sigh of relief that he could drop the façade of joviality, the illusion that all was well between Marianna and himself. But had Goldenthal – no man's fool – really not noticed the strained atmosphere when he and Flair had first come into the house? If he had, he gave no sign. As Curt was showing them to the door Alice suddenly appeared at the bottom of the stairs.

'Alice, I thought I told you that you were to go straight back to bed and go to sleep?' There was barely veiled anger in Marianna's voice. But Alice just smiled her enchanting smile at them all. She knew that her mother could hardly take her to task in front of the visitors.

'But I'm not in the least bit tired, Momma!' She turned her vivid blue eyes onto her parents' unexpected guests. 'Hello, Mr Goldenthal. How are you?'

'All the better for seein' you, sweetheart.' He turned to Flair. 'Isn't she just as pretty as a picture? Alice, this is Garrard Flair. He's goin' to direct your daddy's new picture.'

Alice was clearly very taken with him. She smiled extra sweetly and held out her hand to him. 'How do you do, Mr Flair? Can I come on set and watch the filming when you start your new moving picture? Mr Goldenthal always lets me . . . but Daddy says I have to ask you first because you're the director.'

Flair smiled. 'I shall be honoured, Alice.'

Curt saw them to the door; after they'd driven off in the direction of Los Angeles along the bumpy road, he lingered on the porch awhile, reluctant to go back inside. He was alone again, isolated in his misery and guilt. When he turned back and went into the house Alice had gone to bed and there was only Marianna, staring at him with

353

undisguised hatred, undisguised loathing. The expression in her eyes as she looked at him hurt so much it was like a physical pain.

'I'm going to bed.'

'Marianna.' There was almost a pleading note in his voice. 'We need to talk. We have to talk. Please . . . don't go.'

'We have nothing to talk about, not any more. Not now. Not ever.' How many times in the past had she longed for him to want her with him? The nights when he'd never come home, the nights she'd spent sobbing into her pillow alone. He'd left it too late. He was trying to manipulate her again and this time the hardened, embittered woman she'd become, the woman he'd forced her to be, was out of his reach. Her eyes were cold, unyielding. No hope. 'It's over, Curt. What else is there left to say?'

He tried to speak, but no words came. He watched her helplessly as she turned away, walked out of the room and up the staircase. He knew then that he'd lost her, that there was no turning back. Whatever he did, whatever he said, would make no difference. He had taken her love for granted, thrown it back in her face too many times for her to be able to forgive him. When he'd lied to her so often, deceived her so many times, could he really blame her now if she refused to believe or forgive him?

He stayed alone in the big, empty, opulent room, drinking heavily into the early hours. Then, a little unsteadily, he climbed the stairs to his bedroom, taking the bottle of bourbon with him.

It was palatial, marble-floored, with Moorish arched windows and a massive carved bed. In one corner stood a huge Spanish writing desk. Curt sat down, drew a sheet of paper towards him, then picked up his pen and, his hand not quite steady, began to write. It was too late to reach Marianna. Maybe not too late to reach the friend he'd quarrelled with and turned his back on.

He dipped his pen in the inkwell, rubbed his tired, alcohol-clouded eyes. *Dear Shawn* . . .

* * *

Was his head slowly clearing now, or was it just his imagination? He stared down at the letter. For so long, he'd bottled up all his deepest feelings, his profoundest thoughts, down inside himself. He had wanted to tell Marianna tonight what he had written down here; it was his fault that she'd turned away, that she'd refused to listen. But Shawn would understand. Shawn, Shawn. Best friend. Oldest friend. Shawn who knew him, understood him, better than anyone else ever had, ever would. Shawn would read the letter and know why he had done all the things he had, made so many terrible mistakes – taken Marianna's love for granted, betrayed her with two women who had meant nothing to him – yes; Shawn, of all people, would understand. As he would understand – wouldn't he? – why Curt had left New York so abruptly, so bitterly, without trying to see him again, without even saying goodbye.

A tear ran down his face; he dashed it away. Curt hadn't cried since he was a little boy, and afraid of being in the dark. He unscrewed the top of the bottle, poured just another half measure of bourbon into his glass. One more drink. Just one. Just one more would help to stop the terrible aching deep inside him, the terrible gnawing guilt that nothing else would take away. Just one more.

Four glasses later, he was still sitting there, staring down at what he had written. His head pounded; there were lights in front of his eyes. With shaking hands he folded the sheets of paper, stuck them into an envelope; with great effort, he wrote Shawn's name and address across it, surprisingly straight after the amount of bourbon he had drunk that evening. Then he got up, went slowly downstairs again and out of the house. He had to mail the letter now.

Purposefully, he walked towards the Pierce-Arrow.

She had still been awake when she'd heard him turn out the lights, walk past her bedroom door. He was going back downstairs – why was that? She'd heard the sound of the front door closing, his footsteps on the gravel drive, the Pierce-Arrow's engine as it roared into life; then, a silence that terrified her.

She'd leapt up, run after him. Too late. The red tail lights of the Pierce-Arrow were already disappearing into the darkness; Curt had gone, but gone where?

She stood there for a moment or two in her nightgown, outlined against the night sky; barefoot, hair blowing loose around her, shading her eyes. Then, with a horrible feeling of foreboding that she couldn't shake off, she turned and went back inside.

His bedroom door had been left open a little; his desk lamp was still burning. She pushed it open wider, went inside. That was when she caught sight of the dishevelled desk top, the spilled ink, the empty glass, the bottle of bourbon. Like the glass, it was empty; so he had been drinking again. Tears began to burn behind her eyes; the feeling of foreboding as she stared around the empty room became so unbearable and so strong that she couldn't breathe. He had tried to build a bridge between them tonight, and she'd walked out without listening to him . . . had what he'd wanted to say to her been anything she had really wanted to hear? Maybe. All she could do now was wait for him, so that when he returned she could tell him that she hadn't meant what she'd said, that in spite of everything he'd done to hurt her, she still loved him.

The road curved slightly, then more sharply as he took the bend; the headlights beamed out into the darkness ahead. It was difficult to see now. He could hear the soft, soothing sound of the sea far away to the left, the music of the surf as it rolled back across the deserted sand, smell the fresh, salty, orange-blossom air.

The tears ran down his cheeks; this time, he let them fall. No-one to see his pain, his grief, his anguish, his bitter regrets. Marianna. Marianna. Marianna. The wind ruffled his bright hair, whistled past his ears, but he took no notice. Gene, Elynor, Alice; one day, if they ever found out the truth – about his infidelities, the way he'd used their mother's love as a ladder to climb by – maybe they would forgive him; whatever happened between him and

Marianna when he went back, Curt knew that he would never forgive himself. *Marianna*. Marianna in her white Worth gown, defying her father for his sake. Marianna, pushing her way through the crowds in the Astor ballroom, to plead with Charles Frohman on his behalf. *The Count of Monte Cristo*. That part, that play, had changed their lives for ever. Given him all that he had ever desired, then snatched it all away; the role of a lifetime, that had been a blessing and a curse.

Marianna. Marianna. Marianna in the black Gibson Girl gown, the gown he loved her to wear for him but had never told her why. Suddenly it was desperately important to him that he did. He could see her face, hear her voice from another dimension. The applause rang in his ears from on stage at the Lyceum. Another curtain call, Mr Koenig! *The Count of Monte Cristo*. He walked towards the footlights, took his final bow. The curtains were falling. The bright lights, the audience, the applause were fading now. His eyes tried to focus through the heavy, drunken haze, but he could no longer see where he was going; his hands trembled on the wheel. He had to get back to her, to explain to her, just as he'd explained everything in the letter to Shawn . . . then she would understand, love him again, realize how much he'd come to love her. Faster, faster, before it was too late.

Beneath him, the Pierce-Arrow hummed as it gathered speed; his foot pressed down harder and harder on the throttle until it reached the floor. Surely he was near home: he could hear the spill of the water fountain in the middle of the front lawn. So like the sound of the rushing, groaning sea, it was much closer now. In a moment, he would catch sight of the huge ironwork gates and then, beyond them, the curve of the drive. And his Marianna.

With a flick of the wrist, he spun the steering wheel towards the sounds of the waves as they crashed upon the shore. He was Edmond Dantes again, escaping from the Château d'If; all he needed to do in order to free himself for ever was to find the will, the courage, to jump: Marianna would be waiting. Marianna would listen to him. He smiled as he felt the wheels obey him, skim sharply across the surface of the road; then the waves seemed to rush up to meet him as the Pierce-Arrow plunged nose downwards over the edge of the cliff to the rocks below.

CHAPTER TWENTY-THREE

The symptoms had started that morning, the instant he woke – sore throat, running eyes, a head that felt like lead. Goddam head cold. Shawn had struggled up, uncharacteristically sluggish, groped his way to the bathroom and gulped down a couple of aspirin powders with a glass of tepid water, then gotten himself dressed. He'd glanced at the mantel clock – he was running late now – and realized that because he'd overslept he had no time for a proper breakfast. A couple of cups of coffee later he was hurrying downstairs and into the street, where it was raining hard. He cursed out loud when he realized that he'd missed his tram and he'd have to start walking along Broadway. By the time he reached his workplace it was raining harder than ever and he was soaked to the skin.

'Hey, Shawn!' someone said, mid-morning, after he'd been bent double with a violent paroxysm of sneezing. 'Reckon you'll be spending the weekend in bed, huh?'

'It's just a head cold; I'll be better by then.' But he wasn't. At lunchtime he felt so ill that the boss sent him home and he stopped by Riker's drugstore on 23rd and Sixth for something stronger than aspirin. He was shaking when he reached his apartment, almost too weak and drained to climb the stairs. Marianna's telegram was waiting for him.

He'd sunk down into the nearest chair, his own wretchedness forgotten, trying to absorb the shock of what had happened. Curt, Curt. Though he'd passed at least a dozen news stands along Broadway, not one had borne a hint of the terrible tragedy that was only hours old; as it was, he had only a few hours at most in which to make travel arrangements, pack a bag and head west, before the sensational story broke.

He was dizzy and sweating as he stood on the freezing

station platform, waiting for his train, his own anguish, his own appalling discomfort forgotten. Marianna needed him. Because of her, Shawn had quarrelled with and become estranged from his closest, his oldest friend, something he'd never forget, never forgive himself for, now that it was too late to make amends. If Curt was being buried in three days' time, there was nothing on earth that was going to stop him from being there with her to say goodbye.

It had been Hal Goldenthal who had wired the Koenigs in Minneapolis with the news about Curt's sudden, tragic death, just hours before the story broke in the press. They reached Hollywood half a day in front of Shawn, marginally ahead of the hordes of eastern newspapermen who had been despatched to California by their editors, hungry for sensational details of the accident.

So intense was press and public interest that the studio had hired private security guards to patrol the Koenig house and grounds, in order to keep unwanted interlopers away, and Hal Goldenthal had insisted that the Los Angeles police department deploy men at the church gates on the day of the funeral to ensure that the family had as much protection as possible from the swarm of journalists and droves of fans who had begun to gather outside the studio and the gates of the family home. Goldenthal had met Shawn on his arrival at the local station, and driven him straight to the Koenig house.

It was unnaturally silent; that was the first thing that struck him. So different from the home in Manhattan that he recalled from the early days, with the sound of the children's laughter, Curt cracking jokes, the music from the wind-up Victrola. The memories of all the things they'd shared since they were boys in Minneapolis came flooding back as he followed Goldenthal into the palatial marble hall – so quiet, so empty, so cheerless – and he felt a lump rising in his throat. Without Curt's presence, all the grandeur, the sumptuous furnishings and trappings of success he saw all around him, had no life.

She was standing alone in the palatial drawing room,

dressed in deepest black. For a moment they stared at each other. The change in her appearance – the stunning complexion, the beautiful eyes had vanished – shocked him. This pale, haggard, sallow woman with dark circles beneath her eyes was just a shadow of the Marianna he remembered from New York.

He closed the door, held his arms out towards her, and her face crumpled like a child's. 'Marianna, what the hell can I say to you? I didn't even know what to think myself, when the telegram came. I just dropped everything, came here as soon as I could.'

She threw herself against him, clasped her hands behind his neck as if she was drowning. He was here, alive, something solid, something she could cling to. He was the only real link that was left with the past where she and Curt had been young and happy together, before the clouds had gathered and the unbridgeable chasm had opened up between them. She clung to him as if she would never let go, while she sobbed uncontrollably.

'Shawn, I loved him so. I loved him so much. He walked out of the house that night after we'd quarrelled, and I never got the chance to tell him that I was sorry.'

Shawn held her tightly to him, gently stroked her hair. After everything Curt had done to her, her love for him remained unshakeable, undiminished. While he held her in his arms as he'd often longed to – hadn't he always been secretly a little in love with her himself? – he wished with all his heart that, perhaps, one day, someone would love him like that too.

'Where are the children?'

'Curt's family have taken them for a drive along the coast, to get them away from the reporters and the crowds outside the gates.' She was more composed now, more the dignified Eastbridge the outside world would expect. 'We talked about what would be best for them after the funeral; Jesse suggested they take all three of them back to Minneapolis until things have been sorted out . . . and I agreed.' She wiped her eyes. 'Hal Goldenthal's taking care

361

of the legal side . . . Curt's affairs were pretty complicated, or so he said. He didn't go into details and I didn't ask. I don't think I could handle all that on top of having the three of them here to take care of.'

'Marianna, you don't have to do anything alone.' He came and stood beside her, put his arm around her shoulders. 'That's why I'm here. I have to go back to New York for a few days straight after the funeral, just to sort things out and pick up my mail, but I'll head right back here just as soon as I've done it. I promise you.'

She looked up at him, just a trace of the old sparkle in her eyes; he would never know how much those words meant to her, the knowledge that he was willing to walk away from his home, his career, to be with her when she needed him. Curt had never done as much. Shawn was a lifeline she could cling to. She laid her head against his chest, in her grief and pain unaware of how hot his skin was, how much he was sweating beneath his suit. Hal Goldenthal had remarked how ill he looked when they'd met at the station, but Shawn had shrugged it off, saying that it was just a head cold and he was sweating so much because he wasn't used to the California climate. Besides, in a day or two, with the sunshine and fresh air, he'd soon shake it off.

'Marianna, I would have come before. If Curt had asked me to.' Though the children had written to Shawn frequently since they'd left New York, and he'd written back and sent them gifts on their birthdays, Curt had never contacted him. Maybe now was the wrong time to remind her that the two of them had never patched up that last, bitter quarrel. 'I guess Curt always was stubborn . . . and he had a lot of pride. But it was my fault, too. I should have written him. Maybe I was hoping that he'd come round and write me first. Maybe he was waiting for me to make the first move. Either way, I reckon if he was here now, he'd be just as sorry as I am that we parted company the way we did.'

'Yes.' She had never asked either of them the real reason for that final quarrel, the years of silence and estrangement.

For a moment she hesitated. She'd had her own suspicions, but there was only one way she would ever know for sure. 'I know Curt was unfaithful to me, Shawn.' He looked up sharply. 'More than once. No point going into details now about how I found out. But I know you were his best friend and that you covered for him – out of a sense of loyalty.' He sighed deeply, momentarily glanced away; so she'd known about the other women all the time? 'I want you to know that I don't hold it against you. How could I? You put loyalty to Curt above everything else, and I have to admire that. Even if it was misplaced loyalty. But then, Curt always did have that magic ability to make other people do things for him that they'd never dream of doing for anyone else.'

'He did care about you . . . in his own strange way . . .'

'You knew about Madeline Dupre, didn't you? And the Kopek girl?' He looked shamefaced. 'Yes, I thought so. It wasn't all his fault . . . it was mine, too. I never realized it until now . . . now that it's too late. I couldn't be what he wanted me to be, and I drove him away.' Even to Shawn, she couldn't reveal the truth about Klara Kopek's death; not yet. Perhaps later, when she was stronger, when the pain and anguish were not so keen and raw. When he came back from New York. 'Was that why you and Curt quarrelled? Because he told you about them, and asked you to lie for him?'

'I couldn't bear to think about him hurting you, Marianna. Whatever the reason. I knew just how deeply you loved him – the kind of love any man in his right mind would kill for – and I couldn't stand the way he was just throwing it all away.' He took her hand, and held it tightly between his own. For the first time, she realized how hot he was. 'Neither of them were even a patch on you . . .'

CHAPTER TWENTY-FOUR

Danny Mazzoli had been twelve years old when they'd fished his big sister Sophia out of the Hudson River. He remembered a patrolman coming to the café door in the tiny eating house his folks ran down in Little Italy, and talking to his mamma and pappa in a hushed voice; then the awful, heart-rending sound of his mamma screaming in grief and pain. He hadn't really understood what had happened until later, when his brother Reno had told him. That Sophia, who had quarrelled with Mamma and Pappa over some guy she'd been going with and they didn't approve of, was dead, and she'd never come back again.

No, he hadn't understood what had really happened, not then. It was only later, when he'd met a girl Sophia used to work with upstate, and found out the truth, that the hatred had started growing inside him. A burning, surging, terrifying hatred for the cop who had threatened his sister with a prostitution rap, if she didn't make the false statement he wanted. Sadie Schneiderman, the girl who had worked with his Sophia, the pretty, laughing, lovely Sophia he'd always remember before they'd dragged her poor, battered, swollen, raped corpse from the Hudson, had told him the real story.

'She was scared, real scared. Scared witless of this guy. So we said, come stay with us. The next mornin', she never showed up at the factory for work. Nor the next day, nor the one after that. That's when we started to get worried . . . so come evenin' time, we went down the Lower East Side to find her.' Sadie Schneiderman had hesitated a little then, as if she wasn't sure that she should tell him the graphic details; after all, this was his flesh and blood she was talking about. But he'd made her go on; he wanted to hear it all, every last bit of it. 'She was lyin' there, on the bed, all beat up. Beat up real bad. All her clothes ripped, covered with blood. We took her back home with us, told her to make an official complaint. But she wouldn't do it, even though she knew the guy's name; even though she knew his precinct number. You know why? You can't never prove anythin' against a cop, that's what she told us. You try to get him, he'll get you first.'

Danny had never seen his sister again, after she'd left home; not till they'd fished her body out of the docks. Lots of suicides threw themselves off that point, someone told his mamma and pappa, when they'd gone down to the city morgue to identify what was left of her. Who knew the hell why they did it? Maybe it had something to do with pride – yes, they had a sort of pride down on the Lower East Side – when a good girl from a decent, hard-working Italian family gets raped and beaten and in trouble with the law, sometimes even the most squalid kind of death is better than living with the shame of that. Poor Sophia.

As he'd watched his mamma and pappa sobbing while her poor shabby little coffin had been lowered into a pauper's grave in the local churchyard, Danny had made a vow. He'd find that cop, wherever he was, and, when he found him, he'd do just like it said in the Bible. An eye for an eye . . . a life for a life.

He didn't care how many years it took; and it had taken him some. He didn't mind being patient. When he was eighteen years old he'd got a job as a cart driver for a haulier's company – perfect, for what he had in mind. He'd watched, planned, waited. One day, luck had been on his side at long, long last. When Delucca had come nonchalantly down the precinct steps and begun to walk alone along the street, Danny had whipped up his team and followed him, gathering speed for the final onslaught. But as Delucca had paused to cross the busy thoroughfare, teeming with pedestrians and other traffic, some fool kid had run unexpectedly in front of Danny's horses and he'd been forced to swerve, and in that instant Delucca had stepped back from the thundering hooves and wheels of the cart just in time. True, the logs he'd been carrying had tumbled out, crashing all over the road and knocking Delucca flying – and nobody who'd seen what happened would ever have guessed that it was attempted murder and not an unfortunate accident. But Danny's first plan to get revenge on the bastard who'd caused his sister's death had failed miserably.

Though he was crushed by the falling logs and broke four ribs, an arm and a leg, it didn't kill him.

It had been a shock, an unpleasant shock, when he'd first seen Koenig's death splashed over every billboard in the city, in black letters ten inches high. On his way back to the precinct he'd stopped at the nearest news stand and bought a copy of the evening paper to read more, but there'd been little to read except the bare facts, padded out with pressmen's ballyhoo about the grieving family and Koenig's illustrious career. Few things threw Delucca; but this did. He didn't give a shit how or why Koenig's Pierce-Arrow went out of control and nosedived over a clifftop in the middle of the night, only that, from now on in, he'd be five thousand bucks short every month. No way.

He'd walked around a little, worn away some shoe leather. Fuck the precinct, fuck Chief Rawlins if he was late back on duty. He needed to do some serious thinking. Koenig had been about to sign up for a new picture and, he guessed from reading between the lines of his newspaper, the studio would almost certainly have put some big bucks up front first. Let the heat die down, maybe a month or two, and he'd wangle some unpaid leave and take a little trip down to Hollywood to look up the grieving widow. Born a stuck-up Eastbridge, she'd be anxious to keep the lid on any scandal that'd threaten her dead husband's name, and pay through the nose to do it. Just what he was banking on.

He'd still been deep in thought, still smiling to himself, when the big, heavy cart alongside suddenly swerved violently to avoid something in the road, and the stack of logs it was carrying broke loose and rained down on him, knocking him unconscious to the ground.

Shawn managed to keep how ill he felt from Marianna and
the children, as well as Curt's family, right up until the time
came for him to catch the train back to New York after the
funeral; but driving him in the buggy along the dusty
boulevard through town towards the station, Jesse Koenig
gave Shawn a look of concern.

'You don't look good. You should have seen a doctor
before we left. Gotten something for it. Hell, Shawn, have
you seen yourself? You're burnin' up!'

'It's nothin' I haven't had before; just a goddam head
cold. Half the guys at work have come down with it.'
Though he felt like death warmed up, he shrugged it off.
The climate down here was making him feel worse than he
really was; he just wasn't used to west coast temperatures.
A day or two in bed would have fixed it, if he hadn't gotten
Marianna's telegram and had to leave New York straight
away. Not that it mattered. He'd double up on the medication he'd brought with him and sleep it off on the
three-day train journey back east. He picked up his travelling bag as the buggy drew up outside the station, and
clapped Curt's brother on the shoulder. It had been good
to see Jesse and the others again, a poignant reminder of
times long past, the early days in Minneapolis where they'd
grown up together. 'Thanks for the ride, Jesse. Wish we
could have met up again under happier circumstances.
Your ma's taken it all real bad.'

'We're all hurtin', Shawn. But it'll help, havin' Curt's
kids come back with us to Minneapolis for a while.' Shawn
nodded, then jumped down, fishing in his pocket for his
return ticket. Only ten minutes to wait before it was time
for his train to leave. Dear God, but his head was throbbing
now! Lights had begun to dance in front of his eyes, and he
felt sick to his stomach.

'Just take good care of Marianna till I get back next
week.'

The fog was thick and swirling when the train eventually
reached New York and the passenger cars rapidly began to

367

empty; but Shawn was almost oblivious of what was going on around him. For three days and nights, too ill to make his way to the dining car, he'd drunk copiously but eaten virtually nothing at all. The sheets of the bunk in his cabin, and the clothes he'd left California in, were soaked with perspiration; when the train pulled into Grand Central Station, his temperature was 104°.

Vaguely aware that he'd finally reached his destination, he stumbled up, peered through the window to see where he was, then, with almost superhuman effort as he felt so weak, pulled his single travelling bag from its place on the rack above his head.

The air outside the train was freezing, but he scarcely noticed. The cab he hailed deposited him outside his apartment building on 119th Street, where he fumbled in his pocket to find the fare. The driver looked at him strangely. He stopped a moment to get his breath, willing himself to stand up straight, willing his head to clear.

The single bag felt like lead in his hands. His legs could scarcely bear him up. Got to hurry. A good night's sleep, a visit to his doctor on West 60th in the morning for some proper medication – the pills he'd bought at Riker's drugstore hadn't done him any good at all – sort out leave from his place of work, then catch the late afternoon train back again. Marianna was alone. Marianna needed him.

He had struggled to the top of the staircase, got his key into the lock, when he suddenly collapsed, falling heavily through the door of his apartment and slumping headlong onto the pile of mail that lay there on the mat, Curt's last, poignant letter among it.

She stepped out of the cab, paid the driver in silence, totally anonymous behind the dark, all-concealing veil. Ironic, that in all the days of travelling, then the ride across the city at the busiest time of day, nobody had realized who she was, hardly anyone had paused to give her a second glance; the veil was like a barrier, keeping out the world. That was the way she wanted it. While the billboards and the newspapers screamed banner headlines about Curt's death, his last picture, speculation about how much he was worth, Marianna walked unnoticed among the Manhattan crowds hurrying home from work, rushing past her in their haste to escape from the driving rain.

Amsterdam Avenue on 114th Street, the Episcopal Hospital of St Luke's. She walked inside, showed the telegram Shawn's sister Zelda had sent her four days ago, and asked to be taken straight to him. There was a lump in her throat as she followed the nurse into the gilded-cage elevator shaft, stared through the French Renaissance-style bars as they ascended the staircase well of the Vanderbilt Pavilion. She hated the stillness, the clinical whiteness, the sickly-sweet smell of chloroform and disinfectant that saturated the air. It was her fault that Shawn was here. Dropping everything the instant he'd received her wire about Curt, oblivious of how ill he must have felt, he'd rushed to her side as quickly as he could, ignoring the first stages of the pneumonia that had almost killed him. If anything had happened to him, she would never have been able to forgive herself. Now it was her turn to repay his loyalty.

She sat down slowly beside the bed, shocked at his appearance. His skin was the colour of candle wax. When she reached out and took his hand in hers, it burned like coal, even through the leather of her gloves.

'Shawn . . .'

His eyelids flickered open at the sound of her voice. Weakly, he smiled.

'I only got Zelda to send you the wire to let you know I couldn't get back straight away . . . knew you'd understand . . . goddam pneumonia . . .' He began to cough. 'Who would have figured it? Reckoned I'd just gone and gotten myself another head cold from one of the guys at work . . .' He turned his head, rocked with another violent bout of coughing.

'Shawn, try not to talk.' She leaned towards him. 'I'm here now. I'll stay till you get better . . . then you're coming back to California with me. There's no hurry. The children are in Minneapolis.' She smiled. 'New York at this time of year is no good for that bad chest. You need sunshine and warm air.'

He turned his face towards her. It was a terrible effort even to speak now. 'My sister . . . she's at the apartment, seeing to things. You know the address. If you don't want to stay at a hotel – you know, with people knowing who you are and bothering you with questions about Curt – you can stay as long as you want to. She'll give you a key.' He swallowed. 'Lucky she lives just out of state . . . they got hold of her quickly after the guy in the next apartment found me . . .' He closed his eyes now. 'I told her, I don't want Ma and Pa knowin' I'm in here . . . they'll fuss too much . . . just tell her not to forget that, will you?'

'I'll do anything you want me to, Shawn.'

He looked up into her face, through heavy, drug-laden eyes. He smiled at her. 'You're here, Marianna. That's all that counts.'

A tear welled up in the corner of her eye, and trickled slowly down her cheek. She should have realized how ill he'd really been when he'd come to Curt's funeral; she should have noticed, despite her grief and pain, and made him see her own doctor, stopped him from travelling back. Too late now. 'I'm here because Curt would have been. And because when I got Zelda's telegram, nothing would have kept me away.'

'I always did tell Curt . . . you got yourself one hell of a girl. . .' His eyelids closed, the rasping breathing gently ceased. Marianna stood up in a sudden panic. He was too quiet, too still.

'*Shawn!*' Her frightened voice echoed around the silent ward, bringing a nurse to the bed from the corridor outside. She laid her fingers against his neck, lifted the limp hand to feel for a pulse. Then her eyes met Marianna's dolefully, and she shook her head.

She walked from the hospital in a trance, into the driving rain outside, not knowing, not caring, in which direction she went. People and traffic milled all around her, but she was oblivious of them; no sounds distracted her, nothing penetrated the wall of unbearable anguish, the chasm of utter despair.

She felt drained, numb, hollow; a woman capable only of movement, no emotion. She moved like a sleepwalker along 114th Street, through Central Park, southwards towards midtown and Bowery. An hour or more after she'd walked out of the hospital, she found herself staring at the doors of the Jerry McAuley Mission.

Inside, she sat down on one of the crude wooden benches. Religious slogans decorated the walls. 'Jesus said, If any man thirst, let him come unto me and drink.' 'God is love, for God so loved the world that He gave His only begotten son.' Marianna stared at them, slowly, deliberately, as the anger and the bitterness rose up inside her like gall. No love, no hope, no God. God had perished in the wreckage of Curt's Pierce-Arrow. As long as she lived, she would never believe in any of those things again. If there was a God, he would never have made her suffer this appalling agony, never let Curt be snatched away from her, never allowed someone as good and decent and loyal as Shawn to die.

Two women had come into the mission hall behind her; she watched them go silently to the front and kneel down near the speaker's lectern, heads bent beneath their shawls, lips moving in silent prayer. She looked at them with pity and contempt. No God. The words on the walls were meaningless, the promises empty. She should have known. All her life she had been praying to something, someone, who had never been there.

CHAPTER TWENTY-FIVE

As the automobile drew up at the bottom of the driveway, the children peered from their seats apprehensively. More than six months away from their mother, the home they knew, staying with their grandparents in Minneapolis; more than six months since the terrible accident when their father's Pierce-Arrow had gone out of control, and plunged from the highway into the ravine below. Elynor had never forgotten the sight of her mother's face that morning, when someone from the Los Angeles police department had come to tell her. Then, while they'd been in Minneapolis, the news had come that Uncle Shawn had died of pneumonia in a hospital in New York City. All three of them had been shattered.

Their uncle Jesse Koenig killed the engine and climbed out from the driving seat. Something about him, the profile, the shade of the hair, just the way he moved, reminded Elynor of her father, and she felt the tears stinging at the back of her eyes, the lump rising in her throat. She'd cried herself to sleep so many nights, aching for him; remembering his smile, his laugh, the way he'd walk into the house when he came home from the studio each day and call to them. It was hard, almost impossible for any of them to believe that they would never see him again.

Their uncle Jesse opened the doors for them, and helped out the girls one by one. 'Now . . . your momma's waitin' for you inside . . . so remember what I told you on the way down here. You got to be good for her . . . help her. Not just today or tomorrow, mind . . . but all the time. You got that?' They all nodded, solemnly. 'OK.'

'Uncle Jesse,' said Alice, pushing in front of her sister

372

and clinging to his hand. 'Are we going to stay in this house now that Daddy's gone? Will we move back to New York?'

'That's up to your momma. One of the reasons why we took you back with us after the funeral was so your momma could work out just what she wanted to do. Maybe you will be goin' back to New York. Maybe not. But one thing your momma don't need right now is a whole lot of big questions . . . you all got that?' They all nodded dutifully.

Inside, the house had been transformed in their absence. Upstairs, all the guest bedrooms except one had been closed up, all the downstairs furniture with the exception of the main rooms had been draped in white dustsheets. They were all puzzled. Colleen, looking noticeably sombre, had opened the front door to them.

'Mrs Koenig is in the drawing room.'

The luxurious splendour of Curt's homes had always intimidated Jesse just a little; unlike his brother, he had never felt quite at ease among the rich furnishings and outward trappings of wealth. Like the house on Madison, this one was palatial, expensive, decorated with exquisite and refined taste; no doubt it had been mostly Marianna's. After all, she'd been brought up to it. She was standing by the huge Moorish arched window when they walked in and, instead of rushing to greet them as Elynor and Gene thought she would, she just turned her head towards them coolly and gave them a ghost of a smile. How pale Momma looks, Elynor thought, noticing at once the dark circles beneath her eyes, the tautness around her lips; she looked drained, colourless, as if she was just recovering from a long and serious illness. Their father's sudden, tragic death, then Uncle Shawn's so soon after, had taken a terrible toll.

'Hello, Momma.'

'Hi, Marianna.' It hurt, the likeness between Jesse and Curt; the old feelings buried deep inside her were not quite dead, then, she told herself wryly. She had tried so desperately hard not to think about him, even when she woke in the middle of the night alone and torn with misery; no point in thinking of what might have been.

'Colleen will bring in tea. You must be tired after the drive from the station. I'm afraid the roads are still a little primitive here.'

'I'll say.' She was still not over the shock, Jesse Koenig told himself; anyone could see that, just by looking at her. She'd been so vital, so pretty. He remembered the first time Curt had brought her home and he'd thought how lucky his brother was to have such a handsome-looking girl, and a millionaire's daughter to boot. It must have been a shock to her when F. H. Eastbridge had died and left his fortune to charity. But Curt had left her and the children more than well provided for, surely? Before he left, there were a few things they'd have to discuss; best to wait until the children had gone up to bed.

He sat down. 'Is everything all right? I mean, how have things been?'

'In what respect, Jesse? Nothing's changed from six months ago, has it? I'm still alone, with three children to bring up single-handed.' Her voice held no trace of bitterness, only a curious detachment, as if after all the heartache and the traumas she'd accepted the inevitable. 'I've had these past few months to think about just how I'm going to go about that.'

'You're going back to New York?'

'Why would I do that? Our future is here, in California.'

'I see.' There was a pause while Colleen brought in a tray of tea, fancy cakes and sandwiches, which the three children immediately fell upon. Their mother frowned.

'I see your stay in Minneapolis has brought about a gross degeneration of good manners.' They all stared at her. 'If you can't behave in a fitting way for a civilized drawing room, then I suggest you take your food into the kitchen and eat it there.'

They got up, shamefacedly, and one by one filed out of the room. Gene, the last one to leave, closed the door quietly behind him.

'Hell, Marianna . . . I know what you've been through

with Curt's death, then Shawn . . . but there was no need to talk to them quite so sharp, was there? They've all missed you like crazy.'

'I doubt that. When their father was alive they hardly noticed that I was even here.'

'You can't mean that?' He was shocked. He had never been close to Marianna, never known her well, but he'd never seen her like this before. She was so cold, so withdrawn. Surely she'd be getting over what had happened to Curt by now? Maybe she still couldn't accept it, despite the impression she'd given him when he first arrived that she had. 'All they've talked about these past months was what they'd do when they got back here.'

Marianna smiled, but not pleasantly. 'You don't have to try to pretend to me, Jesse. I think I know my children far better than you do. Curt was the one they were close to. Not me.'

'They need you, Marianna.'

She looked away, out of the window at the setting sun. So many sunsets, so many lonely days and nights since Curt had left her for ever; she must not think about that now. Love had been the bane, the curse of her life. Never again would she allow herself to be influenced by it.

'I'm selling the house, Jesse.' That surprised him. 'I don't think it would be good for any of us to stay here. Too many memories.'

'I understand.' It was her business, not his; but he was a little taken aback. Surely staying here would mean retaining something of his brother's presence, a reminder of the times they'd all been together. But maybe that wasn't the way she looked at it. 'When did you intend putting the place on the market? Will it be easy to find a buyer out here?'

'I don't think that will be any problem. It should all be finalized within the next few days.'

'As soon as that?'

'Jesse, all the major independent studios are seeing the advantages of moving out here. Think about it. They have good weather – something you can't rely on in either New

375

York or Chicago – and labour's cheap. The Trust's long arm of interference doesn't quite have the same bite it had back east . . . Hollywood makes sense. And as more companies move to California, the more valuable real estate and land will be. I'd be willing to bet that within ten years – if you come back – you won't recognize this place at all.'

One thing was still puzzling him. She hadn't mentioned Curt's will, but he must have left Marianna everything. 'With Curt gone . . . I know he must have been pretty comfortable for money . . . why are you staying? You don't know people here . . . all your friends, your family . . . well, they're back east.'

'As it happens, Curt wasn't comfortable for money. That's right. I see that surprises you.' There was bitterness in her voice now. 'Well, I can tell you . . . it came as a hell of a shock to me. Curt always was easy come, easy go, as far as money was concerned. He spent big in New York, then when we came here he bought the house, the big swanky automobile, ponies for the children, not to mention all that imported European furniture he loved so much – it all adds up. He knew he had big earning potential. I guess he thought that there'd be plenty more coming his way . . . except that he died before he could earn it. When I found out after the accident just how little there was left, I realized that I'd have to make drastic economies.' Jesse was speechless for the moment; whoever would have dreamed that Curt would have gotten through so much money? 'As for family and friends . . . you seem to forget that my family disowned me when I chose to marry Curt. Friends? Do I really have any?'

'But all the people you both knew in New York . . .?'

'They were just business acquaintances of Curt's. They didn't care about either him or me. Just how much money they could make by marketing his talent. Only Shawn was a real friend – and he's dead.' It still hurt her, just to speak his name. With Shawn to hold her hand after she'd lost everything that mattered to her, life could have been bearable. But even that comfort had been snatched away

376

from her. She could never make Jesse understand.

'Marianna, you're family to us. I shouldn't have to remind you of that. If you ever need anything, if we can ever help, you know we're just a cable away.' She smiled, but there was no warmth in it. He was trying to be supportive, trying so hard to be kind, but she had never been a part of the Koenig family; they were too different. From the very first time she'd met them, Marianna had never felt anything except a stranger.

'I appreciate the gesture, Jesse. I know you're making it out of loyalty to Curt. But I'm not your responsibility. I have to rely on myself now; my father always taught me that. I never believed him. I always liked to feel that there was someone there, more powerful than I was, who'd watch over me, take care of me if things went wrong. You believe in things like that when you're a child. I know I did. It's only later, when you move into the real world, when you get touched by tragedy and pain – and people you loved and trusted betray you – that you realize there isn't anyone there at all.'

She sounded so cold, so cynical. 'You've changed a lot since we first met.'

'Should I take that as a compliment?' The door opened before he could answer and Alice stood there, holding a blue satin dress.

'Momma, why was this hanging in the closet in my room? It isn't one of mine. And I don't like the colour. Do you, Uncle Jesse?'

'I think it's real pretty, honey.'

'Alice, how many times have I told you that you never walk into a room where grown-ups are talking without knocking first? Go upstairs, put the dress back where you found it. And do it now.' She pulled a sulky face, then disappeared reluctantly without a word.

'You were a little hard on the kid, Marianna. She's just lost her father, for Christ's sake!'

'And I've lost my husband and our best friend! Believe me, I've lost far more than she has.' There was anger in her voice now. She'd intended to ask him to stay until tomorrow, but now she'd changed her mind. His resemblance to his brother was too painfully strong, the reminder of that last night when they'd quarrelled still too vivid for her to be able to forget. A hundred times she'd woken in a hot sweat, always from the same nightmare: hearing the front door close, the sound of the Pierce-Arrow's engine roaring into life, and then the terrible silence. Curt's voice, and the guilt, always the unbearable guilt, were constantly there to haunt her; had he driven off after that last violent quarrel and, in a fit of depression, deliberately steered the Pierce-Arrow over the cliff? He'd been drinking heavily that night, she knew; the glass, the almost empty bottle had been evidence of that. Maybe the amount of bourbon he'd drunk had seriously impaired his judgement, and his death really had been the tragic accident that everyone thought – and she'd forced herself to believe – it was. But how would she ever know for sure? It was the doubt, the single grain of uncertainty at the back of her mind that was tearing her apart. Something she could never talk about to anyone. 'I'm grateful for what you've done. All of you. Taking the children for these past few months gave me a breathing space. But I think it would be better if you left now.'

'I'll do whatever you want me to.' She didn't want him to go, but there was no point in his staying. His presence in her life, in the children's, was only temporary. He wouldn't be here to help her next week, next month, next year, or the year after that. That was the bottom line; she was alone now.

'Why don't you go upstairs and say goodbye to the children?'

They received the news the next morning that their mother was selling the house with considerable dismay; but only Alice, who was adamant that she didn't want to live anywhere else, was ill advised enough to argue with her.

'But, Momma, I'd just hate to go and live someplace else! I like it here and I want to stay!' Her voice took on its familiar truculent, whining note. 'Daddy wouldn't have wanted us to go live in any other house but this one, I know it!'

'I think we all better get one thing clear right now.' Her eyes were colder, harder than they'd ever seen them. They had never seen their mother quite like this before. 'Your father's dead, and nothing is going to bring him back again. From now on, I'll be the one who makes all the decisions . . . so you'd best get used to it.' She looked at each one of them in turn. 'There'll be no complaints. No arguments. And whatever I decide is final.' Her eyes rested on her youngest daughter now. 'Your father was a soft touch as far as you were concerned, young lady; but everything's going to be a whole lot different from now on in. Starting right this moment.' Alice screwed up her face; she didn't like what she was hearing at all. 'You go right upstairs and put on that blue dress. I'll be up when you're ready to fix your hair.'

'But, Momma, I don't want to! I hate that colour blue! I like pale blue, or pink. And I don't need my hair fixed!'

'I don't think you understood what I just said, Alice. When I tell you to do something, you just do it. Right then and there. You don't question it, you don't argue. You just do exactly what I told you to do. Now go straight upstairs, put on the dress. I'm taking you to the studio.'

'Do as Momma says, Alice.' Elynor nudged her sister gently towards the stairs. 'I'll come help you.' But after a lifetime of getting almost everything her own way, Alice found obedience hard.

'Why are we going to the studio, Momma? Is Mr Goldenthal taking us out to lunch somewhere?'

'Go put on the dress. Then you'll find out.'

Alice's howls of pain as her mother dragged a bristle brush unmercifully through her thick, curly hair could be heard two hundred yards away, where Gene and Elynor stood at the end of the drive by the little buggy that Marianna used for transport. Elynor had covered her ears at the worst point.

'That's the trouble with Alice,' Gene said with a wisdom

379

far in advance of his sixteen years. 'Everyone's always spoiled her, 'cos she's so cute and pretty. She can't figure out why everything's suddenly changed now. Momma was the only one who never let her have it all her own way. And she got spoiled rotten in Minneapolis.'

Elynor laid her head against the pony's soft mane and gazed into the distance. When they'd first come here from New York she'd loved it so much; it was all so new, so fresh, so different from the big city. There'd been riding every day and picnics at the beach; barbecues and studio parties, trips in the Pierce-Arrow out of state, when their father would take them to some surprise destination and load them all with extravagant presents; now he wasn't here any more and all their dreams had been shattered. 'Momma's changed so, Gene. It's as if . . . well, it's as if it isn't really her any more. She's so different, from when we first went away. As if she's someone else.'

'She hasn't gotten over Dad. That's what it is, Ellie. She just hasn't gotten over him. Remember what Grandma Koenig told us? When some people have a big shock like Momma, the grief does somethin' to them; they can't handle it. The same as what happened with Uncle Shawn's mom. Didn't his sister Zelda say that after he'd died and she'd cleared everything out of his apartment and sent it back home, his mom put it all in his old room just as it was, and wouldn't even look at it? Even some mail that had come for him right before he died. She just put it all in his old room and locked the door, like she didn't want to accept that he was really dead . . . as if she believed that some day he'd just walk in the front door like nothing had happened.'

'But Mrs Duchovsky's an old lady; Momma isn't like that.'

'She's still affected by what happened to Dad, the same way.'

'How could an accident like that have happened, Gene?' Both of them had wondered, but never spoken about that night, when their father had driven off in the Pierce-Arrow and never come back. 'Daddy was so careful. He was the

380

best driver in the whole world!' She dashed away a tear that had welled up in the corner of her eye. 'You think he missed the edge of the canyon in the dark, and the wheels skidded?'

'That's the only thing that could have happened, Ellie. When it's pitch dark, everything looks so different. Either way, we'll never know for sure.' They both looked up as Alice, wiping her tear-stained face with a lace-edged handkerchief, came out of the house and walked slowly and reluctantly along the drive. Their mother had dressed her golden curls and coaxed them into corkscrews, and two large blue satin bows had been tied on each side.

'Momma's been real mean to me!' She blew her nose vigorously. 'She never took any notice when I told her she was hurting me. I wanted Colleen to fix my hair! She never hurts me when she brushes it!'

'Alice, it's all your own fault. You shouldn't have made Momma so mad.'

'She won't tell me why we're going to the studio. She won't tell me anything!' She gazed back over her shoulder resentfully as their mother came out of the house and closed the door. 'I wish I was back with Grandpa and Grandma Koenig in Minneapolis. It was much more fun there!'

'Only 'cos they let you sweet-talk them into getting your own way all the time! Better do what Momma tells you,' Gene warned.

Marianna ordered her into the passenger seat of the buggy. 'You two. Hadn't you better get back into the house and get on with your studies? I'll bet you didn't get much schoolwork done while you were away in Minnesota?'

'Only a little.'

'Just what I thought.' Marianna lifted the hem of her gown and swung herself up into the driving seat. She picked up the reins. She seemed so calm, so collected, so confident in herself; it was almost unnatural. 'You'd best start making up for lost time, then . . . hadn't you?'

'Yes, Momma.' Would she always be this way, they both wondered, separately? She had always been stricter, more critical and less inclined to spoil any of them than their father had, but the new woman she'd changed into while

381

they'd been away was more than a little intimidating. 'What time will you get back from seeing Mr Goldenthal?'

'I'll be just as long as it takes.'

Hal Goldenthal was studying his production accountants' figures for the last two months when his secretary came into his office to tell him that Mrs Curt Koenig had arrived to see him, with her daughter Alice. He looked up in surprise. He hadn't set eyes on her for weeks now – she'd still be in mourning, and anything to do with death had always depressed him; besides which, seeing Curt's widow only reminded him sharply of how much profit he'd lost since Curt's death. He frowned.

'Have I missed something here, huh? Forgotten some appointment in my diary I should have known about?'

'No, sir. Mrs Koenig doesn't have an appointment. But she is most insistent on seeing you.'

'OK. Show her in.' Goldenthal sighed. 'I guess I can spare her a few moments of my time.' He hesitated. He hoped she wasn't going to break down and start crying in his office. 'If she's still here after . . . ten minutes, say . . . put your head round the door and make out you're remindin' me of another appointment.'

'Yes, Mr Goldenthal.'

She was still dressed in black; not deepest black, more of a dark charcoal colour, but it still made him shudder a little. Maybe it had something to do with the past, his childhood back in the old country, when his grandmother had lain dying and his parents had forced him and his brothers and sisters to stand around her bed until the last moments had come. He could recall it vividly, the sallow, hideously wrinkled skin, the sunken eyes; the hands like birds' claws clutching at the shabby black wool of the shawl she was never without. He shivered, as if someone had walked over his own grave.

'Marianna!' He stood up, smiling his very best professional false smile of welcome, hand extended. 'Say, it's real good to see you! I was gonna call by . . . see how you were doin' . . . but, well . . . I didn't want to intrude . . .'

382

'Cut the baloney, Hal.' He was shocked into abrupt silence. Had he heard her right? This wasn't the Marianna Koenig he remembered. 'I'm not here to listen to your excuses – we both know exactly why in all this time you've never bothered to call. Curt's dead, and all the profit you were expecting to rake in from his next picture has gone down the can . . . why bother with cultivating me any more? Isn't that a little nearer to the truth?'

'Hey, now, hang on a goddam minute, Marianna!'

'Save your breath, Hal. I'm here to talk business. Not waste your time or mine.'

Slowly, he sat back in his chair. What the hell had happened to her since Curt had died? Had his death unhinged her? He glanced furtively at his wall clock opposite; in just eight and half minutes – if he couldn't get rid of her sooner – his secretary would come in and save him. 'Marianna, let me pour you a drink to calm your nerves a little.'

She smiled coldly. 'I don't drink in the daytime, Hal. Surely you remember that? Besides which, I don't need it. My nerves have never been better.'

He laid his hands on his desk. 'OK. Let's hear it. You got a grievance you wanna talk about?'

'I've got a contract I want to talk about. No, nothing to do with Curt. Curt's dead and any contract he signed with you died with him. I'm talking about Alice.'

'Alice!'

Marianna opened the door and called to her daughter to come inside. Christ, those blue eyes of hers and that golden hair! She was the living spit of her father! Goldenthal hadn't seen the girl since she'd gone away to her grandparents in Minneapolis six months ago, and the change, seeing her again, startled him. 'News travels fast in this town. Biograph have just signed Mary Pickford . . . what is everyone calling her? "The girl with the curls." You missed out on that deal, Hal . . . what's happening here at Universal? You losing your grip on the wheel?' She pushed Alice forward, towards his desk. 'Word is, Biograph are set on turning Pickford into a major star. A big box office attraction. Blond curls, blue eyes, picture of innocence . . . they reckon the public will go for it, big time. Trouble is, little Mary's no wide-eyed sucker; she's got a head on those shoulders. I heard on the grapevine that she upped and quit Independent because their production standards weren't to her taste. In short, she's trouble. The kind of trouble producers and studios don't need. Besides which, she's already twenty or so. Even if she doesn't look her age now, she can't go on playing cute little girls for ever.' A sly note came into her voice. 'If you sign Alice, you get the perfect rival to Pickford, but a whole lot younger. Not only that, you get more mileage for your money. In five years' time, Pickford could be twenty-five and fat . . . and who knows if the public will still want to go see her pictures? Who'd even heard of the name Mary Pickford before she came here from New York? But when you put the name Koenig on the screen . . . then everyone knows just what you're talking about.'

Goldenthal lay back in his chair. For the first time, he smiled. Hadn't Curt told him once that Marianna's father had been F. H. Eastbridge, the financier? No-one made five million dollars by not being smart; she was a chip off the old block, all right.

'OK. So I gotta admit . . . I could like what I'm hearin'.' He rubbed his chin thoughtfully. 'I'll need to meet with my script writers, Garrard Flair . . . he'd be directing, of course. Provided we could come up with a suitable vehicle for her . . . yeah, I reckon in a week or so we could be talkin' business.'

'No deal, Hal. We talk . . . and we agree now. Right now. Otherwise I walk. There are plenty of other independents in this town who'd just jump at the chance to sign Curt Koenig's daughter.'

'All right . . .'

'Will Mr Flair be directing my pictures?' Alice spoke for the first time. 'Am I going to be a big moving picture star just like Daddy?'

'Be quiet, Alice.'

'Your momma and me gotta talk about it, honey.' At

that moment his secretary came back into the office as he'd told her to, but he gave her short shrift. 'Mr Goldenthal, your next appointment . . .'

'Yeah, OK. Just take the little girl out with you. Get her some soda.'

The moment they were alone again his smile disappeared.

'I'm willing to sign her, OK? But I need to work out the small print first.'

'Work out just what you like, Hal. Don't bother me with details. Let's talk about the money you're putting up front. I want five hundred dollars a week for the first picture, and forty per cent of the net – not gross – profits. With the pictures that follow on, the salary goes up accordingly. Those are the terms. I get script approval on everything, and I act as chaperon on and off set. No publicity stunts, no unauthorized interviews without my express consent . . . I want full consultation on everything.'

'Marianna, you gotta be kiddin' me! Five hundred bucks a week for an eleven-year-old kid? Hey, now, come on, be reasonable!' Was she out of her mind, or what? 'Carl Laemmle at Independent was only paying Pickford a hundred seventy-five a week, and she had New York stage experience with Belasco!'

'That was more than three years ago . . . prices have gone up a whole lot more since then. Don't try to outsmart me, Hal . . . I've done my homework. I happen to have found out that Adolph Zukor has offered her a thousand a week to star in *Tess of the Storm Country* for Famous Players through Paramount. You're getting a Koenig for half the price.' The new, hardened Marianna looked him in the eye in a way that showed him she meant what she said. 'I would have thought an astute businessman like you would have known a good thing when he saw it . . . and not been fool enough to look a gift horse in the mouth.' She stood up. 'Well? Do you accept my terms or not?' Slowly, Goldenthal nodded. 'Good. I'm glad we understand each other. I'll be here first thing in the morning with my lawyer, Walter Oppenheim . . . I'll see myself out.'

385

'I'm going to be in moving pictures, just like Daddy! I'm going to be a star, so there!' As Marianna came into the house after leaving the pony and buggy with the man she'd hired for outside work, she heard Alice's shrill little voice boasting from upstairs. She walked across the hall and picked up the telephone.

'If you don't believe me, just ask Momma! She's going to get Mr Goldenthal to sign a contract, first thing tomorrow.' She sat on the stool in front of her mother's dressing table and admired her reflection in the mirror. 'I'm going to have hundreds of dollars every week, and I can buy all the pretty clothes I want to. I bet you wish it was you, Ellie.'

'Alice, what are you talking about?'

Alice picked up Marianna's lipstick and started to experiment on herself. She opened the powder bowl. 'It's just what I'm saying . . . Mr Goldenthal said that Garrard Flair is going to direct my first picture . . . he's dreamy! You and Gene can come and watch me on set, and then you'll see it's the truth, won't you? I'll have someone special to take care of my clothes, and make up my face for the camera, just like Daddy.'

Ellie was so used to her sister's outrageous stories that she didn't believe a word of it. 'Alice, why would Mr Goldenthal want you in his pictures? You're just a little girl. He only hires grown-up actresses. Besides, you don't even know how to act.'

Alice's petulant little face flushed with anger. 'You're just jealous, that's what! Because Momma didn't choose you. Well, nobody would . . . you're not pretty enough.'

'You little cat!' Gene said.

Downstairs, Marianna's call had been put through to Walter Oppenheim's Los Angeles office. The line was bad. 'Walter?'

'Marianna.'

'You talked to the Revenue about Curt's bank statements?'

'Sure did.' There was a pause and then his voice dropped in pitch; a sure sign that the meeting hadn't gone well. 'You can see their point, Marianna. The missing forty thousand dollars . . . there's just no trace. Kind of understandable that they're suspicious. Hell, those Revenue guys are suspicious anyhow, they got cause to be, in their line of work.'

'How did you leave things with them?'

'I told 'em the truth. That after Curt died and the will went through probate, you got copies of the statements . . . you didn't know what the cash withdrawals each month meant any more than the bank did. The account was in Curt's name, not yours. Each withdrawal was for the same amount and taken out on the same day every time. In cash, not cashier's cheque. So there's no way of tracin' where it wound up. Not a hope in hell. Trouble is, they ain't buyin' it. The way those guys think, Curt drew out the cash and stashed it somewhere for a rainy day. They can't prove that you knew anythin' about it . . . but they hinted that in the near future they'll be wantin' to talk to you themselves.'

'What the hell is that supposed to mean?' She was furious, outraged. The money that had disappeared from Curt's bank account was as much a mystery to her as it was to the Revenue Service. With everything else she'd had to cope with since Curt's death, the last thing she relished was a battle with the tax authorities; but if it was a fight they wanted, then they could sure as hell have it. 'Get them off my back, Walter. I don't take kindly to being accused of complicity in a revenue fraud, if that's what the son-ofabitches are hinting. Come to think of it, where were you in all this? At the first moment they had the nerve to suggest that I'd been part of something like that, you should have told them that if they didn't withdraw the accusation we'd sue. What do you think I pay you for, Walter? I don't keep a dog and bark myself.' She slammed down the telephone and went upstairs.

Alice and Elynor looked round at her as she came into the room. 'Alice, what in God's name have you been doing to your face? How dare you touch anything on my dressing table!'

'I was only showing Ellie how actresses fix their make-up!'

Marianna yanked her roughly from the stool and dragged her in the direction of the bathroom, while she howled in protest. 'Here!' She was thrust in front of the mirror, none too gently. 'Just take a look at yourself!' She picked up a wash-cloth, soaked it in water and began to rub Alice's face vigorously. 'You look like a painted freak from a circus side-show!'

'I do not! Ow, you're hurting me!' In answer, Marianna added soap to the wash-cloth and Alice screamed louder than ever. 'It's stinging my eyes!' She struggled, but in vain. 'I hate you! I wish Daddy was here to take care of me instead of you!' Marianna jerked her to her feet, then slapped her, hard, across the face. She was so shocked that her mother had hit her – something nobody had ever done in the whole of her life – that she was silent instantly.

'Let's get one thing straight, right here and now.' Her mother's voice was dangerously, terrifyingly soft. 'Your father's gone and he's never coming back. I'm the one you have to answer to. You do what I say, when I tell you to do it . . . and you never argue, you never whine, you never answer back. You step out of line with me just once, young lady . . . and I'll whop your backside good and hard. Do we understand each other?'

CHAPTER TWENTY-SIX

Ironic, that on the very day he was told about his promotion to lieutenant and the news that Chief Rawlins intended to retire, he'd read about Koenig's daughter: that was when the first seeds of the plan had started to take root in his mind.

It had been a shock, while he was still laid up after his accident with the haulier's cart, to see in the papers that Koenig hadn't left anything near what anyone had expected: all those years of high living and extravagant spending had taken their toll. Delucca had cursed. No doubt someone with Koenig's future earning potential had thought that there was no need, at that stage in his career, to worry about saving for his old age – the day after his Pierce-Arrow had plunged over the cliff, he'd been due to sign a seven-figure contract. But every cloud had a silver lining. Now it seemed that the movie moguls had snapped up his daughter and turned her into the hottest property in Hollywood.

Delucca thought about his idea some more, chewed it over; he didn't say a word to Maudie – only about the promotion and Rawlins' retirement – no need to tell her anything more, not yet. There were a few loose strings to tie up in New York, a few enquiries he'd need to make first, before they took the next step. The last thing Delucca needed was her quizzing him, giving him the same stupid sentimental crap about how she could never bring herself to leave her poor, lonely, ailing old mother behind them. Delucca smiled. He had a few plans for the old lady of his own.

He'd saved the newspaper to show her when he judged that the time was right. Like most empty-headed women, Maudie loved to read about movie stars. She wiped her floury hands on her pinafore and sat down in the easy chair by the window, so she could see it better in the bright light.

'She's sure made a name for herself, ain't she, that kid of Koenig's? Couldn't have bin more than eight or nine years old when they upped and left for California before the war . . . now she's a big movie star in her own right . . . more famous than her father was. You see how much they're payin' her for her next picture, Maudie? Two hundred thousand dollars a year. Hell, I wouldn't make that kinda dough in a lifetime – not even a quarter of it!' His voice was indignant, bitter, and with good reason, too . . . wasn't it? Two hundred thousand grand a year for some punk kid with a cute face and big blue eyes to fool around in front of a camera, while a hardworking guy could pound the beat for twenty years or more, dealing with the filth of the back-streets and risking his neck every time he walked down the precinct steps, and be lucky if he made thirty bucks a week. The injustice of it made him want to spit. But Delucca knew how he could get even.

'You know what, Maudie? When I read about Koenig's kid, it kinda gave me an idea. I like the sound of California. That's what we need, a change. A fresh start someplace else. Hell, I'm tired of New York!' She looked up from the article, startled. 'What do you reckon on us moving out, heading west, huh? You like the idea?'

'Roy!' Sun, sea, mountains, fresh air, healthy living; the boys would love it. 'But what about your job, the pro-motion? And Chief Rawlins quitting the force at the end of the year? You've worked so hard for everything, Roy . . .'

'Fuck Rawlins. You think I give a shit about that guy? I just want out, Maudie. Anyhow, I'll still get that promotion . . . except that I'll be a lieutenant in Los Angeles instead of here.' He smiled. 'I knew you'd buy the idea. That's why I asked for a transfer two weeks ago. It came through today.'

Her mouth fell open. 'Roy!' Then a sudden frown. 'But we can't, Roy . . . I couldn't leave Momma . . . it'd kill her if I went . . .'

'I already thought of that, too.' He took a printed brochure from his top pocket and handed it to her. 'Take a look at that, honey. It's the perfect solution. Well, go on. Read it.'

She turned the pages slowly, shaking her head from side to side. 'Roy, it sounds wonderful . . . but have you seen the prices?'

'Hey, it's a paradise for the old lady. Private nursing home, ten miles out of Santa Monica; sunshine, round the clock medical attention, what else could she want, huh? You can learn to drive and go visit her every day if you want to.'

'It sounds a wonderful place, ideal . . . but we just couldn't afford it.'

He smiled again. 'Hey. You let me worry about that. Now, why don't you go tell the boys the good news and start packin' for California?'

Marianna watched closely from her chair on set as Garrard Flair patiently directed Alice in a difficult scene from her latest picture, *The Angel*: her expression was sour. Alice had gradually become more dependent on him, more fond of him than ever, confiding in him and asking his advice when, before, she would have come to her mother; Marianna perceived him as a threat to her authority. And Hal Goldenthal had been unsympathetic when she'd tried, before shooting on the new film began, to get him to hire a different director.

'Flair's wrong for this picture. Wrong for Alice. Can't you see that? She needs a firm hand and he just lets her have everything her own darned way!'

'Marianna, he's the best director in Hollywood! Every studio within a radius of fifty miles would like to get their hands on him. He has a talent for coaxing the best performance out of anybody and that's what I pay him to do.'

'What's wrong with King Vidor?'

'King's tied up with Paramount, you know that. For another six months at least. Besides, Alice likes Flair. There's always been a special rapport between them. And you know as well as I do . . . a contented actress is a good actress.'

'Save it, Hal! You know just what I'm talking about. She's getting too close to him by far, and I won't stand for it. He's twenty-five years older than she is, for Christ's sake!'

'But that's just it.' Goldenthal had attempted to pour oil on troubled waters. 'Girls her age go for the father figure. And Alice more than most. Remember. She lost Curt at an impressionable age. She just sees Flair as a kind of replacement.'

'She doesn't need a replacement. She has me.' A certain coolness had sprung up between them since then. Deliberately snubbing him, Marianna had abruptly declined Goldenthal's invitation to this evening's cocktail party round his pool. Alice had sulked for days on end about it.

'But it's just not fair, Momma . . . I'm sixteen now! Why can't I go to parties? Everyone'll be there except for me.' She'd pouted ominously. Marianna took no notice whatsoever. 'Mr and Mrs Goldenthal, Doug Fairbanks, Mary Pickford; King Vidor and D. W. Griffith. And Wallace Walbrook and the Leopardis . . . oh, Momma, please let me!'

'Christina Leopardi?' Marianna had suddenly become interested. Vince Leopardi was the head of Trident Studios and stinking rich, even by Hollywood standards, and his daughter definitely had the glad-eye for Gene. The party could be turned to good use after all.

'I guess so . . .'

'You can't go, and that's an end to it. You'll stay at home with Elynor for the evening.'

'You mean you're going, and not taking me?' Alice was beside herself.

'That's exactly what I mean.' Marianna wanted to concentrate on matchmaking for her son and the Leopardi girl, not running around keeping an eye on Alice to make sure she didn't step out of line. 'After I've left, Colleen will be told to lock all the doors and keep them locked until I get back. Is that clear?'

'But it isn't fair!'

'Few things in life are. But then, I guess you'll just have to learn that the hard way.'

Alice was still sulking about not being allowed to the party when they got home to the house in Whitley Heights.

'Momma's taking Gene, can you believe that, Ellie? He gets to go with her to all the places I'm invited to. The invitation was for me!'

'Better do what Momma says, if you don't want to make her mad.'

'She was so rude to Mr Flair today, when we came off set. I wanted to stay back to speak to him about the scenes we're shooting tomorrow, and she marched right up and almost dragged me off set, right in front of everyone, so I couldn't. She's with me all day long, just like a shadow – or a jailer! She won't take her eyes off me, even for a single moment.' Alice admired herself in the mirror and smoothed down her long, golden curls; they always photographed so beautifully! 'I'm sick and tired of being treated like a little girl.'

'I get tired of having to tend to your wardrobe and be a chaperone when Momma isn't around. But I don't suppose you've ever thought of that?'

'You're not an important movie star like me, Ellie! You'll always be someone who's just hanging around in the background. I should be able to go where I like, and talk to who I like, without Momma spoiling everything.' She unscrewed the bottle of French perfume Hal Goldenthal had bought her for her birthday, and began to dab it behind her little shell-like ears, not caring that she'd hurt her sister's feelings. 'Mr Flair said I could go and talk to him about my career any time I liked, but Momma won't hear of it. She hates him for some reason. Most likely because he's always paying a lot of attention to me. He treats me like a grown-up, but she won't. I can talk to him . . . I can tell him anything, and he always understands.' She looked round, as they both heard the sound of an automobile pulling into the driveway. 'Who's that, Ellie?'

They both went and looked down from the open window.

'It isn't Garrard Flair, that's for sure.' A man neither of them recognized had climbed out of a black Buick, and was ringing the front door bell. 'Maybe it's someone to bring Momma a message from the studio.'

'No. I don't think so. He's too pale. People who live here get a kind of golden colour from the sun. Haven't you noticed that?'

Alice shrugged; she had already lost interest. She liked fair-haired, handsome men like her father, and Garrard Flair.

'I guess. But I don't think it's anyone important, anyway.'

'Mrs Koenig?' He saw the hint of recognition in her shrewd grey eyes; yes, now she remembered him. Remarkable, since they'd met for only a moment six years ago. 'I'm Roy Delucca . . . a lieutenant in Los Angeles now. We first met in New York . . . around six years or so ago. You lived on Madison Avenue then.'

Marianna had been seated at her desk in the study when Colleen had shown him in, preparing balance sheets to take to her accountant's office in Los Angeles the following morning. What could Delucca possibly want to see her for now? She had a moment of unease, but then as hurriedly dismissed it; if he knew anything about her involvement in Klara Kopek's death, she would have heard from him long before now. Or would she?

'Please take a seat, Mr Delucca. Forgive me, but I don't quite understand why you're here?'

He smiled, and she decided that she didn't like him.

'I was real sorry to hear about your late husband. A tragic accident.'

'Thank you. It was a long time ago.'

'Unfortunate, when he was right at the height of his popularity. So famous. I guess it must have kinda made things real hard for you financially after he died . . . all that money he was earnin'. And then . . . nothin'. All dried up.'

'Mr Delucca. I don't wish to seem rude, but I'm a very busy woman. Is there some special purpose in your coming here to see me? Or have you simply called by . . . a little late, admittedly . . . to offer your commiserations?'

'Business, Mrs Koenig. A little unfinished business.' He was playing a game, but what could it be? Did he know something that she hoped he didn't? She kept her face expressionless. 'See, I'm not sure if you were aware of this . . .but your husband was at one time a strong suspect for the murder of a bit-part actress in New York . . . her name was Klara Kopek.'

'That's an outrageous suggestion!'

'But part of my job is to investigate and weigh up all the evidence.'

'Simply because she was an extra at the studios where my husband was the major star doesn't mean that he had anything at all to do with her death.'

'Did you know he was paying the rent on the swank brownstone where her body was found? Or that he was seen by witnesses running from the house soon after it was estimated that she must have died?'

'I have nothing to say, Mr Delucca. My husband is dead. Even if he had known her, as you claim, he was incapable of killing anyone. And I resent the implication that he might have done.'

Delucca held up his hands as if he was warding off a blow. 'Hey, ma'am . . . don't get me wrong. I'm not accusing anyone of anythin'. Besides, I made in-depth enquiries into her background at the time . . . and she sure was no angel. Quite the opposite, in fact. Trouble is – you know how that old sayin' goes? – if you lie down with dogs, you get up with fleas? Well, that's just what your husband did in her case. Now, I don't want to upset you, Mrs Koenig, by draggin' up things best forgotten, but did you know that they were lovers?'

'Are you deliberately trying to provoke me?'

'No, ma'am. Just to explain the background to what brings me here.' He extracted an envelope from inside his jacket. 'See, the week before Klara Kopek died, your

395

husband took her to a party out on Long Island. Things had gotten pretty wild by the early hours, and some nearby resident rang my precinct to complain about the noise. Ordinarily, disturbin' the peace is a job for police patrol . . . the regular cops. But, well, my chief thought they might have had some bootleg liquor out there, or dope. That's how I came to be sent along.' He was taking some photographs out of the envelope. 'Fact is, never found either of those things. But I did get hold of somethin' else . . . somethin' I found real interestin'.' He smiled slyly as he handed her the pictures. 'Sorry to have to lay these babies on you, Mrs Koenig . . . but they do say that a picture is worth a thousand words.'

The room went blank as Marianna gazed down at the photographs in her hands. Her face burned. She felt sick. They were horrible. Vile. How, she asked herself, as she tried to control her shock and embarrassment in front of Delucca, could a man like Curt have sunk to such depths, allowed himself to be a part of anything so filthy and obscene?

'He was canned out of his mind when they were taken . . . if that makes you feel any better.' It didn't. 'Even the guy who took the pictures couldn't remember most of the things that happened out there that night. Just as well. But when the girl was found dead ten days later, you can see why I had to go talk to your husband? I'd seen the photographs by then. Even if he was ruled out as a murder suspect, publication of those pictures would have completely destroyed his career.' Slowly, she looked up at him, as reality began to dawn at last. 'See, I'm a fair-minded kinda guy, Mrs Koenig. I might be a cop, but I like to see justice done. Now, the way I saw things, why should your husband pay for one little mistake with a Polish tramp by having everythin' he'd worked for snatched away from him? Didn't make sense to me. That's what I told him. I agreed not to show the pictures to anyone who might have bin interested in formin' the wrong conclusions . . . in return for a little financial compensation . . . you get the picture?'

She stood up. 'You were blackmailing him!' It was a

statement, not a question. 'That's why there was almost forty thousand dollars missing from his bank account when he died! And I had the Revenue Service on my back for months after the will went through probate, because they thought it had been syphoned off before Curt died and stowed away to avoid death duties!'

'That ain't my problem, Mrs Koenig.' The sly smile had gone now. This was the real Delucca. 'But those pictures are yours. I got copies. I got the original film. And if you don't want your cute little girl's big movie career cut off in its prime, I suggest you listen good to what I'm goin' to say . . . silence costs. I read about how much Universal are paying her . . . two hundred grand for one lousy picture! Now, I happen to think that that's way too much money for a little bitty girl like her.'

'I want you out of my house right now!'

'Not before we've talked terms, Mrs Koenig. I reckon you wouldn't miss fifty grand of that contract money . . . seems to me, lookin' at this place for starters, you've done real well. Better maybe than when that husband of yours was alive, huh? I read in the papers how he never left much out of all that big time dough he was makin' . . . wonder where it all went? . . . but you can keep your fingers nice and tight on the purse strings now, since the kid's still a minor. Nice touch, changin' her name to Alice Ayres. I like that, it's kinda got a ring to it.'

'I don't keep that kind of money in the house.'

'But you can get it.' He nodded towards the pictures. 'Like I said, you keep 'em. I got the originals. Now, you're gonna be real sensible about this, and talk business. I want the fifty grand up front . . . let's call it back pay for the last six years. After your husband went over that cliff, the payments stopped coming, and after I read in the papers about the will, I knew there'd be no point chasin' you up for what you didn't have. Things are different now your daughter's a big movie star. I did some undercover work for the Trust back in New York, but now that it don't exist no more, I'm kinda what you'd call a little strapped for cash.'

'I could report you to the Los Angeles police department, you do realize that? Extortion and blackmail.'

'But you won't, Mrs Koenig. And we both know why. You're a real smart lady. Real classy lady, too. I could tell that, straight off, the first time I ever met you. I wondered why a guy like Koenig was botherin' to mess around with a filthy little tramp like Klara Kopek when he had a wife like you. Just fancied a little slummin', I guess. I wouldn't know . . . I'm a happily married man myself. Anyhow, like I said, you're a real smart lady. You know if you blow the whistle on me, what happens to that squeaky clean image your husband left behind, and what happens to your daughter's movie career. I don't reckon you'd be fool enough to do anythin' as dumb as that.'

She turned away, went to the study window. The gardener was mowing the lawn and Gene was in the driveway talking to him. She closed her eyes, gripped the ledge with her fingers. After all the pain and humiliation Curt had put her through, he had done this too.

'I can have the money by tomorrow. Same time. Come here.'

'That's real obligin' of you, Mrs Koenig. But that's just the down payment.' She turned round sharply. 'Way I read it, your little girl's earnin' big bucks . . . almost as much as Mary Pickford. I couldn't believe it when I read that that little short ass is rakin' in ten grand a week. *Ten grand a week!* That's more than some guys earn in all of their goddam workin' life!'

'I don't set the rates of pay in the moving picture industry!'

'It's mass entertainment, Mrs Koenig. The theatres buy the films and there are so many theatres they just can't get their hands on enough. Stands to reason. Those movie producers, they must be coinin' it in! Maybe I ought to have gone into movies, instead of bein' a cop. Who'd have thought it? It all started with the goddam nickelodeon.'

* * *

When Delucca had gone, Marianna went into the drawing room and poured herself a stiff drink. She realized that she was shaking, and that Gene had suddenly appeared.

'What the hell do you want?' She needed to be alone for a while, to try to collect herself. The sudden shock of seeing the pictures, of being confronted by Delucca and the past she'd thought was dead and buried, had been too much. Her nerves were frayed and raw.

'I'm sorry, Momma. Colleen said you wanted to see me. I waited till that guy in the Buick left. Who was he?'

'Just a business associate. Nothing to do with you.'

'I said I was sorry. I just wondered who he was, that's all.'

She pulled herself together; now was no time to fall apart. 'I wanted to talk to you about tonight. You're coming to the studio cocktail party with me.'

'What about Ellie and Alice?'

'They're staying put here.'

'Isn't that a little unfair? They don't get out that much; you won't let them. Every other girl in Hollywood has a social life but you block theirs at every turn. People are even starting to talk.' She glared at him. 'It'd be no big deal if they came tonight, would it?'

'Flair will be there. I don't want Alice having any more to do with him than she has to.'

'But why, Momma?' His mother's antipathy to Flair seemed completely unreasonable, almost bordering on an obsession. 'He's a popular guy. Besides being arguably the best director in Hollywood.'

She finished her brandy. 'That's a matter of opinion. I don't want Alice mixing with him off set and that's the end of it, you got that? She's young, she's vulnerable. And take it from me – I know what's best for her.' A meaningful glance in his direction now. 'I know what's best for all of you.' She got up, moved away from him. 'Lay out your best tuxedo for tonight. And when we get there, you'll mix with who I tell you to.'

It was only much later, when they'd arrived at the party and he saw the other guests, that he realized the real reason why his mother had insisted on bringing him. Vince Leopardi's daughter, Christina, caught sight of him across the glittering water of the pool and came smilingly towards him.

It was hot, humid; from the open window, Elynor could hear the buzz of insects, see the red-streaked dusk gradually darkening into a starlit night sky. Poor Gene. At least he knew the real reason their mother had insisted on taking him with her to Goldenthal's cocktail party, and why she'd been equally insistent that Elynor herself and Alice should stay behind. It was not, as Elynor had overheard her telling him, wholly because Garrard Flair would be there, nor because Alice was on set early the next morning and needed a good night's sleep. Elynor was certain it had something to do with the fact that Vince Leopardi and his daughter Christina would be there. Before they'd left, Elynor had told her brother as much.

'Momma's been fighting with Hal Goldenthal again, over the signing fee and percentages on Alice's next contract. She says her pictures are grossing almost as much as Mary Pickford's, and she wants a bigger cut of the net profits . . . he's not too sold on the idea! If she can make him believe that she'd take Alice away and sign her up with Trident, it would make him think twice.'

'Yeah, so why drag me into her scheming?'

'Gene, you know Christina Leopardi's sweet on you. And so does Momma. Can't you see where all this is leading? She uses you as bait to hold out to the Leopardis – what my little gal wants, she gets, is Vince Leopardi's personal motto – so that Hal Goldenthal is suckered into thinking there's an alliance on the cards between Trident and Momma after all.'

'I sure as hell wish she'd leave me out of it!'

She'd smiled. Why was it that somehow their mother always seemed to get her way, however much anyone opposed her? She'd honed manipulative scheming down into a fine art. 'Why don't you just say you're sick and then you won't have to go along with her at all?'

'Because Garrard Flair's going to be there, Ellie. I like the guy . . . he's a real gentleman . . . not like the others. And what he doesn't know about directing isn't worth knowing. I can learn so much from him.'

'Do you know how hard it'll be to try and persuade Momma that you're serious about getting into directing?'

'Yeah, I already figured that, Ellie. But in a few months' time when I'm twenty-one, there won't be much she can do about it, will there?'

'You know Momma.'

Alice had suddenly appeared in the open doorway, a magazine in her hand, her golden hair tied up in rags to ensure perfect corkscrew curls for the following morning.

'I'm so bored, I could go out of my mind! It's so hot in here tonight.' She started to fan her face with the magazine. 'I'll just bet everyone at that party'll be having a great time while I'm stuck here with you!'

'Thanks, little sister.' Ellie didn't glance up from her book. 'The feeling's mutual.'

'You're just jealous, that's all!' Alice had no-one else to vent her spleen on; Colleen was taking a bath and Consuelo was snoring in the rocking chair in the kitchen. 'You'd love to be me, wouldn't you? You'd give anything to have the chance to act . . . but you know it'll never happen, because you can't. Anyhow, you're not even photogenic. You know how important that is? Mr Goldenthal told me. He said the camera fell in love with me the minute my face appeared on screen.'

At last, Elynor laid down her book. She was stung by Alice's cruel remarks, all the more so because she would, it was true, have given almost anything for one chance in front of the camera; but she knew that her mother would never allow it and that her unfashionable looks were against her. Alice was just adding insult to injury, as usual. But she was determined not to show how much her sister's remarks had hurt her.

'No, I don't think I'd like to be you at all . . . you're too unkind, too vain and far too selfish. I wonder what the people who love your films so much would think if they saw you the way you really are? Not much, I'd be willing to bet.'

'I'll tell Momma what you said the minute she comes back! I'll tell her you were hateful and mean to me. You just wait and see!' Alice flung the copy of *Motion Picture* at her and flounced away in a temper, slamming the door viciously behind her, so hard that all the lights and china ornaments in the room shook. Elynor stooped and picked up the magazine, attracted by the page at which it had fallen open: between the Alice she knew and the angelic Alice Ayres who appeared on screen, there was a difference that few people would ever suspect existed. She smoothed down the page, smiled at the handsome face that looked up from it. Wallace Walbrook, Alice had said, would be at the studio party tonight; how much she would have loved to have gone, though doubtless he would not have given her so much as a second glance. Only once, she had actually stood within a few feet of him, and he'd brushed her arm as he'd passed. He was categorized as a 'romantic leading man', and rumour at the studio was that when his contract with Universal expired he was moving to Paramount. Looking at his picture, even if it came a very poor second to looking at him in the flesh, at least had a calming effect on Elynor; now that her sister had gone upstairs in a wild sulk, she would, at least, be able to enjoy the rest of the evening in peace.

She had forgotten her reading book now; she read the caption under the photograph. At the bottom of her chest of drawers in her own room, Elynor had painstakingly collected a whole box of magazine clippings about him and, when she was safely alone, would lock her door and take them all out.

She knew almost everything about him that it was possible to know: that he'd been born in San Francisco, that he was twenty-six years old, that he'd first come to Hollywood in 1918 and been snapped up by Universal after a screen test; he was as popular as Doug Fairbanks and Wallace Reid, with whom he shared a love of golf, dancing and fast automobiles, as well as a first name. Elynor was always stung by pangs of envy when she saw him in publicity pictures with his leading ladies: Jean Hersholt, Mae Murray, Olivia Ray; but whenever she'd seen him outside the confines of the studio, he had always been alone. She was afraid to ask anyone on set personal questions about him, for fear of betraying her romantic interest and being ridiculed; but the one time when she'd actually been close enough to speak to him, her courage had failed her and he'd walked by without giving her a second glance. It would doubtless have been very different if she'd resembled – even a little bit – any of his glamorous leading ladies, or her sister Alice: but she was stuck with the looks she'd been born with, as she was stuck with her mother's strictness, and her own lack of personal choice in almost everything, lack of any personal freedom: her mother even chose their friends.

Her eyes strayed from the smiling face of her idol in the hyped pages of *Motion Picture* magazine to the longcase clock: another hour at least before her mother and Gene returned. She got up, went in search of a pair of needlework scissors and then, with painstaking care, cut out the picture of Wallace Walbrook.

Somehow, Gene managed to escape from the attentive clutches of Vince Leopardi's daughter by pretending that he urgently needed to find the bathroom; when he emerged from the house again, she was on the opposite side of the pool talking to his mother, and their backs were turned towards him. A temporary respite. He sought out the company of Garrard Flair in a quiet corner, away from the others, something he had been trying to do since they'd arrived.

'The trouble with mothers,' Flair observed shrewdly, with a twinkle in his blue-grey eyes, 'is that they never want us to grow up. By continuing to treat us like the children they wish we still were, it gives them a feeling of security – they want to feel that we'll always need them, no matter how old we are.'

'Tell me about it,' Gene said, sipping the forbidden

tequila that his mother had told him not to drink when they'd arrived.

'When they offer you a cocktail, just take it. Hold it in your hand and every now and then touch the rim of the glass with your lips. But don't drink any of it. Cocktails aren't good for you.' She'd been so busy mixing with the other guests that she hadn't noticed Gene had drunk three already.

'I'm sorry to see that you haven't brought your sisters with you. I suppose your mother considered me too dangerous an influence to be around impressionable young girls?' He was laughing, very softly, and Gene warmed to his humour and his easy friendliness. Flair certainly had a way about him; easy to see why Alice had become so smitten . . . despite the fact that he was more than twenty years older than she was.

'I'm afraid Momma can be a little overbearing . . . that's just her way. I think the reason she's so protective towards the girls at least is because Dad's not around to take care of us all any more. Things were always kind of special between him and Alice.'

'Yes.' Flair's light eyes looked brilliant against the golden suntanned face. 'I would like to have directed your father . . . I really mean that. Vitagraph's *Monte Cristo* . . . what a masterpiece that was!'

'Oh, you saw it in New York, then?' The boy was sharp; Flair was more than a little taken aback; he'd need to tread warily here.

'I was passing through New York at the time and everyone was talking about it, so I was determined to see it. I queued up for almost an hour and a half outside the Theatre Unique on 14th Street . . . and it was raining, too.' He smiled. 'I knew when I came out that more than anything else I wanted to direct.'

'It influenced you that much?'

'Yes. That's one of the reasons why I enjoy directing your sister Alice. She's so much like your father to look at, and yet her personality is entirely her own . . . she doesn't have the feel – not yet, anyway – of how a particular scene

404

should go, and she needs to be directed very carefully. I hope I've got it down to a fine art.'

'I wish you'd seen my dad in the stage version of *Monte Cristo*, at the Lyceum. Come to think of it, I wish I had, too . . . I wasn't even born then. Momma said that it broke all box office records.'

Flair looked pensive now. 'Do you find it difficult being the son of a famous father . . . I ask out of pure interest? I mean, do you feel the need to follow in his footsteps, because you think that's what he would have wanted you to do? Someone once said to me that being the son of a famous man is like living permanently under a public monument . . . always in its shadow.'

'I don't want to act . . . I don't think I'd be any good at it. But I've so often seen pictures and thought to myself . . . hell, they shouldn't have done it that way. That's when I first realized how important the director was . . . that he could change a whole scene, alter the entire perspective of a picture if he wanted to. I suppose I also realized that directing is what I really want to do. If I ever get the chance, that is.' He looked beyond where they were standing, half concealed by the spreading bougainvillaea, to where his mother was still talking to the Leopardis. 'I think Momma has other ideas.'

Flair understood. 'Some corporate position in the Trident empire? Seated behind a very large and important-looking desk, but bored out of your mind? Yes, I think I get the picture.' He put down the empty glass on the terrace. 'There comes a time in your life, Gene, when you have to make a stand. It isn't always easy. But you have to have the courage of your convictions . . . tell yourself that, no matter what, you refuse to let anyone or anything hold you back. If you don't, you almost always live to regret it.' God knows, Flair knew what he was talking about. He thought guiltily, unwillingly, of the life he'd lived in out-of-state New York, living with a wife he'd grown to love and respect but could never feel passion for; the escape to New Jersey, then the time he'd spent in England, learning the basics of his craft and forging a new identity, a carefully concocted past. He'd shed his real name of Gerald Fersen along with the boat ticket he'd handed to the immigration official on the other side, and England had been a new beginning. Running away from the past was sometimes easy; it had been easy in practice if not conscience, for him. But what happened if it ever caught up with you?

'I guess you're right. You see, I made myself a promise. When I'm twenty-one, I intend to do what I like. Momma can rant and rave and get mad all she wants – I know she'll try to stop me. But I've thought about it, and thought about it over again. I want to direct. If I turn out to be no good at it and they fire me, well, at least I'll have tried.'

'I don't think that's likely to happen . . . I guess . . . I have a kind of good instinct about you. I've noticed you when you come to the set with your sister. How you watch me, how you watch the cameraman . . . directing is something you need a feel for. Like people. You have to know how to coax the very best out of them. You know, a good director can turn even a mediocre player into a great one; a bad director can make the finest actor in the world look like an amateur.'

Gene glanced up; his mother had noticed that he'd been missing for too long to explain a simple trip to the bathroom; her eyes were roving over the other guests in search of him. Flair had seen her, too. 'I should be making a move myself . . . I have tomorrow's shooting script to look over, and I always like to do that last thing, with a glass of bourbon and ice.' He took out a piece of paper and wrote something on it. 'This is my address and private number . . . feel free to call on me any time . . . I'd enjoy another chat.' He smiled and handed him the scrap of paper with his address and telephone number written on it. Gene took it gratefully. 404 Alvarado Street. If only he had his own transport. 'If I'm not there, my manservant will always give me a message later on. Or you can find me at the studio, of course. At least, until the end of this picture.'

'Is it true that you're going to direct for Paramount after you've completed this movie with my sister?'

'I've always believed that a director has a big advantage if he stays independent . . . *The Angel* was exactly what I wanted, so I agreed to stay on and direct it when Hal Goldenthal made me the offer, though I'd already decided it was time to move on. It just happens that the next one I work on is one of Paramount's . . . but it certainly doesn't mean that I intend to stay with them for ever; a freelance director can afford to be choosy. That way, he always gets the best of both worlds. If you're tied to one studio you often have to accept second best in a whole range of departments – lighting, camera crew, artistic direction – they may, and often do, have entirely different ideas about those things than you have. Paramount are working towards producing fewer but better pictures – I've always believed that quality, not quantity, is best. When you see eye to eye with a studio on all the components that make up a successful picture, you're all working towards attaining the very best . . . hassles cost time, and time is money. Something no Head of Pictures ever wants to waste.'

'I could talk to you all night. I've learned so much from you already.'

Flair laughed softly. 'I think your mother might have something to say about that.'

Gene looked up again and saw that his mother had spotted him with Flair. Her eyes were alight with suppressed anger, her mouth was set; not a good sign. Purposefully, she began to edge her way towards him.

He glanced round to say goodbye to Flair. But he was no longer there.

It was dark when Flair drew up outside the bungalow complex on Alvarado Street; virtually deserted at this time of night, except for a solitary black Buick parked a few blocks down the street. The air was sweet and still pleasantly warm as he climbed out of his blue Cunningham V-8 and stood on the doorstep fishing in his pocket for his latchkey; it was his manservant's evening off. As it dropped from his fingers and fell on the ground, a hand came from somewhere behind him and retrieved it before he could pick it up.

'I think this is yours, Mr Fersen.' He turned round quickly, startled; the stranger had come from nowhere. Had he been the solitary occupant of the Buick that Flair had noticed a moment ago?

'I'm sorry, I think you've made a mistake.' He composed himself as best he could. *Fersen*. Hearing the sound of his real name had shattered him. 'I don't know of anyone with that name around here.'

The man smiled, but not pleasantly. 'Nice try, Gerry. But it won't work. See, I work in the Los Angeles police department. Lieutenant Roy Delucca. But before that, I spent fifteen years in New York.'

Flair's heart sank. At that moment, one of his neighbours emerged from the bungalow opposite and waved to him. 'You'd better come inside.' He let Delucca follow him into the living room, thanking his lucky stars that his manservant would be unlikely to return to Alvarado Street for at least a few more hours. He needed a drink. 'Can I offer you some bourbon?'

'Don't mind if I do.' Delucca sat down on the couch without being asked, and made himself comfortable. 'I'm kinda off duty now . . . didn't want to make this thing official, till I'd talked it over with you.' That sly smile again. 'Make mine straight. No soda. No ice.'

Flair handed him the glass with a slightly unsteady hand.

'What do you want, Delucca? I haven't committed any crime.'

'I don't think the wife and two kids you dumped when you hightailed outa New York seven years ago would agree with that. Come to think of it, if she knew where you were now – and how much you were earnin' as a top Hollywood director – she might just start gettin' greedy. You owe her seven years' maintenance arrears for starters.' He sipped the drink appreciatively; best bourbon he'd tasted in a long while.

'Were you sent down here by the New York police department to trace me?'

'Now, what makes you think that, Fersen? Or shall I call you Flair? Garrard Flair. That sure does have a fancy ring to it, don't it? I like it. It's got style.' As always he was enjoying the game of cat and mouse; he'd scared the shit out of the guy! 'I doubt if that little deserted wife of yours would even recognize you, with that suntan. Leastways, you don't look like the guy in the photograph she gave us when she reported you as a missing person.'

Flair sat down, very slowly. For a moment, he couldn't speak. 'Trouble is, I never forget a face. I seen you down-town, comin' out of some drugstore, and I knew who you were straight away. I did a little diggin', and it brought me right here. You go out somewhere special tonight?' Flair nodded, in silence. He gulped another mouthful of bourbon. 'I figured that. I bin waitin' outside for quite a while.'

'All right. How much?'

'How much?'

'You know what I mean. And I know what you mean. Why you're here, Delucca. You want money to keep your mouth shut. If I don't pay, you contact my wife . . . am I right?'

'If I did that, she'd be sure to hit you with a big alimony suit, you know that?' He smiled again, but his eyes were hard. 'You could go to jail.'

'Don't you think I'm aware of that?' Flair needed a ciga-rette. He lit one. 'I'm not as well off as you might think.'

'Oh, yeah? Well, I reckon keepin' what I know to myself is worth at least ten thousand dollars.' He laughed as Flair looked aghast. 'Price a little steep, huh? Not payin'll cost you a whole heap more.'

'I could scrape that amount together . . . it would take me a few days. But how do I know that you won't keep coming back for more?'

'You'll just have to keep workin' real hard, won't you, Gerry? Oh, you don't like me callin' you that name! Gerald Fersen. Well, you could be right. I guess Garrard Flair sounds a whole lot more classy . . . like that dummy English accent you're talkin' with.' He put down his empty glass.

'It'd come as quite a shock, wouldn't you say, if your swank pals in Hollywood ever found out who you really were . . . and why you disappeared from New York? Now, we don't want anythin' embarrassin' like that to happen, do we?'

Flair was desperately trying to think. 'Don't call here again . . . please . . . if my manservant was here . . . he might get suspicious. Or the neighbours might wonder who you are. Give me a number where I can call you to arrange about the money.'

'Give me a pencil and a piece of paper.' Delucca scribbled something. 'My home number.' The paper changed hands, and Delucca rose to leave. 'One more thing . . . just my own curiosity, I guess. What made you run out on her? You don't seem the type.'

Flair turned away. 'I'd rather not talk about it.'

'Touchy, huh? Look, I understand why some guys do it. We got missin' husbands every day of the week back on my old precinct. Some we find, some we don't. Guys do a runner 'cos they get sick an' tired of lookin' at the same face every mornin', they get sick of hearin' the same old naggin'. Or they see someone else they like better.'

'It wasn't like that.' Flair desperately wanted him to go. 'She's better off without me.'

'I'll take your word for it, Flair.' Delucca opened the door. 'Make sure you get in touch . . . you've got a week, OK? I'll let myself out.'

When he'd gone Flair poured himself another bourbon – a double this time – to knock himself out. He was too upset to think coherently, too upset to go to bed. He wondered how long Karl Sands, his manservant, would be. Perhaps it would be better if there was someone else here with him. When you were alone, you thought too deeply, thought too much. The shock of being confronted, suddenly, by the past he'd thought was dead and buried had been too much for him.

He caught sight of the next day's shooting script lying there on his desk, among the framed photographs of half a dozen leading actresses, all personally inscribed. There was no way he could concentrate on it, no way he could even bring himself to look at it now. He hadn't eaten since lunchtime because of his busy schedule, and the cocktails, then the bourbon, on an almost empty stomach had made him feel a little sick, a little dizzy.

He sat down on the couch and lit himself a Turkish cigarette. From their various places on his desk top, the faces of the actresses he'd directed and dated with their fashionable crimped curls and cupid's-bow painted lips stared out at him, almost mockingly; ironically, his name had been linked romantically with every one of them and more besides, and many men at the studios where he'd worked had envied, even been hostile towards him because of his success with a long line of beautiful women whom he fêted and charmed. Flair, the ladies' man. Since he'd come to Hollywood, he'd got a reputation not only for directing but for never having the same female companion on his arm more than twice. If only they'd guessed at the truth. That the reason he never slept with them, the reason he never stayed with the same woman for very long, was because he never felt the slightest desire for any of them at all.

CHAPTER TWENTY-SEVEN

It had been three weeks or more since Danny Mazzoli had been keeping tabs on who went in or out of Delucca's precinct; another two, before he realized that something must be wrong. There'd been no sign of him. Logically, there had to be a reason. He was either sick, or maybe some other guy with a grievance had gotten to the bastard first; a piece of garbage like Delucca must have made plenty of enemies in his time; could be one of them had already put the finger on him and done Danny's job for him. But he had to be sure.

He gave it another day or so, then started asking questions around town. That was when he'd found out about Delucca's promotion, that he wasn't even in New York City any more. He couldn't believe what he was hearing.

'Got made a lieutenant, that hunk o' shit?' Danny had scarcely been able to contain his fury. After everything that no-good bag of filth had been laying around, he'd gotten rewarded for it. Who said the devil never looked after his own? 'Where? Just tell me where?'

'West coast. California.' The other guy had gone on dealing the deck of cards, looking at Danny through the thick grey haze of cigarette smoke. 'Word is, he's joined the Los Angeles PD. Left town over a month ago.' He'd smiled. 'Why don't you sit in on a game or two, Danny . . . if you've got a few bucks to put up front. Could be doin' yourself a favour. You get lucky, could just pay for your ticket outa here. How about it?'

Maudie had waited up for him, though he'd told her before he went on duty to go to bed; he could see her now through the lighted downstairs window as, when she

412

heard him drive up, she pushed back the net curtain and peered outside. He waved to her and she smiled.

Delucca felt enormous satisfaction as he got out of the Buick and walked up the long flower-lined path to the front of the house; it looked like something he'd once seen in a picture. Detached, plenty of space inside and out, and climbing flowers all round. What a difference from the crummy little apartment they'd had when they first moved to Brooklyn, with the noise of screaming kids and street cars rumbling by, and the neighbours on the floors above and below always yelling. It was true that money talked; he'd made it. From his lucrative little sideline alone he could afford to pay cash for an eight-roomed house in its own landscaped garden, in one of the best suburbs in Los Angeles. But Delucca was smart. He knew that people talked and when people started talking, that meant danger. What if someone someday asked questions about how a lieutenant in the LAPD could afford a standard of living like this? Already, he'd got it figured. But he had to talk to Maudie first. Now, she wasn't too bright on some things, but then she sure wasn't stupid either. He had to put it to her in a way she could accept. Tonight would do as well as any night.

'Honey, you're later than I thought you'd be!' She kissed him. What a difference the money had made, he thought, as he noticed yet another new outfit and the hairdo she'd had done that afternoon at the beauty parlour. 'You had somethin' to eat?'

'I need to have a little talk to you first.'

'You sound like there's somethin' on your mind, Roy.'

He sat down and put his feet up. 'Look, honey. I told you before we left New York about the sideline I had with the Trust . . .'

'Yeah, but they went out of business two years ago. They startin' up again?'

'No. It's just that the money I made from that work, and the bonus they gave me . . . well, you know that paid for a lot of the things we wouldn't have otherwise been able to afford.'

'Sure, you told me already. They paid you big bucks for rootin' out patents law violations.'

'Yeah, well, I didn't know it till a little while ago, but one of the guys involved in the Trust recommended my name to some of the studio bosses here – Universal, Paramount, Famous Players – 'cos they know I'm a guy they can trust to get things done. They want me to kinda work for 'em off the record.'

'I don't understand, Roy. You've already got a full-time job.'

'This is perfect, because it combines the two things. LAPD and keeping an eye out for the studios' interests. See, if I come across anythin' in the job that reflects, say, bad light on any of the studios, I make sure it stays out of the public eye . . . and then everybody's happy. I get paid good dough from two directions, with no-one the wiser. Except the studios and me.'

'You mean . . . suppress things?' He nodded. 'What sort of things, Roy?'

'Well, for example . . . if I pick up some bigshot movie star from an outa-town whorehouse, or some famous actress drunk in a bar . . . I make sure they get home safely, and no charges are made. It's no big deal. Just have to make sure that it's all done nice and discreet. See what I mean?'

Maudie looked a little worried. 'But what about your boss in LA, Roy? Is he in on it?'

'He kinda knows and he prefers not to, if you take the drift? Thing is, what nobody does know – exceptin' the studios and me – is how much I get paid for watchin' the studios' backs. Now, those movie guys have got access to big bucks . . . and I don't see why the hell some of it shouldn't come my way.' Telling people that the luxury house and the new lifestyle that went with it was only possible through the legacy Maudie had been left by an aunt had worked well enough last time; no point in changing the story now. But she understood that already. 'Just make sure you don't let on about it to anyone else . . . especially that goddam mother of yours!'

'Whatever you say, Roy. It's OK by me.'

'Good girl.' He took her into his arms and kissed her. The expensive French perfume she'd bought downtown earlier sure smelled good, and her body was soft and warm. 'Say, you go on up to bed and wait for me, sweetheart. I just got a couple of things to do first.'

He glanced at the clock; Marianna Koenig should be at the Whitley Heights house now. When Maudie was out of earshot, Delucca picked up the telephone and dialled.

'I thought you and Alice would have been in bed a long time ago.' Marianna was irritated to find both girls still up when she and Gene returned from the party, and Alice's cornflower-blue eyes red-rimmed from crying. 'Can't I leave you for five minutes?'

'Ellie was real mean to me, Momma! And she's been cutting pictures out of my *Motion Picture* magazine. I haven't even read it yet!'

'Get up those stairs, get into that bathroom and get cold compresses on those eyes, right now! Do you hear me? When you've done that, you go straight to bed and go to sleep without another word. Do you have any idea what time it is?'

'It's all Ellie's fault. She made me cry on purpose, so I'd have red eyes tomorrow when we shoot the picture. She wants me to look ugly. She's just jealous, because I'm the actress and she isn't.'

Marianna gave her younger daughter a warning look.

'Did you hear what I just told you to do, Alice?'

'Yes, Momma.'

'Then do it.'

'But, Momma!'

'Get up those stairs this minute, before I take a strap to your backside!'

She went wearily into the drawing room and sat down gratefully. It was a strain – on the patience as well as the feet – when you had to spend an entire evening standing round a pool being nice to people you despised. But it had at least been profitable; Vince Leopardi had given her some inside information that she intended to put to full use first thing tomorrow.

'Gene, pour me a drink before you go up to bed, will you?'

'Momma?' Ellie had followed them into the room. 'A man telephoned about half an hour before you and Gene got back. I told him you weren't in.'

Marianna sat up. 'A telephone call, at this time of night? Who was it?'

'He didn't say. He asked to speak to you, and when I said you'd gone out, he just hung up. I didn't have the chance to ask him his name or what he wanted.'

'Did you recognize the voice?' Marianna was alert now. Most callers left their names; she had her own suspicions about who it had been. That bloodsucking bastard Delucca! She'd always hated cops, always distrusted them. No doubt he was ringing to check up on her, to see if she'd got his hush money. Anger made her forget just how tired she was. There was Hal Goldenthal on one hand trying to get away with paying less than the other studios were paying for their major stars; Delucca on the other demanding money in return for keeping his mouth shut over Curt's involvement with Klara Kopek six years ago. She'd had about as much as she could take.

'You two, go to bed.' She needed to be alone to collect her thoughts, formulate some plan. Delucca she could do little about for the moment; only wait and bide her time. Goldenthal was something else.

'Momma, I know it's late, but could I talk to you about something?' Elynor had hung back after Gene had gone upstairs. 'It's really important to me.'

'If it's about you and Alice fighting, I've told you before. You know as well as I do that she's a temperamental little bitch, that she always says the first mean thing that comes into her empty head. She never thinks about anyone except herself, and she never has done. Have you only just learned that? But if you must argue with her, wait until Flair's finished shooting this picture before you provoke her into bawling her eyes out. Do you have any idea what red, swollen eyes look like in close-up?'

'Momma, I don't want to talk about Alice. I want to talk about me.'

'Have you any idea what time it is?'

'This is important to me. I need you to listen.'

Marianna turned away; Elynor could see that she'd already lost interest, that her mind was miles away, probably on something she was scheming to do tomorrow, or the day after that. There was never any time to spare for anyone except Alice. Sometimes, it was hard not to feel bitter. 'Momma, please . . . could you speak to Mr Goldenthal for me? Maybe even Vince Leopardi? If I could have a screen test . . . just for a bit part, I'm sure I could do it well.' That had surprised her mother. 'I've sat on set, I've watched Alice in all her pictures, and other people . . . I just want to try . . .' Her mother's expression was sour; maybe she'd picked her time unwisely after all. But Marianna was always doing things or seeing people, Elynor hadn't had the opportunity. 'Momma, it would mean so much to me if you could help me.'

'So, you think you can be an actress, just like that? You've sat and watched a few pictures and now you know it all. Welcome to the real world! It just doesn't work that way.'

'What do you mean?'

'What I mean is that you just don't have the look. You don't photograph well, you never have. They have a saying around here – the camera loves her – and that counts for more than being the greatest actress or the greatest beauty in the world. There are queues a mile long outside every studio in Hollywood every day of the week, of pretty girls who think they've got what it takes to be a Pickford, a Swanson, a Nazimova. None of them are beautiful off screen – you should know, you've seen them – but in front of a camera they're magic. Why? How the hell should I know? They just are. If you've got one of those faces you don't even need talent to go with it. But you're the other way round; you look better than you photograph. So forget

417

it. You wouldn't even get your little toe in a studio door, whether you're Alice Ayres' sister and Curt Koenig's daughter or not.'

'You're saying that you won't even let me have the chance? That isn't fair! I'm not asking, not expecting anyone to make me into a big time movie star, I just want to act! Surely it doesn't matter if a bit player isn't photogenic the way a leading lady has to be? Momma, please . . .'

For a moment, Marianna was silent; this was a conversation that she did not want to have. Beneath the rock-hard exterior, the tyrannical matriarch's image she'd so assiduously cultivated, there were still vestiges of the younger, softer, emotionally vulnerable Marianna, the girl who'd fallen passionately in love with a handsome Broadway actor who had betrayed her trust and broken her heart. For Elynor, the child who most resembled herself, she had always felt a special, fierce protectiveness; once she allowed her to break free from the maternal shackles, anything might happen, as it had happened to her. She was prepared to do anything in her power to make sure that it never did. This was Hollywood. But not the glamorous, star-studded mecca depicted by the movie magazines and the popular press. She knew the reality underneath the dazzle, the outrageous hype and the lies. True, she was part of it; but from necessity, not choice. Curt had left her alone and, if not quite destitute, perilously close to it. With her trust fund inheritance long gone on his extravagances, with no family or friends – could she ever consign herself and her children to a life of genteel poverty with their Koenig relatives in rural Minneapolis? – she'd done what she had to do. True, Alice with her doll-like innocent looks and little girl appeal had been exploited for all she was worth – golden hair and big blue eyes were all the rage, and set to be for a very long time – but her marketability was not the only reason Marianna had forced her into the acting profession in preference to her sister. There was a hardness, an innate selfishness in Alice that set her apart from Elynor; Alice had all the weapons she needed to survive in a place like

Hollywood, and her mother had always been very well aware of it.

'I'm tired, I've had a long day and an even longer evening. I'm going to bed and I don't want to hear another word about this again, do you understand me?'

'Just give me one single reason why you won't let me have the same chance as you gave Alice?' In her anger and bitter disappointment the words tumbled out that she'd kept to herself but never spoken aloud, not even to Gene. 'Alice can't even act!'

Instead of looking angry, her mother surprised her by merely looking amused. She smiled. 'Has it taken you this long to figure that out? You haven't listened to anything I've said at all.'

Midnight. Impossible to sleep. Flair's manservant had come in a few moments ago, but had not locked up. A look of silent understanding passed briefly between them, and Flair nodded slowly. Yes, he would have to go.

'I'll lock up myself . . . when I come home.' Sands never spoke a word, merely handed him a key. 'Leave the small lamp on near the window when you go to bed. I don't want any of the neighbours to think the place is empty.'

When he had gone, Sands helped himself to his employer's bootleg liquor. The bitter taste helped a little to take his mind off the 'duty' he had had to perform for Flair earlier in the evening, a task he found well paid but disgusting in the extreme. Not that it mattered. He'd worked here for ten months or so and, by now, knew where Flair kept everything of value – his cash, his personal jewellery, his private papers. When the time was right – and it would be soon, very soon – Sands knew exactly what he would do.

The breeze was fresh, bracing, as Flair pushed down harder on the throttle and headed out of town, skirting Los Angeles, the sparsely populated suburbs, in the direction of West Hollywood and Glendale, then turned his Cunningham V-8 further east towards Arcadia Park.

419

The hood of the automobile was down, just the way he liked it when he was tired and his eyes ached; the cool night air, sharp now from the speed at which he was travelling, cleared his head, revived him. He knew that he should never have come tonight because tomorrow was another early start on set; but he couldn't help it. When the anxiety and the fear that had started all over again after Delucca's shock visit this evening had worn off, he was left with that overpowering urge, that deep need that clamoured inside him to be fulfilled, and nothing else seemed to matter.

He slowed down a little now. Main Street, Rosemead Boulevard, more trees, more shrubs, more darkness. The road dwindled suddenly to a rough, unmade track. He slowed even further, coaxing the V-8's wheels gently over the bumpy terrain. From the road leading back to Glendale and Burbank, the tiny wooden one-roomed shack was completely invisible.

He had begun to sweat; he was excited. Excited, tense, eager, ashamed. He felt guilt. Terrible, mind-crushing guilt, the same guilt that had made him leave the wife and sons he'd loved, knowing how much it would hurt them, knowing that he could never go back and live a lie.

His hands were trembling as he climbed from the V-8 and walked towards the shack, partially concealed by the woods, the overhanging trees. There was a small, glowing light peeping from behind the curtains; in front of it, a shadow moved.

Flair took the key from his pocket and fitted it in the lock; the door creaked, then swung open. No need for words. Sands would already have explained to the boy what he was expected to do.

CHAPTER TWENTY-EIGHT

Her first call was on Hal Goldenthal. Imperiously, she swept his secretary aside. She was dressed in original Paul Poiret, expensively imported direct from Paris – impossible to obtain before the end of the war in Europe; Marianna had always had style. He knew by her flashing eyes, her set mouth and her grand entrance that she wanted something – but what was it now? It couldn't be a complaint. With signing fees, salary, fringe benefits and net profits, Alice Ayres was already on almost half a million a year.

'Marianna! You look even more stunning than you did at the party last night. Have a chair.'

'I'd rather have a serious discussion about the terms for Alice's next picture. A subject you successfully managed to avoid talking to me about last night.'

Goldenthal's heart sank. So she wanted more money. Two days ago, they'd been talking about scripts for a new Alice Ayres picture and she hadn't mentioned anything at all; Leopardi had been whispering poison in her ear. It was no secret, he knew, that Trident were trying to flex their muscles in Hollywood and poach major stars from other studios by spreading general discontent. Last night, he'd noticed Vince Leopardi and Marianna spending more time together than with anyone else. So that was it?

'Marianna, sit down. Let's talk about it! Hey, I thought you'd be on set watching the final shoot on Alice's picture.'

'I'm staying right here. Until we come to an agreement. I happen to know how much you're paying your other stars and how much less you're paying my Alice.'

'Say, look . . . Marianna . . . be reasonable! Alice is a big box office draw, sure . . . we all know that! But she's just a kid. No acting background, no stage experience when I took a chance on her . . . we sold her on her name and who she was, and it paid off. I took chances. I stuck my neck out because I was fond of Curt . . . of you. I knew she had the right look to make it big, and it came off. But it was a gamble just the same. Now, you're not gonna deny that? I could have lost money on her. But I gave her her big break. Sure, other people make more than she does – not that I'm supposed to discuss other players' contracts with you, you know that – but they're five, ten years older than she is. Hell, Marianna, the kid's barely seventeen!'

'Stuff the excuses, Hal. I'm not interested. Don't waste your breath.' She moved to the very edge of her chair and leaned towards him, so close that he found it almost intimidating. 'You want facts? I'll give you facts! Pickford got six hundred and seventy-five thousand from First National – when she wasn't that much older than Alice is – plus fifty per cent of the profits on each film she cut . . . and a fifty-thousand-dollar handshake for her mother, for her "good offices". Are you getting my drift? They gave her complete control over production on her pictures – hundred per cent say on lighting, camera crew, artistic direction – and still threw in an offer of two million a year from sales. Four years ago, Chaplin was getting ten thousand dollars a week – a week, Hal – with a bonus of a hundred fifty thousand from Mutual. Now he can ask a cool million from any studio in Hollywood – and get it.

'The list goes on . . . you want to hear more? Lillian Gish, Mae Murray, Barrymore, Swanson, Doug Fairbanks. I've done my homework. The movie theatres and the state distributors are clamouring for Alice Ayres pictures, and you try to short-change me over every deal we make!'

There was little point in trying to reason with Marianna when she was in this mood. All he could do was stall for time.

'Marianna . . . let's talk this thing through, for Chrissake! What the hell's the point in shouting at each other about it? OK. So we can raise her salary, increase the signing fee, take another look at net profits. We can work it out.'

Marianna got to her feet. 'Sure, Hal. We'll work it out. On my terms, you got that? Trident would take Alice tomorrow and she could name her own ticket. Paramount and First National are interested, and when you get more than two studios interested you know as well as I do that the price goes up. So here's what I want before she signs on the dotted line for any more pictures with Universal. Treble the signing fee, the salary, half the net profits from distribution. Plus two hundred and fifty thousand dollars for me. And complete consultation on cameramen, costume, script approval, artistic direction. With the choice of director only made on agreement with me.'

'Marianna, be serious! You wanna bankrupt me?'

She smiled. 'I'll climb down on one clause. I'll settle for a third of net profits in return for two things from you . . . and I want them one hundred per cent guaranteed.'

'OK. What are they?' Alice Ayres' pictures were a goldmine; he knew it, and so did she. No point in prolonging a battle he knew he couldn't win. He'd cast around a little and find some way to recoup the money from somewhere else.

'I don't want Garrard Flair directing Alice in any other pictures. I mean it. And I want a favour.'

'You want a favour, from me?'

'Elynor has some crazy idea about being an actress like her sister. Stamp on it, when she comes to you. As for Gene, I've got other plans for him . . . not with Universal.'

'Vince Leopardi's girl, huh?' So that was her game? Boy, he had to hand it to her. Most women would have fallen apart after Curt died – and she was left high and dry with almost nothing but the prospect of packing up and going back east – but she'd clawed her way up the ladder and made sure she stayed on top of it. She was a bitch, but Goldenthal had to admire her guts. 'OK. You got a deal. But what if Elynor takes it into her head to try her luck someplace else?'

'Let her. I've got all the exits covered.'

Gene moved away from the suffocating heat of the arc lamps, and watched the action taking place on set; was it just his imagination or was there something different about

Garrard Flair today? He had dark circles beneath his eyes and his concentration, usually razor-sharp, seemed superficial, almost wandering. Alice had noticed it, too, and as the filming wore on she became distinctly unhappy; never blessed with an abundance of initiative, always accustomed to having Flair guide her with infinite patience through every scene, she was soon lost. In the end, she burst into tears and stormed off set.

'I was waiting for him to tell me what to do, how I should do it,' she wailed, as Elynor listened in silence. 'But he just kind of stared at me, as if I wasn't there at all! Now I've made a fool of myself and I can't go back . . . I can't face him!' Alice needed a scapegoat. 'It's all your fault, Ellie! If you hadn't upset me so much last night I would have been fine!' She snatched the hairbrush Elynor was holding for her. 'You just can't stand it that Mr Flair thinks I'm a great actress, while you can't even get bit-part work because nobody wants you . . . that's it, isn't it?' A triumphant note came into her voice. 'I came back down the stairs last night, and I heard you whining to Momma about talking to Mr Goldenthal!' Elynor flushed. 'I knew it, all along. You'd love to upstage me, wouldn't you? But you won't.'

'I just might surprise you.' Fighting back her fury, Elynor turned on her heel and walked out.

She kept on walking. Through the lot, past cameramen, dressers, technicians. She needed to be alone, she needed to be away from people. She'd almost reached the studio gates when Gene came running after her.

'Ellie? Ellie, wait!' She stopped. 'Ellie, Momma's looking for you.' He saw her face as she turned towards him. 'What is it, what's wrong?'

'I just had to get out of there. Before I actually hit her.' She leaned against the wall. 'I never wanted to do that before. Maybe she was right. Maybe I am jealous.' She looked away, ashamed of her feelings of envy and resentment. 'She's the one who's been given all the chances, had it all handed to her on a plate. All I want is one chance and nobody will give it to me.'

'Useless trying to talk Momma round. I know. I've tried.'

'I tried to talk to her last night, after you got home. Whenever I do, she always gives excuses. She's too busy, she's late, she has a meeting at the bank, or with her accountant, she has to be with Alice at the studio. That's why I waited up. Much good it did me.' She told Gene what had happened. 'If only I could go to Hal Goldenthal without her knowing, I'm sure he'd give me a trial. If not, I could go to someone else.'

'That's it!' He fumbled in his pocket and pulled out a scrap of paper. 'Last night, I got talking to Garrard Flair. I explained to him how much I wanted to direct. He listened to me. I mean, really listened. He wasn't patronizing, not at all. That's why I like him and – I'll bet my last dollar – why Momma doesn't. Flair's no yes man. It doesn't cut ice with him who you are, like everyone else in this town. He couldn't care less if I'm Curt Koenig's son or Alice Ayres' brother . . . he was just interested in me for myself.'

'You mean he gave you some advice?'

'He knows Momma hates his guts . . . because Alice moons over him. Momma doesn't want Alice taking notice of anyone except herself. But Flair's worked his way up . . . he didn't know a single guy of influence in the moving picture business when he started out, and he told me that he figures being independent – working freelance for any studio who'll hire you – is the best bet. I know he started his career in England. I know things are a lot different there. But it set me thinking, Ellie. He could maybe help me to get started . . . on my own . . . give me contacts.' He showed her the scrap of paper. 'He said to call him any time. That I could always drop by if I felt the need for a chat. If I could sucker Momma into thinking I'd gone someplace else, I'd do it tomorrow.'

'Momma always goes to the bank, then visits her accountant on Fridays. This Friday I know she's got a meeting with Walter Oppenheim too.'

Gene looked hopeful. 'And I know a guy in scenery who

425

offered to lend me his automobile. I'll call on Flair then, and get back long before Momma.'

'Can you ask him about me?'

'I've got a better idea. You come with me. That way we'll kill two birds with one stone. Momma'll never be any the wiser.'

'She will. You've forgotten Alice. If I don't stay home with her, she'll want to know where I've gone.'

Gene thought a little while. 'We could take her with us . . . yes, it would be ideal! You remember how Alice said that Flair had offered an open door any time she wanted, if she had a problem? She'd jump at the chance to come. She'd never tell Momma because, if she did, she'd be betraying herself. Alice is too selfish to cut off her own nose to spite her face. Ellie, we'll never get a better opportunity.'

Elynor hesitated for a moment; absurd, for a girl of almost twenty to still be afraid of her mother. But those who didn't know Momma would never have had the slightest idea . . . If only things didn't have to be this way. But they were. If she and Gene didn't try to break the ties that bound them, both of them would be beholden, dominated by their mother for ever.

'We'll do it.'

Gene was taken aback when their mother raised no objection to his borrowing the automobile for a drive along the coast road; even more, when she suggested that he take his sisters. He and Ellie exchanged glances.

'Alice is tired and upset after everything that went wrong on set yesterday. The fresh air and the drive will do her good. But no speeding, mind.'

'You know I wouldn't do that.' They were both thinking of Curt. 'Anyhow, when you drive slow you can appreciate the scenery.'

'It's all Flair's fault. He calls himself a sensitive director! A real professional would never have left Alice floundering on set the way Flair left her today. He wasn't in control of the picture. He wasn't focused. He just had no idea what he was doing.' There was a sneer in her voice. 'I don't know why the hell Hal Goldenthal hired him! I told him he should have fired him and hired King Vidor instead.'

'Garrard Flair's one of the most highly respected directors in Hollywood, Momma.'

'He just thinks he's a cut above the rest because he's worked in England.' She wasn't really paying attention to them, just collecting her papers and ledgers for her accountant before she went out. 'For some reason he thinks that makes him special.'

'He has a point.' Ellie shot her brother a warning glance; if he championed Flair too far Marianna could well lose her temper and change her mind about allowing them to go out; it wouldn't be the first time they'd all suffered from her complete unpredictability But Gene couldn't help himself. 'In England . . . and Europe . . . countries like Sweden, and Germany . . . the film is regarded more as an art form than just popular entertainment. It's on a par with the theatre, and literature . . . opera, even. They don't go in for things like Bronco Billy, and Keystone slapstick . . . or the Pickford weepies. It's totally different. Once you've directed in Europe, you're really somebody.'

'I shouldn't imagine their production was too high after more than four years of war.'

'Garrard Flair was directing long before 1914. He was telling me about it last night.'

'So that was what he was boasting about? Filling your head with nonsense! What counts is how popular a picture is and how much money it makes. If it doesn't cover all the production costs and make at least fifty per cent profit on top of that, the studio would go out of business.' She looked up as they all heard the sound of a vehicle pulling into the drive; was it Elynor's imagination or had she turned a little pale? 'It seems as if your friend has arrived.' For an instant, she looked suspicious. 'He isn't coming with you on this drive, I take it? He's just loaning you the automobile for the afternoon?'

'That's right, Momma. I'll just drop him back at the studio.'

'See that you don't pick up anyone else . . . I don't want

Alice mixing with the wrong sort of people. Not at her age.' She cast another glance out of the window, then at the clock. 'Well, hadn't you better go? You don't want to keep him waiting.'

They had been gone only a matter of minutes before the black Buick pulled into the drive, and Delucca climbed out of it.

'I don't want you coming here again. Not in the daytime.'

'Wouldn't it look even more strange if I came after dark?'

'I don't want you here at all. But you haven't left me with any choice, have you?' There was cold anger in her voice. She had collected the money from her bank account that morning. Delucca opened the case and looked at it. Hell, but did those stacks of notes look good! And he was raking it in just because Curt Koenig had wanted to stick it up a cheap little Polish tramp! In a way, Delucca could sympathize with how mad that made her; he'd been dead six years and she was still paying for his mistakes. In her place, he'd have felt the same. 'Why don't you count it now you're here?' Her voice was harsh, deeply sarcastic.

Delucca smiled; he refused to be offended.

'Now, I know a real smart lady like you wouldn't be fool enough to try to short-change me. You know what would happen if you tried it.' He stroked the wads of one hundred bills, then closed the case. 'I'll return this to you. So as it's all ready for the next instalment.'

'You've got the money. Now I want you out of my house!'

'Pretty fancy house it is, too. Noticed it first time I came here. Spanish stucco, isn't that what they call it?' He looked around the room appreciatively. 'On two levels, balcony, landscaped gardens, climbing flowers . . . real nice. Real nice. Tasteful is what I'd call it.'

'I don't give a damn what you call it!'

'How many rooms you got here? Ten, at least, judging by the outside. Amazin', how much movie stars get paid . . . I never realized it, not till I started sittin' up and takin' notice, readin' up on the subject. You know, when the nickelodeon idea first kicked off back in New York, folk never realized what moving pictures would mean . . . all that dough! I mean, the whole industry that's grown up in just a few years, worth millions of dollars. It ain't fair, when you think about it. Ordinary workin' guy gets a few lousy dollars a week . . . and some dame like Mary Pickford who looks cute in front of a camera gets a million dollars a year.'

Delucca picked up the money and tucked it under his arm. 'First off, I can see why the guys at the studios didn't give any of the actors' names. I guess they figured that when the public kinda got to like 'em, and they got known, they'd start askin' for big bucks . . . and it turned out just that way. Me, I don't reckon it's right. No-one's worth a million dollars a year . . . not even the President.'

'You're perfectly happy to stoop to the depths of black-mailing to get your cut of it!'

'I'm just lookin' out for myself, Mrs Koenig. That's what we all gotta do in this world. 'Cos if you don't, you can sure as hell bet that nobody else will.'

Marianna stopped him as he reached the door. 'Was that you, ringing here last night?'

'You should have said you was going out for the evenin'. But, no sweat. I just hung up when your daughter told me you was gone. Think I'm stupid?' He smiled that cocksure, infuriating smile that made her want to hit him. 'I'll see myself out, Mrs Koenig. And I'll see you next month. Amazin', ain't it, how quick a month comes round.'

All her hatred and loathing for him blazed from her eyes. 'If I never saw your face again it'd be too soon for me. Now get out.'

CHAPTER TWENTY-NINE

'I know you're a busy man, Mr Goldenthal.' Gene closed
the door to his office gently, and leaned against it. He'd
been biding his time, waiting for a chance to talk to the
studio boss for months; with his mother constantly in his
shadow, that wasn't easy. But he'd struck lucky today. She
was out on set now, having a heated argument with the
director about how Alice should play her scenes; Alice was
having tantrums and hysterics every ten minutes because
the director wasn't Garrard Flair. Goldenthal could
see big trouble looming. Besides, he knew exactly why the
boy was here, exactly what he was going to say. Marianna
had put him wise almost a year ago.

'He's got some fool idea that he could make it in
directing . . . but I've got other plans for him. If he asks, just
step on it.'

'I've noticed the boy around the set, Marianna. He's
quick, he's keen, he's got the instinct for how a scene should
be played. I could always fit him in. Shame to kill all that
enthusiasm.'

'I said I've got other plans for him.'

'He's your son . . . but I sense he could well have what it
takes. Why don't you think it over?'

'Why don't you think this over, Hal?' She'd fixed him
with those steel-grey eyes of hers, and he'd almost shivered.
'If you give Gene a job in this studio, I take Alice away.
There isn't another studio in this town that wouldn't grab
Alice Ayres with open arms . . . and don't you ever forget
it.' He'd known Marianna long enough to know that she
never made idle threats. But he didn't relish being told how
to operate his business, or being threatened in his own
office.

'I could sue for breach of contract if you did that,

Marianna. Not that I'd enjoy it. Litigation costs money and to me going through the courts is throwing money down the drain. I'm all for talking out differences.'

'So sue me. Walter Oppenheim would tie you up in knots in court . . . . he can spot a loophole in a contract with his eyes closed. Don't try it.' They both knew that he never would; Alice Ayres was too hot a property to let slip through his fingers. But he still felt sorry for Gene Koenig, tied to his mother's apron-strings against his will. 'Just do what I say and there won't be any need to talk about lawyers, will there?'

'Have it your way, Marianna. But I think the boy ought to have a chance.'

'I said I had other plans for him. And those plans don't include directing.' She'd swept out of his office and the subject had never been mentioned again. Now the boy was here and he didn't quite know what to say; it was always much more difficult turning someone down when they were standing in front of you face to face.

'Could you . . . would you, give me a chance at directing? Just one or two scenes from one of the smaller pictures? A try out, if you like. I've watched, and listened, studied how other directors work. Garrard Flair's been a big help to me, talking over some of the aspects of the craft. He advised me to try some of the smaller studios . . . no-one was interested, of course. I just feel if I had one chance to show what I could do, someone would take me on, give me that first break that I need to get started.'

'There's a lot of experienced directors in Hollywood, son. Ten years ago, you might have gotten yourself a place. It's much harder today, you know that. Hell, when I first moved out here, Hollywood was just a parcel of land with a few wooden buildings and a dirt road. Hollywood Boulevard was a shambling, drowsy little street of box stores and shingled houses under a few crackling palms and pepper trees! The only public transport was a trolley car that clanged down the eight miles from Laurel Canyon to LA, and actors and actresses from back east couldn't even get a room in town because the local people thought they

431

were shit! You know what the landlords used to put on the FOR RENT signs in their windows? "NO MOVIES, NO NEGROES, NO JEWS." Movies, that was what the locals called film people. They looked down on 'em. Thought they'd eventually up and move out, when the phase for moving pictures passed, like most phases. Even the banks refused to open accounts for 'em. Now, it's all changed in just ten years. Timing. That's more important than anythin' in this world, Gene . . . and you'll learn that the hard way. It's more important than love, money or even luck. If you're in the right place at the right time, you got it.'

'You're saying no, then? You're saying you won't even give me one chance to prove what I can do?'

'I'm sorry, Gene.' It was one of the few things he was sincere about. 'Sure, I'd like to help . . . but there's just no way. Later, maybe. Let's wait and see. Come back and see me in a year's time and we'll talk about it. Things could be a whole lot different then.'

Outside in the corridor, Gene bumped into a girl carrying a pile of costumes, and almost sent her flying. 'I'm sorry. . . I'm not usually so clumsy. Here.' He made himself smile because she was so pretty. 'Let me help you.'

'Is it really that bad?'

'It shows that much? Then I guess it must be.'

'You're Alice Ayres' brother, aren't you? I've seen you on set, watching the shooting.' He carried the costumes for her and they began to walk towards the robe room, side by side.

'That's all you're likely to do, see me watching.'

'I don't understand.'

'I'd love to try directing . . . just a scene or two. Trouble is, nobody will let me.' He gave her a condensed version of his exchange with Hal Goldenthal. 'I don't want anyone to do me any favours . . . I mean, I don't expect special treatment because my name's Koenig, or because my sister is the studio's biggest star. I just want one chance.'

'There are other studios in Hollywood.'

'I've tried most of them. No joy. They say, "No

432

experience, no work." It's a vicious circle. Like banging your head against a brick wall. How the hell can you get experience, prove yourself, if nobody will give you a break?'

'Have you tried Essanay, or First National?'

'Along with half a dozen others. They just didn't want to know.'

'Metro? Trident? They've both got a big reputation for radical policies. My aunt works at Metro in the costume department . . . they're creating some wonderful things for *Salome* with Nazimova, right now. She's working with a new, very talented designer called Natacha Rambova . . . but they've been having problems with Nazimova from the start. Not about the costumes or the set designs, but about almost everything else.'

'I've heard Nazimova's very temperamental. Difficult to work with.'

'She's a nightmare to direct! Trouble is, she thinks she knows everything there is to know about everything . . . she won't let the director guide her in anything at all. Every five minutes she throws her arms in the air and starts screaming, and the cameras have to stop rolling . . . the picture's weeks behind schedule and the production costs have piled up. There's even talk around the studio of the whole thing being abandoned. If it came to that, they'd be throwing away well over a million dollars.'

'And I thought I had problems.' They reached the costume department and Gene handed her the pile of clothes. 'Hey, you haven't even told me your name.'

'Me, I'm just the studio dogsbody . . . you know why I took this job instead of twisting my aunt's arm to use her influence on my behalf over at Metro?' Gene shook his head. 'Because I wanted to make it on my own. I'd like to design, later . . . if I can figure out the right way to go. Trouble is, most of the big costume pictures they make here aren't really my style. I'd like to do something challenging . . . artistic. Create a fantasy wardrobe for a classic in my own style. For the moment, like you, I guess I'm just waiting around in the wings. You've got to have faith, and be ready to jump at unexpected opportunities.'

'That's very profound. And good advice. The best I've had all day.' He smiled. He had his father's smile, and she was instinctively drawn to him. 'If you don't have any other plans, maybe you'd care to join me for lunch someplace? But not here.'

'Yes, I'd like that.' She held out her free hand and shook his with it. 'I'm Susie Costello, by the way. And before you ask . . . Maurice Costello and I aren't related.'

Marianna had just arrived home with a sulking and truculent Alice when the telephone rang. She reached it first. What the hell did Hal Goldenthal want this time, she thought irritably when she recognized his husky voice? If it was to complain about Alice's temper tantrums holding up his precious production, he could look somewhere else to lay the blame: he should have taken her advice and hired King Vidor or Marshall Neilan to direct; all Tod Browning did was rub her up the wrong way. At this rate, the picture would never be finished. But Goldenthal hadn't rung to talk about Alice.

'Just thought I oughta let you know, Marianna . . . Gene paid me a little visit today.' There was a pause at the other end of the line. 'I did like you wanted me to. Told him no way.'

'I'm glad there's something we agree on.'

'I said I'd turned him down, not that I agreed with you.'

'You don't have to agree. Just do it.'

'You could be makin' a big mistake, Marianna . . . keepin' the kid down like that. Just makes 'em want to do things more. You know what headstrong kids that age are like? Plain stubborn.'

'I don't need your advice on how to handle my son, Hal. Just make sure you do everything you can to go on discouraging him.'

'There are other studios he can go to besides Universal.'

'I've already been to them first.' So, that was her game! Should he have been surprised at her scheming after knowing her all these years? She hung up on him without thanking him before he could say another word.

434

She put through a call to Vince Leopardi at Trident on Beechwood and Gower.

'Vince! It's Marianna Koenig. Yes, I'm fine. Just fine. Gene's fine, too. And he'd be delighted to accept the invitation to the party. He'll drive the girls over but not me . . . I'll come on by later, if that's OK with you. A little unfinished paperwork I need to deal with at my accountant's office, and I could be late.'

When she put down the receiver and looked up, Alice was standing on the staircase watching her. 'Was that Hal Goldenthal earlier?'

'He wasn't ringing up to talk about you.' Marianna ignored her and walked off into the palatial drawing room. She opened the onyx cigarette box and helped herself; she'd taken up smoking a year ago.

'I hate Tod Browning and I refuse to go back on set if he stays as director!'

'Goldenthal's choice, not mine. I told him we wanted Vidor or Neilan. He said they were tied up elsewhere. Not much we can do about that, for the moment.'

'You could if you wanted to.' Alice had followed her into the drawing room. 'You make other people do things they don't want all the time. I know why you won't do it! Because I liked Garrard Flair best and you don't want him to direct me!'

'I think you'd better leave the room before I lose my temper, young lady.' Marianna gave her younger daughter a warning glance, and she flinched. 'You can rant and rave and stamp your foot on set, when you're Alice Ayres . . . but don't you dare do it here.'

'I hate you!' Alice turned and ran back upstairs, colliding with Gene as he came into the hall. 'Get out of my way!'

'What's wrong with her?' He came in and sat down.

'She's not happy with Goldenthal's choice of director. She preferred Garrard Flair.' There was a derisive note in her voice.

'Wouldn't it be better to get him back again? He's in between pictures right now.'

'He had too much influence over her for my liking.' She

was pacing the floor, blowing out the smoke in little rings. 'I never trusted him. Just a feeling I always got, and I've never been wrong yet. I like directors who direct, not directors who like giving their leading ladies a little off-set coaching.'

'Momma, Flair's more than twenty years older than Alice, for Christ's sake! He was just a father figure, someone who was sympathetic when she felt nobody else understood her. Isn't that obvious?'

'What's obvious to me is that the last thing she needs is Flair interfering in her life.'

Gene couldn't contain himself any longer. 'Momma, can't you see what you're doing? Not just to Alice, but to all of us? You just can't let us be, live our own lives. You treat Alice like a child. You shadow her, and Ellie, everywhere they go . . .'

'They need to be protected from some of the riffraff that crawls around in this town!'

'You can't lock grown women up behind three-inch doors and high fences for ever! Momma, Alice and Ellie aren't little girls any longer! Why can't you accept that?'

She turned and looked at him. Something about his defiance, the way he seemed to be spending less and less time at home lately, reminded her sharply of Curt, when things first began to go wrong in their marriage. She felt cold fingers up and down her spine. Why couldn't they understand, all of them, that everything she'd done, everything she had to do sprang from her overpowering need to protect them from pain, betrayal, failure? They could never know, never begin to understand the misery and anguish their father had put her through, the isolation and mental agony his infidelities had inflicted on her.

'I know what's best for both of them. You have to believe that. If you don't, it's just too bad. But that's the way things are, Gene.'

'I don't want to fight with you, Momma.'

She stubbed out her cigarette. 'Vince Leopardi rang a little earlier . . . he's having a party out at the Sunset Inn next month. Big affair, half of Hollywood seems to have been invited. I want you to take the girls.'

'What's the occasion?'

'A man as rich as Leopardi doesn't need an occasion. He makes one.'

'Am I supposed to be impressed?'

'If you've got any sense.' His flippancy was making her furiously angry again. Why, why, why did they all have to oppose her? Didn't they understand that after everything she'd been through, she knew best? 'He's heard that you're interested in trying your hand at directing.' It was a lie, but only by its timing; she intended to talk to Leopardi about Gene later. 'As you know, it's not an easy thing to break into successfully. Too many fingers in the pie already.'

'I'm willing to take my chances.' He was immediately wary; why would Trident be interested in him if none of the other studios he'd approached had been willing to give him a trial? Knowing his mother so well, he detected a plot. 'Where did he hear about me?'

'Perhaps from one of the other studios you've been going to behind my back.' So she knew all along!

'Who told you?'

'Does it matter? You seem to forget, Gene, that I hold considerable clout in this town. I've worked hard for it and I use it whenever I can.' Realization dawned and he was furious.

'You don't want me to do anything my way, do you, Momma? You don't think I'm capable of doing anything on my own! It was you, wasn't it? Putting the poison in. Whispering in the studios' ears. Don't hire Gene Koenig! Don't give him a chance! Because I pull the strings around here! How could you do something like this, Momma? Why can't you bear it when I try to stand on my own two feet? Dad would never have treated any of us this way!'

'You don't know what you're talking about!'

'It's all power with you, Momma. Manipulating people. You just can't help yourself, can you? It's that old, F. H. Eastbridge mentality. Money buys everything!'

437

'How dare you speak to me like that!'

'I'm sorry. But you haven't left me much choice, have you? I see what all this scheming's been about now . . . for more than a year, maybe even longer than that, you've done everything you could to hold me back. Because you wanted to move me into position, just like a chess piece on your board. You wanted me to be so disappointed, so devastated when the other studios turned me down, that I'd jump at the chance to work for Trident! Have I got any of it wrong so far?'

'If that's what you choose to believe, believe it. I only have your interests at heart, whether you accept that or not. I do whatever it takes, Gene. Whatever it takes.'

'Momma, you don't have the right to interfere in other people's lives!' Elynor had suddenly appeared on the stairs behind him, but he hadn't noticed. 'That's the reason you stopped Alice seeing Flair, wasn't it? You didn't care that she liked him, that she felt he was the only person who understood her . . . you couldn't bear to see her confiding in someone other than you. You were jealous. And Ellie. When are you going to stop using her as an unpaid chaperone for Alice and let her have a real life of her own? If she gets an invitation, you have to vet it. If she wants to go someplace on her own, you have to go along too. Let go, Momma. For Christ's sake let go before we all end up hating you.' He hadn't meant to go that far, hadn't meant to say it, but now he couldn't stop himself. Years of frustration and pent-up resentment ran free. 'It's Leopardi's daughter, isn't it? She's a part of your matchmaking schemes. Don't bother to deny it . . . I can see the truth in your face.'

'You little fool! What the hell do you know about anything? You haven't even gotten the cradle marks off your backside, and you think you're capable of running your own life! You don't have the first idea.'

'I know when I'm being set up. And that just isn't going to happen, Momma. Tell Leopardi thanks for the interest, but when I accept a job I want it to come with no strings attached.'

'Do you realize what you're turning your back on? You want some lousy director's job when you could have it all? Your own studio. Yes, that's right! Leopardi's daughter could be in the palm of your hand and you can't even see straight. If you played the right game, in ten, fifteen years maybe . . . Trident would be all yours.' She could have shaken him, he was so stupid. 'And you blame me for wanting that for you?'

'You just don't understand, do you, Momma? You and me, we don't want the same things. We don't see things the same way. I don't want to be an empire builder . . . I just want to be happy. OK. I'll drive the girls over to the Sunset Inn if you can't do it. But I'm not staying. I've got my own plans for my life, thank you.'

Her voice stopped him as he turned to leave the room.

'You won't get very far on no money.'

'You don't need to worry about that. I'll find a job. I can support myself. I don't want anything from you.'

'Really? Your efforts haven't been very encouraging so far. Who would employ you? You might just get a job sweeping a bar-room floor, if you were lucky.'

At that moment, Elynor rushed down the stairs to stand at her brother's side. 'Momma, that was a cruel thing to say!'

'I don't believe this conversation has anything to do with you. Will you please stay out of it?'

'You can't turn Gene out!'

'Forgive me, but I thought that was what he wanted. Nothing more from me. Let him go. I shan't try to stop him. Well?'

'I'm sorry, Ellie . . . I have to. I just can't stand living like this any more.'

She caught his arm. 'Gene, please . . . !'

'I'll see you.' He kissed her on the cheek and left the room, his mother's voice ringing after him.

'Forget taking the T Ford. That stays here. You can make it on your own, didn't you just tell me? You won't be needing it. Wherever it is you're going, I'm afraid you'll have to walk.'

Elynor ran outside after him. 'Gene, I know how mad Momma's made you, but please, don't go like this.' She clutched his arm tighter. 'I need you, Gene. If I had to stay in that house with just Alice and Momma, without you, I think I'd go crazy!'

Very gently, he disengaged her hand from his arm.

'Don't you see? It's the only way, Ellie. Momma won't ever let go, she'll never leave us alone to do what we want. Maybe it isn't her fault . . . it's just the way she is . . . that Eastbridge blood. She has to try to run other people's lives, have power over us.

'Do you remember when we were all little, when we used to lie in bed and hear them arguing downstairs, her and Dad? You remember how afraid we were when we heard them shouting at each other all the time? We'd try not to talk about it, because we didn't understand, and we thought if we just pretended it wasn't happening, it would stop. But it never did. It just got worse. And do you know what I think? I think Momma started to try to make Dad do things he didn't want to do . . . that's what they were always fighting about.'

'We can't know that.'

'Can you think of any other reason?' She hung her head. 'Ellie, I hate leaving you . . . but you're not alone. I'm always there if you need me.' He hugged her tightly. 'Just because we don't live in the same house any more doesn't mean I stop caring about you. You've always been special to me.'

'Where are you going? You don't have any money!'

'I've got enough to get a cab when I reach downtown. I'm going to take a ride over to Alvarado Street and see Garrard Flair.'

'You think he can help you get a job?'

'If he can, he will.' He kissed her. 'He's just about the one person I'd trust in this town.'

Christina Leopardi had been lounging by the poolside listening to 'Whispering' on the wind-up gramophone when she'd heard the shrill ring of the telephone inside the

440

house. Too lazy to get up and answer it – one of the servants was bound to be passing sooner or later anyway – her ears pricked up when she suddenly heard her father's voice and the mention of Gene Koenig. Rousing herself into action, she pulled on her satin bathrobe and went inside.

There was a huge carved chair near the telephone in the entrance hall, and she settled herself into it to listen. Her father glanced up, caught sight of her, and blew her a kiss.

'OK, Marianna. Thanks for telling me. Catch you later.' He put down the receiver with a frown.

'What was that about Gene, Daddy? He's coming to my party, isn't he?'

'If I have to hog-tie him and drag him to the Sunset Inn!' Leopardi put his arm around her and they walked together outside. 'No. He's had a little bit of an argument with his mother, and she was just ringing to let me know that he's left home.'

'Left home! What for?'

'Oh, I guess he just wants to stretch his wings a little, sweetheart. I was the same, at his age. Trouble with young men is that they think they know it all. And knowing it all takes time. I should know!'

'Daddy, I want him at my party.'

'I know, honey. Like I said, I'll make sure he turns up. Tell you what, I'll put out a few feelers and find out what he's up to, then I'll maybe have a little talk with him. We'll sort things out.'

'Where do you think he's staying? With a friend?'

'Probably. Nothin' for you to worry that beautiful head about. Leave it to your dad.' He smiled at her dotingly; strange, he'd been so bitterly disappointed when Christina's mother had never been able to give him a son; but he loved her so much that now it didn't matter to him at all. 'Haven't I always gotten you everything you want?'

Flair had seen the black Buick draw up from his window, and his heart had sunk. Had a whole month come round already? The substantial balance of the deposit account he'd held at the National Bank in Los Angeles since he'd

441

first come to California had already plummeted to below half of what it had been this time last year; in between directing films, he was living on his savings. It couldn't go on. He desperately needed to find a solution; but what?

'I got it right this time, huh?' Delucca walked past him as he opened the bungalow door and went into the sitting room unasked. 'It's your manservant's evening off?'

'He'll soon be off on a permanent basis.' Flair looked at him with hatred. 'I shan't be able to afford to keep him on.'

Delucca chuckled. 'Hey, now, you ain't suggestin' that the little agreement between you and me has anythin' to do with that? I told you before. I'm not greedy.'

'That's a matter of opinion.'

Delucca helped himself to the bootleg gin. 'See, I could make things real hot for you . . . on havin' this brew on the premises alone. Course, I wouldn't do that, Flair; I'm a reasonable kinda guy. What's a drink or two in the privacy of your own home?'

Flair opened a drawer in his desk and brought out an envelope. 'This has to be the last. I can't afford to pay you any more.'

'I don't think I quite caught that, Mr Flair?'

'I'm lined up to direct a picture for Paramount, but I don't begin on that for another two weeks or so. I'm living on my savings and I can't do that for long. When I made the withdrawal for the ten thousand, the bank were suspicious.'

'It's your dough, ain't it? You can draw out what the hell you like!'

'That isn't the point and you know it! I've held that account for several years and I've never taken out an amount of that size – in cash!'

'You worry too much. It isn't illegal. So what's the problem?'

'Look. I know you could let my wife know where I am . . . inform the New York police . . . but that would ruin my career and then you wouldn't get a cent more from me. I don't think you'd do that, Delucca.'

'You wanna bet on that?'

'Why blow the whistle on the goose that lays the golden egg?'

'Good point. Now it's my turn. I'll make you a deal.' He lit a cigarette. 'You go back to that bank account and milk it some more. Leave yourself a little dough, just enough to get by. You can always add to it when you get directing again. I'll take one lump sum payment, then we'll call it quits? How does that sound to you?'

'I don't like the sound of it at all. I said, I can't afford to pay you any more. You're not being reasonable, Delucca.'

Slowly, Delucca put down his gin and took the envelope. He flicked the ash from his cigarette onto the rug. 'I want another ten grand. Get it. You got a month. Ten grand, Flair. No tricks. No excuses. Pay up, or I'll give you so much trouble you'll wish you were dead.'

As he drove away in the Buick, Flair saw a cab draw up near the bungalow complex entrance, and Gene Koenig get out of it. He heaved a sigh, ran his hand through his hair; he liked the boy, but at this moment he was the last person he wanted to see. He needed to be alone to think this out.

'I hope it isn't a bad time to call,' Gene said, and Flair forced himself into joviality. He listened in silence to Gene's tale of woe.

'Your mother's a very formidable and determined woman. She knows exactly how to get what she wants. You have to admire tenacity like that . . . even when it works against you.'

'Tell me about it.'

'I'm sure she's only ever acted in a way she thinks best . . . for all of you.'

'I didn't expect you, of all people, to take her side!'

'Gene, I'm not taking sides. I'm just trying to see her point of view in all this.'

What was wrong with Garrard Flair tonight? This was the last thing Gene had been expecting. Didn't he know how much Marianna detested him? 'I was rather hoping that you'd see mine.'

'I'm sorry. I'm a little preoccupied with another problem. But no matter. Can I offer you a drink?' He was

443

amused at Gene's reaction. 'I know, it's not strictly legal. But it won't poison you, I can assure you of that.' He smiled, a little more like his usual self. 'It can often help you to relax. Here, don't take my word for it. If we all did everything exactly by the book, life would be very dull.'

'Thanks, but I don't think I will. I need a clear head to sort out all my problems with my mother.'

'If you want to do that, then shouldn't you be at home talking to her and not here with me?'

'I came here to ask your advice, because you've always listened. I just wanted to ask you what I could do to get a job with a studio. I'd do anything at all, just to pay rent on a room or enough to share with a friend. I know a few guys from around the lot, but I can't expect to park myself on them and pay nothing.'

Flair turned the gin glass around in his hands. 'You really are serious, aren't you?'

'I wouldn't have bothered you tonight if I wasn't. I really do need your advice. You see, I found out the real reason why all the studios I've approached and asked for a trial have turned me down. My mother got to them first. You're smiling?'

'It doesn't really surprise me.' He sat down. 'You see, despite what she's done – and how she appears to you – I think your mother loves you all very much. Otherwise she would never go to such lengths to protect you. Her way of doing that is to keep you all as close to her as she possibly can. It's a mother's instinct.'

'I can't believe every mother acts that way!'

'No, that's true. But your father . . . if you'll forgive me for bringing him into this . . . well, he died a very tragic death. Can you imagine what losing him like that must have done to your mother? It would have affected her very deeply indeed.'

'But she treats us all as if we were possessions. She's stifling us!'

'Love sometimes makes us act that way . . . not easy to understand. When you love someone that intensely, the last thing you want is to see them hurt – in any way. You might do one of two things to protect them from that . . . you either let them go, or you do it your mother's way.' Why was it that Gene had the impression Flair was talking about someone else?

'I can't go back . . . at least, not until I make her understand that I won't let her manipulate me. Use me as bait for Vince Leopardi. Yes, that's right. His daughter's kinda taken a shine to me . . . and what she wants, he gets. Spoiled little rich girl. Momma thinks I'd be a fool to turn the chance down – that if I was real clever I could wind up in fifteen years as boss at Trident. I told her I wasn't interested.'

Flair laughed, softly. 'You have some other girl in mind, I take it? Or do you find Christina Leopardi that repellent?'

'I did run into a girl recently, as a matter of fact. I'd like to see more of her. If I stay with Momma at Whitley Heights, that just won't happen. I know Momma now. I know she's capable of doing anything to get what she wants.'

'Well, I'm glad you came to see me, Gene. There's nothing I can do directly to influence your mother . . . she really doesn't like me at all. But I can be of some practical help. First off, I do have a spare bedroom here. It's only a box room, and the bed probably is a little narrower than the one you're used to, but it is comfortable. The other room is occupied by my manservant and chauffeur – it's his evening off tonight.' Flair poured himself more gin. 'You're welcome to stay as long as you want to . . . until you get something a little more permanent.'

'You're sure? I'd be real grateful!'

Flair smiled; it was the last thing he needed or wanted, but what else could he do? He felt sorry for the boy. 'I'm directing for Paramount in a couple of weeks . . . if you like – and I won't make any firm promises – I'll take you along and see if they'll give you a job of some sort. It might not be what you want . . . but it'll be a start in the right direction.' He smiled. Maybe the company would be good for him; alone, he would only think about his problems, about Delucca, and brood. Having Gene Koenig around for a while would at least take his mind off other, unpleasant things. But there was tonight.

'Gene . . . I do have to go out this evening when Sands gets back . . . around nine or ten . . . just for a couple of hours. In the meantime, make yourself at home. Help yourself to anything in the kitchen that you fancy. And there are plenty of film scripts around, and magazines and books.'

'I don't know how to thank you.'

'What are friends for?'

Delucca had recognized the Koenig kid getting out of the cab as he'd driven away in the Buick; curiosity aroused, he'd doubled back when he reached the end of the block and waited, to see if he came out again. Half an hour, an hour passed, and there was no sign of either of them emerging. Delucca couldn't be sure that the Koenig kid hadn't seen him come out of Flair's bungalow as he was arriving, but he hoped not. He checked his watch, decided it was time to go back to LA. A surprise – a big surprise – was waiting for him when he got there and the desk sergeant told him that a patrolman had arrested a Karl Edward Sands, just a little while ago, in Arcadia Park: Sands had given his address as Alvarado Street, and his occupation as chauffeur/manservant to the film director Garrard Flair. Delucca stared down at the charge sheet with interest.

'Well, you don't say? Guess we'll have to sit on this one?'

'That's what I figured, lieutenant. You better have a word with him first. He's in the cells.'

'Morality charge?' Delucca frowned as he read the entry in the offence column for which Sands had been arrested. 'Indecent exposure or pestering young women?'

'Neither. Soliciting. Not young women, lieutenant. Young men.'

Sands glanced up sulkily when a warder unlocked the cell door and Delucca went inside. He kicked his feet roughly and swore at him. 'Hey, stand up, punk, when I'm talkin' to you!' Sands did as he was told and was shoved roughly against the opposite wall. 'Unless you wanna be in more fuckin' trouble than you already are, cream puff! You got that loud and clear, huh?'

Sands looked worried. 'OK, OK, no need to get rough. I ain't done nothin'.'

'No? A patrolman caught you down in Arcadia Park lookin' for some kid to stick it up, and you call that nothin'?'

'It's not the way you think.'

Delucca looked at him with disgust and contempt. Filth like Sands made him sick. 'Well, well . . . and you work for the film director, Garrard Flair?' Delucca could imagine how shocked Flair would be when he found out about this: he was so gentlemanly, so fastidious. He'd most likely fire Sands the same day. 'Guess he's goin' to be real amazed when we have to tell him we've got you down on a morality charge, huh? If I was you, I wouldn't hold my breath for no reference.'

Sands smiled for the first time. 'He won't be amazed. Yes, that's right. But I can see you are. You see, I was in the park tonight, looking for young boys. But not for myself.' Delucca was speechless. 'They were for him.'

It was well past midnight when Sands returned to the bungalow complex in Alvarado Street, and let himself in with his key. Flair was still up, sitting by the window and waiting for him, nervously smoking a cigarette.

'Where have you been?' He kept his voice as low as he could to prevent it carrying; Gene Koenig was asleep in the other room.

'I ran into a little trouble down at the park.' Sands avoided his eyes. 'A couple of patrolmen, prowling around. I had to come back. Empty-handed.' He shrugged. 'Couldn't be helped. Hell, I'm not riskin' my neck that far!'

'All right.' Flair was tired, tense. He'd needed diversion tonight. Anonymous. No responsibility. The boys Sands picked up for him always provided that. But it couldn't be helped. And having a house guest close at hand complicated things even further. He jabbed a finger in the direction of the spare room. 'We have a visitor. For a few days at least, so keep the noise down.' Sands raised his eyebrows. 'Marianna Koenig's son. He has no idea, so let's keep it that way.'

'You're the boss,' Sands said insolently, and went through to his own room. He threw himself down full length on the bed, and yawned. Jesus H. Christ, this was more comfortable than the cell downtown that he'd been shut up in for hours, after his run-in with the patrolman in Arcadia Park! Looked like he'd struck lucky, too, with a crooked cop hell bent on exposing the suave, refined pillar of the community Garrard Flair, who just about everyone in Hollywood thought was a dedicated ladies' man. What a joke!

Sands pulled off his shoes, turned out the light. He'd done a deal with Delucca but that wasn't going to stop him going ahead with his own plans, the plans he'd already formulated in his mind a long time ago.

A week. Maybe two. And then he was out of here. And he'd sure as hell help himself to what was coming to him.

CHAPTER THIRTY

'It doesn't matter, Gene.' Susie Costello was flattered that, with all he had on his mind, he'd sought her out and was apologizing for something that wasn't even his fault. Ironic, that someone as thoughtful, sensitive, gentle as he was, could possibly be Marianna Koenig's son. After everything he'd told her last night about the past few days, she was surprised that he'd had time to come looking for her at all. 'It's just a party. I'm not invited . . . but it's no big deal. There are a lot of parties in Hollywood that dogs-bodies in wardrobe departments never get to be invited to. We don't take it personally.' She smiled. 'I've lived here for long enough to realize that all they are are grand occasions where anyone who's anyone just get together to outdress, out talk, and outdo as many other people as they can. You can learn a lot just by wandering among the guests with a cocktail in your hand and listening; you don't have to say a word.'

'I'm not going without you.'

'Are you sure that's because you really want me to be there, or because you want to show your mother and the Leopardis that you prefer to choose your own com-panions? I don't like being used to prove a point, Gene.'

'That isn't the way I meant it. When we talked about it last night, I thought you understood.'

'I'm sorry. I guess it's just my inferiority complex.' She touched his arm. 'I think you should drive your sisters to the party – like your mother asked you to before you quar-relled with her – and then leave if you want to. If you don't go at all, it will just look as if you're sulking about what happened between you, and cause bad feeling all round. That would just be childish, Gene. And that isn't the way you are at all.'

'How come you're the expert all of a sudden?'

'I like to think that I'm quite a good judge of character.' She smiled again, and he was more drawn towards her than ever. 'By the way, my offer still stands, if you want to share my humble home.'

'I'd jump at the chance – but I'm thinking of your reputation.'

'I think you prefer slumming it in Garrard Flair's box room,' she teased gently, 'why don't you admit it?' How shocked his mother would be if he moved into Susie Costello's tiny cottage on Sunset Boulevard; not that anyone else would be likely to take any notice. He was too unimportant in the order of things for what he did to make headline news. 'There's even less room at my place than he has . . . but at least you won't have to suffer the cigarette smoke!'

'I came in unexpectedly the other day, and saw that chauffeur of his helping himself from the cigarette box. That's one of the reasons I don't like stopping there . . . nothing I can put my finger on, like I said before, but there's something strange about the guy . . . kind of shifty.'

'Garrard Flair's had three chauffeurs that I know of. They've all left, mostly within a year.'

'I don't know . . . there's something else . . . I didn't notice it, not at first. I suppose I was just too taken up with my own problems with Momma. But he seems to be preoccupied . . . worried about something. I started to feel as if my being there was getting in his way.'

'He wouldn't have offered to put you up if he didn't want you.'

Gene shrugged. 'I didn't give him much choice, did I? I just turned up on his doorstep. I rang the house when I knew Momma wouldn't be there. Ellie said when she'd found out I was staying with Garrard Flair – of all people – she just went crazy . . . especially when she found out on the grapevine that he'd helped me land the job at Paramount. I tried to talk to her – the day I left – but she just wouldn't listen! Flair does. He really understands, just like my dad would have done . . . and that's what I miss

450

most, I guess; having a man around, someone who really listens. Momma won't do that. It's got to be her way, or no way at all. You know what Flair said when I was telling him about Momma and the way she treats us? That it's because she loves us so much, she doesn't want us to be hurt; that's why she doesn't want any of us to leave home, why she won't give us any freedom. In case we get hurt. It's kind of bizarre, but he explained it so well. You know, for a guy who's never been married, never had kids of his own, he understands women and the way they think real well.'

'He should do.' Susie smiled. 'He's been seen out with just about every well-known actress on the Universal lot. And the other studios as well.'

'Maybe that's why I ought to move out . . . I think I might be cramping his style a little.' He touched her arm. He longed to kiss her but he didn't want to rush things between them. 'I know what it's like, when you want to be alone with someone special. Trouble is, if I take you up on your offer – and I do want to – I might just not be able to trust myself.' For a moment they looked at each other.

'I'm willing to take the chance.'

From upstairs, Elynor heard her mother come into the house. From the way she slammed the door and stormed into the drawing room, she guessed her mood was even sourer than the one she had left in. Not hard to understand why. Gene was working in artistic direction at Paramount – a job he'd got through the help of Garrard Flair – and, to add insult to injury, he'd been seen around town with a girl from Universal's costume department.

'Momma?' Elynor had left Alice upstairs in her room, trying on gown after gown for the Leopardis' party at the Sunset Inn on Saturday night. 'Gene rang while you were out.' Her mother spun round furiously. 'He said that if you still want him to drive Alice and me tomorrow night, he'll call for us around seven thirty.'

'I wonder he has the nerve to show his face around here!' She was lighting a cigarette; these days, she rarely moved around the house without one. 'I'm ashamed to call him my son!' She paced agitatedly around the room. What was wrong with Momma these days? She was constantly on edge, snapping at everyone in sight, carping, irritable. 'I blame Flair for this, encouraging him to defy me! Who the hell gave him the right to interfere in my life? First he tried to put ideas into Alice's head, now it's Gene. I called Adolph Zukor about letting him go, but that jumped-up little Jew wouldn't hear of it! Oh no! Flair's his favourite director, Flair got Gene the job on the lot, and he mustn't offend him! Otherwise, if he upsets him, he might not agree to direct his next picture!'

Elynor was shocked that her mother could stoop to such depths. 'Momma, that was a terrible thing to do!' She came further into the room. 'You had no right to try to get Gene fired!'

Marianna, her nerves frayed and raw, rounded on her. Another payment to Delucca was due in a few days' time and Walter Oppenheim had called earlier to tell her that there was more trouble looming from the Revenue Service. 'I can do as I damn well please, young lady . . . and don't you ever forget it! I didn't struggle to bring you three up, give you the best of everything after your father died, to have it all thrown back in my face now!' From upstairs, there was a wail of annoyance from Alice. 'Get up there and help her out of that goddam dress before she rips it! Do you all think I'm made of money?'

Alice's bedroom was littered with gowns of every imaginable style and colour. Elynor began picking them up.

'How can you throw these around like old rags?' Elynor was angry at the flippant way her sister treated everything; her clothes allowance was ten times what Elynor's was. 'Do you know how expensive these gowns are? Besides, it isn't Colleen's job to go clearing up after you because you're too lazy to do it for yourself!'

Alice turned on her spitefully. 'Don't you talk to me that way! I'll throw them anywhere I like . . . and you'll pick them up for me! That's all you're good for. Who's the movie star around here anyway? Not you, that's for sure.' She went on admiring herself in the mirror. 'Do you know how much Momma paid for this gown for me?' Elynor glared at her in silence. 'More than she's ever spent on you, you can bet on that. Not that it matters. Come tomorrow night, people will be looking at me, not you. No-one will notice what you wear.'

'You know, I'm beginning to actually feel a little sorry for you, Alice. You've started to believe your own publicity!'

Alice swung round on her sister furiously. 'Oh, is that right? Well, tell me this . . . whose face is on the cover of *Motion Picture* magazine almost every issue? Who gets thousands of letters from fans all over? So many that the studio have had to take on three secretaries just to answer them? You think that will ever happen to you?'

'I wonder if people would admire you so much if they could see you the way you really are. Selfish, spoiled, and spiteful. I don't think so.'

'You think I care if you call me names? You think it matters to me if you're mean to me? I know why you do it. You're jealous, Ellie. You always have been, you always will be. You just can't stand it because I'm what you want to be. Even when we were little, you were jealous . . . because I was Daddy's favourite.'

'Daddy didn't have favourites. He loved us all exactly the same.'

'That's what you think, but I know different! Why don't you go ask Momma?' She picked up a double row of pearls from her dressing table and held them against her neck. 'If you keep on being so mean to me, I'll get Momma to make you stay home tomorrow night, and then you won't get to go to the party at all. Everyone important is going to be there!' She reeled off a list of Hollywood's best-known names. 'The Barrymores, Mary Pickford and Doug Fairbanks, Richard Bathelmess, Nita Naldi, Mabel Poulton, D. W. Griffith . . . anyone who's anyone! Vince Leopardi sure does know how to throw a party. And guess what else? Mr Goldenthal told me today that a very important producer was coming over here from Europe, especially to have me star in his latest picture . . . and it's all set to be one of the longest and most spectacular films ever! That's right. He's financing the entire production costs himself – so he must be very rich – and he's also choosing his own director to do it . . . it might even be Garrard Flair! Wouldn't that be wonderful? Even Momma couldn't do anything about it. He wants to shoot it in America for lots of reasons, but mostly because he wants an entirely English-speaking cast. And a famous face as leading lady, of course! Mr Goldenthal said that I've got just the perfect look . . . this producer wouldn't even consider any of the other studios because he didn't think any of their actresses were right for the part. This is going to be my biggest role ever!' She smiled smugly in the mirror. 'What do you think about that?'

'I'll believe it when it happens.'

'Jealous again, huh? You just can't stand it that I'm the one everybody wants, can you? Well, if you don't believe me, why don't you go ask Momma?'

'I will.'

'Yes, it's true.' So, for once, Alice hadn't been idly boasting. 'But the deal's not even passed the negotiation stage so far. There's a lot that could happen – go wrong – before it's finally signed, sealed and delivered. I've been in this business long enough not to rely on hearsay.' Marianna was too busy with other things to have time discussing what might or might not happen in six months' time. She was due at her accountant's office in Los Angeles in less than an hour, and there were pressing things to go through before her meeting with Walter Oppenheim. How could she tell the lawyer that the huge discrepancies that not the most astute accounting could cover up were the result of debits for blackmail? All night she'd lain awake thinking, trying to work a way out. So far, she hadn't come up with a plausible idea. 'Sundry expenses' were wearing a little thin now. If the Revenue Service became too suspicious and insisted on an independent audit by their own accountants, how could she explain away a deficit of more than two hundred thousand dollars? Though she was outwardly dismissive about the European picture that might or might not be filmed in Hollywood, it was – if it happened – her only lifeline. With the signing fee and one-off contract that she would be in a position to demand for Alice's appearance in it, she could plug the gaping holes in her account books.

'Who is this European producer, Momma? Has he asked for Alice, the way she said?'

'He wants to film here in Hollywood and the Universal studios are the biggest, with the widest scope and largest technical crews. Also, there's a large pool of independent directors for him to choose from. As far as I know, he hasn't announced who he wants to direct as yet. But, yes, Alice will be starring in the film.'

'She said he might ask Garrard Flair to direct.'

'Not if I can help it.'

'But, if he did, there isn't much you could do. If anything.'

'I think I could persuade him that there are other directors in this town with better credentials than Flair's. Besides, the rumours are that he'll want D. W. Griffith. Griffith has the experience in epics.'

'But not in handling Alice. You have to admit that she isn't the easiest actress for any director to work with. Only Garrard Flair seems to know how to get the best from her . . . and stop her having tantrums on set. I doubt if some foreign producer would be very happy at seeing his production costs soar because his leading lady kept walking off set every five minutes after a slanging match with the director . . . don't you?'

Marianna gathered up her account books and placed them in a briefcase. 'We'll cross that bridge when we get to it. I have to leave.'

Elynor followed her into the hall. 'Have you changed your mind about speaking to Gene when he comes to collect us tomorrow night?'

'I'll speak to him when he learns that he won't get away with trying to make a fool out of me. If I lose face with

455

Vince Leopardi because of his shenanigans with some little nobody from the studio . . . he'd better watch out.' She slammed the front door after her.

The party at the Sunset Inn was already in full swing by the time they got there in Gene's borrowed automobile; lights streamed from every window, from specially constructed poles in the gardens, and even from the trees; Bix Beiderbecke's latest jazz hit wailed like a siren over the cacophony of voices and loud laughter.

'Looks like we're the last to arrive,' Gene said, as he opened the door and helped his sisters out.

'We'd have been here half an hour ago if you hadn't driven the long way round!' Alice slammed the door and stormed off inside. Gene and Elynor looked at each other. It seemed so long since they'd talked – weeks apart seemed more like months – and now she would be on her own again.

'I came the long way so we could kind of catch up on things.' He smiled. 'Guess we'll have to start having sneaked meetings, huh? Just to foil Momma.' His face became suddenly serious again. 'Ellie, I don't want you to worry about me, OK? I know what I'm doing. I'm just hoping that if Flair goes to direct for another studio – if he does move from Paramount – they'll decide to keep me on. There're no guarantees. I knew that when I started out. I think they're pleased with me . . . but since they took me on as kind of a favour to him, I can't rely on them keeping me on the payroll after he leaves. I can't expect Susie to pay for everything . . . hell, I'd rather come crawling back to Momma than have that happen! But I'll do my damnedest to make sure it doesn't.'

'Momma went wild when she found out you'd moved in with her.'

'Yes, I know. Not that she gives a cuss except that it might offend Mr high and mighty Leopardi at Trident.'

Elynor looked into his eyes. 'Are you in love with her, or is it just . . . the other thing?'

Gene laughed. 'I haven't slept with her, if that's what you

mean. But I'd like to.' He laughed, very softly. 'Now I've shocked you.'

'I guess . . . it's a little hard to think of you in that way. You know, being with somebody.'

'I do love her, yes. Not that I could ever explain that to Momma. She'd just say I was wasting my opportunities. Better to go for Leopardi's daughter and get something out of it.' They sat down for a moment, side by side on the running board while the raucous laughter and the Bix Beiderbecke got louder still. 'I can't think the way Momma does. I'm tired of trying to make her listen to what it is I want to do. Do you understand that, Ellie?'

'Yes. But it's easier for you. I can't just walk out the way you did. I couldn't get by. In any case, I don't have anywhere to go.'

'If we had more room, I'd ask Susie if you could come live with us.'

She put her hand on his arm. 'No, Gene. I wouldn't want that. Besides, it wouldn't be fair. You'd do it just because I'm your sister and you felt you owed it to me to help out, but you'd rather be alone. I'd just be intruding.'

He put his arm around her. 'You could never do that. Hey, listen! They're playing "Tea for Two". You should be in there dancing with some handsome movie actor, not sitting out here on a running board talking to me. Anyhow, I've got to get back. Take care.' He kissed her. 'Ellie, don't let Momma get to you. Or Alice.'

'Are you kidding? Ever since Hal Goldenthal told her about this epic that some producer is coming over from Europe to film at Universal, she's been boasting even more than usual. You must know about it. Is it true this man, whoever he is, could ask Garrard Flair to direct?'

'His name is Fritz von Ehrlich . . . and he has quite an awesome reputation in France and Germany. And, sure . . . it's a strong possibility that Flair could be chosen as director.'

'Whoever he chooses . . . it doesn't really matter, does it? Alice will be the star and she'll be more unbearable than ever.'

Elynor walked in, almost unnoticed among the noisy, glittering throng. No-one came to talk to her, no-one bothered to give her a second glance. Against the gaudy, shingle-haired women with their outrageously bright costumes and painted faces, she looked like a little girl lost, pale and insignificant. Here, only wealth and status really mattered; there was no place, no room among the screen idols and movie moguls and their courts of hangers-on, for true art, or true beauty. The entire party – the guests, the bright lights, the background setting – could as easily have come from a studio set, so little relation did it bear to reality. As she invariably did, Elynor found a corner by herself and merely observed from a distance.

She could see Hal Goldenthal and his wife, chatting to the Rudolph Valentinos; Valentino was the new archetypal Latin lover, the star of Paramount's war epic *The Four Horsemen of the Apocalypse*; the scene in which he'd danced the tango with Alice Terry had become one of the most talked-about sequences ever made. She spotted the Leopardis, sipping cocktails with Gloria Swanson and Adolph Zukor, Christina sulky because, no doubt, she had wanted to be brought here by Gene. And there, in the centre of things, surrounded as she invariably was by a bevy of eager admirers and sycophants, was Alice, giggling in mirth at someone's joke that, if Elynor guessed right, she probably didn't even understand. She was making the most of her freedom from her mother's cloying presence; as she watched, Elynor saw her sister catch sight of Garrard Flair across the brightly lit lawn, and edge her way towards him. Then she turned, and saw Wallace Walbrook standing there.

Her heart began to race faster, as it always did whenever she saw him; he was so elegant, so suave, so handsome; to her, perfection personified. But he was not alone. An ultra-slender, heavily made-up platinum blonde with ropes of pearls was clinging to his arm, her exact age undefinable under the layers of powder, lipstick, kohl and rouge. Elynor remained frozen to the spot in her anonymous corner, hemmed in by the other guests, but as she watched them threading their way through the crowd of partygoers and waiters balancing trays of cocktails and exotic canapés, her whole body went rigid with jealousy and shock. Her cheeks burned as Walbrook took the blonde in his arms and in full view of everyone kissed her lingeringly and passionately on the lips. A roar of approval, then wild cheering and hand-clapping went up among the other guests. Pursing her red cupid's-bow lips at the matinee idol, the blonde clasped her hands tightly round his neck and gazed adoringly into his eyes.

Elynor stood there, reeling with humiliation and envy, for a moment unable to tear her eyes away from them. There was a sick feeling in the pit of her stomach. She trembled all over with a terrible helpless anger. Unthinkable now for her to stay here and pretend that she was enjoying herself, that nothing had happened; all the dreams and hopes she'd secretly nurtured for months had been utterly shattered. She'd taken hours preparing for tonight, taken infinite pains with her clothes, her make-up, her hair . . . and he hadn't even noticed her.

'Say, honey, you OK?' she heard someone behind her ask as she accidentally backed into him and almost sent him and his cocktail flying. But she was too upset to answer him, too broken-hearted to care.

She turned away abruptly and began to push her way back through the crowd.

She looked frantically around the sea of faces. She was choking, stifling, drowning in the music and voices. She had to get out, she had to escape from this nightmare. She put her hands over her ears, trying to blot out the deafening noise of the party; she fought back her tears. Then she caught sight of Garrard Flair and her sister and burst through the party guests towards them.

'Mr Flair, would you help me, please? I don't feel well. Could you take me home?' Alice glared at her, speechless with fury. If he drove Elynor back to Whitley Heights, by the time he returned her mother would have arrived at the party, and spoiled everything.

'What's the matter with you?' She was torn between anger and not wanting Garrard Flair to think she was unconcerned about her sister. 'I can't come with you . . . Momma expects me to be here when she arrives.'

'I don't need you to. I just want to go home and be by myself.'

The last thing she remembered from the party besides Wallace Walbrook and the shingle-haired, painted blonde was the band playing 'Kiss in the Dark', and her sister's scowling face as she left on Flair's arm.

Karl Sands drew the drapes in the bungalow and then brought a knife from the kitchen to force open the centre drawer of the desk. It was difficult to open, more difficult than he'd imagined, but he'd spent more than an hour after Flair had left for the party on Ocean Avenue searching for the keys, without success. Flair must have hidden them in a place that he hadn't thought of looking, or else taken them with him. Either way, it made no difference now. With a last fierce thrust, he broke the lock and the drawer came free.

As quickly as he could, Sands rifled through the contents. There were two hundred and forty dollars in ten- and twenty-dollar bills – not as much as he'd thought. But the diamond-headed tie-pin and cuff-links must have been worth a lot more than that. He stuffed the money and the jewellery into his pocket. Nothing else in the drawer worth taking. He picked up an unopened bottle of bootleg gin and went out, quietly closing the door.

Flair had taken a cab to the party tonight, no doubt expecting to drink a great deal and be given a lift back home afterwards. Nothing could have worked out better for Sands. By the time the party was over – probably not until well into the early hours at least, judging by usual Hollywood standards – and Flair returned home, Sands, the valuables, and the Cunningham V-8 would be long gone.

Looking around to see if any of the neighbours might be watching, Sands climbed into the V-8, hot-wired it and drove away. At full throttle, he could be safely over the state border within seven hours.

Flair parked the borrowed automobile at the bottom of the driveway, and she thanked him and ran inside. Though it was the cook's and the maid's evening off, the lights had been left on in the house; Elynor fumbled in her beaded evening bag for her latchkey. She threw down her wrap, ran blindly up the staircase to her room, the tears she'd been holding in check for the entire drive home pouring down her face. But on the landing, she stopped in her tracks. The light was on in her bedroom; the door was ajar.

Inside, she came face to face with her mother. She stared at her.

'What are you doing here? I thought you were on your way to the party.' Her eyes went to the open drawer, the pictures her mother was holding in her hands. 'Those are mine! You've no right to come in here and touch my things!'

Marianna held out one of the magazine cuttings of a suave, immaculate, smiling Wallace Walbrook. 'Alice told me that you'd been cutting articles out of her *Motion Picture* magazine . . . so many, I began to ask myself why. I guess by the look on your face he was there tonight, and you saw him with his wife. Is that why you've been crying?' Elynor was so taken aback for a moment that she couldn't speak. 'I heard an automobile a few minutes ago at the bottom of the drive. You got someone to bring you home because you couldn't stay there and watch him with her . . . tell me if I'm wrong?'

'*His wife?*' A tear ran down her cheek and she dashed it away with her hand. 'But Wallace Walbrook isn't married. I'd have read about it if he was!'

Marianna gave her daughter an almost pitying smile.

'They've been married a year or more. And she's just had a baby. You think those trashy movie magazines that Alice reads would print something like that? They never write the

461

truth about marriages of leading men in Hollywood –
except Doug Fairbanks – the female fans don't like it. If the
fans knew their idol was just the same as any other man,
with a wife and kids, do you seriously think they'd flock to
see their pictures, send marriage proposals by the sackload
to the studios every week?' She placed the bundle of
pictures back in the drawer and closed it. 'But let me tell
you one thing. The worst thing any woman can ever do is
to fall in love with an actor. Give your heart and soul to a
man who pretends to feelings for a living, someone who can
never be trusted to feel them in real life. Lies and fantasy
are their stock-in-trade, believe me. I learned that fact
through bitter experience.' She walked towards the door.
'Take my advice . . . forget about him. Right here and now.
And dry your tears. He isn't worth crying over.' She hesitated for a moment, then handed Elynor her handkerchief.
'I'm leaving now. I don't know what time I'll be back.'

She would have given anything to have put her arms
around her daughter and held her. She understood her feelings only too well; they mirrored her own infatuation with
Curt; she could identify with her misery and pain. But
Hollywood was no place to survive in if you gave way to
emotion, even with your own flesh and blood. She'd got
where she was and achieved what she had by being cold,
calculating and ruthless: there was no other way. To save
Elynor from falling for another man like Wallace
Walbrook she'd had no choice but to be cruel to be kind.

Elynor lay there in the darkness, blinking the hot, burning,
salty tears out of her eyes. They were already sore and
hideously swollen with crying. Her head throbbed so much
that she felt sick. Inside, there was a cavernous, gnawing
emptiness as real as any physical pain, and she wrapped her
arms tightly around herself to try to make it go away.
Tonight, all her girlish fantasies, all her hopes and
dreams had been shattered, and Wallace Walbrook and her
mother had shattered them.

She felt a fierce anger towards him, an even fiercer anger
towards herself. She'd been blind, foolish, stupid. As

462

mindless as the droves of star-struck female fans who went to all his pictures and swooned over his photographs in movie magazines. Childish, unreasonable, maybe; but then childhood was not that far behind her. How Alice would deride her silly little schoolgirl crush that had gradually built into an obsession. How spitefully she'd laugh if she ever knew. Only Gene – intuitive, sensitive Gene – would have understood how much it hurt her, how real it had been to her.

She got up and took out her collection of cuttings from the drawer. For a moment or two she gazed down at Wallace Walbrook's perfect, unblemished, expertly retouched and photogenic face, before she tore every picture she had ever kept of him into shreds.

By noon the following day, the news of Sands' absconding had spread to every corner of the film community, over-shadowing even the growing rumours about his master and Alice Ayres. Marianna had been furious when, arriving at the party at the Sunset Inn, she discovered that Garrard Flair had not only been spotted kissing her youngest daughter in a darkened corner, but had borrowed a roadster to take Alice for a moonlit drive along the coast. Her rage had known no bounds.

'You don't understand, Momma! Elynor didn't feel good, so Garrard borrowed Doug Fairbanks' Lozier to take her home in . . . then, when he came back and you still weren't there, I was so upset about Elynor missing the fun that he put his arm around me to try to make me feel better . . .'

'Just what kind of a fool do you take me for, you lying little bitch?' While nearby party guests whispered and nudged each other, Alice had been frogmarched outside and bundled into her mother's Chrysler. 'You don't give a hoot in Hades about your sister or anyone else except your-self . . . so cut the bull.' The slang had shocked Alice almost as much as her mother's anger. She burst into tears. When Flair came outside after them to try to calm her down, Marianna had turned on him ferociously.

'Save your breath, pretty boy. And the white-toothed smile . . . that famous charm of yours might work on actresses with one-cell brains, but it doesn't work on me!' She pushed him out of her way and got into the automobile. 'If I catch you so much as within spitting distance of my daughter, I won't be responsible for what I do.'

'Mrs Koenig . . .'

'I said, save it, Flair! And get this. If you think you're going to be directing Alice in that von Ehrlich picture at Universal, forget it! I'll see to it that Hal Goldenthal doesn't even give you a job sweeping the studio floor.' Before he could protest, before he could say another word, she'd flicked the engine switch and roared off along Ocean Avenue in a cloud of dust.

Alice had started screaming and sobbing, yelling at her mother that she'd had no right to create a scene at the party, no right to treat her like a child. When they reached home, the noise of their fierce arguing had woken everyone in the house.

'You treated me as if I was just ten years old, in front of all those people!'

'You act like a ten-year-old, you get treated like a ten-year-old!'

'You had no right to talk that way to Garrard Flair! You hate him because he treats me like an adult, because he cares about me, and you can't stand it!'

'How dare you criticize me, after everything I've done for you! Do you have any idea of the sacrifices I've made to turn you into what you are? Alice Ayres, movie star. Your name's up in lights all over this town, at every moving picture palace in America . . . and who have you got to thank for it? Me.'

'You won't let me do anything I really want to do . . . no drives, no dates, no press interviews or parties unless you're there! I can't even choose my own clothes. Or my own friends!' She slammed the door and the glass chandelier shook violently. Upstairs, Elynor sat up in bed and listened. 'You won't even let me have my own bank account!'

'What the hell do you think you know about choosing clothes, or friends, or men? As for the money, I've invested it for you and that's exactly where it's going to stay, so you can't touch it. Invested.'

'It's mine, I earned it and it isn't fair! When I'm twenty-one I'm going to have it all and then you won't be able to do anything about it!' She was silenced suddenly by a stinging slap across the face.

'Don't you ever dare raise your voice to me, young lady. Don't you ever dare question my judgement, or anything else that I tell you to do . . . do you hear me?' When Alice only stood there, sobbing hysterically, Marianna took hold of her and shook her. 'As for Flair . . . you stay away from that womanizer, have you got that? If I catch you driving off alone with him – for any goddam reason – I swear I'll take a horsewhip to your bare backside and whop it till it's raw!'

Alice pulled away from her and ran upstairs, howling like a scalded cat. Elynor heard her rush into her room and throw herself onto her bed. She went out onto the landing.

'Momma, what's happened?'

Marianna looked up. 'She went for a drive with Flair before I got to the party.' Her eyes were harsh. 'I didn't know it was him who drove you back here tonight.'

'There was nobody else there I really knew. He was talking to Alice, and I just went up to him and asked if he could help. He was very kind.'

'Did he try to touch you?'

Elynor was appalled. 'No!' She felt her face reddening. Why was her mother so bitter, so mistrustful of men? Flair had always behaved like the perfect gentleman. 'I felt awful when I found out that he hadn't brought his own automobile, that he was getting a ride back after the party with a friend from the studio. I didn't want to be an imposition. But he said it was no trouble, that he was pleased to help. He borrowed a roadster – from Doug Fairbanks, I think – and drove me straight back here. I said I was very grateful, and I was.'

'That's something you never say to a man. Any man.

That you're grateful to him. If you do that they think it gives them a licence to take liberties.'

'He isn't like that, Momma!'

'This town is full of men like that. Why the hell do you think I won't trust you or Alice out of my sight?'

'Maybe if you did then we could start learning how to judge other people for ourselves.'

'Like Wallace Walbrook, for instance?'

Elynor looked away. She knew from experience how pointless it was to argue with their mother; her way was the only way. Her word was law. Only Gene had found the courage to break free from the maternal chains that bound all of them; but he was a man. Without work, without money, with no place to go, how could either girl survive in a place like Hollywood, where status, wealth and prestige meant more than anything else? Elynor had no illusions, even if her sister did: Alice Ayres might be fawned on, photographed, pampered and spoiled; but their mother was the power behind the throne. Left to herself, Alice was nothing more than a pretty little puppet, and every producer, every director, every movie mogul in town knew it.

Marianna was in Hal Goldenthal's office the next morning, just as the news about Sands' absconding across the state line broke.

'What a pity.' Her voice was mocking as she peeled off her white kid gloves and tossed them down. 'Maybe he'd have been better off staying home last night and keeping an eye on his servant instead of trying to seduce my daughter!' Goldenthal had been at the Sunset Inn with his wife and he knew that Marianna was just trying her old trick of stirring up trouble where there wasn't any. What the hell did she have against Flair anyhow? 'He drove off with her, alone, without my permission. Without even telling anybody. I could have had him arrested for the abduction of a minor!'

'Now just hang on one minute, Marianna . . . !'

'No, you hang on for a minute, Hal! Alice has got some stupid crush on him and he's done everything to encourage her! We both know his reputation with women. Well, as far

466

as I'm concerned he can sleep with every actress in Hollywood if he wants to. But let him step just one foot in my daughter's direction and I'll hit that smooth-talking bastard with everything I've got!'

'Don't you think you've got this whole thing way out of proportion? It was a party. Everyone was havin' a good time, everybody was happy. The way I heard it, Alice wanted to talk to Garrard about the new film and there was too much noise around for them to concentrate. They just took a drive along the coast, that's all. Now, why have you got to make such a big deal about somethin' so small? Hell, Marianna, you gotta let the girls have a little leeway, after all . . . a little male company once in a while. It ain't natural for two good-lookin' girls like that to be treated like they was livin' in a nunnery.'

She banged her fist down on his desk and made him jump.

'You can cut the wisecracks, Hal! You do what you do best. I'll be the judge of what my daughters can or cannot do . . . do we understand each other? Don't forget just how many million dollars Alice's pictures have grossed for this studio, and just how much you'd have left without her as your major star! Am I getting through? Good. Now, as to the real reason I'm here . . . the von Ehrlich deal.' He looked nervous. 'Since we haven't got to contract stage yet, I want to make sure you understand one very important stipulation. Flair doesn't direct.'

'Marianna, I can't give you any guarantees on this one, for the simple reason I'm not responsible for production. Von Ehrlich's running the show, not me. I'm just supplying Universal studio premises, equipment, cameramen and stars. He calls the shots. As far as I know, he still wants Flair to direct and if he insists on that then there's nothing at all either you or I can do about it.'

'Is that a fact?'

'Marianna, I don't think you realize just how important this guy is in the European moving picture industry . . . I mean, we're talkin' about Importance with a capital I. This guy's reputation is awesome, and I mean *awesome*. He's produced classic pictures in Germany, Switzerland, France, England, Canada . . . and the accent here is on classics, not the slapstick and romantic crap Hollywood churns out for the mass media. He knows what he wants, and he gets it. No messin'. You say "von Ehrlich" in Europe, and you're talkin' excellence.'

'Maybe he'll change his mind when he hears what I have to say about Garrard Flair.'

'Look, Marianna. You won't gain a thing by tryin' to stir up trouble. If you hate the guy's guts, it won't cut no ice. Von Ehrlich isn't interested in the whys and wherefores of your personal vendetta against Flair. All he's interested in is his ability as a director. And you've gotta give the guy his due. In that department he's first class.'

'I don't think you've been listening to me, Hal. I said I don't care how you square it with von Ehrlich, but if Flair directs this picture I won't allow Alice to star.' Goldenthal knew she was bluffing; even Marianna Koenig would swallow her detestation of Flair for the opportunity of having her daughter star in an international-calibre picture, and make more money from it than she'd made from any of her films so far. Money apart, only a fool would turn down the chance of working for a producer of von Ehrlich's reputation. He was confident that she'd back down.

'No point in crossing bridges till we come to 'em, huh? I don't even know when von Ehrlich intends to arrive.'

'Surely you're in touch with him?'

'Marianna, von Ehrlich isn't your regular kind of guy. Not from all I've heard, anyhow.'

She looked at Goldenthal suspiciously. 'Are you trying to tell me that he's some kind of eccentric?'

Goldenthal shrugged. 'He's a real unusual type of guy, so I've been told. What I can tell you is that he's fixin' to use that enormous great place up in the hills to live in while he's making the picture. He's already sent orders to the realtor in LA about how he wants it furnished, about the kind of grand piano he wants installed in the music room . . . and that he'll be bringing in his own staff. Like I said, he's a guy who knows exactly how he wants things done.'

Marianna was already rising to the challenge. 'I see. Well, I doubt if he's much different from any of the other men I've had to deal with before. I'm sure he'll listen to reason.' She picked up her gloves and inwardly Goldenthal sighed with relief. Whenever he had a visit from Marianna Koenig, his blood pressure went up. 'Have you no idea at all when he'll be coming?'

'Oh, I guess in a month or two, no more than that. As soon as he's free.'

It was to be almost seven.

CHAPTER THIRTY-ONE

With just fifteen dollars in his pocket after he'd bought a one-way ticket to Hollywood, Danny Mazzoli stepped wearily off the train at the end of his long journey. If you counted New York State and California itself, he'd crossed nine states across the width of America. Ironic, when he thought about it. After his pappa had come to 'the new country' from Italy more than thirty years ago, he'd never once set foot out of New York City in his life.

He stood on the station platform squinting in the strong sunlight, more tuckered out, more thirsty and hungry than he'd ever believed it was possible to be. He could have dropped down and fallen asleep where he stood. The smell of food wafting from the restaurant car had almost driven him crazy in the last twenty-four hours, but he knew that he couldn't even afford the price of a sandwich and a beer. He had no job lined up, not even a place to sleep tonight. But he was here. And so, somewhere, was the bastard Delucca.

Slinging his battered kit bag over one shoulder, Danny handed his dog-eared ticket to a Negro standing at the station gate, and walked on through.

He asked around and got directed to the place where he could find some transport, a trolley that clanged down the eight miles from Laurel Canyon into the heart of LA. En route to his destination, he marvelled at the spectacular scenery, the unfamiliar trees and shrubs, a world away from the filth and grime and frenzy of New York City. At least, he told himself, if he didn't have the price of a bed for the night, the weather was fine enough for him to sleep rough on the beach.

He made for the first bar he saw, and drank down an ice-cold beer; then he got talking to some guys who put him

470

wise about the cheapest rooming houses in town and where was the best place to find a job. This was Hollywood, and Hollywood meant movies and studios. They told him that he'd have no hassle at all finding himself work as a cleaner, a stage-hand or a scene shifter at any one of them. The next morning, Danny had done just that. By the end of his first week he'd been taken on as a scene shifter at Universal Pictures, and found himself a nice little boarding house with three meals a day.

But he never forgot that he was here for one reason and one reason only. To pay back that scum cop Delucca for what he'd done to his sister, for breaking his mother's heart.

Gene had only discovered his copy of F. Scott Fitzgerald's *The Beautiful and the Damned* was missing when Susie had asked if she could borrow it. He'd gone through all his trunks, looked under the bed, even in places where he knew it couldn't possibly be.

'I had it when I was staying with Garrard Flair. I guess I must have left it at his place.'

'Gene, it's no big deal. You can ask him to bring it with him when he comes to the studio.'

'He'll be at home this afternoon; I'll call by and pick it up. Save him the trouble.'

'OK.' They'd kissed, and he'd reluctantly let her go again. 'See you later.'

A strange automobile was parked in the bungalow complex in Alvarado Street when Gene arrived just after four o'clock. Maybe Flair had bought another one to replace the stolen V-8, or hired it, though it looked – with its white body and leopardskin upholstery – more as if it belonged to a woman. Gene was right. When he rang the bell and Flair came to the door, behind him in the drawing room was the familiar face and figure of Alice Terry, one of Hollywood's most famous and beautiful leading ladies.

'Look, I'm real sorry.' He was horribly embarrassed; though how Susie would laugh when he told her later. 'I had absolutely no idea that you had company.' He backed away, hoping that he hadn't interrupted them at a crucial moment. 'I only called because I thought you'd be alone.' He explained about the book. But to his amazement, Flair insisted that he come inside.

'I won't hear of you rushing off like this . . . come in and have a drink. Alice wasn't intending to stop long.' He made the introductions, motioned Gene into the nearest chair. 'When she heard about my temporary loss of transport, she was gracious enough to offer to give me a ride home. But I wouldn't dream of detaining her.'

Gene sat down, a little awkwardly. Was it just his imagination, but was Flair, the dedicated ladies' man, actually giving the actress a subtle hint that he expected her to leave now that he had another, unexpected visitor? Gene felt more embarrassed than ever. He knew that Alice Terry had a house out on Pacific Palisades, and that she had obviously gone out of her way to drive Flair home. He also knew that they weren't working on a picture together: she was being directed by Rex Ingram in a lavish costume drama; Flair was marking time at Universal until the arrival of von Ehrlich. Clearly, she'd made the offer in order to be alone with him when they reached the bungalow complex on Alvarado Street – or was he reading too much into this?

'Really, I don't want to intrude . . . I just thought, since I was passing this way, if you were home I could pick up the book . . .'

'I'll go and look for it. You must have left it in the spare room. But drinks first.'

'You're Curt Koenig's son, aren't you?' Alice Terry gave Gene a regal smile mixed with curiosity: it was a strange sensation, having other people look at you that way because you were the only son of a legend. 'What an actor he was!'

'Yes.' Up close like this, she was not quite as flawlessly beautiful as she always looked on screen, but then someone who worked in the moving picture industry would never have expected her to be. It was truly astonishing what the right clothes and the skill of the make-up department could accomplish. 'If he'd still been here when your last picture showed, I know he would have admired the way you played Princess Flavia in *The Prisoner of Zenda*.' Pride came into his voice. 'The title role was one of his most spectacular Broadway successes . . . second only to *The Count of Monte Cristo*.'

'You've never wanted to follow in his footsteps?'

'That wouldn't be possible even if I wanted to. But I don't.' A glance in Flair's direction. 'Directing is what really fascinates me; I've always wanted to do it. Unfortunately, my mother had other ideas, which is why we fell out about it.'

'This young man shows distinct promise . . . and that isn't idle flattery.' Casually, but none the less purposefully, Flair had picked up Alice Terry's wrap. 'Which is why I'm so glad you called by on the off-chance today. I have a proposition for you.'

'Well, if you two are going to talk shop all afternoon, I'd best be leaving.' Was that a trace of chill in the actress's voice, or just Gene imagining things again? By picking up her wrap Flair had made it obvious that he preferred her to leave – though he would never have been so ungentlemanly as to ask her to outright – and, knowing what he did about the average actress's temperament, Gene correctly deduced that Alice Terry wasn't the kind of woman to settle for only half a man's attention. Flair helped her on with her wrap and then kissed her coolly on the cheek. She smiled, but a little tightly.

'Promise me you'll have lunch with me tomorrow?' The invitation was delivered with masterful timing; her expression thawed a little. 'I won't take no for an answer.'

'Call for me at the studio. I'll be in my dressing room.' Gene waited inside while Flair escorted her to her automobile and waited until she had driven along Alvarado Street and out of sight. He came back and sank down onto the couch with another drink in his hand and a sigh of relief.

'A beautiful woman. But, like all actresses, very demanding.' Strange words, coming from a dedicated ladies' man? 'Unfortunately, in common with most women, they only want to talk about themselves.' Something didn't seem quite right here. Flair sounded almost cynical.

'I doubt if most men would prefer my company to Alice Terry's.'

'I'm not most men.' For a moment their eyes held, and Gene found himself staring at Flair. What, exactly, did he mean by that ambiguous remark? Suddenly, he felt uncomfortable, not a little confused. This was a different Garrard Flair from the man he'd lived and worked with, someone he'd thought of, in the absence of a father, as a substitute, a man who was older, wiser, richer in knowledge and experience. He glanced at the ostentatious array of signed women's photographs on Flair's desk, and then reminded himself of how swiftly the director had got rid of Alice Terry when Gene had unexpectedly arrived. The pictures were displayed like trophies, almost ostentatiously, as if Flair wanted to draw attention to the fact that his name had been linked romantically with not only every one of them but virtually every leading lady in Hollywood, whether he had directed them personally or not. Yet in all the time that Gene had been a guest at the bungalow, Flair had never spoken about them, not even professionally . . . was it only now that Gene had suddenly realized how strange that really was?

Flair had instantly realized his mistake; the words had tumbled out, almost without his thinking. The boy was suspicious now, and that spelled danger. He liked Koenig's son, he was genuinely interested in helping him in the advancement of a directing career; natural talent always deserved to be encouraged and fostered. He was in a perfect position to help him and he intended to do it. Yes, he had to admit it – he was physically attracted to the young man. But he would never, in any circumstances, let him know that. Though he'd tried to come to terms with what he was, those dark urges that sometimes threatened to spiral out of control were still a deep source of shame and self-disgust; by maintaining a normal friendship with another man he could, at least, keep some small semblance of self-respect.

He hastened to repair any damage his ill-chosen words had done.

'Forgive me . . . Alice is a delightful creature . . . if a trifle self-centred. What beautiful woman – least of all a beautiful actress – isn't guilty of a little vanity now and then?' Making light of it, he poured more drinks. 'You're probably thinking that I was a little hasty in encouraging her to leave . . . but I did have my reasons. I wanted to tell you this before the news got out and I knew she'd never be able to keep it to herself.'

'What is it?'

Flair smiled. Yes, the boy's suspicions – if he'd even entertained any – were allayed now. He almost breathed a sigh of relief. 'The von Ehrlich picture. I heard earlier today. I've been given a free hand picking my assistant. Yes, that's right, Gene. I decided to choose you.'

CHAPTER THIRTY-TWO

Garrard Flair was due at the Universal studios sharp at ten. Fritz von Ehrlich was not a man that other people kept waiting. He checked his appearance in the mirror – crisp white shirt, old school tie; checked jacket, *de rigueur* fawn jodhpur pants – the standard working uniform for a Hollywood director. Smartness and neatness were indubitable signs of professionalism and, from all he'd heard over the past few weeks about the European producer with the awesome reputation for absolute perfectionism, first impressions were vital. But he was furious – and not a little alarmed – a moment later when, as he was almost ready to leave for his twenty-minute journey, the familiar black Buick pulled to a halt outside his bungalow and Roy Delucca stepped out.

News – and rumour – travelled fast in Hollywood, whether it was true, good, or bad; he had no doubt at all that Delucca had read that he was directing the von Ehrlich picture, and, more to the point, the salary he was reputed to have been offered to do it. His expression was like stone as he opened the bungalow door.

'I'm sorry, Delucca. Bad judgement. I just don't have time for this.' Flair had always been slow to anger, but the sight of a grinning Delucca on his doorstep, the knowledge that a crooked LA cop held his future, his reputation, and his peace of mind in the palm of his hand, was almost too much. 'I have to be at the studio in twenty minutes and I don't have a single second to spare. Whatever it is, it'll have to keep.'

'Mustn't keep the new boss waitin', huh?'

'Not if I don't want to be fired on the first day.'

Delucca smiled. 'This von Ehrlich guy puts me in mind

476

of my old precinct chief, back in New York City. Chief Rawlins. Hell, I sure did hate his guts.'

'I know the feeling.'

Delucca showed no sign of moving out of his way. 'Well, since you're so pressed for time, I reckon what brought me out here will have to wait. Course, I could always find you on set, if it was real urgent . . .' Flair looked at him sharply; it was a veiled threat. 'Still, maybe you'd prefer to just listen to what I have to say right now, unless you're free this evenin'.'

'Not this evening, either. I'm having dinner with Hal Goldenthal and his wife.'

'Now, that's real nice. Real nice. You won't be interested, then, that the Chicago police have turned up your missin' automobile. A little worse for wear, I'm afraid.'

'They've found it? In Chicago?'

'Just outside Chicago, to be exact. A write-off. And no trace of Sands.'

Flair sighed. 'I see. I don't suppose you'll ever find him. And I'll never see the other property he stole from me again.'

'Looks that way. But then, I don't figure it'd be to your advantage if we found him. Whether he still had the stuff or not.' Flair frowned. 'See, er . . . what I never did tell you was that a coupla weeks before Sands skipped state in your V-8, he got himself arrested.' He grinned, as Flair's face turned white. 'In Arcadia Park . . . you know the place?'

'Vaguely.' He was feeling very nervous now.

'Well, a patrolman picked him up for soliciting . . . you still with me? Reckoned he'd spotted Sands in the park before. A lot of times. When I got round to questioning him, he told me a very interestin' story, Flair. That he was actin' on behalf of someone else.'

'What are you implying?'

'I think we both know the score here . . . and that it's time for you and me to stop playin' games.' Flair stepped back into the bungalow, let Delucca come inside. His legs felt a little weak; arriving at the studio on time suddenly paled into insignificance. He had to sit down. 'You know that enticin' male minors for immoral purposes carries a real stiff penalty in this state? You have any idea how long you'd go to prison for? And how bad that oh-so-respectable name of yours would stink if this got out? Yeah, I reckon you do.'

'Sands was a liar. And a thief. Nobody can dispute that. He betrayed my trust!'

Very slowly, Delucca took out a cigarette and lit it.

'I don't think you're in much of a position to take the high moral ground on this one, do you, Flair?'

'And you? A bent cop on the take?' His voice was bitter. He was angry now. 'I wonder what your captain would say if he knew that for the last year you've been blackmailing me?'

'I've always looked out for myself. Watched my own back. And, sure, I've taken what's on offer. Bootleg liquor. Dough. Women. Why not? When you play everythin' in life exactly by the rules, it all gets a little dull. But there's one thing I ain't never done; one thing that makes me want to spew when I look at someone who does. Some guy posin' as a pillar of the community, when he spends his free time fuckin' young boys. Now, that's somethin' I don't reckon on at all, Flair. And I don't reckon Hal Goldenthal or that new boss of yours would reckon on it either.'

'So what are you saying? You want more money from me to keep your mouth shut?'

'I guess I am.'

'No way. I'm not paying a cent more than I'm paying you now. I mean that. You've bled me dry. Do you know how much my savings account at the bank has dwindled to? From almost a hundred thousand dollars, it's less than ten.'

'Now you better listen to me, cream puff! If you want to go on workin' in this town – if you don't want to spend the next ten years in jail – you'd just better get smart!'

'You know, for a cop, you're not very intelligent, are you? All I have to do is deny Sands' allegations . . . he's not even here to testify about what he says I had him do for me. Even if you found him – and I doubt that – I'd deny anything he accused me of. Think about it. Would the

478

charge stand up in a court of law? A liar and a thief against a man of my reputation? Would any court take Sands' word against mine?'

'You're pretty damn sure of yourself, ain't you? They might just think twice about it when I subpoenaed the wife you ran out on seven years ago and heard what she had to say! I wonder what that'd be, Flair, when she realized the real reason you hightailed it and left her on her own to bring up your two kids was because you couldn't fight the urge to fuck other men instead of her?'

'You bastard!'

'I guess I just pulled out the ace in the pack, didn't I? You'll pay. You're too fuckin' fond of your own hide to do anythin' else.'

Flair found he was shaking with emotion. 'I loved my wife! How could I expect filth like you to understand that? That's the reason I left . . . disappeared . . . because I loved her. I couldn't stand the thought of hurting her any more than she was hurt already. It would have killed her, if she'd found out.'

'Then I guess you'd just better make sure she never does.' Delucca grinned; he'd found Flair's weakness. Something he cared about even more than his reputation. 'We wouldn't want her and those kids of yours to ever find out what you really are.' He went towards the door. 'I won't keep you any longer, Flair. Not when you're in such a hurry to meet your new boss. But don't you forget . . . you and me have got another meetin' real soon. Make sure it's all in used twenty-dollar bills.'

Flair went straight to his drinks table and poured himself a double bourbon. He was instantly sorry; Goldenthal and – even worse – von Ehrlich would smell the liquor on his breath, and all the trouble he'd gone to to create a good impression would be wasted. He checked his watch: he was already running almost fifteen minutes late. He grabbed his keys and rushed out to his new roadster. However fast he drove he would never reach the studio by ten now. How would it look to von Ehrlich when his director turned up on set late and stinking of liquor?

One thing he knew for sure. He couldn't go on this way, living on an emotional precipice, living a life of guilt, a life of lies. When the filming was done and over with and von Ehrlich had finished with him, he knew exactly what it was that he would, that he must, do.

Marianna had dressed Alice stunningly for her first meeting with the enigmatic Fritz von Ehrlich, glad now that she'd persistently ignored her ceaseless whining to have her long, lustrous, golden hair fashionably shingled. Though Hal Goldenthal hadn't delivered copies of the shooting script – there would be another two or three weeks of rewriting before it was ready – the character that Alice would play was a girl who became an opera singer in Vienna, and the part required her to have long hair.

'I could have worn a wig! Nobody would have known!'

'It wouldn't be the same! Nothing photographs like real hair, you should know that by now! Hold still!' Ignoring the screams of pain that had reached to the furthest corners of the house while she'd brushed, combed and then coiled it into a sleek, elegant French pleat held in place by ebony and diamond combs, Marianna had pushed her younger daughter onto her dressing-table stool while she'd painstakingly applied her make-up in front of the mirror.

'I can do it myself, Momma! I can fix it the way I want to look.'

'Keep your mouth shut or I'll smudge the lipstick!'

'Maybe I need just a little more kohl for my eyelids . . .'

'Stand still!'

The sky-blue voile tunic, over a silk and taffeta under-skirt embroidered with tiny clusters of blue beads and seed pearls, set off Alice's china-doll complexion to perfection. Marianna smiled as she surveyed the result of the last hour's work, satisfied at last. She called to Elynor to fetch her sister's hat.

'Momma, I think the blue silk turban we saw in the French milliner's in LA was much better than this two-tone cloche . . . it's too tight around the front and it makes my head ache after I've worn it awhile. I wish there was time to drive into LA and change it.'

'Be quiet and put it on. No, not like that! Like this! Don't you ever pay attention to anything I say?'

Two doors along, Elynor had been left to her own devices; her appearance was only of secondary importance. Eschewing the bright, popular pastel shades that her sister loved, she'd chosen a light charcoal georgette two-piece with a matching straight-cut jacket and wide-brimmed hat, her long dark hair parted in the middle like a ballerina and coiled at the nape of her neck. It was another half-hour before Alice was ready and came downstairs, and she was even more petulant than usual.

'Momma's going to try to get Fritz von Ehrlich to fire Garrard and bring in another director,' she whispered harshly, glancing over her shoulder towards the stairs. 'But I'm the star of this picture . . . I should have the final say about who I want to direct. Momma's real sore because she wanted to have a meeting with him as soon as he arrived from England. But Hal Goldenthal told her that he couldn't be reached and he wasn't seeing anyone until this morning.'

'I bet that pleased Momma.' Their mother was a woman who always demanded that she get her own way in everything, and she usually did; but Elynor was beginning to suspect that von Ehrlich was going to be a force to be reckoned with.

'She was as mad as hell!' They both fell silent as they heard her coming down the stairs.

Marianna snatched up her purse, ready to do battle at the studio. Flair would direct over her dead body. And this von Ehrlich and Hal Goldenthal had better realize that she meant what she said. No D. W. Griffith, no Alice. They were her terms and she refused to yield an inch.

'Well, what are you both standing there gawping at me for? Go and get into the automobile.'

They came face to face, suddenly, as they entered the Universal studio lobby together, and he came from one of the opposite doors. Marianna stared at him, almost affronted, not quite able to believe her eyes.

'What the hell are you doing here? I thought you were working at Paramount?'

Gene smiled. 'Hi, Momma. Yes, I was there; but not now. It was only temporary, just to pay the rent. I'm here for the same reason as you are . . . the von Ehrlich film.' She was furious, just as he'd expected her to be. 'You see, when Garrard got chosen as director for it, he was told he could pick his own assistant. Since we'd worked together at Paramount and he was impressed with what I'd done, he picked me.'

'We'll see about that. Since I'm on my way now to make sure von Ehrlich fires him, he won't be in a position to choose you as his assistant, or anyone else. I'm afraid you're going to be out of a job!'

Elynor could tell by her brother's face – a kind of mischievous look in his eyes she knew well – that their mother was in for a surprise. Just then, a stage-hand burst through the door.

'Hey, Gene . . . I just seen von Ehrlich arriving . . . he's gone into Hal Goldenthal's office! Say, this guy is weird, I mean, *weird*! Listen. Some of us boys were out front when this big black limousine draws up, and he gets out of it! Hell, he was six six, six eight, maybe taller . . . shoulders this wide . . . !' He held his hands apart to demonstrate. 'Long black coat, black hat, gloves . . . just like some goddam undertaker, no kiddin'! I never seen his face . . . he's got hair this long,' he touched his shoulders, 'dark red, all fallin' over his eyes. He sure was creepy! Sure as hell wouldn't like to meet *that* guy in the dark!'

'Momma, that isn't true, is it?' Alice looked startled. 'He isn't really like that, is he?'

'Of course not! I've never heard such utter nonsense!' She pushed her daughter in the back and propelled her in the direction of Hal Goldenthal's office. Elynor turned to Gene.

'You put him up to that, didn't you?'

He grinned. 'You'll find out soon enough.'

'Gene, I've missed you so much!'

'I've missed you.'

'But you've got Susie. Lots of friends. You can come and go as you please. You drive. You've got a job, your own money. I don't have any of those things.'

'Ellie, when this picture's finished and I've got more money than I need, let me help you.' She looked up hopefully. 'I've been thinking about you, ever since I left. You'll suffocate, staying with Alice and Momma. You have to break free.' He paused, as they wandered through the busy set together. 'Why don't you go to Grandpa and Grandma Koenig in Minneapolis?'

'Gene, I don't know . . .'

'Please, Ellie . . . listen to me. We've got to talk now because with the way Momma treats you and Alice there mightn't be another chance like this . . . think about it. You have to make your mind up. Momma wants to control everything, everyone around her, like she was directing a play, and you deserve more than that. A life of your own. Ellie, you've got to make the break!'

'It isn't that simple, Gene. Not when you're just a woman.' She wanted so much to believe him, to convince herself that it might be possible. 'I can't do anything . . . I'm not clever like you.'

'That's rubbish and you know it! You're smart, you're bright, you're pretty. And you learn fast. You could do almost anything you want to do. All you need to do is take that first step . . . what do you say?'

'Only a brother would say all those things to me!'

'Not true. Hey, you remember that Christmas in New York when Uncle Shawn bought Alice a musical box that played tunes from the *Merry Widow*, and you did a song and dance in front of all Momma and Dad's guests?' Elynor smiled. 'You said you couldn't do it, that you were too shy, that you were scared you might sing the wrong note and make yourself look a fool . . . but you did it, and you were great. You got to tell yourself that whatever it is, you *can* do it. It's all mind over matter.'

'Gene, things were a little different then! I was only eight years old!'

'Nothing's changed . . . you're still the same underneath. Listen. If everybody thought that they couldn't do things and didn't even give them a try, where would we all be? If Hal Goldenthal hadn't decided to walk to America from Lithuania, if all the independents hadn't had the get up and go to up sticks and move out west, if Mary Pickford hadn't had the neck to ask First National for a million bucks a year . . . where would they all be now? That's the way you got to start thinking! Think ahead, think big, think positive. Hey, come here . . .' He pulled her by the arm. 'We've got some time yet before Momma's finished doing battle with Hal Goldenthal and von Ehrlich . . . take a look in here.'

'What's this little room used for? And what are all those lights?'

'This is the testing room. Screen testing room . . . want to have a try? Hey, come on, it'll be a gas!'

Elynor peered into the ten by ten space uncertainly.

'It's more like an execution shed!'

'That's what everybody says. But testing for the movies is different from auditioning on stage. You mustn't have any outside distractions, and directors are looking for different things. Remember, you don't have the advantage of being able to express yourself just by speech . . . because, as yet, they haven't invented sound. Miming a scene is very important . . . but you must never go over the top. Look, I'll show you.' He led her inside and closed the door. 'This is Momma, pleading with Fritz von Ehrlich to fire Garrard Flair! Just watch.' Gene hung his head, threw his arms wide apart and went down on one knee, then rubbed his eyes dramatically to parody a woman crying. Within a few seconds, Elynor was hysterical with laughter.

'Gene, you're wicked!'

'I'll just bet Momma's on the warpath right now, threatening everyone in sight. Do you know, I think Hal Goldenthal's always been a little afraid of her?'

'But didn't he tell Momma that this isn't his picture?'

'He did, and he's right. If it was, do you think Garrard Flair would be director and I'd even be within a mile of a Universal set? But this time, I think Momma's bitten off a little more than she can chew.'

Elynor still wasn't sure. 'Have you ever known Momma not to get her own way in the end?'

'No, but there's always a first time. Come on, do you want to try a screen testing or not?'

'I don't want Alice or Momma to see me, because they'll only make fun.'

'You might surprise both of them.'

Elynor stood a little uncertainly in the claustrophobic little square, while Gene gave instructions. Didn't she remember one of the scenes from their father's film of *Monte Cristo*, when Mercedes was brought the news that her lover had disappeared, the night before their wedding? That was the one that he wanted her to do. In the space of two minutes, she had to portray despair, anguish, misery, desolation, then reluctant acceptance that the man she loved more than anyone in the world would never come back again. That was the easy part. When she remembered the night their father had driven away into the darkness in the Pierce-Arrow, and had never come back again, it was no longer difficult, no longer even necessary to pretend. When Gene called 'Cut', the tears she was wiping from her face were real ones. She had only enough time to come out of the testing room and put on her hat again before the doors leading from Hal Goldenthal's office burst open and their mother stormed out in a fury, pushing Alice in front of her.

'Gene, I'd better go. It doesn't look as if Momma's had much success in getting rid of Garrard Flair or you ... I've never seen her so angry!' When she looked at him he was grinning. 'You knew, didn't you? That von Ehrlich would turn her down?' He began to laugh, very softly. 'You've met him?'

'You could say that.'

'But what they were saying about him ... he isn't really like that, is he? Gene?'

485

He nodded in the direction of the door their mother had just come out of. 'Why don't you look for yourself?'

A man, followed by Hal Goldenthal and half a dozen production assistants, suddenly appeared from the corridor, and walked across the set. He was tall – the tallest man Elynor had ever seen in her life – and exactly as the stage-hand had described him. His long, unkempt red hair flowed down to his shoulders, fell across his eyes, and even from this distance Elynor could see the pale auburn shadow around his lower face of two or three days' growth of beard. He was dressed from head to foot in black, and towered over everyone around him. As he walked past the assembled crew to the opposite door, the entire studio fell silent.

'That is Fritz von Ehrlich?'

'That is Fritz von Ehrlich.'

It took Elynor more than a few minutes to recover from her astonishment. 'I think you're right, Gene. About Momma. This time, I really do think she's met her match.'

'That man is insufferable!'

'Momma, I don't like him . . . he's real creepy!'

'Be quiet and let me think, will you?'

'You've got to agree to what he says, Momma!' Alice was near hysterical all the way back home at the thought of her mother refusing to sign contracts unless Garrard Flair and Gene were fired. 'If you don't sign, they'll call your bluff and then I won't be in the picture at all! Alice Terry'll get it instead! It isn't fair!'

'I told you to be quiet! And who said I was bluffing?' The argument continued when they reached the house at Whitley Heights. 'Use your brain for once . . . if you've got one! Do I always have to do all your thinking for you? Who does von Ehrlich need most . . . Garrard Flair or Alice Ayres? There are a dozen other first class directors in Hollywood he could sign up for the picture . . . but no stand-in for you!' She looked triumphant, almost smug. 'He just wants to see how far he can push me. Well, I'll show him whose nerve is going to break first. And it isn't going to be mine.' Marianna had poured herself a large bourbon on the rocks to calm herself. Though she would never admit it, even to herself, the half-hour she'd spent with von Ehrlich in Hal Goldenthal's office had been the most uncomfortable of her life. Eccentric, intimidating didn't even begin to describe him. 'If I give in to him now, I'll never be able to have a say in anything else, once they start shooting. Costume approval, script changes . . . he'll expect to control everything!'

'He is the producer, Momma,' Elynor said. Alice swung round on her in a fury. 'I don't like him! He didn't even smile at me, not once . . . and he never even shook hands when Hal Goldenthal introduced us. He was sitting in this great big chair behind the desk when me and Momma went into the room, and he just stared at us through all that long, untidy hair . . . he gave me the shivers!' She put her arms around herself as if she couldn't bear to think about it. 'He's got real scary, staring eyes, and they kind of bore into you so you have to look away. You didn't see him close up, Ellie. If you had, you'd have seen for yourself.'

'He's a freak, that's what he is!' Marianna was beside herself. She lit a cigarette and paced up and down. 'I'm not losing this goddam contract, not a contract worth over a million dollars!' With the proceeds, she could get Walter Oppenheim to pay off the Revenue and settle with Delucca in one fell swoop. But standing down on Flair as director – not to mention her wayward son – went hard against the grain. But what other choice was there?

'Momma, please ring the studio and tell them you'll agree to their terms. You have to!'

'I've got a better idea.' She was smiling now. 'I couldn't say what I wanted with you and Hal Goldenthal standing there. I'm going to ring von Ehrlich and go see him out at that place of his in the hills.' She pointed her finger at Alice threateningly. 'Don't you dare step out of this house while I'm away.'

Garrard Flair had been relaxing in his sitting room with a drink and a copy of the film script when the telephone rang. Expecting Hal Goldenthal or even von Ehrlich, he had been surprised to hear Alice's voice on the other end of the line. She was clearly in a highly emotional state, after von Ehrlich's uncompromising attitude, almost on the point of crying. 'Alice?' He couldn't believe that her mother knew she was ringing him, of all people. Marianna Koenig must have gone out. 'Are you all right?'

'Garrard, you've got to talk to von Ehrlich . . . make him understand that Momma doesn't mean what she said today! Promise me!'

'Alice, will you calm down? Is she there in the house with you now?'

'No, she went out. That's the point. She's gone to see him!' She started crying again. 'I'm scared that she'll just get mad . . . you know the way she does . . . and spoil everything for me! He isn't like Hal Goldenthal . . . he isn't like anyone! I tried to tell Momma that she won't be able to get her own way this time, but she won't listen! She knows how important it is to me to have you direct this picture, that it means more to me than anything else. But I just had an idea.'

'An idea?'

'If you could work it that Gene didn't get to be your assistant on the picture, it might calm her down . . . then she'd feel that she hadn't lost face with von Ehrlich.' Flair was appalled. He'd known that Alice was petulant, difficult, selfish, but not how much; she was happy to sacrifice her own brother's advancement in order to score points with her mother. 'Garrard, are you still there?'

'I'm sorry, Alice. I won't do that. Gene stays.' He heard her sharp intake of breath at the other end of the line. She couldn't believe that he was actually refusing her. 'It would be completely unethical. Besides doing him a gross injustice. He has a great deal of talent . . . and a very promising future . . . something that should be fostered, not cut off in full flight.'

'But he can get another job with another studio! You could fix it for him, you've worked for every major studio in Hollywood.' When he didn't answer straight away she thought she'd succeeded in winning him over. If only she could be there in person, how much easier it would be! Alice had never met a man in her life – except that peculiar von Ehrlich, of course; but he didn't count – who had failed to be enchanted by her wide-eyed little girl charm. 'Garrard, *please* . . . for me . . . this means so much to me.'

'I'm sorry, Alice. There aren't many things I wouldn't do for you . . . but getting Gene fired is one of them. Working on a picture with this much prestige attached to it is just as important to him as it is to you.'

'Now you're mad at me.'

'No. No, I'm not mad at you. I don't think you realized what you were asking me to do, that's all. I'll see you tomorrow.'

'How could you even have thought of asking him to get Gene taken off the picture!' Elynor was appalled at what she'd overheard. 'Of all the mean, self-centred things you've ever done, that was the worst! You should be ashamed of yourself, Alice!'

Alice turned on her. 'Just who do you think you are, listening to my private telephone conversations? This is nothing to do with you. Anyhow, whatever happens, Momma will fix it. She'll talk von Ehrlich round, I know it. She always makes other people do whatever she wants. And I can, too.'

Elynor didn't even want to stay in the same room with her after what she'd tried to do to Gene. 'I think this time you're both going to be very disappointed.'

The rough-made road looped its way like a river, twisting and winding, undulating, thread-like, through the hills, presenting an awesome, breathtaking panorama from the summit above. Marianna slowed down, turned on the headlights; up ahead, she could see the tall, gold and black iron railings of von Ehrlich's gates.

The huge mock Tudor mansion lay sprawling across the circular courtyard with its flowerbeds and central fountain; in the oncoming dusk, lights from the mullioned windows beamed across the billiard-smooth lawns and, in the stillness, she heard the exquisite notes of a Liszt piano concerto, masterfully played. Stepping out of her automobile, she was so struck by the beauty of the playing that for a moment she was unable to move.

An elderly Englishwoman came in answer to her ringing at the door. She gazed beyond her, to the flagstone floor, the rich oak furniture and the golden glow of the lights that gently illuminated the entrance hall.

'Is Mr von Ehrlich at home?' The exquisite piano playing could be heard more clearly now. She wanted to stand and listen to it. 'My name is Marianna Koenig . . . we met this morning.'

'Please come inside, Mrs Koenig.' The woman stood back, opened the huge arch-shaped door wider. 'I'll enquire if Mr von Ehrlich can see you.' The music continued while Marianna stood there, waiting; surely, it was a Victrola and not von Ehrlich himself at the keys? Only a pianist of concert standard could possibly play so exquisitely. But when the woman returned and led Marianna into an enormous and sumptuously furnished room with paintings, china, mirrors and coloured glass lights, Fritz von Ehrlich, still dressed from head to toe in sombre black, sat at the keyboard of a classic Bechstein grand. He stopped playing immediately she appeared, and looked at her, but did not get up.

'Good evening, Mr von Ehrlich. I'm sorry if I'm in any way disturbing you.' His face – what she could see of it behind the curtain of unkempt red hair – remained expressionless. The cold eyes made her feel distinctly uncomfortable. 'I think we need to talk.'

'We talked this morning. I made my position about the production perfectly clear. Nothing has changed.' He stood up now, and she saw that he was so tall that his head was only fractionally lower than the ceiling. 'We have nothing further to talk about.'

'You're not an easy person to conduct business with, Mr von Ehrlich.'

'I could say the same about you.'

'I came here this evening so that I could talk to you in confidence. And tell you something that I found very difficult to talk about this morning in front of my daughter.'

'Which is?'

'The reason I want you to take Garrard Flair off this picture. You've only just arrived here in Hollywood . . . so you won't be aware of his unsavoury reputation with women.' Was that a ghost of a smile on von Ehrlich's lips? She couldn't be sure. 'My daughter is totally besotted with him! She's a young, impressionable girl . . . and easily led by someone like Flair, who's so worldly, and more than twenty years older than she is. This is a small town, and I don't want to throw them together any more than is absolutely necessary . . . and that's difficult enough as it is. Having him direct her in this picture, working closely together every single day for weeks on end . . . I want to avoid that at all costs!'

'I would have thought that the danger of his seducing her on set would be almost non-existent.' Was he laughing at her? She was unable to detect even a spark of humour behind those unnerving eyes. His face was still expressionless. 'Besides, the impression I formed this morning was that your daughter prefers Flair to direct her, rather than anyone else. Experience shows that when a rapport exists between an actress and a director, both give their very best. That can only be beneficial to the entire production.'

'That's exactly the point I'm making, don't you see that? I urge you to reconsider.'

'Then I regret to say that you've had a wasted journey, Mrs Koenig. The decisions I've made about the production stand. Garrard Flair directs. If you don't wish your daughter to screen test for the part of Marguerite, you can give me your answer by tomorrow. I shall quite understand.' Marianna frowned.

'Screen test for the part? Nobody said anything about Alice having to take a screen test this morning!'

'If you recall, you left my office before I could go into detail about anything.'

'My understanding from Hal Goldenthal when this

491

project first came up was that Alice was to be given the leading part!'

'Not quite. The arrangement between myself and Universal is for exclusive use of their studio, technical equipment, crew, and any players I might require. *Might* require. He did suggest your daughter for the lead role, yes. But after meeting her this morning, I'm not at all sure she's right for the part.'

Marianna was aghast. 'You can't mean that? Alice Ayres is one of the biggest box office attractions in Hollywood!'

'That isn't at the top of my list of essential criteria. I don't think you're familiar with my productions, Mrs Koenig . . . otherwise, you would know already that I judge films by artistic merit, not by the short-term popularity of cheap, mass-market rubbish that's forgotten within six months of production.'

'But my daughter is Universal's top star!'

'I'm not disputing that fact. What I'm telling you is that I have serious doubts about her suitability for this particular production.'

'When you've tested her for the part in the morning, I know you'll change your mind.' She realized that she'd already lost her battle over Flair; but that hardly seemed to matter now. This was a situation she didn't like at all. With the Revenue Service and Delucca breathing down her neck, she could see the prospect of a million dollars fast slipping away from her. 'When can you let me have a copy of the shooting script?'

'I think you're putting the cart before the horse, Mrs Koenig. There would be no point in giving you the script before I've watched her test.'

There seemed nothing left for her to say to him. His housekeeper came to show her to the door. She turned back as she was leaving the room. She glanced at the piano. 'As I arrived just now, I heard you playing . . . at first, I thought it must be a Victrola . . . you play beautifully.'

'Thank you.' He inclined his head.

'Liszt . . . I always loved Liszt. Brahms. Chopin. But Liszt was my favourite composer. We always had a grand

492

piano in the house, when I was a girl.' She smiled, with just a trace of sadness. Seeing the Bechstein, hearing the music, had reminded her; so long ago it all seemed now. 'I loved to play, but my father said that it disturbed him. So I was never allowed to use it when he was at home.'

'You no longer have one?'

'Yes, but I never play now.' Von Ehrlich was watching her intently. 'I haven't played for years.' She looked at him, for the first time glimpsing something of the real man behind the enigmatic façade. 'You're very gifted. I didn't realize that you were a man of so many talents.'

'You flatter me.'

'No. Flattery is merely a sop we bestow out of politeness on the ungifted. To compliment you on what is simply a fact, is just speaking the truth. Goodnight, Mr von Ehrlich.'

She arrived back at the Whitley Heights house in an unusually subdued mood. She went into the drawing room, sat at the grand piano that Curt had bought her so long ago, looking down at the keys. The melody that von Ehrlich had been playing went round and round in her head; tentatively, her fingertips touched the keys.

'Mrs Koenig?' She looked up at the sound of Colleen's voice. 'There's someone coming up the drive . . . do you wish me to let him in? It's very late.'

'Do you recognize him?'

'A gentleman in a black Buick, ma'am.' Colleen paused. 'Miss Alice is in the bath right now . . . but she said that she wanted to see you the moment you came back.'

'I don't want either of my daughters to come in here while I'm talking . . . do you understand?'

'Yes, ma'am.'

'I thought I told you never to come here unless we'd already arranged a time?' she said to Delucca after he'd been shown into the room and they were alone. 'I don't want anyone in the house to start getting suspicious.'

'A little edgy tonight, aren't you, Mrs Koenig? This is just a friendly social call.'

'Forgive me if I don't invite you to stay and have a drink with me.'

Delucca grinned. 'I understand how you feel, Mrs Koenig. I mean, I know the life that drop-dead handsome husband of yours led you was no picnic . . . all those bit-part players and actresses on the side . . . me, I never did figure out why he did it. I mean, with a beautiful wife at home, why go out to play?'

'Did you call here to tell me something specific, or is there some other reason for this unexpected pleasure?'

'One million dollars' worth of contract, that's what's brought me here. The von Ehrlich movie contract you said you were signing today.'

'If that's why you've come, then I'm afraid I'll have to disappoint you. I've just got back from seeing von Ehrlich a few moments ago.'

'And?'

'My daughter isn't a hundred per cent certain to be signed for the picture. He won't make a final decision until she's screen tested tomorrow.'

Delucca's smiled vanished. 'Is it just my imagination, or do you kinda not seem as upset about that as I figure you oughta be?'

'Take it any way you choose, lieutenant. Whichever, if he casts another actress, there's absolutely nothing I can do about it.'

'You said your daughter was gettin' the part for sure! That's what it said in all the papers!'

'It's what Fritz von Ehrlich says that counts.' She got to her feet. 'My daughters know that I went to see him tonight. They'll be down here in a moment. I think it would be better if you left now.' God, how she detested him! He shot her a warning glance before he went.

'Don't ever try to double-cross me, lady. Because if I have to, I'll use those photographs. You might have the copies . . . I've got the original film.'

'If you ruin my daughter's career and blacken her

father's name, your little additional source of monthly income dries up with it. I think you're forgetting that.'

'I haven't forgotten.' Delucca shook his head. 'But I think William Randolph Hearst and his newspaper would just love to get their hands on that film . . . moral crusades and diggin' dirt on famous names are his stock-in-trade.'

Elynor watched the man leave the house from her bedroom window; she was trying to place him, wondering who he might be. He looked like an official, perhaps someone from studio security. Neither she nor Alice had ever asked questions about anyone their mother invited to the house. But as Colleen had let him out of the front door and he'd spoken to her, Elynor had heard his voice and remembered where she'd heard it before. That evening on the telephone. Her mother had seemed anxious, almost agitated, when she'd told her about the call. Elynor wondered why that should be.

When she went downstairs, Alice was already there in her dressing gown, on the verge of another tantrum after what their mother had told her.

'He said what? That I have to be screen tested? Only nobodies have to have screen tests . . . who the hell does he think he is?' She was working herself up into a frenzy of rage. 'I'm Universal's biggest star, doesn't he know that? Doesn't he know about anything that's happening in Hollywood?'

'He's the producer and what he says goes. You'll just have to accept that.' Elynor came into the room and Alice turned on her.

'Who asked you anyhow? Why don't you go back upstairs and go to bed?'

'If you feel so strongly that you're being slighted, why don't you tell him tomorrow at the studio, instead of taking out your frustrations on me? It isn't my fault.'

'He can't treat me this way, Momma! Hal Goldenthal said I was going to star in this picture . . . he promised, he did, you know he did!'

'Go to bed, both of you.' Marianna turned away, walked

495

out onto the terrace. The cool night air fanned her face, soothed her mind. She was tired, but she knew that even if she went to bed she wouldn't sleep. There was so much at stake, so much to lose. Everything she'd worked for, schemed for, suffered for. Unthinkable, to let anyone snatch it from her now.

CHAPTER THIRTY-THREE

Gene Koenig had come to the studio almost two hours before most of the crew due on set had begun to arrive. He wanted to run the little piece of film that he'd taken of Elynor the day before, and then surprise her with it when she came later in the morning with their mother and Alice. Susie had come early with him to the studio, too.

'I was told a week ago by the Head of Department that von Ehrlich is a fanatic for absolute punctuality. I don't want to make an enemy of him as well as your mother.'

He snatched a kiss. 'Momma doesn't hate you. What she hates is not getting her own way . . . a trait my sister Alice has inherited in full measure.' He was concentrating on setting up the projector in the darkroom. 'You know, I only found out last night that it isn't a hundred per cent sure that she'll be cast for this part . . . Hal Goldenthal got his wires crossed over it. I saw the correspondence. When he offered Universal's full star roster along with the studio for von Ehrlich to shoot the film in, von Ehrlich wired him that he accepted. But what he didn't add was the rider that he might not need every player on the Universal payroll.'

'It's a three hour screen epic about an opera diva, Gene . . . can you really see your sister Alice being comfortable in a role like that? For one thing, you'd need to have incredible staying power . . . even with Garrard Flair directing her, do you think she'd have the patience to portray the character with all the intense detail that hallmarks von Ehrlich films? He'll be on set, watching every second of shooting, remember. Even most of the men find him very intimidating.'

'He sure is a strange kind of guy!'

'From all the rumours going around this place since he got here, your mother's first meeting with him didn't go down too well at all. Looks as if even she found him a little too awesome to handle.'

'The trouble with Momma is that she takes it for granted that everybody's a pushover . . . this time, I guess she came unstuck big time. Hey, look at this!'

'That's Elynor?'

'Sure is. Well, what a surprise!' Gene could scarcely believe what he was seeing in front of him. 'All this time, everyone was telling Ellie that she wasn't photogenic, would never look good up on screen. But just take a look at her now . . . the way she uses her eyes, her hands . . . she's a natural! Just like my father. . .'

'Gene, if she comes to the studio today you've got to show her this!' They both spun round suddenly, startled, as the door to the projection room clicked shut and a long, tall shadow fell across the screen. Gene stood up.

'Mr von Ehrlich!' Susie got to her feet too, and stood a little way behind him. She hid her surprise; he was so tall he had to duck when he came through the door. 'We didn't realize you'd got to the studio so early, sir.' He turned off the projector. 'I'm not due on set for another half-hour or so, until Garrard Flair gets here. Is there something that you'd like me to do?'

'Who was that girl on film?'

'Oh, my sister . . . Elynor. She came along with Momma and my sister Alice yesterday. While they were talking to you and Mr Goldenthal in your office, we just did a little fooling around.'

'Rewind the film. Turn the projector back on again.'

Gene and Susie looked at each other. 'OK. But there's nothing else on here.'

'I don't want to see anything else.' As Gene re-ran the short test over again, von Ehrlich's pale, penetrating eyes were transfixed on the screen. 'Why haven't I seen her before? Why wasn't I told about this? This girl is magic.'

'Elynor isn't an actress, sir. She's never acted in her life.'

Von Ehrlich spoke to Gene without taking his eyes from the projection screen for an instant. 'As soon as Flair and

Goldenthal come into the building, I want them both in here.'

'But, you can't be serious? She isn't even an actress!' Goldenthal was shocked, barely able to take in what von Ehrlich was telling him. Had he completely lost all sense of reason? 'Elynor Koenig's never acted in her entire life! However well she comes across in a two-minute test strip, you can't pluck someone like that out of total obscurity and star her in a major picture like this!'

'Are you offering me the benefit of your advice, or are you telling me what I can and can't do?' The pale eyes stared out at him from beneath the curtain of dark red hair, and Goldenthal broke out into a nervous sweat beneath his hundred-dollar suit. 'You seem to have forgotten one very important fact, Goldenthal. I have sole production control over this picture, and everyone who works on it or in it. If any actress is worth a million dollars, then you're looking at her.'

'But she isn't up to a task like this! She has no experience, no acting background, she won't have the first idea . . . I thought you intended to sign up a major Universal star for this? You can't get any more major than Alice Ayres, believe me!'

'Alice Ayres is a pretty little china doll whose entire range of acting movements consist of looking right, looking left and looking straight ahead. She couldn't even lift up a knife and fork the right way without a director telling her how to do it. The one reason why you've been able to turn someone without a shred of real talent into a star is because you cashed in on the vogue for golden-haired, blue-eyed dolls who look sweet, vacant and nothing else – and on her father's name.'

'I can't believe you just said that!'

'If you can't believe it, then there's something wrong with your hearing as well as your eyes.' Goldenthal looked up into von Ehrlich's face and knew that he'd lost. 'I want Elynor Koenig for this film, otherwise I withdraw every cent of financial backing, and the deal's off.'

Elynor had no idea what was happening until Gene rushed to meet her at the studio door.

'Your face is flushed! What's the matter?'

'Ellie . . . I don't want you to ask any questions, not now. I just want you to come with me.'

'Where to? I have to wait here for Alice and Momma. They're in Hal Goldenthal's office, and they'll wonder where I am.'

'I don't think so. He'll tell them.'

'He'll tell them what?' People working on the set were staring at her, and she didn't understand why. 'Where are you taking me?'

'To meet someone who wants to meet you.' At the end of the corridor she recognized the door of the projection room where Gene had taken her yesterday. Today, she could see several other people inside. She stared at the unbelievable sight of herself up on screen as Gene led her into the room. Then, the towering figure in black that she recognized from the day before as Fritz von Ehrlich bore down on her from the group of men, and she felt her face grow hot. The pale eyes staring at her through the curtain of untidy, dark red hair, seemed to see straight through into the window of her mind. Did he really know what she was thinking?

'How do you do, Mr von Ehrlich?' Her voice was a whisper. She held out her hand. When he took it, she trembled. She couldn't stop looking at him; would he think she was unutterably ill mannered to stare like this? But she couldn't help it. Close to, his skin was covered in tiny, pale red freckles; his chest, visible through the open neck of his black linen shirt, was thick with coarse red hair, but there was something about him that Elynor found strangely, almost compellingly attractive. Beside a man like von Ehrlich, sleek, bland, matinee-idol types like Wallace Walbrook, whom most women found devastatingly handsome, seemed pale and insipid. 'I'm not quite sure that I understand why my brother has brought me here.'

Von Ehrlich pointed to the projection screen. He lifted a

huge, freckled hand and removed the tortoiseshell clasp that held back her hair, and it fell down around her shoulders like a glistening cape. Her mother's hair. All the other men turned to look at her.

'This is the girl I want to play Marguerite. No-one else will do.' He looked down at her from his enormous height with a ghost of a smile on his lips, amused at her astonishment. No-one had ever seen him smile before. 'Will you do it?'

Danny Mazzoli had been helping to lift a particularly cumbersome piece of scenery on the Universal backlot when a door about a hundred yards away suddenly opened and a man came out, smoking a stub of cigarette. For a moment he couldn't believe his own eyes, couldn't move at all. Roy Delucca, right there in front of him! If the other stage-hand who was holding up the opposite end of the chunk of scenery hadn't shouted at him to look what the hell he was doing, Danny would have dropped it in surprise.

'Hey, Mazzoli, what the fuck you think you're doin'? You tryin' to amputate my goddam foot or somethin'?'

He stood there, watching, still in disbelief, as Delucca tossed down the cigarette stub on the floor and ground it with his heel. When he'd first reached Los Angeles and got himself a room and then a job, he'd made it his business to find out exactly where the cop station was downtown; there was only one for the whole LA district, so that part was easy. That was where Delucca would be; but he worked staggered hours. Danny knew that, logically, Delucca must sometimes work alone, but finding out when that was, and when he was with a partner, was something else. All he could do was bide his time, play a patient waiting game. He knew all about being patient. But when he'd caught sight of the bastard just now it had taken all his patience and all his self-control not to drop the piece of scenery he was holding, and run after him. A taste had risen in his mouth like bile. Holding on to the reins of his spiralling anger, he just stood there, staring after him.

'Hey, Mazzoli! You still work here, or what? We gotta get all this stuff shifted before we knock off!'

'Yeah, yeah . . . I heard you.' Slowly, reluctantly, he turned away, grasped his end of the piece of scenery more tightly. 'I just thought I saw a guy I used to know, that's all. But it was someone else.'

Garrard Flair had had a terrible day. When the news about Elynor Koenig broke, Alice had gone into violent hysterics, and had been bundled into her mother's automobile and driven home to Whitley Heights. A doctor had had to be called to give her a sedative, so enraged was she over what had happened. The instant her mother had left to collect Elynor from the studio, Alice had got out of bed and was on the telephone to him.

'Garrard? You've got to do something! Elynor's stolen my part in this picture!' She was sobbing, almost incoherent from the effects of the medication and pure rage. 'Von Ehrlich doesn't know what he's doing! Hal Goldenthal told Momma months ago that that part was mine!' He tried to calm her down, say anything to attempt to pacify her, but she was completely out of control. 'I won't let her. I won't just stand by and let her take everything from me that I've worked for, everything I deserve to have!'

'Alice, please . . . you're upset.'

'I have to come over and talk to you.' She started crying again. 'I must see you, tonight. No, it won't wait. I've already called a cab. Nobody will know I've been to see you . . . when Momma comes back and sees my bedroom door shut, she'll just think I've gone to sleep. I need to be with you, Garrard . . . you're the only one on my side, the only one who really understands!' He'd put down the receiver after agreeing with the greatest reluctance, full of misgivings. But there was nothing he could do.

It was almost dark when Delucca drove slowly along Alvarado Street and stopped the black Buick within a few yards of Flair's bungalow. The drapes hadn't been drawn yet, and the moon was quite bright; he could make out two figures in front of the window. Looked like Flair had himself a late night visitor. Delucca flicked the engine switch and took out his cigarette case. Might as well enjoy a smoke if he had to wait awhile. He'd been seated behind the Buick's steering wheel for almost twenty minutes when, finally, the bungalow door opened and Flair, with a slim, blonde young woman, came out. Alice Ayres.

They stood at the end of the path for a few moments in earnest conversation; then Flair kissed her and she threw her arms melodramatically round his neck before walking off very fast in the direction of Sunset Boulevard. Delucca stayed where he was until he saw her, in the distance, flagging down a cab.

He hung around cautiously for another moment or two; then, checking that nobody was watching, he got out of the Buick and went quickly up the path to Flair's front door. A Victrola was playing a popular tune, 'Indian Love Call', somewhere in the distance. One of Maudie's favourites.

'Well, well,' he said mockingly, when Flair opened the door to him and he walked inside unasked. 'Quite the ladies' man, aren't we?' He sniggered. 'I wonder what little Miss Goldilocks would say if she and that bitch of a mother of hers knew the real deal about you?'

'You really are the lowest form of life, aren't you?'

Delucca's expression instantly changed. 'You carry on like that, Fersen – Fersen, I think I like that name better – and the price might have to go up. Think about it.'

'I have.' This was a different Garrard Flair from the usual, ultra-polite-even-under-extreme-provocation Flair that Delucca was accustomed to; there was something harder, more positive about him now. 'I've decided. I'm not giving you another cent.'

'I'm not sure I heard that right.'

'Then I'd better say it again. I'm not paying you any more. Not a solitary dime . . . I've made my mind up. When we've finished shooting this picture, I intend to go back to New York and settle things with my wife. She may hate me and despise me and I may never see my sons again . . . that's just a chance I'll have to take. It'll be her decision. I'll make a lump sum payment to her, then go back to direct in England. I worked there before, I can look up old contacts. And even if I don't get paid a quarter of what I can earn here, the peace of mind will be worth the sacrifice.' Delucca just looked at him, as if he was trying to decide whether he was bluffing or not. All his instincts, all his experience with men told him that Flair meant what he said. 'But before I leave, I shall make a visit to the District Attorney ... I think you can guess what I intend to say to him. I don't expect to see any of the money I've lost again ... that would be too much to hope, wouldn't it? But if I can stop you putting just one person through the hell you've put me through, it'll be worth it.'

He hadn't noticed that Delucca's hand had slipped unobtrusively inside his jacket. 'Now, I don't think it'd be very wise of you to go and do a fool thing like that ... do you? It just wouldn't be good for your health.' As Flair half turned to take a cigarette from his silver cigarette box on the side table, Delucca pulled out his handgun and shot him at point blank range in the back.

He took a handkerchief from his inside pocket, wiped the door handle clean, then walked out of the bungalow towards the parked Buick without glancing back.

CHAPTER THIRTY-FOUR

'You little fool!' A savage slap across the face from her mother's hand sent Alice reeling halfway across the room. She staggered up, eyes wild, hysterical and defiant at once. 'Do you have any idea what you've done?'

'It's all her fault!' Alice glared at her sister with hatred. 'She stole my part in von Ehrlich's film! Everybody said that it was mine and then she came along and took it away from me! If it hadn't been for her I would never have gone to see Garrard last night!' Spittle ran down her chin; she looked as if she was possessed. 'I needed him, I had to talk to him . . . he's the only one who understands! You never cared about me! Only Daddy cared about me . . . he was the only one who really loved me for myself!'

'Be quiet at once and take control of yourself! Have you seen what you look like? If the police arrive and see you like that, they really will begin to believe that you had something to do with Flair's murder!' Marianna had been beside herself since the shocking news had broken that day; last night, she'd caught Alice coming back from Flair's Alvarado Street bungalow only minutes after she and Elynor had arrived home from the studio, and there had been a furious argument. Now, everything seemed to be falling around her in chaos, and she was gripped with a terrible sense of foreboding and fear; a neighbour of Flair's had seen Alice arrive at the bungalow just after eight, when Flair had opened the door to her . . . the last time anyone else had seen him alive. Though Alice swore that she'd left before nine o' clock, nobody had seen her. When Flair had failed to turn up on set the next morning, von Ehrlich had sent someone from the studio to Alvarado Street, and his body, with a bullet hole in the back, had been discovered lying on the sitting-room floor. Within the hour, the whole town was alive with rumour and counter-rumour.

'I can't talk to the police when they come.' Alice had started sobbing again. 'I can't talk to anyone. I'm too upset, can't you see that? I loved Garrard. He loved me. He would have stopped her stealing my part in von Ehrlich's film . . . what reason would I have to kill him?' She stopped talking abruptly as they heard the sound of an approaching automobile. 'Momma, tell them to go away and leave me alone, I can't see anyone today . . . I can't see anyone at all!'

Marianna's frayed nerves were taut and raw. She grasped her younger daughter by the wrist and shook her roughly. 'You listen to me, do you hear? You've got to talk to them. You've got to tell them exactly what happened, just as you remember it.' As Alice tried to break free from her iron grasp, she shook her again and grabbed a handful of her golden hair. 'I swear if you don't pull yourself together and do what I say right now, I'll fetch a pair of scissors and hack every last bit of this off!'

'No! I won't let you touch my hair!'

'Then do as I tell you!' Marianna looked up as the door bell rang. 'Elynor, go let them in.'

Elynor sat quietly in a corner while they questioned Alice; she was watching and listening to one of the detectives in particular, very carefully. Though he'd introduced himself to her mother as if they'd never met, she was almost certain that she recognized him; surely he was the man who had come to the house once before? His voice, too, seemed familiar: the mysterious voice on the telephone that night asking for her mother. Could she possibly be mistaken?

'Mrs Koenig . . . if you want your lawyer present while we question your daughter, go right ahead and call him. We'll wait.' Alice was almost in a state of collapse.

'Momma, get Walter Oppenheim, please!'

'That won't be necessary, lieutenant.' Marianna ignored Alice's pleading completely. 'My daughter will be happy to answer any questions you want to put to her. I assure you, she has absolutely nothing to hide.'

506

In between frequent breakdowns and sobbing, it took Alice almost an hour to blurt out her story. 'I telephoned him first, to tell him I was coming straight over. I had to do it while Momma and my sister were away.' She wiped her nose on the back of her hand. 'I knew Momma wouldn't let me go and see him. She didn't understand.'

'He was alone when you got to the bungalow, Miss Koenig?'

'Yes.'

'And he didn't mention while you were with him that he might be expecting anyone else?'

'No. We just talked about what had happened that day. He said he'd see me tomorrow, and then he walked with me to the end of his path. Somebody must have seen us together!' She was becoming hysterical again. 'He kissed me goodbye and I said I was going to get a cab on Sunset Boulevard. If you find the driver, he'll tell you it was true!'

'We already have, Miss Koenig. He confirms you flagged him down at nine or ten. Unfortunately, that doesn't really prove a thing. The autopsy confirms that Flair was killed sometime between eight and nine.'

'My daughter doesn't have access to a gun of any kind, lieutenant. Even if she did, I doubt if she'd understand how to fire it.'

Delucca kept his face impassive as he played out the charade. 'In my experience, Mrs Koenig, mothers don't necessarily know everything there is to know about their daughters. I'm sorry, ma'am. But I have to ask these questions.' He turned back to Alice. 'Were you and Garrard Flair having an affair, Miss Koenig?'

'No!'

'Were you in love with him?'

Alice gave a small, covert sideways glance towards her mother. 'Yes. And he loved me. I'd never do anything to hurt him, I swear it! He was the only person besides my father who ever really cared about me!' A tear ran down her cheek. 'He was the only one who understood how humiliated I was yesterday, when Fritz von Ehrlich gave my part in his film to my sister!'

For a moment there was no sound in the room at all except the noise of Alice crying.

'Do you know if Flair was seeing any particular woman? I understand he had a reputation as quite a ladies' man?' Delucca wanted to smile at that. If only they knew. 'Was his name linked with any particular actress at the studio?'

Alice shook her head. 'Lieutenant.' Marianna went and stood behind her in a gesture of solidarity. 'If this is leading in the direction that I think it is, I will call my lawyer. But I can tell you this. Since he arrived in Hollywood, Garrard Flair's name has been linked with every leading actress he ever worked with. Except my daughter. Last night aside, I would never permit her to be alone with him. Just for the record . . . I wholeheartedly disliked the man.'

'I know why you hated him!' As soon as the detectives had gone, Alice suddenly came to life. 'You were jealous, because he loved me! You were afraid that when I was old enough, I'd leave you and marry him! Then I'd have all the money from my movie contracts to myself! That's all you ever cared about, wasn't it, Momma? The money. You can't stand not to have everything your own way . . . that's why you were always fighting with Daddy. I'll just bet he got to hate you as much as I do because all you ever think about, all you've ever cared about is yourself!'

'You've got no right to talk to Momma that way!'

Marianna suddenly felt very calm. Somehow, she'd always known that the moment would come when she would tell them the truth about their father. The truth that was necessary. Without another word, she went and fetched the photographs.

'Her name was Klara Kopek. She was your father's mistress in New York City.' They both stared, unable to believe their eyes. 'These pictures were taken at an orgy on Long Island. He didn't even know, not till afterwards. A few days later, someone found her dead . . . in the house he was paying the rent for.

'Right up till the time he died, he was being blackmailed because of these . . . easy to see why. If the truth had come

508

out, not only would his whole career have been ruined – he could have faced a charge for first degree murder. He wasn't guilty . . . but that didn't really matter. The scandal would have clung to his name for the rest of his life. He was still paying more than half of everything he earned for these when he died. Maybe that's why he did it. Drove his Pierce-Arrow over the top of the ridge. Maybe it was guilt because of you, because of me. But when I was left all alone with the three of you to take care of, I couldn't take the easy way out.' Her eyes were hard. No time for weakness now. 'I've made more sacrifices, done more things to keep a roof over your heads, than any of you will ever know!' Her voice rose in anger. 'So don't you ever, *ever* tell me that all I've ever thought about is myself.' She turned to Alice. 'As for von Ehrlich's picture . . . you could never have played that part anyway. The minute the news broke that you'd visited Flair on the night he died, your career was dead.'

'I don't think I can do it, Momma. I just can't. I'll have to telephone the studio and tell them I can't make it on set today.'

'You can do it. And you will.' Her mother's voice was harsh, concealing her own deep-rooted pain. Elynor's career was the life-line, the one remaining thing that had to be preserved at all costs, no matter what. 'After Flair's murder, Alice doesn't have a career. I told you that, more than a month ago. Hollywood will forgive anything of its stars except getting found out.'

'But his death was nothing to do with Alice! He had other visitors that evening before she arrived.'

'But he was still alive after they'd left. She was the last one who saw him before he was killed.'

Elynor was trying to compose herself. Production on *Marguerite d'Augur* had been held back for a month because of Garrard Flair's death, but she was still in a highly emotional state after the shocking revelations about her father's secret life. Didn't her mother understand that it was impossible for her to go on as if nothing had happened? 'The inquest verdict was murder by person or

509

persons unknown. How can anyone possibly connect Alice with that? There was no evidence, not a single shred. No motive. There were even rumours around the studio that his chauffeur Sands had come back and killed him. Yes. Accusations had got as wild as that!'

'Whatever the truth is, it doesn't matter now. Flair's dead. What does matter is that you have to do this picture, whatever you feel like . . . we need the money, Elynor. I never told you this before, but you might as well hear it all first as last. There are large discrepancies in my revenue returns . . . discrepancies that they want to know about. They think I've been salting away large sums from Alice's contract earnings, not declaring them. I've been playing a cat and mouse game with them, ever since your father died. Taking from one account to patch the holes in another. That strategy won't work for ever.'

'Just what are you saying, Momma?'

'At the end of this shoot, Hal Goldenthal will offer you a contract with Universal. You'll take it.'

Shooting had almost finished for the morning. With a dozen others, Danny was waiting around for the director to call 'Cut!' and then he and the rest of the stage-hands would begin moving the scenery ready for the afternoon shoot.

Out of earshot, out of camera range, he watched the action in front of him with a mixture of admiration, curiosity, and wonder. What a beauty, what a lovely girl that Koenig kid was, with her big, expressive grey eyes and that mane of dark hair, and what a talent! All the guys on the set thought that this von Ehrlich was weird because of how he looked and the way he dressed, but he knew his business all right when he'd cast for this movie; even someone as ignorant about motion pictures as Danny was could tell that. The girl was a natural. And no matter how many times he asked her to go over a scene, or even a line of dialogue, she bore it all with the greatest patience, always gracious and polite to anyone who had anything to do with her, unlike that spoiled little brat of a sister who never came to the studio any more and who, Danny had heard on the Universal grapevine, stayed home all day having hysterics because she hadn't been given the leading part.

Danny leaned against a pillar, a rolled-up newspaper under his arm; he aimed to read through the headlines during his morning break. Garrard Flair's murder had been a terrible shock to the entire film community, and everyone was avidly following the case from the executives down to the humblest stage-hand. It was a mystery, that was for sure. Some of the guys Danny worked with reckoned the killer must have been a jealous lover, Flair's rival for one of the many actresses whose names had been linked with his; others said it was that runaway manservant of his who'd stolen his Cunningham V-8 and some valuable property, and must have had some grudge against him that no-one knew about; maybe nobody would ever know for sure. Hal Goldenthal had sent a typewritten announcement to everyone on the Universal lot about Flair's sudden death, saying that the Los Angeles police would be visiting the studio to take statements from anyone who had seen or spoken to the dead director that day, but so far Danny hadn't seen anyone he knew being questioned.

It was then, just at the end of the scene when von Ehrlich had called for a short break in shooting, that he suddenly caught sight of a group of strangers in long coats and hats, who he instinctively knew were nothing to do with the filming or the studio at all. Cops. That was when he saw Delucca.

He was mingling with the crowd, notebook and pencil in his hand, strutting around in that arrogant, smartass way he had – how many times had Danny watched him go up and down those precinct steps back in New York City? Delucca had a face, a walk, an attitude that you just didn't forget. A terrible burning rage suddenly erupted inside Danny, and he realized he was trembling. The thought of what Delucca had done to his Sophia, his sweet, gentle, innocent Sophia, of the degradation and shame his cruelty and his brutality had brought her to, all at once came flooding back and completely overwhelmed him. He forgot everything else except why he was here, what he'd followed him to do. That he'd sworn to be patient, careful, cunning, that he'd do what he had to do and never risk getting caught until he'd done it. All he could see in front of him was the man responsible for his sister's battered, bloated body and his mamma and pappa sobbing their hearts out beside the pathetic little pauper's grave. The family hadn't even been able to afford a decent headstone. Nothing left of her, not even her name.

Delucca was now standing directly beneath one of the heavy scenery hoists, two thick ropes that held a massive piece of painted wood by either side. Danny didn't hesitate. Fate might never again hand him a chance like this one. He darted towards the nearest ladder and scrambled up it to the top, then pulled out the knife he carried in his back pocket and had never been without since he was fourteen years old; you never knew when you'd need to defend yourself down the filthy, dangerous alleys in the Lower East Side.

His fingers shook. His heart raced. But as the blade sliced through the thick coils of rope that held the scenery in place and it hurtled downwards towards the ground, Delucca suddenly stepped aside. To his horror, too late to do anything but watch helplessly, Danny saw Elynor Koenig standing in the very spot where Delucca had stood a second ago. But only moments before it crashed down and splintered into pieces before her eyes, von Ehrlich had seen it coming and rushed forward to pull her to safety.

'You're sure you're all right now?' He handed her the glass of brandy. He laid his huge hand on her shoulder, and she instantly felt calm. This was the extraordinary effect von Ehrlich had on her, something she found it impossible to explain, even to herself. All she knew was that when he was there she felt safe, in the best possible hands. Only her father had made her feel that way; but von Ehrlich must be about thirty-three, thirty-four; nobody knew. Hardly a father figure. But was this the way her sister Alice had once felt about Garrard Flair?

'I'm fine, really. It was just the shock.' She'd taken the glass from him and realized that she was still trembling. 'If you hadn't pulled me out of the way just in the nick of time, you wouldn't have had a leading lady.' She suddenly realized what she'd said, and was astonished to find that she felt a stab of bitter disappointment; that was why, of course, he'd reacted so quickly. Without a leading lady the production would have been held up – maybe indefinitely – while another actress was cast, and Elynor knew just how astronomically costly that would be. Von Ehrlich was no fool.

'If you don't feel up to it, we can break shooting for the rest of the day. It's up to you if you want to continue.'

She smiled, masking her real feelings. It had pleased her so much to think of him rushing across the set to rescue her from injury, or something worse, but her practical mind had given him a less romantic motive, and it spoiled everything. She was just being foolish. 'It's better if I go straight back on set.' She put down the glass. She was unused to drinking spirits, and the brandy had made her feel slightly giddy. 'Everyone else is waiting, and I'm holding the production up. I know that can be extremely expensive.'

It was von Ehrlich's turn to smile. 'That isn't my prime consideration.'

'It always is for other producers . . . especially Hal Goldenthal.'

'I'm not "other producers". And Hal Goldenthal has nothing at all to do with the production side of this picture.'

He was looking at her through that curtain of untidy, dark red hair and she found the way his eyes seemed to bore into her thoroughly disconcerting. She felt her cheeks start to grow hot.

'As I said, I'm sure I'll be all right now.' She got up, still a little unsteady after the shock of what had happened. The top of her head barely reached to von Ehrlich's shoulder. 'I wonder just how that piece of scenery came loose and fell?'

That question was already foremost in von Ehrlich's mind, and he meant to get to the bottom of it. The instant shooting had finished for the day he intended to question studio security.

'Whatever, whoever caused it to fall . . . I shall find out.'

'Someone deliberately hacked through both safety ropes, Mr von Ehrlich.' Chief of studio security was holding out both pieces of the severed rope in his hands. No doubt about it . . . whoever did this meant to do someone a permanent injury . . . you can see that for yourself. That goddam thing weighed a ton; falling straight down, from the height it did, it would have flattened anyone standing directly underneath it.' The man looked grave. 'Question is . . . why would anyone want to do a thing like that? You reckon somebody is trying to sabotage the production?'

'If they'd wanted to do that, they would have done something equally drastic long before now. No, I don't think so.' This was something personal. Though he was furious at the very thought of the danger Elynor Koenig had been in for that crucial instant, common sense told him that she had not been the target; to have sawn through both ropes would have taken several minutes, even with the sharpest of blades. Elynor had only changed her position and moved into the line of danger in the final few seconds. The question was, who had been standing on that same spot before her?

'There were a handful of stage-hands standing around . . . and one of the detectives from LA, taking statements from various people about Garrard Flair. Yes, I remember now. I was talking to him just before he walked along the back of the set on his way out. He said he was Lieutenant Roy Delucca.'

Delucca. Von Ehrlich's astute, logical mind worked cog on cog. Delucca had come to the studio to ask questions about Flair's death and someone had deliberately attempted to flatten him with a lethal piece of scenery; whoever he was, he must have been a studio employee and equally he must have been afraid that Delucca's investigations were getting a little too close to the truth.

But something still wasn't right here; an important piece

514

of the jigsaw was still missing. The only studio employees who had been standing close enough to tamper with the ropes above the spot where Delucca had stood had been humble scene-shifters. If von Ehrlich's theory was the right one, why should any one of them have hated Garrard Flair enough to kill him in cold blood? It was a mystery.

Von Ehrlich frowned.

'I want from Personnel the name of everyone who was standing in that vicinity when the scenery fell. Have them on my desk in half an hour.'

Danny had almost panicked and run away after his second attempt to get Delucca had failed; but somehow he'd managed to keep his head. Luck, at least in one thing, had been with him. He'd been able to scramble back down the ladder and mingle with the crowd without anyone noticing. Why should they? With everyone's eyes on the action happening on set, no-one had thought to glance up to where Danny was hiding in the beams, giving him time to get away. But he was badly shaken. If the scenery had fallen on Elynor Koenig he would never have forgiven himself; what he'd done had been stupid and desperate, and he swore never to make the same mistake again. He should have stuck to his original plan – getting hold of a gun, and lying in wait – that was the way to do it.

CHAPTER THIRTY-FIVE

With Flair dead, von Ehrlich took over direction on the picture himself, and Elynor astonished everyone with her masterly portrayal of the doomed opera diva, releasing flights of brilliance from a source deep within herself that neither she, nor anyone else, had even suspected existed. It was her father's amazing dramatic talent, born all over again. From extreme nervousness and shyness in front of the camera, under von Ehrlich's sensitive, expert tutelage, she gradually emerged like a butterfly from a chrysalis: at the end of each working day when, with von Ehrlich, Gene, and Hal Goldenthal, she viewed the day's footage in the projection room, she could hardly believe that the image on screen portraying every facet of emotion with such spell-binding realism could be her. Few people on set – except Gene, who knew her so well, and the astute von Ehrlich – would have guessed that, beneath the deceptive exterior of professionalism, the strain of having to force herself into a frame of mind conducive to work each day, after the terrible upheavals at home and the revelations about her father, was beginning to take its toll on her. In one scene, there had been no need for Elynor to simulate bursting into tears; remembering those ugly, shocking, humiliating pictures of her father, it had been easy to do it.

Mid-morning, during a break in shooting, Gene sought her out.

'Is the stress of living at home and having to cope with Alice getting a little too much for you?' He held her hand. 'Ellie, you know you can always tell me.' Knowing how much he'd idolized Curt, how much he'd looked up to him, Elynor knew that she never could. Gene would be shattered. Pointless, purposeless to destroy his illusions about their father now. 'I know just how taxing a picture like this is, believe me. A three-hour epic is no picnic. Alice could never have stayed the course . . . even if she'd had the talent. We both know that.'

'I'm all right. Just a little tired, that's all.' She made herself smile. 'She scarcely even talks to me now . . . when I come home, she locks herself in her room.'

'It isn't your fault.'

'She said that I came along and stole her picture. If you look at it from her point of view, I suppose I did.'

'That's nonsense and you know it!' For the first time, he sounded impatient. 'When Momma first took her to Hal Goldenthal, they sold her on Dad's fame . . . on the blond-haired, blue-eyed little cutie pie that was all the rage. Every studio in New York and Hollywood had a resident Mary Pickford lookalike . . . and Pickford's the only one left. Fashions change, Ellie. Why, in ten years von Ehrlich says we'll have talking pictures – maybe even sooner than that – and half the stars in Hollywood now won't even exist. Can you imagine an audience swooning over John Gilbert's high falsetto, or Clara Bow's Brooklyn twang? But when the time comes, you'll do it with flying colours.' He could still feel the tension in her. 'There's something else, isn't there? Something you're not telling me?'

'It doesn't matter.'

'I'm not leaving here until you do.'

She looked at him. Part of the truth, part of the reason for her unhappiness, it was possible to tell him. Perhaps sharing it would make her feel better. 'Momma says that after this picture is finished, Hal Goldenthal will want to sign me up for Universal.' She hesitated. 'I don't want to do it, Gene. I'd hate it. Those pointless, plotless things that Alice used to do. Absurd love stories, impossible coincidences. I think of acting in those kinds of pictures and it makes me go all cold inside. Momma would say that it's just the rewards that matter, that nothing else counts. I can hear her now: art doesn't pay the bills. But I can't help thinking that if Daddy had never quit the stage, everything would have been different. Going into moving pictures . . . it kind of cheapened him somehow.' She came within a hair's breadth of revealing the truth, but she drew back, afraid to go on. 'When I look back . . . all the bad things that happened to us happened after we moved out here.'

'You got discovered by Fritz von Ehrlich.' He was smiling at her.

'Yes.'

'After the first shock of meeting him . . . I guess there are very few people who don't find him intimidating . . . you start to see what lies beneath the surface, and your perception changes.' Out on set, the crew were beginning to reassemble. 'I've learned so much from just watching him . . . you know? The way he does things, the way he draws every ounce from other people. When I watch him directing you, it's like . . . how can I describe it? Something very special is happening, right in front of my eyes, and I don't even know what to call it.'

'He's asked me to have dinner with him this evening . . . at his house out in the hills. There's a scene he says might be difficult tomorrow, that we need to work through. I was thinking exactly the same thing myself, except that I didn't have the courage to suggest it.'

'You're not afraid of him, are you?'

'It's strange. . .when we're on set, and he's directing me, I feel . . . just as easy as I do now, sitting here with you. But off set . . . it's just . . . different, somehow. I don't know how to describe it.'

'You should be honoured, being invited to his place. No-one else ever has been. He lives there alone, except for his chauffeur and housekeeper. Do you know he brought them with him all the way from England? He's a very private person.'

'That's why I feel a little uneasy about going there tonight. As if I was intruding.'

Gene winked at her, to lighten the moment. 'Tell me if he bites.'

The huge house lay in the depth of the hillside, like a jewel in the palm of a hand. She had never seen it close to, and the sheer size of it astonished her. So much for one man.

Inside, it was as beautiful as she had imagined any home of a man like von Ehrlich would be.

Elynor concealed her nervousness by walking slowly round the massive drawing room and studying the pictures. 'It's so still, so peaceful here . . . as if we weren't in Hollywood at all. Is this like your house in England?'

'Very similar, yes.' He was pouring two glasses of red wine. 'Why don't you sit down? You look uncomfortable. Are you?'

Elynor blushed. 'I'm sorry . . . I didn't mean to stare at you.' It was somehow so different between them, off set, away from the cameras and the lights. 'It's just that . . . I think that you're a very remarkable person.'

Von Ehrlich sat down at the grand piano. Without speaking, he began to play, and the beauty of the melody and the exquisiteness of his playing echoed around the room, seemed to fill every corner of it, and inside her head. She got up and walked over to him. 'I wish I could play like that . . . I had no idea that you were so gifted.'

A ghost of a smile behind the pale eyes. 'That's exactly what your mother said to me.'

'My mother?'

'The evening she came here – when I first arrived in Hollywood – and demanded that I dismiss Garrard Flair.' He was amused rather than angry.

'I'm sorry. I'm afraid my mother has always been used to getting her own way. Ever since my father died . . . when she had to take care of all of us. She's so used to making demands on Hal Goldenthal, and having him do exactly what she wants, that she sometimes forgets herself. I think she knows in her heart that this picture was never right for Alice.'

'Why did she never let you act before?'

'Alice was always the important one . . . the one with the golden hair and big blue eyes . . . I didn't really stand a chance. She always looked so angelic, so adorable. And those looks just happened to be the height of fashion in movies. People never bothered with me. Momma always told me that I didn't have the right look to be an actress,

519

that I just wasn't photogenic. Secretly, I was very envious when she got Alice into films. I wanted it so much to be me.' He had stopped playing. Unsuccessfully, Elynor had been trying to place the composer; was it Mozart, Chopin, Liszt? 'That's why I can never thank you enough for giving me the chance to prove to myself that I could do it.'

'Why thank anyone at all? You've simply inherited your father's charisma and talent.' He smiled, taking her a little by surprise because he smiled so rarely. On set, almost never. 'There's something troubling you, isn't there? I sense it. Would you like to tell me what it is?' She looked away, caught unawares; if only that were possible. 'Elynor. I'd hoped you and I were more than actress and director. More friends than simply two people who work together. Talk to me.' She let him draw her gently down beside him on the piano stool, where to her consternation and embarrassment, she burst into tears.

He didn't take her hand to comfort her, didn't draw her sympathetically against him as Gene would have done; she could hardly have expected that. But as he just sat there listening quietly to her, she found his presence more reassuring, more strengthening, than any overt display of emotion would have been. Without speaking a single word, he passed her his handkerchief.

'It . . . started with Garrard Flair's death . . . when the police came to speak to Alice.' She wiped her eyes. 'She was violent. Abusive. Hysterical. She always did have another side . . . like my father, I suppose.' She had to glance away. 'We never knew, any of us, about things that he did when we lived in New York . . . his private life.' She closed her eyes tightly, to shut out those hateful, ugly pictures. 'There was a girl he met – an extra – at the Vitagraph studios . . . Klara Kopek. Momma told us that Daddy had taken a house for her at Washington Heights . . . that he paid the rent. Then one day someone found her dead, and the police questioned Daddy. If it had come out about his affair with her, the scandal would have ruined his career. Not only that, he was a strong suspect for killing her, even though he'd been filming out of state at the time she was murdered.

520

'If the police had really thought he was guilty, they could have arrested him on strong circumstantial evidence . . . I guess he managed to convince them that he wasn't.' Elynor hesitated now; this was the hardest part. She knew how much von Ehrlich respected her father's reputation and it went against all her instincts to tell him anything that would change that. 'Just before this girl died, Daddy took her to a wild party on Long Island . . . and someone took photographs of them together . . . horrible photographs . . .'

'Are you telling me that he was being blackmailed because of them?'

She nodded. 'After he died, Momma discovered that a great deal of money in his private bank account had simply disappeared. Then the Revenue thought that it had been hidden away deliberately, to avoid death duties and taxes. She staved them off when Alice started starring in Hal Goldenthal pictures . . . but when the Flair murder story broke and it came out at the inquest that my sister was probably the last person to see him alive, Momma knew that that was enough to finish her screen career.

'Momma's never admitted it to any of us, but I think she's still paying someone for those pictures. She has the prints . . . but the blackmailer must have the original film. I was afraid to talk to her about it; Momma's never been an easy person to confide in. It was always so much easier to talk to Daddy . . .' Her voice fell to a whisper; there was a lump in her throat. What did von Ehrlich think of Curt Koenig now?

'And do you find it just as easy to talk to me?' For the first time he touched her hand, and a strong physical thrill ran through her, in spite of her emotional distress.

'Yes.'

'So tell me everything. Then I'll tell you exactly what we can do about it.'

She looked up, hopefully, gratefully. 'I think someone is still blackmailing Momma over the pictures . . . because even now the Revenue are still not satisfied with her accounts. There are just too many holes in them, and, despite outward appearances, she's always desperately short of ready cash. It doesn't add up. When this picture is finished and you leave, Momma is almost certain that Hal Goldenthal will want to put me under contract to Universal ... she's counting on the money for that. The trouble is, I don't want to act in Universal's pictures ... not after working on a real classic like this with you. You see, it's made me look at everything differently ... all this time, I've envied my sister for what I thought she had; but now I realize that it wasn't what I would have wanted. Her films are so cheap, so badly performed, so forgettable. Yours are like my father's stage performance of *Monte Cristo*. Unforgettable. I don't think that I could ever compromise, even for Momma's sake.'

She gazed up into his face; he had pushed his long, dark red hair back; he was looking down at her. Their bodies were lightly touching. She wanted him to take her into his arms so badly now that it almost hurt when he didn't.

'Is there anything else?' He was looking at her searchingly; could he read her mind? She felt suddenly acutely embarrassed at her secret feelings towards him; wasn't it a joke on set that the leading lady always fell in love with her director? It was as much a shock to her that she'd inherited not only her father's talent but his passionate nature as it was clear that von Ehrlich did not reciprocate her feelings.

She pulled herself together with some effort. 'There was one thing.' At the back of her mind was the detective in the black Buick; he was a safer subject than her infatuation with a man who – in a few weeks' time – would have left California, almost certainly for ever. 'I could have been mistaken ... voices can get distorted on the telephone ... and it was late, I was tired. But the detective who came to question Alice ... I just felt that I'd heard him, seen him, somewhere before. One night, when it was very late – Momma and Gene had gone to a studio party – there was a telephone call for her.' At the word 'detective' von Ehrlich had suddenly become noticeably more alert. 'It was a man's voice ... not a west coast accent ... and when I told him she wasn't home he just hung up before I could ask who it was. Momma seemed agitated when I told her later. Then, not long afterwards, she had a visitor at the house; a stranger I'd never seen before. I only caught sight of him as he was leaving; I only got a brief glimpse of him from behind. But he did drive a black Buick, I'm sure of it. Then, at the studio the other day – just before the scenery fell – I saw him again. It was the same lieutenant who came to interrogate my sister after Garrard Flair died. I couldn't swear to it, but his voice sounded strikingly similar to the voice that night on the telephone. A Brooklyn accent.'

Von Ehrlich stood up; was he beginning to see the faintest glimmer of a light? It was just too much of a co-incidence, surely? From the list of stage-hands' names Personnel had left on his desk, one had stood out from all the others. Every man except one was a native Californian – Danny Mazzoli was from New York City. So, it seemed – if Elynor was right – was Detective Roy Delucca. Suddenly, everything was beginning to fit.

'I have to make some telephone calls. I'll do it now.' Elynor, too, stood up. 'Come into my study with me . . . I want you to hear what I say.'

Danny had quit his room at the downtown boarding house and had slept rough for the last few nights; instinct had taken over after the first blind panic had subsided. If he risked turning up for work he might be asked awkward questions, and with Delucca sniffing around the studio about the Flair murder, things could get much too hot. No, it was safer this way.

He had the gun, all the ammunition he needed. It'd take only one well-aimed shot to finish that bastard off for good. Then nothing else mattered.

He hid it inside his jacket, spent his last few dollars on a three-course meal, then went into the nearest church to light a candle for his mamma and pappa and his sister Sophia.

CHAPTER THIRTY-SIX

It was one of the final scenes, and Elynor had never been so nervous; for the first time since shooting on the picture had started, she questioned her ability to give a convincing performance; she was terribly unsure of herself. Unlike any other scene in the film, she was playing it not to a co-star but to the camera alone – how could you simulate love, need, yearning, to a mere machine? She felt sick, anxious, her legs were shaking a little as she walked from her dressing room onto the set where everyone was already waiting. The big question was: was she actress enough to bring it off?

After more than a dozen retakes, when she was already working herself into a desperate state at her failure to do the scene, von Ehrlich stood up. Although his face betrayed nothing at all, she sensed that he wasn't angry with her; as he always was on set, he was cool, patient, silently encouraging. He went and stood behind the camera.

'Do it again. But this time, say the words to me.'

She took a few moments to compose herself, to push every other thought from her mind. Only the scene was relevant. She walked back into position on set, and turned to face him. What would she do after he had gone? He was never coming back – he had never made any secret of his preference for Europe – when the picture was finished in a few days' time they would never meet again. That thought brought tears into her eyes and a lump in her throat that had nothing to do with theatrical make-believe. The words and actions that poured out of her until the end of the scene might have been in the script; the emotion was real.

As von Ehrlich called 'Cut!' and the electric tension all over the set suddenly eased, Elynor stood there wiping her eyes while everyone down to the humblest extra and stage-hand broke into wild applause.

Delucca had been in his study at home enjoying a bootleg gin and reading the evening papers when the telephone rang. Smiling, he'd picked it up, expecting Maudie's voice: she was staying overnight at the private clinic where her mother was, and he'd told her to ring him that evening to let him know what time tomorrow she expected to be back. But when he put his ear to the receiver it wasn't his wife on the other end of the line; his smile faded.

'Roy? Trouble.' It was his buddy from the downtown police precinct in LA. He sat up. 'Got a whisper this afternoon that somethin' about you was goin' down in the DA's office . . . some kind of internal enquiry . . . somethin' to do with the Koenigs.' Delucca swallowed; under the expensive new suit, he broke out into a nervous sweat. This sounded heavy. 'I don't know no more than that, except that they're sendin' a couple of guys round to see you tonight, from the DA . . . a sealed report came in earlier from your old precinct office in New York. Just thought I'd put you wise, OK?'

Delucca slammed down the receiver, rushed to his wall safe and emptied it of everything he could carry, cursing his bad luck. He swore foully as his shaking fingers clawed at the handle of his desk drawer where he kept a handgun and ammunition. His sense of self-preservation came uppermost. No time to ring Maudie, no time to write a note of explanation for when she returned. That fucking bitch Marianna Koenig had sung to the DA and they were on their way now for him, baying for his blood. Well, when they got here they'd find he'd been long gone.

He had a full tank of gas in the Buick and, in a few hours at most, he would be safe over the state border into Mexico.

He'd been watching the house for more than a week now, ever since he'd left the studio and gone into hiding. He only moved at night. Mrs Delucca had just gone away. Perfect. He felt sorry for her; yeah, she deserved a little pity. But for that bastard he could see moving about inside the house now, Danny Mazzoli felt no shred of pity at all. An eye for an eye.

He didn't care if they caught him afterwards. He didn't care about himself. All he wanted was justice. When he'd done what he'd come here to do he'd try to make a run for it – maybe they'd get him, maybe not. He could hole up somewhere on the studio backlot till the early hours and then train-hop out of the state. No point paying rail fares twice. He was sweating a little, even in the warm, scented night air. But he felt calmer than he'd ever felt in his life. As Delucca came out of the house carrying a small travel bag and walked towards the black Buick parked in the driveway, Danny Mazzoli took out the handgun he'd gotten from a downtown store just a few days ago, and fired.

Elynor had been at Hal Goldenthal's house on Ocean Avenue with her mother having dinner when he'd been called away suddenly to answer a telephone call. While he was gone, Marianna had made small talk with his wife and Elynor had toyed with the food on her plate, trying in vain to muster something of an appetite so that the Goldenthals wouldn't think she was rude. But every mouthful stuck in her throat tonight. When they'd arrived her heart had sunk with bitter disappointment at discovering that von Ehrlich – whom she'd expected to be there – had declined Goldenthal's invitation. She was so upset that she had scarcely said anything all night, despite dark looks from her mother. Tomorrow, yes, tomorrow; she must get to the studio early to see him before he cleared his office and left for good.

Mrs Goldenthal was trying again to bring her into the conversation.

'You know, my dear, I wish I'd been on set to watch that final scene from the picture . . . Hal says in all his years in this business, he's never witnessed anything like it. He said you acted as if you were inspired.' Elynor smiled modestly. 'Now, although Hal promised that we wouldn't discuss movie business tonight, I can let you both into a little secret.' Her voice lowered conspiratorially; she glanced towards the door. 'He's got a very special offer to make you in a day or two . . . but I can't say more now. He'll tell you all about it.' At that moment Goldenthal burst back into the room, and they all turned round.

'Hal! What's the matter?'

'Trouble. Down on the studio premises. The police want me to go down there now. Some guy we employed as a casual worker a few weeks ago has gone crazy and shot a cop outside his home, and now he's holed up in one of the storage sheds with one of my nightwatchmen as hostage!' They were all horrified; nobody spoke. 'They told me that von Ehrlich's already gone down there, to try to persuade the guy to give up his gun.' Elynor turned pale. 'Seems like he gave the DA's office some dope on this cop who got shot tonight, and the name of the other guy who did it. Don't ask me what's goin' on! Sorry about this, Marianna. Gotta go.'

Elynor jumped up from her place at the table, ignoring her mother's expression. She wouldn't dare try to stop her, she wouldn't dare create a scene in front of the Goldenthals.

'I want to come with you!'

She climbed out of the automobile behind Hal Goldenthal and stared at the astonishing scene in front of them; like something from a Keystone movie. There were uniformed cops everywhere, and a crowd had gathered outside the studio gates, alerted by the swarm of policemen and the flares.

She caught sight of von Ehrlich at once; with his build and height he stood out more than head and shoulders from the rest of the crowd. In the light of the flares his long, straggly, unkempt hair glowed red in the night. She pushed her way through the wall of people, desperate to get to him.

'What are you doing here, Elynor?'

'Mr Goldenthal just got a telephone call; I wanted to come with him.' This wasn't what she wanted to say to him at all. He was staring straight ahead, to where an officer with a megaphone was bawling out some garbled warning to the man hiding inside the storage sheds. She wanted him to turn and look at her, to listen to what she wanted so much to tell him. That she'd been devastated when they'd arrived at the Goldenthals' tonight and he hadn't been there, that she couldn't bear the thought of him leaving California tomorrow and never coming back. That she'd never felt this way about anyone in her life. But now she was with him, she was tongue-tied. He was so remote now, so strange, so enigmatic; did she really know anything about him, what he was thinking, feeling, at all? She fell silent. Maybe she shouldn't have come.

'After you gave me Delucca's name and I rang the DA's office, they asked me to go there in person and tell the DA himself what I knew. So I did. I told him exactly what you told me.' He looked down at her now, but briefly. His eyes went back to the closed door of the shed where Danny Mazzoli was hiding. 'They sent some wires to New York, did some digging. Delucca was transferred from New York City. And he led the case on Klara Kopek's death . . . it was never solved. When I mentioned blackmail, they looked at his bank account; and they found it very interesting. Large deposits of cash on a regular basis, from two different sources. They match withdrawals taken from your mother's and Garrard Flair's personal accounts.'

'Delucca was blackmailing Garrard Flair?' She was amazed. 'I can't believe it! But why?'

'We don't know the answer to that, not yet. Maybe nobody ever will. Flair and Delucca are both dead. But we can be almost certain of one thing . . . Danny Mazzoli was taken on as a stage-hand at Universal, and he was there on the set when the scenery crashed down; he was after Delucca. He must hate him pretty bad, to have followed him all the way from New York.' There was a sudden shout, and the doors of one of the storage sheds came open. Two figures were slowly emerging.

Elynor grasped von Ehrlich's arm. 'He's holding the gun to the watchman's head! Do you really think he'll use it?'

'He's already killed one man tonight ... do you think one more would make any difference? He knows what he's facing. If you were in his place, wouldn't you say that you might as well be hung for a sheep as a lamb? Maybe, just maybe, I can change his mind.'

Before Elynor could answer, before she realized what he was doing, von Ehrlich had stridden from the spot where he was standing and made his way through the cordon of police.

'You can't! He'll shoot you!' Frantically, she tried to push her way after him but one of the uniformed officers caught her by the arm and held her back.

'Better stay put, miss. Things are set to get real ugly here. That guy's gone loco. Just look at his eyes.'

The captured nightwatchman had sunk to the ground on his knees, trembling with fear; standing over him, Danny held the handgun to his head. Ignoring the chief of police who tried to stop him walking through the barrier, von Ehrlich made his way slowly, steadily, unblinkingly to within a few feet of where Danny and his hostage stood.

'Keep back, you hear me? Keep back or I'll fill him full of lead. Then I'll kill myself!' His voice rang out into the night; shaking, hysterical. He began to cry, uncontrollably. His gun hand shook. 'That cop, he was responsible for killin' my sister ... he beat her up, he beat her real bad. She was so ashamed of what he'd done to her that she threw herself in the river ... he defiled her, you know that?' He dashed away the tears with the back of his hand. 'If anyone did that to your sister, wouldn't you hate his guts? Wouldn't you do anything in this world just to get even?'

Von Ehrlich took another two steps forward, and the crowd held its breath. Elynor could scarcely bear to look.

'Yes, I do understand. How you feel, and why you've done what you've done. But this man hasn't got anything to do with Delucca. You don't even know him.' Von Ehrlich held out a huge, freckled hand towards Danny Mazzoli. 'Let him go, Danny. Let him go home to his family. And give me the gun.'

Elynor felt the policeman's hand relax its grip on her

arm, and she suddenly broke free. Danny Mazzoli had shoved his terrified hostage to one side, and was pointing the barrel of his gun directly at von Ehrlich's chest.

'*No!*' she heard herself scream, her voice choking with fear and desperation, and at that very same moment von Ehrlich reached out and took the gun from Danny Mazzoli's hand.

CHAPTER THIRTY-SEVEN

Hal Goldenthal was not a happy man; Elynor Koenig was no Alice Ayres. On the day after the von Ehrlich picture had finished he'd called her into his office and laid a deal that every actress in Hollywood would have killed for right on the line. Three pictures a year for the next five years, with special bonuses and a generous share of the net profits; a deal her mother would have been proud of sealing. But what did he get for all his generosity and trouble? A turn-down. He'd been so shocked when she'd said no that he'd drunk down three double bourbons one after the other, without ice. It was clear that the girl was just plain crazy; maybe that business with Danny Mazzoli the other night had simply unhinged her. She'd been acting strange ever since the last day of the picture. 'Elynor, I don't think you realize what I'm handin' you on a plate here . . . or do you suppose that if you hold out on me for long enough one of the other studios will make you a better offer? They might; but none of 'em can top my net profits bonus . . . it's more generous than any deal I ever made for your sister. Get smart. Never hang around for what might happen . . . a bird in the hand . . . you know that old sayin'?'

'I'm sorry.' Why did she feel so desperately unhappy, after the months of elation while she'd worked with von Ehrlich? It was a common reaction, Gene had assured her with a cheerfulness she could not share, after completing a very long and very demanding schedule. But she knew better, in her heart; von Ehrlich was on the point of departing Hollywood for ever, and she couldn't bear it. 'I don't wish to seem ungrateful . . . please don't think that. The truth is . . . I don't think I'm cut out to be an actress.' That really had shaken him. 'I just feel as if every ounce of talent I might have had has all been drained out of me. Can you understand that?' She guessed not. But when did Hal Goldenthal ever understand anything except greed and profit? She could see his point of view much more clearly than he might think. Almost to a man, almost to a woman, every current major Hollywood star came from backgrounds ranging from circus, vaudeville, or burlesque: dangling two-million-dollar movie contracts in front of them was supposed to produce a miraculous effect; around these parts, money was the universal language. Could this be the daughter of rapacious, grasping, scheming, conniving Marianna Koenig? No wonder Goldenthal was having trouble believing his own ears.

'If you don't act, what the hell are you going to do for the rest of your life? Just wait till your mother hears about this!' But to his astonishment, even that threat had failed to move her. Goldenthal had a hunch that, if he'd got down on his bended knees and begged her to sign with him, she would have still said no with a firmness that even he recognized. This definitely wasn't a lady for changing her mind. And the instinct honed by nearly twenty years in the moving picture business told him that here was one actress who wasn't motivated by money.

'I actually decided a week or so ago that when the picture was finished and I'd said goodbye to everyone, I would go and live with my grandmother in Minneapolis. I'd feel closer to my roots, somehow. Something I've never felt since we came here. At least, not since my father died.' It still hurt to talk about him; even her memories of him had been shattered by those vile, hateful pictures. She tried to blot them out of her mind.

He leaned back in his chair; what was there left to say? 'I haven't told Momma about it, not yet. I'm on my way to do that now.' She hesitated. Was she about to change her mind after all? Anything was possible with a woman. 'When you see Mr von Ehrlich, will you please tell him that I said goodbye? There wasn't much opportunity, not earlier. And then he just disappeared. I looked all over the studio for him, but I couldn't find him.' That sounded like von Ehrlich.

'I'll tell him.'

The instant she was gone, Goldenthal was reaching for his telephone.

'How dare you turn down a two-million-dollar deal with Hal Goldenthal!' Her mother's rage was terrifying. 'Who the hell gave you the right to refuse that kind of money without even telling me first?'

'Momma, please, listen to me!'

'Listen to you? Have you completely taken leave of your senses?'

'I didn't turn down the offer lightly, please believe that.'

'You're not turning it down at all!' Elynor had never seen her mother so angry. 'Do you have any idea how many years clawing my way to the top it took me to get even half that kind of money for your sister?'

'It isn't about money, Momma. That isn't the most important thing to me. I want to be happy, whatever I decide to do.' Though she was tired and upset at not seeing von Ehrlich before she left the studio, Elynor knew that she had to stand her ground. 'That's why I think I should spend some time in Minneapolis, trying to sort out which direction I ought to travel in. Please, try to understand that.'

'Try to understand? That you think you're just going to turn your back on two million dollars and a five-year movie contract with Universal and walk out of here?'

'Hal Goldenthal didn't understand. And nor do you. Momma, being in this picture we've just finished has meant more to me than anything I've ever done in my life. I always wanted to act, but you would never let me. You said I had the wrong look, that I'd never be right in front of a camera, that I had no talent. I accepted that. But then Fritz von Ehrlich saw me and he chose me – out of every other actress in Hollywood – and I can't tell you how being chosen by a man like him made me feel. That's exactly why I couldn't sign with Hal Goldenthal. The difference between the picture we've just finished and the kind he produces is like comparing a circus act to a Frohman production on the New York stage. There is no comparison. My heart just wouldn't be in it, Momma. I'm sorry.'

She turned and walked up the staircase, went into her room, fighting the urge not to cry. Had von Ehrlich thought so little of her that he'd forgotten her as soon as the filming was finished? Had he seen her only as an actress and not a human being – despite what he'd said to her about friendship? Perhaps. After that evening when she'd poured out her innermost feelings and thoughts to him – something she had never done to anyone, not even her brother – she'd hoped that, at the very least, he might have regarded her as a friend. But he was, after all, widely known among the film community as an eccentric. Clearly, nobody really understood him at all.

She took off her hat and shoes, lay down on her bed and closed her eyes. She rolled over and buried her face in the pillow. Desolation overwhelmed her. Then, as the hot tears began to pour down her cheeks, she heard the sound of her mother turning the key in her door. Shock, fright, made her sit up at once. She leapt from the bed to the door and tried to open it. But it was locked fast.

'Momma? Momma! What are you doing?'

'I've locked you in and locked in you'll stay till you come to your senses! In the morning, if you're ready to sign contracts with Hal Goldenthal, I'll ring him at his office and he can have them drawn up straight away.'

'Momma, you can't do this to me!' Frantically, she rattled the handle and pummelled the door with her fists, but it made no difference. 'Momma? Are you there? Let me out!' But the only sound she heard from the other side was her mother's footsteps going back down the stairs, and then silence.

It was almost dark outside her window. Elynor had sobbed her heart out until she had no tears left. She had sat crouched on the floor behind her bedroom door pleading with her mother to open it, but the whole house was still swathed in silence. Then she had heard the noise of an automobile coming from the road into the drive.

She staggered up, stiff after hours of sitting cross-legged on the floor; she tried to see who it was from her window, but the courtyard at the front of the house was in total darkness, and her room was on the wrong side of it; almost impossible to get a proper view. It could only be Hal Goldenthal.

She leaned against the door, straining her ears for the sound of voices; she rubbed at her sore and swollen eyes. Her mother had obviously carried out her threat of telephoning Goldenthal at the studio, and he would have come straight over with the contract, all ready for her to sign. Clearly, her mother took it for granted that she would capitulate.

She stood back as she heard the sound of approaching footsteps; her mother's. They stopped outside her door and the key turned in the lock. The door swung open. For a moment they stared at each other in the sudden rush of light.

'You have a visitor.' Strange, her mother's voice was harsh; not what she'd expected. 'He insists on seeing you.'

'Who is it?'

'Why don't you go down and see?'

Without another word, Elynor walked past her and went to the head of the stairs; she caught her breath, her eyes widened with disbelief. Her visitor was not, after all, Hal Goldenthal.

'*Elynor?*'

Her face lit up, her heart leapt with joy as von Ehrlich stood there looking up at her.

'What are you doing here?'

'You left the studio before we could talk properly today ... Hal Goldenthal gave me your message. He said that you asked him to thank me and say goodbye. Surely you didn't think that I'd just pack up and go without seeing you first?'

'I didn't know what to think.'

'I'm leaving for England tomorrow ... you already knew that. But what I came here to ask was, will you come with me?'

Alice suddenly appeared behind him in the hallway. 'Momma, what's going on? What is he doing here?' She had never forgiven von Ehrlich for giving the role of Marguerite to her sister instead of her. She glared at him, then turned her spiteful gaze onto Elynor. 'Momma told me about the big movie contract Hal Goldenthal offered you today, and that you turned him down! I suppose you think his pictures aren't good enough for you now? Well, why don't you go with him,' she nodded bitterly towards von Ehrlich, 'if he wants you to? I hate you for stealing everything that was mine and I'll never forgive you! Never!'

Elynor glanced back at her mother with pain in her eyes; then she came down the staircase and stood beside von Ehrlich. She looked up at him and smiled, slipped her hand into his. Just the touch of his fingers made her feel safe, and strong. She looked sadly at her sister.

'If you think a movie contract is the most important thing in the world, then I pity you.'

Inside his chauffeur-driven limousine, she turned to him as it sped smoothly along the deserted coast road and towards the hills. She couldn't bear to look back. 'I'm so glad, so grateful that you came . . . when I refused to sign the contract with Hal Goldenthal, Momma flew into a terrible rage and locked me in my room. I'd never seen her that way before! I was really afraid of what would happen if she didn't get her way.' She didn't want to start crying again; she put a hand up to her reddened eyes, realizing how awful she must look. But von Ehrlich didn't seem to notice. 'When I heard the automobile, I just assumed it was him, that Momma had told him to get the contract and come over. It must have been a shock to her when she opened the door and saw it was you.'

'She refused to allow me to see you when I first arrived.' A trace of amusement had crept into his voice. 'Until I told her that I wouldn't leave until you came down.' He reached into his coat pocket and brought out an immaculately laundered handkerchief. 'You didn't really believe that I'd leave without seeing you again?'

She looked down at her hands. She wanted him to take her into his arms and hold her so much. So much. But whenever she found herself alone with him she was cursed into being tongue-tied and shy. Was all he felt for her friendship? He'd asked her to come with him to England, but was that for purely professional reasons because he knew that her mother stifled her, controlled her life? She'd already told him that she had no interest in acting in Hal Goldenthal's crude mass market pictures, no matter how much money he offered; working with von Ehrlich had introduced her to real dramatic art. Was she misconstruing his intentions entirely? He had always been such an enigmatic figure to her, revealing so little of himself, that even after all these months she wondered if she really knew him at all. 'I'm glad that you didn't leave without seeing me again. Because there was something I wanted to tell you. I wanted to tell you weeks ago, when I first realized it was happening to me. But I didn't have the courage.' She gazed up into the face behind the curtain of dark red hair. 'You see, I think I'm in love with you.'

He smiled. Then he began to laugh, very softly.

'Do you think I hadn't guessed that? On the last day of filming you weren't acting for the camera, were you? You were saying all those things to me.' He reached out, stroked the side of her face gently. 'Why else did you think I came here tonight to fetch you? I wanted to say that I feel exactly the same way about you.'

He led her into the vast beamed hall, then took her hand and led her to the top of the enormous stairs. The wall lights glowed soft and golden in the bedroom. Silently, he closed the door and drew her into his arms. There was no need for words. He slipped her silk shift down across her shoulders and let it fall to the floor, then he kissed her lips and fire raged through her.

She ran her eager hands over his body, across his hugely muscled arms; the coarse red hair on his chest tickled her skin. She wound her hands in his hair and clung to him. She never wanted him to let her go.

He smiled at her as he laid her down gently, almost reverently, on the counterpane of the enormous bed.

'Do you know just how beautiful you look, lying there with all your hair loose across my pillows? Tell me what you're thinking?'

'All this and Heaven too.'

'Has she gone with him for good, Momma? Isn't she ever coming back?'

'Go to bed, Alice.'

Alice followed her mother into the huge drawing room. 'If she goes back to England with him, then Hal Goldenthal can give her contract to me. She only stole what was rightfully mine in the beginning!'

'I said, go to bed.' Colleen had come into the room to take away the tray. She had something in her hand. 'Hal Goldenthal won't offer you a contract . . . you already know the reason why. We've been through all that.'

'But it isn't fair!' Alice's high-pitched voice rose to a shout of protest. 'Why won't you talk to him, call him at home? When he finds out that Elynor's gone away to England, he'll want me to come back. I know he will!'

Colleen was still in the room, waiting to speak to her. Marianna poured herself a brandy and soda. 'I don't think somehow that Hal Goldenthal will want to be hearing from either of us any more. And the sooner you accept that your career's over, the better for both of us. Only fools cling on to hopeless dreams.' Her voice was bitter. She sat down on the couch, cradling the glass in her hand as Alice rushed out of the room crying hysterically.

'Is that right, Mrs Koenig, ma' am? That Miss Elynor won't be coming back?'

'No, she won't be coming back.'

'I'll pack all her things away in the morning, then. In case she sends for them.' She laid down a bundle of letters beside Marianna. 'You haven't seen the mail today, Mrs Koenig. I'll leave it here for you to look through.'

'Goodnight, Colleen.' She put down the brandy and soda, idly leafed through the pile, all bills except one. She frowned, then sat up. The postmark was Minneapolis, and it was much thicker than all the rest. Unfamiliar with the small, neat hand, she tore it open impatiently. Zelda Duchovsky's signature was at the foot of the single page.

. . . Momma died in her sleep a few weeks ago, and I found this letter together with all his other things, in Shawn's old room . . . after we lost him, I had everything in his apartment boxed up and sent on to Momma . . . but she could never bear to look at any of it . . .

Marianna looked down in stunned surprise at the second, unopened envelope that Zelda's letter contained. In Curt's tall, sloping, unmistakable hand, it was addressed to Shawn in New York. She broke it open and looked at the date. Curt had written it on the night he died. Slowly, incredulously, Marianna unfolded the pages and began to read them. There was a lump in her throat. Tears suddenly sprang into her eyes. How long had it been since she'd been able to cry? Curt had never intended her to see this letter, which was why she knew that everything he'd written in it was the truth. *I love Marianna.* She stared down at the words, touched them with her fingertip. Curt hadn't lied to her, after all.

They lay curled up in each other's arms on the rug before the fire, when von Ehrlich's English housekeeper came to say that Miss Koenig's mother had arrived at the house. Neither of them had noticed the lights of her automobile, nor even heard it coming along the drive. Elynor sprang up at once, visibly upset. She clung to von Ehrlich's arm.

'Fritz, I don't want to see her! Please, don't let her come in.'

He put his arm round her protectively. 'There's nothing she can do to hurt you, not now. Why don't you hear what she has to say?' He made a sign to his housekeeper to show Marianna into the room. 'I promise I won't leave you alone with her unless you want me to.'

'All right. But I'm not going back with her! I never want to go back!' Why couldn't her mother leave her alone to live her own life now? Didn't she understand how unhappy she'd made her all these years? She gripped von Ehrlich's arm more tightly. 'She's come out here to try to make me change my mind, and I won't do it.'

'No, I haven't come here to ask you to come back.' Elynor turned towards the door, where her mother had suddenly appeared. She looked from one to the other. 'Thank you for seeing me. I apologize for calling here so late. But I do have my reasons.'

'What do you want, Momma?'

Marianna glanced at von Ehrlich. 'Do you think that Elynor and I could have just a few moments alone? I would appreciate it.'

'Whatever you've come to say, I don't want to hear it. I want to stay here, with Fritz. I want to be with him.'

'Yes, I understand that.' Her mother surprised her by smiling. Elynor noticed that her eyes were red. Surely she hadn't been crying? For a moment, Elynor was taken aback. 'I do assure you, I haven't come here to try to persuade you to change your mind about leaving for England. That really isn't any of my business now, is it? I give you my word that I'll leave as soon as you've heard me out. But hear me out first.'

For an instant, Elynor hesitated; then she nodded at von Ehrlich and he quietly left the room. He looked back at her when he reached the door. 'I'll be just outside if you need me.'

They stood there after the door had closed, looking at each other. Her mother made no attempt to come towards her.

'What do you want to say to me, Momma? That you're sorry you locked me in my room? I was your prisoner. Do you have any idea how that felt? Would you have kept me there till I agreed to do what you wanted? Would I still be there now if Fritz hadn't come to the house and insisted on seeing me? You tell me, Momma.'

'I had no right to do what I did. And I haven't come here now to give you any excuses. You can hate me if you want to. But maybe when you see everything around you falling apart, when everyone you ever loved is taken away from you, you sometimes don't see straight. That's the way it was between your father and me.'

'What do you mean, Momma?'

'Maybe one day I'll tell you my whole story . . . from the beginning right through to the end. But now isn't the right time to do that; it would take too long. I just wanted you to know that in spite of everything I've ever done, I do love you, Elynor. When I stopped you doing things in the past, it wasn't because I didn't want you to be happy. I was afraid that you'd be hurt by other people, just as I was. But when I saw you and him together through the window tonight, I was glad that I came . . . even if you refused to see me. I know you're in good hands now.' She turned to leave. There was no parting kiss, no final word of goodbye. The door behind her opened very softly, and von Ehrlich stood there waiting. 'He's a man you can trust, Elynor. Go with him. And, if you can . . . forgive me.'

EPILOGUE
Beverly Hills and Lake Winnipesaukee, 1933

Elynor was crying silently as she finished the final page. From the connecting room, Fritz came and sat down beside her. Wiping the tears from her eyes, she handed him the manuscript.

'I never knew. I never guessed. Not even a tiny part of everything that happened.' She looked at him. 'Why didn't she tell us? Why didn't she trust any of us enough to confide in us? I could understand why she never did when we were children . . . but later . . . she was willing to risk us hating her for what she did without giving us the chance to understand . . . why, why did she do it?'

'Your mother wasn't a woman to do things without having her reasons.' Von Ehrlich looked down at the manuscript, knowing exactly what Marianna Koenig had delivered into their hands. Had that been her purpose, when she'd written it, to bequeath to the daughter she'd wronged the most but loved the best, a posthumous film script of her extraordinary life, right from the very beginning? Somehow, he thought not.

'Fritz, what shall I do? Before we leave should I show it to Alice? To Gene? I think they both have a right, as much as I do, to know the truth.' She turned to him. 'Wouldn't Momma have wanted that?'

'If she had, she would have made it clear to Walter Oppenheim that the package was for all of you. But that is the one thing she didn't do. Think what her reasons were. She knew Gene would have wanted to make a full-length feature film from it . . . the director in him . . . he could never have resisted it. And Alice, living in lonely splendour with her dogs and cats? Your sister always preferred to remember the past as she liked to think it had been, rather than what it really was.' He turned the pages; words, names, sentences, flew up from them and caught his eye. 'What was it she said to you on that last night she ever saw you?'

'*Maybe one day I'll tell you my whole story.*'

'The story's been told. She trusted your judgement, Elynor. Do with it what you think you should do.'

New England was always so glorious in the autumn, with the carpet of fallen leaves, red and russet, orange and gold. The breeze was strong now, a little chilly. Elynor shivered as she held Fritz's hand and they walked towards the pebbled shore of Lake Winnipesaukee, her mother's childhood haunt, the place where, Elynor knew, she had once been happiest.

Her footsteps faltered a little as she fought the clumps of grass, picked her way across the rise and fall of the grey, craggy rocks towards the little jetty; it looked old and fragile, neglected and moss-strewn, now. Was it the same jetty, she wondered, as she stood on the very edge of the shore, watching a seabird overhead shriek as it circled in mid-air searching for its prey, where her mother and her childhood friend Luke Waad had launched their little fishing boat? It no longer mattered now. As peaceful, as silent as the churchyard, this place that her mother had loved so much was as fitting, as perfect as any memorial stone.

Von Ehrlich watched her as she opened the little box of ashes – the remnants of the manuscript she had watched burn last night – and, as the wind circled around her, blowing her long, loose, dark hair about her face, cast each handful inside it onto the waters of the lake.

THE END